The Obsidian Shard

By Kristy Nicolle

Queens of Fantasy Saga
The Ashen Touch- Book 6

First published by Kristy Nicolle, United Kingdom, December 2018

QUEENS OF FANTASY EDITION (1st EDITION)

Published December 2018 by Kristy Nicolle

Edited By- Jaimie Cordall

Adult Paranormal/Fantasy Romance

Disclaimer:

This e-book is written in U.K English by personal preference of the author. This is a work of fiction. Names, characters, businesses, places, events and incidents are either the products of the author's imagination or used in a fictitious manner. Any resemblance to actual persons, living or dead, or actual events is purely coincidental.

ISBN: 978-1-911395-16-4

www.kristynicolle.com

For My Leeah,

Who knew my tether to this life would be a leggy redhead with a love
for little red British phone boxes?
Thanks for being my person.

Oh, and if I haven't said it before, I'm super sorry I threw up in your
Official Stylist of Mortaria jacket that one time.

Here's to the endless adventures to come,
both fictional and factual.

PROLOGUE

HAEDES

DIAMOND PILLARS RISE ON either side of my slim figure as I enter the Olympian Council Chambers, throwing light in rainbow hues across my pale and flawlessly restored skin. As my polished black shoes echo out into the cool air, mist plays around the hem of my suit trousers and a rope of anxiety knots itself tight within my stomach.

Wasting no time as Thane catches up to me, ready to have this over and done with, I move to take a step forward, squaring my shoulders.

The eyes of Kanaloa, who is talking with Ava nearby, fall on me, surprised as they widen in kaleidoscopic and multicoloured hues. She's dressed in a tribal robe that falls asymmetrically across one shoulder, complimenting her voluptuous body. My gaze runs rampant over her, smouldering and unapologetic. Her hair, beaded with seashells, rattles as her head snaps quickly from me to Thane, who overtakes me in only two steps, beckoning me forward wordlessly with her angular fingers.

I keep my head up, shoulders relaxed, expression dead on my face, striding straight across the lobby between the offshoot corridors in lapis lazuli slick with quartz froth and onyx boasting gold spittle on both my left and right. They lead to The Circle of Eight council chamber and the long unused Nexus council chamber. Neither of these locations, though, is why I'm here.

Unfortunately.

My ceremonial Nexus robe pinches in at the waist, velvet brushing against the simple black suit jacket beneath as I move within its slimming confines. After much deliberation, I decided to go with an entirely black suit, black shirt, and startling white tie, complementing the ridiculous outer robe Thane had insisted I wear. Apparently, it makes me look like I mean business, not that anyone should doubt it. There's only a handful of reasons I'd ever step foot in this godforsaken

1

temple of hypocrisy, and none of them are unimportant by even Apollo's wild imagination.

The mist coating the floor gathers as the train of my black and white skeletal robe drags across the stone. I misstep, momentarily unable to see as the fog thickens leading up to the stairs that will elevate me to the Aetherial Court. I trip, falling sideways, only just catching myself on a half pillar supporting a pair of gold scales.

The Kindred Scales.

They wobble, vibrating and causing the few surrounding Gods and Goddesses observing me to give a sharp inhale, gasping. It's over-dramatic; I mean these scales are purely symbolic. If they weren't, I'd question laying them out right in the centre of such a public and politically fraught space.

Sighing, my cheeks flush hot as silence falls over the space like ice water. I straighten myself yet again, clear my throat, and turn back to the throngs of Gods and Goddesses who have started to appear, seeping through the doors like an unwanted and noxious chill.

"Yes, I am back. Thank you for your warm welcome. Now— if you could all go and take your enormous noses and stick them back in your own business, that would be most appreciated," I call out into the silence, cocking a cobalt eyebrow and narrowing my eyes as they flash momentarily scarlet. The people staring disperse, some conducting, some convecting, and some simply scurrying out of sight as I scorn the entire room with my gaze.

"Well, that was— aggressive," Thane comments, rolling her eyes as she stands, overly erect, at my spine.

"Oh, I'm sorry. Did I come here to be stared at like a fucking blue-assed baboon in a zoo?" I demand, anger rising fast in my narrow ribcage, trapped barely beneath delicate layers of velvet and fine cotton as I shoot her an infuriated glare over one shoulder.

Thane doesn't respond at first, letting the silence spread out between us as she begins her ascent up the staircase carved from diamond veined through with amethyst. It's so over the top I almost want to be sick, but I restrain myself, mainly because I need to look seriously badass if I'm going to go toe to toe with Zeus after all this time.

"I didn't realise you had hair on your ass—" She smirks, looking back over her shoulder after a moment, and I almost laugh, tension broken for merely a second.

Unfortunately for me, her face turns serious yet again, all too soon.

2

"Hurry up, lunch hour is almost half over already!" Thane hurries me as she reaches the top step, and I sigh a little too loudly. She scowls. "Hey, I wouldn't have to rush you if it hadn't taken you like ten years to decide on a tie!" she exclaims. I say nothing, fresh hot nerves with a side order of utter loathing seeping slowly into the pit of my stomach.

Reaching the top of the staircase, I note the gold bannisters flanking the long corridor that leads down to the shimmering diamond doors of the court. We take no pleasure in our surroundings, simply walking through them as though we were anywhere else in the world.

With every step closer to the entrance, my heartbeat becomes louder in my ears, and my teeth begin grinding harder against one another, jaw ticking with anxiety. I haven't exactly been invited, and the entire reason we're here during lunch hour is because there was no way in hell Zeus was going to let me schedule an appointment.

Reaching the end of the corridor, Thane pulls me to face her by my lapels, licking her thumb and polishing the side of my lip before giving a satisfactory nod. The grey storm that lies beneath her eyes, which has been dull and lacklustre ever since her return, sheens momentarily, deepening to charcoal as her pupils become billowing dark clouds, heavy with anxiety and anticipation.

"There." She tilts her head to one side, black hair wild around her face, before she gives a final nod and spins me toward the doors. She stands still at my back, palm on my shoulder as if I'll convect right out of here or try to run away. However, if I were going to do that, I never would have bothered getting dressed up or dragging my ass here in the first place.

It's truly amazing what I'll do for a room with a tranquillity pool.

Swallowing, I allow my eyes to wander with reluctance up the grandiose height of the doors, lips puckering in irritation. They're ridiculous. So heavy only Zeus or Ares can open them and obscenely shiny to the point where, when they move, you need sunglasses. Still, I guess that Zeus gets a kick out of having to open the door for everyone. Stupid ass.

Raising a hand gloved in black velvet, I knock, knuckles ringing out in pain as they contact the too-hard, pristine facets.

"Speak!" Zeus' voice rings out, deep as rolling thunder and all that jazz. I give a small exhale before cringing like I've just stubbed my toe.

"It's your brother. You know— the one you don't like?" I call as a collective murmur rises from within. A few moments pass, but I don't try to open the doors. I merely wait, not stupid enough to let them see me struggle.

"Well, are you going to open the door, or what?" I exhale the words in a gust of agitated and clipped syllables, left eye twitching.

"Why don't you come on in?" Zeus calls through the solid stone, laughing, and I roll my eyes.

"You know I can't do that. These doors are too heavy! Now let me in, or I shall start singing!" I threaten, hands balling at my sides. I hear another deep chuckle come from inside, followed by several sniggers.

"Come back when you are worthy to move them!" Ares calls, voice higher in pitch than his father's but no less unmistakable. It sounds like steel ringing on steel, like the echo of a battle cry in the traumatised memory of some long-fallen veteran. I hear them all burst now into pathetic breathless giggles and turn to Thane yet again.

"You see? You see what I have to put up with?" I hiss through gritted teeth.

She frowns but gestures for me to move forward nonetheless.

Rolling my eyes and balling my fists, I convect into the chamber.

It hadn't been my intention to make things uncivilised, but apparently my brother has the maturity of a twelve-year-old schoolboy, so here I am, forcing my way into his stupid company anyhow.

I reappear upon amethyst veined through with gold. The flames recede around me, and I find myself unable to tame the glare that lands full force on my brother, sitting in the centre of a crescent moon dining table piled high with food. The sniggers die upon my arrival, and I take a moment to stare at The Aetherial Court in all their ascendant pomposity.

My eyes are drawn, as always, not to Zeus on first inspection but to his wife, Hera. She sits behind gilded platters of fruit and fish, hair a sumptuous caramel with strands of solid rose gold intermingled among the rest as it falls over her shoulder. Her eyes are pale lilac, enormous, and her face is fierce. Her body is draped in a conservative lilac gown and adorning cloak, which caresses the rounds of her shoulders as she sits on Zeus' left-hand side. I smile at her, but she doesn't return it, looking instead to her husband.

Typical. My brow falls into a glower as my eyes narrow, and I clear my throat.

"As I was saying—" I begin, but I'm interrupted by Zeus before I can go any further.

"I hope it's important. You're interrupting lunch." He gestures to the feast that's been laid atop the white marble of the table's lunar arc, and I feel the eyes of the other court members resting on me, judgementally.

"Well, I wouldn't want to intrude on your oh-so-important—" I look down at the central platter, the one in front of Zeus, and my eyes widen as saliva rushes across my tongue. "Wait— is that— a Kaleidoscope Salmon?" I demand, fixated on the fish. Each scale is its own light prism and sharp as diamond. They're impossible to catch for exactly that reason— or so I had thought.

"Why yes, it is. Atargatis has been using the services of a new fisherman. Atlas is his name. It's her you need if you'd like one of your own. Is that all?" He gets to his feet, biceps bulging against platinum lightning-shaped cuffs as he leans forward on the table. His silver beard glistens with matching platinum strands as I scowl, increasingly nauseous as I note he has, as ever, refused to put on a goddamn shirt.

"No, that is bloody well not all!" I exclaim, crossing my arms over my own civilised pectorals.

"What is it Haedes?" Aphrodite asks, her voice the pulled strings of a thousand heavenly harps. I've been trying to avoid looking directly at her, but after all these years, I suppose it's finally time. She sits, sandwiched between Hera, the wife of the man who relentlessly pursued her for years, and Apollo, her asexual shield.

"I thought you'd already know." I assert, taking a step closer to the table. Aphrodite's irises tinge pink as she stares at me, but I try not to act surprised. She brushes her golden hair, which shines like the sun, behind one ear, several of the strands coated with white gold shimmer and almost flawlessly reflective in the too-bright light of the room.

Before she can answer, I turn almost a full ninety degrees on the spot, moving to gaze directly into the deep galaxies that lie behind Nemesis' irises.

"You can't tell me you haven't noticed a shift in The Crucible?" I berate her.

Her black hair glints, midnight blue in tone as her head tilts, observing me with a morose expression. Crystals trapping pure starlight are woven amongst her inky tresses and tinkle as they hit the heavily beaded navy of her diamond-encrusted cloak. She blinks slowly, pursing her lips, an observatory silence falling over the room.

5

I watch Hecate shift uncomfortably beside her lover, placing a phantasmal and pale hand over Nemesis's as her nose wrinkles, the pink sugar of her scattered freckles vibrating with her deep exhale. However, Nemesis' expression remains blank as her own freckle constellations remain steadfast, marring her skin with the ancient stories of the heavens.

"Bring it up." I gesture to the ceiling overhead where a blanket of tumultuous clouds stirs with intermittent lightning, courtesy of Zeus. She sighs, glaring at me, but relinquishes by waving her long fingers, nails lacquered silver catching the light. I watch as the shifting ceiling overhead changes, a projection of The Crucible cloaking the room and turning it dark.

As the shadow falls, the pinwheel of souls spreads like a tentacled star from a singular central point. This is the place where my soul had been forged, but isn't what I'm interested in. The centre of The Crucible is always the same because the souls which fall from it are immortal and unchanging, the most powerful among us. It is the spokes I'm most preoccupied with as I gaze up, the light of thousands of mortals, their lives but flashes in the hot pan of eternity, falling over my face like an immensely important disco ball.

"There." I point to one of the spokes, which is dimmer than the others, less densely populated. "You know why I've returned. An old friend of yours has been scheming; she's taken control of Mortaria, and therefore the flow of sinners' souls moving through it now lies under her rule. Put simply, as I know may be more your preference, she's fucked us royally." I exhale, watching as Zeus laughs.

"Always so overdramatic, Haedes." He tuts, raising a golden fig to his lips and setting the delectable juices free of the shimmering skin with his too-white teeth.

"Excuse me? *Overdramatic*? The entire underworld has fallen into the hands of our enemies— or more specifically *your* enemies— though why they hate you so much is of course, as ever, a mystery." I reek of sarcasm, eyebrows fighting the urge to cock, eyes destined to roll. "You didn't even notice?" If I sound incredulous, it's because I am.

Zeus shrugs.

"Pandora isn't the threat you think she is. She's merely a pissed-off Titan. It's not my fault that you can't keep control over your own dominion. I don't tend to check on The Underworld. Especially seeing as how you claimed you needed no council to help you rule. I figured you'd have it handled. Besides, I do have my own hands rather full with a situation in Aetheria as of late, a situation that you are entirely responsible for." As the words fall from his lips, he takes a large hand and places it around Hera's shoulder, possessive as ever.

I recall that night, the night I'd been banished as I promptly ignore his final comment. He claimed it was because I failed his stupid test, but I've always known deep down it was because Hera had tried to seduce me to get revenge for yet another one of my brother's classless infidelities. I wonder now, staring at her, if she has thought even once that she chose the wrong brother or if she just used me to hurt him. I certainly would have treated her better than Mr Manwhore over there.

"Look, I don't want to be here asking for your help. But as it is, if we don't do something soon, the walls between dimensions will fall. She'll tip the balance. You and I both know it, and you also know what that means— The Island of The Blessed will no longer be a prison," I explain, and Zeus gives me a deadpan stare, his baby blue irises every mother's dream. He had always been the pretty one, the strong one, after all. Rhea's favourite.

"I am aware! I am the King of The Gods!" He balls his fists and slams them down on the table, causing a platter stacked high with untouched apples from the Othrysian Orchard to topple onto the floor. I pick one up in my gloved palm as it skids to a halt at my feet, polishing it against my velvety breast before taking a bite.

"And you're doing nothing because?" I enquire as I chew, more desperate than I want to be. Our irises blaze into one another's, and I feel my heart start to race involuntarily, but before the moment can escalate, a high-pitched and melodic cough rings out into the air, distracting us both.

I spin, twisting to face Apollo as the roots of my hair tinge scarlet.

"Yes?" I spit, glaring at him.

"I would like to remind you that you *were* warned this could happen—" He looks tired as he sits back in his seat, foot propped upon his knee. His white poet's shirt is embroidered with silver honeysuckle and he's wearing too tight jeans. A myriad of rainbow-coloured hair protrudes messily from beneath the wide brim of his hat as he cocks his equally bright eyebrow, taming a smug smile that pulls, without subtlety, at the corner of his lips.

"Oh, don't even get me started down that road, asshole," I growl, watching his pearlescent irises dilate with pleasure before turning back to Zeus.

7

"The way I see it, if you had let Sephy take her rightful place here, this wouldn't be happening. So, it's your fault. Your fault I resurrected her, your fault Pandora went on this vendetta in the first place," I announce.

Artemis stares at me, harsh face incredulous.

"So— *you* hold no blame in any of these events?" she snorts, long raven hair glistening with gold as her doe-like eyes turn wicked with malice. Her tiny stature has become no less ferocious with age.

"Of course, I do. But it's not just me! And I'm asking for your help. We at least need to remove Pandora so that souls may start moving through Mortaria again. And as you can see, I have no power to facilitate that from here." I don't want to sound desperate, but I am concerned they don't realise the severity of this.

"You're proposing we go to war for Mortaria? With what army?" Ares asks, running his fingers through the bronzed strands of his dark wiry beard. His dark chocolate eyes gleam; the idea of bloodshed clearly appealing as the veins of his arms rise closer to the surface of his skin, bulging hot.

"I'm not proposing war. I'm proposing going in and taking out the main players, you know, with subtle finesse if you can imagine such a thing. Once that has been achieved, then we can attempt to re-establish some control," I suggest.

The Crucible still spins, a stark white shower of light overhead.

Eight pairs of eyes stare at me before exchanging colourful glances filled with a full spectrum of mixed emotions.

"Look. I did my duty for centuries, without falter, without hitch. Then this crazy bitch turns up, travelling with that stupid box you tempted her with, and everything goes to shit. You don't have to like me. I sure as hell don't like you, but this is your responsibility! Might I remind you that you have enemies trapped beyond walls that will fall should she succeed?" I make my final argument with a flourish of one hand, Hera's eyes meeting mine momentarily before flitting to stare at some invisible focal point behind my left shoulder.

"And what of Lucifer?" Hecate asks me as Zeus ponders the predicament, running his fat fingers down the edge of his jaw before resting them close to the cleft in his chin that I always thought looks like an extra, under-evolved asshole. I twist my head to face her, pursing my lips.

"You care now?" I demand, watching as Nemesis moves to clasp Hecate's hand as if she's the victim here. I bite the inside of my lip

8

before moving to chew the soft inner flesh of my cheek, unable to hold my tongue.

"She's my daughter," Hecate whispers, pink freckles and albino skin looking fragile as her pinkish irises glint like puddles of diluted blood.

"You might have tried remembering that when you banished her for something that wasn't her fault. Whatever happens to her now— well, I hold you solely responsible," I spit, receiving a full-force and hate-filled glare from Nemesis.

I sigh.

These bitches deserve everything they get.

"Well?" I turn to Zeus, eyes narrowing. "I don't have all day."

"I will send Hercules. He will bring order."

Oh, for fucks sake. Hercules? Just what I need. Let's add fuel to the fire by putting your biggest fan in a room with the son who lists 'hating my father's guts' at the top of his secret resume.

"That's your big solution? Send Hercules?" I almost burst out laughing, Ares shifting uncomfortably in his seat at the mention of his half-brother's name.

"And what of your daughter? Where is *she* in all this?" Zeus inquires, a smirk painting itself upon his face.

"You leave her out of this. If she's not worthy of a place among us, I don't see why she should have to sacrifice for the cause," I bite out, fierce in my defence of the redhead who had stolen what was left of my heart against my consent.

"I see," Zeus mutters, platinum eyebrows rising on his broad forehead.

"What's that supposed to mean?" I bark, biting when I know I shouldn't.

"Nothing. It's just classic Haedes' isn't it? Do you remember when father used to take us to the Crystal Colosseum across the border?" he asks, eyes glinting with malice. I lick my bottom lip, taking another bite of the apple still clutched, with skin now dented, in my tense palm.

"Not something I'm likely to forget. My own father taking me and my asshole siblings to fight to the death," I mutter. Zeus smirks.

"Ah, but you didn't fight, did you? You used to convect home to mother. I'd call that cowardly, and I can see now not much has changed. You have made terrible decisions with far-reaching consequences, and now you are running from them. Crawling back to me. Not wanting to get your own daughter involved in the mess you created. So, I, as ever, will sacrifice my offspring, to fix your mess. But know this— you, my brother, are a joke among us." With this final sentiment, he shoots Hera a smile over his shoulder, but she doesn't return. I don't want to stay to watch the reactions of the others, so I clench my fist, letting the apple drop from my palm and thud upon the crystal floor as I convect out of the room.

"Send Hercules. I'll be watching."

My words echo out as I disappear in a plume of humiliated smoke.

READY TO MEET THE NEXT QUEEN OF FANTASY?

KEEP READING FOR A SNEAK PEEK OF INDIGO DUSK- BOOK 1 IN THE THIRD TRILOGY OF THE QUEENS OF FANTASY SAGA OR DOWNLOAD KAIRI'S STORY HERE!

I

SCREAM IF YOU WANNA GO FASTER

SEPHY

THE EARLY SUMMER RAIN hits the rooftop of the downtown apartment block like blistering shrapnel. It drips down my face, off the fan of my eyelashes, and onto the rough black leather of Xion's jacket.

Peering down over the edge of the rooftop, I'm grateful for the sparse moonlight as the hairs on the back of my neck stand up.

They're here.

I don't know how I know, but after four weeks of standing on rooftops just like this one, watching, I find their presence unmistakable. As a bolt of lightning strikes without mercy, slicing across the sky, I feel my heart gear up to race; a sensation I've come to rely on this last month.

It's addictive. Not as addictive as sex, but since I vowed to stop sleeping with Xion because, according to him, he's in love with me, it'll do.

Narrowing my eyes, I ball my fist at my side and continue to stare down into the alleyway on the left side of the building, the rain creating an unfortunate and blurry haze. I should be cold with the sudden night-time downpour, but I'm not. My skin is blazing, breath scorching as it escapes my hot, plump lips. My fingers caress the calloused skin of my palms, hardened from four weeks of intense training and kickboxing in my old ballet studio whenever I get the chance. I thought the end of the world would be a rain of fire, a real phenomenon, but as it turns out, it's just a whole lot of extra bodies on the slab at Chicago Morgue and even more confused cops.

That's where I come in.

I can't take back Mortaria, but after three days of restless nights and avoiding Xion, who was permanently camped out in my room waiting to *talk*, I've concluded that I can't just sit on my ass either.

So, here I am, waiting for some poor schmuck to come stumbling into the wrong place at the wrong time.

As if he's heard my internal monologue, the schmuck in question potters around the corner, hood pulled up over his head, trajectory nothing short of a meandering river. He's clearly drunk, which is no surprise at this hour. Anyone sober would also have the common sense to stay home and lock their doors, especially after the citywide state of alert that's been broadcast across every major news channel due to the unsolved homicide rate going through the roof.

I watch him, inhaling deeply as I hear it, the feral growl of a Banshee that even the rolling thunder cannot disguise.

A sudden but anticipated scream signals it's time for my debut, so I close my eyes, allowing a plume of blue flames to rise around me, compressing the humid air. I convect from the rooftop and reappear directly between the Mortarian predator and its human prey.

"Run," I bark over one shoulder at the man, glancing back only long enough to glimpse a pair of dark terrified irises and wide pupils beneath the hood of his rain-speckled parka.

He turns, moving to bolt from the alley, but as I listen for the continuation of his footfall amongst the rain, eyes still trained on the hulking silhouette of the approaching demon, I hear him stop.

Before I can turn to yell at him again, the Banshee before me crouches down low, the white glow of its eyes becoming distinct amongst the blur of the rain as it prowls closer, ready to pounce.

I raise my hands, summoning The Eternal Flame to both palms in a rush of explosive power that promises to remain forever in wait within my veins. The Banshee is alone, a pleasant surprise seeing as so often they're in packs of at least six or more lately, and it moves back from me as I widen my stance, hair sticking to my forehead in sodden tendrils as my cognac irises shine out into the dark.

"Bad dog," I pretend scold it, just as I would Cerb when he's chomping down on one of my brand-new Jimmy Choo's. Sassy and powerful, I stand there; a lone blaze amongst the downpour of the night. I guess it's sad, a cliché of epic proportions, but I have to get my happy on somehow.

It growls, still unsure as it remains rooted to the spot now, not daring to come closer. I roll my eyes, unimpressed with the poor effort, tossing the flame in my palms into the rain and watching as the beast catches light seconds after it launches into the air. Its screams echo out among the flash of lightning and slash of rainwater on hot concrete.

I watch it burn, the light from the blaze illuminating my face as I gaze into it. Turning slowly on the spot, I partially eclipse the slowly diminishing flames charring the corpse behind me.

"I told you to run," I snap, as the eyes of the man widen even still. His dark and plump bottom lip is trembling, only just visible beneath his hood in the weak moonshine.

"But— but — you're a *chick*? What the hell, girl?" he slurs, tottering back on his thick rubber soles.

"Well, you're quite the detective. No shit I'm a woman. What was it that gave it away?" I cock my hip to one side, leather pants damp with rain, ready to walk away from him before he recognises me from the papers.

"But— I don't need no woman saving me! I didn't ask you to! What if my boys hear about this? I'll be done!" he calls out as I turn, making me pause.

Blinking slowly, I twist back to glare over one shoulder.

"I should've let you get eaten," I decide aloud, shaking my head.

"What are you, some kind of superhero?" he demands, desperate for a reason to justify my strength and his weakness.

I smirk.

"Nope. Not a hero. Now go home. It's too late for a little boy like you to be wandering around alone. Next time, there might not be a chick around to save your stupid ass," I insult him, tired of the conversation but reminding myself that gagging random strangers is wrong. In theory anyway—

The man still doesn't move, so I look down at my palm, letting blue flame flicker to life. It wouldn't kill him, but he doesn't know that.

His eyes widen, thick bone structure and broad forehead exposed as he turns on the sole of his too-white, high-top sneaker, and his hood falls around his shoulders. I stand, stance wide, unflinching in the downpour with a hand full of flame until his quickening tread dies into silence.

Exhaling, I let the fire extinguish, flexing my fingers and stretching my neck from the left to the right. I'm tense, tenser than I should be, but my usual stress relief is off the table, so I guess I'll have to stick with saving sexist morons until further notice.

Speaking of morons, as I'm about to turn to make sure that the Banshee's charred remains have been washed away by the rain, the sound of an engine grows closer. It usually wouldn't catch my attention, but I know that purr, that rumble. It's the sound of an Aston Martin Vanquish.

Ugh, I curse, stilling as the silver car pulls up beside the alley. The window rolls down, and from within the confines of the car, a familiar pair of metallic gold irises glare out at me.

"Sephy, what the hell are you doing? It's pouring! Get in the freaking car!" he calls, causing my defences to fly up immediately.

I won't be told what to do, especially not by him, not after the entire reason I'm stuck in this restless limbo is because he couldn't keep his goddamn mouth shut.

"I'm busy, come back later!" I shoo him away, but as I turn my back on him again, I'm startled as he rams his hand down on the horn. The sound explodes into the street, causing doors to slam and windows to open in the moments that follow.

"Hey! Turn that fucking thing off! I'm trying to sleep up here!" a pissed-off resident calls from above before a window is loudly rammed shut in protest.

"Xion! Stop! I'm trying to be covert here!" I hiss.

"Get in the car!" He pushes open the door closest to the alleyway, and I watch as his fingers linger, a silent threat, over the car's horn.

Sighing, I storm angrily through puddles, letting the water splash up and into my boots, chilling my feet. When I reach the car, I lower myself into the heated leather seat before slamming the door shut.

"Happy now?" I demand, glaring at him through the raindrops clinging to my lashes.

"Ecstatic," he mumbles, knuckles white on the steering wheel as we pull away from the curb with expensive effortlessness.

He doesn't look at me as I put my seatbelt on, or when I cross my arms over my breasts, or when I sigh super loudly to express my rage. Instead, he simply fiddles with the dial on the stereo, pulling up a local radio station and humming along, oblivious, to the beat.

I don't respond, sitting back in my seat and watching the windscreen wipers work frantically in silence. Xion finally looks across at me as I turn from him, staring out of the window with listless disinterest.

"You know I wish you'd stop stealing my jacket. You have hundreds. I own that one. That's it," he reminds me, and a lump forms in my

15

throat. It's just a jacket, but more than anything, it smells like him, a subtle reminder of what could have been that I've been refusing to relinquish.

"It just looks good on me, that's all." I shrug, looking across at him. Even in the current weather, he's only wearing a black round-neck t-shirt and jeans, the same thing he'd worn the day we chopped down The Hollow. "Besides, I told you to go shopping. You're the one who hates sales assistants and what you claim is 'the hassle' of the mall." I remind him of the argument we'd had after Jules informed me he'd washed the same single outfit of Xion's every day for two weeks.

"Look, that's beside the point. It's *my* jacket. I want it back. It's not like you're my girlfriend or something. You don't have any right to it." His words sting like a slap across the face, but I don't falter in my response. I deserve it I suppose.

I take off my seatbelt after we slide around a corner, slipping the wet jacket off and tossing it at him as we head toward the city centre down roads far more desolate than usual. It lands over his head, as I intend, leaving raindrops trapped and sparkling in the oily darkness of his hair. He grasps the material in one fist and pulls it away from his eyes in a fluster so he can continue driving.

"Nice," he spits, throwing the jacket into the compartment between our seats, jaw tensing as he refuses to stare at me yet again.

I sit back, not bothering to put my seatbelt on, feeling a chill run rampant up my arms as the familiar warmth and pomegranate scent of his jacket leaves my skin.

We race through the streets, and I keep my eyes trained once more on the window, which is veined slick with rivulets of summer rain. Beyond, I stare out into dark alleys, seeking the bloody red eyes of a Succubus or the slithering undulations of a camouflaged Gorgonian. I could be considered paranoid, but I'm troubled by their abundance to say the least.

When Pandora had taken back Mortaria, I thought that would be the end of demons feeding in this world. Turns out that despite gaining back their hunting grounds, they're appearing more regularly than ever before, which to me makes no sense at all. It's one of the many things that isn't Xion keeping me up all night, wondering.

The song on the radio ends, fading into the worried voice of whichever unlucky and underpaid college graduate is reporting at this godforsaken hour of the night.

I watch as Xion's irises flick to the neon green of the stereo, suddenly alert.

"Breaking News! Yet another gruesome crime has been committed tonight, as Police are called to the scene of a local packing warehouse where several sets of remains have been uncovered— stay tuned to receive updates as they become available." As the announcement ends and the jingle of the station takes over, my eyebrows rise on my forehead and Xion and I catch one another's gaze across the car. I shift in my seat, stomach in tumult under the curious nature of his stare.

"Know where I can find a packing warehouse?" he demands.

I smile, glad that, for just a moment, his icy approach to me has thawed.

"Shouldn't be too hard. Just head west, and keep your eyes and ears peeled for the sirens."

As the rain diminishes into a miserable drizzle, we finally find the warehouse we're looking for. The car is filled with the heavy sound of *My Chemical Romance* as Xion pulls onto the curb a small distance from the police cars that leave red and blue flashes bouncing off the metal frame of the building's immense, rigid shadow.

"Ready?" he asks, taking off his seatbelt and moving to place his hand on the door handle.

I examine him, glad for his improved mood.

Ever since that night, the night Thane took her own life and everything went to hell, things have been awful between us. I knew this was a possibility, but Xion assured me he could handle it. Turns out, he'd turned full-on emotional masochist and decided to say the one thing I can't get past, the one thing I can't ignore. And so, I have not only lost my physical connection with him, but our friendship seems to have all but withered as well.

"Ready!" I smile back at him with enthusiasm before stepping out into the night.

Slamming my door, I look over the low roof of the car as Xion grabs his jacket, throwing it over his shoulders without a second thought. A chill creeps through my thin black sweater as I notice Xion's nostrils flaring, inhaling deep as the leather of his collar closes around the stubble of his throat.

Promptly ignoring this, I turn on my heel and make my way around the bonnet of the car, exhaling heavily as the scorching alabaster of my skin fights the cool damp of the surrounding air. I don't wait for Xion to lead the way, instead taking off along the sidewalk.

Police officers mull around the scene, trying to look busy by holding blank reporter's notebooks. They don't know anything— I mean, how could they? But I suppose they need to at least look like they're earning their paychecks.

As I approach a stream of unattractive yellow and black tape, I am met head-on by a female cop with a full head of dark voluptuous curls slicked back to the base of her neck.

"Excuse me, ma'am, this is a crime scene. You can't be here," she says, not looking at me as she continues to stare at her blank notepad, pretending to be busy.

Xion catches up to me, and I watch his eyes narrow as they fall onto the officer. I reach into my bra, pulling out one of the cards Jules had given me, courtesy of Colonel Sandy Toe.

"Actually, I can." I pass it to her and watch as her eyes widen in surprise at my face.

"Hey— aren't you—" She looks like she's seen a ghost.

Xion coughs beside me.

"I assume everything is in order?" he prompts, interrupting her as she looks down at the piece of glossy card between her manicured nails.

"Uh— yes, one moment." She turns, walking off toward the crime scene, and I swear she exhales, glad of finally having some purpose which isn't make-believe.

I look to Xion, confused.

"What was that about?" I ask, and he glares at me.

"She was one of the cops who came to the estate. You know, the night you were—" he trails off, and I roll my eyes.

"Brutally murdered? It's okay. You can say it." I shrug, and his mouth twists into a puckered grimace as he runs his hand back through his hair, dislodging shimmering rainwater.

The scent of pomegranate wafts, so I take myself out of the situation and duck under the police tape, not waiting for the officer to return. As I tread forward, I'm only too glad of air that has become sour, infected with the scent of death, the scent of the feed.

"Everything good?" I ask the officer as I pass her and another male cop at the entrance to the warehouse.

"Seems to be, I don't know why they're sending private investigators though. We do have this handled." She frowns, almost as if my

18

presence has insulted her personally. It's not her fault, not really. She's just got a veil pulled over her eyes like most of the world.

She's lucky.

I'd kill to go back to before this nightmare began, when my biggest problem was getting Jules and Peter off my back about the family business.

This certainly wasn't the family business I had expected to find myself afraid of taking over, I muse as I enter the chasmic warehouse.

There are crates wrapped in plastic everywhere, peppered with blood spatter dripping cold onto the floor. The smell is only too familiar, fresh blood and ichor. I frown, finding not what I expect as I look around at the floor, now a murderer's dot-to-dot of body parts.

"Several victims—" I muse aloud, looking over my shoulder to Xion, who frowns down at the scarlet fluid, splattered and pooling every-where. There are shards of bone, its jelly smeared like the yellows in Van Gogh's *Starry Night* all over the concrete of the floor.

"You know what's weird?" Xion asks me, crouching down close to one of the piles of remains and leaning in. He gives a sniff, and I shoot him a grossed-out stare as bile rises in my throat, the venom of mortal weakness.

"You, sniffing the bodies like they're a bouquet of fucking butter-cups?" I guess. His eyes narrow, expression deadpan as his molten irises diminish in shine.

"No, look at all this—" he gestures to the mess, and I blink a few times, seeing what he means.

"This is bad," I begin, sighing. "They've left so much — mess — it's almost like they're getting so comfortable hunting here now they don't feel the need to take everything they can get from a single kill." Shaking my head, dread begins to drip, slowly, into my stomach. "What does this mean?" I ask him, watching as he straightens and plunges his hands deep into the pockets of his jeans.

"It means that the worlds are beginning to bleed into one another. Right now, that's because of Pandora's free use of the box, but soon— the walls between this dimension, Mortaria, and all the others will fall." He shudders, and I bite down on my bottom lip.

"Hell on earth," I comment, eyes widening slightly as they rest on the brutal murder scene at my feet.

Mortals don't stand a chance.

"The problem is, the more people who are murdered, the bigger the potential imbalance. She's slowly killing enough mortals to single-handedly tip the scales of good and evil." Xion lowers his voice as he takes a step closer to me, looking deeply into my eyes.

"So— we keep doing what we're doing. We double efforts on patrolling, maybe start getting Lucifer or The Furies involved?" I suggest, desperate in even considering setting them loose. Xion only shakes his head.

"That's not the answer Sephy. You can't protect the whole world on willpower alone."

"Hey, I'll have you know I'm extremely stubborn!" I quip, trying to make light of the conversation and steer it towards something other than what everyone is so sure is inevitable.

They want me to fight for Mortaria. Maybe die trying.

They want me to be the hero. To save the fucking world.

But— that just isn't me.

Xion is so jaded by his feelings for me, so blind to who I really am, he has no clue how much of a bad idea me attempting to save anyone truly is. I have barely been able to save myself and, arguably, have failed even in that. I'm so different than I was when we'd first met; there's barely any of the original Sephy Sinclair left in residence. The problem is, I don't know if that's for the better, or more likely, the worse.

"So, what do you think of all this?"

We're interrupted by the male cop, who has been inching closer for several minutes, trying to hear what we've been saying.

"I think this is some kind of animal attack," I say quickly, watching as Xion flashes me a look of warning.

"I see, well, that's what we figured. I don't know what animal could do something like this though— and I grew up in Alaska, so I've seen animal attacks before." He shrugs, so I copy him, keeping my face carefully impassive.

"I'm just telling you what I think, and I'm a specialist in these kinds of crimes," I retort, forceful, placing a hand on my hip and moving to walk past him.

"Wait? You're going?" he's almost whiny, like as we go, so goes the entertainment. I nod without giving him the courtesy of a verbal acknowledgement, and Xion follows me past his increasingly suspicious gaze.

Wanting nothing more than to brush him off, I begin walking at a brisk pace across the wet concrete and duck once more under the hideously yellow police tape. Leaving the scene behind, I can't be entirely sure I won't be revisiting it in my nightmares.

I don't hold the tape for Xion, dropping it behind me and making my way back to the car, awfully tempted by the thought of convecting to an island on the opposite side of the planet and never coming back.

"Hey, wait up!" Xion calls after me.

Spinning, I want to yell or tell him to fuck off and go back to being Mr Frosty, but something about his expression, the way he goddamn cares, stops me.

"What?" I whisper, both my breath and bravado doused by his sudden proximity.

"Are you okay?" he demands.

I shrug, unable to find the words to answer.

"Ready to go home?" he presses, placing an arm across the top of the car door to stop me opening it.

"Is that a fucking trick question?" I snap at him.

"Um, no? Why would it be?" he asks, ignorant, and I roll my eyes.

"Well, of course, why wouldn't I want to go back to the house with three raving pent-up feminists and a bereaved devil who is addicted to raiding my spice cabinet for her next fix?! The only person back at that house who is partially sane right now is Jules. Why the hell do you think I'm out on the city streets every chance I get? I like my spa tub, Xion. I like my bed too. I wouldn't be out here unless I found being there unbearable," I burst.

He places a hand on my shoulder.

"Okay. I'm sorry," he whispers, brushing a loose strand of hair back behind my ear and leaning in, kissing me on the cheek.

What is this? A truce?

I shudder at his touch, at the pain that comes from remembering what had been between us.

Mistaking the gesture for cold, Xion sighs slightly, taking off his jacket and passing it to me.

"Come on, let's go for a drink," he decides as I take the rough, damp leather in my palm.

I stare down at it.

"You were right; this is yours. Here, take it. I never should have stolen it in the first place. It's not like you have another." I try to give it back to him, but he shakes his head, goosebumps noticeably rising on his forearms.

Walking around the bonnet of the car, he opens the driver's side door, looking at my curious expression over the rain-speckled roof as he throws me the lopsided grin I've missed so much.

A shrug rolls over him as his tension seems to all but dissolve.

"It looks better on you anyway."

IN TOO DEEP

XION

THE AIR IS STICKY and electric as we both get out of the car, finding the rain has finally subsided.

"It feels like forever since I last parked here—" Sephy remarks, her fiery red hair damp as it hangs limp in a high ponytail suspended from the top of her skull. I stare up at the immense height of the glass sculpture centre, finding the abstract silhouettes of the artwork inside unsettling at best. It's not surprising. I've been on edge; we all have. I guess if I'm being honest, we had expected the apocalypse to be well underway by now, and this waiting around is just— paranoia-inducing to say the least.

Locking the vehicle, we both make our way out of the parking lot, and the atmosphere turns thick and sharp between us. Silence used to be comfortable for us, but now it is filled with the echoes of those words, the words I let loose.

"*Sephy— oh God, Sephy— I love you so much.*"

Do I regret it?

No.

Do I wish she'd stop running from me every single chance she gets? Yes.

"Huh. Weird—" she interrupts the line of thought that's become cyclical in my mind, doomed to be repeated over and over as I lie awake at night, staring up at the ceiling within the stone-cold sheets we'd once set ablaze.

"What's weird?" I demand, turning to look down at her as we keep a competitive pace over the concrete sidewalk.

"There used to be dozens of homeless people around here. I mean I get that the city is on high alert because of the attacks, but these people— they had nowhere to go," she explains, and I inhale as an awful thought materialises.

"You don't think— well, I mean if Pandora was looking to recruit people quietly, homeless people would be perfect. Nobody would notice they were gone," I suggest.

"That bitch really needs to suck a lemon and die," she grumbles, and I can't help but smirk at her like the smitten idiotic fool I have become.

After a few minutes, we reach Retropolis. There's no bouncer on the door tonight, no queue flanking the building. I mean it's late, but not too late for partying. The reason for the abandoned city streets though doesn't escape me, because when I've come down here in the last few weeks, hoping to deflect Sephy from the masses of horny men she seems to attract like moths to her oh-so-alluring flame, the place has been dead.

No pun intended.

It would seem that Chicago has gotten the message of The Underworld loud and clear.

Once the sun sets, nobody is safe.

Up in the club, Sephy and I take our usual seats, hers a neon lime barstool and mine flashing a too-bright magenta, which really isn't my colour.

"The usual?" Simon turns and addresses me. Sephy chortles.

"I haven't been here in a month, Simon, I'd hardly call it the usual." She's being confrontational, drumming her nails on the bar in an irritating and unceasing rhythm. I realise she reminds me of Haedes as she crosses and uncrosses her legs for the hundredth time, fidgeting within the confines of my leather jacket. She's restless, looking for a fight, and I know exactly what she would be doing right now to cure that restlessness if I wasn't here. The thought makes me irrationally angry, possessive, and pathetic in the single notion that someone who isn't me might assume to try and make her theirs.

"I wasn't talking to you," says Simon, narrowing his eyes as his lips twist into a smirk, pupils darting to me and turning lime as the club lights continue to phase through a rainbow spectrum.

"Wait— *what*?" Sephy's head snaps to the left, eyebrows quirking on her forehead as her eyes become suspicious slits.

"You're not the only one who likes Retro music." I make the excuse, knowing full well she isn't going to buy it.

"This isn't the only club in Chicago that spins the oldies you know!" she exclaims. I shrug.

"It's the one I knew about. I'm not exactly a local." I brush her off again.

Of course, she's right. There are hundreds of other venues I could have chosen, but none of them would have allowed me to make sure she wasn't getting herself into trouble. After all, the last guy she had a one-night stand with murdered her, so if she wants to blame it on my feelings for her, then she can shove it right up her—

"What's his usual?" she chortles to Simon, who pulls out a fancy glass bottle and a tumbler, setting it down in front of me.

Her face contorts with amusement as he pours me an orange juice, adding a cherry and ice with a tiny paper umbrella just because he's decided he suddenly enjoys my utter humiliation. I look down at the tiny umbrella, contemplating stabbing him in the eye with it, but then sigh out, realising my rage isn't directed at him at all.

Fuck it. I take the umbrella and stick it behind one ear, smiling at Sephy and deciding to own my fanciful and fruity drink as I take a dainty sip.

Simon pours Sephy a whisky with the customary duo of ice cubes, and I watch her trying to contain her laughter but failing dismally.

The truth is I'm not mad about the drink, or Simon. I would happily sit here with this drink, letting Sephy laugh at me, if she and I were still engaging in— sex? A relationship? Demon friend-with-benefits type liaisons? Whatever you'd call it.

As it is, I haven't touched her in weeks, and for someone who re-pressed their sexual urges for so long, I'm having a hard time shoving them back down where they belong. It makes me on edge, makes me want to hit things, makes me want to take her the way I know she likes. But I'm a fucking gentleman, so until she says otherwise, my hands are tied in the least kinky of ways. I realise as her lips purse together and her laughter ceases that I'm staring at her and have been for longer than I should.

"You know I fucking hate you right now," she reveals.

I cock an eyebrow.

"It's because you know I work this umbrella better than you ever could, isn't it?" I try to keep the mood light, but the truth is my heart is hammering in my chest.

"No, it's because you and I had a great thing going, and you ruined it," she blurts as though the mere presence of alcohol in front of her has unlocked the truths she keeps so carefully hidden.

I roll my eyes.

"I didn't do anything. You're the one who—" I begin, and she downs the whiskey in front of her in a single gulp before ordering another. I steel myself for the conversation in front of me, knowing it's not going to be pleasant.

"I told you. I told you about the feelings. I said to you, '*Don't let this get serious. I can't take that kind of risk.*' It's not like I was acting all gooey and shit for you," she complains, scowling at the mosaic mirror in front of her and avoiding eye contact altogether.

"Oh, I'm sorry, Miss— *When I look into my future, all I see is you—*" I bat my eyelids and bring my hands up to cup my chin, the bristle of my thick stubble rubbing against my palms.

"Yeah well, at least I'm not trying to replace you already—" The words fly from her lips, confrontational, and I see her for what she is. Exposed, hurting— jealous maybe?

What, does she think that I've been coming here to pick up other women?

I almost spit juice as I cock my head.

"Are you fucking insane? I've only been coming here to stop you getting it on with some other dude!" I blurt, and she flushes under the disco lights, the music in the background seeming to disappear altogether as we reach the ugly truth of it all.

I don't want to sleep with anyone but her.

She doesn't want me to sleep with anyone but her.

"So, let me get this straight. You think I'd say I love you—" I begin, but she covers her ears and begins humming loudly. I sigh, exasperated.

"*Laaa laaa laaa*— I can't hear you!" she yells at me, eyes wide and posture stiff, uncomfortable at yet another confession. I grab her hands, pulling them from her ears, and raise my voice over the incessant wailing now pouring from what I have always considered, until now, a sweet pair of lips.

"You honestly think I'd say that and then come find another woman? I don't want another fucking woman. I want you, dumbass!" I find myself screaming the words, a cathartic release I hadn't known I truly needed until right now. Her lips falter and then purse firmly as her cognac irises diminish in their furious blaze, the gaze between us all-consuming. I turn away, unable to get lost in her because I know that her next instinct will be to run.

But she doesn't.

Instead, she simply says, "I have a question for you."

"Go for it." I shrug, taking another sip of orange juice and letting it run, tart, down my throat.

"If you had to choose between saving my life and saving the lives of hundreds, maybe even thousands— what would you choose?" Her eyes become intense at the core, and I feel her stare, boring into the side of my face like a pneumatic drill as I ponder this for a moment.

I don't know what she wants me to say.

What is it with her?

Why is everything always some kind of fucking test?

If I say her, then I'm morally reprehensible; if I don't say her, then she might conclude that I don't really love her at all.

Women!

As Haedes had once told me, you can't live with them— and that's about it.

"Well?" she pushes me for an answer, bringing the glass of renewed firewater to her lips and drinking deep as she glances at me sideways over the rim.

"Well, for one thing, I'd expect you to save your damn self. Being able to convect and throw fire and all that—" I announce, attempting to avoid whatever it is she's trying to insinuate.

"Xion! That's not the point. Answer! My life or the lives of many strangers?" She scowls, swallowing too fast and causing a small hiss to escape her lips.

"This is such a bullshit question," I grumble, still not wanting to answer. She crosses her legs.

"See, that's what you don't understand. Haedes— he had to give up everything he loved for the cause of some higher calling. I'm not going there. I've lost enough. Look at Luce. She couldn't choose the greater good, and it's doomed us all." She places the glass down on the bar and looks miserably into its depths.

"So, you're saying you love me?" I whisper, too hopeful.

"Are you fucking crazy? I'm saying even if I did— which *I don't* — it doesn't fucking matter! It's a surefire way to put you six feet under! I'm not going to be the one responsible for that. The world doesn't give a shit about happily ever after. About tying crap up in a neat little bow.

What's the point in even trying? Everything just falls apart anyway—" she concludes, never more serious.

Blinking slowly, I ponder her words and realise that she will never allow herself to fall for me, not now, not ever. It isn't even her fault. I also come to realise, in a single second, that I no longer give a shit about having feelings for her. If the world is going to hell, I would rather burn for her than alone.

"I—" I look at her, reaching out and placing a hand on the small of her back and biting my bottom lip.

"Xion— don't do that stupid face at me," she growls.

I refuse to move.

"Look, why do you give a crap if I love you? You clearly don't reciprocate, right? I don't see why it should stop us enjoying each other. I'm not going to ask you for a commitment. I promise. I just—" I trace her bottom lip with my thumb, wiping away a single drop of whiskey and licking it off as words fail me.

"So, you're saying you don't give a crap that I don't love you back? You're not upset?" she sounds incredulous, fidgeting atop the barstool and uncrossing then re-crossing her legs yet again. I smile slightly at her dumbfounded expression, adoring the hope kindling in the back of her eyes. I don't want to waste any more time being apart. Not if everything is going to hell. Not if it really is the end.

"I can't love you just for me? I've never felt like this— I'd rather die being with you than survive alone. Honestly. I don't want to go back to before— before I knew you. Everything was so empty— so endless. Please don't make me go back to that. I miss— *it*. With you." My eyes roll over her figure, caressing the curve of her, taking in her long legs and savouring every inch of damp exposed skin.

"You miss— *it?*" she bites her bottom lip too, staring up at me from beneath wide fans of black lashes that she knows I can't resist.

Adrenaline floods my system.

"More than anything. Sephy— what if it's really the end? What if none of it really matters?" I ask her, thinking back to the blood and ichor smeared all over the warehouse floor.

"Xion. I don't— I just—" she stutters, hesitant even still, and so I do the only thing left to do. I plunge forward and I kiss her, tasting cinnamon and whiskey melding into one upon my tongue. She groans despite herself, and I end the kiss abruptly, looking down into her eyes as she stares up at me, never having seemed so innocent.

"I don't want to waste any more time. Call it screwing around, fun, a relationship, friends with benefits— *I don't care*, Sephy. I just need this. I need you. If not, what's the point in fighting for any of this? What's the point in trying to survive it all if I'm not going to fucking live while I'm at it? I'll take the risk, shoulder the burden. I don't care if you never love me, but I want to be the one who gets to hold you, whether that be in the flames of the apocalypse or not. I don't give a fucking damn anymore." I'm out of breath by the time I finish the rant, and I watch as she sighs, moving to stare at Simon who is watching us both, transfixed.

"What the fuck did you put in his drink?" she demands, eyes wide. They both burst into laughter.

The night continues, and we both fall into silence as she finishes off more drinks than I'm sure is sensible. She doesn't look at me for a long time, simply sipping and thinking.

Finally, she turns to me.

"I'm sorry," she whispers, and I stare at her, shaking my head.

She looks so guilty but, nonetheless, more content than I've seen her since four weeks ago when I first made my feelings known.

"I'm not, and I never will be. No matter what happens," I vow.

SEPHY

He says he's fine with it. With all of it. With me not loving him— with us screwing around.

What the fuck am I supposed to say to that?

I'm too exhausted to fight the urge to be with him as well as trying to keep everyone around me at the manor from falling apart. So, I guess we're back on again. I mean he has a point. If the world goes to hell, it won't matter who I'm sleeping with. Life is short.

So— this is fine?

This is fine. *Right?*

Sleeping with a guy I'm somewhat addicted to who is in love with me— who I can never love back.

Oh yeah, this is totally fine.

About as fine as a shitstorm in the middle of hurricane season.

But— fuck it, right?

He says it's fine.

So, it's fine.

Is it though?

Fine, I mean—

The conundrum spins around on repeat in my head as I continue to sip drink after drink. I've been on the hard stuff quite a lot lately back at the estate. What with Xion becoming a permanent fixture in my suite and The Furies deciding to use the low-hanging chandelier in the main lobby as target practice, a good drink is the least I deserve.

Tolerance for liquid spirits heightened, me and Xion have been sitting in silence for quite a while, simply drinking and listening to the music when the song changes.

Both our heads turn to the DJ manning a booth at the far end of the deserted space before we look at each other, eyes sparkling and lips unable to stop themselves from curving into matching smiles.

"Would you like to—" Xion asks, and I grab his hand without answering, pulling him down off the bar stool. I've been here with him before, and alone, but we've never actually taken to the dancefloor together to, you know, dance. My last altercation with Xion here had led to him hauling me out of the club fireman style— from what I remember anyway.

A perfect fusion of Kygo, the artist responsible for our last dance upon the top of his apartment building during a spark shower and, unbelievable as it is, Marvin Gaye have come together, giving us an upbeat remix of *Sexual Healing*. This could not be more perfect.

He raises his arm as both our faces are speckled over with pure white light from the disco ball. I spin beneath it, beckoning him. He catches me as I pull away and yanks me back toward his body, bringing his lips close to my ear and audibly inhaling.

"Come here you," he growls, tone a low rumble as I bring my long fingers up to splay out over his heart, knowing full well the scar in the shape of my palm still lies beneath.

Why had I done that?

Branded him?

I try not to think about it. After all, it's such a permanent mark for somebody who will inevitably be a temporary attachment.

30

Our feet dance, effortlessly coordinated despite Xion's usual lack of grace or finesse. I press my torso, hot, into his rigid abdomen, looking up at him as I snake my arms around his neck and then let myself bend backwards, flashing him my cleavage as I do so. I inhale as I meld back into his solid silhouette, letting my fingers wander up the back of his t-shirt and causing goosebumps to rise, unstoppable, along his spine.

The song is overwhelming, with everything around us dissolving under the weight of the way we readily touch each other after such long refrain. I sigh, closing my eyes and feeling my long lashes tickle the very top of my cheekbones as I bite my bottom lip and continue to sway. Turning, I try to avoid kissing him as I know I won't be able to stop, but he catches me, pulling me so my back is flush against his chest and his arms are tight around my waist. He bends down, kissing my shoulder and breathing, slow and heavy, into the crook of my neck.

I'm terrified, terrified that he will get hurt, more terrified that I'll have to truly give this up forever, but what I'm terrified most of is letting this night slip away without taking full advantage of our sudden openness.

I want him. All of him.

It's been too long, which makes me undeniably angry, not just at him for saying the stupid words that caused all this trouble, but also at myself for running yet again.

I don't speak, afraid that words might only shatter the sexual tension growing between us as I press the curve of my ass into his crotch, continuing to swing my hips to the intoxicating beat. Making my decision, I grab one of his hands from around my waist and turn on the spot before letting the flames of my desire consume us both right there.

We rematerialize, leaning against the passenger side door of my car, and I immediately begin to kiss Xion under the hot and heavy blanket of the night's dark clouds.

I was serious when I said I had no desire to return to the estate until it was absolutely necessary, but that doesn't mean I'm going to deny myself what I crave either.

The world around us is silent as the sound of my pounding heart and rushing blood fills my head. He tastes, as ever, like pomegranate, but this time, there's a too-sweet edge of cherry juice upon his lips, causing my tongue to flick out in a gentle caress, hungry.

"Sephy—" I hear him say my name, not in the groan I had hoped but in confusion.

"Shh— please don't speak. That never ends well, and I want to— *you know*—" I whisper against his lips. I hear him sigh and lean back slightly, looking into his confused eyes.

"I want to — I just — isn't this a bit public?" he asks, and I cock my eyebrow.

"The car has tinted windows," I remind him, looking at the dark glass on which he's leaning.

"In— *in the car*?" he looks like I've just offered him the keys to a candy store and I nod, laughing at his over-amorous grin.

He pulls me back to him, cupping my chin and moaning into my open mouth as I feel his abs tense and his erection grow with anticipation. I grind my hips into him, pinning him to the passenger side door, urging him on as the caress of his skin washes away the chill of the night.

We must kiss without stopping for at least five minutes, and everything disappears, that is until the car alarm goes off in a deafening and unapologetic screech, causing us both to jump and then burst out laughing.

At least it isn't a Banshee.

Sex with one demon present is enough.

Xion takes the keys from his back pocket and unlocks the car with the impatient stab of a button. I take his hand from my waist, leading him around the hood with a provocative stride and opening the driver's side door before lowering myself into the driver's seat with a dirty grin.

I position myself as I have done a few times before, promptly kicking off my shoes and throwing them onto the passenger seat as I wriggle out of my leather pants. If I'd known I was going to be getting my exhibition on, I might have gone with a skirt, which in my opinion is the only justification for wearing one.

Hindsight is a bitch.

I push the seat all the way back, the way I would if I was eight feet tall and trying to fit behind the wheel comfortably, before reclining the plush leather seat and pulling off Xion's leather jacket. It goes into the pile with my pants and shoes, and with a final swoop of my arms over my head, I'm sat in the driver's seat in only a black lacey thong and matching bra.

"Get in—" I call, looking up at Xion and tracing his body with my eyes, having missed his hard-cut lines, his unrivalled definition.

He doesn't hesitate, crawling into the footwell of the car, the steering wheel uncomfortably close to his back, before unzipping his fly and pulling his boxers down so that I can see him, fully exposed now, as he climbs on top of me.

He slams the door shut as he goes, and all bets are off.

In the enclosed space of the car, we become enveloped in not only one another but in our own private world where nothing can hurt us except each other, where nobody else exists. The only things that do exist are the heavy panting, groans, and moans which escape us in moments of unstoppable surrender.

It starts gentle, him moving my panties to one side and easing into me as I spread my legs and pop my feet on the dashboard. He kisses my collarbone and the top of my breasts, but soon, within the confines of the hot leather and the proximity of our gently perspiring skin, things start to become desperate, angry even.

He thrusts so I cry out, giving me all I can take as his left hand rests on my breast, squeezing tightly, and the other presses hard against the tinted glass of the car window. I watch his knuckles turn white out of the corner of my eye as he crushes me into the leather of the seat, unforgiving and merciless in his constant and unending punishment of the deepest part of me.

It's delicious, exactly what I wanted, and so I dig my fingers into his back, only spurring him on further. I let my hands run the course of his torso as he backs away, kneeling as upright as possible and watching me, towering over me as he takes me stroke for stroke, the hardness of his pelvis hitting me in exactly the right spot but not quickly enough to send me over the edge.

It's torturous, excruciating, and I dig my nails into his ass, pushing him into me, selfishly craving my release.

As I'm about to climax, mouth forming a wide 'O', he stills, causing me to cry out in frustration.

I open my eyes from where they've been screwed up, but what I see isn't what I expect.

Looming over me now is not Xion but the demon inside of him. His skin is scorched charcoal, and his shirt has ripped where he's transformed. I'm so close I'd barely noticed the change, but as he looks at me, eyes glowing orange and molten-looking tattoos shedding light over my trembling body, I can feel he's gotten even wider, even harder than before.

I don't know what he expects me to do.

To stop maybe, to be scared?

I'm not.

I want my damn orgasm.

"Well, what are you waiting for?" I demand, impatient as I place my fingers between my breasts and unclip my bra from the front. The flimsy black lace falls aside, exposing me, and I see him become practically feral as his scorched ashen lips plunge to my puckered skin, causing me to cry out. Running my fingers through his thick black hair, I inhale the scent of smoky pomegranates before forcing his lips up to mine and tongue kissing him so tightly he can't pull away. I embed my heels in his muscular back, bringing my knees up, determined to find my release.

I kiss him one last time before laying back fully in the seat and letting him lean over me, smashing into me repeatedly with slick, hot ease until the waves of pleasure become a dark and dangerous ocean for me to drown in.

I come.

Finally.

In a torrent of brutal pleasure, my muscles ripple around him, pushing him over the edge too. I watch as a demonic growl escapes his charred lips and his entire body becomes hard as rock, teeth bared, lips pulled back, eyes wide, his pupils dilating with the shock of what we've just done.

The last thing I feel before I pass out in ecstasy is him emptying himself, scorching, into me.

The last thing I hear is smashing glass.

3

OUR HOUSE

SEPHY

AN EARLY HOUR'S CHILL seeps in through the broken window beside Xion as I wrap his jacket around me and we speed consistently toward Forest Glen. I stare at the shattered glass, then at his bloody, pale knuckles hanging relaxed over the steering wheel, trying to contain a smile.

His eyes flick to examine me with absolutely no subtlety, so I turn away, enjoying the silence as every single muscle in my body tingles, held happily hostage by the aftermath of clenching and releasing so pleasurably beneath him.

As we creep closer to the Sinclair Estate, an inevitable wave of anxiety begins to extinguish my happy glow, the foreboding nothing short of an underreaction.

My house has descended into madness.

I mean I'd say hell, but I'm pretty sure that was more organised.

I put my feet up on the dash, no longer needing to deeply inhale the leather to smell pomegranates, mainly because I'm both suitably and happily drenched in both his sweat and scent. It wafts from my hair, from between my thighs, from the crook of my neck where he sighed my name, from my lips that he claimed repeatedly and unmistakably his. I reach up to touch them, finding the flesh plump and raw, a state I've sorely missed.

"How was she when you left?" I ask him suddenly, realising that I can't run from things at the estate any longer by focusing on the unstable and fleeting fantasy of us. I've put off coming back here for as long as I can, but now as we gobble the miles, I know I need to prepare myself.

"The same," is the only response Xion gives. I watch as his facial muscles tense, jaw becoming rigid with words and emotions unspoken. I know Luce's current condition is affecting him worse than anyone; I mean she's been his only family for as long as he can remember.

I don't pry; don't want to shatter the calm that we've finally found after everything as the rest of the drive passes in a blur of building anticipation and an equally unpleasant anti-climax. I always feel this way when I return to the estate, mainly because when I leave, I psych myself up for this epic fight and, on my return, realise my struggle on the streets isn't making a single bit of difference.

The electric gates of the Sinclair Estate whir open as we turn onto the alabaster gravel of the road flanked by two identical copses of trees. I used to find comfort in this small forest, in the way I could always get lost in it and escape the scrutiny of my uncle, but for some reason, now the shadowy spaces between the trees have become foreboding, ominous even, and even peering into the darkness from afar gives me a paranoid tingle that creeps like slow freezing water up my spine.

As the drive down the long gravel road, which moves on to cut through the ever-luscious lawns, concludes, I look out over the grounds.

It's still out there in the night, quiet even, which unnerves me deeply. I'm not used to the quiet here, not used to peace, not anymore.

Xion parks the car outside the house lazily, and we both twist in our seats, turning our backs on one another and the events that have passed inside before exiting the vehicle. The lights inside the main house are still on, blazing out onto the white of the surrounding gravel and turning it phantasmal. I look up at the immense contrasting darkness of the building, letting a small sigh escape my lips as we head back into the trenches.

The towering dark wood of the double doors creaks as Xion pushes them open after we clamber up the mocha stone steps, and I find myself confronted by an underwhelming scene to say the least.

There's no fighting, no weapon throwing that I can discern; the only thing of note is Jules sitting laid back on the couch with his feet on the coffee table, pinching his nose while holding an ice pack to his forehead, and the smell of rotting egg.

"You're back," he announces, nasal tone relieved as I close the front doors behind me. Striding across the black and white chequered marble, I examine him, finding a large amount of blood on his usually flawless white suit shirt and a tampon stuffed up his nose.

"What the hell happened?" I demand, peering at him as I weave through the many couches and slump in an armchair next to him, staring and unapologetically curious.

"Oh, this? Well, since you asked. The Furies decided to practice ambush tactics at the top of the staircase. I fell. I also borrowed one of your tampons for a little damage control. Hope you don't mind—" He glares at me, removing the ice pack and revealing an enormous swollen black bump on his forehead.

"I uh, don't even want it back— it's yours to keep and everything," I volunteer, peering at the blood-soaked wad half dangling from one of his nostrils.

"You're too kind." He gives me one final glare before tilting his head back once again and sighing, clearly pissed. "Did it even occur to you when you offered this place to three archaic feminists and the devil that maybe they're not suited for this dimension?" Jules asks me. He doesn't look directly at me though, just at the ceiling as his words, laced with disdain and incredulity, echo into nothingness.

"Nope." I sigh, knowing it was a rash decision but unsure of what else I was supposed to do. I couldn't exactly set them up at the goddamn Hilton, could I?

"What's that smell?" Xion asks, breaking the silence surrounding the unspoken question I'd been hoping to avoid. Jules tilts his head forward, glaring at Xion who already knows the answer, but before he can retort we are interrupted by the sound of Cerb barking frantically and then, another sound— horse hooves.

"Uh, Jules? Where exactly are The Furies?" I demand, words spilling from me fast.

"I've been a little busy you know! Why don't you put a bell on them?!" he huffs, and I twist in my seat as fear pools in my gut.

From the left wing of the house, Cerb appears. A brown and black fluffy blur, barking at the top of his lungs. I move to call him, but before I can so much as inhale, he's already gone. Moments later, I see why. Nightshade comes thundering across the marble, her hooves smashing into the floor as Erin and Ericka urge her onward, weapons drawn high into the air, after the Leonberger.

My eyes widen as Xion's expression becomes a mix of shock and awe.

Acting without thinking, I launch myself to my feet before convecting so I'm five feet in front of the horse. The flames spook her, and she rears up, tossing both Furies from her back in the process. I raise my hands into the air, trying to calm her as she whinnies, hooves narrowly missing my face as she lands back on all fours with a thud. Blowing hot air from both nostrils, she shuffles restlessly from foot to foot.

"Xion, take the horse outside!" I bark, fury rising like hot venom in my throat as I thrust the leather of her reins at him. He doesn't argue, taking them from me and leading Nightshade from the main hall with an uncomfortable grimace that instantly tells me he isn't a huge fan of horses. I'm not surprised. I mean he doesn't exactly have the finesse riding requires.

"What the hell are you doing?!" I yell, looking down at the two women splayed on the marble floor beneath the scorn of my gaze. If I wasn't so pissed, I'd probably smirk as Erin is wearing a white shirt that says *The Future Is Female* and Ericka is sporting the same style, but which reads *#FREETHENIPPLE* across the front in unapologetic bold font.

"We were merely practising—" Erin begins, but I cock my head, trying hard not to unleash some serious firepower in the middle of the hall.

"You stay away from my dog and my horse! You hear me? They're not weapons or toys for your amusement! Got that?" I yell, a wave of sudden exhaustion falling over me. The two Furies get to their feet, posture rigid as their faces remain expressionless. There is no guilt there, and it's often I wonder if they have room for any emotion except the fury that's braided itself into every part of them. Without it, they would surely cease to be.

"Understood." Erin nods, eyes flicking to Jules without apology.

"Go to your room and go to bed. It's three in the morning. And make sure you take Erlea with you, I don't want to find her slicing up perfectly good fruit again with her Katana." I sigh as the strength in my voice falters, fatigued from my sudden outburst. The two women walk in bare feet and without shame from the lobby.

I look back to Jules, shaking my head.

"Fun never stops around here, huh?" I try to dissolve the tension between us, but Jules' bloody nose and throbbing temple make it harder than usual. I continue, "I'm sorry. I know you didn't ask for any of this. I know it's shit— but I don't know what I was supposed to do. If I'd given them over to Colonel Footface, they'd probably be getting split open on some slab for crazy ass tests right now. I can't do that to them. It's my fault they're stuck here." Guilt pulls at me again and Jules' eyes soften as he sits back down on the plush couch behind him.

"It's not your fault," he sighs, taking the ice pack from his head and slumping, an unusual pose for him for sure. I can see now the exhaustion that's overcome us both as his head hangs low for a few seconds. He looks up at me after about a minute, green eyes dull in the tungsten glow of the overhead chandelier.

"If I hadn't been brought back to life we wouldn't be in this mess," I remind him, and he shakes his head.

"You didn't ask to be brought back to life, Sephy. The fault here doesn't lie with you."

"Then why do I feel so guilty?" I ask, biting down on my still-plump bottom lip.

"Because, despite yourself and what you'd like everyone to believe, you aren't the kind of person who doesn't give a damn." Jules' words strike something within me, something resistant which makes me want to argue back, to tell him he doesn't know me as well as he thinks he does, but before I have the chance, familiar heavy footfall is approaching. I turn to see Xion, a nervous Cerb trotting slowly in his wake.

"Is she okay?" I demand, and he nods, grimacing.

"She was pretty spooked, but I got her locked away— I don't know what they were thinking." He shakes his head as Cerb pads from behind his knees and moves over to me. I bury my fingers in the spot he loves behind his ears, looking into the enormous brown eyes and trying to help him find some semblance of calm among our new madness.

"I don't think that thought is something they put into much of anything. They're ancient beings running off pure fury," I remind him, and he nods.

"Jules, I need you to make some calls. Firstly, I need you to find some temporary accommodation for Nightshade—" I announce.

Jules looks surprised.

"Seriously? But— she's yours." He looks hesitant, knowing how much of a stress killer riding can be for me.

"She is mine. My responsibility. She can't stay here while The Furies and Luce are living here. If tonight is proof of anything, it's that she deserves to be somewhere where she can feel safe. Not be taken out for training exercises by the three incredibly angry stooges," I remind him, and he nods, looking sad. "Secondly," I continue, "I need you to get the window of my Vanquish fixed."

His eyes widen.

"What happened?" he asks, removing the tampon from his nose gently and dabbing at his upper lip, checking for blood flow.

"Nothing serious. Just a demon, you know, the usual." I brush off the question, but my answer isn't technically a lie either. I just don't think he needs to know that the demon was Xion and that he and I were fucking at the time.

"Unfortunately, I do know." His expression is deadpan, and I almost want to laugh. I used to ask him to bring me my breakfast, run me a bath, and show out my one-night stands. Now he's cleaning up after demons and trying to wrangle The Furies. If it wasn't so hilarious, I'd probably feel sorry for him, but as it is, I can only bring myself to be uncontrollably amused.

As I move to get to my feet, a sudden yowl startles me. My eyes locate the source in seconds, finding Beelz walking the length of the bannister with untouchable feline elegance. Cerb's ears prick at the sound, but he doesn't move. Sometimes, I think he's far too used to the panther for his own good.

"Come to steal more steak, have you?" Jules demands, looking directly into the tangerine glow of the panther's eyes.

"Wait, she didn't steal the Kobe, right?" I enquire, feeling suddenly desperate. I've been looking forward to Kobe steak and eggs, which I've been promised, all week.

Jules looks aggravated as he turns to me.

"Damn it!" I cuss, crossing my arms over my chest and puffing out hot air from my cheeks.

"I left it out to marinate, and the damn panther took off with it into the woods." Jules purses his lips, anger simmering just behind the surface of his eyes. Arguably he's more pissed about the steak than being sent flying down the stairs, which I can't help but find borderline hilarious.

"How did she get in the kitchen?" I ask, suspecting the answer.

"How do you think?" He cocks an eyebrow.

"Is that what that god-awful smell is?" Xion demands, picking up his line of questioning from before we were so rudely interrupted.

"Yep. She's been in there for hours, and I'm not going in there again. You know what happened last time." Jules glowers at Xion.

Unfortunately, all of us remember only too well what happened the last time Jules had tried to reclaim his kitchen from Luce. He had been found, bound and gagged, in the pantry with cow's blood smeared across his forehead and both cheeks. He hasn't taken Luce fresh towels since. Not that she would use them anyway. Ever since Thane left, she's been acting more animal than anything else.

"I'll go and get her out of there; I'm starving anyway," I promise him, placing a hand on his knee and giving a quick squeeze as I get to my feet.

"Come on, Xion," I call behind me, knowing I'll need him too if we are going to successfully negotiate with Little Miss Sunshine.

"There are sandwiches in the fridge," Jules informs me as I flash a quick smile over my shoulder.

He goes back to icing his head as Xion and I make our way under the overhang of the upstairs landing and toward the woman who had both saved and simultaneously doomed us all in a single careless act.

The kitchen had once, long ago, been one of my favourite rooms in the house. There are lots of cupboards, so a young me also found there were lots of places to hide from Peter. I remember once I'd gotten so engrossed in the book I was reading he hadn't found me for almost twenty-four hours. The police were called and everything.

I wonder now, as I step into the room and my boots click upon the continuation of black and white chequered marble, if he was really as frantic as he seemed. Had his desire to do away with me and claim the Sinclair Fortune been alive then? Or just a malicious twinkle in the depths of his far more youthful and less jaded eye?

The space is enormous and hasn't changed at all. It's entirely lined with thick walnut cabinets topped with coffee-coloured marble. Copper pans hang from the ceiling upon various racks, and beneath their ominous shadows, I find her, standing beside the kitchen island erected in the centre of the room.

My eyes scan her first, her dark matted hair looking like it hasn't been brushed in weeks. The baggy cotton round-neck hanging off her reads 'I've been to hell and back and all I got was this lousy t-shirt' and is paired with black leggings that are a little too big and her bare feet, which like the rest of her too white skin are mapped dark with black spidering veins running just beneath the surface. My eyes jump next to the kitchen, to the source of the smell.

On the hob, a solitary saucepan sits, smouldering.

Walking across the room, I go to remove the copper saucepan from the heat, but as I approach, I find myself face to face with the entire set of designer kitchen knives that Jules adores like they're his own children.

They hover, silent and malicious in the air just inches from me, a threat no doubt.

Xion exhales audibly behind me as though he's not sure Luce has even noticed he's here.

"What are you doing here?" she asks, voice hollow.

I stare at her, unable to take my eyes off the hovering blades for longer than a few moments. She hasn't moved her gaze to so much as look at me and, instead, is simply staring down at whatever it is she's contemplating on the kitchen island. I stare at her hands and find her fingers coated a deep burgundy, the colour of fresh arterial blood.

"We wanted to see if you needed any help," Xion replies, treading slowly over the marble floor and approaching her as soundlessly as he can manage.

"No. I'm fine," she mutters the lie like an incantation. The lie she always tells when she's teetering on the edge of dark oblivion. At this point, she might as well say nothing at all because all we hear is pain and denial.

"Let Sephy get to the hob, Luce. You're going to cause a fire," Xion warns her, placing a hand on her bony wrist as he leans over the kitchen island between them. Luce looks to me, finally, eyes chasmic. She blinks, and the knives clatter to the floor, making me startle as I release a breath I've been holding captive for at least a full minute.

She turns back to Xion, face stony.

"Happy now?" she demands, going back to staring at whatever it is she's holding in her hands.

I waste no time, rushing to the hob as swiftly as possible and looking into the depths of the smoking pan. Inside, a solitary and blackened egg lies, the water it had been boiling in long since gone, the shell charred and the stench unbearable.

I remove the pan from the stove, quickly shoving it into the nearest basin and blasting cold water into its scorching depths. Turning the ceramic rings off on the countertop using the touchscreen, I quickly move to Xion's side.

I find what Luce is playing with to be disturbing, but it's not the worst thing I've seen her do. In her hands lies the mangled corpse of a hare, flayed and bare between her fingers as she picks out its bones from between muscle and sinew.

"What's that for?" I ask, unable to stop myself. I'm not sure if that's because I'm more curious or afraid at this point.

"I am trying to get a prediction, to see how long it will be before Thane returns to me," she says calmly, the first time in weeks I've heard her utter Thane's name without hysterics or violence.

"With rabbit bones?" I ask her, and she nods, not replying as she uses her nails to prize open the poor thing's ribcage.

"Where have you two been?" she asks, dreamy in tone as though she's not even in the same room as us anymore.

"Demon hunting. There have been more attacks," I reply, and instantly regret it.

"Demons? Did they leave anything behind?!" She's eager now, dying for her next fix.

"Like what, a calling card?" I chuckle, trying to lighten the mood.

"No, bitch. Like things I can actually use. Bones, fur, teeth— even an eyeball would be more useful than the crap you've got lying around in this ridiculous excuse for a kitchen," she snarls, and I find myself having to bite my tongue. I could take her in a fight, I'm pretty sure, and some of the time I'm wondering why I haven't just handed her over to the guys with the pretty guns and let them deal with her attitude.

"No, and even if there was, I wouldn't bring them to you. You're not supposed to be using magic. Isn't that why Thane left?" I demand. Luce's eyes widen, nostrils flaring.

"No, impotent child. Thane left because you went and got yourself murdered by whoring around like the slut you are, and me being the gracious entity that I am, I saved your sorry life. That's why Thane left. Because of you." She is baring her teeth by the time the final word falls, and I momentarily consider throwing myself across the table and beating the shit out of her stupid ass face. Imbued with darkness or not, there's no need to be a bitch.

"Oh, hell no! Why don't you just fuck the hell off! Get out of my kitchen before I put you in the ground!" I exclaim, allowing my fingers to twitch and The Eternal Flame to materialise in my calloused palm.

She eyes me, and for a moment, I expect to have to convect out of the way of a barrage of flying kitchen knives. However, as Xion looks at her, his eyes now pleading, she merely walks from the room without another word.

After her footsteps have died into silence, I let the flame in my hand extinguish, muscles taking a few minutes to relax as I look at the disembowelled rabbit in front of me with disgust.

"She's getting worse." I look at Xion with a frustrated expression, eyes dark as his molten gaze rises to my face.

"I've never seen her like this. The Luce I know—" he begins, but I cut him off, placing my hands on my hips.

"Is gone. She's *gone*, Xion. And I don't know that it's safe for us to be living under the same roof if she's going to continue down this rabbit hole of self-destructive behaviour and denial. She's using magic even though it's bad for her, and now that Thane is gone, I'm not sure she has any intention of stopping," I theorise. He nods.

"You're right. But I think her being stuck in the house for so long might be part of the problem. If she had somewhere to direct her rage, maybe—" he begins, but I shake my head, causing his next words to die on his lips.

"You want me to set her loose on the city? Are you nuts?" I almost laugh, and he shrugs.

"I just think—"

"Look, I took a huge risk telling Colonel Bunion Brow that I had her under control, that she wasn't a threat. The last thing we need is her killing some taxi driver for looking at her two seconds too long. She's not stable enough to be let loose on the city. She's barely stable enough to boil a freaking egg," I remind him, gesturing to the pan in the sink. "Not only that, but if I take her out hunting and she starts collecting parts for her morbid pet projects, then my credibility with these military morons is shot to hell." I'm ranting now, my nostrils full of the smell of burned, rotting egg and too-fresh animal blood.

"Okay, okay. I get your point. I just— I don't know what to do," Xion admits.

"Me neither. This isn't exactly something that I studied in my degree. Nowhere in the classical studies curriculum at Oxford do they teach you how to deal with The Devil addicted to alchemy. Though, I should probably write them because that would have been way more useful than how to date stupid pottery," I muse, as ever, trying to keep things light. I mean, if I focus on how bad things are, on the potential apocalypse, I'll probably just drink myself to death and be done with it.

"Anyway, I'm starving. Do you want something to eat?" I ask Xion as my stomach gives an audible rumble.

"Yeah, that would be nice. Jules said there were sandwiches in the fridge," he reminds me, a small smile tugging at the corners of his lips.

"Ah, right, so he did." I turn on my heel, striding over to the double doors of the brass-finished refrigerator and yanking them open with delayed enthusiasm.

"Son of a bitch!" I exclaim, immediately furious.

"What? What is it?" Xion asks, brows rising sharply on his forehead. "Luce didn't leave you any surprises in there, did she? You know— of the dead variety?" he asks, and I shake my head.

"No. It's worse. Much worse." I sigh, scanning the fridge with a horrified expression. "Someone's eaten all the goddamn sandwiches."

Is nothing freaking sacred?

4

SMOOTH OPERATOR

PANDORA

HIS FINGERS SLITHER, SMOOTH and effortless, through the dark velvet of the sheets. I stare up into his green reptilian eyes, palm pressed against the cold flesh of his chest where his heart beats beneath my fingers, too calm perhaps.

Placing his knuckles on the edge of my jawbone, he strokes the side of my face, head on the pillow next to mine, gazing at me with half-interest.

"Satiated?" he asks me, his voice a low, deep hiss as it hits the cool air of the surrounding room.

"Yes." I swallow hard as the word falls from my lips and into the bed we're lying in. Secretly, I'm never sated. Not now I've discovered what real sexual pleasure feels like, what two bodies can create together when they meld in all the right places and work as one. He showed me, opened my eyes with his fingers and tongue, and I, in turn, have allowed him to claim me in a way no man ever has. It wasn't expected, and though I have the sneaking suspicion I'm falling in love with him, slowly and deliciously, neither of us ever speak of feeling. We don't need to. Everything he and I could ever say is spelled out, unmistakable, in black and white, across my skin as I shudder and shiver beneath the expert bite of his fingertips.

He sits up on the side of the bed, tearing away the warmth we've kindled as he pulls back the sheets and dangles his long, spindled legs over the edge of the mattress. I reach out to touch his spine but hesitate, knowing I must remain cautious despite everything. I don't want to. I want to surrender to this single sacred thing, somehow flourishing within my very own hell. Yet, I am not naïve enough nor careless enough to fully relinquish the defences I've built over so many years.

Pulling back my fingers, I close them into a fist and allow them to rest over my breast as I roll onto my side and watch Gorgon dress. The way he moves has become a fascination of mine. His effortless and swift gait might as well be liquid smoke. His steps are always silent, his breath always perfectly controlled within his narrow ribcage. He slides into his clothes like a snake re-adopting shed skin, flawless and without pause as the layers of cotton and velvet come to once again encase him.

As he buttons up his black shirt with disciplined haste, a knock at the door startles us both, the hypnotic spell his motion casts over me broken.

He strides, waiting only until the final button on his shirt is neatly settled between his pectorals, and opens the door, revealing a mortal servant in a grandiose and practised motion, slick as oil.

"Yes?" he barks, tone clipped. His narrow shoulders barely eclipse the servant from view, and I watch as he peers over Gorgon's shoulder. The man is curious, and I meet his gaze while pulling the sheets around myself, smiling at him. I'm not ashamed.

Why should I be?

"There's a visitor for Her Highness—" The scrawny looking mortal blinks once, then twice, dark eyes shimmering with an all-engulfing fear that pleases me immensely.

"Who is it?" I demand, interested beyond what I would admit.

Who would dare come into my kingdom unannounced? Have they not heard that Mortaria is now mine? That the demons once again feast on what is rightfully theirs?

"I— I don't know. I told him to wait to in the throne room for you," the servant replies, pushing his thin lips into a hard and uncomfortable line.

"You didn't ask his name?" I query him, tone sharp. I sit bolt upright as my face becomes marred by a deep frown, observing his fear.

"He said you wouldn't come if he told me his name," the servant admits, turning slightly green like he might be sick.

"Well, my curiosity is piqued. I'll be down in a moment," I respond, shooing the mortal with a fluttering of my long fingers and turning my back on the door as Gorgon closes it quietly.

"You're not concerned?" he enquires. I shrug.

"Why should I be? I have armies of demons and five extremely powerful Demon Lords on my side. I have very little to fear, wouldn't you agree?" I ask him, brushing the knotty tendrils of my inky black hair back over one shoulder. Getting to my feet, I let the sheets fall to the mattress.

I walk, nude, over to the closet on the opposing wall, quickly selecting a simple, shimmering onyx gown and an intimidating black overcoat to top off the look.

"One can never be too careful, Pandora. After all, if I know anything at this point it is that snakes are everywhere." His comment causes me to raise my eyes from where they have fallen to the gown pooled in a puddle of glistening fabric on the floor. I step into it, the stretchy material hugging all my curves as I pull it up over my shoulders.

"What's that supposed to mean?" I bite.

His eyes caress me with silent contentment.

"Just that I want you to be careful. Taking a kingdom is one thing, keeping it is quite another." He sounds wise, but I'm wondering if he's not trying to make me doubt myself. After all, if it weren't for my instincts, for my plans and my careful observation of the powers that had once ruled this place, we wouldn't be here.

"Thanks for the advice, but I can handle myself," I retort, placing the coat over my shoulders and letting the narrow cut slim my silhouette, smoothing my curves and creating an air of invincibility, of untouchable godly grace, around me.

"Very well, and so I leave you."

Gorgon gives a curt nod, turning on his polished heel and exiting the chambers within the blink of a double-lidded eye.

I turn to the mirror hanging over the mantle, flattening my dishevelled hair and giving myself the once over before nodding with narcissistic satisfaction. I turn, and with a final glance back over the edgy and well-defined line of my shoulder, I leave the chamber. As I depart, the sheets upon which Gorgon and I played for the last hour or so remain messy in my wake.

I stride down the corridor; the place lit bloody courtesy of Barbas and Abraxis. I can hear the scuttle of Phobias, and yet where exactly they're dwelling overhead remains a mystery.

At the end of the long expanse of smoky quartz that glides beneath the train of both my skirt and overcoat, I turn right, making my way towards the throne room. *My* throne room. Mortals bow their heads in respect as I pass, and I try extremely hard not to give them evidence of the glee this sparks inside. I hold my head a little higher, my shoulders straighter, and make my strides more grandiose as they open the throne room doors and I make my entrance, sweeping around the corner without pause.

The person waiting for me inside the throne room isn't who I expect.

"Well, this is a surprise," I announce, banal tone ricocheting against the chasmic high ceilings with razor-sharp intent. It has been made to look as though it is billowing with the indigo clouds of dusk, every now and then a lightning fork splitting through the stone, a momentary and entirely faux fracture.

"Really? I thought it would be obvious I'd show up at some point. After all, I am Zeus' messenger boy." Hercules cocks a far too well-groomed eyebrow, blue eyes sparkling like the eternally burning Aetherial sun.

He's sitting in my newly commissioned throne, made from the splintered and jagged remnants of what had once been The Hollow, head thrown back over one arm as his too-muscular body struggles to fit into its narrow dimensions. He looks uncomfortable, but I don't know why this occurs to me as an observation because it's not his throne to sit upon. He should look damn uncomfortable.

"So, you've come to what? Deliver a threat from the almighty bonehead?" I cross my arms, cocking one hip as I mentally tally the numbers of both mortals and demons I have at my disposal. Hercules might be an extraordinary being for a Demi-God, but he's still only one person. I could have him torn apart in seconds.

"Actually, I was sent here to kill you." he pulls an underwhelming manmade broadsword out from his thick leather belt as he gets to his feet, voice perfectly calm. He places the flat edge of the blade into his enormous palm, examining it in the now violet light.

"I see." I exhale, opening my arms to him. "Well, I suppose you had better get on with it then. Not that it won't end in your immediate demise." I invite him to end me, to carry out the orders of the father I know he loathes.

He looks up from beneath the feathered strawberry blonde strands of his fringe, a cunning smile marring his stereotypically attractive masculinity with a cruel and unexpected edge.

"Oh, I'm not going to kill you, but thanks for the invitation. Not that I need it." He continues to smirk, too white teeth stark against the shadows. I laugh at him, pushing my wild hair behind one ear, a slight and intentional blush flooding my face.

"Of course, you need it. This is my kingdom now, Hercules, in case you haven't noticed. If you lay so much as an unwanted finger on me, I'll have you ripped apart by more demons than your pitiful mind can imagine," I threaten him, lips pulling back over my teeth in a snarl. He cocks his head, expression underwhelmed, and laughs.

"Oh, I've noticed. In fact, I might be the only one. Nobody in The Higher Plains seems to be very concerned. I mean they sent me all by myself. So, you're obviously not much of a threat, are you?" His voice is incredulous, amusement running deep.

I ball my fist, letting my nails bite into the soft white flesh of my palm. Worried my anger will make me reckless with my words, I don't even reply.

"Anyway, I wanted to warn you. To help you if you like. I don't see that there's much of a problem with someone other than my father or one of my uncles ruling this place, but the issue arises when that person is stupid enough to think she has mustered the undying loyalty of The Demon Lords," he explains, and I stalk past him, allowing my shoulder to knock into his solid mass as I head for my throne.

"What do you mean?" I ask, curious despite my better judgement. I cross my legs beneath the shimmering black fabric of my long sheer skirt as I take a seat in the high-backed throne, facing him.

"You don't have the power to keep control over Mortaria. You're not a God, or even a Demi, you're a failed Titan relying on the power of others for security. You want to take revenge on my father; I get it. He probably has it coming, but your agenda is not the only one with potential to come to fruition through your actions," he informs me. I frown.

Does he think I'm stupid?

"I don't know what you're implying—" I begin, but he cuts me off, a bold move for someone standing uninvited in my throne room.

"That much is painfully obvious. Even to me, a lowly Demi-God. I am simply trying to warn you. You might succeed in taking down the walls between dimensions to get your revenge— but do you honestly think you'll get that far? The Gods of Ancient won't bow to you, for they have no gratitude, only lust for power. And their children, The Demon Lords, will certainly kill you before you have a chance to set foot in The Higher Plains. They're using you. You are a pawn, don't

50

you see?" he announces this like it's some big reveal, some plot twist in a novel I have not seen coming.

I shake my head, lips twisting into a smile.

"So, if you think I'm so ill-equipped for this, that I'm a pawn, why not kill me and be done with it? Why not take down the Exilia with that sword of yours? Are you not Hercules? Son of Zeus?" I whisper, watching as the confidence in his eyes flickers like my words have almost won in snuffing out his spirit. His biceps tense, revealing his weakness, and I smirk.

He knows he cannot take back this place single-handedly. He knows the demonic presence here is more powerful than anyone, including him, expected. I've flummoxed them, a darkness they had not seen coming, and Zeus hates his brother so much I doubt he will listen to what Haedes has to say on the matter. He will use this to inflate his pride, to make his brother look weak, and to exaggerate his failure. Because in his mind I truly am no threat, that much is clear. Little did he know his son would soon come to learn of my great power as well. Even if he would never admit it.

So, he finds himself in a predicament. He must return with results, with answers, a hero, and yet he also cannot tell them the truth. This being that he is not strong enough to carry out the deed in question.

So, his alternate solution is what?

To negotiate with me to save his stupid reputation.

It would almost be funny if it weren't so unbelievably sad.

The great Hercules, bargaining with me, the shunned and fallen Titan, to save the reputation he holds with a god I despise.

It's a disgrace, the personal crap that dictates the fate of our universe. You'd think by now the gods would have learned not to let personal feelings of grandeur and egotism get in the way of doing what's best for the fate of everything they hold dear. But alas, no. The man in front of me is trying to strike a bargain, trying to kindle a fear of betrayal in me so that he doesn't have to go snivelling back to his father a failure. He proves yet again that he isn't worthy of a place among them.

Pathetic.

"You cannot cause me to self-destruct. I am more than aware of the dangers which lie in my advisory court," I admonish.

His jaw tenses.

"So, you're just going to kill off mortals one by one using your stupid box? Tilt the balance? Seems rather underwhelming as a plan of revenge if you ask me." He's panicked now, not visibly, but I can tell. He's trying to make me question myself, so I will become fearful, paranoid even.

"I have stoppered the flow at the spring of souls. It won't be long now," I announce, peering down at my dark lacquered nails and trying to act casual. "Besides, why do you care? Even if you did stop this, even if you did succeed in taking back Mortaria— who would rule it then? Do you honestly think that after everything, this will be the one act that earns you a place in The Higher Plains as a Titan? You will never be your father's equal; no one can be, especially not in his eyes, not even his brothers." Now it's my turn to once again rattle the confidence of the man before me. A small smile threatens to crack my formal demeanour as he balls his fist at his side, making his bicep pop beneath the skin.

"And so, what do you suggest that I do?" Hercules asks, sounding almost truly curious as he shifts on the soles of his leather boots.

"I don't care what you do. I am simply trying to level the playing field so that power and magic are delivered to the righteous and not to the entitled. Zeus has sat upon his throne looking down at everything and everyone for far too long. I thought that you would be the first to see that and agree," I provoke him, uncrossing my legs and leaning forward as my fingers slide down the jagged wooden arms of the chair, catching against the grain. "You are not a victim unless you allow yourself to be. If you truly wish to claim a place in The Higher Plains, then you must take it upon yourself. If you wait for your father's approval, then you will be waiting a long time."

I allow silence to fall between us as he sheaths the sword in his left hand.

"And if you achieve your goals, take down my father— will I be welcome then?" Hercules asks me, and I cock an eyebrow, heart pounding in my ribcage at this most exhilarating turn of events.

"Don't you think that would hurt your father?" I theorise, and he smirks.

"But of course," he replies.

"Then I should think you'd be very welcome," I retort, and he nods, thoughtful now as he runs his fingers through the featherlight gold of his hair.

"Well, I have delivered my warning. What you decide to do with it is up to you, but I am serious about The Demon Lords, and The Gods of Ancient. I hope you have something up your sleeve. Without some serious power in your corner, and by that, I mean running in your veins, you are nothing more than a pawn in an extremely long-held universal game between the descendants of Uranus and of Gaia. If you are to succeed, you must prepare to be betrayed at any second. That is the way of The Demon Lords. It always has been, and I don't think that's very likely to change." He turns on his heel to leave, but before he can reach the double doors at the end of the hall I call after him.

"And what will you tell your father of Mortaria?"

"Whatever I have to to buy you some time," he replies without pause or falter, footsteps continuing to ring out heavy against the floor.

After the echo of the double doors closing has rippled into silence, I'm left pondering his words. I allow the throne to partially cup my back with its unforgiving design, unable to relax even though I am alone. He's an unlikely ally for sure, but it makes sense he would hate Zeus more than anyone, especially after what happened to his mother at the hand of Hera.

I had thought, when he first began warning me, he had become a mouthpiece for The Aetherial Court. But after the end of the conversation, I'm now beginning to wonder if he's not right.

What power do I truly have over The Demon Lords?

If they choose to betray me, to turn on me— what power do I truly have to stop them?

As I sit, looking out over the empty throne room, lightning flashing on and off as Phobias crawl from one end of the ceiling to the other, it appears, causing the hairs on the back of my neck to rise in synchronised plight. I peer over one shoulder, checking behind the throne for listening demons.

Slithering like a poisonous snake in long grass, paranoia takes hold.

5

THE STORY

LUCE

THE IMPACT OF EACH chill raindrop hitting the veined flesh of a single leaf echoes, slow, sharp, and hollow. I peer up from beneath my hood to where deep black clouds billow; each one defined by a golden streak penetrating the narrow cracks struggling to divide the heavily blanketed sky.

The scents of the earth's wet carpet, curtains of lush, rain-soaked flowers, and of damp moss pillows rise from the floor in a mushroom cloud of sensory intoxication, drowning me in pungent reverie.

I let my toes bury into the moist dirt beneath my bare feet, turning in slow motion as the edges of my form blur like a watercolour painting. It's like I'm suspended within a clear jelly, preserved and yet utterly exposed to the world beyond, unapologetic and magnified, the ultimate forgery.

It is dark, my gaze falling upon the thick tree trunks that ring the grove, causing the space to turn shadowy and welcoming. I find myself soon fixated on the plants that weave amongst one another, creating a beautifully deceptive tangle.

Hemlock. Belladonna. Mandrake. Jimson Weed. Black Nightshade.

Another eye would have missed them, too distracted by the bloody burgundy petals of the enormous velveteen roses to notice the surrounding poison or the adorning thorns.

But not I.

For I don't see poison but power.

The world around me trembles as I reach out, pale fingers extending like the legs of a spider fighting for life against the sole of a mortal boot.

"Lucifer." My name slices through the air in the softest of cuts, simultaneously a caress and a slap as rain trickles, lukewarm now, down the back of my neck.

I spin, the once curvaceous edges of my now hardened body dissolving and reforming as I still, facing her.

I blink once, twice.

I know this isn't real.

And yet— I don't care.

What is *real*?

Taking a single step forward, the soles of my feet are caressed by the sodden organic matter slowly blanketed by the dark velvet of the cloak trailing in my wake.

As I approach, it washes over me. A tidal wave of nostalgia, simultaneously crushing and healing me in the single moment that hangs between us, a dense and noxious ecstasy.

Blackberry and pine. Just like it has always been, my poison, my tonic, curls in tendrils of inescapable bliss. It climbs up my nostrils and nuzzles deep into my brain, an unsuspecting key for the door I've vowed never to re-open.

Memories flood me, gushing like the hot blood from a freshly severed carotid. It's irreversible, and I let a small sigh escape my lips, the pleasure of the release undeniable even to me, a long-awaited climax.

Her eyes are deeply stormy, beckoning me into the madness within her, into the conflict we have always known. The unbearable distance between us, how to close it, how to brace for the storm that our love conjures every single time our gazes connect, how to come out the other side in one piece.

She holds out a hand, spindled fingers beckoning to me as the rain continues to fall, heavier now than ever. Her wicked halo of black hair captures each raindrop, turning the light through tiny globular prisms and throwing a rainbow of colour back onto my face. It exposes the black of my hair, of my eyes, of the dark veins spidering too close to the surface of my skin, as lacking and dull compared to her ethereal beauty. She really is a Goddess. More so than I could ever be.

I reach out to touch her, to take her fingers, but she side-steps me, a mischievous grin possessing her angular features, no sound passing her lips.

Spinning on the spot, my cape flares around me in an opening rosebud of slow-moving velvet shadow, finding her now flush against the tangle of poisonous vines, leaves, and the stark bloody crimson of one of the blooms.

I think she might pick one for me, a reminder of our last date at the Exilia. The night that had gone so differently than I had originally intended, but she doesn't. Instead, she backs into the tree behind the ominous knot of poisonous plants and gazes at me, lowering her chin so her lashes become more visible than ever. She blinks, slowly, each eyelash vibrating under the weight of her intent as her eyes rise again to mine and she bites her bottom lip, slight colour rushing to each of her sharply cut cheeks.

She beckons with her gaze, and so I tread, slower than I should. I get close to her, so close I can practically taste the wound of her open lips, but as our faces come only inches apart, she looks down, eyes suddenly emptying of all emotion.

The vines tangle around her wrists, around her legs and torso, then around her throat.

I panic, but no motion follows the rush of adrenaline as it hits me and my heart begins to pound, blood rushing in my ears.

No. This is the only reaction I can muster as I stand, watching the thick and lethal vines close in around her fine porcelain skin.

A growl pierces the air, startling me as the trance of this place loosens its hold. I pirouette, coming face to face with the orange glow of Beelzebub's irises, shining out, pinpricks of hope in the dark.

I move to command her to free Thane, but before I can, she leaps from the thick moss-carpeted branch, her shadow flying over the dark form of my cloak as she launches herself through the air.

I spin, following the glisten of her rain-strewn, silken coat as she passes high overhead but realise too late the intention of this beast was never to defend at all.

Her claws protrude instantaneously from within the thick pads of her paws; aiming directly for the throat of the person I love most in this world.

I go to move but find myself glued to the spot, suspended once again in that crystal clear and magnifying medium, trancelike as I watch the panther set about ripping her to shreds.

I want to scream out, but my lungs are empty. I want to move, but my feet are rooted to the spot. I can't even blink, held hostage to the situation by my own body, my own mind.

Her screams die, along with the rest of what she had once been.

Beelz turns, licking her lips, a knowing glint in one eye, as the blood runs down, soaking into the soil of the dark grove, an alchemic baptism of death in my very own dark church.

I awaken, floating five feet off the bed, flat on my back with a splintered shard of wood from what had once been The Hollow clutched between my palms.

My eyes fly open, and I allow myself to fall slowly back through the space between the mattress and me, gazing up at the ceiling in a comatose and inexpressive moment. As I descend, I am fully submerged back into reality. If that's what this really is.

It's hard to know anymore, what with how Delyria's Kingdom of Illusion, of delirium, captures all five of the senses so completely within its sphere of dark influence.

When my back is flat against the bloodstained white satin of the comforter, I sit up, eyes falling immediately to the pale skin of my forearms. My hands, still covered in the dried blood of the hare, are gloved burgundy to the wrist, but I continue to let my gaze travel to where the delicate skin of my upper arm has been ripped open. I inflicted this myself, with the wood of what had once been my ticket out of this godforsaken realm. Not that Mortaria is any better right now, well, at least not for most. I have no idea how I would fair, being surrounded by demons, with so much dark power so close at hand.

I wave a hand over the snagged and torn flesh, healing the wounds with what little magic I have left from the wooden shard in my hand and leaving only rivers of dark dried blood behind. It's desperate, I know, clinging to something like a piece of wood, but this piece of wood had been grown and showered in the blood of Haedes not so long ago, and it is perhaps the very last ounce of potent magic I have access to.

That's the problem with alchemy – unlike light magic, blessings – alchemy makes you a thief. The power you amass is stolen, not given willingly, which means that you are always scrounging for the next ingredient, the next raw ounce of power that can be transfigured into a consumable medium.

This, what I'm doing here, is messy; it's crude. Hardly appropriate for someone of my lineage, but it's all that is keeping me going, keeping me sane, keeping me hopeful that I'll somehow be able to reach her, to make her come back to me.

I stare past the chair that I haven't been able to bring myself to move, to the bay window looking out over the world beyond. The sun is setting, meaning I've been in my magically induced trance for well over twelve hours.

The sky is deep indigo veined through with clementine light, empty of all life, a sign that I am, as ever, alone in this place. Rage fills my chest like poison as I get to my feet, swallowing hard.

How could she do this?

Leave.

After everything.

And without so much as a goodbye.

Bitch.

A tear trickles down my cheek, salty and unwanted as it dissolves upon my lips. I sweep it away fast with a single flick of my tongue.

Staring down at myself, I find I'm still in the same clothes I'd been wearing yesterday, and the day before, and the day before that.

It's less magnificent than the billowing black cloak from the trance, underwhelming. Everything in this dimension is underwhelming, from the way mortals box themselves into tiny rooms with low ceilings and thick walls, to the utter lack of imagination which plagues every waking hour they suffer.

Claustrophobia threatens to choke me out as the moments pass endlessly, days of grime, sweat, and murder making my skin crawl.

I ignore it.

Taking a final glance through the glass pane across the room I find the last dying rays of sunlight dissipating across the sky, throwing it into a mess of magenta and deep purples.

Turning on my heel, my heart lead inside the steel of my ribcage, I make my way into the bathroom, switching on the too-fluorescent light and walking over to the sink.

I turn on the faucet, letting icy cold water purify my skin as the crimson mask of dried blood peels away slowly. I watch it, moving down the drain the wrong way, something I'm no longer even aware of doing.

I gaze up into the egg-shaped mirror opposite, its surface flawlessly pure, clean.

I wish I could say the same for myself. My eye sockets have become caves of grief, lit only by the single spark of light reflected by the glassy onyx surfaces of my eyes. My hair is matted, my skin a yellowish grey rife with grit, dirt, and lack of rest. I don't sleep anymore. Instead, I fall into trancelike highs that last days at a time, sometimes longer. They take me away, allow me to find solace, to stretch my soul in the shadows to which it has become so accustomed, of which nobody approves.

I hear them through the wall as I turn off the faucet, hands still speckled bloody in the creases of my knuckles. The groans of ecstasy, the way he calls her name like its gospel. The way she cries out beneath the weight and force of his passion.

The two of them should be slaughtered where they sleep.

Even I can see the love between them goes both ways, and yet they refuse to revel in it, instead fleeing like pathetic school children afraid of the real world.

Sighing, I'm unable to bear the sounds of their ravenous fucking through the wall any longer.

I glide over to the bed, slipping the shard of The Hollow into my back pocket before pulling on some leather boots.

I exit the room in loaded silence and leave nothing but that same silence behind.

My feet carry me faster than I intend along the corridor, past the door that is dismally failing to contain the moans of passion growing ever louder. I glide down the staircase, finding the hall abandoned. My gut floods with relief. I don't want to have to deal with The Furies—and especially not Jules with his judgemental and superior gaze.

I don't understand it because out of the two of us, he is the mortal, not I. He should be cowering before me, not sticking his nose up in the air.

I rush across the monochromatic floor, wishing the state of my soul was so neatly arranged; black here, white there. Instead, it has become an inevitable mixing palette for an artist who paints only in greys and will tolerate only the most melancholy, tortured subjects.

The night air hits me as I step out of the house, the steps underfoot sheening the colour of too-weak coffee under the moonlight.

I don't have any keys; don't have the intention of needing any either. I should be able to hotwire a car. With my magical skills, I can't imagine getting an engine running will be that hard.

However, as though fate knows I need to flee, to take off into the encroaching night and escape the prison this place has become, I find a silver car parked on the gravel with a broken window. The keys remain in the ignition, almost as though some higher power is begging me to take it.

I slip into the driver's seat, allowing the broken glass of the window to slice open my palm. I sigh out, the pain a welcome distraction from the heavy heart I've been carrying around like a bastard child; the remnants of a love that should have never been and would never last. It's a cold reminder, this fleshy mass within my chest, this lump of cold tissue, that perhaps someone like me doesn't deserve to love at all.

Perhaps I was made only for destruction.

I pull out the splintered dagger of The Hollow's last remnant before I turn the keys in the ignition, resting the grain of the broken tree against the slash left behind by the shattered window. I feel the burn of the power held within it fading as the very last of it seeps into my skin, into my blood, igniting my nervous system and lighting up my brain with an explosion of dark fireworks that blossom dangerously in the abyssal sky of my consciousness, eclipsing all sense and reason.

I sigh out, relieved that I no longer have to feel, have to bear this pain. Even the minutes between waking and now have been unbearable.

As the engine of the car roars to life, I begin to see the energies of this world sparking into view around me. My hand blurs as I place it, stubbornly bloody, onto the leather of the steering wheel and push down on the gas, heart racing, urging me to keep moving forward.

I reach a high speed as I pull onto the straight and narrow driveway, the world outside the vehicle becoming an indistinguishable blur of muted colour and fast morphing shapes.

Smashing through the gates as I exit the grounds, the car turns on a surface area the size of a pinhead, causing the tyres to squeal as I take off into the night, high as a kite.

I'm woken by the sound of rain slashing down against the windscreen and the smell of damp but fresh smoke filling my nostrils, temple throbbing.

I blink once, then twice, finding my forehead resting against the cool leather of the steering wheel and my gaze fixed on my knees. Everything aches, and the world continues to blur around me like a bad dream as I sit up, raising gentle and slow fingers to my forehead. The white flesh has split like the skin of a too-ripe peach, and blood drips down into my dark brows.

What the fuck happened?

I don't remember—

All I know is that I'm somewhere in Chicago, my head hurts, and apparently, it's raining.

I hadn't bothered to put on a seatbelt so open the car door. It grates, metal on metal, shedding broken glass onto the concrete beneath like dead mechanical skin as I step out into the rain of the night.

How long have I been unconscious?

I stand gingerly, the world around me spinning too slowly as everything distorts, hazy. Turning, I try to counteract the oncoming motion sickness and find, to my surprise, that it's not really raining at all.

My eyes fall on the smouldering wreck of what had once been a silver sportscar. The hood is crumpled beyond recognition, and the source of the downpour becomes quickly evident as I find I've crashed into a bright red fire hydrant. It showers this part of the sidewalk in chill water, a geyser of uncontrollable fury tempted by my disregard and blatant disrespect for physical laws.

Taking one look at the scene of the accident, I find people on the other side of the street, standing by an ornately twisted steel fence. The harsh metal spikes reign in the natural and wild intentions of the park, a sure threat to the pathetic urban sprawl of the surrounding manmade atrocity.

I need to get out of here before the police show up, or worse, A.D.A.M.

This isn't exactly proof that I'm no threat to society.

I stumble, legs humming and muscles tight with tension, across the street, not bothering to look for oncoming traffic as the too-bright streetlights blind me, causing me to raise a hand. I don't have a hood, or I'd pull it over my head to obscure my identity. Instead, I'll have to make use of speed and stealth to avoid recognition or blame.

I reach the park in under a minute, world still spinning. The dark shadows of trees leer over me, their imminence overwhelming.

I scurry along the path made from concrete, a sick scar on an otherwise preserved piece of the natural world, finding myself out of breath as my head continues to weep blood.

Once I'm far enough away from the road, I find a bench and slump down onto it, not feeling the heat or chill of the night air on my bare arms as I fold them over my chest. I let the darkness blanket me, watching the thrumming shadows of natural dark magic seething through the wildlife that silently teems on all sides, breathing fast. My head continues to throb, and as I search my person for the remnant I've been clinging to, I realise it's gone. I perhaps have just enough magic left to heal myself so wave long fingers over the gaping wound just above my brow and feel the sting as the skin begins to weave itself back together.

As my buzz fades, dregs of magic scream through me, all that's left making me burn.

Suddenly, I'm caught off guard, jumping slightly as a stranger appears from the dark mass of trees in front of me.

"Please! You have to help me! I'm starving. Do you have any money? Anything you can spare to help someone in need?"

He comes into the dim light cast by the sliver of moon that dangles overhead, eyes dark and glassy with desperation. He's wearing ragged jeans and a dark hooded sweatshirt, which appears to be stained by some kind of bodily or alcoholic fluid. I tilt my head at him, allowing the darkness that has infiltrated my mind to recede from the windows of my irises, eyes returning to their once innocent and ghostly powder blue. I stare a moment, unmoving as I take in the details of his form. He's got a threadbare backpack strapped to his shoulders, and while I'm eyeing it, I notice that just below where he's rolled up the sleeves of his sweater, he's covered in scars. The kind of scars you only come by from injecting yourself with liquid bliss.

I begin to think the hold of the magic is growing in potency once again as his outline shudders but then realise he's shaking like a leaf caught in a hurricane. His skin is pale, eyes embedded deep into dark caves inside his skull. It's a familiar sight, one I find in the mirror.

I don't have much magic left, not really, but I have enough for one last minor act. I wave my hand, and within it, a roll of one-hundred-dollar bills appears, transported straight from the safe that Jules thinks I don't know about underneath his bed back at the estate. As if locks and secret six-digit codes could ever keep someone of my power out.

Taking a single bill from the roll, I pass him the rest, stowing the cash in my bra.

"Are you fucking serious?" The man gapes at me, his dishevelled and dirty blonde hair blowing slightly as the leaves around us rustle.

"Take it and go. Before I change my mind," I bark, voice hoarse for some reason. He looks down at the money in his dirty fingers and then back up at me.

"Thanks."

As I watch him turn and leave, I have the unmistakable urge to follow him, to hunt his private life, make prey of his secret habits and behaviours. I get to my feet after waiting for him to turn the corner, knowing I don't want to go back to the estate. It's too crowded, too loud, too— unremarkable, and I tire of it.

I suppose this is as good a form of entertainment as any.

I follow the man out of the shadows of the park, exiting into the centre of the crude metropolis via a gate opposite where I'd entered. He walks for a while, past jewellery shops, coffee spots, and bars. His pace is hurried, unfaltering, and laced with desperate longing. I've seen steps just like this once before, on a street just like this one in yet another city I can't tell apart from all the others.

They had belonged to Alex Johnson.

I close my eyes, allowing my body to trail my target on autopilot as I'm taken back to that day, all those years ago, the very last of my high allowing me to make the memory crystalline as though it were yesterday.

1958

Detroit

The sun is just falling over the top of the Detroit skyline as I turn to Haedes, sighing into the muggy air of the city. Car horns and sirens blare around us, the background noise of evil working itself into the hearts and minds of the masses.

"Everywhere is closing up for the night, and I still haven't found anything I think she'd like." I feel my heart fall inside my chest. Thane bought me the most beautiful pair of pearl and ruby earrings for my birthday, and I don't want to disappoint with my gift for her. We've been together so long it gets harder every single year. I mean she's not exactly the material type either.

I want something different, hence why I'd convinced Haedes to bring me shopping in a mortal city. I could have had the sinners make me something, but she's seen it all before, and I want to impress.

"What about a suit?" Haedes asks me, brushing his long pale fingers through the cobalt slick of his hair and staring with longing into the window of a tailor's shop as we pass.

"She doesn't need clothes. We have a personal tailor back in Mortaria. Plus, there's no imagination in that—" I inform him.

"I don't get what the big deal is. You buy each other shit every single year. You both know you love each other," he complains, and I scowl at him.

63

"You've never really been in a long-term relationship— so I don't expect you to understand. And no, Aphrodite doesn't count," I retort, feeling his words sting me. He doesn't understand the fact that I will never stop finding new ways to show Thane how much she means to me. This thing we have, it's forever, and that means trying and compromising until one of us is no longer breathing.

Haedes opens his mouth to protest, but before he can get out so much as a whiny syllable, he's shoved aside by a topless man who comes out of nowhere. I catch his eyes as he passes; they flash bright orange, unmistakably demonic as his mortal features ripple in and out of existence as though his body is one of those new-fangled colour televisions on the fritz.

My head snaps sideways, following his motion as Haedes scowls, brushing down the black velvet of his suit jacket without subtlety.

"Come on!" I exclaim, hurrying after the figure that continues to bowl through the crowded sidewalk, his pace desperate as his skin morphs from alabaster to charcoal and back again. People gasp and yell as he continues to thunder through them without apology, knocking them off course.

Gift forgotten, I chase him the length of the street, but when I come to a corner, I lose him. I gaze desperately from left to right, spotting a tangerine glow for only a second within the dusky shade of an alleyway to my right.

I turn, striding silently into the shadow, and find him crumpled on the floor, sobbing.

"Stay away!" His voice is broken as I bend, trying to get a closer look at him.

He has golden eyes now, all trace of the demon within him gone.
But how?
There's no such thing as a demon-human hybrid.
It doesn't make any sense.
I watch him for a few minutes, the way his fingers claw at his skull as if he's dying to crack it open and let himself spill over the pavement.
My heart wilts, pity filling me.

The rest, as they say, is history. Xion spent the next month in a prison cell beneath the Exilia, per his own request, while I tried to discover a way to separate him from his darkness. It became apparent over time that the darkness within him was born there, and therefore, separating him from it entirely would kill him by making his soul less than whole, less than it needed to be to survive.

I continue to pace the sidewalk, anxiety flooding me for a reason I can't discern, watching the man I'm stalking turn into a nostalgically familiar dark alley. I stand at the mouth of it, peering into the shadow. I can't follow him any closer because he'll see me, so I guess that's the end of that.

As if, yet again, a higher power wants me to continue my stalking, a random woman exits the apartment building flanking the left side of the alley. I move swiftly, like shadow, and slip in between the glass doors only seconds before they seal shut behind her.

Once inside, I climb the stairs, letting my legs burn as I ascend too slowly, floor by floor, to the very height of the apartment block.

I take the emergency exit to the roof in stride, letting the rusty metal door slam loudly behind me and not caring who I wake in the process.

The breeze is slightly more chilled up here, and it ruffles the matte tangle of my dark hair as I move closer to the edge, staring down over the alleyway below like a bird of prey.

The man I'd given the roll of cash exchanges it for white powder that is passed from hand to hand in stark and deliberate motion, fingers of both parties fumbling, hungry for what the other is offering.

I watch him as his dealer leaves, transfixed as he slumps against the wall opposite the building that I'm observing him from.

It takes a while, maybe hours, maybe minutes, of me perching, watching over the edge of the building, but eventually, something invisible changes.

He stills, limp like a ragdoll for ten minutes, maybe twenty.

I tilt my head, squinting, curious now more than ever.

Turning my back on the scene, I make my way back down the stairs, the building passing me in a blur of banal decorating choices, and walk out into the Chicago night before turning deliberately into the alleyway.

Staring down at him, I realise he's not high; he's dead.

His gaze is glassy, eyes fixed open, mouth slightly parted as if he's taken one last ecstatic inhale.

I could have stopped this, could have prevented this man's demise. I could have refused him the money he'd used to buy the chemical bullet that had ended his life in a single blissful kill shot. But I didn't— because I felt *sorry* for him. I empathised with him.

If I saw Xion now in that same alleyway, I would have encouraged him to embrace his demon half, to use the power he'd been born with to force his will upon the world. He would have lived a life of regret— of shame.

But I hadn't done that. At the time, I'd used the single shard of Obsidian Haedes had gifted me a few years before to draw off some of the darkness. I had used it to tether him to the stone, using the pendant he's worn ever since.

He had asked for help, and I had given it, willingly and without second thought.

As I stare at the dead man, at his lack of expression, the meat sack that has become nothing more than back-alley trash, I realise that I'm staring into the future.

My future.

Tears prick my bottomless dark eyes.

Thane was right.

It is, I feel, time to ask for Xion to return the favour I had done all those years ago. The truth has never been clearer to me than it is now, as I feel suddenly more alone than I ever have.

I need to ask for help.

For perhaps the first time, I want someone to save me.

6

EVERYTHING IS ALRIGHT

<u>SEPHY</u>

LEFT. RIGHT. LEFT. RIGHT.

Inhale.

I see him climbing on top of me in the dark, this stranger who will end my life, but am powerless to stop him.

Exhale.

Left. Right. Left. Right.

Glass explodes from the back wall of this very ballet studio, raining down in a brutal onslaught of jagged shards.

Inhale.

She looks down on me, through the intermittent gaps between the bars of my cage.

Exhale.

I claw my way up through the earth, suffocated by the world, desperate to return to death but unable to surrender my beating heart.

Left. Right. Left. Right.

Pounding paws, hungry jaws, getting closer and closer as I stand in the dark colosseum, waiting to die.

Inhale.

He kisses me. I burn. Unwillingly. Heart in my throat, I choke on the words that flit in and out of dark spaces every time we touch, dangerous and inconceivable.

Exhale.

It is with this final rejection of breath from my lungs that I smash my knuckles into the punch bag so hard that it flies from the chain suspending it from the ceiling. The metal ring atop the thick hide filled with sand chimes out as it breaks and the bag sails straight into the mirror, smashing the glass.

The sound haunts me, takes me back to where this all began.

It's dark in the ballet-turned-training studio. The light from the fluorescents overhead would only reveal me to myself, so I keep them turned off.

I wonder now if what Luce is experiencing is something fated for me too. How do you kill monsters, demons that just keep coming, without becoming one?

I'm already incapable of love. Unable to do what I need to for the greater good as fear splinters my perception of who I have always secretly hoped, deep down, I would be.

The hero. The badass.

But I'm not. I'm selfish and I'm afraid.

No true hero would be afraid at a time like this. They'd be too busy doing everything in their power to save the oblivious people of this world. Too busy being honourable, being righteous.

It's funny, because the most righteous, honourable man I've ever met is half demon, half monster himself, so perhaps it is not the demons that are the monsters at all. Perhaps it's the human cowards like me, too afraid to step up and do what's right.

Is it a demon's fault that he exists?

No.

No more than it is my choice to be standing here once again instead of six feet under among insects and hungry roots.

But humans— humans have the choice. They can choose darkness or light, and instead of coming out shining like a knight in well-polished armour, all of us merely end up a muted state of guilt-ridden grey.

Then again— a well-polished suit of armour has never seen battle.

So, what do I know?

The lights overhead flick on, so I spin, startled as I instinctively summon a ball of scarlet flame to my palm.

I raise my hand, letting the flaming projectile loose sooner than I intend. Jules ducks, flawlessly fluid in anticipation of my reaction.

"Oh shit, sorry! You startled me," I apologise, watching as he observes the flames extinguish fast, leaving a large scorch mark on the fraying silken wallpaper.

"Any reason you're training in the dark?" he asks me, and I shrug.

"Helps me focus, I guess," I lie, and he quirks an eyebrow.

"I can see that." He gestures to the broken mirror behind me, the punching bag slouched against it like a corpse.

"I guess I got a little too into the zone." I flush.

He closes the distance between us, black cotton pyjamas swallowing the light of the room and making his outline definitive, taking my wrapped hands in his.

"You're bleeding," he notes, looking deeply into my eyes, his irises green and grassy. I've never really investigated them before, but for some reason, in the still of this silent night, I find myself lost in the unexpected tide of his relentless caring.

I blink once then tear my gaze away, finding two of my knuckles split and weeping blood beneath the white fabric of my wraps. I sigh; I thought they'd toughened more by now. Turns out I'm still undeniably mortal underneath it all.

Vulnerability sweeps across my flesh as my heart begins to slow in my chest, and blood cools beneath my skin.

"I'll get the kit, hold on," he orders, spinning on the ball of his slipper and gliding from the room with perfectly composed elegance.

I turn on the spot, looking at my reflection in the jagged mirror, the surface of which is cracked like molten rock, smouldering with my gaze.

I'm not the girl who had walked into this room with the weight of Adam Sinclair's legacy upon her shoulders. My eyes are deeper somehow as though the sheen of my cognac irises has diminished, but the colour has become more intense, the fire within them warmer, more ferocious. Beneath my sports bra, my abdomen is taut, any softness gone. My arms are roped with veins which have risen close to the skin, my skeleton clad in tight muscle, flesh still marred by the scars of my murder and the consequential autopsy that will never truly be gone.

Jules interrupts my self-assessment as the return of his padded tread grows louder across the varnished pine of the floor.

"Here, sit," he says.

I drop to the floorboards underfoot, compliant as I cross my legs in front of me.

Jules unravels my boxing wraps, revealing two enormous splits over the top of the second and third knuckles on my left hand. I watch him open the green medical kit beside me, bringing out antiseptic wipes and bandages.

I stare at him, trying to distract myself from the fast and sour sting of the antiseptic, eyes resting upon the enormous black egg protruding from his forehead.

My heart wilts, and suddenly I'm taken back to a moment nineteen years ago.

I sat on this same floor, staring at Jules in this same fluorescent light. He'd been tying my brand-new ballet slippers up my calves over powder-white tights.

I examine him in my memory comparing him then and now. His hair has thinned and is greying, lines etching themselves into his face in a permanent and unerasable protest of time.

How old must he be now— fifty? Maybe sixty? Within the confines of his flawlessly tailored suits he seems unchanging, but now I examine him as he slowly wraps my limbs in white bandages as he had once done baby pink silk, I find him mortal. Find him fragile.

"Jules—" I watch him wrap the final length of bandage around my hand, fastening the end with medical tape.

"Yes, Sephy?" he asks me, not looking up.

I reach up, not sure what's come over me. Now that the rage has gone, the frustration too, dissolved by both sex and violence, I find myself like fine china teetering on the edge of a crooked shelf, an earthquake threatening destruction in minor seismic quakes.

"What is it?" he presses me, brow furrowed as I touch the side of his face like a child feeling the stubble of a real man for the very first time.

"I want you to go." I exhale, tears coming to my eyes.

"I beg your pardon?" he demands, sitting back on his haunches, spine perfectly erect as his eyes steel with resistance.

"You didn't sign up for this. None of it. You deserve to live out the rest of your life how you want. Not in my service. Not like this. I'll give you as much money as you think you need. Whatever you want. Take the jet. Just get out of here. Before it's too late." I'm set on my decision, knowing I can't watch him suffer because of my choices. He should be laying on a beach somewhere, Mai Tai in hand. He deserves it more than anyone.

Breathing out slowly, he gets to his feet. Offering me a hand.

"Come with me," he whispers, and I can tell the gesture has deeply touched him. I place my bandaged palm into his, and he pulls me to my feet. Together, we exit the training studio. The father, as ever, leading the child.

"Where are we going?" I demand as we stride across the lobby.

"I have something to show you." Jules is ominous in his tone, not giving anything away.

"Why are you even awake?" I ask, swallowing my hurt at the thought of him leaving.

"The Furies have the room next to mine," is his only reply, and so I sigh, guilt growing.

Jules leads me through the once again immaculate kitchen, unlocking the door to the attached apartment he's lived in for as long as I can remember.

I've never been in here before, not ever, and my curiosity grows as I step awkwardly into his personal space.

"Nice— I, uh, like what you've done with the place." I look around at the interior. It's barren of any personalisation, a simple apartment with a small living room, kitchenette, and bedroom. Stepping through the warm space, I notice the one thing he does have is a rack at the end of a modest double bed. Here, at least fifty suits hang, each as identical, as sharp, as the last. I smile.

The walls are bare, but on his nightstand, I notice two photographs in silver frames. One of them I haven't seen in years, not since it was first developed.

The photo catches my eye because of the shock of red from my hair, which is swept up into a bun. I remember it because Jules had looked so uncomfortable during the event itself.

He is holding one of my pale, thin arms, gangly against the rest of me, which seems to be all legs and very little torso. I'm standing on one foot, spinning as he helps me practice how to spot. As Jules begins to fiddle with the rug beside the bed, I can't help but pick it up.

He's looking at me, and though his body in the frame is rigid, uncomfortable, embarrassed even, the look on his face is purely enraptured by the child in front of him. I look at my face too, at the way my too-large mouth engulfs the rest of my face, spreading in a wet and toothy smile, the freckles I make sure to cover now plain as day across the bridge of my nose like chocolate sprinkles.

In this single image, I see the truth of my life.

He has always been more to me than anyone. More of a father than my own, more of a friend than anyone could have claimed otherwise.

He doesn't deserve to die for that loyalty.

The second photo isn't as attention-grabbing, but as Jules gets down onto his knees and they give an audible creak, I pick it up, placing the other back where I found it.

This one is more official. A young Jules surrounded by his A.D.A.M. unit. Or so I assume. Would they even allow him to keep photographic evidence that such a team exists?

Before I can think on this anymore, my attention is pulled back to the present by a large thud.

"What the hell was that?" I demand, flustered in returning the photograph to where I found it before spinning to face the wall next to the bed.

"Oh, don't worry about that. It's just The Furies. They practice knife throwing at the wall when they're bored," he informs me. I scowl. "Anyway, that's not why we're here. Come on."

He gestures to the floor, and I squint as he touches a whorl in the wood of one of the floorboards, no different from any of the other surrounding walnut. A panel slides out of place, leaving a gap in the floor. I hear a collapsible pair of wooden steps unravel in a staccato of squeaking hinges as the otherwise invisible trap door is revealed.

"Down you go."

He holds out a hand, which I take as he helps me lower myself down through the square opening in the floor and into the darkness below. There is no light that I can see, so I allow the Eternal Flame to flicker to life in my hand, causing the cellar below to illuminate.

Within moments, Jules follows me down the ladder with a torch procured from seemingly nowhere, casting further illumination upon the contents of the space.

"Guns?" I take in the heavy artillery propped on a rack, ordered from smallest to largest on my left, and leaning lazily against the raw brick of the house's foundation. Crates of what I assume to be bullets are stacked into tall wooden towers next to the matte black of the many gun barrels, which boast an array of different lethality and size.

"Keep walking—" Jules shines the torch further down the length of the surprisingly large storage space. It had originally looked the size of any other room, but now I can see it sprawls, almost like its own building, beneath the parallel over-world of the house.

My footsteps echo out on the bare concrete as I continue walking forward, finding the flame in my palm and the torchlight reflected back at me and curved multiple times, jaded against glass.

"So, this is where we keep the wine and all my whiskey! Wait—you keep alcohol next to the guns? Whose idea was that?" I snort, smirking as the underside of my face is illuminated a hearty orange by the crackling tendrils of fire.

"Your mother's. She said if we were ever in the situation to need such heavy arsenal, we'd also need a stiff drink," he reveals, and I laugh. I definitely inherited her sense of humour, that's for sure.

"Keep walking," Jules encourages.

I let my eyes flit reluctantly from the endless racks of expensive wines and valuable spirits.

Leaving them behind, I continue taking step after cautious, measured step, the space around me empty until it isn't. Suddenly, the cellar narrows into a corridor, and from what I can see, that corridor ends in a heavy-duty door that boasts a dull matte steel and hinges thick as a gorilla's thumb.

"A post-apocalyptic survival bunker? Aww Jules, but my birthday isn't until October! You shouldn't have!" I gush, teasing him, but this time his face doesn't reflect my humour back at me. Instead, it remains grim as the torch turns the lines around his mouth dark and the whites of his eyes phantasmal, haunted by a memory that coagulates like clotted blood just beneath the surface.

"Come," is all he says, voice cracking as he grabs my hand and pulls me closer to the door with unexpected urgency. My heart starts to race, palm becoming clammy beneath the thin weave of my newly applied bandages. I breathe deep, the smell of dust and dry, musty air filling my nostrils, turning my throat acrid.

"Jules—what the hell is going on?" I demand, my unease becoming evident as I try to tug my hand from his grasp. My knuckles twinge in protest as he tightens his grip.

"Once I show you what's behind this door— it will change how you view me, Sephy. Are you ready?" he asks. My lips part slightly.

I'm not ready.

Not ready to have the one true hero in my story tainted by bloodshed, cruelty, or whatever else it is he has to confess.

"No," I reply, stomach fluttering as bile rises in the back of my throat.

Jules sighs, but without pause, he does what I wish he wouldn't.

Unlocking the door, he lets it slowly open with a metallic groan, revealing a darkness inside I never wanted to see.

As the door swings back, it takes a few moments before automatic and too-bright white lights whir into life. It's a more sterile, pure glare than I've ever seen, almost surgical in its unforgiving illumination.

The air inside is cold, a hint of iodine, alcohol, and the unmistakable metallic tinge of blood rife within the history of its makeup.

I take a step forward as Jules steps to one side of the door frame, allowing me to enter. My cautious tread reveals my hesitance as the sweat coating my body starts to cool, leaving me with goosebumps plaguing my bare skin.

"What—" I scowl, trying to take in what's before me.

It looks like some kind of theatre, a crude one I'll give you that, but there is an unmistakable focus on a single point within the room. The space is enclosed on all sides with melancholic slate grey concrete, flawlessly smooth as though it was only poured yesterday.

I stand at the top of a staircase, exposed to the spectacle, confused.

As I cock my head, feet unwillingly dropping from one stair to the next, hairs stand to attention up the length of my back. Then, I realise what it is I'm staring at.

"This is where— this is where he did it? My father." I look back over my shoulder to find Jules standing, staring down at me with a devastated expression, at the top of the staircase.

"This is where we did it, yes. This is where we performed the tests. Where we kept him—" His voice echoes around the cavernous room, which sinks deeper into the earth than the cellar leading here. A concrete coffin almost. The walls are suffocating, no windows, no doors. Plush leather seats are gathered in a semi-circle around the main event, looking utterly wrong and out of place.

I walk through the centre aisle they create, stopping before my reflection and placing my hand upon the dirty glass of the empty tank, an altar of cruelty in a church of mortal greed.

"It's so small—" I comment, examining the cylindrical container. The smell of stagnant water mixed with disinfectant rises from the innards of the receptacle, taking me back to the moment of waking, confined, just like the Merman must have been.

"We didn't want him to have anywhere to hide. The Mer, they're fast. Faster than you can imagine in the water," Jules explains. I look back at him once again as I hear his footsteps reach the last step of the stairs as he descends after me.

"So, you— you stole his tears?" I recall, morbidly curious despite myself. I feel a little sick, heart unceasing in a too-fast palpitation as I stand, dwarfed by the enormity of such inhumane acts.

"That was the original intention, yes. But— once your father re-alised that the Merman we captured had something else far more valuable for us to study, he began ordering me to conduct physical examinations, tests."

"For what?" I ask him, and he sighs, eyes hollow.

"The source and limitations of the Mer's immortality. Your father wanted to bottle it, make it marketable, perhaps even make use of it himself to escape his Mortarian fate. Once he had the Merman's tears bottled and sent off for scientific study, so we could recreate them, he wanted me to push the limits of the creature's ability to heal— to survive," he explains, causing me to swallow hard.

I look to my left, finding dull, iodine-splashed metal tables upon wheels, chains for restraint the only real remnant of the pain that has passed here. On my right, medical equipment lays rusting, untouched, with both lethal and painful promise, in the light.

"So, you tortured him?" I ask, numb.

Shuffling on the balls of my sneakers, I turn in a slow circle to give him a hard stare. My breath comes in stifled wisps, rationed as though I don't deserve to breathe deep, to calm myself.

Not within this place, not after what he did.

"Unequivocally. Yes. It is my biggest regret," he admits, sitting on one of the padded chairs, bending so his elbows rest upon his knees and looking up at me, ashamed.

"Why are you showing me this?" I ask him.

It's awful, terrible, more disgusting and cruel than I'd ever imagined, making me want to burn the vast piles of money which came as a result, but why does he feel it necessary? Why now? Why after all this time?

"Because I need you to know. I need you to see why I owe myself to the world of the mythical. I assaulted one who is blessed, one of The Circle of Eight's chosen. For that, I will always be guilty, and I will always put my life in harm's way to maintain the balance between worlds, it is my penance. How I live with myself," he confesses, eyes flitting between the tungsten-rusted tips of the scalpels and the dirty glass of the tank behind me.

I frown.

"Are you really telling me that you have no desire to get as far away from this place as possible? Because I never figured you for a sadist."

I cross my arms over my chest, becoming unwillingly emotional at his loyalty, at his conviction. He'd have made a wonderful father. If he had been mine, perhaps I wouldn't be so much of a coward.

75

"I'm telling you, darling girl, that I am in this with you. Until the very end. No matter what that means," he announces, getting to his feet.

"And what if I want to run?" I ask him as he places his hands on my shoulders, causing me to be suddenly aware of how isolated the enormous space of this chamber makes me feel. It's as though all humane contact is a million miles away, unable to ever penetrate the thick concrete.

"Then I will be carrying your bags." He pauses, taking a deep inhale. "But you won't run."

"Why is everyone so sure of the fact I'm going to get myself involved in all this? It's not me. It's not who I am. I'm not a hero, or a saviour, and definitely not a queen. I just want to be normal." I shrug, imploring his sympathy with my gaze. He laughs.

"You never were, and you never will be. You're extraordinary. It's why I love you," he leans forward kissing me on the forehead, and I feel myself relax for the first time in weeks, the chill of my surroundings miraculously retreating if just for a moment.

I don't know what to say now, so instead, I change the subject, unsure of how to deal with such unexpected and candid emotions.

"Why are you keeping all this stuff down here anyway? Why don't you just get rid of it or at least clean it?" I ask him, placing my hands on my hips and spinning from left to right as I scan the contents of the room yet again, still shocked. I mean, I knew this event happened but seeing it in person gives it a new and much darker resonance. As though the ghosts of screams have been waiting here to penetrate my bones, planting themselves in my marrow and reminding me of how my family fortune was built.

"If I'm ever unsure about my calling to protect, I come here. It reminds me that I once chose to use my power to be cruel, to torture." He looks misty now as though the past events are playing behind the screens of his pupils, an inescapable reminder of what he's done.

"Well, you're still my Jules. No matter what. We're family." I promise him. We stand staring at one another, our gazes tender even still in the dark, guilty shadows of both our personal and familial past.

7

THE MIGHTY FALL

SEPHY

I STARE AT MY reflection, stone-cold sober, in the window of what had once been my ballet studio as Jules sweeps broken shards of mirror into a dustpan.

Looking beyond the pallor of my own expression staring back at me, I peer out into the dark of the night, eyes flitting from the unnerving darkness of the thick lines of surrounding trees and landing on the empty driveway.

"Wow, you really got the car taken care of fast," I comment, appreciative of his efficiency as I find the space where Xion and I had parked the Vanquish now empty in the dim light of the waning moon's last remaining sliver.

"Huh?" Jules looks up from where his grassy green eyes are fixed on the varnished pine floorboards, scouring the space for missed shards of glass. I fold my arms across my breasts, double-checking the car really is gone before I reply, observing a thin layer of sweat which has made the bald round of his head slightly shiny.

"The car— it's gone. I assume you had it towed, or moved to the garage, right?" I guess, and his brow furrows deeply as his irises flicker fast from left to right, scanning my face for any inkling of a bad joke.

"Uh— they weren't coming to collect it until the morning." His voice is slow and cautious as though he's approaching a hungry lioness in a suit made from a nice cut of raw sirloin. My heart falters in its beat, my attachment to the car not clear to me until this very moment. I wonder now if I should have been slightly more careful with The Mean Machine.

"So— where is it?" I ask.

78

He places the dustpan and broom against the wall and walks over to stand beside me, staring through the window. Our reflections stare back at us, side by side, as we squint into the dark.

"Did Xion take it out?" he asks me, and I shake my head. When I'd left him, he'd been passed out in bed after a marathon sex session.

"I don't think so—" I murmur, cocking my head closer to the glass as Jules dives into his pocket.

"What is it?" I ask him as he picks up the phone and shoves it close to his ear.

"Taxi driver at the front gate," he answers in a clipped tone, bordering on formality as he hangs up.

We both stride from the room together, and as Jules moves back past the stairs, toward the control centre of the house to open the front gates, I make a sharp turn left and head for the front doors. I open them, unsure of what to expect. My first thought is a flashback to the black SUVs that had busted in through the front gate. Then I doubt myself. With those at their disposal, why would A.D.A.M be using a taxi? Not only that, but if it's the same person who took my car, why haven't they driven it back?

After a few cold moments of anticipation on the front steps of the house, a pair of headlights break through the blanket of dark thrown over the world by the humid yet remarkably chill night. The taxi, tyres crackling against the gravel of the driveway, pulls up to the front of the house slowly as I stare at it as though it offends me, pausing only a second before the back door opens.

Out steps Luce.

"Thanks," she passes the driver what looks like a hundred-dollar bill, which is way too much, but he doesn't argue. Snatching the money and turning the wheel, he quickly reverses before pulling back up the driveway and disappearing through the electric gates at great speed.

Luce looks awful; an enormous cut on her forehead barely healed— the kind you'd expect from someone who has been smashed headfirst into the steering wheel of an Aston Martin. *My* Aston Martin.

"Where the hell is my car?" I demand, crossing my arms again and cocking an eyebrow, unimpressed in every regard.

"Why, I'm fine, thanks for asking—" she mumbles.

"Luce, where is my car!" I stamp my foot like a child about to throw a tantrum, channelling Haedes through and through.

"I, uh— I got into an accident. Kind of," she explains, and I blink slowly, a long exhale escaping my frustrated lips. It's not the answer I wanted, but a part of me is surprised it didn't come out of her in a feral snarl.

"What the hell are you playing at? That car wasn't yours to take, and besides, I don't recall telling you that you could leave the estate," I chastise her, inhaling deeply and trying to calm myself with the scent of the damp surrounding forest. I know it's harsh, but she's risking her safety for seemingly no good reason. She better have one hell of an explanation.

"I'm not a child," she spits, standing in the driveway.

And there's that attitude again—

I stare at her, noticing that she's more like herself than I've seen her in a while. Eyes powder blue like new moonlight on fresh snow, posture relaxed with her hands hanging limp at her sides.

"You could have fooled me," I retort, brushing a free strand of hair behind one ear and steeling myself for the argument that no doubt lies ahead. "Why did you leave? It's not safe for you to be wandering around the city, for anyone." I add this final sentiment, knowing that it's hardly Luce's safety that concerns me. I'm more worried about the poor souls she may have run into on her travels.

"I needed to get some fresh air— some perspective," she adds, and my eyes widen. She sounds almost like she's come to her senses, which worries me immensely.

Is this a new calm before an even greater and more ferocious storm?

My temper is frayed beneath my cool composure, my posture chill and gaze glacial as my irises sweep her form, any pity I might once have felt gone.

"And?" I ask her, not sure if I want to know the answer.

Has she killed someone?

Am I going to get a phone call about my car being involved in some random hit-and-run?

I'm pretty sure A.D.A.M isn't going to like that, and if that's the case, what argument can I possibly make that she's not a threat to this world, that I have her under control?

"I need help." The plea comes out in a voice I haven't heard from her in weeks. Her usual tone is high-pitched, full of superiority, and yet utterly void of human emotion. Now, however, her syllables are no longer clipped but flow from her like a tumbling bolt of uncut raw silk.

"No shit," I retort. "Come inside; it's late," I order her, preparing even still for the fight, the resistance, and the madness I'm so used to from her. I ball my fists out of habit, ready, but none comes. Instead, she strides straight past me and into the house without so much as an inkling of protest, silent as a shadow.

Turning on the spot to follow her through the double doors and into the lobby, I find her silhouetted meek against the bright light of the crystal chandelier, her frame not holding the intimidating sense of power it did only yesterday as I'd stood, unblinking, in front of a set of floating kitchen knives.

I ascend the mocha stone steps, slick with rain, making my way into the entryway and closing the doors behind me. As I spin to face the room, I find her sitting, and looking at her shoes, on the third step of the staircase.

At the sound of my approaching footsteps, she raises her gaze, sparkling with unshed tears, to find mine.

Should I feel pity for her?

I don't.

"Sephy— I can't do this anymore—" she pleads, and I sigh.

"You don't have a choice. None of us do. You drank from The Well; this is the consequence." I'm unfeeling in my response in the face of her vulnerability, the last few weeks of her irrational and entirely uncivilised behaviour irking me even still.

"Please— I need your help. *Please*," she begs, and I cock one eyebrow as her plump lips part, her next words falling from her in a torrent of fresh fear. "I don't want to die."

"Yeah, well you should have thought about that before you played god and forced me back into this world. There's nobody to blame here but you." I shrug, standing over her so her pale skin is darkened by the imminence of my shadow.

"I know that, but I'm afraid. I'm afraid I'm going to kill myself if I carry on this way. I can't stop," she informs me, and my heart flutters slightly beneath my ribcage. These are the words I've been wanting to hear from her for the past month, the confession Xion and I have been waiting for. Yet now it spills from her like blood from an unstoppable, deep wound, I can't help but be suspicious of her intent. Is this a new form of self-mutilation, self-destruction, we haven't been prepared for?

"We all warned you, Luce. Thane too. What's changed?" I watch as she wrings her fingers nervously upon her knee, her foot tapping an incessant and frustrated beat on the onyx velvet of the runner that falls the length of the stairs.

"There was this man in the city— I gave him money. He was so desperate I—" she stutters, and I frown, cutting her off mid-hesitation.

"Money? Where did you get that from? I haven't given you any money?" she looks ashamed, and I know that she must have stolen it from me.

Perfect. An addict and a thief.

I stare at her, my gaze a flaming projectile that scorches her right through with disdain.

"Anyway— I gave him money. Then I followed him. He— he bought drugs— and then he died. Just like that. With a smile on his face. I've dealt with death my whole existence, but I've never seen somebody trade life so willingly. What's worse— I recognised that desperation. I see it in the mirror every day," she admits, running her dark fingernails through her matte onyx locks, her pupils wide in the inescapable light showering the room tungsten.

"So, what exactly do you want me to do? I'm not really sponsor material, and I doubt there's a Dark Magic Abuser's Anonymous group around here—" I'm bored of the conversation, not wanting to get my hopes up too high.

"There's this shard. It's made from obsidian. I used it to draw off part of Xion's darkness all those years ago. I need you to do the same for me. This magic isn't tied to my soul like it is to Xion, so it should be easier than when I did it to him," she explains, the solution seemingly simple, and yet I feel like there's a catch. Is this a trick? Does she want the obsidian for something else? I've heard addicts can be resourceful manipulators when they need to be. Is this all an act?

Sensing my lack of belief, she adds, "I need this darkness out of my system if I can ever hope to heal from this."

"Where is this shard?" I enquire, a slow cold pool of dread filling my stomach drip by drip as each breath passes my lips.

"It's back in my alchemy chamber. In Mortaria," she explains, and I laugh, the sound of it ringing from the walls in loud and unmistakable peels.

"Are you fucking joking? You want me to go back into goddamn demon palooza? Uh— no. Not happening." I shake my head, a smile tugging at the corners of my lips with the absurdity of it all.

She must have hit her head harder than I thought when she crashed my goddamn car that she didn't ask to borrow. I mean, I know I trashed The Mean Machine, but now I think about it, I did at least ask first.

"You're saying you won't help me? After everything?" Luce's eyes narrow, pupils dilating slightly as the darkness within her threatens to present yet again.

I stand firm.

"That's what I'm saying. I'm not risking my life for this. You decided to go down this road. You do it. I have people relying on me here." I think about Jules, about Xion and The Furies. Right now, they need me. Luce had her chance to avoid all this, and she said no. I don't see how that's my problem to fix.

"I can't. I can't convect like you, and The Hollow is gone. You know that." She balls her left fist as it dangles past her hip, and I watch her muscles tense beneath the baggy cotton of her shirt.

"How convenient for you," I bite the inside of my lip, rage reaching boiling point. Luce gets to her feet, widening her stance on the stair and baring her teeth.

"How dare you!? How dare you stand there and act like I'm the dirt beneath your feet, like you have the right to deny me anything? You are nothing alone. The only reason you are blessed with your miserable existence is because I willed it so. The only reason you have a demon boy toy to fuck is because I saved him. How dare you deny me after everything I've done for you. You miserable spoiled bitch!" Her entitlement hits a final nerve, and I summon a ball of fire to my palm.

"Get the fuck out of my house," I threaten her, holding the ball of flame high above my shoulder as she stands.

"Make me," she doesn't budge, taunting me, daring me to challenge her as though this is what she's been waiting for all along.

"I said, *get the fuck out of my house, bitch!*" I scream this at the top of my lungs, letting the flame loose as it soars toward her. She ducks, the flame hitting the stair behind her as she darts faster than I expect so she's up in my face, so close I can smell the rancid death on her breath.

"I shouldn't be so surprised. After all, what chance did I have of getting help from the famous Sephy Sinclair, murderess of those she loves? I mean even your parents didn't stand a chance. No wonder you don't have a family. No wonder you're all alone." She spits the sentiment, slamming into my shoulder with the bony round of her own and storming from the house and out once more into the night.

I don't know where she's going, and I don't care. My heart pounds in my chest, unexpected hurt spreading through me like easy catching wildfire.

As the front door slams shut in her wake, tremors of angry sound fly out into the room, causing the chandelier to shake. I exhale a heavy breath, unwanted tears filling my eyes.

XION

I'm stirred from the depths of an exhausted sleep by doors slamming somewhere in the house. I sit bolt upright, heart racing as I launch over the side of the bed, untangling my sleepy limbs from the sheets. Glancing back over one shoulder, I know what I'll find before I lay eyes on the barren left side of the four-poster. She's gone, of course. She never stays once we're done.

I scramble for the clothes I shed earlier, pulling the black round-neck shirt over my head and stumbling into my jeans without hesitation. Straightening as I zip my fly and button the pants, I yank open the door of the suite, storming out into the corridor and picking up pace. I run the length of the hallway until I turn the corner and enter the openness of the landing, slowing only slightly. Urgency refuses to loosen its hold as I rush to the , letting my clammy fingers slide over the polished round of its wooden circumference.

Below, Sephy peers up, and our eyes meet. The warmth from before, when I wrapped her in my arms and traced her skin with careless fingertips, is gone. Replaced instead by a furious blaze, her cognac irises glow intense, the colour of whiskey.

"What on earth is going on?" I call, leaning over the bannister, breath coming in quick, cold inhales which chill the delicate tissue of my lungs, fluttering beneath the thick bone of my ribs.

"Luce." Sephy sighs out, turning a half circle on the spot as though lost and pulling her long fiery locks down from the high ponytail in which they've been captured. Her hair falls in a flaming waterfall, brushing her shoulders and licking the bare pale skin of her back. I want to bury my face in it, feel the silken tendrils consume me, but

I know right now I must, yet again, put all that aside and do what is right.

Unfortunately for me, what is right and what I want never seem to line up. Ever.

She turns back to look at me with hesitation, so I round the bannister and take the stairs two at a time, quickly closing the distance between us as though it's a fatal wound.

I put my palms on her bare shoulders, and it's then that I see something else buried deep behind the furious glaze of her irises. As the heat diminishes and she stares deep into my face, I see that she's hurt. Her eyes shine, not with fury, as I originally thought, but with tears.

Sephy isn't the kind of girl who just cries for no reason.

"Calm down. Tell me what happened?" I order her, letting my palms brush against her upper arms, giving a delicious friction that I hope will calm her into compliance.

"Luce— she took the Vanquish and went out into Chicago. I think she got into an accident, but she wants help *apparently*. I don't know. I don't know what to think. She's turned around so quickly; I think it might be a trap. She said something about a shard of obsidian she used to draw off your darkness. Said that we could do the same thing to her—" she explains, and my eyes widen. My lips part, and something in my gut blooms. I don't acknowledge it, too afraid to be hopeful after everything.

"Where did she go?" I enquire. Her eyes flicker to the door as her dark lashes flutter delicately.

"She stormed out—" Sephy replies, crossing her arms across her sports bra, abs tensing visibly as she bites her bottom lip.

"Why?" I ask.

She sighs, a wave of guilt rippling across her features only momentarily before disappearing as her features harden.

"We got into a fight," she explains, eyes dulling as they drop from mine to the floor. "I don't want to risk going back into Mortaria for this shard— if it actually *does* exist. We barely got out alive last time, and that was before the place was swarming with demons. Besides, I don't even know if what she's saying is true. What if it's a trap? She's an addict— I just can't trust her right now."

I cock my head. It doesn't sound like something Sephy would get overly emotional about. I let an eyebrow rise, querying her further with only my look, and she sighs, running nervous fingers back over her scalp. "She kept saying how I owe her, how I'm only alive because of her— how it's no wonder I wouldn't help her because all I'm good for is murdering those close to me. I told her to get the fuck out." The confession comes as a single, overdue, and breathless exhalation, and I blink several times. Her eyes glisten. "She's not exactly wrong," she breathes.

I take my thumb and run it along the line of her jaw, brushing her hair behind her shoulder, the defiance in her having melted. Tilting her lips to mine I allow myself to kiss her gently, not passionately or in a manner that might indicate lust, but gently so she knows that I care.

"Don't listen to her," I whisper against her lips, and she leans forward, placing her forehead on my shoulder and letting her eyelids fall, blanketing the fire and starving it of fuel.

As we stand, slumped against one another, exhausted, an uncomfortable cough breaks the thick silence.

"Miss Lucifer— she is skirting the edge of the estate. The cameras caught her. She's merely out among the trees," Jules informs us as I take an alarmed step back. Sephy stiffens in posture, and we both turn to face the butler, who stands, still in his pyjamas, at the foot of the staircase. His expression is endeared, and I wonder what exactly I'm supposed to make of that.

"She's not lying about the shard," I add after a moment's deep thought, turning to Sephy. I grab the pendant hanging around my neck and whip it from beneath the fabric of my shirt.

"This— this is part of it." I shake it in front of her face. "She separated me from a lot of the demonic power in me. It saved my human soul— my life." I remember the alleyway, how I looked up from the shadows of that place and found her, blonde hair, blue eyes, staring down at me like a God-sent angel.

"So, she's not trying to trick me?" Sephy queries, biting her lip with nerves, and I shake my head.

"Well, I don't think so. I could be wrong—" I muse, and Sephy frowns.

"What if she wants to take the power in that shard as her own?" Sephy asks me, eyes wide and fearful. It's moments like this one that make me sure deep down she loves me. That I've occupied one of the many luxurious suites within her heart where Jules has become caretaker, clearing the cobwebs and dust that have settled over a lifetime of loss.

"The shard cannot be used to imbue dark magic, only store it." I remember the same fear clutching at me, how Luce had assured me that by splitting the stone and creating a pendant, the demonic power I was shedding couldn't be used by another.

"How do you know?" she snaps, still paranoid, which I honestly understand after everything. I mean what kind of a person would you have to be not to be suspicious?

"Lucifer told me that the reason she made this pendant was not only to allow me better control over the darkness still left in my soul but also because, if she'd left the obsidian tether whole, anyone could have absorbed that part of me. It would have killed me. My darkness wasn't acquired; it was woven into my soul when I was conceived. It cannot be truly separated from me, not in the way the darkness she absorbed from The Well can be," I explain. Sephy takes several steps away from me, slumping down on the bottom stair and putting her head in her hands as my words sink in.

"So, this could work?" she asks, looking increasingly nervous. I shrug. Jules looks down at her, resting his pyjama-clad elbow on the edge of the bannister, and then back to me, listening intently.

"I don't know. But in theory—" I let my mind wander; the possibility of Lucifer returning as she had been is tempting to say the least. But would she be as she had been? Or has her dabble with the dark changed her forever?

"You think I should go, don't you? Risk my life to get this shard?" she barks, almost accusatory in her tone.

"I think that in the current situation, having Lucifer back to her old self could be an asset we can't ignore," I admit.

"Ugh. You are so annoying," she grumbles. I can't help but smile.

"I only annoy you when you know I'm right. Regardless of whether she's an asset, she's family. I know she'd do the same for you. So would I. If we can take this risk and it helps her, I think it's worth it," I conclude, and Sephy snorts.

"Of course, *you* do. You're not the one who has to go in there and get the damn thing. Besides, Luce is practically your mother—" She waves my opinion away as if it doesn't matter and Jules clears his throat. Sephy looks back up to him.

"What?" she snaps, and he flinches before straightening inside his pyjamas and steeling himself as he replies.

"I'm just thinking— if you could get her under control, it would go a long way in showing A.D.A.M that you are capable of more than they give you credit for," he suggests, and she laughs.

"Like I give a shit about them— I could torch them all and smoke sausages over their remains before they could even lay a hand on any of you." She's confident, the ferocious spark returning to her eyes as she shakes her head.

"Look, it wouldn't be hard. All you must do is convect into the alchemy chamber, grab the shard, and convect back out. Nobody even has to know you're there," I remind her, and she rolls her eyes.

"Wow— just like taking candy from an extremely powerful and well-defended baby." She scowls, probably feeling like we're ganging up on her.

"Look, you don't have to go. You don't. It's your choice, but this might be a simple fix for one of our many problems. Not many of them even have fixes, let alone simple ones. It might help—" I express, imploring her with my gaze.

"Fine. Let me think about it. Just go and get little miss Queen of Darkness— I have questions." She sighs, and I nod, turning on my heel and wasting no time reaching the front doors. Before I reach them, however, she calls me, and I turn back to look over my shoulder.

"What is it?" I ask, watching her face turn sad.

"I'm tired of all this. Don't you ever get tired of all this shit?" she asks, earnest, and I frown.

"More than I thought possible," I reply.

Sighing out with a gentle smile, she rests her chin in her palm, bored.

"Maybe one day we can actually — I don't know — go on a proper date?" she suggests, and my eyes widen, the pull to her strengthening with every single word hitting the air between us.

"I'd like that," I reply, and she smiles at me, her eyes becoming sleepy, almost childlike in their dull sparkle, the shimmer of dreams, of hopes, rising like a new sun behind the horizon of her gaze.

Returning to my objective with a reluctance I often feel, I pull open the door without pause, stepping out beneath the star-studded blanket of the night, hope taking root like a weed.

It isn't as hard to find Luce as I thought, because as I make contact with the defiant grass blades of the lawn, I hear her crying, the sound pitiful and heart-wrenching.

I've seen her angry since Thane left, seen her violent, but I've yet to see her cry. My breath catches in my throat at the sound as I approach, finding her shadow by the edge of the trees, clinging to Beelz on the grass. The amber glow of the cat's eyes grows as I get nearer and a low rumble, half yowl, half warning, emits from her chest.

"Luce?" I whisper out into the darkness, keeping a small distance between us just in case.

She doesn't reply, not verbally anyway, just looks up from where her face is buried into Beelz's neck, her powder blue irises shocking me.

She looks halfway like herself again, the black hair causing the rest of her to appear ghostly in the sliver of moonlight struggling to illuminate either of us.

"What do you want?" she mumbles, wiping beneath her eye with her bare forearm. I take another step closer, finding her forehead split partially open and marred by dried blood. It must be from the crash.

"I want to help. Sephy, she wants to know more about the shard. We all do— we want to help you," I announce, nervous as her eyes glaze, and her gaze drops into the floor.

"I don't deserve it," she whispers, and I feel my eyes narrow as frustration rears in me like a spooked black stallion.

"Get up. Stop with the self-pitying crap. I won't have you destroy yourself." I'm firm now, tired of all the emotional turmoil from not just Luce but Sephy too. It doesn't have to be complicated; it's actually very simple, at least to me.

Luce is family.

We don't let family suffer, especially not when there is an easy fix like this one. Luce is shocked, looking up at me, eyes wide, as if I'm a saint delivered from the heavens.

"I don't want to die—" she sobs, tears falling fast down her cheeks.

"You're not going to die. Get up." I grab her arm now, tired, exhausted, unable to return to my empathetic self.

"I don't want to go back in there. She's mean!" Luce resists, tugging her arm from me. Beelz watches us, ready to intervene if things turn ugly.

"Do you blame her? You trashed her kitchen, her car, you've threatened her and Jules. Of course, she's not going to be happy about you now coming to her and asking her to risk her life!" I exclaim, losing my temper as the pendant around my neck cools slightly.

"I saved her life!" she exclaims, eyes threatening to dilate to black.

"So? That doesn't mean you get to treat her like shit! What was the point in saving her if you're going to do that?" I demand, trying hard to control myself as my voice escapes me in a hiss.

"You don't understand!" she exclaims, and I lose it. I feel my flesh ripple from olive to charred jet as I launch forward and haul Luce, yelling bloody murder, over my shoulder. She pounds against my back with her tiny angry fists, scratches at me with her dark pointed nails, but I don't care.

I'm done negotiating.

I walk back to the house with her screaming at the top of her lungs, contemplating knocking her out just for some peace as I open the front doors of the house and stride in, throwing her like a ragdoll to the floor.

Sephy and Jules stand opposite me and we stare down at her as she smashes her fists into the marble like a small child having a tantrum.

I nod to Sephy, eyes blazing a bloody orange as I relish the feel of my tattoos swirling within the crevices of my molten flesh.

Sephy paces around the flailing woman and bends down fast, grabbing Luce's chin in her hand and forcing her to meet her gaze as she holds her eyes hostage with her own. Firewater meets a glacial lake with an angry hiss, and they stare into one another, unblinking for longer than is normal.

It might be brutal, but I don't find it unnecessary any longer. This thing with Luce, with the darkness, it must end. For nobody's sake more than her own. If the world is really coming to an end, to a final awful crux, to Ragnarök, we need all the help we can get, and nobody owes the world more than her.

If it weren't for her, for me, for Haedes, we wouldn't be here. I'll never forget that, and I can no longer stand by and watch her self-destruct if she herself has come up with a solution to fix it.

I owe her, if nobody else does, even if it means she might hate me forever.

Sephy narrows her eyes, jaw firming up beneath the flawless porcelain of her skin as she glares into Luce's furious expression.

"Now—" she says, no fear or waver in her tone, mind set. "Tell me about the shard."

8

HEAVEN'S ON FIRE

PANDORA

I STARE AT THE volumes packed into shelves along the curved brick wall of the Alchemy Chamber. My finger traces the worn leather bindings, dislodging dust that is sent cartwheeling into the stale air of the long-abandoned space.

What am I looking for? I wonder, not entirely sure what it is I'm even doing here.

Power. I need power. My tongue flicks out to caress the plump, cracked skin of my bottom lip. It's rough from where I've chewed on it as my nerves have grown into an undeniable phantom, possessing my body with a frantic energy where before there had been what seemed like an unshakeable confidence and sense of calm.

My eyes flick from the volumes over to the shelves at the farthest end of the tower, jars of ingredients, life energy stolen, which if combined in the right way can provide power— but it's never going to be permanent. Hercules is right; I need to find a way to imbue myself with real magic, need to feel it running in my veins where nobody can steal it from me.

Frowning, I turn my back on the shelves of what I now deem to be useless stacks of crinkled brown paper and pitiful ink, smeared by those not powerful enough to live, only to record.

My eyes fall over the pedestals ringing the outside of the room, housing nothing but junk or what someone with a soul might consider sentimental trinkets in an elevated and exaggerated state of importance.

Sighing, I move to the door, opening it swiftly and almost walking straight into Anubis who is on the other side, head cocked to where the wood grain had just been.

"Oh, it's you!" she exclaims, not sounding relieved. I quirk an eyebrow.

"Expecting somebody else?" I snap, looking into her face with an irritated expression. Without the sun, the ageing of her skin has begun to pick up again, and it is noticeable. Where before the flawless tan of her flesh had exuded a golden glow, it is now dull, her dark eyes sunken into her skull.

I wonder if she's been sleeping or, instead, pacing the floors, wondering about how to free her son, Osiris, who is lying in one of the many cells of the vast dungeons below.

"No, I just— I don't know. I thought maybe it might be one of The Demon Lords." She stands awkwardly as though I am a welcome alternative, a relief.

I frown.

Does she really feel me that little of a threat?

The thought irks me.

"I'm heading down to the dungeons. Are you coming?" I ask, watching her eyes spark with predictable, but nonetheless satisfactory, hope.

"You considered my request?" she enquires immediately, voice rising in pitch.

I snort.

"Why would I? Your son is a traitor. Traitors belong in a prison cell." I dismiss her with these three simple, clipped sentences, the scent of her perfume, a rich concoction of myrrh and rosewater, causing my nostrils to widen and my stomach to turn. Her eyes narrow, jaw tensing under my gaze, but she says nothing. I observe her posture stiffen, breath shallow and controlled within the slimming confines of her white and gold gown. If I were being cruel, I would comment on how it looks very much like a death shroud, a form of fashionable foreshadowing perhaps?

I turn on my heel, descending the spiral staircase fast and leaving Anubis to retreat into what had once been Lucifer and Thanatos' suite. As she opens the door, I hear the echoes of her jackal's barking chase me as I continue to increase the distance between us.

They cease as the door slams angrily in my wake, and as I reach the bottom step, I hear a familiar voice take its place. I still, pressing myself against the inside of the tower's crystalline wall, hiding instinctually.

"You think she's no threat?" Abraxis' deep voice rumbles through the air, causing it to tremor as my withered heart speeds. My fingers crawl, tracing the same stone that chills my back, looking for purchase as my blood begins to roar in my ears, a pertinent reaction to the person replying.

"I think she has the potential to be a great many things. A threat? Perhaps." Gorgon's confidence in me causes me to flush, hand rising to rest just above my breast like a schoolgirl thinking of her latest crush.

"Is that why you're sleeping with her?" Abraxis demands, and I hear Gorgon stutter, failing to reply. "Gorgon, I'm the Demon Lord of Lies and Illusion. It is written on your soul. Her stench is all over you." Abraxis laughs, and I narrow my eyes, left eyelid twitching uncontrollably.

"That is none of your concern," Gorgon hisses, and I smile.

"Whatever. Just make sure you know what you're doing with her." Abraxis delivers his warning, and I hear Gorgon inhale sharply, can almost feel the crinkle of his thin lips as they pull into a smile.

"I know exactly what I'm doing. Actually, there's something I wanted to talk with you about. A surprise for her—" As Gorgon begins to speak, I hear Abraxis hold his breath.

"Come, let's discuss this somewhere else," he decrees, blunt in his deep and definitive sense of authority. I wonder if he knows I'm listening, can sense my presence, smell my '*stench*', but before I have a chance to listen on and continue to wonder, the two have disappeared swiftly, their synchronised footsteps dissolving into distant silence.

I wait a good three minutes before peering around the edge of the curved wall encasing the spiral staircase of the tower, brain flitting between feeling flattered at Gorgon's loyalty and wary of Abraxis' contempt. My paranoia creeps, ever slow but unmistakable, from the mist of my mind's deepest recess. It has tendrils, has roots and hungry vines that bury deep into my memories, breaking them apart like loosely packed earth and worming into every word that's ever passed between me and The Demon Lords. If only there was a way to see the truth of it all, to rise above mere perception and to know the universe as it is, like a god.

A thought occurs to me as I contemplate taking a walk around the perimeter of the Exilia and checking on the demon hoards crowding the gates, pining for their masters. So, instead of moving to descend yet more stairs, I take a sharp left and stride at speed toward the dungeons.

The high ceilings of the narrow corridor have eyes, dark and deep, staring down at me as the hairs on the back of my neck involuntarily stand to attention. I try to ignore them, but my own eyes cannot help but sweep upward every few seconds as the sound of scuttling legs and dripping jaws chases me down the length of the corridor.

Reaching the dungeon entrance, I push open the thick wooden doors, which in no way match the rest of the décor, and flit down into the dankness of the labyrinthine tunnels. They are lined on all sides with damp cells made from mould-infested cobblestone and sealed off with wrought iron bars, peppered through with rust that will continue to spread like metallic cancer, weakening them with the years. This is perhaps one of the only visible signs here that time is not at a standstill.

As I pass Osiris, who has crawled closer to the bars in case it is not I but his mother who approaches, he looks up at me, walnut-coloured eyes hollow and disappointed. I kick a small stone at him, violet eyes flashing dangerously in the low light.

"Now, now, don't heckle the prisoners." Barbas' sharp tone slices through the dank air between us, curling around my shoulder like a hungry hyena and making goosebumps rise across the side of my neck.

"I'll do what I please, thank you," I bite back, finding his edgy silhouette leaning against the bars of the cell I've come to visit. "What are you even doing here?" I try not to sound too curious, but he still smirks at my intrigue.

"Indulging my curiosity—" he whispers, eyes glinting wicked.

"Curiosity?" I ask, watching him examine the ragged nails which complete his spindled fingers. I inhale deeply, the smell of old urine and body odour ripe in the air like sour fruit that's been fertilised by a heavy layer of cruelty and confinement.

"Haven't you ever wondered what Fate has to fear?"

Feeling my brows rise, I realise I've never really thought about it.

"I'm sure you'll tell me." I refuse to act interested, as ever, keeping my face mostly inexpressive. My dead eyes, the firm line of my lips, the pointed cheekbones and unflushed demeanour forge the crucial and impenetrable links of my personal chainmail.

"I would if there was anything to tell." Barbas' gaze becomes irritated, eyes scrutinizing my face as I spot a small spider crawling among his long silver hair, weaving a web between strands.

"They fear nothing?" I sound more surprised than I intend and watch as he visibly stiffens with defensive dissatisfaction at my assessment.

"I suppose that's what comes of knowing the most probable outcome before it happens." Barbas' voice seems too relaxed when contrasted with his body language. This is the second time in recent history he's been unable to instil terror, and I cannot help but wonder if he's losing his touch.

As if reading my mind, he slinks forward, lips spreading salaciously like a tiger about to pounce on its next meal.

"As for you, my dear, it might be time for a stiff drink. Your paranoia is showing." He saunters past me, rancid breath catching in my nostrils as the half-threat half-whisper tickles my right ear. I push my hair back as he passes through the long corridor behind me before making his way nimbly up the stairs toward the exit.

I exhale as I hear the door close behind him; unaware of how stiffly I've been holding myself while in his presence until he's gone. I scowl, hating him and his ability to make me transparent.

Hercules, it seems, is being proven more correct with each encounter I endure within these hallowed halls.

Turning on the spot, I lay eyes on the reason I'm here, finding the three elderly figures hunched on crooked yet somehow identical wooden stools within the cell. I found them wandering the halls my second day in residence, wondering if they'd missed the memo that Haedes no longer runs this wretched place, or if they had some kind of inside knowledge that led them to expose themselves. They're tricky despite being old and infirm, mainly because, as has been confirmed by Barbas, they fear nothing and nobody. It has never been more clearly demonstrated than by these three old crones that knowledge truly is power.

"Pandora, what a pleasant surprise." One of the women, the blind one, acknowledges my presence, unnerving me.

I watch the three women collectively turning a spinning wheel, feeding straw into the contraption. The thing creaks, wood on metal causing a ghastly cry of protest. From the other side, I watch a shimmering fibre that is not entirely natural looking appear, woven fast. It glistens in the low light, gold perhaps?

No, that's the stuff of fairy tales. It must be something else.

I clear my throat, ignoring the quick work of their withered fingers and trying to get to my point.

"I'm here for information," I announce, and the blind woman stares at me again, mouth quirking at some joke I'm not privy to as she blinks slowly with unseeing eyes.

"We know. Do you know who it is you're talking to, dear?"

"Don't underestimate me, old woman," I hiss, fingers wrapping too tightly around the bars between us.

"We never under or over-estimate anybody, pet. We see with clarity; it's what we do. And you know if you want information, I could go for a nice cuppa, two sugars and lots of cream." The deaf woman, who looks more withered than the other two, gives me her demands. I watch the mute old woman sign the words to her, fingers smacking loudly against one another, so she knows what I'm saying. They flash me a collectively gummy smile, and I tense at their insubordination. It's as if they think they're on vacation.

"It is not your place to demand anything from me. You are my prisoners," I remind them, the incessant clacking of the ancient spinning wheel jarring on my last nerve.

"Someone is a Debbie Downer," the blind Fate tuts, not turning to face me as she grabs more straw from a pile beside her.

"A real grumpus—" the mute signs passionately to her deaf sister, causing them both to laugh, silver wisps of hair falling from their high buns like thin and flighty smoke. "Such a pretty girl. Such a shame—" she continues on her own behalf. "You know you really should smile more. And take your hair up off your face. No use hiding behind that fringe now, is there?"

"Enough!" I bark, rattling the bars between us. My fury becomes uncontrollable as the three women smile with unshakeable calm, glancing quickly at one another.

"Oh, hush. Stop being such an anger ball! The answer is right in front of that pretty nose of yours!" The blind Fate announces, and I frown.

"What? What do you mean?" I snap, and the deaf Fate watches the mute beside her quickly sign.

"The only solution to your problem has already been within your grasp once. But you gave it to another—" she speaks, and my mind whirs, retracing my steps.

"It's a shame it isn't here right now— I'd even take my tea from it. Not quite fine china but as you know, desperate times—" The voice of the blind woman flicks a switch within my head, and I find the problem illuminated by a sudden and obvious solution.

97

"The chalice?" I query aloud, and they nod in synchronised time. They smile next with gaping mouths, the corners of their lips moist with gathered spittle.

"But of course, dear." The red eyes of the blind Fate remain unblinking, fixed now on her handiwork.

"I'm — I'm not — I'm not worthy. I am merely a Titan, and my immortality — the sun —" I protest, and all three of them turn to me, giving me a look of mighty disapproval.

"Whoever is putting these ideas in your pretty head? Not worthy? Have you even *tried* to drink from The Well, child?"

My eyes widen, chest filling fast with something like pride.

"I was too afraid— Lucifer said it would kill me," I whisper, voice a sliver of what it had been only moments before as I begin to wonder, in awe of my own stupidity.

Have I been worthy all along?

I've always known I was different, special even, but this?

Is it destined? Fated?

"And you believed her? Pfft." The deaf Fate shakes her head, her mute sister continuing to gesticulate vowels, consonants, and concepts in a flurry of handwork.

"Such low self-esteem for such a powerful beauty. Whatever has the world done to you?" the blind woman asks.

"I suppose my confidence has been a little broken since the thing in The Higher Plains with Zeus," I admit, feeling the vault where I keep my emotions contained open ever so slightly. It is a box of unspeakable horrors, of terrors and self-doubt, and it is opening voluntarily of all things.

"So, what are you waiting for? Go and get the chalice!" They encourage me, and I realise fast that there's no time to waste.

Turning on my heel, I look back over one shoulder.

"Right, I'll do that. Thanks. I guess it must still be at The Well," I relinquish, not recalling retrieving it after Lucifer had drunk deep and been transformed, made whole, at my hand.

I can't believe I had fallen for her playing on my low self-esteem and feelings of failure.

She will pay for that, and soon.

The old women, who have been far more helpful and willing than I anticipated, give a collective wave, toothy smiles wide and gaping.

Returning the expression for only a fraction of a second, I pick the box out from my innermost jacket pocket and allow the smile to vanish before taking off to claim my rightful fate.

The deep burgundy of the sky falls over Mortaria like a bloodstained shroud, the remnant stain of the once presiding Haedes, who has long since been put out to pasture. There are no clouds, no stars, no sun. Nothing but barren, deep merlot from here to the horizon. I stare at it, an intoxicating reminder that the land now belongs to me.

No chill breeze, as ever, and yet the air stirs just enough for me to notice as I stare into the walls ahead, which are infested with scarlet twisting vines. I study them, the vice grip of nature trying to suffocate the architecture of this unnatural monument, erected where it doesn't belong.

I feel them as I take a single step forward, my pupils full of sanguine lust, peering out from within the shadows of the place. They scurry, too fast for my eyes to catch, behind the dark outlines of crooked, scraggy trees, their branches seeming to crack the sky as they protrude upward in edgy and blatant protests of the earth from which they've sprung.

I don't want to waste any time, and so ignoring their spine-tingling presence, taking long strides toward the entrance of the small plot of land that surrounds The Well. The archway casts a shadow over me as my heels impact the stone, the change from soft ruddy soil to hard blood-spattered rubble causing a stir among the demons I know await inside. It makes sense that they would want to be close to the source of their power.

As I enter the arena where Lucifer and I had battled, I remember that night, watching her bleed an innocent dry. It is here that I find them, circling The Well, protecting their heritage like loyal guard dogs. I'm surprised to find a mix of demons, not only Succubi, which I would expect as the Sanguine Forest is their feeding grounds, but Banshees, their shoulder blades rising in mountainous peaks around the valley of their spines. Gorgonians undulate in and out of existence too, their camouflage almost perfect, almost flawless, but not quite as the kaleidoscopic blur of rot and leaves causes them to adapt with every single slither. There are no Abraxians, probably because Abraxis has convinced them they are too good to need such proximity, but Phobias hang lazily in the shadowy corners, webs spun around them like armour as they watch on.

I look at the demons, each species coming to notice me within seconds and pausing in their clockwork motion around the ancient site. I raise my chin, looking down my nose at them, expecting the same façade of loyalty as I have procured from their masters, but I receive no such courtesy. The hissing of forked tongues and the baring of jagged teeth rumbles through the air, a warning of the coming storm.

The bodies of the guards that once kept this place for the power within the Exilia alone are still strewn across the floor, their skeletons stripped dry and their bones soaked red by the soil. I left them here like confetti from the celebration of my victory, but now I will utilise the weapons they have left behind.

I lunge, feeling the eyes of the demonic Kindred follow me, launching into action as I clutch at a rusty blood-soaked sword, pulling it from a skeleton's dead grasp. Finger bones creak and then explode, flying outward as I wrench the thing free, blood and soil coating my pale skin with a grim chill.

A Banshee catches my intent, launching itself into the air and heading right for me.

I roll onto my back, hair flying around me like wicked tendrils of ink suspended in dark water as the sword finds itself impaling the beast fast. Blood spatters from the chest wound, baptising me with murderous intent as the Banshee falls, dead, on top of me. Shoving it to one side, I push myself to my feet, feeling the crunch of dead leaves flattened beneath my boot.

I can hear them approach from my left and so pirouette, my sparkling sheath of a skirt twisting itself around me like a tornado. I slam the sword into the ground, skewering an approaching Gorgonian in the process, and then use the blade to pick up the flailing body, now a dull and slimy mould colour.

I thrust the sword back, the entrails of the Gorgonian spattering my hand as the body is flung from the length of the weapon and into the wall behind me with a dull thud.

Striding sideways, crouched, I place one foot behind the other and allow my violet eyes to catch the vermillion of surrounding forest and sky.

A Succubi launches forward, pale spindled fingers outstretched, but I step back, balancing on one foot and raising the other like a crane before slicing the head of the Succubi clean from its shoulders. Its fingers narrowly miss my throat as they fall through empty air, and the body crumples to the floor like a sad puppet with no master. Breathing in the rank air of the place, I find myself unafraid, adrenaline coursing through my veins and reminding me of the days when I had soared above Aetheria, the days when I fought with righteous and misguided intent.

I stare at other demons glancing, almost as though they're sentient and not rabid, at the dead bodies of their kin. Cocking an eyebrow, I expect them to continue the attack, but they don't. Instead, without masters, without orders of restraint from The Demon Lords, they retreat. They climb the walls of the place, trapping claws between crags of cobblestone and leveraging themselves to safety on the other side of the site's weak boundary.

I smile.

The Fates were right. I am worthy, worthy of their loyalty, worthy of the dark.

I let bones, leaves, and metal clatter underfoot as I approach the mirror surface of The Well's dark magics, the simple stacked cobblestones of its structure in no way doing the power within justice. I scan the floor, finding the skeleton of a kid strewn opposite me amid curling burgundy leaves. The blade I'd given her to do the deed is brown with dried blood, laying on the floor, dull and unremarkable among the debris, quite the opposite of the act itself.

Treading around the circumference of The Well, I find it on the floor. Bending, I grasp the scarlet-coated silver in my palm, the scent of it rich with iron.

As I examine it, my heart drops. It's cracked, the metal dented by the tread of many demons, the stones smashed to pieces.

The chalice is useless, the power that had been imbued in the murderous glint of the rubies and the abyssal dark of the onyx gone along with their smooth facets.

I spin, launching the cup over the top of The Well and letting it clatter against the wall, causing several remaining Phobias to scuttle away and off into the surrounding forest. My rage bubbles close to the surface as my nails bite into the pale skin of my palm.

The Fates said— they had said that I was worthy— so what now?

I look deep into the flawless black mirror of the water's surface, wondering, daring, as pride and confidence swell within me like a storm cloud about to burst.

Closing my eyes, I lean forward so both palms are splayed over the bloodstained stone at the edge of the structure, staring down into my reflection, draped in gossamer shadow.

My face, the same now as it has ever been, is surrounded by jet black hair and boasts, ever still, the violet eyes which give away the fact I had been chosen. I'd been chosen by Hera for greatness. So then, why should this not be my power to consume?

I ponder this for a few moments, grinding my teeth, exhaling and inhaling deeply as I steel my nerves.

Such low self-esteem for such a powerful beauty. The Fate's voice echoes in my head as I take a final exhale and extend a single finger to touch the surface of the abyssal pool.

I gasp, recoiling, my flesh burning, bubbling from the contact as a feral hiss explodes from my lips, nerves exploding with agony like the branches of a tree set alight.

The pool of the ancient magic only ripples twice at the contact, but otherwise remains undisturbed, unchanged by my presence.

They lied— *wrinkled old bitches.*

This is not my power to take.

I am not worthy.

So— where do I turn next?

9

SYMPATHY FOR THE DEVIL

SEPHY

I PLACE MY HOOD up over my head, loose red strands of hair swept up by the force of the rising air from the flames. They diminish as I stand, firm in stance, heated tongues dissolving in a plume of smoke upon the roof of Xion's apartment building.

I stare out over Mortaria, eyes widening as I take several slow steps toward the edge of the building's flat rooftop. I kick a loose piece of stone with the toe of my boot as I reach the low-hanging ledge, all that now stands between myself and thin air.

The last time I stood here, Xion and I had been about to dance underneath a night sky weighted with a heavy crimson hue; the threat of an oncoming spark shower. He had twirled me beneath the cascade of falling embers, something kindling between us that would ultimately be the catalyst to our inevitable destruction.

I let out an uncontrollable sigh, my go-to reaction for any deep thought involving him and me, me and him— *us*, if you can even call whatever the hell we are that.

Mortaria boasts the same dark sky as it had that night, but now it isn't because of the imminent flood of scorching tears from the bloody heavens. Instead, it's because where the sun had once been, an enormous black spot hangs in the sky like a shadow of grief, the land mourning for the loss of its one true king.

Haedes and I hadn't been close. I mean, honestly, we barely knew each other. Regardless, and without my consent, something within my chest aches at the thought of him being gone from this world. Is that because now the desperately hopeful eyes of his followers fall to me to restore everything to the way it had been? Or is it because he and I had been more alike than I had ever anticipated?

Perhaps – I wonder as I look out over the land, surveying what has changed and what has stayed the same – that is what terrifies me about the burden of this place. I have seen what it took from Haedes, and I have already lost enough for one lifetime.

This place is somebody else's problem now, no question in my mind.

My eyes connect with the horizon, the sky dark and empty, the air still as ever, and yet— the hairs on my arms stand to attention, and I have the unexplainable urge to flee as quickly as possible.

From here, they look like fire ants, swarming in the veins and arteries of the diseased city. Banshees screech, voices rising in a sick and ear-piercing tribute to the new power here.

I scan the place, the dark shard of the Exilia Multum rising in an unapologetic and blade-like suddenness into the air, the silhouette of it as doused in shadow as it has ever been.

Something is different, but it takes me a full two or three minutes of standing, crouched over the ledge of the building, to work out what.

The River Styx no longer runs through the land like a flow of phantasmal lifeblood. Instead, the paths where it had once carved through the dark land are but a scorch mark, a bruise of what it had once been.

So— the river isn't flowing.

What does that mean?

I don't know the answer, but I know it can't be good.

Scrunching up my nose, I take a deep inhale of stale air, my usual sense of humour dampened by the harrowing decline of what I once thought of as not beautiful but sublime.

It made me feel small, this place. Made me feel like my own problems were considerably unimportant in the scheme of the universe. Yet another reason I don't want to take on the universe's problems as my own. They belong on the shoulders of a pure-bred god, somebody trained, somebody prepared, not on the shoulders of a feisty orphaned redhead with a whiskey problem and a thing for fast cars.

Showtime. I think, channelling Haedes as I turn my back on the cityscape and ball my hands into fists.

I let the blue flames rise, disappearing seamlessly from beneath the dark and heavy weight of the now-empty sky.

I reappear within the cylindrical confines of Luce's alchemy chamber. I've had potions from inside here before, but I've never actually stepped foot into its stale darkness. The scent of odd concoctions, of long evaporated incense and lush but poisonous succulents hits me, and I stand, distracted by the shelves on the curved wall farthest from me. Jars of powders, dried leaves, and worse, *body parts*, call to me as I let curiosity overwhelm.

I'm distracted from my quick mission as I tread over the cobbled weave of the floor, finding stains from what had once been spilt with urgency beneath my boots. The place is dark, the torches long since extinguished, so I click my fingers, summoning The Eternal Flame to light the room as an orange glow explodes like a new sunrise, casting long shadows upon the walls and floor.

The flames flicker, reflecting over and over in the tiny glass cylinders of each vial labelled in spidering scrawl. I peer into their depths, finding papery thin iridescent wings, glistening teeth, claws, hair, and bones. It seems humans aren't the only ones who take mystical parts for what they need.

A single vial catches my attention more than the others; I don't know why, but inside I find several glistening scales, magenta in hue.

I peer at it, watching the surface of what I think are small pieces of Mermaid scale catch the light, turning it iridescent peach and tourmaline with blue sheen as I turn the vial in my palm.

What is it about this that made my father— Adam Sinclair, into less than a human being? Did he take scales like these to sell to the highest bidder or worse?

I move to place the vial back on the shelf but knock another vial, containing some kind of white shimmering powder, from the corner of the shelf in turn.

I reach out to catch it but drop the one I'm holding without thinking as I reach for it, a reaction performed on instinct. It falls to the floor, a loud and ear-shattering smash following in quick succession as the glass explodes out like a firework from the tiny focal epicentre of my imminent demise.

Shit. Shit. Shit!

I spin on my heel, scurrying over to the pedestal Luce had described and lift the glass bell jar encasing what it is I came all this way to find.

I hear someone coming, so yank the sliver of obsidian, which looks like it could have been a spearhead before the piece Xion wore around his neck had been taken, from the pedestal. I slip it into the back of my waistband, feeling the cool and jagged facets of the pearlescent black crystal press hard into the soft skin of my lower back.

I turn just as a key swivels in the lock of the door and extinguish the torches with a wave of my hand only seconds too late. I stand with my hands balled into small fists in the dark, waiting for the intruder to expose themselves.

My heart slows in my chest as I allow my breathing to regulate, blood cooling and fingers unfurling to twitch at my sides as Anubis stands, tall and willowy, silhouetted like an immense statue against the light of the landing outside.

"Hello, Anubis." I greet her without warmth, glad now that I have the chance to look her in the face.

She's the reason we're all in this situation, and I contemplate killing her. I don't know what it is that stops me, but I continue to gaze at her as her tongue sweeps across her voluptuous bottom lip.

"I assume you're here to take back the throne," she guesses, stepping in through the open doorway, eyes sunken dark pits. She looks weary, her skin lacking its usual radiant sheen, her shoulders stiff with tension. I don't know why she's tense though. She's sitting pretty from where I stand.

"You assume wrong. As usual." I glare at her, and both her threaded brows rise in twin peaks of surprise upon the once-flawless landscape of her face.

"Then why did you come back here? Are you stupid? Why would you—" she exclaims, looking over one shoulder with paranoia sparking like wildfire, infectious, behind her rich chocolate irises.

"I came back here to help the woman you destroyed," I reply, glaring at her and crossing my arms over my chest. She doesn't appear to want violence, just a nice little chit-chat. I wonder why I continue to indulge her. I should be getting out of here.

"So, you're not trying to take back Mortaria? I think you're lying," she goads me, and I can't help but find her tone condescending. The old me would have snapped, would have been so easily baited, but I know her now. She always has a motive.

"I don't want to sit on a throne, least of all here. My concern now is the people of the mortal world, so don't worry. You're safe. Though you deserve to be burned to a crisp. I think though that perhaps I'll let The Demon Lords and Pandora dispose of you. A little bit of karma after everything," I retort, a twinkle blooming in one eye.

I turn, ready to spin into a plume of flames and disappear with the same swagger my father once had, but before I can, I hear her clear her throat.

"W—Wait—" she stutters, voice hoarse and more vulnerable than I ever recall hearing it before.

"And why on earth would I do that?" I ask her. I would usually have sarcastic retorts, but this entire place is making my skin crawl, the proximity of so many demons known in my marrow. I'm worn down, and I don't have time for games, least of all hers.

"Because— you're a good person," she replies, tone cautious even still, reluctant perhaps. I spin back on one foot, hair pluming around me as my hood falls from my head, and burst into a high-pitched, incredulous laugh.

"How did you figure that? I think you've got me confused with someone who gives a shit about you. As it stands, I'm too busy clearing up the mess you made with Lucifer to give a damn what you have to say. Even if I was a good person, Anubis, I'm not a stupid one," I admonish, narrowing my eyes.

"How is Lucifer?" she asks me.

I laugh again, almost choking.

"Oh, I'm sorry. You care now? Why don't you just fuck off!?" I turn back to leave yet again, but before I can, I feel her long fingers gripping my shoulder, pointed nails digging into my skin through the leather of my jacket.

"I just— I think your father would be disappointed if you were not to succeed him, Sephy."

"I think you're full of crap—" My voice trails off as I turn back once more, slower than before. Why does she care so much? Is it a trap? Something to goad me into launching war on the demon hoards? Is she trying to get me to tip the scales?

As I peer into her eyes, taking in her face in its exquisite detail, it hits me. Of course, Anubis doesn't care about the scales. The reason she wants me on the throne is much closer to home.

"Pandora— she didn't tell you she was going to turn out the sun, did she?" I demand. Anubis looks immediately uncomfortable.

"No."

I think about this for a moment. The Demon Lords are immortal without it, and, well, I don't know about Pandora. Either way, Anubis lost big despite her alliance.

"So, let me get this straight— you want me to risk life and limb, so you don't start to age like a real mortal?" I must sound even more incredulous than before because I watch her begin to chew the inside of her cheek. As I breathe in the rich scent of her lacklustre skin, I think even she must know she sounds pathetic.

"It's not just about me. What about Osiris? He helped you. You owe him—" She begins her plea, but I press my index finger to her plump lips, pushing her back from me.

"Uh, no. I don't *owe* anybody. What the hell is it with you gods and keeping some kind of tally with this shit? I do what I want, when I want. As far as I'm concerned, your son made his bed. He can lie in that sucker." I think on him, on the way he'd warned us of what was happening so we could run to save both Luce and Thane.

Still, though, I cannot forget that he must have stood by while Anubis schemed with Pandora for months. Even if he is innocent, which I doubt, he may still hold alliances with his mother, and I can't risk her poisoning any more of the people I care about with darkness, crappy Egyptian appetizers, or otherwise.

"So, you're just going to stand by and let the universe burn?" she asks, a crazed look in her eyes as she stands still as a sarcophagus left within a deep dark tomb, waiting endlessly for a verdict that might never come.

"Shouldn't you have thought about that before you lit the match? I'm no firefighter, Anubis. I don't put out blazes in case you haven't noticed. I revel in them. Pain, destruction, even death is what's forged me into who I am. Now, I don't know who you think that is, but it's not a hero or a queen."

"Your father would be disappointed—" she snarls, and I laugh at her.

"I think he'd be proud. Choosing fine whiskey and good sex over responsibility and bloodshed. I think that's exactly the kind of thing he'd do."

"He sacrificed everything to keep the balance intact— you don't understand," she whimpers, staring over one shoulder. "You have to—"

"I don't have to understand. I'm not going to get involved. End of story."

I turn to leave.

"What about Osiris?" she asks desperately as I hear what she has only moments before; footsteps approaching up the spiral staircase. Yet again, I turn back over my shoulder, feeling like I've been here before. Now though, I end the conversation on my terms, keeping control of her in the only way I know how.

"I'll be in touch," I taunt her, knowing that a sliver of hope can be more painful than none, and that more than anything, I want her to hurt. I want her to burn for everything she's done.

As two familiar faces skid around the doorway and Anubis spins to meet them, I make my exit, convecting in a thunderous roar of flaming scarlet fury.

IT'S NOT ENOUGH

XION

THE HOT WATER FROTHS around me, fragrant bubbles rising into the steam from the depths of the sunken tub as I sit, arms spread along the length of one side, lost in thought.

Everything has happened fast, too fast, and I'm left feeling worn down from it all. I can see it in the others too, especially Sephy, her sarcastic flair somewhat diminished as though it's taking everything she has not to fall apart, that making light of it all might just push her over the edge.

The scent of lavender, an obvious choice given the absence of any single calming influence in my life, blooms thick into the air, leaving a thin mist of floral musk over my skin. I let my eyes fall to where the outline of her palm remains, scorched into the blanket of olive skin just inches above my heart. I close my eyes, letting myself float, if for only a second, in a reverie of broken shards, the memories containing her that are both stunning and jagged. The emotions associated with these memories are held in my grey matter, riddled with synapses, delicate and fragile compared to the razor edges of these recollections, a lethal beauty threatening to shred it all.

"Are you— is that *lavender*?" her voice creeps, mocking, over my shoulder. I twist, water sloshing around my chest, and find her at the edge of the bathroom, staring out of the window into the sunrise, legs casually crossed as she props herself against the marble countertop at her spine. The floral perfume from the tub intensifies in a wave, unleashed by the motion of the water.

"Uh— yes. You're back," I comment, spinning and resting my chin atop the damp downy hair of my forearms, staring up at her dark outline, her silhouette somewhat edgier than it had been before.

"You know— lavender is a little girly, even for you," she taunts, turning to the mirror behind her and examining her reflection. She bends over the basin to get a closer look, presenting the curve of her ass to me, a ripe peach that needs biting into.

I watch as her jacket slips up her back as she stretches, a flash of dark stone catching my eye.

"You got it then?" I ask, and she spins to face me again, rolling her eyes.

"Duh. Who do you think you're talking to?" She smirks, mouth quirking up on the left side and causing her cheek to dimple ever so slightly. I return the sentiment, reminding myself that she's not the kind of person you ever want to underestimate.

She pulls the shard from the back waistband of her pants, holding it up to the light and turning it over.

"I thought it would be— *bigger*," she teases.

I cock my eyebrow.

"Never judge a demon by the size of his tether, Persephone." Her full name slips from me, but she doesn't correct me. I'm surprised. She hates being called by her full name.

"All right, Mr Floral Bloom. I apologise— now, would you like some cucumbers for your eyes, to help those bags? A relaxing facial mask with sea minerals, perhaps?" She sticks out her left hip, running her tongue along her bottom lip provocatively. I give her a death stare.

"There's nothing wrong with lavender. I like it," I retort, inhaling deeply as though I've been presented with a full rack of ribs.

"Pfft, and to think I thought you were all masculine intensity. With your giant swirly flaming tattoos, bulging muscles, and facial hair the consistency of a freaking shoe brush! You're just a giant pansy!" She flips her hair in nonchalant amusement.

"Don't make me remind you what I'm capable of—" I growl, letting my knuckles turn white on the edge of the tub.

"Want an orange juice? I'm sure Jules can rustle up some little pink umbrellas—" she taunts me, eyes sparkling, a rare good mood for her these days when the world seems to be wearing her down slowly, hour by hour.

I lift myself up and out of the tub, sloshing water everywhere as she bolts for the door. I catch up to her as I bound from the bottom marble step, spinning her to face me and pushing her into the dark grain of the bedroom door, my dripping naked body flush against her as the hot water seeps into her clothes and the carpet below.

Running my tongue along her jaw, I bite down hard on my bottom lip, heart racing, the demon straining within the cage of my torso to be set free. If I didn't want to ignore the fact entirely, I might even think that the demon half of me has a thing for her too.

Dismissing the thought as fast as I can, I take her earlobe in between my lips, whispering in a feral, breathy exhale.

"Persephone— don't you know by now never to goad a demon?" I demand, my lips spreading into a smile against the nape of her neck. She sighs, the cinnamon spice of her breath twisting around my form like a python, making my heart ache and my soul constricts with need. From her, the question simply falls.

"Why the hell not?"

Half an hour later, we emerge fully dressed from the suite, calm and sated as blood cools in my veins, both of us smelling of lavender. She holds the shard tight in her palm as we adjourn down the corridor, passing the record room on our left where I'd first given her the book on The Demon Lords and moving directly to the suite that once belonged to her parents.

"Ready?" She sounds anxious as I raise my free hand to the door, the other locked with hers, a desperate attempt to continue the mood between us I know will soon evaporate.

Everything right now is a chronic ache, so the few moments we steal alone I cannot help but want to dedicate to animal instinct, if not for the fact that we seem to physically meld so perfectly after so little time, then to simply remove ourselves from the situation outside the door of her suite altogether.

If I was a selfish person, I would have asked her to convect us far away from here long ago, to a beach with crystalline aquamarine waters and powder white sand, a place where we could surrender always and let go of the responsibilities that seem ready to crush us both flat.

The sound of my knock shatters the dream that I know for me, honourable stupid me, is impossible. I couldn't live with the guilt; I'm just not ignorant enough to be able to turn my back on my responsibility to everyone here, especially Luce.

The door doesn't open, no sound exuding from within, so Sephy impatiently twists the golden doorknob and lets herself inside. I follow her, not sure what to expect. Within the duck egg blue walls of the expansive suite, Luce is staring out of the bay window, sitting in the chair in where we'd found Thane dead. Her legs are curled up beneath her, and her head is resting against the high wings of the silken upholstery, eyes vacant but no longer black. The sun catches their glassy sheen in its orange newness, turning her irises into flaming glaciers of despair, slowly melting as drops of grief freeze her facial expression into one of catatonic absence.

Sephy, never one for finesse or subtlety, slaps the shard of obsidian down on the small coffee table in front of her as she continues to stare out over the grounds without acknowledging us. Beelz stirs at her feet, staring up at Sephy with a pissed expression. She hates being disturbed during naptime and honestly seems to have missed the warmth of the yellow sun in this dimension.

"Got the shard. Let's do this thing," she announces, standing with her arms crossed and stance wide. She's wearing a black tank top and one of her favoured pairs of leather pants, bare feet pale in contrast. Her red hair sheens fiery in the new light of day as she stands in the falling rays from the window, an almost holy glow emitting from her sun-dappled skin.

Luce doesn't move.

Sephy reaches out, bopping her on the nose like she's pressing an on button, and I cannot help but laugh. At the sound, she stirs.

"You're back—" she says, voice hollow and tired.

"Yep, had a nice little chat with Anubis before a couple of Demon Lords busted in. Got out just in time," she explains, and my expression turns automatically stony at the mention of Anubis. I hadn't thought to ask how the trip went because she'd returned successful in the retrieval.

"What the hell did she want? Did you fight?" I ask, curious, as Lucifer gets to her feet and picks the shard up with listless dreaminess from the glass table in front of her. I watch her as she approaches the stark gold light of the window, raising her face to meet its rays and exposing her pale skin to its light before raising the shard to examine it.

"She wants me to take the throne of Mortaria." Sephy sighs at what she clearly views as an incredulous notion, putting her fingernails out in front of her and examining them carefully.

"Um— *excuse me*?" I almost choke on my own intake of breath.

"Oh yeah, she's a complete twatwaffle. Surprise, surprise. Can we move on?"

Sephy looks bored, pushing a luminous red lock of hair behind one ear.

"But why—" I begin, thinking hard. Then it occurs to me as my eyes flit over to Luce, leaning against the right curve of the bay window, the obsidian shard casting an odd oily shadow over her face. "The sun— she's ageing, isn't she?" I can't help but stifle a laugh.

"Ding, ding, ding!" Amusement flits across Sephy's face like the campfire hand puppets of children.

"I guess she didn't think about that before she got Haedes killed— idiot." I tut, wondering now if all of this could have been avoided if she had only been content with her life as it was. I suppose, when I think about it and my eyes trace the dark outline of Luce's matte black hair, a lot of things could have gone differently that would have prevented this from happening.

"She wanted me to get Osiris out of there. I told her to go to hell. I just can't trust him," she announces, and my brow furrows uncontrollably. It's a shame. Another god on our side wouldn't be a bad thing, but one you can't trust could also be lethal.

"Good point," I agree, and she smiles at me as if looking for my approval. It's odd, her doing that. She never seems to need the approval of anyone, least of all me. Is she losing that confidence she's always seemed so full of?

"So, that's it right?" Sephy snaps at Luce, head jerking in her direction.

"Yes— this is it," Luce confirms, dropping her hands and letting the shard rest against her leg, jet black in the shadow.

"Right, well I'd best let you get on with it then." Sephy claps her hands together. "Is it too early to start drinking? I haven't even been to bed yet— so let's say no?" She looks at me expectantly, interrupted by a small mousy cough from Luce.

"But I can't do it— I'm the one having the magic pulled out of me. I need— I need someone else to do the ritual," she explains, and I watch Sephy turn nuclear.

"What?! None of us has that kind of power! I don't even know how to do a ritual like that— I mean what kind of effect is that going to have on the person performing it?" I can tell she feels misled, slighted, as her fingers instinctually curl into fists.

"I—" Luce begins, but Sephy interrupts her.

"Don't you dare say you don't know!" she exclaims, and so Luce shrugs, saying nothing at all as she turns to look out the window, eyes glazing.

"God fucking dammit!" Sephy curses, snatching the shard from Luce and turning to me.

"I need a goddamn drink. Come on—" she growls, storming from the room.

She's clutching the shard so tight I fear she might shatter it with only her grasp as I trail her down the corridor.

"Jules! I need a drink!" she yells down the stairs to where Jules is sitting on the sofa in the lobby, sipping a cup of tea. He gets to his feet, cup clattering audibly against the fine china saucer, sweeping promptly across the lobby as she charges down the black runner, feet furious in their small pounding beat.

She collapses into the seat where Jules was just sitting, exhaling heavily and putting her head into her hands. I take a seat in an armchair beside her, watching in tense silence as she visibly shakes for several seconds.

"*God fucking dammit!*" she suddenly screams, her hair lighting on fire at the tips. I knew she could do it, but I've never seen it. She's never been angry enough.

"Calm down," I whisper and her head snaps toward me with such ferocity that I fear she might internally decapitate herself.

"Calm down?!" She looks like she might throw a ball of flaming inferno right in my face, so I put up my hands, trying to show I mean no harm.

"Look, I know it's been hard," I begin, and she snorts, shaking her head furiously.

"Hard? My dissertation— that was hard. Learning to ride side-saddle when I don't have a goddamn ladylike bone in my body— that was hard. This isn't hard Xion. It's impossible." She pauses for breath, getting to her feet and pacing, frantic as she drags her fingers through her hair. "Even freaking Anubis, the one who put Pandora in charge in the first place, wants me to take the fucking throne— I can't do it. I won't!" she exclaims.

I exhale heavily, seeing her point.

"It's okay— I understand. You don't have to. Nobody is saying that—" I try to calm her, but she spins to face me, turning on me like a rabid dog that is about to begin foaming at the mouth.

115

"Except they are though, aren't they? Everyone is giving me this goddamn *the universe is in your hands* look, like it's so inevitable. I'm not a fucking save the world type of girl. I'm a goddamn drink yourself stupid and party 'til the early hours girl. I don't need this crap! Why is this happening to me?!" She yells this last part, vein throbbing beneath the thin pale skin of her forehead.

Jules swiftly returns with a tray, a bottle of single malt and two glasses containing a duo of ice cubes. Sephy spins, hair flaring out in wicked scarlet tongues, and yanks the spare glass – the one he always adds in case I want to join her – from the tray and hurls it over my head. It hits the wall at the opposite end of the entrance and shatters into a million pieces as she grabs the bottle off the tray next, forgoing the other glass entirely. I watch, ducking just in case, as she unstoppers it and takes a swig, reminding me of Thane only one month before.

I hear her swallow, a small sigh of relief escaping her lips, as Jules sets down the tray and turns to her.

"What's going on?" he asks, looking at her with disapproval and concern mixed into one tight expression.

"I got the shard, but now it turns out Luce can't do anything with it. She says somebody else has to perform the ritual. It's been a complete waste of freaking time!" she explains with furious speed, and I feel my sense of irritation growing too. Sephy risked a lot going to get the shard. The least Luce could have done was mentioned that someone else needed to perform the ritual afterwards.

"You need someone to perform a ritual? Like putting magic into the obsidian?" Jules enquires, thoughtful, and Sephy snorts.

"Yeah, why? Know somebody?" she chortles, but Jules' face remains deadpan and unamused.

"Actually, I do—" he replies, words slow and even. Sephy plops the bottle of whisky down onto the tray, which vibrates with the sudden clang of glass on silver.

"But?" she asks, sensing his hesitation. She cocks her head, gaze impatient, and crosses her arms over her breasts as Jules lets out a sigh.

"But— you aren't going to like it."

PANDORA

The vermillion hue of the room, cast bloody once again by Abraxis, reflects from the dull silver flatware before me. It's shaped like curved bones, each piece of cutlery a sick work of art. I let my gloved fingers reach out and touch the hilt of the knife, the blade embedded into where the articular cartilage would otherwise reside.

My eyes rise, falling next along the length of the silken cloth runner, arms moving to caress the rough grain of my throne, which has now been placed at the head of the long banquet table. Anubis sits, stone-faced and unmoving at the tail end, and behind the high back of her rustic-looking wooden chair, Barbas and Abraxis appear, the last to join the gathering as the doors of the throne room click neatly closed behind them.

They both take their seats on my right as my eyes linger over the spread of food, prepared and laid before me like a vast and fruitful landscape. It spreads the entire length of the table, which has been crafted from the parts of the Hollow which were left over from my throne. The wood remains bloodstained in parts, where the fluid had crept up the roots and into the trunk of the tree, a reminder of the sick kingdom over which I preside.

The banquet is my idea, something left over from my days in Aetheria. We had thrown so many magnificent feasts, platters stacked high with glistening and multihued fruits, meats, and vegetables, wine flowing in a never-ending torrent like the blood from the mortal wars from which we had ascended. It was a game, or at least a part of one, made ritual by the Sephilim King. We had invited those we feared might swerve in their loyalty, watching them as they ate and interrogating them with a single question for every decadent mouthful. You can tell a lot about someone when they're eating, especially in company. Doing two things at once tends to cause slips where usually there would be none, and the wine serves best to loosen tongues and lower defences.

I know we have limited supplies in the underground pantry since the fleet of trading ships manned by sinners now lay motionless, ghosts in the harbour, but this had seemed worth it. Seemed necessary even.

I'm wearing an aubergine tulle gown with a billowing skirt that pinches in at the waist and falls off both shoulders, revealing the pallor of my collarbone protruding just beneath an onyx and amethyst choker clasped at my throat, a gift from Gorgon. I have a suspicion that the onyx has been retrieved from the remnants of Haedes' hourglass, though of this I cannot be sure. My arms lie in my lap, covered in black silk gloves that climb to my elbows, hiding the burn upon my hand from The Well.

"Shall we eat?" I query, looking to the five Demon Lords and one salty Titan who glares into thin air opposite me. Gorgon is on my left, sitting beside Lilliana who has kept an empty place between them. Here, two of her favourite Banshees sit, lying in the space half covered by the table's shadow, like dogs waiting for scraps. On my right, Katerina sits primly, with Abraxis between her and Barbas, who sits beside Anubis, scanning her face with interest. I wonder how much fear he's savouring from her right now; he's always said that those of a mother for her child are the ripest, the most delicious, the best to satiate.

"Let's eat," Katerina admonishes, reaching out to help herself to one of a few steaks piled beneath a cloche directly in front of me. The blood from its rarity pools on the bone-white china plate before her, coagulating slowly.

"I'll take some of the suckling pig—" Abraxis reaches out to cut himself a piece of the animal splayed out, a whole pomegranate wedged between its lips, feet tied at both ends so it looks like it's mid-leap in the centre of the spread, surrounded by piles of caramelised brown apple slices.

"Cut me some too," I command, and he nods, not feeling it appropriate to acknowledge me any other way as his knife spears into the thick skin of the hog. I watch as Lilliana grabs some chicken legs, the ears of the Banshees at her side pricking, drool dripping ever so slowly from their jaws to the floor. She also helps herself with outstretched fingers to buttery mashed potatoes, green beans, pork, and gravy, but seemingly either hasn't noticed the cutlery before her or simply has no intention of using it. She eats with her fingers, food getting stuck in her wild dark locks as her hands fly from table to mouth in a rabid frenzy. I cringe with distaste, raising my plate so Abraxis may lay several neat slices of pork onto the china as everyone else helps themselves. Everyone that is, except Anubis.

"Would you like some steak, Anubis?" I ask, keeping my face impassive. She folds her arms across the white shroud of her gown, which twists like silken bandages flecked through with gold leaf around her breasts, shaking her head.

"Not eating?" I cock an unimpressed eyebrow as the Demon Lords turn to her, watching as they take eager cutlery to task, eating as though they've been starved as their eyes dart between us without so much as a pause of their masticating jaws.

"I will not, cannot feast while my son starves below." Her voice rings out like a warning shot as my eyes narrow, pupils dilating as I take in her piously defiant face.

"You will eat. We all need our strength if we hope to unleash The Gods of Ancient once more." I lower my eyes as I pick up the goblet in front of me with a gloved hand, sipping the red wine from its depths slowly as I examine her over the golden rim.

"Anubis has no problem finding the strength for conflict— I assure you," Barbas' voice crawls through the air like a noxious gas, heavy with fatal intent.

"Something to share with the group?" I enquire, placing my goblet back down on the table and picking up my cutlery to begin on what is now a heaped plate thanks to Katerina, who has taken it upon herself to load mine for me. A steaming steak leaks fluid into the space where the pork lies beside several sticks of buttered asparagus, so I start on that first, the metallic tang of the rare cut swirling around my tongue as I chew and swallow, eyes intently resting on Barbas' hollow face.

"Well, it's just that Abraxis and I burst in on Sephy Sinclair snooping around in the alchemy chamber upstairs," Barbas announces. My eyes widen, my next bite paused only centimetres from my lips, dripping warm juices onto the plate below.

"What?! Why didn't you say anything?" I bark at Anubis who flinches as though the pitch of my voice is a weapon in its own right.

"I didn't think it was exactly dinner conversation—" she makes the excuse.

"You're not even eating dinner. What was she doing in there? Tell me!" I grab the piece of steak off my fork with hungry teeth, chewing rapidly as she shrugs.

119

"I assume she came to retrieve something. I can't be sure though. I had barely set foot in the door when these two came charging in and spooked her. She convected out before I had a chance to question her." The reply slips seamlessly from her tongue, woven so fast and so intricately it's obvious to me now she is a master seamstress of lies. She fabricates one story after the next, agenda never clear to anyone. Perhaps even she knows not what her intent truly is.

"So, Sephy Sinclair has been sneaking around the Exilia—" I mutter, mind now preoccupied as Lilliana throws a chicken bone from her plate to the other side of the hall. The Banshees charge after it, clattering into one another as they leap into the air in pursuit of this pathetic morsel.

"Yes, but I doubt it's anything to worry about," Anubis adds, and I feel one eyebrow quirk on my forehead, my mouth twisting into a grimace.

"I don't think that's your place to say," I retort, leaning back into my throne and taking another deep drink from the goblet beside my plate.

"Anubis is right, Pandora. Sephy Sinclair is not a threat. She is but one Demi-Goddess against five Demon Lords, a demon and mortal army, and two Titans," Abraxis asserts, and so I turn to Gorgon, who has until this moment been silent.

"What do you think?" I ask him, and he looks up, assessing each of the faces in turn.

"I think Abraxis is right. It's probably a trap, maybe something to lure one of us out into the mortal world, get us surrounded and vulnerable. Worry not." He licks his bottom lip, which is slick with grease. "Besides, we looked through that chamber, Abraxis and I, it's just a lot of junk and raw ingredients," he concludes and so I nod, unsatisfied even still. I feel the box, weighted in the pleated folds of my tulle skirt, and reach for it gingerly, placing my silken fingers atop it, insecure.

"You're probably right," I say sweetly, smiling into Gorgon's slit pupils, which glitter, admiration and adoration melding into a glassy shine. His gaze is intense, and yet something within me still isn't convinced. Paranoia uncurls like a serpent in my gut, hissing and spitting, defences raised.

I must do something.

Quickly, I form a simple plan, not wanting to waste any more time than I must to put my increasingly wary mind at ease.

I will journey to the mortal world. I need to know what the Sinclair girl took. The Demon Lords are wild cards enough, and despite my calm demeanour, I don't think I can truly trust them. The last thing I need is Haedes' brat scheming too.

"So— tell me," I quickly change the subject, attention falling back to my food, decision made. Taking a deep breath, I plaster on a gracious smile, "How are you all?"

II

HOW WILL I KNOW

<u>SEPHY</u>

"YOU'RE FUCKING KIDDING ME—" I say it again, like a record stuck on repeat.

"No. Not kidding— you've been saying that for the last half an hour," Jules remarks, exhaling heavily and leaning forward so his elbows are propped on his knees.

"Because I still can't believe that you're not fucking joking—" I put a hand on my forehead, rubbing my left temple and letting my pupils bounce between Jules and Xion. Both their expressions are deadly serious, worrying me immensely.

"I think it's a good idea," Xion announces and I glare at him.

"Of course, *you* do. He didn't try to get you murdered!" I protest, disdain for my Uncle Peter rising to the surface of my subconscious like an egg gone rotten.

"He performed the ritual on you as a child. He separated you from your powers and stored them in the opal blade all those years ago. He might be the best person to help," Jules explains.

I pout.

"Or, he might be a giant stinky asshole who won't be setting foot in my freaking home ever again."

"Giant stinky asshole? What are you, four?" Xion exclaims, a smile tugging at his lips despite his attempt to remain stoic.

"Yes, right now, in the case of my traitorous Uncle who got me murdered, I am. I am four. Because even four-year-old me knows that's a stupid ass plan, and I will throw a goddamn tantrum the size of a nuclear blast if you two don't admit that you're goddamn joking right now!" I stomp my foot on the floor, scowling and wrinkling my nose in absolute distaste of my only living relative.

"Okay, okay— I understand why you feel that way. Anyway, we don't even know where he is," Xion concludes, slumping back into the clutch of the armchair and sighing out as though this is such a tragedy.

"Actually—" Jules interjects, and my head jerks sideways again to glare at him. I've been doing that a lot lately, no wonder I wake up with neck ache. I mean, it could be that, or it could be that I've been giving very generous head to a demon half-ling I suppose. Either way, I need to call my chiropractor.

"Oh please— you haven't been tracking that loser?" I snort, disbelief clutching at me. Jules sniffs a little, straightening as he holds my eye contact.

"I have a tracking device on the bottom of his car. You didn't honestly think that after what happened I was going to let him disappear off the radar?" he chastises me, and I roll my eyes.

"You know stalker looks creepy on you. I'm just saying. It's not flattering."

"It looks a damn sight better on me than dead looks on you," he comes back, his smart mouth surprising me as his emerald eyes shimmer with victory.

Touché Jules. Touché.

"Sephy I really think—" Xion begins but I hold up a hand.

"I know what you think."

I throw it around in my mind for a moment like a piece of shattered glass with jagged edges on every side, regaling my options and realising that, as ever, there's no way to avoid getting cut.

What I want doesn't mean a damn thing.

Exhaling a heavy breath, I'm tired of the conversation so throw up my hands.

"Fine, go find him. But if he so much as looks at me funny I'm torching him to cinder, extra crispy," I mutter.

Xion leaps to his feet.

"We'll get going right now," he looks to Jules, who nods, rising from the chair opposite me.

Xion retreats up the stairs, taking them two at a time, to get what I assume is his jacket and shoes, and Jules adjourns to retrieve what I can only pray is his most powerful shotgun.

I slump back into the chair, eyeing the untouched bottle of whisky and debating downing the entire contents. I turn to look out the window, finding the early morning sunlight streaming in without care and pooling upon the monochrome stone of the floor. I determine after only a single minute that being drunk in front of my scheming asshole of an Uncle doesn't sound super appealing, mainly because I would look awful in an orange jumpsuit. It'll clash with my hair.

Fresh hot rage simmers in my bloodstream, the thought of everything that's happened making my muscles twitch with anxiety. He tried to have me murdered, his own niece, for money. For bits of paper. He was willing to trade his flesh and blood for fast cars and a nice apartment with a balcony overlooking the sea.

Fuck him.

I get to my feet as Xion and Jules return.

"You're not coming with us?" Xion enquires, and I shake my head.

"I think it'd be for the best if I wasn't there," I admit, watching him smirk a little.

"Good idea. We'll be back as soon as we can. Look after Luce." His expression turns stern and, for a moment, my rage begins gathering again, directing itself at him. I'm not a fucking babysitter.

"Yeah, yeah. Get out of here." I shrug, taming my temper as the two of them head for the exit, the crack team forged from the only two men in my life who have meant anything, going to hunt down the man who should mean everything, but who tried to have me killed.

Happy families. I sigh to myself, restlessness trickling like an itch through my thighs and down the length of my arms. I turn, knowing there is only one way I am going to get it to stop, heading for the ballet studio and not looking back.

Left, right, left, right.
Peter's stupid ass face, judging me at the bottom of the staircase.
Right, left, right.
Peter's lying ass as he denies everything, my fingers buried in his hair, the temptation to end him ensnaring my mind.
Left, right, left, right.
Jules drawing a shotgun from behind his back, aiming it directly at my uncle.

I pause as a smile taints the focus upon my face, leaning forward, heart pumping rapidly and lungs sucking in and releasing air with furious urgency.

"What are you doing?" Her voice travels over my shoulder, dreamy and clouded with fatigue. I spin, finding Luce propped weakly against the doorframe.

"What does it look like?" I snap, edges sharp after her less than well-thought-out plan which could have gotten me killed. Again.

"Wasting your energy—" she retorts, voice not angry but simply honest in her assessment.

"Look, I'm busy. What do you want?" I ask, staring down at my knuckles and trying to ignore the intensity of her stare.

"I don't feel good," she replies, swallowing hard.

"Nobody does right now. Shit happens," I reply carelessly, turning my back on her.

"No, Sephy, I really—" her voice trails off and I turn back, hesitant to get involved in what is probably a play for attention.

As I glance back, I find her slumped on the floor, staring at her hands. I take several steps forward, faster than I expect as an unexpected urgency clutches me.

"What is it?" I ask her, serious now as I drop to my knees, getting on eye level with her. She raises her hands in front of her eyes, which shine out in a powder blue, observing them as they tremble. I cock my head, hair falling over one shoulder as I take them in my palms, trying to stop her shaking.

"What's happening to me?" She's breathless, and I gaze at her, concerned.

"I think you might be going into some kind of withdrawal," I guess, but the accuracy of my assessment surprises me.

"I ran out of The Hollow—" she nods, and I frown.

"What do you mean?" I demand, suspicious immediately as a frown forms, hardening my expression. A sigh-like gasp escapes Luce, and she begins to explain.

"I've been using the fragments, the splinters left from it to tide me over. There's a lot of magic in that thing, Haedes' watered it with his own blood you know—" she explains and pulls out an arm, laying it flat so I might take a look. Along what used to be flawless pale skin, there are now jagged scars running in uneven lines from the crease of her elbow where she's opened veins and taken in what doesn't belong to her.

"Shit, Lucifer—" I rub my forehead, breath caught in my throat. She looks awful. "Come on." I put my arm around her shaking shoulders, smelling blood and God knows what else in her hair, convecting us fast from the floor of the studio and up into what is now her room.

When we reappear, I shift her onto the bed, and she looks up at me, eyes wide.

"I wasn't joking when I said I needed the magic." She shudders like someone has poured ice water into her veins.

"You don't *need* it. You're just coming down from it. It'll pass," I say, determined to stay calm even though I have no idea what's going to happen.

"Where's Xion?" she enquires through chattering teeth.

"He and Jules went to find someone who can perform the ritual with you and the shard," I explain, and her eyes widen.

"Thank you, Sephy. I mean it. Thank you."

She's childlike as I push her back down onto the pillows beneath the quilted headboard, shifting her shuddering legs up onto the mattress and covering her with a blanket. It doesn't seem to do any good.

She curls up onto her side, the foetal position, pulling the blanket up beneath her chin.

I look at her, seeing what Thane had seen, why she left.

"You know—" I begin carefully, not wanting to cause another shouting match. "I can see why Thane didn't want to be around for this. It's hard when you love someone, watching them suffer," I admonish and her eyes narrow as she stares at me, not moving.

"How do you know? You've never loved anyone," she retorts, and I shrug, thwarted. She's not wrong.

"True—" I concede, and she glares at me, her expression deadpan.

"Oh, come on. You can't be that deep in denial. I've been wired as hell, and even I can see that you love Xion," she says, almost spitting the words but lacking the energy to follow through.

"How do you know?"

"It's clear as day."

"Not to me," I snap, and silence falls between us as she continues to tremble, her brow becoming slick with perspiration. "How did you know you loved Thane?" I ask, watching as her lips part, and then she stops a moment, thinking hard.

"People think it's the sexual attraction, the lust— the way your skin ignites whenever they touch you. But— it's not. At least not for me. For me, it's the relief. Whenever she held me, I felt safe. Felt like nothing in the world could touch me. It was like coming home." Her eyes sparkle with fresh tears, and her body clenches, hunger pangs for the dark melded with chasmic grief and newfound loneliness.

I am taken back to the deep exhale, followed by a stark inhale of his pomegranate musk, the way I slumped into him in the hall downstairs, the way every time I see him I unwillingly unravel.

126

"I see."

I watch her as she examines me through half-closed eyes, silence falling over us.

Peering around the room, I remember what had been before the fire. My mother and father, letting me climb into bed with them on Sunday mornings. My mom reading to me in front of the fireplace. I felt safe here, like this room was a private island that only my parents and I had access to. I miss them, and it makes me realise that Luce is right; love is deeper than just the physical. I suppose that's why I'm so resistant to the idea. Trust is weakness; it's giving the other person the ability to hurt you and trusting them not to. It might not even be their fault, that pain. Letting someone in, you open yourself to the grief of losing them forever, of forgetting how you ever existed without them before.

I turn to Luce, staring down at her pitiful shuddering mass, her eyes spilling tears onto the pillow beneath her like salted memories. I feel sorry for her, for the first time. She had loved Thane, opened herself to that mortal wound, that critical blow, and taken it full force— right to the heart.

I know, looking down at her, that I have made the right choice in keeping my distance from Xion as much as I can. Luce is wrong because even though the possibility, the ingredients for love might be there, I simply refuse to give his presence, or lack thereof, the power to destroy me. I can't. Surrender isn't an option, and for me, surrender to love is more of a risk than surrender to the enemy.

I can't be reliant on anyone, not anymore. Not when everything is teetering on the edge of oblivion and I'm the only thing standing between the Demons of Mortaria and the unsuspecting mortals of Chicago.

There is no place for love here, only the fight.

XION

Jules continues to glance between the phone, which is suctioned to the windscreen of the black Jeep, and the road as I sit in the passenger seat, silent.

"Do you really think he'll agree to help us?" I ask, voice a deep rumble.

"I think he'd be extremely stupid if he doesn't. Besides, one call to Sephy, and she'll be there threatening him with a faceful of fire. I'm not worried." He doesn't seem it either, his hands relaxed on the steering wheel, clad in black leather driving gloves.

"You really believe in her, don't you?" I ask him, curious about their relationship now more than ever. They aren't just butler and employer, and I doubt they ever have been. There's something deeper. Perhaps Jules is one of the only people who can help me get an unbiased perspective on where I stand.

"I do. She's extraordinary." His answer is simple, and I can feel his pride warming the interior of the otherwise chill car. "Don't you?" he counters, taking his eyes off the road and scrutinising my face.

"Of course. As you said, she's extraordinary." My response is lacklustre at best, but talking about the emotions I feel for her is almost as exhausting as enduring them.

"You would be a fool not to be in love with her, Xion." The statement takes me by surprise.

Am I really that transparent?

Jules' eyes flick between me and the road yet again, waiting for me to deny it.

"I don't know. I think often I'm a fool to even contemplate it. I can't seem to help myself though," I admit, and he gives me a sad smile.

"What makes you say that?"

"She can never return that love. I know that. She's too scared of being vulnerable. I can't say I blame her; she's been through more than anyone should ever have to go through. She's so young—" I think about her sarcasm, about the seriousness and the hurt it hides. She might seem like a fun time girl, but deep down she's more mature, more broken than anyone who didn't truly know her would ever realise.

"She might not ever tell you, Xion. But you have to know she's fallen for you. I've never seen her like this with anyone. She's— she's home with you." The sappy sentiment doesn't have me fooled, and yet, I wonder.

"I don't want to ever cause her pain. I'm afraid that in the end, one of us will end up dead for good, and the other will just be broken. Maybe she's right to keep her distance," I admit, and he shakes his head.

128

"She can't have you that blinded— if anything ever happened to you, Xion, it would devastate her. There's no running away from that. You've gotten under her skin whether she admits it or not. She's already vulnerable for you. You're already a weakness." I am stunned by his candour, but he knows her better than anyone else. So perhaps what he's saying is true.

"She'd never tell me that. Never admit it." I chew my bottom lip and he laughs.

"Does she have to? The Sephy I know goes through men like they're disposable. Not since you though, notice that? She isn't the kind of girl who will tell you; she's the kind of girl who will show you. If you ask me, that's far more genuine. Don't you think?" he asks me, and I contemplate this hard. I'd written it off as fear after what happened with Brad or an addiction to the fact the sex is so good.

"I guess—" I mumble.

"Look Xion, I'm not saying she's easy to be with, but if you're worried about her not feeling the same way, don't be. I've known her forever. She loves you. Trust me."

I don't reply, and we both sink back into silence as the world outside whizzes by in a vivid early morning blur. My hopes are raised, despite the fact I know they shouldn't be, and I feel a pool of what could be warm melted chocolate sprinkled with cinnamon settling in my gut.

We track down the glowing green dot with ease. It's stationary, and we soon discover it's parked on the road outside a block of completely unmemorable flats. It's not that far from where I'd tracked down Brad, though in a slightly less dodgy part of town even if it's only a few blocks north. The early morning heat rises off the concrete underfoot as Jules and I exit the car. He has on a long overcoat, a ridiculous garment for this kind of weather, but when I see the bulge under his left arm, I know he's only wearing it to conceal the gun he's carrying. I pull up the collar on my leather jacket, plunging my hands deep into the pockets of my jeans and steeling myself, ready to throw a punch, or several if I have to. Maybe I'll even go demonic. I'm sure Sephy would enjoy that story immensely.

We walk up a shitty garden path, which has been laid crooked, dividing the two halves of the overgrown front lawn. There's rubbish among the foliage, empty beer bottles, discarded takeout containers – a definitive and sharp decline from the grandeur of the Sinclair Estate, that's for sure.

Good.

He's lucky he's not in a fucking prison cell for the crap he pulled.

Jules approaches the entrance, which is locked to non-residents, looking at the list of names beside many steel buttons before stabbing one with a gloved finger.

"Hello?" Peter's voice crackles into existence, like a ghost from beyond the grave, as Jules leans in toward the speaker.

"It's Jules. I have a cheque here for you and some boxes of your things," he lies, glancing sideways at me. He waits several moments, the silence from the speaker keeping us both in suspense, before the door buzzes and the lock clicks open.

"A cheque?" I query, impressed.

"Well yeah, I didn't think he was gonna want to see the guy that perp-walked him off the estate at gunpoint for a couple of dog-eared old books—" he elaborates, and I nod. He's smarter than anyone gives him credit for. Especially when it comes to manipulating people.

We ascend four flights of concrete steps stained with what could be alcohol and scattered with the dog ends of cigarettes, the trash continuing to please me immensely. Reaching apartment eleven, I let Jules knock as I remain hidden by the doorframe on one side, guessing that if he sees me he may not be so hospitable.

"Peter, it's Jules—" Jules calls through the wood, which is peeling green paint. Before he has a chance to continue, the door sweeps open, revealing Peter and a handgun, raised directly in Jules' face. I smirk, reaching out from the left-hand side and taking the gun in my palm, ripping it from his grasp and bending the barrel almost in half before throwing it down the length of the corridor. Jules smiles contentedly.

"I knew I had a good reason for keeping you around—" He throws out this comment casually, walking straight past Peter, who nearly falls over at the force of both our shoulders colliding with his on purpose.

"What do you want? Where's my money?" he asks, and I laugh, the sound entirely hollow.

"There isn't any, numb nuts. You don't honestly think we'd give you cash after what you pulled?" I give him an incredulous look, plunging my hands deep into my jacket pockets to try and remain calm in appearance. I hadn't seen him after Sephy had discovered his role in her murder, and I don't want him to know that merely looking at him causes my hands to form fists. I examine him as we stand, the three of us crowded in his tiny apartment.

He looks tired, bags under his eyes and grey hair dishevelled. The place he lives in doesn't appear much better either, with a worn blue carpet carrying on the trend of the stairs with multiple stains, and plain white walls that boast not a single painting or photograph. I take a seat on the threadbare beige couch behind me, finding the cushion uneven and lumpy beneath my weight.

Peter stiffens visibly inside his crumpled white dress shirt and jeans as I make myself at home, his glasses reflecting the awful halogen bulb overhead.

"Then why are you here?" he demands. Jules places his hands behind his back, posture perfect as he stares, unblinking, at Peter.

"Actually, we're here because we need your help," he explains, stone still on the spot.

Peter laughs, the entirely forced sound grating on my nerves.

"Pfft, and why the hell would I help you?" He's incredulous, but Jules remains unshaken, no humour in his gaze.

"I can think of several reasons. Some honourable, some less so— Honourable choices include helping the niece you got killed," Jules explains, and Peter looks to me, swallowing.

"And the less honourable options?" Peter presses for an answer, so I get to my feet, picturing what I'd like to do to his stupid ass. This notion alone is enough to cause me to transform as I grab a hold of his shirt collar with my now charred fingers.

"Think of it as payment for me letting you live," I growl, the glowing orange of my irises reflected at me in his lenses.

"Or— I could just give Sephy a call and let her finish what she had going on with you back at the estate— she could be here in around— what do you think Xion? Like thirty seconds?" Jules suggests as I release Peter from my grip, watching as he stumbles backwards a few paces toward the door.

"I'm thinking more like ten—" I retort, watching the fear behind Peter's irises grow, his mouth falling slack.

"What— what do you want from me?" he whimpers.

Jules looks suddenly appeased.

"Great choice, Peter. Co-operation is definitely the best option." He claps his gloved hands together and I wonder if he wears them just for driving or if it's a conscious decision to avoid leaving fingerprints behind. "We want you to come back to the estate with us and give some guidance on a ritual of sorts. We believe you have experience. After all, you did place Sephy's powers into that opal knife. You know,

131

the one that you got her killed with?" Jules reminds him less than gently and Peter looks concerned, running his hands back through his hair.

"But— that ritual nearly killed me. I couldn't do it again, not even if I wanted to," he explains. Jules takes a measured step forward. I inhale, watching the two men, the scent of spirits rife in the air. Peter has clearly been drinking.

"Who said anything about you doing the ritual? We just need your advice. Then, you are free to go," Jules admonishes, looking kind of sad at this prospect.

"That's it? You just— you just want my expertise?" he asks, and Jules nods with definitive authority.

"Yes, well, it's not as though you ever had much more to offer, is it?" I want to laugh, watching the twinkle in his eye. He's enjoying this far too much, not that I blame him. It's giving me a kick of joy too.

"Oh, and by the way, don't think about trying to pull anything funny. Sephy isn't the only one living at the estate right now. Lucifer, you know, the devil, is also currently with us, and The Furies— you know, the ones who hate men with a passion," Jules reminds him, and he frowns.

"What's going on?" Peter demands, suddenly looking concerned. "Is— is there something going on in Mortaria?" he asks, taking off his glasses and cleaning them in that utterly irritating way he does on the bottom of his crumpled shirt.

"Well, I suppose if you call the apocalypse *something going on* then sure—" I retort, watching his eyes widen. "I guess you could consider that another honourable reason to help us, saving the world, or dishonourable if you're considering it to save your own worthless ass." I shrug, nonchalance bordering on ignorance. I mean, the apocalypse sounds scary, like bloodshed and rain of fire and all that stuff, but so far anyway, it's been a bit of a let-down. Not that I should complain.

"You're serious. It's really — what — the end of the world?" Peter's eyes pop from his face in alarm as I confirm his fears only too readily.

"That's what apocalypse means," I reply, his mortality annoying me immensely.

Turning to face the exit, I place a heavy hand on his shoulder, steering him toward the door. Jules moves forward so he's at Peter's spine, giving no room for escape. We move to leave the apartment, one weasely traitor in hand.

"And there's nobody who can stop it?" he demands, looking back over his shoulder at us both like we're crazy.

My eyes meet with Jules', and we share a knowing glance, hearts heavy.

Oh, there is, we both think.

She just really isn't happy about it.

12

SUNNY DAYS

SEPHY

I LOOK INTO THE bathroom mirror, steeling myself for what I know is coming. Xion called, telling me they're on their way back, traitorous asshole in tow.

Great. I exhale, wondering why it is that life seems to work out so fucking shitty for me. I mean I can't even get away from the uncle who got me murdered, and what's worse— now I have to go and play nice.

Well, nice as I can.

I drench my face in cold water, hoping that the chill helps me gain some kind of control over my temper, and as I'm towelling myself dry, I hear the front doors open, voices echoing from the high ceilings and all the way through my suite's open door.

Showtime.

I put on my best '*I'm trying to ignore the fact that you got me murdered*' smile and hesitantly leave the room. The further I get down the corridor, the quicker my pace becomes. If I'm going to do this then I want it over with as quickly and painlessly as possible, and preferably without me torching anyone in the process.

Even if they do deserve it.

As I break out of the narrow corridor and onto the airy landing at the top of the stairs, my eyes fall on him, tumbling down every stair before hitting him full force with the full momentum of my disdain.

"I'd say welcome— but you're not really, at all. The only reason you're here is because I care more about my family than people I hate with the power of several ferocious and long burning suns— got it?" I announce, voice bouncing with nonchalance off the walls as I descend each step with definite and harsh steps.

Xion's face softens when the word *'family'* falls from my mouth. I guess that's what they are now, all of them, including Luce. She's like the bat-shit aunt, who always turns up to the Christmas party absolutely smashed off her face and tries to get all the young adults smoking weed with her out back by the dustbins. You know she's trouble, know she's a bit odd, but she's part of the family, so by God, you invite that crazy bitch anyway.

"Nice to see you too, Persephone," Peter grumbles, taking off his stupid glasses and predictably moving to clean them on his untucked shirt. It's a wonder to me at this point whether they're ever actually dirty or if it's a device he uses to avoid having to hold eye contact with people.

Lying dick.

"Right, shall we get this shit over with?" I ask, gesturing up the stairs.

"Yes, I uh, need to get a few things from my office. I still have the supplies from last time." Peter's eyes shift uncomfortably between us as Jules stiffens at his side, face pinching in distaste.

"What? Just in case you wanted to strip me of my power again?" I demand, and he looks uncomfortable.

"I, uh, it was a precaution," he mumbles, and I roll my eyes.

"Whatever dude."

I storm up the stairs, wishing with every passing second that his betrayal didn't sting quite as much as it does. We've never been close, not even remotely, but the fact my last blood relative decided I was worth more dead than alive kind of rubs me the wrong way even if I'd rather it didn't. Nonchalant Sephy is way cooler, way more intimidating than emotional wreck Sephy, that's for sure.

Reaching the landing I take a right, Xion catching up to me and placing his hand upon the small of my back. I shrug away from him, not wanting Peter to see my only potential weakness.

"Are you alright?" he whispers in my ear, bending down and allowing his lips to brush past my hair.

"I'm fine. Just— well it's not exactly a reunion I wanted, is it?" I snap, and he shakes his head, eyes full of pity. Right then I consider punching him, though whether that's because I'm mad at him or the whole situation is beyond my grasp at this particular moment. I recall storming down this same corridor only a handful of weeks before, my blood hot with whisky and my mind consumed with the smoke from my temper's unending blaze. I really wanted to kill Peter. Perhaps more so than I've ever wanted to kill anyone. More than Pandora when I'd been captured. I guess that's the thing about betrayal; I can't be mad at Pandora for trying to use me, to kill me, because she doesn't even know me— but Peter, he held me as a newborn, watched me disintegrate after the death of my parents, and even still, he had decided my life, his sister's only child, wasn't worth more than the Sinclair fortune. Worth no more than a stack full of pretty printed paper and a handful of cold metal disks. That was what he was trading the last remnants of his supposedly beloved sister for— and I just don't fucking get it. Perhaps I never will, but then again, that's good. At least I'm not a traitorous prick.

I pass the bookshelf where '*Paradise Lost*' stands out precariously to me even now. There's nothing different about it, and to anyone else, it wouldn't even be of note, but I know it's the lever to the secret room. The thing that started my freefall into a world of secrets that should have died with my parents.

As I reach the door to Peter's office at the end of the corridor, I wonder what my life would be if I never picked up that knife, if I listened to Xion and backed away, had gone back to bed that night and nursed my hangover like anyone sensible.

I'd be a lot less stressed, still think of my parent's death as an accident, and never would have had to deal with the enigma that was Haedes or the crushing weight of Luce's addiction. I never would have crawled out of my own coffin in the pouring rain, broken beyond recognition. And yet, as I enter the office and turn to find Xion, as ever, by my side, I'm not as sorry as I thought I'd be that I didn't listen to him. For all the pain and suffering, I've also had moments which have formed me anew, changed my perception entirely, and shown me who I really am, and many of those are because of him.

For that, I'll always be grateful.

Peter and Jules enter the room slowly behind us, Jules one step behind my uncle as though he's worried he might escape. I mean I guess he could try, but I can convect, so if I want him here, he's staying.

"Right— so you did this ritual. What did you use?" I'm interrogative, and Peter raises a finger, treading carefully around the desk that separates us, moving closer to the back wall. The shelves are lined with books, and I watch him with half-interest, trying to keep my cool. He pulls one out, the spine reading '*Dante's Inferno*', and the third shelf on the left, which makes up a third of the room's rear wall, swings back.

Predictable, I muse, wondering why I hadn't thought to check the bookcases in here before. Peter is nothing if not a creature of inanely boring habit. I mean even the cleaning of his glasses is routine.

"Come on." He beckons me forward, exhaling heavily as I follow him.

Walking toward the now shadowy doorway, my feet hit bare concrete as I cross an invisible threshold. The heels of my shoes echo as I summon The Eternal Flame to me, illuminating what would otherwise be dank shadow as the smell of musty pages and stale air fills my nostrils. Spider webs and dust have infected almost every corner and are illuminated a dull silvery grey in the light of The Eternal Flame as the miniature library within is revealed.

"What is this?" I snap, angsty as he places his hands into the pockets of his ill-fitting jeans.

"Just books on the occult, the supernatural— none of them make much sense on their own, but I've been a collector ever since things between Adam and Haedes started. It's hard to get full sets in the mortal world though— and even if you can find them, they're entirely out of my price range," he confesses, looking hard done by but eyeing the flame that crackles in my palm, nevertheless. He turns slowly to face the shelves, silver hair turned bronze by the tungsten light of the flame, staring upon the bookcases stacked with thick leather-bound volumes. It makes me wonder about him, seeing the hunger in his eyes as I take several steps forward to examine his flickering profile. I have always thought he just wanted my money to spend on luxuries, but was he seeking something more potent than fast cars and French chateaus? Magical power perhaps?

As I'm pondering this, he darts forward like he's spotted what he wants, yanking out a wooden chest with a heavy steel lock that's barely discernible from the books surrounding it. Sagging under what he perceives as immense weight, he puts the chest on a small wooden table beside a dust-covered armchair resting in the corner, the faded brown leather seeming cold and unloved.

I turn back to Jules, who is leaning against the doorway; stiff in posture as he watches the events unfold like a hawk. He raises his eyebrows as though to ask, *'Are you alright?'* without even so much as a word. I shrug at him but smile reluctantly. I'm not all right, not even slightly. My life is a complete joke and every single day I feel less and less equipped to deal with the undying intensity of every single moment. I just want it all to stop. Even for five goddamn minutes.

Unfortunately for me, there is no intermission in the apocalypse, so here I am, tired as all hell but still standing, even if my attitude is less than heroic.

Peter takes several steps back after slowly running his fingers along the wooden joins of the chest, keeping an eye on me with wary sideways glances. He shuffles past me, the atmosphere between us increasingly awkward, lifting a silver candlestick peppered with dust that adorns yet another table at the opposite end of the small square chamber. Beneath the candlestick, a dull key sits, and I lean in with my flaming palm to get a better look.

Peter swipes it from the grain of the walnut and places the candlestick back where it was, fumbling between myself and Xion in the claustrophobic space as he returns to the chest. He takes a seat in a leather chair beside it, exhaling heavily before he turns the key in the lock and pulls back the lid, revealing the contents.

Inside is a jar of what looks to be white shimmering glitter, a book, and some herbs.

"So, you will need to place this in a circle around the subject to draw out the darkness in her." He gestures to the jar of white powder as he hands it to me. Our fingers touch, and he noticeably grimaces as I take the jar in my non-flaming fingers. I examine it, no clue what it is but sure I've seen something similar in Luce's alchemy chamber.

"Then what?" I demand, impatient.

"Then, you speak the ritual after the space has been cleansed of any pre-existing magic by the sage." He takes out the thick and ancient-looking volume and then hands me a stick of the dried herb. I inhale fondly, the smell reminding me of the boarding school I attended back in England.

"That's it?" I press him, wondering why on earth Luce hadn't been able to explain this to me herself, but he only glares at me.

"I almost died performing this ritual, so no. Not really." He looks immensely annoyed at my words, as if he has any right to be anything but humble. Xion snorts, crossing his arms over his chest.

"Well of course you did. You're mortal. Mortals have no right playing with magic. Only the blessed or mortals infected by darkness stand a chance of being able to wield magic, and even then, it takes years of training. I'm amazed you're around to tell the tale." He's enjoying berating Peter, and I wonder at this moment, as Peter's face takes on a kind of childish affront, if Xion might be my favourite person in the world.

"Maybe I'm stronger than you think—" Peter bites back, and Xion laughs under his breath.

"Or maybe you're just lucky," he retorts, and I smile at him, grateful for his support in the hating of my only remaining relative. He looks at me, cocking his head. "I think it's probably best if I conduct the ritual. I have darkness in me already—" he begins, but I shake my head in defiance, mind made up.

"No. You're already connected to the shard. What if you end up absorbing all that darkness yourself, or tearing your soul apart?" I remind him.

"Tethers are strange things. The power can't be absorbed by me because the shard is broken, because of my pendant. Luce made sure that nobody could get to the darkness inside— well unless we somehow figured out how to meld the pendant and the tether together. I don't even know if that's possible but—" He's rambling now, imploring me to allow him to take the risk, but I shake my head.

"No, still not happening. I'm going to do this. I'm not risking it. I don't even want you in the room,"

"But you're half mortal too, Sephy! Luce did this before, and she's a full-blown god. I still remember her after, she looked awful for days," he exclaims, eyes glowing molten gold in the darkness as his body tenses.

"I'm doing it. That's that." I retort, and he goes to bicker with me, to defend his right to put his life at risk yet again. However, before he can get out another word, I simply say, "No, Xion. I can't lose you."

Placing a soft hand on his shoulder, I watch him unravel.

Peter looks between us with an interested gaze as Xion's hard expression slowly melts.

And so, it is settled.

LUCE

I'm shuffled from where I lie shivering upon the bed upstairs to a chaise longue in a room I've never been to on the ground floor. It's smart, connecting both me and Sephy with Gaia as much as possible,

139

but with every stair, I feel my bones threaten to shatter, the glass of them cutting me to ribbons on the inside.

A man I've never seen before, with silver hair and round-rimmed glasses, accompanies us as we adjourn to what appears to be a kind of lounge with walnut floors and deep scarlet upholstery. The walls are peppered with fine art, or what I believe to be through blurred vision, framed in gold. Everyone does their utmost to ignore the stranger like he's no more than a bad smell.

A wide window rising from floor to ceiling looks out onto the prim lawns of the estate, and the bright midday sun shines mercilessly down on me, making me sweat. I think about asking Xion to close the drapes, which frame the pane in crimson silk, but then my scorching flesh turns chill once more, so I stay silent, basking and glad of it.

"Why didn't you tell me she was like this over the phone?" Xion snaps at Sephy, who towers over me, looking down with pity in her gaze. She and I haven't had the easiest relationship lately, so I know I must look bloody awful if she's feeling sorry for me. I rest my clammy palms over my stomach, head lolling to one side.

"Would it have made a difference? As far as I'm concerned, you were already doing the one thing we can to help her," Sephy retorts, looking tired as she holds an enormous leather-bound volume in her palms. I recognise it immediately, *The Principles of Power*. I remember now, using the same book to cast the darkness from Xion, back when I thought myself pious and good.

I should have mentioned it to Sephy, had her grab it when she was back in Mortaria, but my mind is so full of warring opinions that I'm barely able to form words, let alone recall a single ritual I performed a lifetime ago, and so it is only now that the details return to me. The smell of sage rises in a fog of nostalgia from the recesses of my memory, the sprinkling of aether. I remember all these things now, wondering how I could have forgotten as my mind is jogged into crystalline recollection.

I wonder if perhaps, as dark magic and alchemy is running in my veins, wiring my thought processes, and sparking life into parts of my brain that had long been turned dark, I've forgotten the struggle of wielding this kind of magic from before. I've forgotten the carefully chosen words, the ingredients, and the precise conditions required to summon meagre offerings.

As I remember that pain, that never-ending routine of jumping through mystical hoops, the researching of every single aspect, of gaining power by single handfuls at a time, I panic.

"Sephy, I'm not sure this is the right thing to do—" I say quickly, biting down on my bottom lip so hard that blood floods across my tongue. Her eyes narrow. The smell of the sage wafting in the air, a purifying entity, is making me antsy, the darkness within my blood screaming.

"Erin, Ericka, Erlea!" She calls for the Furies, who I hadn't even known were here, and they return her glance with knowing but vacant eyes. Taking small steps forward, two of them grab a wrist each with the third fastening my ankles against the soft weave of the fabric beneath, holding me down to the chaise longue without mercy.

"I'm sorry, Luce, but this is happening." Sephy glares at me, and Xion drops the aether in a circle around the chair where I'm lying, not making eye contact as if he might go weak at the knees or something equally as pathetic.

She stands over me, drawing something from the back of her waist-band.

The obsidian shard glints pearlescent in the downpour of sunlight, lethal with its jagged edges.

Xion steps back, the circle around me complete, before looking to Sephy.

"Now, you go," she commands him, not looking up from the pages of the book in her hands, studying the words as he looks between us.

"All right, I'll be just outside if you need anything—" he vows, noble as ever. I struggle against the three women pinning me down, fruitless in toil.

"So, I just read this?" She looks at the man with silver hair being watched by a hawk-like Jules.

"Yes. I suggest you sit on the floor. It'll ground you—" he adds, and she nods, folding her legs beneath her and resting the width of the volume on her knees. I stare at her, the Furies holding me down silently, suddenly wishing her dead.

"Don't do this—" I hiss, serpentine.

"Too late," she retorts, looking down at the crinkled paper in her lap and beginning to speak the words I haven't heard in what seems like forever.

141

I know them, but I can't hear them. The second her voice hits the air, I feel it; like my blood is being distilled, torn into its constituent parts. It's left screaming and raw like acid within my veins.

I struggle, the pain agonising and turning each second into an eternity. I feel The Furies holding me down, the sunlight turning my skin to what feels like dry, brittle ash. Twisting, writhing, I find Sephy looking at me without mercy as her lips continue to move, each syllable resulting in a breathless and inhumane exaltation of excruciating pain.

"You'll regret this, *bitch*," I gasp, heart pounding like it might arrest within this unbearably frail carcass.

I feel the chaise longue disappear from beneath me and know that it's coming. Delyria's dark kingdom is encroaching on my psyche, maybe for the last time.

My body hovers in mid-air, rising, as I let my eyes roll back in my skull, a sad smile on my lips, and everything goes a welcome black.

The world opens up above me, smoky greys and dark crimsons bleeding into a mass of looming and heavy sky. The wind whips around my shoulders and when I stare down at myself, I find no longer the baggy shirt and leggings I was wearing but a billowing gown of white, grey, and charcoal tulle. It falls off my shoulders, leaving the pale skin of my breasts spilling atop the corset.

Above me, dualistic suns, one scorching crimson and the other pale blue, hover, slowly rotating around the same orbit, dancing with one another. Clouds of burgundy, aubergine, and jet swirl underfoot, the heady scent of burning rose petals filling my nostrils and causing my pupils to dilate.

I stare around, rich mist swirling around my ankles, bare feet poking out from beneath the abundance of skirt. My dress trails around me like a plume of fog transitioning into dirty smoke from the clouds underfoot and up toward the sky.

He steps forward, form materialising from nothing, and the ram's horns adorning his broad forehead capture the red and blue light of the dual solar presence, releasing it dull, cloaked in the shadow of dark keratin.

"Welcome, beautiful daughter." His oily irises turning hues with the two-tone light become smaller, his pupils dominating as he takes me in.

He's wearing a long overcoat, the high collar closed with a lime green clasp that looks like a reptilian eye. Beneath it, a waistcoat of charred dragon scales wraps around his broad torso. A black cotton shirt clings to him, tucked into slim-fit pants that graze the floor, accentuating his height and the girth of his upper body. My heart flickers inside my chest like a flame without the will to burn. It's tired, exhausted from the fight between the part of me that came from the God before me and the part I clung to for so long, the safe part.

"Why are you here?" My voice is lost as the wind carries it from me in no more than a whisper. From the edge of the cloud I can see that the world burns below us, smoke rising and billowing from a blood-soaked land.

"Only you can answer that, Luce—" He uses the name reserved for family, for friends, the name Thane had invented for me all those years ago, disrupting my view of the world below as I'm compelled to stare at him once more. He takes a step forward, the light darkening as his shadow grows closer and closer.

I want to take a step back but find myself rooted to the spot, breath trapped within the bone cage inside of me, refusing to move. He takes my spindled fingers in his, his enormous hands fading in and out of scale at the wrist, the natural armour of his skin turning my stomach. I let my head hang back as he loops one hand around my waist and become limp like a doll, a puppet even, all energy gone from my limbs.

"Dance with me, pretty girl—" he commands, tongue flicking out with snakelike speed to moisten his bottom lip. I hear an organ chime from nowhere, the noise catastrophically gothic and making the hairs on the back of my neck rise in synchronised plight. My black hair trails, loose and wild down over my shoulders as I continue to hang in his grasp, letting him have his way with me. I have no fight left to give, surrendering entirely to his will.

He sweeps me across the clouds, plumes of ashen greys and arterial crimsons flying up in the wake of our nimble footwork. He glares down into my eyes, a wicked malice contorting his face as he twirls me, never letting me leave his grasp. I let him lead, letting my feet trail beneath the tulle of my wide skirt, my breathing slow even still as we glide across the hellish skyscape, a piano joining the organ and making my eyes flutter. It's a dark lullaby, a father's arms rocking me, waltzing me to sleep as he never had.

I tilt my head to one side, glaring up at him through half-glazed eyes, watching as he remains fully erect, the perfect gentleman. Our steps become faster, mine trailing his, unable to break the stare between us. The music that has accumulated to a dark and gothic waltz reaches its climax, and as he smiles at me one last time, he twirls me out from his body.

His hand slips from my waist, and as I move from his embrace, the clouds beneath my feet become little more than thin air. I fall, and he sees me going, grabbing onto my wrist with his enormous hands, hair falling wild around his face, eyes desperate and sad.

"Lucifer, don't let go!" he pleads as I dangle beneath the layer of rich-coloured clouds, my heart now hammering, breath coming in disappointing wisps.

I don't want to let go, but I can't hang on—

"I can't—" I sob, feet flailing beneath me in the open space of oblivion.

My fingers slip, the heat from my blood making my hands slick. One moment he has me in his grasp; the next I'm gone, falling through the smoke and bloody mist of the sky, descending too fast to be able to stop it. I watch as his face disappears above me, leaving only the desolate sky behind.

I crash into something solid, more clouds, a plume of lavender mist flying up around me as this new ethereal platform breaks my fall. It doesn't hurt, not really, not compared to the pain that shoots through me at the sight of her. When the smoke clears, her hand extends toward me, pale skin marred— just as I remember— by a spattering of pale pink freckles.

"Mother—" I whisper, finding her pink eyes angry as I stand before her. The white silk of her robe billows in the wind, her hair flowing out from her head in a wild halo of pink and cream curls. She's so beautiful, her skin like an artist's canvas before the first drop of a masterpiece, so full of potential.

Her full lips part slightly, and I think she might say something, but instead, she walks forward without a word, putting her arms around me and pulling me to her breast.

I inhale the scent of patchouli, of white roses, and of baby's breath, and I'm home. I feel my eyes becoming wet as my body goes limp yet again in her embrace. I smile at her, but she shakes her head, placing her hands on my shoulders and giving a firm shove. I fall backwards, the clouds no longer there to catch my fall, descending toward the flaming world below.

As I stare up into the sky, the smoke gathers, forming ocean-like waves.

A single roll of thunder echoes, and a solo of a fork of lightning illuminates everything that had once seemed so complicated as simple.

I dissolve into ash as I tumble to the earth, set free by the mercy of hellfire below.

13

Hungry Like the Wolf

PANDORA

SKIRTING THE EDGE OF the copse of trees that lines this so-called grand manor home, I peer out from behind a large trunk made rough by flaking chunks of bark.

I expected security, but under the high sun of early afternoon, an eerie half silence falls over the lawns, the only sound the thick blades of grass rubbing against one another in the breeze like bows on silent cello strings.

Looking left then right, the box is still clutched in my palm. My black leather corset and deep aubergine velvet pants hug me tightly, causing sweat to bead at the base of my neck. I haven't missed the sun's tyranny, and so exhale, wiping my brow before scurrying quickly across the lawn, eyes and ears taking in the tiniest flicker of sound.

Nothing.

Does she view me as that little a threat that she doesn't even feel the need to have someone on watch? Or perhaps she knows that I'm no match for her any longer—

I *must* find out what she stole.

Slamming my spine, flush, into the brick wall outside the closest window, my breath comes in shallow wisps beneath the boning of my corset. My usual composure unravels and I wonder if this is entirely self-inflicted. Hercules made sense to me, his fears that I will be unable to control The Demon Lords justified, and it is this logic that's driven me here in what could be considered an illogical and dangerous act.

Is this what he wanted?

What Zeus wanted?

It is too late to ponder this as I hear a groan emit from the window on my right-hand side, the flowerbeds beneath my feet trampled as I carelessly lean in for a closer look, risking my anonymity.

The crimson drapes framing the window topple to the floor in waterfalls of rich silk, giving me adequate cover to at least glimpse what's going on. I watch, heart frantic in my chest as I narrow my eyes, trying to work out what it is I'm seeing.

Lucifer hovers in the air, horizontal and straight as a board, while Sephy Sinclair sits cross-legged on the dark wood of the floor. She's got a book splayed open in her lap, and I watch her lips move, the sound barely penetrating the thick glass between us.

"I beseech thee to remove this power— to make her what she once was—" My brow furrows at the insinuation, watching as Lucifer's body trembles, parallel to the floor and anchored to one spot by three furious women.

The Furies.

I lick my bottom lip, mind reeling at the possibilities they present.

They would make great assets to my team, and I already know they hate Zeus.

Sephy gets to her feet as I lean out too far, desperate for more information, and then recoil slightly, exhaling in relief. That was too close. I hear a bang as the book falls to Sephy's feet, and upon observation discover that she looks almost drunk. As she takes several shaking steps forward, a breeze with no discernible source lifting her fiery red curls from her shoulders, I see it. A glint of obsidian, the solitary shard clutched hard in her palm.

Could it be?

Gorgon told me all the dark tethers had been destroyed.

I watch on, leaning a little closer and holding my breath so I can peer once more beyond the drapery undetected.

She slices into Lucifer with the jagged edge of the obsidian, letting blood run down from the newly made slit in the hovering woman's wrist. Lucifer cries out, a delirious moan escaping her lips and echoing out into the room. The Furies continue to attempt to anchor her to the furniture to no avail, her black hair tangled around her like onyx vines. She shudders, Sephy continuing to chant but careful not to disturb the glistening circle of white aether that surrounds her. I snort. That stuff has plagued me most of my immortal life, and I can't even count the hours I've spent trying to get it out of my hair,

147

my feathers— it just, gets everywhere, like goodness, like mercy, like weakness.

Lucifer's body trembles once more as though she's hovering over the epicentre of an invisible earthquake. I feel it before I see it, the hairs on the back of my neck standing on end as Sephy falls to the floor, the shard still clutched in her palm. The darkness seeps into the clear air, her skin giving up its mapping of black veins, her hair turning a holy white blonde once again.

Sephy watches on, looking as though she's about to sigh in relief, but then Luce's suspended silhouette shudders. Something within her fights, refusing to let go of what could be black ink as it plumes into flawlessly clear air, hovering above her. It remains there as if it's unsure of what to do, where to go.

"I beseech thee to remove this power, you absolute fucker!" Sephy screams as if cussing will aid her in any way.

At her words, the power splits, a sliver returning into the mouth, eyes, and ears of Lucifer's hovering figure as though she's no more than a floating cold corpse atop a calm sea.

The remaining darkness, the darkness I had put into her, lurches, heading straight for Sephy as she throws up the hand clutching the shard, presenting it as an obvious target. She grasps it, knuckles turning white as her arm tremors, the facets of the ancient stone absorbing the darkness I'd forced upon Lucifer little over a month ago.

Sephy goes limp, collapsing, and Luce falls gracelessly back down to the chaise longue beneath her, her body impacting the upholstery with a sharp thud.

She does not wake.

The Furies look at one another, one of them picking up a lock of her hair. It's not white but silver at the root fading ombre into to a black tip. I wonder what that means, wonder why the darkness within her seemed so hesitant to leave. Could it be that she didn't want to relinquish her hold on the power?

I lean back against the wall, glaring out over the lawns, the box still hot in my palm from arrival.

She had given up the power from The Well— and so now it was there for the taking.

Anyone could absorb it—

I could absorb it.

My lips curl into a smile, fate having twisted to fit my needs, to aid me in my quest.

I leave the brick wall behind me, creeping across the lawn once more and making my way back into the forest, box in hand and ready for me to make my return to the Exilia, destiny intact and plan in tow.

The Exilia towers overhead, intermittent lightning flickering across my face as it bounds within the smoky facets of the quartz ceiling. I stride with purpose, head held high, heart beating fast. I know I need to get that shard. The only problem is that I'll need the aid of The Demon Lords, one last time.

"Pandora— and *where* have you been?" His voice echoes out from the shadows as he takes a silent step forward.

"Abraxis, what are you doing skulking around here?" I bark, brow furrowing and lips pursing in extreme distaste for the man before me.

"You didn't answer my question—" he whispers, voice as threatening in low decibels as it is in booming summons.

I straighten.

"If you must know, I've just been to The Sinclair Estate." I exhale, knowing there's no use in lying to him.

"After we all so rightfully agreed that there was no point? I thought you were a team player, Pandora— seems I was mistaken." His thick lips twist into some semblance of a smile as he runs his fingers back through his greasy black hair, cool in demeanour as ever.

"Yes, well, where are the others? I want them to know what I've discovered," I ask.

His irises sheen, clementine and curious.

"They're resting. It's been so long since they last ate so much. They're in the throne room. They had the mortals prepare a lounge, so they might nap," he informs me. I begin to climb the skeletal staircase with haste, turning my back on him so fast I can imagine he is left looking rather affronted.

I hear his footsteps following me and so smile to myself, knowing I've made him wonder about the nature of my findings. I get such a thrill, holding these once powerful Lords in my palm and making them dance, a master puppeteer if ever there was one.

Striding across the open lobby, I catch the eyes of several mortal guards. They drop their gazes immediately, pleasing me immensely. As they open the double doors to the throne room, I clap my hands three times, the sound echoing out too loud for the slumbering Demon

Lords to ignore. They jerk awake, bolting upright from where they've been slumped over many a chaise-longue or curled up in random armchairs. Lilliana is hunched into a ball on the floor like a dog, her mouth open with drool pouring out. They all face one another, a stark indicator that none of them truly trust the other either.

"Rise and shine! I have news!" I call, voice melodic and over the top in its joy. The Demon Lords groan, collectively rubbing foreheads with long tense fingers and wiping their eyes with the backs of dirty palms.

"What is it now, Pandora?" Barbas' voice drips thick and cold with spite. I wonder what he dreams about when he slumbers, if he has sweet hallucinations or tumultuous nightmares.

"Well, I'm glad you asked. I have made a rather wonderful discovery." I rock on the balls of my feet as The Demon Lords fidget into wakefulness, straightening collars and the straps of old ball gowns, pushing hair behind ears damp with the sweat of sleep, and glowering with undying hatred at me, the supposed intruder. I don't know why they're so angry. It's as though they're merely children.

"What is it?" Gorgon demands, unfolding from the confines of a narrow-backed armchair upholstered in black velvet. His legs uncurl from beneath him like water, eyes wide. He's the only person in the room who seems to give a damn.

"One of the dark tethers, it survived." I let the words spill from my lips, eyes sparkling and gut giddy with moths fluttering incessantly at the prospect of my victory, a light upon which they will flock and feast.

"I beg your pardon?" Barbas demands, leaning forward and propping his dagger-esque elbows onto his even more angular knees. He narrows his eyes as though he thinks I could be lying.

"It's what she stole. The Sinclair girl!" I exclaim, almost jumping up and down.

"And how do you know that?" Katerina is suddenly interested from the chaise longue on which she's sprawled, the rusty silk of her gown pooling on the floor to one side as she twists to face me, propping herself up on a jagged elbow. I watch her carotid throb just beneath the thin skin draped over her throat, seemingly vulnerable even though I know it's anything but. Her crimson irises dilate, tracing my gaze, and momentarily consume my train of thought as I become lost in their endless pits of sanguine terror.

Blinking hard and breaking her gaze, I will myself to continue.

150

"I went to The Sinclair Estate, watched her pulling the darkness from Lucifer with it myself," I announce, crossing my arms over my corseted breasts and inhaling, chest puffing out with pride.

"You went to the Sinclair Estate? I thought we concluded that would be a bad idea," Barbas interjects.

I glare at him.

"Did you not hear what I just said? A dark tether is still in existence, Barbas! This could be huge for us! We could singlehandedly tilt the scales in a night with that kind of power and the ability to deliver it how we see fit." My fury stirs at his short-sightedness.

"*We*?" he snorts, straightening. "You're hardly entitled to that power, Pandora. It was entrusted to *us* by the Gods of Ancient," he sneers.

I clear my throat.

"Yes, and you've done *so* well with it," I counter, glaring at him.

Lilliana interrupts the stare between us, rising nimbly to her bare feet.

"You truly believe it's a dark tether?" she enquires, voice barely an awed whisper, and I nod.

"I do. Ask Abraxis. He'd know if I was lying." I turn to the man standing behind me, watching the exchange with reserved interest. I challenge him with an intense violet glower, willing him to speak.

"She tells the truth," he simply states, folding his arms and exhaling a sigh. "Regardless of the fact she did so without our permission or knowledge, we cannot deny the significance of what she discovered during the trip," he adds though I feel it is to appease me more than anything else. "I, however, will not be adding my demons to the mix if you're wanting to launch an attack. There seems little point. My son will detect their origins immediately, so the stealth I would usually add to the brew will be utterly useless," he insists, though I doubt it's his real reason. He's just a goddamn lazy coward.

"And what of the rest of you?" I assert pressure, not wanting to waste any more time. Katerina nods her assent, as does Lilliana, making me feel slight relief at their wordless loyalty.

"I will help," Gorgon adds after a moment's terse silence.

I expect no less.

Barbas, on the other hand, cannot be so easily swayed.

"I feel rather inclined to sit this one out if you don't mind," he adds, and I roll my eyes, cursing him internally. I don't know what it is about Barbas, but he and I never quite see eye to eye. Perhaps it's because he sees my fears, knows that I'm attempting to get the shard for personal gain more than that of the collective, but regardless, I can't find the will to care. The Banshees, Succubi, and Gorgonian forces will be more than enough to decimate the estate and everyone inside. It will be easy.

"I want us to assemble forces where they can be seen. Then I will be able to estimate how long it will take to transport them via the box," I announce, spinning on the ball of my foot so that my hair flies out around my shoulders in a sharp flurry of well-kept tendrils.

Soon, I will have the power I seek, and even better, I will be able to make The Demon Lords who don't intend on aiding my cause kneel at my feet. Abraxis and Barbas will be sorry they didn't help in this quest; I know they will.

I storm from the room; the frantic pace of the three allying Demon Lords close on my heels as I take a sharp left. I ascend the ramp to the west wing of The Exilia where the balcony overlooking the length of the main road resides, knowing it will be favourable as a position from which to appear powerful.

Passing a bedroom encrusted with tourmaline and chocolate diamonds, I note only a barren fireplace leaves the interior cold and dark as the wine stain of the sky beyond the balcony peeps through the fluttering drapes. The darkness makes the entire room appear rusted in hue, and I briefly allow myself to wonder who it belongs to before returning to my overwhelming intention to dominate.

Finding the narrow double doors at the end of the hallway surrounded by mortal guards on either side, they open before I even have to ask.

I stride straight through, the stale air filling my nostrils as the wide balcony on the opposing side of the library beckons. Dust sheets are pulled up over the shelves of countless mystical volumes; the collection of a lifetime, though I doubt magically imbued. Not that it means they can't be useful. Once this is all over, I'll have to begin reading through them all, attempting to lock away as much valuable knowledge as possible to ready myself for a war against gods that have aeons more life experience than I could ever hope to achieve.

"I want this room cleared and returned to a state where it can be used properly," I demand of the mortals whose glazed eyes peer into the room after the last of us, Katerina, has stalked past them.

"Of course, Your Highness." I hear the response but don't bother to acknowledge it.

My time is becoming undoubtedly ever more precious with each passing day, and so I turn to the Demon Lords. They stand, still now, at my back, staring around the room as Mortals remove dust sheets and rearrange furniture beneath our unimpressed collective stare.

"I want you to summon them. We must begin transporting now if we are to have enough forces by mortal nightfall," I explain.

Taking a moment to watch them, I stop in motion as one of the guards spins as though he's been slapped, eyes widening suddenly as his forehead creases beneath the mop of his dark, lank hair.

"Yes?" I spit, unamused and surprised by his pause.

"Oh, uh, nothing. My apologies." He stutters as my gaze pierces right through him like a set of knives set free from the hand of a practised assassin.

I turn at this, throwing open the French doors leading to the wide balcony spreading the length of the west face of the Exilia and stepping out into the muggy Mortarian air. The Demon Lords follow, and before I know it, I'm surrounded by demonic howls, hisses and the whispers of Katerina that will resonate within the blood of her Kindred.

I stand, surveying the dark scorched coil that was once The River Styx, the immense sanguine darkness of the sky overhead, the endless black of The Sea of Shadows kissing the endless horizon to the South.

It's beautiful, this place. Not conventionally, but it truly is a gothic, dark, and murderous masterpiece.

I sense paws hitting the earth in an oncoming rumble, hear the collective hiss of snake tongues on the wind, and smell the hungry, bloodstained, gnashing teeth and rusty breaths of Succubi ready for a fresh kill on the approach.

I smile, like a proud mother, admiring her despicable child.

SEPHY

I stir from sleep, the scent of pomegranate rising into my nostrils, a rhythmic stroking of rough fingertips upon my cheek bringing me back to consciousness.

"Mmm," I moan, allowing a few more minutes of dreamless dark to cocoon my mind before I open my eyes.

When I finally do, I'm met by a golden glory, the molten depths of his heated gaze only inches from my face.

"You are so beautiful when you sleep—" he whispers, catching me off guard as a sarcastic reply catches in my throat but won't go any further. The room around us is still, warm, and flooded with candle-light, the gossamer drapes of the four-poster muting the glare of the flickering flames and casting a warm glow upon his stubble-speckled skin.

The urge to retort grows, but before I can move to sass him, his thumb comes up to graze my bottom lip, eyes hooded heavy and his thick dark lashes falling to flutter against the sturdy architecture of his cheeks.

"Luce—" I begin, but he shakes his head, a soft laugh rumbling up from his hair-smattered chest that lies bare and flush against my left side.

"Shh—" he takes the thumb that has been stroking my bottom lip and silences me with it, something having overtaken him while I've been unconscious.

What is he doing?

"Xion, I—" I begin to protest, but his mouth comes down on mine, sealing my fate as his hand traces the length of my neck, burying into the thick tangle of my red curls and tugging, causing my mouth to tilt up as he climbs on top of me.

This isn't us. Isn't desperate. It's slow, civilised— excruciating. Animal lust is all but vacant from his stare as I fall into the dark abyss of his pupils, finding warmth to wrap my racing mind inside, calming my heartbeat and my fears as he presses his forehead against mine.

"No more talking," he whispers against my lips, inhaling me deeply as his hand travels down the length of my body and creeps back up toward my breasts beneath the flimsy black cotton of my shirt. He takes his leisurely time, pulling the thin lacy cup of my bra down and taking a nipple between two gentle fingers. He kisses me on the cheek, keeping eye contact as he caresses, making my back arch beneath him.

"There—" He smiles, biting his bottom lip and revelling in my pleasure.

I run my fingers back through his hair, letting my nails graze his scalp as he turns so his cheek fills my palm.

154

What is he doing? I want to ask him, but a part of me has been indefinitely silenced, pinned to the spot by the intention in his stare that goes far beyond what either of us could ever say.

He lets his hand slowly slide from my breast, the rough callouses of his palm causing goosebumps in the wake of his touch as it slides to rest flat on my stomach. Reaching down with the hand still buried in my hair, he unclips my bra. I rip my t-shirt off, letting the bra slide off the bed as I throw it carelessly to one side. He pulls my jeans off next, then my lace thong, leaving me an exposed mass of glowing peach flesh in the warm ambient glow of the suite.

He takes off his jeans in a single motion, unleashing his erection without pause, and then pulls back the sheets for me to slip inside. I wonder why he's doing that. We never actually get into bed— never. We're always crudely unapologetic; bare asses rising and falling, chests heaving and groans exploding from our lips, careless of who might know we're fucking like rabbits just behind my bedroom door.

He gets into bed with me, curling his arm beneath my neck and cradling me as he climbs on top, positioning himself between my legs and then relaxing, his erection making itself known between my thighs, throbbing and scorching against the wet of my trembling skin.

I'm ready, so what's he waiting for?

Why the hold-up?

I kiss him, lurching up and slamming my lips into his, groaning and trying to urge him into action. He grabs my hands, which clutch the side of his face, pushing them back beside my head.

"What's the hurry, Persephone?" he demands, biting that pesky bottom lip again as I remain splayed, bare, and wanton beneath his thudding heart.

"Well, you seem more than ready—" I gesture downwards with my eyes, and he chuckles, his laugh deep and raw, eyes alight with mystery.

"What?" I snap, impatient.

"I want to try something different. Want to see you—" he reveals. I give him a crazed look.

"See me? If you were any closer to me, my nipple might put your eye out!" I protest, and he shakes his head.

"No. I don't want to fuck you, Persephone," I feel disappointed by his admission, and he catches the dismay in my eyes.

155

"I want this— I want it to be different. Nobody needs to know. Just this once—" he begs me, and I feel myself confused one moment and terrified the next.

"Xion please, I don't—" I begin, but he places a hand to my cheek, stroking down the length of my jaw and then neckline, making me mewl with need for him.

"Please— just this once— I won't tell anyone. I'll never even bring it up again," he vows, eyes full of desperation. I feel myself become exhausted, surrender inevitable as the toll of the ritual still hangs over me like a dark cloud.

I don't say anything, don't reply. I simply lie back down against the pillows and reach up for him, curling my hands around his neck, heart beating a punishing rhythm, screaming against my ribs for me to put an end to this.

"I'll make it good for you, I promise—" he vows, kissing me on the forehead and then on the lips, the smell of him washing the hesitance in me away within seconds.

"You better—" I whisper, unable to believe my willingness to relinquish all control to him. "Or I'll toast your ass like it's a marshmallow." He takes this as both permission and challenge, smiling down at me.

He places both hands softly on my breasts, disappearing within seconds under the sheets, spreading my legs and pinning me down so I can't move. His enormous hands caress my inner thighs, making me sigh out as I try not to think about what this means. What it means to him— or to me.

I'm trembling, breath coming in shallow wisps like the ghosts of everything I vowed never to do, never to let him do to me.

I feel his hot tongue make contact, and he kisses me *there.*

I whimper, eyes rolling back in my head, and he spreads my legs wider, caressing me at all angles, making figure eights with his tongue and bringing me closer and closer to the edge. My muscles clench as he reaches a frustrating and unwarranted halt in his oral motion.

Crawling back up the length of my body, his scorching flesh flush with mine, he enters me, oh so slowly. He stretches me wide, filling me and making me moan as he comes up to kiss me. I taste myself on his tongue, the salt and the need melding with his scent to intoxicate me as he slowly begins to thrust. He looks down upon my face; the waves of his pleasure visible like a tide of molten gold, crashing repetitively into the onyx shores of his pupils as they dilate, taking me in. His lips shudder at the connection between us as he continues to tease me beneath the sheets, taking his time and kissing me without pause.

I stare up at him, mouth popping open as I get closer and closer to climax, he slows yet again— right as I'm on the edge.

Stilling, he bends, kissing me and causing my blood to boil, scorching and hurtling through my veins like an unstoppable wildfire that only he can cultivate and set loose.

"Xion— *please*. I'm so close—" I nudge him, and he smirks.

"I am well aware—" He goes back to kissing me, running his lips down the length of my neck as he begins again, making small shallow thrusts into me, just enough to make me groan, ecstasy rippling out from the point of contact and consuming my every thought as I writhe and sputter.

He grips my chin between his fingers, holding my face in place as he gazes down into my eyes, searching— searching for something.

"I want to watch you unravel for me, Persephone—" He uses my full name yet again, which I had never enjoyed hearing until the moment it first passed from his lips in a ragged whisper and speckled me with goosebumps, his voice becoming fast, rough, and erotic.

I go to respond, to lower the tone, to make the atmosphere between us less emotionally fraught, less meaningful, but before I can, he thrusts, a sudden and deep promise that soon I will fall apart beneath his fingers, beneath his mouth.

He watches me, eyes wide with each and every stroke, as he cradles me in his arms like I'm the sun— central to his universe.

It mounts, slowly, and I cannot help but let the moans fall from me like an avalanche of fast-melting hot snow, caught between the chill of wanting to keep him out and the burning need to have him closer than I've ever wanted anybody.

My body clenches around him, and he smiles, staring into the depths of my eyes in a way nobody ever has.

A smile overtakes me, and something like love blooms at my core. I shudder, wracked with excruciating pleasure beyond any orgasm I've ever experienced.

"Xion, fuck! Oh, Xion!" I cry out, a gush of hot, slick release coating him as his biceps become solid beneath my touch and his pupils dilate. The veins on his neck become prominent, and he bites down hard on his bottom lip, giving one final thrust into my thrumming body. He climaxes in a sudden and shocking groan, emptying so hard inside of me it almost hurts.

"Fuck!" he hisses between clenched teeth, gaze unfaltering even as he collapses on top of me.

The silence falls like a heavy blanket— the aftermath of this tenderness here too soon.

What just happened here?

I've never experienced anything like this— not in the entire time I've been alive.

I stare at him, breathless, and he peeks out from the thick tangle of my hair beneath his cheek.

"I—" I begin but he shakes his head.

"No. No words. Don't say anything. No labels. No fear. Just— just kiss me," he begs, and I blink several times slowly, feeling for the first time like sticking around for the aftermath of us.

Us.

Like a sickness, I feel my heart flutter beneath my breast, hammering against his in perfect time. I stare into his eyes and stroke my fingers through his hair, kissing him slower than I've ever kissed anyone, my stomach and chest aching in a way utterly unfamiliar and terrifying.

What have you done to me?

The Sephy I know would be making wisecracks, pulling on her shirt, pants, and shoes, and striding from the room. I wish I was— wish that was me.

And yet—

The Sephy I am couldn't bear the pain of moving from this man's embrace— not for anything.

Not for the whole fucking world.

14

POUR SOME SUGAR ON ME

SEPHY

I SLEEP DEEPER THAN I have since I crawled out of my own coffin. Wrapped securely in a blanket of warm pomegranate musk, soft skin, and dark chest hair.

I float, careless, free.

A knock at the door startles both Xion and me awake. The room spins, cloaked in darkness as I jerk upright, skin scorching hot to touch, the drapes still drawn around the bed.

The candles have long since extinguished.

What time is it?

I can't have slept through the night— can I?

As I untangle myself reluctantly from Xion's embrace, he sits up, eyes bewildered like a deer caught in headlights. I look to the window. It's dark outside, the moon low in the sky and casting a puddle of weak white light onto the carpet. It's probably not even midnight— so, why the sudden intrusion?

I stroll through to my closet, slipping on a pair of silk boy shorts and matching camisole, trying not to think about the fact that my entire body is still humming from whatever the hell it is that's passed between Xion and me.

Don't even think on it. Not for a second. No labels. I remind myself of the promise he'd made and run my fingers back through the fiery tangled mass of my bedhead, which probably resembles a dead cat after everything Xion did to me.

I pull open the door, too bright light flooding through the narrow crack as I peer out into the corridor outside.

"Jules?" I scrunch up my face, light painful to my unaccustomed eyes as I shield them with one hand. I take in the scene slowly, Jules, backed by the three Furies.

Uh oh. This can't be freaking good. I muse, still half asleep and groggy as all hell.

"What did you guys do now? Do you know what freaking time it is?" I yawn, allowing my eyelids to flutter slightly. Leaning haphazardly against the edge of the door, I find the wood feels good, cool against my cheek.

"Do you? It's only ten thirty. Besides, that's not why we're here—" Jules informs me, his expression unreadable.

I shake my head, placing my hand flat on my forehead and sighing.

Christ, I really needed that sleep.

"So— what is it?" I ask him, stifling another yawn as I note the anxious eyes of the three women behind him. My senses sharpen after a moment, anxiety flooding the place in my stomach that unfurled this afternoon, relaxing for the first time in months.

"The Furies, they say can sense something— and Cerb, he's been barking his head off downstairs, scrapping at the door, that kind of thing. I think you should take a look," he explains, looking nervous.

"All right let me just put on some goddamn knickers first," I grumble.

Jules gives me an apologetic smile as I close the door on him, pressing my back against it and fighting the urge to slide down its length and go back to sleep on the carpet. It looks pretty soft, after all.

"What was that about?" Xion demands, flinging his legs over the side of the mattress and parting the drapes with a hand as he steps, naked, into the moonlight falling through the window. He's silhouetted, highlighting the lines of definition cut through his muscle, making me even more desperate to return to bed.

"The Furies and Cerb— Jules said they can sense something out in the grounds. I'm gonna go take a look." I sigh, watching as Xion closes the distance between us.

"Are you okay?" he asks me, placing a warm palm on the cool round of my shoulder.

"Mhmm—" I give him a weak, sleepy smile and he kisses me on the forehead.

"Thank you, for that." He gestures back to the bed and I nod, too groggy to want to make sense of my emotions. Besides, I have potentially bigger problems, so it's going to have to wait.

At this acknowledgement, I feel slightly relieved, blinking once, twice, and then a third time, trying to rattle myself into some kind of alert state. We stare into one another's eyes, savouring the last of our privacy, but too soon, the moment has passed. Xion hurries to put his jeans and t-shirt back on, and I head over to my closet to find something more appropriate to wear.

We dress in silence, me putting a black tank and my favourite leather pants on over fresh underwear and then pulling on a worn pair of metal studded Doc Martens.

"Those look like shit-kicking boots," Xion observes playfully, and I grin at him. "Expecting trouble?"

"Oh, they are—" I assure him with a wink, "—and when are we not expecting fucking trouble?" I remind him, a small and sad laugh escaping my lips.

"Well, I guess it is the apocalypse," he retorts, and I pucker my mouth, impatient.

"Yep, so let's hope it starts hurrying the fuck up. I'm sick of this waiting around crap. It's driving me insane! If the world is gonna go up in flames, I'd rather it be sooner than later, get it over with, ya know?" I admit, and he nods in awkward agreement as we hurry, only just fully dressed, side-by-side, toward the door.

You know what they say.

Careful what you wish for.

Everything in the lobby is still except for Cerb, who is frantically running from the window on the left side of the doors to the window on the right side, scrapping at the glass with his paws. His nails click on the marble as The Furies watch him, heads darting from left to right like they're at Wimbledon.

Jules turns as the sound of our footsteps reaches him, green eyes darker than I've seen them in a while. Concern lines his forehead, deeply etched into his skin as he swallows hard, Adam's apple dislodging the tight collar of his suit shirt.

"How's Luce?" I ask before he can start talking about anything else. Not knowing about her state after the ritual is nagging at me. He looks slightly sad, eyes dropping to his shiny shoes, toecaps reflecting his morose expression back up at him.

161

"Still out of it. It may very well be best to put her upstairs again, just in case," he suggests.

I think of the wide window in the downstairs lounge and how I'd left her lying asleep in front of it, exposed, before looking to Xion.

"Can you take care of that? Don't forget to take the shard up with you, too." I remind him, having left the Obsidian Shard clutched in Luce's unconscious palm as if the proximity of the darkness she had given up might help her wake faster. It was a silly, superstitious move but it felt right, more so than keeping it with me and close to Xion anyhow.

"Sure, be careful out there, okay?" He gestures to the lawns sprawling around the estate, dissolving too fast into the shadow of the night. His fingers linger momentarily on my shoulder, and I feel his hesitation to leave, but he goes nonetheless.

As he departs, I turn to The Furies who are still watching Cerb and fidgeting anxiously on the spot. Jules sighs, but before he can speak, I address the giant murderous elephant in the room.

"So, where's Peter?" I glance around for him, and Jules purses his lips.

"I called him a cab. He left ages ago. Figured you wouldn't still want him here when you woke up."

"And that's why you're the man, Jules." I compliment him, but before long, the wide smile dies on his lips and he turns to look out of the window, brow furrowing.

"I can't sense anything myself, but I'm not, you know—" He shrugs, changing the subject too fast to the morose, and I exhale heavily, chewing the inside of my lip as a shiver runs up my spine. I watch the Leonberger bounding and frown, he's not a bad dog, and he never barks for no reason, so something is definitely going on.

"Okay." My eye catches the glistening glass facets of the whisky bottle on the coffee table between the couches on my left, right where I'd left it what feels like forever ago.

Jules eyes me then stutters, shame overcoming him.

"I was going to clear that up. I've just been a little distracted." I smile at him, shaking my head and waving a casual hand.

Like I give a shit about mess after everything he's done for me.

"Oh, no. I don't want you to. I'm taking this sucker with me—" I explain, and he gives me a curious stare, tilting his head to the left.

"What do you mean? Might not be the best time for a drink, Sephy. We need you sharp." He sounds like a military man in this sentiment, making me laugh.

"Oh, Jules. Don't you worry. I'm as sharp as a lemon juice coated pin in the eye. I have something different and entirely more fun in mind." I grin at him, striding over to the bottle and picking it up in a quick lunge toward the coffee table. I'm trying to diffuse the tension, willing my relaxed air to remain with me as long as possible. The Furies and Jules stare at me, and suddenly I realise that I'm kidding myself. Playtime is most certainly over.

"Right, then. Let's go look." I try to stay calm, but anxiety quickly takes root in me like a far-reaching and potentially fatal disease. My mind moves quickly, running through the worst-case scenarios, but none of them seem to make any sense.

Why would anyone be attacking now?

After all this time?

Is it because of my little visit to Luce's alchemy chambers?

Fucking Anubis.

Just when I think I can't hate that chick anymore, she goes and proves me goddamn wrong all over again.

"We'll be here." Jules swallows hard, and I observe The Furies as I pass them, fingers wandering toward their respective weapons. My muscles instinctively tense as I inhale, steeling myself for a fight.

I don't take the front door, instead convecting toward the back of the estate in a sudden and ferocious eruption of blue flames. Through the window behind me, I can see Xion picking up Luce and wrapping her listless arm around his shoulder, preparing to move her. I knock on the window, laughing as he almost shits himself at the sound, blowing him a quick kiss before flitting off into the night, uncharacteristic giggles caught fast in my throat.

The sensation isn't immediate, but as I move further away from the puddle of warm light that surrounds the main house, the breeze ruffles my waning sense of confidence even further. There's something there, wafting through the fast-moving air and lacing it sickly sweet— ichor.

Awesome. My fingers tighten around the lid of the bottle in my hand as I force myself to keep putting one foot in front of the other.

I narrow my eyes, un-stoppering the bottle of whisky and inhaling as the scent of it stings my nostrils. Taking a quick swig— *for courage—* I tell myself, I find myself painfully aware of my surroundings as I creep closer to the line of the trees, the hairs on the back of my neck standing to attention. There's definitely something there; a heavy breathing masked by the night's chill, the shifting of shadowy warm masses in the dark, avoiding the moon's illumination by only a sliver.

So how many?

One, two, three?

A whole pack?

I upend the bottle of whisky, not up for wasting any more time, breaking into a light jog and letting the brown liquor glug as it falls noisily from the bottle, soaking the grass and causing it to glisten gold. I run along the length of the trees as far as I can before it runs dry, wanting to gauge exactly what it is I'm dealing with. It might be a small enough number to take on single-handedly, but I need to make sure none are left hiding in the trees, waiting to surprise me, and a single handful of flame simply isn't going to cut it with the size of this forest.

After the bottle has spilt its last fiery drop, I throw it carelessly onto the grass, cocking my head as my hair is whipped from my face by a sudden chill gust. Then, leaning forward, I stare between two thick tree trunks into the dark.

I inhale, then exhale, clicking my fingers and summoning a palmful of Eternal Flame, holding my breath.

I stand a second, hearing the sudden crack of a nearby branch, and toss the ball onto the trail of whisky I've left in my wake. The fire catches within seconds, scorching the grass black as it spreads in a neat line, illuminating the edge of the trees.

I tread back, shocked. Just inches from me, the white eyes of a banshee stare directly into my face. A screech erupts from its lips, making the air around me feel as fragile as glass ready to shatter, the sound ricocheting inside my ears like a rogue bullet.

Keeping my cool, I throw a palmful of flame through the wall of flickering fire between us, hitting it right in the face and watching as it burns.

Get off my goddamn property! I think, satisfied, but then it happens.

The same screech, the same cry of hunger, of desperate bloodlust, but this time it doesn't come from merely one Banshee. My head snaps to the left, hair flying around me, skin flickering between ghostly ivory and the orange of a winter banishing hearth, eyes wide, heart beating so fast I worry it might burst through my chest.

I see them, the source of the ferocious violation of sound, but there aren't six. There are at least several hundred packed into the dense greenery of the forest, a rabid army with white and scarlet eyes staring out at me, teeth bared, exposed, and hungry. They fill the entire forest, another pair of white eyes coming forth from the shadow to replace the beast I've just set alight.

I stand, facing them.

Watching.

Waiting.

What are *they* waiting for, anyway?

My mind can only find one conclusion.

A command from Pandora and The Demon Lords.

This is not the attack I had expected. This is a full-out invasion— a crucial battle in a bigger war that's come out of nowhere, a plan to turn what has always been my last sanctuary into a slaughterhouse.

I stand, rooted to the spot, paralysed with shock and growing terror.

Moments pass, the breath of the demons coming in slow motion, until a thought forces me forward into motion.

Xion, Luce, Jules, The Furies—

My little dysfunctional family.

I have to protect them, have to stop this.

As I turn on my heel, I feel the mass stir at my back and begin to head back toward the house in a full-out sprint, mind whirling in a vortex of distress. The Resurrection Flame rises in cobalt tongues around me, swallowing me from the night as I convect back inside the house, the only thing I can manage to think being—

Well, shit.

I skid in a blur of flames back into the lobby, the thick rubber soles of my boots squealing hard against the marble.

"Weapons at the ready! Incoming!" I shout, watching Xion, Jules, and The Furies scatter. Xion takes the stairs two at a time, heavy tread bunching the runner at the edges.

"What is it?" His voice is one long exhale.

I look over my shoulder, heart racing. Now I've seen them, exposed them, we might have mere seconds before they're upon us.

"Hundreds of them, Banshees, Succubi, God knows what else." I pant, looking desperately into his face as his pupils widen.

"Oh, shit!" He runs his fingers through his thick hair, frustrated, "But— why *now*?" he asks, and I watch as Jules returns with several boxes of ammunition and one of his many shotguns, presumably from down in the basement.

"Not caring at this particular moment, too busy trying not to die—I'll worry about that later!" I frown at him, staring out of the windows to where the demons, now passing the threshold of the firelight, are beginning to lurch closer. The ground gives a barely noticeable rumble, the vibrations indiscernible if you didn't know they were from demons, but I know. I've been here before.

I look to Cerb, who has trotted over and is sitting at my heels, waiting for instructions, chocolate brown eyes huge with unmarred innocence as whines escape between his bared teeth.

"Cerb! Go!" I point up the stairs, and he charges toward the landing, paws scuffling and ears flapping as he goes, turning a sharp left at the top and heading toward my suite. I've never thought I'd be so glad I got Nightshade moved from the grounds either because there's no doubt in my mind that hungry jaws wouldn't cease in ripping her glorious well-muscled body to pieces.

"Sephy, behind you!" Jules exclaims.

I spin, just in time to hear the window shatter and have my field of vision invaded by the first of many Banshees launching itself toward me. I duck, unable to muster The Eternal Flame before it makes impact. As I ready myself for a scrappy brawl on the floor, a gunshot rings out and the Banshee falls on top of me, dead, instead. Blood leaks out between its milky glazed eyes, dripping off its snout and trickling, warm, down the side of my face.

"Somebody help me, for Christ's sake!" I exclaim, stuck glaring up at the ceiling while Jules and Xion stare at my splayed and Banshee-covered body.

As my voice hits the air, they fly into action, hauling the dead demon from on top of me and tossing it to one side. Scrambling to my feet, shattered pieces of glass fall from my hair, tinkling to the floor. I attempt to wipe the thick globule of blood from my cheek, but it smudges. Unfortunately, I don't have time to worry about it as The Furies reappear from their room, more weapons clutched in their hands, eyes narrowing in on the targets that can be seen fast approaching the shattered window. Erlea throws a spare broad sword to Xion that he catches effortlessly in one hand before beheading a Succubi that's just managed to breach the exterior wall.

We're too close here, and within seconds, we'll be overrun.

I stare around the room, making my logistical analysis as quickly as I can, blood roaring like a beast of its own, rushing to my brain and pounding in my ears.

"Jules, Erin, and I will take the landing. The rest of you keep the bottom of the staircase from getting overrun. Go!" I bark, the orders coming from me in a natural and hurried flow, leaving no room for questions.

Spinning on the ball of my foot, Jules, Erin, and I hurry up the stairs, feet a dull clatter upon the velvet runner. I take a central position, looking directly down the length of the staircase with Jules on my right, propping his shotgun over the bannister, and Erin on my left, pulling her bow from her spine and grabbing an arrow from the leather quiver strapped to her muscular thigh.

I watch on, breath coming too fast, as Xion, Erlea, and Ericka spread at the bottom of the stairs, our first line of defence, as the second window breaks.

Then, en masse, they are upon us.

Succubi use their long limbs to skitter across the floor, claws leaving permanent indents in the stone as Erlea takes down a line of three with one swift swing of her katana. Blood, thick and red, spatters the marble and is left dripping from the blade and down her arms, peppering the pale skin of her face as she looks up at me, smiling. I meet her gaze, one full of hate, of fire, but before I have a chance to make any kind of gesture, like even a simple thumbs up, I hear glass breaking from other locations on the ground floor.

I summon The Eternal Flame to me as quickly as I can, taking out several Banshees clawing at each other to gain access through the gaping window pane, the first of them launching toward Xion as those in its wake become trapped by a fortunate bottleneck.

He takes out the demon fast, sweeping its front paws from beneath it with a swift kick and then shoving the steel blade into the space between its ears. As his sword is wrenched back and my flaming projectile hits two of the Banshees making their way toward him through the window frame straight on, brain matter and skin fly across the floor, turning it slick beneath Xion's feet.

Demons pour in from the left and right wings of the estate within seconds of the first line of the breach, clambering up the walls and skidding across the lobby floor, trying to get as close to their targets as possible, hunger flashing in their soulless eyes.

Xion spins, almost skidding on a glassy puddle of demonic guts, but regains his balance just in time to find the two screaming Banshees I have just targeted ablaze. He watches as they burn, the fire from their bodies catching on the drapes surrounding the window as they stumble back. Too soon, though, he's confronted by more bodies to skewer as the demons close in from all angles.

The front doors begin to shudder, demons fighting one another to gain access to us on all sides, and Succubi and Gorgonians slither in through the west and east wings via ground-floor windows they've presumably broken through with ease.

I should have had this place converted into a fortress, not freaking redecorated.

Ericka throws daggers left and right, and as she turns to take out a Gorgonian climbing the wall, shimmering in and out of camouflage as it goes, Jules' shotgun goes off, splattering Succubus brain all over the far wall in a psychotic impressionist's dream.

The drapes are now fully ablaze on the right side of the double doors, which tremor with increasing ferocity, the sound of paws slamming against the wood and scratching claws falling into the din of battle cries, last exhales, and the spilling of bodily fluids. These are the audible components that make up the increasingly depressing white noise of the scene.

Suddenly, a blaring siren begins to wail. I turn to Jules, eyes wide, and he quickly uses his shotgun to shoot out the smoke detector on the left-hand wall, silence falling in a thick and welcome blanket after the bang of the bullet leaving the barrel echoes into nothing.

I watch as the flow of demons through the window, now framed by roaring flames, trickles to nothing, and quickly toss another ball of flame to the corresponding drapes on the other side of the door. Watching the rich silk catch alight, the flow of beasts slows a little more.

As they realise that both windows are now a dangerous path of entry, the front doors begin to splinter at the hinges, the increased mass behind the only remaining security in the house making it buckle within only seconds.

"Sephy, if those doors don't stand up, we're never going to make it!" Jules yells, taking aim and shooting a Gorgonian hanging haphazardly from the chandelier. The bullet takes out the demon, but it also takes down the lighting fixture.

"Watch out!" I cry, as Xion, Ericka, and Erlea scatter, narrowly escaping the path of the chandelier as it crashes loudly onto the floor and lands dead centre atop a Succubi that's been fighting its way toward the stairs.

Xion continues to slash at the demons, falling into a dodge roll and coming up close enough to slit the throat of a Banshee that's decided to launch itself from the east wing of the house and into the centre of the lobby. Its body slumps to the floor, but as I watch it fall, I find the corpses stacking up, walling us in against the staircase.

The door groans, and after a sharp splintering sound slices through the air, the doors collapse inward, crashing to the floor as a nightmarish hoard of oncoming beasts crosses the threshold and begins to charge right toward us over the top of it. The lines are seven demons across with more coming from the forest in the distance even still.

Shit.

"Xion! Get Luce! We have to get out of here!" I scream at him over the cacophony of death, of the fight, watching as the demons destroy furniture, dislodge pictures, and carve up wallpaper in their attempt to grasp flesh.

"I'd love to—" he exclaims breathlessly as he backs up a few stairs, ducking as Erin hits a Succubi right between the eyes with a practised throw of one of her many daggers. "But I'm a little busy— I don't think we can just leave!"

I look around at the fighting, overwhelmed.

He's right.

There is no way the Estate is salvageable, not without all of us giving our lives.

"It's okay. I know what to do— get Luce and get out!" I shout, eyes reflecting the flames billowing thick smoke as they crawl ever closer to the ceiling, the state-of-the-art sprinkler system nowhere to be seen thanks to Jules' careful aim.

"Sephy, what now?! What do we do?" Jules shouts, turning with eyes wide as he grabs his shotgun and hits a Gorgonian straight on with the butt of the gun. It falls, quickly engulfed by the crowds of demons encroaching on us with every single second.

Smoke fills my nostrils, billowing in enormous clouds toward the ceiling of the room and crawling toward us with nowhere left to go.

Xion hurries past me with one final look back over his shoulder toward the demons, which have flooded the property and outnumber us at least fifty to one. He bolts past me, running down the corridor toward my parent's old room as I widen my stance and look down over the demonic invasion. The frothing teeth, the gnashing jaws, the rabid breathing. The killer instinct is the only one that matters.

"Sephy! What do we do?!" Jules cries again, and I exhale, taking one last look around at the home I've come to love.

"Jules! Get everyone to the cars! Go! I'll be right behind you!" I exclaim.

There's only one thing left to do, only one option that seems likely to get us out of this in one piece.

It's time to light it up.

PANDORA

I watch her from the shadows, the wails of death and sighs of final exhales creeping up the corridor outside like spectres of the battle raging below. The door muffles it, but I know what's happening, know the bloodshed taking place only metres from where I'm standing. And yet, everything in this room is so calm, serene almost. It's as though this is a sign I'm exactly where I'm supposed to be at exactly the right moment.

I walk briskly to her bedside, the shard glimmering in her limp grasp as though the facets within are ablaze from the dim orange lights illuminating the room with a soft, homely glow. Taking a deep breath and holding it, I slowly slip the shard from her grasp and into my own but don't feel the rush I expect, heart falling slightly with an underwhelmed sadness. I don't know what I'd been expecting, but nothing wasn't it.

Exhaling, I watch as she stirs in sleep again but does not wake.

Still, it's mine now, and soon I will be sucking it dry and taking the darkness within it for myself, no matter what.

Staring down at Lucifer, her eyelids tremor, eyelashes fluttering as she flails in a troubled sleep. I envy even such fragile peace, the peace I will know only once vengeance has been grasped within my palms and savoured.

Will it be so tenuous as this?

Her mouth is slack, and as I hang here over her, I wonder if we could have been friends, she and I. It seems unlikely, but I think that together we could have done great things. Terrible no doubt, but undeniably great, nonetheless.

Hearing footsteps approach, I panic a moment, moving into the ensuite and propping the door ajar behind me only seconds before he bursts into the room.

"Luce come on! We have to go!" The demon half-breed's voice is urgent, and I hear the padding of paws at his heels, a deep rumble emitting from the throat of what I assume to be Lucifer's pet panther. While I've been watching over her, the beast has been scraping outside the door like a stupid house cat I've been only too happy to ignore.

Standing in the dark of the bathroom, I observe them through a crack in the door as smoke begins to billow in at Xion's back, thick and grey. The smell of burning reaches me.

Xion picks her up in a single fluid motion, her body unresponsive and limp in his arms as he carries her as though she were no more than a ragdoll.

He doesn't so much as glimpse my way.

The air heats slightly, drying noticeably around me, and I clutch both the box and the shard in my palms, holding them close to my chest. The power of each object alone is to be respected. Being in possession of both— it's practically godlike.

I could sneak away, could retreat, but a small part of me wants her to know who did it. Needs her to picture my smiling face as she recalls who destroyed the calm of this place and took her only remaining home from her. She has caused me suffering, gotten in my way at perhaps every opportunity, so how can I possibly pass up the opportunity to rub her demise at my hand in her face?

I listen intently as Xion's hurried footsteps fade into nothing, leaving everything behind them without a second thought. Neither had noticed the shard was missing, which I suppose isn't a surprise as there is rather a lot going on. My distraction has been a stroke of genius, playing out at exactly the correct moment and having the exact effect I'd hoped for.

I hear it then as I breathe a sigh of relief a little too soon, the rumble of the panther approaching. Through the crack in the door, I glimpse its piercing orange gaze, glowing through the thick gunmetal grey of the smoke-laden air.

"Beelz, come on!" I hear Xion call after the animal and stand stone still, staring at it and trying not to blink, to breathe. In this moment, I become a pale marble statue, a monument to my willpower and patience.

Seconds pass, maybe even minutes, but eventually, the panther turns and follows its master with a hesitance bordering on knowing, leaving me alone in the dark.

I exhale, relieved, as its paws fall into the din of crackling flames and Banshee cries, the song of death consuming this place as the foundations groan and the wooden floors creak, protesting the growing appetite of the heat that devours it oh so slowly.

A smile crosses my lips as I hurriedly slide the panels on the box in the sequence I know by heart, ready for my grand entrance down in the lobby. I want to look into that brat's face as her world comes crashing down around her.

Clutching the shard, the portal whirs into life within the cramped confines of the small bathroom and I step inside, giddy like a child, knowing now for certain that I have succeeded in becoming the architect of all her misfortunes.

15

FEVER

XION

"BEELZ, COME ON!" I call back over one shoulder, the smoke from the main lobby rolling in thick and fast now. The panther's tread can be heard catching up to us, so I charge, headfirst, into the swirling tendrils ahead, my heavy footfall causing the wooden floorboards beneath my feet to protest.

Déjà vu takes a firm hold over me as nostalgia threatens to overwhelm.

"Xion?" Her voice is a rasp, bubbling up into a cough as her eyelids flicker open, lashes thick with moisture from her stinging eyes. The flames climb the walls around the landing, charring everything in their path and leaving an acrid smell behind.

"Luce. It's okay. We have to get you out of here." I look down into her face, coughing a little myself as my lungs begin to fill with smoke, my inhales getting deeper in a desperate plea for air. I should've known it wouldn't be the last time I would be standing in The Sinclair Estate surrounded by rising flames.

"What's happening?" She looks around, eyes wild, but I refuse to cease in my bid for escape. She bounces up and down in my arms, long legs jostling over my elbow.

"Pandora, she sent a demon hoard— they're attacking the estate," I whisper. She coughs yet again, pale weak fingers covering the sag of her limp mouth as she stares at the stormy billowing greys trapped against the ceiling.

"Xion— it's a distraction— what is she here for?" she demands.

I look at her, eyes widening.

Something to take down Sephy perhaps?

The obsidian shard would be useless to her, and besides, it's on Luce's person. I look her up and down, but can't see it. She must have stashed it somewhere personal for better security.

My mind flits next to the opal blade, the memory of Sephy grasping it with triumphant and a deviant twinkle flashing behind her cognac irises rippling like the recollection is a stone skipping across the surface of my consciousness.

We stored it back in the hidden room, behind the bookcase, after everything that happened in Mortaria. It was perhaps Sephy's biggest weakness, and I can't leave it to chance that someone with ill intent might pick it up.

"Luce— I—" I stutter as I come to a break in the smoke, finding Jules about to descend the staircase.

"Can you stand?" I ask her, tone rising over the crackling of flames. She nods, eyes glassy.

I set her down on bare feet, watching as she sways a moment, eyes sunken deep with exhaustion. Her silver hair almost becomes lost in the blaze, and I look to Sephy, who is proudly torching everything she can reach with inexhaustible handfuls of fire. Sweat trickles down the side of my face. The bannister is ablaze, the runner on the staircase and the marble beneath perhaps the only parts of the room she hasn't yet targeted.

"I have to go and get something— I'll be right back. Jules, take her!" I call to him and watch as he extends out a hand to her. She takes it, and the two of them head down the stairs toward the flaming mass of demons below, the shadow of Beelz flitting in and out of the smoke as she prowls in their wake.

I don't know how they're going to get out, but I hope they do. The Furies meet with them as I make a final effort to stare down through the flames consuming the bannister, watching as they set about hacking through scorched limbs and screeching vocal cords of perishing demons, which flail like burning dancers, to get to the doorway.

Skidding around the corner, I sprint up the hallway, boots bunching up the carpet as the heat from the landing encroaches against my spine. Pulling back the copy of *Paradise Lost* in one swift motion, I dart inside as the bookcase swings forward, trying to clear my lungs with a deep cough, eyes watering profusely.

The opal blade glints in the flickering fluorescent spotlight overhead, a sure sign the fire is beginning to affect the electrics.

Closing the distance in two long strides, I smash clean through the glass of the newly installed security case. My knuckles scream in protest, the hilt of the knife filling my palm as I yank it toward myself and glass tinkles to the floor.

Gotcha. I smile to myself, proud of my quick thinking about something that could easily have been forgotten.

Leaving the room, I seal the bookcase behind me, running back down the length of the corridor and out onto the landing, ready to get the hell out of dodge.

The problem is, when I reach the landing, the main portion of the wooden floorboards in front of me is ablaze, the runner having finally caught light. It blazes higher and higher, the nature of its deathly charms no mystery to me. As I back up, realising that a window might be a better option for escape, the floorboards beneath me begin to splinter. This flame, The Eternal Flame, could destroy my soul in a manner of seconds, and so I peer back over my shoulder, finding the landing ready to disintegrate right beneath my feet. I have to move, but one step in the wrong place and it could all be over.

Backing away from the blaze, I peer over the bannister on my left and find Sephy, hoping to signal her.

I find her, eyes wide, fists balled at her sides as she stares at someone I can't see directly in front of her, distracted.

I don't know who, but I can guess.

That expression is *never* a good sign.

SEPHY

Her eyes peer out at me from beyond the wall of flame I've just created, separating me from the doorway using only the demon corpses piled up between us. Their violet depths flicker peach and then demonic scarlet, her gaze unwavering as a smile twists her lips.

The marble floor is refusing to catch light, which, under most circumstances, I'd be grateful for. Not today though. The flames rise, my once semi-peaceful home victim to beastly havoc on all sides as demons pour forth like an unending supply of misfortune from the depths of hell, coming back to bite me in the ass. I torch more bodies, building the wall up a little higher as they collapse on top of their comrades. There'd been no other way to hold them back as they flooded through the door, but I figured convecting would be an option anyway so wasn't too worried about blocking my only exit. The next line of demons back up behind the flames, wallpaper curling beneath the fire, which is slowly licking at the ceiling overhead. Sparks fall as the flames climb, landing in my hair and sizzling against my scalp, the room filled to the brim with smoke and demons.

There are so many, and I'm only one person.

"Well, I hope you enjoyed my little home makeover—" Pandora snarls, her voice rising in an irritatingly high pitch above the roar of the fire. The smoke stings my eyes and makes them tear at the corners, sweat beads on my brow, on the back of my neck, my palms slick and hot as I take out more demons. I don't drop eye contact with Pandora for a second as she simply stands there, a serene smile amongst the chaos.

"You'll never be Ty Pennington!" I yell, recalling many nights tearing up with a pint of ice cream as I pondered how many people I could help similarly with my millions. She gives me a confused look, pleasing me immensely.

I stare left, then right, faltering as I hear his echo out from somewhere close.

"Sephy!"

I can't find him through the wall of demons.

They just keep coming.

"Behind you, darling." She tosses a familiar looking box up into the air carelessly, like it's a baseball, gesturing behind me as I turn to peer over one shoulder.

Xion is trapped at the top of the staircase, the wooden structure growing more unstable by the minute.

What the hell is he doing up there?! He's the last freaking person you want standing on top of an unstable landing, which is also on fire. *Shit!*

The wood beneath his feet makes an audible groan as he goes to take a step back, legs only just visible through the flaming bannister. I turn, looking at her, wanting nothing more than to end her right here and now.

Stupid heavy-footed bastard! He's going to fall to his death! I curse his lack of grace, knowing that his escaping the rising flames on his lonesome is less than likely.

"You could save him, *or* you could kill me. Looks like you're in another one of those delicious "this or that" decisions you seem to so successfully attract." Pandora laughs. I watch as she picks up a sword, the one Xion discarded earlier, from the floor at her side.

The metal glows white hot as she stares at it, lips pulling back to widen her smile, face aglow with the flickering fire consuming the house around us as we stand, motionless, among the ruin. The blade twizzles in her palm, her eyes widening as they come to rest on my face once again.

"Or—" she poses the question, "—I could kill you both and be done with it?" She pops open the lid of the box in her palm, sliding the panels like a Rubik's cube prodigy without even looking.

From within, three Banshees spring, heading directly over the wall of flame in an enormous leap, paws out-stretched and claws un-sheathed, aiming right for me. I stare into the jagged-toothed jaws, saliva strung from incisor to incisor, hungry.

I'm about to summon my weapon to me, to add yet more fuel to this already blazing fire, but before I can, an enormous brown mass leaps in front of the demons, smashing into them and knocking them aside. Cerb has come from seemingly nowhere, having had the good sense to flee my room from the smoke, and has given me the split second I need. The cost, however, is one I couldn't have predicted.

The banshee gets to its feet, shaking its head, matted fur unmov-ing and damp with sweat, bearing its teeth as its packmate joins in ganging up on what would usually be considered the intimidating silhouette of the Leonberger. I have to make a choice, and if I don't make it soon his sacrifice will be for nothing.

Heart sinking, I make my choice.

Convecting backwards, the blue flame engulfs me, bright among all the scarlet. I reappear, the wood audibly splintering beneath my additional weight as I grab onto Xion.

Bracing myself, I pray that the floor holds just a few more seconds, before tensing my fists in the cotton of his shirt and convecting. We disappear from the building only moments before the staircase falls in, taking some of the interior lobby walls with it.

We fall onto damp grass, surrounded by demons, at the edge of the lawn. Panting, our chests rise and fall, competing for air as our heads hang close. My eyes meet his, the smell of burning increasingly over-whelming as the dim moonlight pales in comparison to the nearby blaze.

"Get to Jules. Get the cars ready— I have to— I can't leave them alive. Once they're done here, they'll just move on to the rest of Forest Glen," I surmise, rolling from his chest and onto my feet.

I find the demonic eyes glowing out from the dark, piercing the night, circling us like predatory lions, but I don't have time for this fight.

I shoot Xion a single firm glance, signalling he's on his own, before the flame consumes me again, leaving the newly distracted demons and a circle of scorched grass behind.

I re-emerge exactly where I plan to. The cellar. An idea blooming inside my mind like a wicked and catastrophic mushroom cloud.

I look at the boxes of ammunition, the wine, the guns, and know what I have to do to clear the estate for good.

I won't be leaving even one demon alive. I can't risk it, can't put the residents' lives in danger.

Hurrying over to the racks of drink, all that can be heard overhead is the ring of shattering glass and the groans of the house that fights, even still, to remain standing.

Once I'm finished, I convect yet again, knowing I have very little time, back to where I'd been standing before. I find Cerb, surrounded by Succubi and Banshees, miraculously still fighting.

Pandora orders her demons to continue their assault and I watch as they leap forward, finally too many for my lone fighter. I can hear his cries echo in my ears, making my knees weak and my eyes narrow.

These are cries that will haunt me for years to come.

No.

Pandora smiles at me through the flames, through the sounds of whining and the gnashing of teeth against what I assume to be bone.

No. No. No!

My eyes fill with tears, smoke so thick I can hardly stand it, unable to move as the fire encroaches on all sides. I don't have enough time to save his remains, don't have enough time to say goodbye, to avenge his murder.

Cerb saved my life— and lost his instead.

That fucking bitch.

She will pay for this.

I do the only thing I can think of, flipping her the bird and then convecting from the house, nerves raw, temper frayed, and heart shattered.

There's nothing left for me here within the four walls of this now ticking time bomb, not anymore.

I reappear in the garage, the doors of the structure being rammed against by the rabble on the other side. Claws and teeth scrape against the corrugated iron, ringing out in a sharp and ceaseless warning.

"Let's move!" I exclaim, looking to the group slumped against the sides of two different cars, waiting. The Furies and Luce scramble, Xion and Beelz nowhere to be seen.

Jules is sitting in the driver's seat of his black jeep, and the Furies pile into the back behind him. Luce climbs in my jeep, which sits right beside the one Jules is driving. It gleams an identical black, driver's door wide open, keys in the ignition, waiting.

"What about Xion? What about Beelz?" Luce exclaims, and I shake my head at her. Her eyes are sunken, terror evident in the spark which burns intense and fast behind her icy blue irises.

"We better hope to God we find 'em on the way. I don't have time for a discussion."

Storming forward, I'm unable to stop for even a second. If I think too hard, I'm going to fall apart.

Jules gives me a startled look as I sprint around the bonnet of his car, my boots dispersing thick detritus and slivers of charcoal across the concrete floor, the smell of burning ever rancid in my nose.

"Remember how we talked about what a party it would be with all that wine and gunpowder in the basement?" I cock my head at him as his eyes widen, mouth popping open.

"*Everybody in the cars! Let's move it people!*" he bellows out over his shoulder, turning on the engine of his Jeep with a single jerk of one wrist and slamming his door shut.

My hair, which is peppered with ash, bounces on my shoulders, leaving a trail of the stuff behind me as I rip open my car door and launch myself into the driver's seat. Luce slams her door shut with less than full strength as I turn the keys and push down hard onto the gas, placing the gearshift into drive.

I can feel the demons just outside the garage door so ram one foot on the break and the other on the gas, listening to the tyres as they squeal upon the bare concrete of the garage, the scent of burning rubber coming in through vents as white smoke plumes around the vehicle, encasing us in fog.

"Hold on!" I call back over my shoulder, hearing the audible click of Luce's seatbelt as I take my foot off the brake, allowing the car to fly forward.

The bonnet smashes through the flimsy metal of the automatic doors and we fly, engine roaring, headlights drenching the lawns before us, out into the night.

We impact the grass, and the suspension takes the brunt of it, but I still feel my ass bouncing out of the seat. I can see Jules in my rear-view mirror, following close behind as the car jostles beneath me. However, my attention doesn't stay fixed on his steely gaze for long.

Smoke is escaping from the upper-story windows of the estate now, an eerie orange glow tipped with black billowing edges emanating from the building like it's possessed. I try not to think about the burning bodies of demons and my beloved dog still inside.

Godammit.

If I ever accused you of disloyalty, Cerb— I'm sorry.

Tears threaten to obscure my vision as the car jostles from left to right, manoeuvring the terrain as my headlights illuminate demonic eyes by the hundreds. Some dive out of the way, but some are smashed aside by the bonnet. I hear the splintering of the glass in the headlights as I careen straight into a Banshee's skull without even flinching.

The demons toward the back of the lawns remain despite the oncoming vehicles and their stark, full-beam headlights, getting in the way and causing me to weave from left to right.

I look for Xion, finding his orange swirling tattoos glowing neon against the black of the night, his eyes flashing like two clementine beacons as he rips the jaws of a banshee apart, breaking its skull into two with his bare hands and leaving it for dead at his feet.

I screech to a halt on the wet grass, dew flying up beneath the wheels.

"Get in!" I scream, calling out of the window as I wind it down, the smoky scent of destruction leaching into the car's interior.

Xion leaps over a Succubus, pushing its face into the grass as he yanks open the passenger side door and falls into the seat, breathing heavily.

"Hurry!" I exclaim, and he rolls his eyes.

Soon he'll see why I'm in such a damn hurry, and who'll be rolling their eyes then?

Slamming the door shut, his breathing is rapid, chest rising and falling as it had beneath me as I'd saved his life. I push down on the gas again, spinning the steering wheel hard to the left and making my way towards the gravel driveway. About a hundred metres away, it happens, shattering the glass in the back window of the jeep and causing Luce to scream as she searches the darkness for Beelz. Glass shards hit the back of my shoulder as the Jeep finally thunders back onto the even layered stones of the drive, slowing down only slightly as I look back over my shoulder to watch the action. As the vehicle slows, Jules overtakes me from the left, having accelerated even more at the sound of the explosion.

It comes from seemingly nowhere, but I know differently as a fuck ton of gunpowder and the Sinclair's private collection of fine wines and whisky goes up in a ball of flame, blowing any remaining glass from the structure and taking out the primary architectural support.

The ground shakes, the foundations crumbling under their in-flamed weight as the interior collapses in on itself like a neutron star.

Turning away, I slam down on the accelerator.

Racing forward, the car gets closer and closer to the metal gates, tyres crunching fast over gravel, and I watch in the rear-view mirror as the home I've always known is demolished under my very own firepower.

The explosion has startled the demons, causing them to stop, to stare at the bright orange and yellow ball of flame as it consumes the debris of the house and the sky above it, flaming detritus setting numerous small fires that quickly spread across the lawn too.

Slowing ever so slightly in front of the gates behind Jules. I exhale, leaning forward and resting my slick forehead on the sleek leather steering wheel.

"Take that, you fuckers," I mumble, staring down at my knees, heart hammering as something within me shatters.

The gates open, too slowly given the adrenaline coursing through me, as I pull forward, moving from the estate for what could very well be the last time.

I follow closely now in Jules' tracks as The Furies stare out of the back window in front.

I can feel Xion staring at me, his molten irises boring into the profile of my face. I can't stop looking back in my side and rear-view mirrors to glance at him though, not able to give him the reassurance that I'm alright.

I'm not alright.

The sight of my last true tie to my parents, to my childhood, is engulfed by flame, dissolving into ash along with my childhood dog's remains, the sudden and unexpected loss consuming me in an emotional inferno as well.

We drive, one jeep in pursuit of the other, for almost half an hour before suddenly Jules indicates, pulling off the freeway and into a truck stop. Nobody in the car has spoken a word, Luce and Xion simply staring with blank faces out of the windows while I chew on my bottom lip, trying not to either cry or punch something extremely hard.

We pull along a short length of road lined with well-kept hedgerows before coming to a large parking lot peppered with fast-food restaurants, coffee shops, diners, and gas stations. I park in a space behind the other Jeep, getting out of the car and into the cool night air, exhaling heavily as Jules walks toward me.

His arms envelop me right in the middle of the parking lot, under the fluorescent floodlighting, and I steel myself, knowing that I can't fall apart. Not yet.

"Thank God you're alright—" He sighs, taking a step back from me, hands still on my shoulders, and staring. I know I must look a sight. My bare arms are streaked black with soot, the same deep char embedding itself under my nails. My hair fans out wild and unkempt from my face as I brush it behind one ear, hand shaking.

Christ only knows how my face looks at this point.

"I didn't know what else to do, Jules. I couldn't leave any of those demons alive—" I'm suddenly rambling, the deep guilt from destroying the home my parents had loved so much eating at me.

"You did the right thing, I have no doubt." He comforts me, a streak of black across his forehead. I'm staring at it when the other car doors open, and people pour out onto the starkly lit and cracked concrete of the lot, distracting me.

"Beelz, I can't leave her behind Sephy— my tether—" Luce is the first one to speak, and Jules nods.

"Don't worry, I'll make some calls. We will find her," he assures her, suddenly the real adult, the real lynchpin in this situation. I just stand

182

there, staring into the fearful eyes of The Furies as they come closer, weapons still clutched close to them.

"Are you alright?" Xion puts a large hand on my shoulder as he paces around Luce from where he's been leaning on the hood of the jeep.

I exhale.

"Cerb, he saved me. He's dead—" Tears rush to my eyes, and Xion's face fills with grief.

"I'm sorry— he was a good dog." His reply is lacklustre, like he doesn't know what to say.

"He was the best dog, Xion. The *best*." My glare is intense as he nods in agreement. My heart beats like a lead hammer inside my chest, threatening to destroy everything inside of me with the weight of its own grief.

"I know." Xion leans in to kiss me on the cheek. I turn away, at utter emotional capacity.

I'm standing in the middle of a truck stop with no home, the clothes I'm standing in, and two cars. Not only that, but the lives of everyone here now rest tenuously in my charred hands.

How the hell has it come to this in only one night?

"What do we do?" Erin asks me, her rich skin glistening in the light that puddles over us, banishing the surrounding dark.

"We go to a hotel, and we get some sleep. Then— we decide what to do together in the morning." I make the decision hastily, but as I do, my stomach rumbles and my head becomes cloudy.

"I think we should grab some food first." Jules looks at me with concern.

"Got any cash on you?" I ask him, eyeing the McDonald's across the lot. The golden arches have never seemed so appealing.

"Sure, I have spares of all your cards and some cash in the glove compartment of my car." He says it like it's nothing, but I know that it's entirely possible he's been anticipating the worst for weeks. Or *maybe* he's just always this prepared. Either way, I'm grateful.

"Okay, I'm starving. Let's go and grab some fast food and then we will head over to a hotel. Any ideas which one?" I ask.

Jules clears his throat yet again and I stare at him. Expectant.

"I think it would be a good idea to grab a room near O'Hare International. We have the jet there, and you don't know where our next move will take us. Couldn't hurt—" he suggests, and I nod furiously. The thought of jetting off somewhere sounds utterly appealing; especially if that includes never looking back.

"Okay, I'm feeling McDonald's. Any objections?" I demand, staring at the group, who shrug.

Xion grabs my hand, but I pull away yet again, trying to focus on moving through the next moment, the next minute.

We walk in a cluster across the parking lot and step up onto the curb, the fluorescent lights from inside the chain restaurant blanketing all of us. Lucifer looks pale as a ghost as I open the door and allow the mess of sooty bodies to pour inside ahead of me.

Jules jogs to catch up, a wallet and plastic bag full of cash clutched in his palm.

"It'll be okay, Sephy—" he begins, but I raise a hand. He doesn't know that. Nobody does, and I don't have time for hopeful lies.

"Let's just get something to eat. It's been a long night," I state, letting him take the door from me as I slip into the off-white tiled interior of the building.

The smell hits me, and my stomach opens into a desperate chasm.

The Furies and Lucifer stand with a pale-faced teen looking out over the counter at them with curiosity. I can't say I blame him. Luce isn't even wearing any shoes.

Taking a deep breath and relishing the smell of cholesterol in a bun, I lick my bottom lip, closing the space between us. The Furies stare at me, and Luce cocks her head, staring up at the illuminated menu hanging above the counter. I glance around, finding several customers pausing mid-bite, staring at us, or more particularly, at the sword sheathed even still to Erlea's back.

"Couldn't you have left that in the car?" I snap. "People are staring!" Then I look down at myself, at the soot and ash still clinging to me.

Okay, so maybe it's not only her they're staring at.

I feel exposed here among the ordinary with such unpredictable and powerful women.

"Okay, what is everyone having?" I exhale, knowing immediately that I'm going to be having several Big Macs at least. I mean I just fought off a demon army. I deserve it.

"I have a question—" Erin looks to me, eyes wide and innocent as the boy behind the counter continues to watch us, fascinated, as he leans over beside the till. Sipping a little too slowly from a cup of soda beside him, his gaze wanders slightly, transfixed. Now I look carefully, he's staring at Luce, not that I blame him. Even under the hideous fluorescent lighting and surrounded by tacky plastic booths, she looks like a goddess slash supermodel. He's probably hiding a boner underneath the countertop too, poor guy.

"Yes, what's the question?" I hurry her, sighing and feeling impatient to order. I'm starving.

Erin's forehead creases with serious concentration, and she looks at me deadpan in the face, abs tensing as she rests a hand on the dagger stashed in her belt. Pausing before she speaks, she cocks her head, curly thick hair bouncing in a dark halo as she examines the menu yet again.

"What—" she asks, turning back to me, eyes sheening, "—exactly, is a chicken nugget?"

16

RED

SEPHY

THE AUTOMATIC DOORS OF The Hilton at O'Hare sweep sideways silently, a gush of cool air from the lobby's air condition blanketing each of us in turn as we enter. We present as a rabble, a cacophony of different styles and attitudes, exhausted, worn down, and defeated as we trudge across the too-bright scarlet carpet. I watch eyes turn to us as I exhale heavily, sluggish and tired after the Big Mac I'd consumed in all of five bites, ravenous for every single one.

"What are you looking at?" I hear Erlea snap at a doorman who apparently lingers too long on her face, eyebrow cocked beneath the brim of his hat, guilty in his curiosity.

"Don't worry everyone, Comic-Con!" I call out, smiling with a little too much enthusiasm to the few people scattered around the lobby at this late hour.

Please God let them give us a room. I pray silently.

I approach the lengthy, pine check-in desk, the person behind the counter a woman with cropped caramel hair. Her eyes, which I assume have been previously glazed at the inactivity of the late hour, gleam with amusement.

"Comic-Con? I didn't know they were in town— who are you guys supposed to be?" she asks me.

I smile at her, uncomfortable as my legs ache, fatigue hitting me.

"Uh— an assortment— you know— from films and stuff," I mumble, and she looks disappointed.

"So, what can I do for you?" she asks, and I turn, looking to my posse and counting as my lips move but no sound comes out.

"I'm gonna need— Four rooms. One family room and the rest as double rooms." I look back over my shoulder and Jules slips the credit card into my palm as he comes closer to my spine. He watches Luce stare around the lobby as though she's never seen anything like it; her tired face focused for only long enough to appreciate the scale of the place.

"Okay give me a second—" The receptionist chews on her bottom lip, glancing every few seconds to Xion and giving a slight smile. I contemplate throwing myself over the counter and grabbing her by the hair— but then I notice, Xion isn't even looking at her. He's staring at me, eyes full of concern, instead.

Well, what do you know—

"All right, I've got the rooms available— how long will you be staying?" The question lingers in the air, highlighting the fact that I have no idea.

"Uh, two nights," Jules answers, placing a hand on my shoulder.

I visibly relax, posture sagging beneath his palm.

"All right— and how will you be paying?" Her fingers tap a wicked melody on the keyboard in front of her as miniatures of the changing screen flicker in her glassy irises.

"Credit card," I respond, and she pulls up a card machine, placing it on top of the varnished pine of the countertop.

The group stands, bored, as I shove in the card and the receptionist notes down the necessary details. I almost hear a collective sigh of relief as she procures a multitude of key cards.

"Which is the family room?" I ask, and she procures a silver keycard instead of a black one with a too-cheery smile. I pass it to Jules, twisting to find him directly behind me even still.

"You'll have to show The Furies how to get into their room. I'd do it but I'm low on patience. Here's yours." I pass him a black keycard too, and he nods.

"What's your room number?" he asks me, and I stare at the room number on the card I randomly pick for Xion and me.

"Uh— six hundred and sixty-six."

I roll my eyes.

"I'll come and check on you in the morning. I think we all need to sleep before we discuss anything further," he suggests. I nod, giving a faint and strained smile, turning to shepherd the three weapon-toting women over to the elevator.

"Here you go, Luce—" I pass her the final keycard and watch as she takes it in her palm, interested.

"What's this for?" she demands. I exhale.

"It's a key. For your room," I explain, and she shrugs.

"Oh— thanks." She's dream-like even still, eyes betraying the level of exhaustion that runs deep, like a crevasse, splitting her apart inside.

Making our way over to the row of elevators, one of which has just swept Jules and The Furies to the upper floors, I hear a plane taking off somewhere nearby. I blink; sounds, smells, and lights overwhelming me entirely. I cannot help but hope my room is somewhat quieter than this.

As the elevator arrives and the metal doors slide open to reveal the empty box, Luce, Xion, and I pile inside, selecting floor six as our destination. As the doors sweep closed, a commercially banal tune blares out without apology over the speakers. Luce hums, swaying slightly as though it's some kind of ritualistic chant, and I catch Xion smirking at her. I, however, don't have the energy to find anything funny.

The elevator pings as it reaches the correct floor and we pile out into the narrow corridor carpeted a still bright crimson and framed by cream walls adorned with golden sconces. Striding fast, I make short work of the distance to our designated rooms. Finally, I'm swiping the card in the door lock— watching as Luce copies me, and all of us disappear behind the heavy pine doors.

In the privacy afforded inside, I debate bursting into tears, mourning everything I've lost. The energy for this evades me as my mind swims in a concoction of exhaustion and grief, images of flickering flames and the sounds of Cerb's final whimpers echoing between the walls of my skull.

Xion comes close, as though he wants to wrap me in his embrace, but I step back, turning from him and throwing the key onto the bedside table, pulling off my boots and collapsing onto the bed.

I don't remember what happens next, whether Xion joins me or whether he watches me as I sleep.

I'm too exhausted to care.

Heat pours onto my skin as I surface from the darkness of sleep. His arm is slung over my waist, his breath tickling the back of my neck. I stir, rolling over and dislodging his arm as I lie back on the pillow staring up at the ceiling. Everything hits me at once. The violet gaze of Pandora, the flickering flames, the blasting of glass from what had once been my home. Demons now roam the estate, treading only feet above where my parents lie, buried in the soil.

My breath comes in heavy, nauseating waves, filling my lungs with the disgusting realisation that now I must move forward. Must decide what to do next, where to go from here.

Where do I want to be at the end of the world?

The question haunts me as Xion slowly finds consciousness beside me, moaning slightly as he opens his eyes, retinas scorched by the too-bright sunlight flooding in through the large window, the surrounding drapes left undrawn.

"Morning," he mumbles, staring up as he remains curled to face me, head denting the pillow beneath him considerably.

"Mmm," is all I can come up with, still staring at the ceiling.

"What are you thinking about?" he whispers in my ear, a playful smile tugging at the corners of his lips. It irritates me. He might be able to enjoy pillow talk, but I can't. Not even slightly. My mind is whirring around in cyclical torment, chasing questions I already know the answers to, answers I refuse to acknowledge.

"Murder," I reply, trying to quell the atmosphere he's attempting to cultivate.

"Okay then. I take it you haven't had any coffee yet?" he guesses, and I don't reply, still looking up at the ceiling, still numb.

As he looks at me, admiration evident and annoying me immensely, I run through it in my head, the attack—

What was she after?

"Hey— uh, why were you upstairs— you know, when the staircase was on fire?" I blurt abruptly, mouth a serious line as exhaustion tugs at me even though I've only just woken up.

Apparently, I need a vacation.

He rolls over, reaching to grab something off the nightstand on his side of the bed as I prop myself up against the wooden headboard, still fully dressed in last night's clothes.

As he rolls back, I catch a glint of it in the light and sigh.

"You went back for *that?*" I exhale, exasperated, and he nods.

"Of course, it's a big weak spot for you. I couldn't risk that Pandora was looking for it." He hands me the knife and I balance it on my index fingers, looking into the opalescent surface and feeling my mouth twist into a pucker of thought.

"What about the obsidian shard?" I query, and he shrugs.

"Luce has it—" he replies, uncertain as his voice dissolves into silence.

"You sure about that?" I probe, impatient.

"I guess—"

"You guess?"

"I was a little busy trying to make sure none of us got incinerated. So yes— I'm pretty sure," he snaps. I can only nod curtly as endless numbness continues to eat away at my insides.

"Sephy— are you alright?" he asks, eyes full of more caring than I deserve. I nod again. Simply unable to form words about how I feel. How has everything gone wrong so fast? Or has it always been heading this way, and I've just been too in denial to see it?

"She must have been in those woods for hours, just transporting that many demons here—" I muse, and Xion's face shifts into a grimace.

"I agree with you there— it's worrying. I mean, what's stopping her from doing that in the middle of Chicago and tipping the scales right then and there?" he asks, astute.

I narrow my eyes, biting down on my bottom lip as something occurs to me.

"She's waiting for something— but *what*?" I murmur under my breath as Xion reaches up and places a hand on the side of my face, trying to calm me. I shrug away, getting out of bed and placing both my feet onto the worn carpet beneath, standing and stretching upward.

"Sephy— are you— did I do something wrong?" Xion asks me, and I spin to face him, suddenly furious.

"Are you fucking kidding me? My home and my childhood best friend just got torched to a cinder! This isn't about you! For fuck's sake, Xion, get your head out of your ass. I have a few more things to worry about right now than whatever the fuck is going on with *us!*" I spit, infuriated by his lack of perspective.

Everything in my world just tilted dramatically on its axis, and I'm still reeling. I don't have time for emotion. I have to figure out what to do next, and fast, before more people die.

"Sorry— you're right," he replies, voice no less tender, and sits up in bed, swinging his legs over the side of the mattress and standing. Walking over to the window, he leans against the sunlight-dappled pane, watching as a plane soars into the sky from the runway of the airport.

We stand for a few moments in silence before I head into the bathroom and lean over the cool ceramic of the basin, taking a long hard look in the mirror. My skin is still charred in places, my hair wild and my eyes wide, scared.

Usually, I have some kind of a plan, but right now my mind is just flatlining. Not even one year ago, I was just like anyone else— and now, *now what?* I have to do something. Have to stop more people dying. But I'm no ruler, no Queen, I know that.

A knock at the door disturbs me as I bite down once more on my bottom lip and so walk across the cool relief of dark tiles and into the hall, peering through the peephole in the door and finding a distorted Jules with a huge head and tiny body peering back at me.

I unlock the door, propping myself against the frame and running my fingers back through my hair, finding a streak of soot I hadn't noticed on the underside of my forearm.

I need a goddamn shower. Not to mention I didn't even check to see what state I'd left the hotel's pristine white sheets in.

Screw it, let them charge me.

"Hey," I breathe, and he smiles in return, holding up a shopping bag.

"I took the liberty of grabbing everyone some fresh clothes from the strip mall down the street. Hope that's okay?" he asks, and I look down at myself, at the clothes that smell of burning hair.

"Have I ever told you you're my hero?" I relinquish, watching a twinkle bloom in the deep emerald pastures of his irises.

Well, at least one of us is keeping our shit together.

I stare at him, feeling something is different, but I can't put my finger on it. Then I realise. He's not wearing a suit. Instead, he's wearing a black blazer with a black polo shirt underneath tucked into dark jeans. I didn't even know he knew what the word casual meant.

"You look snazzy," I compliment him, and he does a twirl, bags still in hand. I presume they contain clothes for Luce and The Furies.

"Why, thank you. Anyway, I booked us a table for lunch at the restaurant downstairs in an hour. I'll see you in the lobby around then? I tried Luce before you guys, but she didn't answer. She must still be asleep," he elaborates.

"Thanks. I'm kind of— out of it," I admit, and he blinks sympathetically, a sad smile overcoming his face like he doesn't quite know what to say. I hate it, the pity in his stare.

"Oh, and tell Xion— I couldn't get him a plain black t-shirt in his size. They only had— well, you'll see— I thought you could use a laugh." He waves a casual hand, dismissing himself as I close the door.

"Jules brought us some clothes," I announce as Xion continues to look out of the window, head snapping toward me as my voice hits the air.

"Can you also call Luce's room next door and tell her about the reservation? I want to make sure she's awake," I request, flinging the bag of clothes at him.

"I'm going to take a quick shower," I tell him as I watch him rummage through the bag. He pulls out a bundle of black leather, which I assume is mine, and then grabs a long-sleeved, black, muscle-fit shirt, holding it up and rolling his eyes.

"What?" I ask with half interest, and he turns it around, eyes half affronted, half amused.

"I'm going to fucking kill Jules!" he exclaims.

I squint, reading the shirt he's holding out from across the room.

'This does not count as a sass-quatch sighting.' It reads in bold white print. I snort, bursting out into uncontrollable belly laughs, tears gathering at the corner of my eyes. My smile makes Xion relax slightly and he gives an amused smirk too.

The seriousness of everything happening subsides for a single second, but it's enough. Enough to remind me that I must keep moving forward, that my house is insured, that one day, perhaps I'll return— Sasquatch in tow.

And Cerb— I'll never forget him.

As I try to stifle my entirely inappropriate giggles, I head back into the bathroom, eyes still tired but lit with a new sheen.

Jules was right; I needed a laugh.

LUCE

I'm naked, bare feet soaked in the soil, bathed in blood. My skin is rampant with goosebumps, the porcelain shade of it picking me out stark and exposed against the landscape.

The sky overhead is stained charcoal with intermittent and terrifying forks of lightning flicking across the expanse like the tongues of hungry snakes. Thunder rumbles, making the air vibrate against my bare skin, chilling me as an icy rain begins to fall. The drops soak my silver hair darker in shade, droplets rolling like heaven's tears down from my shoulders and over my breasts, dripping from my erect nipples and making me shudder.

I don't bring my arms up to cover myself, nor do I try to rub warmth into my body. I know, as I stand here shivering, shaking like a leaf in a hurricane, that I deserve this. All of it.

Taking a step forward, my toes sink deep into the blood-coated soil, and rain begins to fall like bullets, ricocheting from my skin, a baptism of natural fury.

I'm standing in a burnt-out forest, the trunks of what had once been lush trees standing, a now charred testament to the torment they've withstood. The trees are equidistant, abnormally so, and I find the pale lines of lightning damage crawling down their bark, scars of the pain they have seen. My own body does not bear such scars, my skin perfect as ever now that the darkness marring it is gone. I, however, am far from flawless. My scars are internal, forever, and I cannot claim to be the same person I was before taking the Chalice of Uranus to my lips.

I keep walking, step after blood-soaked step, blood creeping up my ankles as I sink into the sodden earth, making my way through the burnt outline of what had once been a thriving forest. As the lightning flashes, I see it, a pair of brown eyes, large and innocent, the bleating of that which I have stolen echoing in my ears. It scampers between the trees like a phantom of my conscience, flitting in and out of my memory, the holy deliverance of a moral cut so deep I cannot even begin to justify the cause, cannot even begin to suture it closed with excuses. I have none. Not anymore.

Another strike of lightning licks the underside of charred clouds like a force starved of the fire it so desires.

They illuminate, hanging from the twisted and dark branches of the electrocuted trees by a single rope, a rope braided from my once golden hair.

Their feet dangle, swaying in the howling wind as their dead eyes stare into me, blame etched into the glassy surfaces of their eyes.

I pause, staring up at them, dwarfed by what I've done, unable to reach any of them, unable to cut them free. I don't know these people, but I've killed them. I've dunked their fate into a glaze of death and unavoidable suffering, hardening them into something unrecognisable, something unsalvageable.

It's my fault.

I stare around me, turning on the spot. Every tree around me is decorated with these sick baubles of death, corpses swinging limply in the downpour of icy rain that steals my breath from my lungs as my eyes fall on their lifeless faces.

Turning, I don't know what else to do but run. The mud is thick and scarlet beneath my feet, and with every step I sink further into it, like I'm being slowed, held back, by the weight of such despicable acts and choices.

I fly through the forest as fast as I can, breasts heaving up and down, taught skin of my stomach tightening with the strain of my abdominals beneath as I charge endlessly forward, no destination in mind. I must get out of here, and as I refuse to cease running, I notice that every tree I pass is host to yet more hanging corpses, strange and rotten fruit with not a single hint of temptation emanating from the saggy skin, heavy with decaying sour juices.

Finally, something changes, the trees cease, and I come to a lake. It's not large; I can see all sides, and as the lightning flashes yet again, illuminating the glassy still surface of the water, I find it arterial crimson beneath the clear weep of the storm overhead.

Blood.

A lake of blood.

I see her, knowing she would be here somewhere, my heart pounding. The boat is tiny, a small wooden rowboat. She stands, motionless on its bow, staring at me from the centre of the lake.

"Thane—" Her name comes from me like a prayer I know will not be heard, let alone acknowledged. I take a step as she beckons, then another, lowering myself into the chill blood only too willingly.

As I get closer, I see her not as I know her, at least not for years. She's a child, her face full of innocence and not yet marred by our love, by the toll it has undeniably taken. She's small, her form jagged and unable to fill her clothes properly, just like I remember. Her hair is long; she had always hated it that way, but her mother had insisted she look respectable in the presence of so many gods and goddesses. Her eyes are mirrors of my despair as the blood rises around me and I continue to walk toward her. It laps at my torso then at the bottom of my breasts, slowly coming up to my chin as I start to swim out to the rowboat illuminated by the single gas lamp clutched in her young hand.

I approach the boat and she stares down at me, her eyes bloody as they reflect the sanguine water at me. Her mouth contorts, head shaking as she turns, and the boat begins to move away, lightning illuminating her silhouette as she drifts further into the distance.

I claw at the surface of the water, thrashing, trying to swim closer to her.

As I struggle, something cold, fleshy, grabs my ankle, pulling me back. I writhe, trying to stay afloat. Another cold fleshy mass grabs my free ankle and tugs, pulling me under.

I look up to the grey of the sky, knowing that my ambivalence, my judgement, my sense of who I am, is forever scarred by what I've done. I want to fight, want to continue to struggle, but as I stare around and find young Thane has gone, I give in. Hopelessness coming far too easy.

I let them take me, pulling me beneath the surface that shortly returns to a reflectively seamless calm, a flawless and undisturbed mirror of the storm raging overhead, as I disappear into its bloody depths.

It's as though I was never there at all, just an aberration which nature has finally righted.

Blood fills my nose, my mouth, my ears, the taste of it cold and metallic, flooding every orifice as I sink deeper into the pit, endless and deep as my guilt, below.

I startle awake, chest rising and falling in the dark clammy air of the room. It's not my room, not even the room at the Sinclair Estate I've come to call some semblance of my own. This room is utterly unremarkable. Cream walls, cream sheets, banal wood furniture, and a noisy air conditioning unit sputtering in the corner. A painting, a copy of thousands of others, of a single tree on a hilltop, stares at me from the opposing wall as I blink once, then twice, mind taken back to the thick braided golden nooses that adorned charred branches in my dream.

It hadn't been Delyria's grove, this time it had been my subconscious, my guilt, which has so completely disarmed me.

My body aches like someone has taken too much of my blood and my head whirls even still, missing the potent dark magic which kept it sharp, kept it slick for the past month. I feel like something's missing inside, like a void has been opened that I'll never be able to fill.

My fingers twitch, wanting to be busy, wanting to brew and concoct, but I know I can't. Those days are over.

My silver hair tumbles over my shoulders as I run my fingers back through it, getting up from the mattress and padding across the downtrodden carpet. Drawing the curtains, I allow light to stream through the enormous window and find my reflection staring, ghost-like, back at me.

I prop myself against the glass, looking at my face, the pale skin, the blue eyes, my hair perhaps the only indicator that I'd been in too deep, and now nothing will ever be the same. Beyond my face, planes take off into the sky, and I wonder what it must be like to be able to fly. I envy Pandora that, the freedom which must come from the ability to soar off into the sky, to get far away from your problems at any given time. Then— I remember. There's no getting away from my problems because they're inside of me, like a disease-riddled deep through my marrow, twisting around my skeleton and constricting, causing pain with each and every breath.

I *am* a problem.

I can see that now as I stare down at my bare feet and shuffle on the spot. People warned me; they'd tried to help, but I knew better— I was better— than them. I didn't listen, and now I'm marred forever with the blood of billions soaking my hands and seeping into my skin, my heart turning cold.

I have doomed this world.

As I look around the room, something occurs to me.

The walls seemed stifling before, but now they make me feel safe. Perhaps that's why mortals do it, box themselves in. Perhaps it makes them feel less vulnerable than they really are.

I miss Thane.

More than I ever imagined, and now that the darkness is mostly gone, my heart is shattered. The pieces are apple red ceramic, and they cut into me, making me bleed endlessly into my chest. I cannot die, so I know this must be my torment, my punishment.

I know some remains, some of that power. I clung onto it as best as I could, much to my own disgust, and it had wanted to stay. I have a problem, an addiction, a vice. I am more mortal than I ever thought, not in body but in mind and soul.

I am *weak*.

The phone rings, startling me and breaking my melancholy as I let the summer sun burn down on me like an ant beneath a magnifying glass.

I don't answer it. Letting it ring until silence falls once again. I'm tired, weak, and everything I have always known is changing. I have never felt so lost— so human.

As I ponder this, a knock comes at the door. I guess whoever it was that was calling wasn't content to leave me with my misery, so I wander across the room, opening the door too slowly as I exhale in a heavy and weighted sigh.

"Yes?" I demand, finding Sephy in a bathrobe, hair swept up in a large white towel, in the hallway outside.

"Sorry— I did call. I just— Jules has some fresh clothes for you. We're going to grab some lunch down in the restaurant in half an hour. I think you should be there." She extends the invitation, eyes nervous as she crosses her arms over the thick white towelling wrapped across her breasts.

"Okay. I'll be down. Which room is Jules in?" I ask her, and she gestures to a door three rooms down on the opposite side of the hall.

"That one— he did try to knock." She's stuttering, taking in my appearance and biting down on her bottom lip.

"Uh, yeah. I was asleep," I admit, and she nods, giving a weak smile before she turns to move back to her room.

"Sephy—" I call to her.

She looks back over one shoulder.

"Yeah?"

"I'm sorry about your home, and Cerb," I admit. Her eyes become sad, and yet there's a warmth there toward me that hadn't existed before.

"Oh, before I forget. You have the shard, right? Xion said it was with you?" she asks me, and I frown, thinking back.

"No— I thought you had it. When I woke up, it was gone." I explain, my heart thudding a little harder against the inside of my ribs.

"Hmm." She looks concerned, and I know immediately that she doesn't have it.

"Is that what she came to the estate for, do you think?" I ask her, and she bites her bottom lip yet again, eyes blazing with something almost like fury.

"Perhaps," she replies, brow furrowing.

"Anyway, I'll get dressed. I'll see you in a few." I close the door, not waiting for her to respond as silence blankets me, a welcome relief.

I tread into the bathroom; the tiles cool against my feet as I turn to the oval mirror mounted behind twin basins.

I'm a mess, my skin too pale, my eyes sunken into my skull, gaze vacant as though I'm not really there.

I wish Thane was here to hold me, but she isn't. I have to be the one to pull myself together this time, no more hiding from my mistakes, from my weaknesses. I have always been thought of as a threat, and I've proved them all right. Now I have to prove I can overcome this, that I can still be the person Thane had fallen in love with all those years ago.

I turn the shower on next to me, letting the cold-water pound down on the floor of the cubicle as I strip.

I step under the showerhead, letting the ice water cover me, gritting my teeth against the pain. It cleanses me, washes away what I've done.

What matters now is what I do next.

I continue to stand under the assault of the shower, not allowing myself comfort as hot tears fall down my cheeks.

Scolding myself, I sniffle, steeling myself against my pathetic inadequacies.

I don't deserve to cry.

Not this time.

I did this to myself.

17

I'LL NEVER BE FREE

XION

WE STAND IN THE lobby, not talking, waiting for The Furies. Jules looks at me with a worried stare, and Sephy huffs as she paces back and forth. Luce's face is the picture of ambivalence, but she looks undeniably more put together than I've seen her in a while, plus she keeps frowning at the slogan printed across my chest.

"Finally!" I hear Sephy breathe a sigh of relief as The Furies approach us across the lobby, exiting the elevator amongst a crowd that shoots them curious and even disturbed glances. As they move closer, I see why.

"You brought weapons? This is lunch!" Sephy hisses.

Jules has made them change, so they're all wearing identical skinny jeans and different coloured t-shirts which make them appear more curvaceous and less edgy. Nonetheless, Erlea still has the enormous Katana strapped across her spine, Ericka is toting her bow with a quiver of arrows buckled in leather around her thigh, and Erin has several daggers stuffed into the denim waistband of her jeans.

"You didn't think to mention that we don't bring weapons to the table?" she asks Jules, eyes blazing with heated agitation and social anxiety. I can almost see her carotid begin to throb with increasing speed beneath the pale flesh of her throat, blood pressure spiking.

"I didn't think I had to." Jules shrugs as she runs her fingers back through her hair, taking deep breaths.

"Come on, Sephy. Let's eat. I'm starving," I coax her, placing a gentle hand on her shoulder as she spins atop the scarlet carpet. She shrugs away from me as if now she can't stand my touch. We had been so close, so connected, and now I feel as though I'll never be able to touch her again.

The reason why isn't lost on me.

She's distraught, not that she'd admit that in front of everyone, but the loss of her home has affected her worse than I would have imagined. It's only a building, but perhaps it means more to her, represents the last security her parents could deliver from beyond the grave. Now, that sanctuary, that safety, is gone.

She leads the way through to the hotel restaurant where the décor changes suddenly from stark scarlet carpet and bland beige wallpaper to highly polished oak on every surface. The wood panelling adorning the restaurant on all sides seems to melt into the hardwood floors as though the entire room has been carved from one single cube. A bar rises from the floor in the same oak grain, the sheen of it an almost pristinely reflective chocolate hue. Hanging above, several televisions show the latest sports or natural disasters, and hundreds of wine glasses hang from their stems, twinkling in the starry mood lighting of the place. On the farthest wall, I find a single glass panel, looking out over the airport beyond where planes taxi for take-off and after landing.

The others gather close to the podium at the entrance to the dining room, and I find my eyes drawn to an enormous tank in the centre of the flawlessly laid tables. It's filled with lobsters, and bubbles rise intermittently from the crystal-clear depths as they sit at the bottom, teeming in a restless mountain of shell and claw. I think about the fact that it's someone's job to keep it clean, someone normal. Sephy says she wants to be normal, but I'll never understand why. Normal seems pretty boring to me. Even before I knew about my half-demon heritage, I had longed for adventure, for the blood rushing in my ears and the din of war.

"Do you have a reservation?" A waiter with square-framed spectacles and slicked brown hair asks, breaking my internal monologue. His pointed nose has become a slope for him to stare down with the slightest disgust as his eyes trace over each member of our party in turn.

"Yes, Sinclair," Jules announces, clearing his throat and putting his hands into the pockets of his blazer, a somewhat awkward motion for him. It's weird seeing him in jeans, seeing him in anything that's not a suit actually—

"Welcome to the Hilton at O'Hare International. Here you will find a light lunch menu, a fully stocked bar, and a more comprehensive dinner menu which can also be prepared for lunch at your request.

Specials today include lobster, which you can choose yourself from our central tank, and is served with a green salad and a rich butter drizzle." The waiter is dressed in all black, forehead misted with a fine film of perspiration as he leads us, stepping backwards, toward a table. It's like he lives for this moment, the moment when he's centre stage, and his words fall out in a torrent of practised annunciation, gaze daring anyone to interrupt. If he knew who he was dealing with, he wouldn't be so self-assured.

Lucifer hurries across the room, gliding past Sephy and Jules as the waiter stops near a large circular table dressed in crisp white linen and adorned with clean-cut crystal. She takes a seat in a simple oak dining chair, looking up at the rest of us expectantly.

I take a seat after Jules and Sephy draw chairs from the table in unison and tuck themselves beneath the drape of the tablecloth. As I sit, I realise The Furies are no longer right behind me and crane over my shoulder, dread settling over me like the chill slow-moving mist of a fifties horror flick.

"Hey, where did they—" I begin but then falter in my words as my eyes locate them.

I can't believe what I'm seeing so blink, wondering if I might be mistaken.

I am not.

As my eyes widen and my mouth opens to call to them, Sephy, Jules, and Luce all turn to see what it is I'm looking at. Words fail me.

Erin and Erlea are lifting Ericka on their shoulders. She has her bow drawn and is loading the arrow in the centre of the dining room, pulling it back so it lines up against her lip as she aims down into the lobster tank.

Sephy launches up out of her chair, which flies back further than it should, as I observe the staff behind the bar watching with interest. Nobody moves to stop them except Sephy. Everyone just watches, too surprised by what they're seeing to so much as whisper in protest.

Sephy goes to yell, to make a scene as she rushes out from behind the table, but it's too late as Ericka lets the arrow loose, shooting it into the depths of the water at close range. It hits the bottom fast with a clunk that echoes, causing the glassware on two surrounding tables to tinkle. She's lucky she doesn't puncture the tank, causing a leak or worse at such close range. Instead, her two honorary sisters lift her up and she leans over the glass, dunking her torso into the tank and reaching in for the Lobster she's just skewered.

Triumphant, she raises it above her head, the surface of the water in the tank sloshing as she comes back up for air. Sephy storms across the room, unable to believe what it is she's seeing, and hisses into the ears of each woman in turn, knuckles turning white at her sides as her fingers scrunch into fists.

I don't know what she says, but whatever it is isn't placid as the eyes of each woman go wide in turn before they trail behind her, faces hard in expression, toward the table. Ericka's hand wraps around the body of the dead lobster that hangs, limp and dripping onto the floor.

After everyone has taken their seats and Ericka has placed the skewered lobster, still sporting the arrow she shot it with, onto the table, the waiter returns with menus.

"I'll have the lobster," Ericka demands, twisting back and passing him the limp crustacean without so much as a pause. He takes the creature in his hand, no longer superior but speechless.

"Lord help me—" Sephy murmurs, bringing the menu up high to hide her face as she pores over the choices as though she's taking an exam. She's flushed, as is Luce, and the waiter cannot stop staring at the three women across from them.

"Problem?" Jules asks the waiter, giving him a firm stare as the lobster drips cold water onto the pristine polish of the waiter's black shoes.

"No— I— I— This is—" he stutters, teetering between outrage and utter speechlessness as Luce smiles up at him. Dazzling him with her glacial blue irises and porcelain skin, she speaks in a sweet innocent tone.

"Well, you did say choose it yourself," she giggles.

"So—" I begin, looking at Sephy as our starters arrive, being placed over each diner's left shoulder by several well-manicured hands. I'm having crab cakes. The most expensive thing on the appetizer menu. I mean I guess it's the least I could do after The Furies decided to go shooting in their lobster tank.

"Yes, Mr Sass-quatch?" Sephy prompts, taking one of her crab cakes and bringing it to her lips on one of the tiniest forks I've ever seen.

"The shard— Luce, do you have it?" I enquire, looking at her and finding her shoving bruschetta into her mouth like she's never seen food before.

"No. I already told Sephy. I thought you guys had it," she reveals, breathing deep between bites. I haven't seen her enjoying food like this in a long time.

"You did?" I look to Sephy, surprised.

Why didn't she tell me?

Doesn't she realise what this means for me?

"Yeah— I was going to bring that up. I just—" she begins, but Jules interrupts.

"You know I don't mean to blow my own trumpet, but my crab cakes are far superior to these! Not only that, but who serves them with this sauce? The presentation leaves much to be desired as well." He's outraged, and Sephy smirks, laughing slightly as she struggles to swallow.

"Don't worry Jules. Nobody is replacing your five-star Sinclair Estate cuisine." She lays a hand atop his in comfort, and he snorts.

"I should hope bloody not. Look at how *limp* this lettuce is!"

"Getting back to the topic at hand—" I begin, taking another bite of my crab cake and chewing thoughtfully. I can't see what Jules is complaining about. I think they're delicious and a large improvement on yesterday's meal.

Sephy interrupts my distracted, hunger-laced thoughts.

"Yes, I was waiting until we were all together. The shard was obviously what Pandora was after. Xion salvaged the opal blade before the explosion." Sephy doesn't make eye contact with anyone, keeping her stare trained fast on the food in front of her.

"But why does she want it? She can't do anything with it— isn't that right, Luce?" Sephy demands, voice growing higher in pitch. Luce nods, and I watch her shoulders slump slightly.

"Well yes. She can't use it to administer dark power— but maybe— maybe she doesn't know that." She looks at Sephy and then at me.

"So, what, we just let her go?" Sephy enquires, the hint of hope in her voice unmistakable.

"I don't think that's an option anymore. You're a loose end even without the fact that Xion has the other piece of the tether and aside from the fact the shard is tied to him implicitly. I don't know if there's anywhere you could run to that she wouldn't eventually follow," Luce says, brow twisting into a heavy furrow.

"I'm not scared of her. I'm not running." Sephy sounds determined as she pops the final crab cake into her mouth, cheeks flushing red with what could be either anger or fear, though at this point, I'm not sure.

"It's not about being scared, Sephy. All it will take is for her to catch you off guard, catch you sleeping or in a moment of weakness— and you're a dead woman. And that's if the hordes of demons don't kill you first." Luce's tone is grave now, and for a moment, all that can be heard is the scraping of silverware on porcelain.

"So, what are you—" Sephy begins, eyes flashing wild, but something catches her eye then, causing her mouth to fall open and her face to go slack. I twist, turning to see what it is she's focused on. I find it and stare too.

Behind the bar, one of the televisions is showing what remains of The Sinclair Estate— it isn't much more than a pile of rubble. The group remain silent as the report goes on to scan the lawns, showing not a single demon left within the grounds.

My heart fills with relief for a moment, and then the conversation slowly picks back up, Sephy's eyes flitting now and again to the television with morose interest. She takes a deep drink of ice water from the glass in front of her, closing her eyes as her chest visibly rises and falls.

"I'm saying that the question isn't where you run to. It's whether you run into the battle or away from it." Luce's words hit Sephy like a slap across the face, and she visibly flinches before setting her glass down a little too hard on the table. Water sloshes up and over the side, a damp patch spreading on the fine tablecloth.

"So, what? That's it? I'm it? No fucking way. No. Why the hell aren't The Higher Plains— the gods up there — doing anything? I'm not worthy of a place among them apparently, so shouldn't it be *them* fixing this mess? Isn't Pandora doing all this because of Zeus? Why should I have to be the one to sacrifice myself for his stupidity!?" she slams her fist down on the table, causing diners walking past the table to startle before shooting her disgusted glares as they pick up pace. She doesn't even spare them a thought, glaring with unceasing intensity across at Lucifer, teeth bared.

"Sephy, I don't think— If they were going to act, I believe it would have happened long before now. Maybe there isn't anything they can do. Their power here is restricted. They aren't allowed to screw with free will." She bites her bottom lip, regret lacing her expression. Sephy shrugs, eyebrows rising on her forehead.

"So, what? This is entirely my problem now? I've been doing just fine keeping the streets of Chicago safe. Don't you think that's enough?"

She's furious, not that I blame her.

"It's not enough. We need to stop this at the source— or we stand the risk of being picked off one by one. It may have seemed like it, but after yesterday, it's clear we haven't been forgotten. We're still targets." She looks to Jules, frowning as she finishes her appetizer and wipes her voluptuous lips with a napkin,

"I agree with Luce," I acknowledge reluctantly, and Sephy shoots me an outraged look. It pierces me like a dagger flying across the table between us. Jules shifts too, uncomfortable among the tension as he watches us intently.

"Not that my opinion has any real weight here, but I don't think running from this is going to work anymore. We have to do something, even if the cost is high." I watch as Sephy's face contorts, crumpling with misery. She gets to her feet.

"Well, it's nice to know that you're all good with sending me to get slaughtered at the hands of evil villains. Thanks for the fucking support." She turns from the table and storms out of the restaurant, not looking back. The Furies watch her go, fidgeting nervously, as waiters come and clear our appetizers away.

I look first to Jules then to Luce.

They both appear surprised, which alarms me. What did they think was going to happen? She's already been through hell, been dead and clawed her way back against her consent. Why on earth would she want to do that for people who don't give a damn about her?

"Xion—" Jules gives me an odd stare, and I slump in my seat.

"I'll go make sure she's okay, but I'm not forcing her hand on this. She must come to whatever decision it is she's going to make on her own. I won't influence her." I say this last part wondering if I even could influence her. She's stubborn, feisty, and she knows her own mind.

I can't say I blame her. If I were her, I'd want to run too.

I mean, who on earth willingly goes to war for gods who have shown you nothing but disrespect?

Unfortunately for her, we're running out of both time and options.

The clock just keeps on ticking, and as much as I'd like to stop it, to stand still with her in a vacuum, I can't.

I jog down the corridor toward our room, half expecting Sephy to be waiting outside because I have the only key.

Instead, though, I come face to face with a scorch mark on the carpet outside our door.

It's taken me at least ten minutes to make it to this, the correct corridor. I exited the elevator on two identical floors, which weren't the right one, desperate to reach her and not thinking clearly as my mind filtered through the many possibilities of what might happen next. I wonder why it is that hotels have this eerie quality, whereby every floor is seemingly a mirror image of the next, but shake off the thought, knowing I have far more pressing concerns.

I steel myself, not knowing what I'm going to find behind the door of room six-hundred-and-sixty-six, but slip the keycard into the slot of the locking mechanism regardless and press my weight against the wood of the door before I step inside.

The room is quiet, shadows falling short through the drapes, which I'd left drawn as we'd departed for lunch. I stare out into the bedroom, but she isn't there.

However, light creeps notably from beneath the bathroom door on my right.

I slowly close the front door behind me, pressing it shut so it emits a mere subtle click rather than a slam. Then, taking a single step toward the bathroom door, I twist on the handle, half expecting it to be locked.

It isn't.

I step inside, finding the shower curtain drawn around the bath. I grab a fistful of the PVC and yank it back, finding Sephy lying, fully dressed, in the empty bath. In one hand, she's holding a tiny bottle of Jack Daniel's, and on her left, there's a force-induced fissure, an indent from a tiny, enraged fist, in the ceramic tiles of the wall.

I look down at Sephy's knuckles; they're bloody atop her leather pants.

She glares at me.

"What do you want?" she asks, miserable as she brings the miniature bottle of whisky to her lips. Glugging messily, she crosses her feet, still encased in heavy boots, atop the silver faucet at the other end of the tub.

"I came to make sure you were okay."

I sit on the edge of the bath and she rolls her eyes, typically Sephy.

"Why do you care? Worried I'll end it before Pandora can do it for me?" she spits.

I cock an eyebrow.

"Can we please stop acting like I'm not the guy who doomed the world to resurrect your stubborn ass, please?" I ask, voice low, and she snorts, the sound coming thick and hot from the back of her throat.

"So, what? I owe you for services rendered? I didn't ask to be here, you know! As I have said only about a million times before."

I shake my head.

"God, you're so fucking blind. Of course, I don't want you to go to war for Mortaria. I wouldn't have brought you back if that's what I thought you'd end up doing. Why do you always act like everyone is so against you? Can't you see that we're trying to support you? Trying to keep you alive?" I feel the truth spill from me, hurried and desperate, and she shakes her head furiously.

"How exactly is encouraging me to go to war in a hell dimension crawling with demons trying to keep me alive?" she snaps, taking another swig from the now nearly empty bottle.

"We are suggesting you bite this problem in the ass before it bites you in yours, Sephy. This isn't about Mortaria. It's about protecting you. You think I brought you back from beyond death, so you could spend the rest of your life running?" I implore her. I want her to take this seriously, but a small chuckle escapes her lips, and I know that isn't going to happen.

"You brought me back because you think, for some insane reason, that you need me. I was just fine where I was." The words sting me, but I can't deny she's right. I was selfish.

She catches the agony behind my eyes, the poison of the truth of what I've done, of my ignoble motives, and exhales heavily, the weight of everything visible on her sagging shoulders. "Look I'm sorry, but I don't want to risk losing any more people. I— I'm not strong enough." Her head lolls backwards so it's resting against the cool rim of the bath, bloodied fist balling in her lap. She winces slightly, and my heart deadens in my chest at her surrender.

"The thing is, Sephy, I'm not sure running is going to save anyone— not anymore. Pandora has the shard now. If she chose to destroy it, I'd die. You know that, don't you?" I swallow hard.

I hadn't wanted to bring this up, but she somehow believes that ignoring this problem is going to make it go away when the reality for me is playing Russian roulette with a part of my soul held at gunpoint.

"I didn't— I mean I guess I should have figured. Why didn't you say anything?" she mumbles, eyes wide and full of a new kind of fear, the kind that threatens tears. It's a new look for her and one that I never want to bear witness to again.

"We've been a little busy. I was about to mention it, but you stormed out—" I explain, and she traces the broken tiles on her left with her fingertips, her pupils tracking the ginger motion, no longer wanting to hold eye contact.

"So, what are you saying?" she asks me, chewing on her bottom lip. She seems so unlike herself at this moment, almost like she's forgotten who she is.

"I'm saying that I want you to fight for your life. For all our lives. I've never thought of you as the kind of woman who would flee in the face of death. You've already been there with not only your own experience but losing other people. You're still here. You can do this. You're the strongest person I've ever met. I want you to fight. I want you to take the risk. For *you*. You deserve a life, a beautiful, exciting, long life. Don't just lie down and take this. You'll lose something whether you fight or not. I want you to live, Sephy, and you can't do that if you're running for the rest of your life."

I reach out to touch her, placing a hand on her knee, and she stares at me, the fluorescent light of the bathroom turning her ghostly pale, her expression haunted by the loss in her past. She is silent, head hanging back even still as she considers my words.

"I put the universe at risk to give you another shot at life, to give us another chance. Please— don't waste it. I want this, whatever it is, to have at least a shot at lasting." I plead with her, and this time she frowns. I've crossed a line, made it about me now, and I'm convinced I've made the situation worse. "If you want to run, I can't go with you. I want to, but I must go and retrieve that shard. I can't walk around wondering if she's going to end my life— it'd be torture." The decision is final for me because I know I couldn't bear to watch Sephy constantly looking over her shoulder, waiting for the end of both of our lives, either.

"Can you give me a minute? I need a minute—" she asks, eyes flicking to the door beyond the shower curtain, begging for my departure. I nod, breathing deeply and wondering if I've gotten through to her at all.

All I can do as I exit the bathroom and launch myself onto the bed, body going limp, is hope and wait.

SEPHY

I'm furious, knuckles throbbing and blood racing around my body, hot and rabid.

How can he do that? Use our— whatever you call it — to try and scare me into going on this suicide mission?

The thing that really pisses me off though is that it's working.

I am scared — more scared than anything — of losing him. Of having to carry on without him to come home to.

Apparently, I have more feelings than I bargained for.

Figures.

Was it that night, the sex? It was almost— *visceral*, the response I'd had to him, not just in body, but in mind, in soul. It wasn't a kind of closeness I'd knowingly wanted, but soon I realised it was something I've needed for longer than I want to admit.

I think about him, about his gold irises, about the way he looks at me.

Nobody has ever looked at me like that.

I stare at the cracked tiling from where I punched the wall in a fit of rage, of frustration at the fact there seems to be no escape.

Maybe that's because there is no escape.

How do you run from someone who has a magic box that allows them to find you within seconds?

This is so fucked up.

I can't do this.

I'm going to get myself and everyone around me killed.

But then— as Xion said, isn't that what will happen if I don't act anyway? I've been waiting for the end to come for so long, waiting for the rain of fire, the apocalypse. Have I just resigned myself to all this as inevitable?

Running is the long game, the long torturous game, which will end in bloodshed and pain— that's what they're trying to say. All of them.

So, I guess it must be true.

I wasn't like this before my murder. I wasn't a coward. I'd been a fighter. I clung to life by my fingernails and stood up against odds stacked steeply against me just for a shot in hell at survival.

What the hell happened?

Had one night, one man, one blade— really convinced me that I'm doomed to die, not once but twice? More importantly, have I been sitting down and taking it?

I clawed my way back from hell all those months ago and found myself on the cusp of a good life. A full life. A life my parents would have wanted for me, and a life I was excited to begin. Then— everything changed, and I concluded that nothing means anything because the end— the end is unavoidable, so why bother?

Right?

I ponder this for entire minutes, the only sound the cold droplets falling from the faucet hitting the leather of my pants in funereal time.

But that's the thing, isn't it— I still have to exist in this body— still have to wake up every day and breathe in and out, even if the end is just on the horizon. I've been forced back into this life. Allowed to live by a force unnatural.

So— then why am I not fighting to make my existence what I want it to be?

Why am I letting some bitch with terrible fashion sense dictate my misery?

A rush of shame overcomes me as I think about Haedes. He shut down too— stopped fighting after losing my mother. But then— then something changed with him after I'd come, uninvited, into his life. He'd staked everything to bring me back; so had Xion— and Luce. Luce lost the love of her life because of it. All of them had risked loss so I could have a chance at something real. They had put their hearts on the table— for me.

Have I convinced myself that gamble means nothing?

If I run, if I become her prey— then I guess it does.

Haedes death, Luce's darkness, Thane's broken heart— they've all given up so much, despite the fact I hadn't asked them to, to give me a chance.

All this time, I've been adamant that I don't owe them a damn thing, but the truth is that I don't owe them. How can I ever repay an act that has led to this much death, this much heartache and pain, for my benefit?

Without them paying that price, I'd never have been in Xion's arms again, never have learned the depths of Jules' devotion either.

This world, it might not be utopia, but there's love here in spite of everything. Perhaps if there wasn't, there wouldn't be hurt either— wouldn't be hate— wouldn't be evil.

Maybe you can't have one without the other.

Maybe.

The thoughts, philosophical and deeper than I intend, spin around in my head, forming a cocktail of passion mixed in with the zest for life I've been missing, coming from nowhere.

Perhaps losing my life in pursuit of the chance to live it the way I've always wanted is the only option I have left.

I didn't choose this, but I guess in life we don't choose. We get given the hand we're dealt, and we do our best with it.

Besides, I guess if I die, it won't matter anyway.

I get to my feet, climbing out of the tub and staring at myself in the mirror. I place the empty Jack Daniels bottle on the side of the sink, mind made up, finally.

I'm terrified, hands shaking and breath coming in shallow wisps, but perhaps, after the numbness, the resignation, this means I'm finally coming back to myself.

I exit the bathroom, and Xion sits up upon hearing the door open, his eyes fixed on me as I enter the bedroom.

"You, okay?" he asks me, face a map of his growing concern.

"Yeah. I think I finally am." I give him a small smile, crossing my arms over my breasts and taking a few steps deeper into the half-light of the room.

"What are you thinking?" He presses me for an answer with his stare as I near him, placing a hand on the side of his stubble and tilting his chin so he's staring up at me.

"I'm thinking that running is no longer an option as much as I wish it was. You were right." I bend and kiss him, heart pounding as he kisses me back, slow and sweet.

"I was right?" His voice is quirky as I pull back from him, narrowing my eyes.

"Yes. But don't get used to it. I'm sure you'll be saying something incredibly stupid any second now—" I tease him, and he chuckles.

"For the record, I think that Pandora and The Demon Lords should be shaking in their boots. I've been on your bad side, and it's not somewhere anyone wants to be." His gaze is determined, and I chew the inside of my cheek, anxiety becoming cancerous, riddling every part of me.

"We will get through— won't we? I mean there's a life after all this crap, there must be— right?" I ask him, looking for promises I know he can't make despite knowing better.

"Yes, and it's filled with sunny beaches, cocktails, and you in tiny bikinis—" he replies, taking his hands and tracing the curve of my body, making me shudder.

"And you?" I add, nervous, and his face contorts into the largest smile I've ever seen. I take in every detail of him. He really does have a beautiful smile.

"Where else would I be? I'll need someone to adequately berate me about my fruity drink choices." His laugh is a rumble, exploding from his lips and making his chest shake as his smile continues to illuminate his face.

"I'm guessing there will be many tiny umbrellas—" I muse, a smile dancing at the corners of my lips.

"Well yes, but just for you, mind." He brings up a finger and traces my jawline. My knees go weak, and I want to surrender to the desire to crawl into bed with him. However, I have a lot to do before I can even contemplate losing myself in him. If I want this to last, for us to survive, there's no time to lose, no time to rest.

"Speaking of beaches—" I have decided on the course of action I need to take next, but announcing it makes it real. Real and insane, but real, nonetheless.

"You've decided where we're going next?" he guesses, and I nod, pushing my lips together into a thin hard line.

"I have—" I reply, shifting on the balls of my feet as he grips my hips, stare unwavering as he gazes up from the edge of the mattress.

"So— tell me. Where's the next stop on the mystery tour?"

Leaning back and placing both hands behind his head, his shirt pulls up to expose the cut muscle just above his groin. His happy trail, sprinkled with hair, peeks out just above his jeans, tempting me as the scent of pomegranate wafts through the air between us.

"I hope you packed some suitable shorts— they're pretty particular about them— or so I hear—" I whisper, pushing my hair back behind one ear.

"We're heading to Bermuda?" He looks insanely excited at the prospect of sun, sea— and, more than likely, me in tiny bikinis.

I nod, knowing that this is going to be the furthest thing from a vacation and yet unable to stop myself smiling at the mischievous glint in his eye.

"We're heading to Bermuda."

18

A DEMON'S FATE

PANDORA

MY HEART IS SWOLLEN in my chest, pride coursing through my veins like alcohol. In small amounts, it can lower inhibitions, fuel desire, and even give you a sense of confidence unlike any other. But in too large a dose, it can be deadly, an Achilles heel in liquid form.

The portal whirls, fizzling into the dusty air of the library as I step out upon hardwood floors. I find mortals buzzing around the edges of the room, removing dust covers and cleaning away cobwebs, frantic like flies.

"Pandora, you've returned." Lilliana's voice echoes into the increasingly large space, her voice bouncing from surfaces which have long since been covered. She's examining the mortals with semi-interest, feet curled beneath her tattered skirt within the confines of a silk-upholstered armchair. Her cheeks are flushed, noticeable when you consider her usual ghostly pallor, and stained with the remnants of what must have been tears.

"I retrieved the shard," I announce, holding the crystal up to the light that flickers from warm and newly lit sconces peppering the midnight blue walls.

"I am aware. Many of my children perished for your cause," Lilliana almost spits it as an accusation, but at the very last moment, she loses her nerve, and the consonance of her final word falls flat and dull like a rudimentary blade that's missed its mark.

"What did you think was going to happen?" I enquire, tilting my chin as I close the panels of the wooden box in my palm without even looking. I slip the box into my too-tight pants, letting the edges bite through the material and into the thick muscle of my upper thigh.

"I thought you would take more care— more tact. My children are not fodder for your personal vengeance," she snaps. At these words, Katerina turns from where she's pondering the bookshelves behind me, the rustling of her rusty skirts the only indicator of her presence.

"And neither are mine." She glowers, fingers roughly tracing over spines of books and disturbing layers of dust as she goes. She nears a mortal cleaning a crystal vase, which has been utilised as a makeshift bookend, eyes dilating vermillion and lips spreading wide to reveal her too-sharp incisors. I wonder how long it's been since she tasted fresh blood— perhaps not as long as I would hope.

I mean I've noticed the odd mortal going missing, but I've not questioned her about it. They are, after all, easy enough to replace. It never seemed like an issue to me before now as I watch the mortal man shuddering, the crystal vase trembling within his fingertips. I guessed they fell victim to the Succubi or Banshee at the two women's command. But now— now I wonder if it's not their personal self-restraint I should be worried about.

The picture of Katerina's eyes looming over me from the dark shadows beyond the four-poster bed of my new quarters while I sleep makes my heart flutter, hairs on the back of my neck standing on end.

I scan the room, looking for Gorgon, but find he is no longer among us.

"Where is Gorgon?" I ask Katerina, voice higher and sharper in pitch than usual. The high ring of it distracts her as her bloody irises retract and she turns, focusing in on my face fast. The mortal she was approaching looks between us, setting the vase back where he found it and leaving the room.

As the door opens, the fleeing mortal reveals the very person I am looking for.

Gorgon slides past him with slick elegance, not missing a step as he crosses the library's threshold.

His eyes are drawn to my palm with immediate effect, the glassy surfaces of his lime irises shimmering as he fixates on the shard. I wrap my fingers tighter around it, the edges digging into the flesh of my palm.

His lips twist into a smile.

"You did it—" he breathes, something like wonder twisting around his sentiment like a vice intended for my heart. I smile, unable to stop myself, pride swelling once again like a rabid high tide.

"Indeed."

His eyes widen as they rise to my face, pupils dilating as he takes me in like my magnificence is too much for him to behold.

"I have a surprise for you." He bites his bottom lip, the announcement escaping him in a whisper as awe continues to ail him.

"For me?" I press my palm, shard still flush against it, into the place above my breast, flattered and curious.

"Come with me, Your Highness." He bows slightly and offers me an open palm with extended fingers. A giggle falls from my lips, the schoolgirl in me pert and breathless for what will happen next.

I loop my arm through the crook of his jagged elbow, our silhouettes falling side-by-side, angular masculine edges against voluptuous feminine curves. He sweeps me from the room, eyes falling every now and again to the oily sheen of the obsidian. The gasoline tint of the stone is held too easily captive by the black of his abyssal pupils.

We stroll together, like two lovebirds in early spring, through the terror-riddled halls of the Exilia for which so much demon blood has already been spilt. His steps are somehow still silent, even against the slick flawless crystal underfoot that clicks beneath my heels. His suit is velvet, and I run my fingers down the length of his sleeve, shuddering as we turn the corner into the entrance lobby.

My eyes fall to where the River Styx had once flowed, but now only a dry and barren riverbed, carved through stone, remains. It's an ugly dark scar through the smoky crystal that forms the space, my arid coat of arms on what had once belonged to someone else.

The lightning continues to flicker in and out of existence across the ceiling as we turn beneath the gargantuan cut facets, heading for the throne room.

Curiosity piqued, I watch as Gorgon gestures at the two mortals on either side of the double doors. They spring into action, pushing them open and revealing what lies inside.

Abraxis, Anubis, and Barbas stand in the centre of the space, and Gorgon lets go of my arm, falling back as the doors close behind us, blocking my exit.

"What is this?" I demand, watching as the group of three people who quite possibly want me dead step aside, looking up to the platform on which my throne is usually perched, central to the space.

It's been moved, standing now to the right, but that isn't what catches my eye. What pulls my focus and leaves my mouth hanging slightly open is the enormous set of wings hanging on a stand where my throne used to be. They're crude, made of scraps of metal, ugly even— and yet to me— to me they are *everything*.

I take hurried steps, closing the distance between myself and the pair of wings as fast as I can, slipping the shard into my back pocket before forgetting about it entirely.

"Do they— do they work?" I ask, looking over them. The jagged steel emits a dull silver glimmer, layers upon layers of metal feathers soldered together so they lay flat against one another like that of a bird— or a Nephilim.

"They do," Anubis replies, watching me carefully. Her face is unreadable as I stare between her and the mechanical wings.

"How can these things possibly work? Surely, they're too heavy—" I muse, circling them like a hungry lion, desperate for answers. The sooner I have them, the sooner I might look down over the world once again.

"I told you she'd like them—" Gorgon says, a smile twisting his lips wide as he brags to Abraxis and Barbas. The two of them, neither one my biggest fan, watch on in silence.

I would wonder what they're thinking, but the prospect of flight again, no matter how unorthodox the method, is too tempting to resist.

"I had these retrieved a long time ago from the Sea of Shadows. Muerta— she enchanted them with an odd magic. Voodoo she calls it. It was a gift for a sinner who was trapped here— a sinner called Icarus," she reveals, and I cock an eyebrow.

"But why—" I begin, and she smiles, continuing and clearly enjoying the attention of being centre stage once again.

"His father— she was in love with him," Anubis reveals, the white silk of her gown trailing in a fluid puddle of fabric behind her.

"But Muerta is married—" I frown, confused.

"Indeed. So, when she kissed Daedalus, he blackmailed her. Told her if she didn't help his son Icarus escape this place, he would reveal her infidelities to Yama." Anubis smirks now, examining her gold lacquered nails. The smile creases her skin, casting shadows from wrinkles that had not been there before. I wonder if I too will start to age so quickly without the Mortarian sun— not that it matters now. Once I have absorbed the darkness from the shard, I'll be immortal once again.

"But— no Doppel body can survive outside of Mortaria," I scoff, and she nods.

"Exactly. But Daedalus didn't know that. Muerta was so heartbroken that she did as he requested but told Icarus to fly high towards the sun for the best chance of escaping undetected. Being so close to that kind of heat, the solder of the wings turned molten, and he fell into the sea. Nobody knows what happened to him after that— but he never rose again," Anubis finishes the story, and I clap my hands together.

"A wonderful tale. Perhaps you should make it into a bedtime story for children— Have you ever considered librarian as an occupation?" I smirk, looking at the wings with new hope rising in me.

Anubis doesn't respond, face going slack, her dark eyes dead pools of hard black crystal in her head. It gives me a kick of pleasure.

"Well, what are we waiting for? I want to fly again! Right now!" I exclaim, looking to Gorgon who rises in two rhythmic steps onto the platform.

"And so, you shall," he whispers in my ear, making me shudder as waves of electric pleasure roll down my spine.

He circles me, taking straps and fastening them around my corseted torso. I thought the wings would seem heavy, but as they are strapped to my back and stabilised with yet more straps around my shoulders and finally my waist, I find them a lot lighter than I had anticipated.

It must be the magic.

"What now?" I ask, turning and almost swiping Barbas in the face with one of my wings, not the least bit apologetic or sorry as he staggers backwards out of the way.

"Now, we go outside." Gorgon takes my hand and together we walk, my breath bated and blood running hot with excitement, through the double doors and out into the entrance hall. We continue onward, ignoring the incredulous looks of mortals. The wings probably look ridiculous, but if they enable me to take to the skies once again, I can't quite find the will to care. Also, this will be a gift nobody can take from me, not as the gods of The Aetherial Court once had. They made me a Titan, a reward in their eyes — that much was true. But they stripped me of my last ounce of what masqueraded as freedom. The only thing that had kept me sane in my holy union with the Sephilim King.

I can hear the others in unsubtle pursuit and find Katerina and Lilliana just outside the throne room doors, eavesdropping on what was going on inside, before they join the procession. The Demon Lords and Anubis follow in my wake, my shadow immense beyond the span of my wings. Gorgon has given me perhaps the best gift I've ever received. I'll have to make it up to him later.

We take long strides, following the scorch-mark of what had once been the river curling through the dry soil impacted with demon tread and littered with bones. I look up at the sky. To the enormous expanse of it, the warm wine-coloured blanket covering this world and what had once been the sun — now an ominous black speck— a bruise on an otherwise flawless horizon.

"So now what?" I ask Gorgon as we reach a flat expanse of dirt leading away from the Exilia and out into the surrounding land.

"You've flown before— you tell me." He crosses his arms, encasing his narrow chest, greasy hair plastered against his creased brow.

"Well— I'd hardly attempt a standing take-off in these. I guess maybe a run-up?" I suggest, and he shrugs.

"You're the expert, my Queen."

That, my dear Gorgon, is the *correct* answer.

I spin on the ball of my leather boot, not caring for the people around me as they dodge out of the way of my new metal prosthetics.

I go to start the sprint, but before I can, I hear Gorgon clear his throat.

"You might want to give me that shard before you take off— I'd hate for you to lose it," he suggests.

My heart wilts.

Is this just a distraction?

I shake my head, not able to find a word to convey both my anger and fear in a way that won't blow up into a fight. I don't want to fight right now; I want to fly.

With my heart becoming heavier by the second, I take off, jerking forward in long unpractised strides with the wings clattering behind me. I don't know what to expect, how they work or even if they will work. Perhaps this is a ploy to get me killed so The Demon Lords can be rid of me once and for all. But then, don't Gorgon and I share something— *special*? After all those hours of writhing together like serpents hidden among the sheets. Does all that mean nothing?

I realise then that I need to focus on myself.

What do *I* want?

My feet stagger, one in front of the other, picking up speed as my weight impacts the dry earth beneath. I can't stop running now.

Why?

I stare up at the sky, and I know. I know I want to feel the rush of the wind against my face, the sight of an endless void above me and the pitiful below.

As I reach a kind of plateau in pace, heart racing, eyes watering against the dry air that rushes me, I feel my feet leave the ground.

Suddenly, I'm free.

The wings shudder, the metal of them grating slightly as the wind lifts under them, and I'm in flight. They move magically, but they're still undeniably mechanical in sound.

This isn't effortless; it isn't a blessing. This is real. This is hard, heavy, a thing birthed from the earth and forged in the fires of this place, in the will of one man to save his son from the sins of his past.

I ascend fast, the world below becoming a speck, becoming inferior to my might in every regard. I feel the shard in my back pocket as I soar through the bloody void, the heavens of hell spinning around me in an endless sanguine blur, and know that I must act quickly once I return to the Mortarian soil. No one can be trusted, and I can never forget that.

The rush of air clears my head of emotional shrapnel, and I remind myself that I'm here for revenge, here to cripple Zeus. I must not be distracted by what had placated me to the whim of that very same god for aeons, nor the touch of another.

For now, though, I smile, letting the gift of flight carry me over the city, over The Ashen Waste, and toward the fiery imminence of Mount Mallum. As I glide through the air, I cannot help but admire the hordes of demons, what would soon become the scourge of the earth at my beck and call, below.

Upon my return from unholy flight, I find them gathered on the soil beneath me. I don't need to wonder what they're talking about because I already know.

How will they use the shard?

That is the question on everyone's lips. The question itself makes me smile. Funny how two people who had no interest in retrieving it in the first place think they have a say in how it's used now I've triumphed. I'll soon show them that the shard is mine; that the power inside belongs to no other than I.

The wings spread, catching air beneath them and slowing my descent as I fall, not so gracefully, to the ground. The weight of them pushes me down too hard, and my knees buckle beneath me as I fall into a half-crouch atop the earth, wings balanced precariously on my shoulder blades.

The group turn to face me upon my return, smiles plastering their faces, filling in the cavernous holes in their skulls that would otherwise reek of betrayal, of self-serving agendas.

I don't smile back at them.

"How was it?" Gorgon asks, taking several fluid steps forward and offering me a hand as I straighten.

I don't take it.

"Wonderful. But now, I have more important things to attend to." I unclip the wings from me, letting them fall with a thud to the ground and walking away from them fast. I let my palm rest on the back pocket of my pants, feeling the shard beneath the fabric, flush against me.

I stride over the dirt, past the crowd of watchful eyes, and back toward the Exilia. I sense them begin to follow me but ignore them, knowing now I need to act as fast as I can. I need this power to be mine, and I can't risk waiting any longer.

Reaching the entryway, I pick up the pace, heading not up the staircase and into the throne room as they might expect but back to the library, my stride rhythmic. My heartbeat is heavy and insistent in my chest, and as I push both the library doors wide for a memorable entrance, I find myself staring out over Mortaria through the open balcony doors on the opposing side of the room in only three large strides.

"Pandora?" Anubis' voice is riddled with concern. I turn, cocking an eyebrow.

"Yes?" I ask, eyes wide and innocent as I'm silhouetted against the bloody sky.

"What— what are you planning?" she asks, and I smile at her evident unease.

"I intend to absorb the power in this shard for myself. I'd say I've earned it. You all have your powers, your magic. Now it's time I claimed mine." I watch as Barbas' left eye twitches and Gorgon's eyes narrow. Katerina and Lilliana don't react other than to cross their hands in front of them in synchronised time.

Abraxis takes a step forward.

"You don't have any right to the dark magic within that shard. Those dark tethers were gifted to The Demon Lords by our gods. You have no right to it."

He repeats this sentiment as though it will have any impact on what I intend to achieve.

"I'd say I have more right to it than any of you. I'm the reason we are here. I'm the reason this shard is filled with Lucifer's dark magic in the first place. I'm the reason your Kindred once again prowl the land that's rightfully theirs." I list my accomplishments as they spread out slightly, forming a semi-circle around me. I take several steps back, nowhere left to go but the balcony.

"Pandora, you can't handle dark magic like that— you aren't chosen." Barbas' face remains dead, even his skull shape boring to observe in the half-light of the library. I reach back, pulling out the shard from my pocket and clutching the jagged crystal in my palm, holding it up so they can see.

"Who are you to tell me what I am?" I ask him, lowering the shard and using one of the edges to slash a long vertical gash up the inside of my arm. I wait for the rush, for the dark promise to be unleashed within my blood. The Demon Lords and Anubis stand, frozen and waiting.

Blood drips down onto the floor, the shard's outermost edge glinting crimson. I wait. One minute. Two minutes.

Nothing.

Abraxis and Anubis share a knowing sideways glance, which I easily could have missed in the dim light that blankets them. I stand, making another gash beside the first, a hiss escaping between my grit teeth, heart racing and blood boiling as it bubbles from beneath the surface and trickles in crimson rivulets down my arm.

Still nothing.

The Demon Lords turn and exit the room, leaving me standing there on the balcony, blood dripping to form a small puddle at my feet.

I stare at the shard, stare at my arm, fury evolving quickly within my veins like an unexpected storm.

What is this? Is it a fake? I took it from Lucifer myself, watched as her darkness had syphoned into its dark facets against her will.

So maybe— maybe it isn't the shard at all.

Maybe it's me.

Despair crashes over me in a wave, fury following quickly like a brutal undertow as I storm from the library and down the corridor toward the entrance hall once more. Only one day ago, I would have gone to Gorgon for advice, maybe even Katerina or Lilliana, but now

I've seen the fear in their eyes at the prospect of me gaining power equal to their own.

After everything I've done for them, they still can't bear the thought of me becoming their magical equal. I guess I should have known.

When I reach the entryway, I storm past the throne room doors, the eyes of mortals tracking my path as I head for the dungeons, shard still clutched in my hand as blood continues to drip in a spotty trail upon the crystal floors.

Proceeding down the narrow corridor, I make a sharp right, ploughing through the wooden door and taking the steps down into the dark underbelly of the Exilia two at a time, breathing rapid in my throat and seeing red everywhere I look.

Disappointment, the ache of yet another failure after my experience at The Well, threatens to overwhelm, but I instead focus on my anger, rushing to the cell I seek and slamming my open palm into one of the metal bars. The steel vibrates, the sound of impact echoing out into the cell as the residents startle, waking from where they had been snoozing upright, unnatural seeming for three elderly women upon wooden stools.

"Wake up!" I snap, watching as groggy white and scarlet eyes flutter into view from beneath too-thin flesh veils mapped blue with veins.

"Pandora, what can we do for you?" The blind Fate asks, voice little more than a wisp of smoke among the dank.

"Why didn't this work?!" I demand, shoving my still bleeding arm and the shard up against the bars. The clang of crystal on steel rings out, harsh, causing the woman to jump.

"What is it?" the deaf Fate asks, withered skin sagging from her bones as she shifts behind the spinning wheel between us.

"As if you don't already know. It's a dark tether. A remnant from one of the weapons gifted to The Demon Lords by their Ancient Gods," I spit, impatient.

"What are you trying to do? Absorb its power?" the unseeing woman asks, and I cock my head.

"No, I'm standing here bleeding onto the floor because I thought I'd mount it as a nice pendant. Of course, I'm trying to absorb the dark power! Are you stupid as well as ancient?" I feel like screaming, the walls of the entire Exilia closing in around me and making me feel small.

"Why are you here?" she asks, folding her craggy hands in her lap.

"It didn't work!" I scream, slamming the stone into the bars of the cell yet again. None of The Fates jump this time. Instead, they merely stare.

"I'm sorry—" she replies, and I debate calling a mortal to unlock the cell so I might throttle her.

"Don't be sorry. Tell me how to fix it!" I exclaim, running fraught fingers back through my hair that's now wild around my face, my chest rising and falling too fast, pushing out hard against the boning of my corset.

"I cannot do that. Darkness is tricky. There are hundreds of reasons it could be unusable as a source of darkness. And besides, even if we did know, we wouldn't tell you," she sneers, unholy in the darkness.

I ball my fist, flesh breaking open like the skin of dark berries over the sharp edges of the crystal.

"You know how to fix this. If you don't tell me, I'll have you murdered—" I hiss, spit flying from between my desperate lips.

"Go ahead, at least if we're dead, we would have access to a good cup of tea. Not only that, but our first port of call would be Zeus to tell him what a bad girl you've been," she threatens me back, and I snort.

"He would never let you back into The Higher Plains." I glower, eyes flashing as my blood begins to clot, thick and cold around the self-inflicted wounds climbing my arms.

"Ah, but you already took care of that, didn't you, Pandora?" The deaf fate smiles, her crooked teeth stained a disgusting brown as strings of drool spread between her gaping lips.

"I beg your pardon?" I spit, and she smirks.

"Surely, you can't have forgotten that it is not only Zeus who has the power to grant access to The Higher Plains. All of Cronus' sons possess that perk. And though Poseidon might be too busy with the drama of his marriage to protest Zeus' choices, you made sure that Haedes was yet again able to grant us passage home," she reveals, and I feel my heart drop.

If The Fates return to The Higher Plains, then Hercules' lies will no longer stand up to The Aetherial Court. They would most certainly come down on me with their Sephilim Armies, their fleet of Draconians on dragon back—

I shudder at the thought, not of death, but of losing to Zeus. To having what I'd once been become the source of my final demise.

I have no choice but to let The Fates live, rotting in this cell for the rest of their days. I have no power over them, and no threat I can make will change that. The only thing I can do is keep them locked up to stop them causing more problems.

They are of no use to me.

Fury courses through me, and I want to throw the shard at the floor, to watch it shatter into a hundred pieces.

Why is nothing ever simple?

Why must I suffer?

Why has the universe decided to watch me flail and burn under the scorn of an unjust god?

I didn't ask for this.

I wish Hera left me dead, let me move on and be reborn as something new, but she took me for herself, blessed me, and made me a soldier. Made me fodder for her cause. Made me a servant of a master I never wanted nor asked for.

I want to thrash out, craving violence and the contact of bone on bone that only comes through the whirling of angry fists.

Instead, though, I pocket the crystal, steeling myself and vowing that if it takes everything I have, everything I am, even if it consumes my final breath, I will get my revenge.

Dark power or not.

I turn and leave the dungeon, drifting, melancholy, back up into the main Exilia and wondering how much more I must sacrifice to bring justice to the heavens.

19

PEOPLE WILL SAY WE'RE IN LOVE

SEPHY

I'M LAID BARE UPON the scorching grain of the Bermuda sand, eyes closed, letting myself burn beneath the early morning sun. I stir, eyes fluttering open as I hear the rush of the waves crashing into the nearby shore. Gulls cry out, piercing the salt-laden sky like razor blades.

Xion is beside me, arms slung across my midriff. I'm wearing a baggy white t-shirt and a pair of bikini bottoms underneath, fiery red hair trailing over my shoulders and framing my face as the sun kisses it warm.

"Xion?" I'm so relaxed here, so at peace, I don't want to break this tranquil spell, but I need to see his eyes, need to know this is real.

Letting my head loll to one side, my cheeks flush with anticipation.

I look into his face, and those metallic gold eyes stare into mine, unblinking.

Cold.

It takes me a minute to work out what I'm seeing, but once I realise, I crawl back in panic, heart racing in my chest.

He's dead.

His corpse falls face down in the sand as I scramble from beneath it, staggering to my feet, mind racing.

He's untouched, not a speck of blood or sign of bruising anywhere.

I don't want to stare anymore, can't bring myself to touch him to make sure, but I know it as sure as I know that war and darkness lie just over the horizon.

Xion is gone.

My feet fall one behind the other, toes catching my ankle as my eyes refuse to look anywhere but at the body.

I turn, first instinct to run back up to the beach house, to get help. It might not be too late; he might just be in shock—

I tell myself these lies, trying to make sense of everything.

I fail.

Nothing makes sense.

Nothing about this will ever make sense.

I race up the path formed of smooth pebbles laid into the powdery white sand, tearing toward the Sinclair's Bermuda property, sun beating down and punishing my fair skin as I ascend the left side of the grassy dune.

The entire place is walled with glass and open space living areas and an enormous kitchen can be seen inside, though barely as the windows are tinted dark. All seems still until I glimpse it within the midst of teak and minimalist modern furniture. A glimmer of blonde hair, catching the tropical sunlight and holding it hostage until it sheens with solar intensity.

I fall into the revolving glass door, weight causing the pane to rotate on a central axis as my hot soles meet the cool grey marble of the floor, relief from the heat barely registering.

I'm too late.

Luce is strewn like sleeping beauty across the long couch, which is upholstered in fabric peppered with green palm leaves in a myriad of watercolour blurs. Her eyes are icy glass mirrors, reflecting my horror back at me, and her hand drags against the marble of the floor beneath the couch, lifeless.

Jules is sat in a chair beside the landline on an antique carved teak table, posture as ever perfect but somehow wrong. His mouth is agape like he's shocked by something no longer there, his body stiff and eerily proper.

Rigor Mortis.

How did this happen?

How long was I asleep?

I stumble into the kitchen, my heart the only sound I can hear as I find the three Furies fallen like autumnal leaves across the floor, limbs twisted, eyes wide open, mouths slack.

Dead.

They hadn't even reached for their weapons, and I find quivers of arrows still full, a katana untouched, and the hilts of knives abandoned by the expert hand they have always known. The entire scene is eerily bizarre, wrong even.

I spin, feeling eyes on me, and find her out on the deck facing the ocean, serene.

Her dark hair tumbles down her spine as she turns slowly on the spot, the salty air of the tropics disturbing the loose black tulle of the gown she's wearing. It falls to the floor as free moving as shadow itself, pooling light around the ankles of her bare feet.

Her violet eyes meet with mine, thick lashes framing them dark, pupils lit with a murderous spark.

She glances down into her open palms, motion slow, fingers splayed, pale skin marred with fine cuts. She holds them out from beyond the windowpane so I might see, the rush of the tide mute now behind her.

The shard. Or what had once been, lies in her cupped and bloody palms, tiny slivers of the crystal all that remain.

She smiles, what would be a beautiful expression if I didn't want to throttle her.

"Sephy—" The whisper is a challenge, falling far too quiet into the panicked air between us.

She's still, tranquil, even now. Even beneath my murderous gaze.

"Sephy!" My name floods the house again, bouncing from the walls and shattering the glass of the windows as I place my hands over my ears. It's her voice, but it does not seem to come from her.

Pandora stares at me, eyes unblinking as her lips move yet again.

This time though, it isn't her voice that comes, but Xion's.

Relief floods me.

"Sephy, it's time to wake up!"

I shoot bolt upright with a start, the sound of the ocean filling my head as I find my palms closed into fists and gritty with sand. The grains cling to the sweat running down my forearms, persistent and rough. I exhale heavily like I've just been shocked back to life.

"Are you okay?" Xion's voice echoes in my ears like he's too far away, just a blip on the horizon.

I try to get my bearings.

I'm lying on the beach in surf shorts and a black bikini, a small way from the same Bermuda property I've just walked through in my dream.

I always forget exactly how much property I own and the fact that it's all just sitting around, fully stocked with clothes and everything I could possibly need on the off chance I decide to stay. It is one of the most useful perks of being an heiress, especially when you're on the run from a psychopathic ex-Titan.

Jules' agitated voice is raised but muffled by the glass walls surrounding him as he paces the living room floor over and over. I allow myself to be hopeful, wondering how the phone call he insisted on making is going. Not that I should. His outrage says everything.

The flight had taken six hours, and I hadn't slept for a minute of it. I didn't even bother to close my eyes and try. My mind was racing with half-cocked battle plans, strategies, and a slew of worst-case scenarios. I'd had what could not be considered a small amount of whiskey on the flight as well, not that anyone can exactly blame me. It was an attempt to calm the nerves, which I have well and truly shredded to ribbons. It's almost as though a careless child has been running amok in what had once been the tightly woven strands of my life with a pair of extremely sharp scissors.

The dream showed me what I knew was likely.

Those I love dead because of me and my failure to protect them from Pandora.

God, I hate that bitch.

"Sephy? What is it?" Xion's voice breaks through the panic, which rises like slow thick bile in my chest, threatening to drown me from the inside.

"Uh— nothing. A bad dream. It's fine." I get to my feet, needing to move, needing to calm myself. I can't look at him right now, not without seeing his lifeless corpse.

He lies back on the sand, and I find my pale skin flushed red as I stare down at my arms instead of at him. My complexion is good for many things, but long periods out in the sun isn't one of them.

The shouting from the beach house has ceased, and the heat causes my panic to grow, parasitic and unstoppable.

I head inside, steps faster than I intend as I leave Xion splayed out on the sand, basking like an extremely hairy Mermaid. The house rises in front of me and I peer hesitantly through the gargantuan panes of glass into the airy lounge.

Jules is still pacing, looking down at the phone in his palm, and Luce is saying something to him I can't quite hear. I look around for The Furies, but I can't see them anywhere, breath catching in my throat accordingly.

Cool air rushes over me as I enter the house and immediately look at Jules.

"Where are The Furies?" I demand, tone clipped and riddled with obvious concern.

"They're asleep. I think the excitement of the flight wore them out." He shrugs. I run my fingers back through my hair, not smiling at his response. My breath comes in icy wisps now, my eyes darting to the deck beyond the kitchen unwillingly and half expecting to find her there.

Jules stares at me; my stiff posture and fast-moving chest, lips trembling slightly as I try to reclaim some semblance of calm.

"Are you alright?" he enquires, and I nod. The action is a definitive lie. I'm not fine at all. Not even slightly.

Turns out, I have no idea what I'm doing.

"What did A.D.A.M have to say?" I ask, taking several steps, barefoot, across the chill grey marble and leaning haphazardly against the arm of the tropically patterned couch. Luce gazes at me as I perch, eyes full of unspoken curiosity.

"They say it's not their jurisdiction." Jules lets out an enormous sigh and a deep crevasse of irritation forms between my eyebrows.

"Are you fucking kidding me? This is about the fate of the mortal world. How the hell is that not their jurisdiction?" I'm on my feet again, outrage pushing me to stand despite the world that refuses to stop spinning around me.

"I just spent the last ten minutes yelling that at them. You don't need to tell me," Jules grumbles, setting the phone down on a teak table pushed against the far wall. He sits down on the chair beside it, the chair he'd been sitting on in my dream.

I look to Luce, unable to let myself linger on her face.

"So— I guess it's just us then." I breathe, livid. She gives me a sad smile.

"It would appear that way. What do you think we should do?" she asks me, both her and Jules' eyes expectant.

My heart races. Pulse heightens. Pupils dilate.

They continue to stare.

I open my mouth to speak, but no sound comes out, and despite the air conditioning unit not thirty feet from me I feel my blood boiling just beneath the surface of my skin. My ribs become a prison, lungs unable to expand as I see their faces, dead-eyed, before me. My cheeks scorch with colour, my heart rate pounding a deafening techno-beat in my ears.

It wasn't only a dream. I know that. It was a warning.

I don't know what else I can do. I'm on an island, surrounded by water, in a world that will soon be surrounded by demons.

Shit. Shit. Shit.

My pulse is too high. I'm too warm. And for some reason, turning and running seems like the best option.

I flee from the house, Jules and Luce calling after me, no doubt confused as all hell.

My feet pound hard against the uneven yet smooth rounds of the pebbles forming the path down to the beach, but soon that is behind me too.

My heart refuses to slow.

I'm hyperventilating, the sound of the surrounding world lost on me. All I can hear is my own panic closing in.

I'm going to get everyone killed.

I don't have a plan. I don't have even the beginnings of a plan. I don't have the numbers— don't have the arsenal—

Shit. Shit. Shit!

I bend over as my feet slow, my body giving out, palms clutching my kneecaps as I suck in the too-warm, too-humid air. I've gone as far as I can along this particular expanse of powdery sand, jagged rocks slick with sea spray blocking the path ahead.

My hair falls around my face as I hunch over further, the sun burning into the back of my neck as I stare, eyes watering, down at the ground.

I don't hear him approach, but I feel him ground me as his palm comes to rest on my shoulder.

"Sephy— breathe—" Xion's voice is a husk of a whisper, his eyes too sad as they stare at me. I don't need his pity so look away fast.

I don't know what I need.

But again, I know it isn't pity.

"I'm trying—" I mumble, misery rife in my tone.

"What is it?" he asks me, and I straighten, giving him an incredulous look.

"Oh, I don't know. It might be the fact that I'm going to war with no goddamn help and absolutely no idea what I'm doing! I'm going to get everyone killed!" I blurt, eyes stinging as they fill with tears against my consent.

"Okay— *okay.* Just stop a minute." Xion rubs my upper back in slow, deliberate circles, causing my heartbeat to unwillingly slow.

"I don't have time. We're running out of it. You're running out—" I gasp, thinking of Pandora's clawed fingers clutching the shard, the crystal connected to his soul.

Usually, at this point, fury would be coursing through me, but it isn't. The anger is almost entirely diminished by the chill of my fear of failure. The stakes are higher than I'd ever want to play if I had a choice.

But I don't. Not really.

"Look, I know it's overwhelming. But let's break it down. What do you need? We came here because of the devil's triangle, right? The only other way into Mortaria without using your convecting powers now The Hollow is gone."

"That's right," I whisper, voice weak. The sound is almost entirely extinguished by the rush of nearby waves.

"So— we need a boat?" Xion suggests.

Yes, we would need a boat.

And weapons.

And armour.

And more bodies.

"Sephy, breathe. One step at a time— you *can* do this," Xion reassures me. All I can do is continue swallowing the zest of the sea air, thick with salt.

"Okay. I need weapons. And not just swords. I need proper artillery. Guns— maybe even grenades and other explosives. I also need armour, the good stuff—" I think out loud, breathing rate slowing with each word.

"Right. Okay. So, we tackle the obvious stuff first. Getting a boat here— getting the weapons and armour we need. That's the first step." He makes it sound so easy. Like this isn't a suicide mission.

"Do you have a boat?" he asks. I shake my head.

I had a boat once.

A few years back I'd gone on a trip around the coast of South Africa in a brand-new yacht. It was beautiful, all cream and aqua metal soldered in sleek lines down the body of the vessel.

It had been named *Firecracker*.

Unfortunately, though, the weather had changed unpredictably and within only hours. The storm had been terrifying though I'd been drunk for most of it. The captain lost the boat to the waves, and we both ended up being airlifted to shore to top off the entire experience.

Safe to say I'm not the biggest fan of the ocean.

I stand on the beach for a second as I banish those memories, closing my eyes and then opening them again, turning to him.

Somehow, I've returned to some semblance of calm, and I know that's only because of him.

"Thanks," is all I can say.

He takes my hand in his, intertwining our fingers and looking out to sea, eyes so hopeful it hurts. He's tanning already, his olive skin darkened considerably over the few hours since we've landed. I envy him that.

"You're in this with me, right? No matter what?" I ask him, not about us but about the war that's coming. It's a stupid question, and I know the answer. But for some reason, I need to hear him say it. Why is it that I refuse to trust my gut with him, refuse to relinquish to what I know is true?

He would die for me.

And I hate him for it.

I remember his face, the dead eyes of his corpse in my dream, and I know why.

I can't open myself up to loss again. My heart is already broken beyond repair.

"Where else would I be?" He smiles, the left side of his mouth twisting upward into an adolescent smile. He looks young in the sunlight, almost carefree. As if he's somehow let go of all the worries that have been weighing him down over the last few months. I wish I knew how he does it because I'm pretty sure I'd be able to focus a lot better without all this anxiety.

I turn and begin to walk away from him, back up the beach in the direction I've just come, wishing I was stronger. I've pretty much just had a full-blown panic attack, something I know I don't have time for. I have to toughen if I'm going to lead these people to war. My weakness is their weakness, and I don't have the luxury of that anymore.

I sweep my hair up off my neck, damp with perspiration, moving now with direction and purpose. Suddenly, I want the numbness I felt after returning from death to sweep over me. I hadn't felt connected to life so had nothing to lose by risking it. That kind of careless ambivalence is a luxury I just don't have anymore, either. I'm mortal, and I care, no matter how hard I try not to.

"Hey, where are you going?" I hear him call after me, his jeans rolled up to just below his knees, hands stuffed in his pockets.

I twist, looking back over my shoulder, realising that to stand the best chance, I'm going to need to bargain with someone I'd rather not.

I mean I have the money to procure pretty much anything, but something tells me that this particular organisation is going to have weapons that haven't yet been released into the mainstream market.

"I'm going to call back A.D.A.M. I need more firepower, and they're going to give it to me."

"Hello?" the voice is clipped, official, bored even.

"Well, hello there, Colonel—" I put on my best good girl voice, biting my bottom lip as I twirl the landline cable around my index finger like an 80's teenager.

"Persephone. I can only guess why you're calling. I already told Jules, Mortaria isn't in my jurisdiction." I roll my eyes at Jules, who smirks, sitting on the arm of the couch where Luce is still lying, watching the two of us with the beginnings of a smile teasing the corners of her mouth.

"I was thinking you could do me a favour actually." I'm cocky, listening to him clear his voice at the other end of the line.

"I don't do favours. I'm a military Colonel, not Santa Claus," he replies.

"Sandy isn't short for Sandy Claus? You mean you don't have Rudolph stashed in some air hanger in area fifty-one? I better call that reporter from the airport and tell him I made a mistake—" I feel a glimmer of amusement sparkle behind my eyes, and Jules shakes his head, smirking.

"Goodbye, Miss Sinclair." His tone is unamused and metronomic, a drone.

"Wait, look. I'm in a bit of a bind here. But the way I see it, me going into Mortaria benefits us both," I begin, and hear nothing for several seconds except the crackle of the line.

"And how do you figure that?" he demands, interested even though he doesn't want to be after only several seconds.

"Are you telling me you don't want the mortal hostages Pandora abducted returned?" I ask him, eyes flicking to Jules.

His expression relaxes slightly, and I smile.

Got ya.

"Pandora has mortals— you mean *living* mortals, in Mortaria?" he queries, surprise rife in his tone.

"Oh, you didn't know that? I figured with your military intelligence you'd have already identified and numbered them like cattle." Jules places his head in his hands, cringing. I know it's overkill, but I love screwing around with these official types. It just makes me happy.

"No. I was not aware of that particular fact—" His voice trails off as though he's lost in thought.

"So—" I begin, shooting Jules a thumbs up and doing a victory dance, shaking my booty from left to right.

"What do you need?" he asks, and a wide smile spreads over my lips as I halt, propping myself against the table and biting my bottom lip, examining my nails like I'm on hold with the salon.

"You got a pen and a piece of paper?"

LUCE

We stand on a wooden jetty protruding out over the crystalline Atlantic waters. The breeze and open sky calm me, and for the first time in a long time, I feel relatively put together. I'm alive, sun-kissed, and free from the darkness that held me within its clutches. I had been undoubtedly more powerful, more useful, but I had also lost what made me myself. My ability to deem right from wrong.

It's been twelve hours since she hung up with the Colonel, and as we stand, the four of us silhouetted against the setting sun, a speck, then two, appear on the opposing horizon.

They speed toward us, growing bigger and flanked by a blur of fast-moving white sea spray, bouncing on top of the waves like low-soaring sea birds.

"Here they come," Jules breathes at Sephy's side. I watch her visibly ball her fists and straighten.

I stare at her, respect flooding me. She saved me, and now she is risking it all to save everyone else. She's not the most likely hero, but she's exactly what we need.

Haedes' daughter is alive and well in spirit as well as body, *finally*.

The cold remnants of death do not cling to her any longer, and the fire that once held permanent residence in her eyes has returned without falter or flaw. Her cognac irises blaze in the dying sunlight as the roar of the boats grows ever louder.

We step forward across the sea swept planks of wood making up the jetty, water calm beneath us, the smell of salt encircling us like lost spirits from the beyond.

Reaching the end of the platform, we wait, a few more minutes elapsing before the swarm of black, military-grade speedboats descend on us like bees, their interiors abuzz with hive activity.

The honey— the sweet nectar she's requested doesn't gleam; instead, it is stocked high in wooden crates packed with straw, dull matte black and gunmetal grey peeking out between wide set slats.

"Miss Sinclair," the Colonel addresses her, launching himself off the side of the boat and landing upon the jetty with a thud, both feet impacting hard against the wood. I feel the barnacles clinging to the underside recoil, terrified.

If only they knew his first name was Sandy.

"Mr Claus," Sephy addresses him, not offering a hand or any kind of physical welcome, merely standing with her fingers clutching her hips, eyes glistening at the sight of the heavy artillery he has in tow. She's like a kid at Christmas, not that I should know, but it's an expression. I've never had a real Christmas— except for the year Demi Sinclair stayed with us.

The memory isn't given a chance to form as the Colonel doesn't pause in his response, unsurprisingly one for efficiency above all else.

"I should think so with the turnaround you gave me for this amount of firepower." He tuts, the black matte of his uniform taking in the dying sunlight and giving nothing back, the world's natural beauty perishing fast upon his military insignia.

"So, keys—" Sephy opens her hand, palm up, staring at him without humour now.

"Wait. There's something we must discuss first."

I watch her exhale.

Had she known this was coming?

"We found something that belongs to *her* at The Sinclair Estate." His eyes flick to me and, if I'm not mistaken, I glimpse fear at the root of their darkness.

"Oh?" she asks, and he pulls a radio from his belt.

He presses down a button on the side, speaking clearly into the crackle emitting from the speaker without pause.

"Corporal you there? We are *Go*." He sends the order, and from within the radio, an enormous rumble erupts only seconds later.

A growl.

"Beelz! What did you do to her?" I exclaim, taking several steps forward and feeling my fingers tense, becoming claw-like in only seconds.

"Oh nothing— *yet*," he adds, malice twisting his expression as he positions me for checkmate. Beelz isn't just a pet; she's the guardian of my tether. Her survival on this plain and mine go hand in hand.

How could I have left the estate without her?

I should have stayed behind and looked for her.

"We have a job for you—" he announces, placing the radio back on his belt as it falls into silence. Soldiers bustle around us, tying up the boats and emptying some of the weapons from one into the other.

I stare at him, eyes narrowing, but Sephy answers before I can come up with a reply.

"We told you already we'll get the mortals out and back to this realm," she snaps, impatient.

"See, that's the thing. We don't want them here. We need you to— *dispose* of them. They've seen too much. It's too much of a risk. You understand that, don't you?"

My brain short circuits at the request.

"Are you fucking *kidding* me? I'm not murdering innocent people so you can keep your boss happy!" Sephy exclaims, flipping her fiery locks over one shoulder in the way she's so used to. Xion leaps into the conversation, where before he's been but an observer, stepping forward so he's right beside me.

"You can't be serious? You can't ask her to do this!" he protests.

"I'm not asking *her* to do anything—" The Colonel's gaze falls to me from where before he'd been observing Sephy with unfounded authority, a small and rage-inducing smirk taking over his face.

I look at the boats full of weaponry, armour, things we desperately need. Lives are bound to be lost, as is the way with war for universal balance. I'm also, I must remind myself, far from innocent in all this.

Perhaps this is the true cost of what I've done, coming back to bite me in the ass. More people will die if we don't win this fight, and we need these weapons to do that. So, I am now in the position of sacrificing the few to save the many.

If I had let Thane go, back in The Sinstone Mines, then I wouldn't have this same dilemma now.

I could dwell on the guilt, but when I really think about it, I wonder if I can be more consumed by it than I already am.

If this is the price I must pay to right what I've done, then I'll pay it. I'll bear the pain.

"Alright," I agree, and Sephy spins, looking back at me with a shocked expression.

"It's okay Sephy." I give her a forceful look, hoping that I give her the impression I have some trick up my sleeve.

I don't.

"So that's settled. You'll dispose of the mortals, and in exchange, I'll leave you with this—" He gestures to the boat, which is becoming stacked ever higher with weapons loaded from its counterpart.

"I want my panther back when this is all over, or else you'll see why they call me the devil," I hiss at him, feeling the ferality of darkness flicker back to life within me for only a second.

Xion stares at me, blinking slowly.

Jules steps forward without pause.

"Get the hell out of here," he says simply, and so we watch the men turn from us, watch them climb back into their now empty speedboat, twice as heavily manned as before, and disappear silently onto the horizon, none of us saying a word.

The only sign they were ever here is the boat they left behind and our mutual pissed-off expressions.

"So, on a scale of one to ten—" Sephy looks back between us, her eyebrow cocked.

"About as comfortable as a broken glass enema," Xion retorts.

"Yeah—" she says, sighing out, eyes resting on the outline of the boat floating beside us. The victory is more underwhelming than any of us has expected. "—that's what I thought."

20

DRESSED TO KILL

XION

THE SKY OVER THE Atlantic has long since fallen into the clutches of a deep and humid night, the waves growing increasingly restless with each passing second.

We waste no time getting to work, taking a quick inventory of what's been left behind by A.D.A.M within the slow bobbing confines of the military grade speedboat. There are a ton of wooden crates, each identical except for the varying dimensions, and as I step up and into the boat, I'm overwhelmed. Had Sephy really asked for all this?

I mean, I knew she was worried but—

"Is this a *bazooka*?!" I exclaim, tentatively lifting one of the wooden lids just enough for weak moonlight to illuminate the contents.

"Yeah— should be. One of them at least," Sephy adds, peeking over the side of the boat from the jetty. My eyes widen.

"And what exactly are you planning on doing with this?" I gesture down at the enormous barrel.

"Wouldn't you like to know?" She winks at me, tongue flicking out to wet the side of her mouth. "When you find the armour, throw it over here. Then we can get suited and booted," she commands without second thought, ignoring my obvious surprise and changing the subject fast. She's proving herself to be a natural born leader, even if she denies wanting any part in being the person looked to in a crisis.

"Hey, you three; come give me a hand." I gesture to The Furies, who have just approached the shore end of the jetty. I don't know what they'd been doing during the hand-off with A.D.A.M, and I'm not sure I need to.

The three of them make pace, bare feet padding on the slick wooden planks, quickly reaching the side of the boat and climbing into it with me without another word. Sephy watches us with interest as we continue to sort through the boxes.

"So— am I the only one who was surprised about the whole mass murder thing?" Sephy asks.

Jules laughs.

"I wasn't. But then again, I'm used to their political etiquette," Jules confesses, his arms folded with palms resting lightly on the bare skin of his wrists, bald head shining dull in the moonlight.

"So, you were expecting them to ask us to just kill all those helpless people?" I don't try to hide my disgust, opening another crate and discovering several grenades inside.

Jesus Sephy— I eye the criss-cross black plastic encasing the hand-held explosives, pins balancing in a way seemingly far too precarious in the top of each one.

"I was expecting them to— what's the term that they always use on the official report— *flush* the knowledge from the system. That many people having seen what they've seen— if it got out, mass panic and hysteria would follow," Jules sighs, looking tired of explaining A.D.A.M and their stupid policies.

"As opposed to the mass hysteria and panic from the apocalypse they're refusing any part in because it *'isn't their jurisdiction'*?" Sephy retorts, using air quotes and mimicking the Colonel in a low and overly superior tone.

"Hey, I didn't say their logic made any kind of sense— that's bureaucracy at its finest for you, and besides, they didn't ask *you* to kill anyone."

He turns to Luce, eyes sad.

"I know you feel like they're holding this over you, with Beelz. But we can find another way to get her back. You don't have to do this—" He touches her arm gently, and she shakes her head, silver strands of hair ghostly in the night's weak pearly light.

"I understand where they're coming from. You know that Haedes and I spent years making sure that our own dealings with the mortal world were kept on the down-low to avoid this exact problem. A.D .A.M might be going about it in a rather brash fashion, but we can't let those mortals reintegrate into society," she says, and my eyebrows rise on my forehead.

When did she become so callous for the greater good? Wasn't it her lack of ability to choose the greater picture over the personal one that had put us all here in the first place?

Then again, I'm just as much to blame as anyone.

I watch as Luce turns and moves silently back toward the house, slowly retreating into shadow. Things are awkward for a moment, but as ever, The Furies can be counted on to distract.

"Hey, what's this?" Ericka holds something up to the moonlight, and when I turn to answer her, I feel my heart stop.

"Don't goddamn touch that! Put. It. Down!" I exclaim, making her jump. I worry she'll drop it so snatch the grenade from her palm, breath coming in a staccato of terrified wisps.

"Oh yeah, I'm sure you're so much better at handling this shit with care— Mr Sass-quatch," Sephy smirks, trying to joke with me, as I place the grenade back among the straw of its crate with as much ginger care as I can muster.

This really isn't the time for jokes.

"Okay. Everyone out of the boat. I'm gonna go through this myself. Out!" I demand, pointing for the three women to move as far away as possible. They give me looks of joint sulk, but I ignore them, turning instead to the task at hand.

"I would be able to tell you how most of this stuff works—" Jules offers his help, and I nod, still not looking up.

"I thought you hadn't worked for these guys in years?" Sephy confronts him, suspicion flitting ill-disguised across her face.

"Oh, true. But I still get the newsletter," he replies. Nobody has an answer to that, or the energy to ask more questions. We simply stand for a moment as the air stills around us, silent.

"All right, but just you! Everyone else on the dock," I sigh. Frustration has caused my t-shirt to become dominated by large sweat patches, and even in the night's cooler air, I can feel perspiration dripping down the back of my neck too.

Jules climbs into the speedboat, fingers immediately moving for some flatter boxes toward the floor. Beside them, I notice several canisters of what I assume is either gasoline or petrol for the boat itself. I guess Sephy wanted accelerants to compliment her pyromancy. It's smart.

"This will be the armour, I think. Can't flat-pack assault rifles—" he muses, passing the boxes to Sephy with gentle care.

She pulls a small knife out of her cleavage and begins to pry open the tops of the wooden crates that have been nailed shut.

"Looks like Kevlar to me. Good call." She opens the crate fully, revealing several garments. I could be wrong— but they look like corsets.

"Well— I did tell him I didn't want to look like G.I Joe," she mutters, bringing out some other bits of clothing and looking down at them.

"Shoes!" Jules calls, tossing boxes this time over the starboard side of the vessel. Its bow points directly at the house around half a mile up the beach, still bobbing as we work onward into the night.

After around an hour and a half, we've finally taken a full inventory. One Bazooka, much to Sephy's dismay, fifty small grenades, twenty Colt AR 15 semi-automatic high-powered rifles, and three canisters of accelerant. There are also a few handguns, one of which I recognise immediately as a Smith and Wesson Model 29 revolver. I know this because Dirty Harry was on repeat for months at a cinema I used to frequent back in 1971. You couldn't get away from Inspector Callahan back then.

Sephy, unsurprisingly, quickly claimed the gun as her own.

"Oh my God, I can't believe they actually got me a Smith and Wesson!" She hops from one foot to the other, excited like a little girl as her red hair bounces on her shoulders. "It's so *shiny!*"

"Wait— you requested that enormous thing? *Why?*" I sound incredulous but also can't hide my amusement at the image of her tiny hands clasped around the enormous gun.

"Oh, don't tell me you've never seen Dirty Harry! Clint Eastwood is hot as fuck!" she exclaims, a wide smile making it seem as though she's forgotten what is about to happen.

In only a few hours, we'll be headed back to Mortaria, and it'll be crawling with demons.

"I love that movie," I confess, rubbing the back of my neck with one hand.

"Me too." Sephy blushes, and for a moment, everything feels odd, like I don't know her at all.

I know how quickly she unloads a flaming projectile; know how she takes her whiskey after sex, but other than that? What do I really know about her? Favourite colour? Food? Book? Movie—

As I stare at the girl in front of me, her porcelain features lit by the night sky above, she seems a bigger mystery than ever before.

And yet— I love her.

How is that possible?

We've known each other such a short time, know so little about one another other than how we fight, how we fornicate— but I'd die for her.

"Is that everything?" Sephy asks me as though she's repeating herself. She might well be; I tend to zone out when I start questioning everything between us.

"I think so. We just need to get changed. Have you ever shot a semi-automatic rifle before?" I ask her, watching her face intently.

"Pfft!" She laughs, confident for only seconds before the sound slowly trails off and her face falls. "Nope."

"I'll show you." I keep things straight to the point, clambering down from the boat and bringing the last of the boxes with me. I have clothes here for Jules and me while Sephy is carrying the female attire bundled in her arms.

"Ready?" I ask her, and she nods, turning and taking off back towards the house.

I know the truth in her lack of response. She's not ready. None of us are. How can you be? Going to hell is no picnic, going to war *for* hell— well, it's practically suicide.

I zip up my leather jacket, which comes up high under my throat. It brushes against the stubble that crawls down from my jaw, confining my broad chest. It's fashionable and, most importantly, lined with Kevlar. If it'll stop bullets, I have no doubt it might also protect against a Banshee's claws or a Succubus' jaws, perhaps even some swords and other low-grade weapons as well.

"Ready?" Sephy asks me as she steps into the open living space.

I stare. I can't help it.

She's wearing a black corset, black leather pants, and a bolero that buckles high under her chin and rounds her shoulders with glimmering gold protective pads. She's got a sheath slung low around her hips, and a sword runs the length of her left leg, the opal blade holstered to the outside of her right. She's wearing knee-high boots, corset-laced from ankle to knee, with thick black platform soles that must be at least two inches high.

Her bright red hair is pulled up into a high ponytail off her face; it's an odd look for her. Normally when she goes into Mortaria, she wears something hooded, to hide her identity. Not today though. Today she's returning to reclaim what's hers, loud and proud.

"You look like a badass," I compliment her, and she smirks.

243

"Why thank you. I guess Corporal Sandy has the fashion sense his name would suggest. I'm impressed."

Reaching into her back pocket, she retrieves two leather gloves and pulls them over her hands. They entirely cover her fingers, but wrap back around her wrist, leaving her palms clear for pyromancy.

"You don't look bad yourself." She gestures to me.

"Yeah, I'm surprised. Pretty fashionable for being Kevlar reinforced," I comment, pushing my hands deep into the black khaki pants. In my left hand, an AR-15 hangs, waiting for me to show Sephy how to use it. It's alarmingly casual how I handle something that can cause so much devastation so fast.

From behind Sephy, The Furies emerge from the corridor that leads to several ground-floor bedrooms. They're all wearing leather pants too, but their shirts are made from leather straps that have been bandaged around their torsos in varying arrangements. Erin's dark hair is braided close to her head, and Ericka and Erlea's hair is French braided down their backs in two equally long braids. They're toting their usual weapons, not that I'm surprised. I can't think that Sephy would trust them with assault rifles in her Bermuda beach house.

Luce appears a few moments later.

"Well. It fits—" she expresses, and we all move to stare at her.

She's wearing a leather dress coat, which rises to right under her chin. She has the same boots on as Sephy and leather pants which disappear beneath the billowing tails of the jacket that accentuates her every curve. Her silver hair falls over the black, stark in contrast, and her light blue eyes pop from her face, taking us in as we collectively gawp. She looks more like Luce than she has in a long time.

"What? It's just a coat." She scowls, walking past Sephy and plopping herself down on the couch. Jules smiles at her, the expression almost painful. Nobody knows what to say to her. I mean I know she's back now, but— there's something different. As though some of the darkness she couldn't let go— a kind of snake's skin she couldn't shed.

It would always be a part of her now.

"No sitting. We've got to go." Jules is antsy, his black trousers and leather jacket hanging from him, far looser than mine. It's odd seeing him casual like this. He almost looks like one of those bounty hunters you see on reality TV.

"What's the rush? Excited to walk into a fiery inferno of death and bloodshed?" Sephy crosses the room and nudges him playfully. He shakes his head.

"We want to get this thing done. I'm tired of waiting around. The anxiety is going to give me a stroke," he says, more forward than I'm used to hearing from him.

"I need Xion to get me acquainted with the AR-15, and then we're good. Luce— how exactly does this portal thing work? Xion said it's why the Bermuda Triangle is nicknamed the Devil's triangle. You made it into a gateway, right?" Sephy enquires, and she nods.

"Yep, it'll be a rough ride though. Ships around here always get swallowed by accident. Once we go out there and I speak the passcode, there's no turning back," she explains, and I watch as everyone nods, listening intently.

"A passcode? Really? How mythical and epic—" Sephy chortles.

"Well, it had to be something trade ships could use to access the portal. Blood magic wasn't going to work. Mortal blood is about as useful as toilet water," Luce explains and Sephy looks mildly offended. "Not only that but the portal we're going to use isn't the only thing mystical around here— there's pocket dimensions and all sorts. It wouldn't surprise me if there are whole cities hidden away below the surface," she muses, loosening her high collar as though it's choking her to the point where each breath is a struggle.

"Right—" Sephy mumbles. I watch her posture slump a little, and I can tell she's getting nervous.

We could continue to stand around here all day, dreading what's to come— or we can just keep moving forward, meeting the inevitable head-on.

"Come on, Sephy. Let's go, and I'll show you how to handle these guns real quick. You guys lock up and, we'll meet you at the boat," I suggest, and everyone begins to move, tired of worrying about what lies just beyond the horizon and even more tired of waiting.

The night opens above us into an expertly woven canvas of diamond stars and an opalescent, low-hanging moon. The high tide rushes the shore, lapping at the sand in a gentle caress. She leads me down onto the beach, not looking back as we pass sparse grasses interspersed with a thick spattering of rocks and shells.

When we're both standing on the sand, she turns to me, gaze hard as steel, set on moving forward like a bullet from a gun after the trigger has been pulled in haste. It's something I've missed in her, the intense desire to fight, to triumph, no matter the cost.

"Let's do this." She keeps her eyes trained on the gun in my hand, all business.

245

"Right. Okay, so you know the basics, I assume. Keep the thing pointed away from your face and in a safe direction, finger off the trigger until you're ready to shoot, yes?" I query her with a single cocked eyebrow and she rolls her eyes.

"Yeah, yeah. I'm not a total noob. I've just never used a semi-automatic before." She flips her long ponytail over the shoulder of her bolero, the gold shoulder pad glimmering brightly in the moonlight as it takes in the dull sheen and turns it sharp, angular.

"Okay, well. Take the gun—" I hold it out to her, and she snatches it from my grasp, every one of her movements rushed, frantic even.

"You clear the chamber by pulling back the charging handle." She carries out my instructions without so much as a pause. No round flies from the gun, indicating that the chamber is empty.

"Now, lock the bolt in place with the bolt catch—"

She does this, handling the AR-15 like she's stroking a feral kitten. "Put the safety selector on safety. Just above the pistol grip." I point to it as I round her, walking so I'm peering over her shoulder. She stiffens as my chest pushes flush to her back.

I pass her a loaded magazine from one of the deep pockets of my new khaki pants as soon as she's finished doing what I've asked. It's almost strange, seeing her this compliant.

"Load the magazine into the mag—" I say, but before I can finish, she's clipped it in place. She's far too comfortable with all this. It makes me wonder where she got her experience handling guns.

Maybe Jules taught her?

"And now we close the bolt and pull the charging handle back—" I show her, coming close so my breath tickles her ear. I feel her shudder in front of me.

She shifts the weight from her left to right as I hear the bullet enter the chamber.

"Disengage the safety?" she prompts me, her voice a husk. I can't tell what she's thinking, but I can feel my own body becoming extremely alert at her proximity. The humidity makes my skin clammy, the breeze only just strong enough to ruffle my hair. I breathe in the salt of the sea air, the scent one I'm not familiar with but enjoying more than I want to admit.

"Yes, now point that way to shoot—" I place my hands on her hips, and I feel her inhale sharply as I turn her ninety degrees clockwise so she's facing down the length of the sandy expanse.

I look out over the ocean, wondering if perhaps it's the conquerable endlessness that makes me feel so at peace here. I feel almost free as if the past doesn't exist here, as if I'm simply a man, no demon, with no dark past, just me.

Alex.

"Okay, so, finger just beneath the safety, elbow pointing down to the ground." My fingers stroke her outer arm, nudging it into position. "Feet apart." I kick the inside of her boot so her right foot is forced out, shoulder width apart, trying to focus.

I place my hands now on her wrists, breathing heavy into the crook of her neck as I guide her hands to position the stock just to the edge of her pectoral.

She holds the handguard with her free hand, and I direct her to a target. It's the trunk of a palm tree just down the beach from us. She aims too high.

"No, aim just below with this—" I whisper, feeling the weight of the gun through the back of her shoulder, pressing into me.

She aligns the sight, a natural in all things except apparently love.

"Can I shoot now?" she asks me, the scent of cinnamon pluming from her as she turns her head to the left.

I inhale sharply, holding her from behind.

"Disengage the safety— and then shoot," I breathe, shifting my weight so I'm pushing into her behind, giving her something to lean against.

I hear the click of the safety being turned off then feel her stomach muscles tauten as she inhales, I inhale too, bated breath caught just beneath her jaw, her long tendrils of fragrant hair tickling the side of my face.

She presses the trigger and the rifle shoots off several rounds, kicking back into her shoulder. As the casings fly from the chamber, I feel her exhale, like a weight has been lifted from her.

She turns to me, re-engaging the safety and clearing the chamber by pulling back on the bolt.

"Okay, I think I got it— Thanks." She doesn't make eye contact with me, but I notice the goosebumps climbing down her arms, her dilated pupils, the way her lips are slightly parted as she sucks in air. She's burning, just like I am, at our proximity.

"Hey, Sephy?" I push my lips together in a firm line, blood leaving them fast.

"Yeah?" She looks up at me now, pointing the AR-15 barrel-down toward the sand. I hear the slosh of the waves lapping against the shore and the slight humid tropical breeze in the silence that follows as I stare at her.

"What's your favourite colour?" I blurt, feeling ridiculous. She cocks an eyebrow.

"Black— same colour as my soul. Why, what's yours?" she poses the same question.

"Orange— like your hair." The answer slips from me in an overly sentimental gush. She smirks, lightening the tone before she even opens her mouth to speak.

"Could've fooled me. I didn't think you knew any other colours existed but black, what with your wardrobe choices." She snorts, obviously uncomfortable all of a sudden.

"It's nice here. Maybe — maybe we could come back — you know after this is all over?" I suggest. She frowns.

"Xion, please don't."

She looks unmistakably bereft.

"Why not? Can't I want to come and spend time with you here without it being the end of the world?" I ask her, and she shakes her head.

"I can't think about it. I can't even acknowledge there might be an after. Hope is lethal. You should know that better than anyone." She blinks fast, pursing her lips as a divot forms between her eyebrows. Her face is ghostly pale in the moonlight, taking me back to her deathly complexion after the resurrection.

"So, what— we just accept we're all going to die?" I ask her, and she shakes her head, biting down on her bottom lip and shuffling on the spot.

"No. I just— I need to get through this day, and then the next— and then the one after that. Maybe, maybe one day I'll look up and realise I've made it. But until then— I can't make plans. Least of all with you." Her words sting, but I can see she's barely holding it together so don't push it.

"I'll make plans for the both of us. Then, when we come out the other side, I'll surprise you," I vow, and she smiles, tilting her head at me and staring, blushing like a schoolgirl.

It's sweet, innocent even, and I can't help but smile right back at her like an idiot.

"Thanks—" she mumbles.

I step forward, placing a slow kiss on her forehead. She doesn't relax, the tension evident as ever in her shoulders as she leans into me ever so slightly.

"No. Thank you. I've never wanted to survive so badly before. It's because of you— even if you don't realise." I try to make the moment deep, sentimental, but she steps back as if my proximity has become quickly painful for her.

"Yeah, I guess you need me around. How else will you know how girly your lavender obsession is?" she quips, shooting me a cheeky grin though it doesn't reach her eyes that continue to sheen with undiluted sadness. I know there's no use forcing things between us, know there's no use trying to make this into what I want it to be.

Perhaps then, as I stare at her, that resistance is what makes me love her so much. She won't be cornered or forced into what I want her to be, so in the moments when she's right there on the same page as me, looking into my eyes and being all I need her to be, it means so much more.

"Shall we do this then?" she suggests, reluctant as she sighs, and I nod.

Together, we walk back up the length of the beach toward the jetty and the others.

I know she can't think about the future, about us.

Unfortunately, it's all I can think about.

21

BEYOND THE SEA

LUCE

SEPHY AND XION GROW closer, a semi-automatic rifle clutched in her palm. They walk at ease, as though one has always been beside the other. It makes me sad.

I'm leaning back against the starboard side of the military-grade speedboat. It bobs beneath my partially distributed weight, my knee-length dress coat fluttering around my legs. Crossing my heavy knee-high boots atop the damp wooden planks underfoot, I try to appear casual.

Despite my outward appearance, my mind is whirring. Sephy hasn't mentioned a destination for this little journey back into Mortaria, but I have more than a few ideas.

Jules gets ready to cast off from the jetty, and The Furies examine various parts of the vessel they're standing in, faces illuminated by the stark neon lime of computer panels that are embedded into the gunmetal grey control desk at the bow of the boat.

"That was quick—" I mumble.

Xion shrugs.

"She didn't need all that much instruction. Girl's a natural." He claps Sephy on the shoulder, smiling down at her. She doesn't return the expression, face pale and ambivalent. I can see the fear, stirring like a growing shadow behind her pupils as loose tendrils of her hair are lifted by the sea-scented breeze.

The three of us board the boat, heavy boots loud against the metal deck beneath.

"Hey, Sephy?" I ask as Jules starts the engine. He has a metal joystick sheathed in thick leather in his grasp and looks over the flashing dash in front of him as we begin to pull away from the shoreline.

"Yeah?" she responds, leaning back so she's sitting on the port side across from me, her hands clutching the steel railings that rim the entire outer edge of the vessel.

"Well, have you thought about where we are going once we get into Mortaria?" I ask, and she purses her lips.

That's a no then.

"I didn't get that far. I still don't know if we're going to make it to the mainland. Isn't the Sea of Shadows crawling with demons?" she asks, voice rising against the growing roar of the engine as we take off over the water, gliding as if we are merely skimming the surface of a frozen lake. If it weren't for the thick spray coating the back of my clothes, I'd think we were flying.

"Yes. But I had a thought. We're gonna need an army, right?" I ask her, uncrossing my legs as the boat hits maximum velocity. Jules turns to me, bringing two fingers to his lips and capturing my attention with a high-pitched whistle.

"So, I just keep going until I reach the coordinates?" he calls, and I nod, hair whipped back from my face, breeze rushing over my ears and turning them chill. His eyes are half closed against the onslaught of the sea air as he turns back to continue steering us over the frothy cresting waves of the Atlantic. The further we get from the shallows, the feistier they seem to become.

I look out over the ocean, knowing the spot well. The Devil's Triangle is merely a nickname for the area, but what we're looking for is an exact spot where the three points of said triangle centrally converge. It's here, and only here, that the portal can be accessed. If we are even a few hundred feet off it won't work. We've done our best to keep the entrance as hard to access as possible, though even I can't deny we've had more than a few ships cross over and never find their way back.

"Let me know when we get there!" I exclaim, voice straining after only a few minutes of trying to talk over the whirring machinery that continues to launch us forward across the vast expanse of water.

"So, what's your idea? I'll take any help I can get. You think you can get me an army?" Sephy enquires, eyes glinting under the spread of stars. Her high ponytail is caught up in the speed of the boat, the length of it trailing out behind her like ribbons soaked bloody.

"Well, I was thinking, and I think we should head for Golgotha down the river. There's underground accommodation there, and if you relight the beacon, then we should be able to start raising some

Doppels again, even without the sun. We'll need the numbers to fight for us," I muse.

"That's a good idea. Golgotha it is." Her gaze hardens, satisfied, before turning to Xion. He nods, approving of the idea as well. My heart swells a second, more than it has in a while, so much so that I'd almost forgotten it was capable of anything other than grief.

"Thanks for— trusting my judgement," I say, voice swallowed by the slosh of the waves and the smacking of water against the sides of the boat. Sephy doesn't reply, so my eyes drift left, resting on the spines of Erin, Ericka, and Erlea as they stand steadfast to the rear, watching the rotors blend the seawater into a dense, salty foam. I can't see their faces, but they look surprisingly serene, clutching their weapons to them and staring out at the heavens birthed on the horizon.

The sky soars overhead, a thick dark skin of beauty, masking the harsh realities of the world below.

"We're here!" Jules calls, cutting the engine.

We bob atop the waves, none of us speaking for a few moments as we simply bask in the lush silence broken only by the shifting of the ocean.

"So, what now?" Sephy asks, pushing herself so she's standing straight, staring at me.

"Now, I announce the passcode." I get to my feet, looking up at the sky. We're surrounded by water on all sides, the moon the only light source as the computer panels on the dash have gone dead. Everything is still; everything is waiting for me to speak.

"Open sesame," I call out, loud, into the air.

"Oh, for Christ's sake!" Sephy snorts, and I glare at her over one shoulder.

"What?" I demand, but she can't wipe the smile off her face.

"Cliché much?" she teases me.

"I can guarantee I used this as a passcode before any sorry mortal, Sephy. What can I say? I'm a trend starter."

I wait for her sarcastic retort, but none comes as she's distracted by a sucking noise rising from the surrounding water.

Suddenly, as if the heavens have been listening, the ocean begins to move. Not like during a storm, but mythically, magically.

The water swirls, rising, and my knuckles empty of blood as I grip onto the railing behind me. It's been a while since I entered Mortaria this way, centuries even, and yet I've not forgotten the unpleasantness of the experience. Not one bit.

Clouds draw in overhead, eclipsing the watchful constellations and darkening the scene as the moon is all but erased from the sky. The pull of the water is soon greater than any of my fellow passengers expect as they too cling onto the edges of the boat, which is tossed from wave to wave as though it were no more than a child's rubber duck at bath time.

"What's happening?" Erlea yells, tone clipped as her braids are blown sideways, caught in the wind. Rogue pieces of hair dampen with the rising sea spray flying up into the air, becoming stuck against her forehead.

"What she said!" Sephy cries out, staring directly at me as the boat undulates, caught in the beginnings of the portal now.

It won't be long.

"It's okay; this is how the portal opens!" I call back, gripping ever harder onto the starboard side of the speedboat and watching as lightning strikes, illuminating a newly formed blanket of clouds overhead, hanging thick and impenetrable.

The water is rabid now, a sucking, groaning, tumultuous animal wanting to devour us whole.

The boat is caught in its hungry clutches, and I know that there's no turning back.

This is it.

We're going back to Mortaria.

It's as though, at this thought, the portal becomes even more desperate to consume, the ocean's waters being pulled anti-clockwise and making it appear as though someone has pulled out the plug of the seabed, intending to drain it dry.

The cacophony reaches its crescendo as we are tossed from left to right, dragged unceremoniously forward, and drenched in icy salt water over and over.

Fish are upended, flying into the boat, slapping to and fro upon the deck, drowning in the night air. Erlea spears several before any of us have the chance to try and return them to where they came from, the blood almost immediately washed away as though it never even spilt.

The whirlpool shifts, getting faster and faster as the boat tilts, causing all of us to hang on in any way we can as we move closer to the centre of the portal.

Xion's got his arm around Sephy, his other hand taut on a rope knotted fast around the railing behind him. She's got a hand raised, shielding her eyes from the continual onslaught of seawater, red hair a dank shade of auburn. She clings to Xion by the fabric of his jacket, arms peppered with goosebumps from the cold.

"Hang on!" I cry, looking out over the bow.

As we're pulled at increasing speed down into the eye of the whirlpool, water continues to batter us on all sides, the front of the vessel rotating so it's now pointing directly into the abyss below.

We all brace ourselves, The Furies clinging onto the weapons crates, which have fortunately been fastened down with multiple ropes, and Jules clinging to the joystick as if he could even attempt to steer us any longer.

Screams fill my ears as the darkness consumes us, and all we can do, as ever, is hang on for dear life as we are dragged kicking and screaming back to hell.

XION

Groans fill the humid air as I stir, face down on the metal grain of the deck. It tastes like steel and salt; a fact I wish I didn't know.

"Ow—" I exclaim, cheek throbbing where it impacted the floor.

"Well— that sucked." Sephy staggers to her feet, one eye twitching with pain as droplets of saltwater fall from her leather pants.

"I feel like I got thrown up by the sea," I moan, pulling myself to my feet and pushing my sodden hair back from my forehead. It lies wet against my skull, seawater trickling slowly beneath the collar of my jacket.

"Well— maybe you all should have thought of that before you hacked down The Hollow," Luce suggests, the most composed of any of us. She flattens her sodden silver hair to her skull, shaking the tangled mess like a wet dog. Her pale cheeks are flushed, but otherwise, she continues to lean against the railing, casually observing our pain.

"Hey, I could have convected here— kind of wish I had now. But I thought I'd be a team player, you know, for morale." Sephy scowls, dishevelled.

"Inspiring—" I can't stop smirking.

"Hey, shut up. At least you're not the only one who looks like a drowned rat—" We start to bicker, but Jules quickly interrupts us.

"This is—" he breathes the words like they're sacred, leaning over the computer console and staring out over the horizon.

I forgot. He's never been here before.

Following his gaze, I find a pristine black mirror sprawling in all directions, its crystalline surface so still it looks like glass.

"That's—" I frown. It seems wrong somehow.

"There's no tide. It's because of the sun. We have— or had — solar tides, because the mass of the sun is closer to the atmosphere here than it is on Earth. I guess that's what you get for having a synthetic sun," Luce ponders as we float upon a sea of what could be liquid sin.

The wine-coloured sky spreads from horizon to horizon, like an arterial blood spill.

"It's so dark," Jules comments.

"It's not usually. Usually, the sun never sets, it's actually kind of weird, not having night or day—" she explains like a weary tour guide. The butler only continues to gaze with wide eyes, pupils fully dilated as though he's struggling to take it all in.

"Jules, we should move—" Luce prompts him, and he shakes his head as though trying to break a physical hold that the view has over him.

"Right. Sorry. Let's hope everything still works after that— little entrance," he mumbles, flicking several switches. The dash flickers into life, stuttering momentarily as it warms up, the computers illuminating Jules' face in a haunting green light, a stark contrast to the surrounding dark.

He turns the key in the ignition, taking his hand and wrapping it around the joystick as the engines burst into life with a roar. The water around us ripples, the flawless reflective sheen disturbed by us and us alone.

The boat launches forward, away from the horizon on which we've materialised, reaching top speed in only seconds as the tideless expanse offers no resistance. The gunmetal grey steel of the boat slices through the surface like a pair of ice skates on a frozen lake, precise and effortless.

My hair is blown back from my face yet again, the humid Mortarian air cooler than usual but no less packed with moisture. I feel the water on my skin begin to evaporate and stare at Sephy as she looks out over the side of the boat.

"What's that?" She points to a small island, yet more black, barely discernible amongst the onyx of the water below.

"I don't know. An island I guess— Nobody has ever really explored Mortaria outside of the city limits. It's never been important. I mean with the way the demons suffered after the sinners colonised and The Gods of Ancient were overthrown, I suppose Haedes just figured there was nothing out there," I guess, standing and steeling myself against the breeze.

"Huh— weird," Sephy's response is laced with curiosity unsated, but she doesn't question any further. I guess she has too much to worry about to allow herself to wonder.

I look back over my shoulder, to where The Furies continue to stare out over the back end of the boat, watching the waters fly beneath us like air. I can't help but wonder, as they stare at the horizon, what exactly lies on the other side. The portal brought us there, sure, but there must be something out there other than just more water, right?

"There it is!" I hear Jules call, his jacket ruffled by the speed of the vessel as we race closer and closer to where he's pointing. In the distance, I watch as the Mortarian coast, The Obsidian Shores, comes into view. The Sanguine Forest and the steep cliffs that leave no option but a sharp drop into the waters below are off to the right, the red of them more noticeably scarlet than ever before now the sky is dark.

We all fall silent, the atmosphere between us tense as we approach the coast, the cliffs crowding the ground obsidian sand rising and towering high above. Usually, you'd see horses and carriages journeying along the clifftops, but no longer.

As we inch forward, the engine slows to a low purr, and Luce's eyes narrow in a squint. She turns to Sephy.

"Sephy— what happened to the river?" she demands, and Sephy's eyes widen.

"Oh shit! I didn't even think about that. I saw it when I came to get the shard, but I didn't think—" she murmurs, looking angry at herself as her eyes blaze with sudden frustration.

"You mean the river—"

256

"Is all dried up and crusty, just like Pandora's fashion sense? Yep."
She smirks at her own joke, but Luce looks seriously concerned.

"This is bad. She's really serious about tipping the scales. We might
have even less time than I originally thought— and what's worse—
we can't get to Golgotha on foot. Not with all this," she gestures to
the weapons, still stacked, damp and sea-weathered, at my spine.

"Okay, so what do we do?" My voice is deep with hope that this can
be solved quickly and quietly.

"Pandora— she doesn't have the power to actually stop souls coming here— so my guess is she's probably stopped the flow at the
source," she muses, jostling slightly in place.

The engine of the boat promptly dies as we reach the mouth of the
river.

"But— isn't this the source of the river?"

Luce shakes her head.

"Partially. The seawater mixes with the flow from the Spring. If
not, there isn't enough water volume for proper flow through," Luce
explains.

Sephy squints at the crenulations of land, breathing calm and
steady.

"It looks like she's blocked off the mouth there too—"

Luce and I peer in synchronised time over the bow of the boat,
finding a makeshift dam there.

"I mean it wouldn't be as hard as usual to stop the flow— there's no
tide —" I theorise.

"What a mess," Luce whispers, guilt evident in the depths of her
dilating pupils.

"Look, I'll go and get rid of that dam. Then I'll go to the spring
and get things moving again. You guys, sit here and wait for me—
and don't touch anything." Sephy winks, clicking her fingers before
disappearing into a plume of scarlet red flames and leaving the metal
beneath my feet suitably warm.

I see her reappear near the mouth of the river, watching closely
as she sets whatever it is blocking the water's path unceremoniously
aflame. Smoke rises, and I follow its path through the air, consumed
by the stillness of the world around me.

This isn't the Mortaria I know.

As if my thought has prompted fate to rain down yet more pain,
more problems, a sudden and unmistakable clang rings out into the

air. The boat lurches from where previously it had floated, serene, upon the motionless mirror of the water.

Jules, Luce, and The Furies stagger sideways, before regaining their balance with clumsy and surprised countermotion.

"What the hell was that?!" Jules calls out, face draining of blood.

"Cthulhu." One of the many names of Leviathan's chosen Demon Lord falls from Erin's lips, causing us to turn and stare at her. Seconds pass, and ripples can be seen forming circles around the boat's circumference.

The Furies draw their weapons, and Jules moves to the crates behind us, ripping them open without care and handing us guns.

"Be careful you don't accidentally hit the boat. I don't need a sinking ship and a sea-full of demons below—" Jules orders, and I can tell he's both used to issuing orders like this and more nervous than I've ever seen him. I know he fought demons before, has seen the mystical, but the man is now encapsulated in a world that isn't his own, a world that belongs once more to them. They have the upper hand, and he knows it.

I load an AR-15, following the sequence of the steps I'd shown Sephy what feels like a lifetime ago in expertly practised motion. Fluid, fast, trained. The chamber gives a click as a bullet is loaded inside and I flick the safety off.

Looking to the shadows which encircle us, I stare at Luce, The Furies, and then finally, to Jules.

We have no choice but to hold these things off until Sephy returns. We can't lose the boat or the contents. Not if we hope to succeed somewhere down this very dark and twisted road.

Placing the rifle up and into the groove between my pectoral and shoulder, I look down the sights, aiming at the shadows beneath the surface.

"Let's go to work."

22

DON'T YOU FORGET ABOUT ME

SEPHY

FLAMES RELINQUISH THEIR TENDRILS from my body as I reappear within the Sanguine Forest. It's the third attempt I've made at finding The Spring of Souls, seeing as I've never been here before, and I think I've finally got it right.

The sound of Banshees rings loud in my ears, my stomach a pit of bottomless anxiety. I am painfully aware of it all; the beat of my heart, the rushing of air into my lungs, the sharp edge to the breeze, the snapping of individual twigs, and the rustle of bloody leaves.

Paranoid, I spin on the spot, squinting into the shadows cast long by the surrounding trees, finding dark shapes moving among the many trunks, bark black and cracked.

I knew this wouldn't be easy, but I guess I hadn't thought about exactly how many demons I'd be facing. I thought the estate had been overrun but standing here with my boots sinking slightly into the ruddy earth, I come to realise, comparatively, that was child's play.

I turn my focus to the task at hand, finding what I'm hoping is the spring in the ground only several feet away. It's not much to look at, a jumble of rocks stacked precariously on soil scattered with organic vermillion debris.

I thought it would be some kind of monument, but as ever, I'm underwhelmed by the mystical.

I hear the hesitant tread of a demon approaching and realise I'm going to need some cover.

I *can* unplug this thing.

I take a deep breath, shake my head as if this will physically clear my muddled thoughts, and act.

Standing in the centre of the naturally occurring ring of trees, I hold out both palms, casting a line of flame to the ground at the edge of the grove. I create a makeshift half-border between the trunks behind me, flames rising and crackling, smoke twisting high above the sanguine canopy overhead and transforming the air around me thick with an acrid and metallic singe.

I wanted this to be stealthy, undetected, but something tells me that with this many hostile entities in the vicinity, I'm going to need to use my pyromancy skills to full effect. That means my attempt at any kind of subtle entrance has been firmly shot to shit.

So, I guess it's time to announce my return— I muse, body eclipsed by the surrounding crescent of flame, a small sigh of what could be relief escaping my lips.

Ghostly white eyes and equally bloody chasms stare through the fire, biding their time until they're ready to make the leap over its hot flickering tongues, to leave their fatal mark on my flesh.

Impatient now, I storm forward, closing the space between me and the blocked spring, kicking scarlet leaves out of my way and setting about moving the stack of rocks. I heave them, veins popping beneath the thin veil of my skin, muscles taut and defined, as I throw the first boulder to my left. It thuds on impact, rolling a few times before stopping just inside the voluptuous curve of the firewall.

I sense more demons gathering, the hairs on the back of my neck standing to attention, so work as quickly as I can. I haul the boulders one after another, sweat bursting from my skin and rolling down the back of my neck in protest of the growing heat.

As I'm moving one of the last boulders, I catch a shadow descending overhead, cloaking me, in my peripheral vision. Turning, the rock tumbles to the ground, and I'm suddenly face to face with a Phobia that's dropped down from the overhanging tree branches, a thick, sticky-looking black web attached to its back end.

I reach out, grabbing its two front legs in swift time, acting on pure instinct and without thought as I pull the two appendages free from its body with a shoulder-wrenching yank. Blood, thick, cold, and black in the half-light of the wine-stained sky spurts from the arachnid torso as it falls, flailing, to the floor.

I set it alight without a second thought and head back to work.

As I do so, I realise that my anxiety is dissolving.

I'd once been so afraid of a single demon, and now I'm surrounded and still carrying on. Funny how what was once grotesque is now my new normal. Just another day in the life of Sephy Sinclair.

I shoot a few fireballs up into the canopy overhead, causing whatever other demons are hanging there to hopefully scatter, and watch as the entire leafy blanket goes up in flame.

Whoops.

I'm finally at the last remaining boulder and so haul it up before throwing it behind me and toward the blazing crescent.

As the last stone is dislodged, I see it.

A small sputter, a trickle, then a gush. The eerie glow of The River Styx's soulful waters runs through the soil at greater force than I would have expected, probably because of the backup.

Glancing over my shoulder, I find the demons encroaching now, a Banshee leaping through the flames at my back, its dripping teeth bared in a snarl.

I don't pause, watching as it crouches to pounce.

I let it, twirling on the spot and waiting to feel my foot impact against its chest in a spinning back kick, sending it flying. I smile, content as it lands with a high-pitched thud among the blaze, writhing, and then begins howling, fur catching light.

Booyah.

I see more demons coming to take its place, not only from behind me but from in front of me too. Their eyes are numerous, hungry.

Time to get back to the others.

I smile into their demonic faces.

"Sephy, out." I flash them the peace sign, causing them to falter as the movement comes, unexpected, startling them like they expect me to summon The Eternal Flame.

The blaze of convection swallows me in the split second they're distracted, right before they close in, taking me back to Jules, Xion, Luce, and The Furies. My very own not-so-happy go-lucky band of no-good meddling kids.

I reappear beside Xion, the sound of gunfire ringing loud in my ears. The boat is not the tranquil vessel I left behind. Instead, it is now being tossed from left to right by barely visible shadows lurking beneath churning water.

"What the hell?" I exclaim, the semi-automatic causing Xion's shoulder to judder with recoil beside me. He turns his head slightly, shooting me a sideways glance before refocusing on whatever it is he's aiming for.

"Kindred of Cthulhu," he bites out, eyes steely as they squint into the darkness.

A tentacle flies up from the depths, thick as a beanstalk, heading right for us, all slime and suckers.

It nears the boat, the girth of it alone threatening to fully submerge one side. Luckily for us, Erin lands an arrow central to one of its topmost suction cups, causing it to recoil momentarily.

On the starboard side behind me, something with reptilian eyes stirs, slamming into the hull, pushing us closer and closer towards the tentacled terror.

We need to move, and fast.

I glance around the deck where Jules, Luce, and The Furies are staring hesitantly over their shoulders at me, wondering what I'm going to do next.

It catches my eye, matte gunmetal grey beneath the railing on the opposite side of the deck; a petrol canister slick with the seawater tossed up over the side, first by the portal and now demons.

I make a dive for it, grabbing the handle and unscrewing the cap, throwing it to one side, careless, and shoving Xion out of the way.

"Move!" I bark, upending the canister into the water and watching as the thick contents glug from inside and spill, forming a puddle of unassimilated gunk that refuses to meld with the sea.

"Jules, start the engine!" I call back over my shoulder.

I hear the roar of it only moments after the echo of my voice has died, relief flooding me.

"Go!" I shout, clicking my fingers and letting a spark jump high into the air. It fizzles, falling fast before it hits the surface of the petroleum puddle I've just unloaded.

In a single moment, the entire thing catches light, flames flickering into sudden and unapologetic existence, the blaze blanketing the demons beneath. I could swear I hear them screaming, the sound inhuman, but it could be the squeal of the engines and the froth of the water coming together in a sick harmony. Perhaps it is only in my imagination that a tentacled monstrosity feels real pain at my hand, let alone acknowledges it.

I dash to the other side of the boat, boots struggling for hold on the sea-slick metal, grabbing another petrol canister and pushing past The Furies who stand steadfast, looking out over the back of the boat.

I let the contents pour from the canister yet again as I tip it upside down without pause, peppering the waters in my wake like fatal and explosive breadcrumbs.

I don't want to be followed.

I let loose another spark, setting a thick trail of fire ablaze behind us, and watch as the ripples of the demons below the surface die away.

They're gone.

For now.

The smell of petrol is thick in my nostrils, coating the back of my throat too. My hair whips back from my face as I turn to look out over where the river is now flooding the dry barren crack in the earth it left behind. The gush from The Spring of Souls meets with the ravenous sea water as it screams down the dry riverbank, reclaiming what's been lost.

Xion is staring too, Jules gripping the joystick with white knuckles as the ocean before us surges from the motion of the boat, filling the mouth of the river over and over with salty froth like the foaming jaws of a rabid dog.

Luce looks at me, nodding in approval as her icy blue irises capture the flames eating into the darkness we're leaving behind. Something like respect sets the lines of her face into definite and unwavering appreciation as she pushes her silver hair behind one ear.

The unending tilt and sway of the boat are enough to make anyone sick, but as we move into the narrow confines of the river, I find myself caught up in the memory of waking up on this same river with a shitty hangover courtesy of Haedes.

I smile, the image of me spinning on a barstool coming back in a rush of neon lights and lowered inhibitions, Xion's disapproval a blur before my eyes.

Demons move from the dark shadows of the forest which encloses the riverbank as we approach, interrupting my nostalgia, and I set to igniting the ruddy earth on either side of the swelling current, buying us some cover as the eerie white water rises higher than I've ever seen it. The river is rabid, moving fast and raising the boat so we're nearly at the same height as what had once been steep banks.

Up ahead, the rising water levels have swept up numerous Gondolas from the depths of the dry and cracked riverbed that's spent several months exposed. They swirl now, obstructing our path, fast-moving wooden projectiles.

"Move!" I bark, needing to be in several places at once as Xion replaces me on the starboard bow. He begins to fire into the rising flame of my makeshift defensive walls without falter, aiming for the slinking forms with glowering eyes and wide gaping smiles, barely visible now in the shadows beyond.

I lose my balance momentarily, but Erlea catches me by the wrists, helping me to stand upon the shifting deck. I feel like I'm in one of those walkthrough carnival fun houses, except it isn't fun, and there's no acne-ridden teenager looking bored senseless who holds the power to make it all stop with the simple flick of a switch.

I twist, not having time to thank Erlea for catching me as I clamber up next to Jules.

"Incoming!" he yells, visibly flinching as the surging river tosses several gondolas up into the air. I raise my palms without second thought, launching dense flaming projectiles into the once elegant boats and watching them smash into pieces as they fall back into the ravenous clutches of the river. The shards of wood bob, disappearing beneath the bow of the speedboat, swallowed by our relentless momentum.

"Woah—" Jules is staring at me, so I wink at him. I guess he's never seen me fight before, not really, not like this.

I feel a rush of confidence at his impressed gaze, my anxiety gone as I remember who I am. I'm the girl who has bad memories of a hangover on this river because of drinking with her father, who also happens to be Haedes, God of the Underworld. If anyone belongs in this hell hole, I guess that would be me.

We thunder down The River Styx, water flowing clean over the banks in some places and lapping hungrily at them in others. I continue to light the space flanking us where I can, but we're moving so fast it's almost impossible to get complete coverage.

Demons start to slip through, and I watch as Luce pulls back on the string of a military-grade crossbow, letting an arrow fly loose and accurate before launching several daggers at targets that I can't see.

Xion's face is taut as I continue to light up the world around us, destroying more gondolas and even a few demons who've been swept up in the rush of the river's return to power.

Then, Luce calls out.

We're coming to a bend in the river, a meander. On the far side, I see the outlines of fields of endless headstones rising from the previously flat expanse. The river's backlogged speed has gotten us here quicker than I'd expected.

"Sephy, we're here!" Luce points up ahead,

Her face is concerned, pupils dilated.

I see then what she's gazing at as I squint into the sprawling darkness of the mass graveyard.

The place is crawling with demons.

Not that I should have expected anything else.

Inhaling, I turn and move to the crates full of weapons on the port side of the ship, flipping off one of the sodden wooden lids and rummaging inside. I grab the handle of the semi-automatic, biding my time as we approach the meander, boat unstoppable.

"Jules, you're gonna have to dock this thing. I'll cover you." I bark, the sudden sheen of his bald head moving the only acknowledgement that he's heard me.

I look next to The Furies.

"Come on ladies!" I gesture for them to follow me, allowing the air to compress into a scorching fire and then relinquish fast as I rematerialize upon the soil.

The gun is already loaded, luckily for me, and I wonder if Xion had the forethought to load these before we set off.

Thank God for forethought.

I flick off the safety and empty a magazine in a few short seconds, hitting several demons close by and causing them to crumple to the ground. I let the gun drop to the floor, spreading my palms and letting the flame flow from me like fine wine. It drenches everything, setting the ground alight, igniting the yew trees that line the bank and devouring the corpses of the demons, souls and all.

Cover laid, The Furies approach to meet me. The clattering of their weapons rings in my ears and is drowned out only slightly by the smashing of their heavy, practised tread growing louder with each passing second.

There're demons everywhere, and I slam my foot down hard, sensing the Gorgonian before it has a chance to wrap itself around my leg, smashing its skull beneath my foot. Blood and bone explode outward in a sick and fatal firework.

Xion opens fire from the boat behind me, and I turn to find him taking down several Banshees heading directly toward him, bullets peppering their flesh and tearing the air apart with ease.

Luce helps Jules kill the engines and prepare to anchor the vessel, jumping out over one side and dragging a thick rope toward one of the many metal poles. They protrude, ugly and unnatural, from the riverbank, presumably where the gondolas docked when waiting to pick up new Sinners before all this had happened.

Xion is at my side before I know it, the scent of pomegranate subtle amongst the stench of burning flesh but undeniably there.

"Sephy, go and light the beacon—" he says breathlessly, gesturing toward the enormous, charred metal dish standing atop what I can discern as a steel man bent double in pain and bearing the entirety of its weight. The thing is central to the graveyard, and there's still about two hundred metres between it and me.

"You got it," I reply, looking back to The Furies.

"Cover Jules and Luce. Xion is coming with me to the beacon—" I yell, voice barely audible over the cries of dying demons and the crackling of Eternal Flame.

Xion flanks me, skin rippling to charcoal beneath the tight confines of his jacket, eyes aglow with the adrenaline of the fight. He belongs here too, in the middle of a warzone. Just like me.

I jump forward, weaving expertly through the line of fire stopping several of the demons, the flames tickling my shoulders a moment as I bring my scorching hot palms down onto the skulls of two encroaching Succubi. They buckle beneath my assault, bursting into flames as their flesh bubbles beneath the direct hit of my scorching hot death grip.

I lash out, powerful and high on adrenaline, on the rush of death, as I break open a Banshee's jaws with my bare hands. It's just like I'd seen Xion do at the estate, and I've been wanting to try it since. As I expected, bone snapping from bone gives me a rush of satisfaction, the demon crumpling to the ground before I set it alight and watch it burn.

"Sephy come on!" Xion hollers, pointing toward the beacon as a smile tugs at my lips. There's a clear path now, flanked on either side by piles of dead bodies, fur, and scales matte with dried blood. They keep coming— relentless, but I have the fleeting chance to get up there and relight the beacon now.

I take it.

I convect the distance, spinning on the spot before the flames have fully left me and kicking a Succubi in the face. Its long claw-like fingers swipe through thin air as it falls back, narrowly missing a chance to bury them in my calf, and I wonder how exactly it was I knew it was there.

Must have been instinct.

Gazing into the dark depths of the charred beacon, a simple bowl atop the steel carved shoulders of a broken man, I wave my fingers, summoning The Resurrection Flame to me without falter.

Once upon a time, I found using my powers almost impossible. But now, now it's second nature, and I'm not sure I'd feel like myself without them.

Instantaneously, the beacon ignites a bright cobalt, a blaze of intention pluming thick with smoke.

The announcement of my presence burns stark into the sunless sky overhead as the battle continues to rage on all sides, demons relentless even still.

I look up through the smoke, giving myself only a second to fixate on the dark jagged silhouette of The Exilia Multum where I know she's watching.

I'm here, and I'm done running, bitch. Come at me.

PANDORA

I pace around the library, skirt sweeping over the wood of the floor. I've showered and changed since my unsuccessful attempt earlier with the shard, forearms now clean of blood but unmistakably scarred with my failure.

The shard is sitting atop a black marble pedestal, which I retrieved via mortals from the alchemy chamber upstairs, and is encased in a glass bell jar for examination. I circle it, a predator assessing its prey. Mortals watch on from the sconce-lit corners of the room, observing me with reverence and half-interest.

Gorgon stands, opposing me, posture stiff as he strokes his silken jawline with a long and indecisive index finger.

"I don't understand it—" I mutter, eyes jumping from the shard to his face and back again.

Hearing the doors to the library open on my left, I glance up, finding the rest of the Demon Lords walking through the doorway to join me in my speculation. I grimace internally. I can't think clearly with them watching me.

"Any luck?" asks, tilting his head as though he pities me. It stirs something within me, something vile and furious uncoiling fast in my gut, something not befitting someone of my poise and power.

"Not yet." I smile, the words forced between my teeth that grind together with frustration.

"Well, we have news," Abraxis announces. Barbas smiles as he tilts his head, noticeably observing the sliver of stone beneath the glass jar. As he approaches it, hands outstretched, several of the mortal guards I've assigned with this most important task step forward, blocking his path.

"No touching, Barbas. That shard is mine," I remind him in a low growl, a warning. I turn back to Abraxis, catching Anubis gazing upon me with bright eyes, a change in look for her of late.

"What is it?" I demand, the side of my face burning as Barbas glowers at me. I ignore him.

"Go to the balcony." Raising a slender arm, golden bangles clatter against one another as Anubis extends a jade-lacquered fingernail to the double doors that remain open behind me.

I spin, skirt flaring out from me in a floral layering of floor-length velvet petals. Striding, I make my way out onto the curvaceous confines of the crescent balcony, standing at the epicentre and gazing out over Mortaria. The sounds of demons are as ever rife in a cacophony of airborne melancholia and pain, but I tune them out with a practised ear. Soon, I see what it is The Demon Lords are so coy about.

"The beacon, it's lit—" I exclaim, finding the blue flame blazing into the otherwise dark shadows of Golgotha. The graveyard sprawls, endless, to my right just before the haze of the horizon blurs the landscape into a thin and distant line, any landmark beyond it entirely indistinguishable.

"And—" Abraxis is at my back now, hands folded in front of his pelvis as I turn to look over one shoulder. His proximity is unwanted, to say the least.

I gaze over the city, noticing what it is I've missed immediately. Perhaps it's because I've seen The River Styx aglow amongst the landscape for far longer than it has been barren.

Rage sputters into existence, a harsh dry blaze that catches between the chambers of my heart, boiling my blood and turning my breath ashen in my lungs.

"How is that possible?!" I spit, scowling at him.

"I'd say you fucked with the wrong Demi-Goddess. She's back, Pandora. Sephy Sinclair has returned." He sounds almost victorious as I spin on the spot, slamming both palms into his solid, muscular chest and watching as he moves back a step, raising his hands in a flimsy and entirely voluntary surrender.

"I will end her!" I ball my fist at my side, sharp nails digging into my palms as my heart races within the corseted confines of my gown.

"Woah, woah! Now hold on. That would be doing exactly what she wants you to do. She clearly wants the shard back. Why risk coming here otherwise? She's only reappeared because of your actions, which we did warn you about by the way—" Gorgon slides across the floor, feet silent as they glide over the woodwork, closing the space between us. He places his hands on the bare flesh of my shoulders, sending an involuntary shudder, rampant, down the length of my spine.

"So, what are you saying?" I growl, watching the other Demon Lords hiding the beginnings of smiles and smirks at the way he's touching me.

"I'm saying that your rage is going to make this easier for her than it should be. You need to stay here and guard the shard, and you need to figure out how to unlock the power within it, which she clearly doesn't want you to have. If there wasn't a way— well, she wouldn't be here." The man before me speaks sense, irritating me immensely.

"I can't just let her infiltrate the city," I argue, words slipping out between fast clenched teeth.

"Of course not. So, send— send Abraxis and some of his Kindred. They can assimilate with mortal soldiers and come back with a status report for you," he suggests.

Abraxis smiles.

"I would be happy to assist. Given that I didn't give you the benefit of the doubt with regards to your retrieval of the shard last time around." He bows his head, worn leather jacket bulging against his obscenely large pectorals.

"And do any of you have any idea why this shard won't allow me access to the darkness inside of it?" I look around at them. Each one has only a blank stare in reply. Anubis and Abraxis share a look, and then their eyes snap back to me.

Something within me stirs, something like instinct.

They know something.

"Why don't you go with Abraxis, Anubis? What better way to prove your new allegiance than by killing those who you once thought of as family?" I suggest.

"I don't see why not. If— you consider letting Osiris go free," she bargains, and I shrug.

"Whatever, we will see how well you fair, shall we?" I watch as her irritation grows evident, teeth chewing visibly on the inside of her cheek.

"Fine." Spinning, she flounces away on one heel, leaving the room and taking Abraxis with her. Lilliana, Barbas, and Katerina go with them, retreating from the library and out into the shadow-casting corridors beyond. I wonder if they came along merely to see me lose my temper at Sephy Sinclair's return. Have I disappointed them with how easily I'd been able to put aside my rage and return to logical thinking? I suppose that's one of the many differences between them and me.

Gorgon looks at me, a sly smile tugging at the corner of his thin lips.

"You look thoughtful—" he says, taking long fingers and stroking the edge of my shoulder.

"I am. I need to borrow your Kindred." I turn to him, eyes wide, lashes fluttering. He straightens, looking down the length of his full nose at me.

"Of course, but why?" he asks, and I smile. Kissing him softly on one cheek, I inhale the earthy scent of his skin made sharp by the unmistakable citrus zest of lime.

"Because it's time, dearest one, that we find the truth of where the loyalties of those among us truly lie."

23

MERCY MERCY ME

LUCE

I WIPE THE BLOOD from my fingertips. It cools with each moment that passes after the death of the demon it belonged to.

We've finally cleared the space. It's taken almost two hours of constant killing, the insistent crunching of bone against bone, the repetitive recoil of a rifle, and gunshots littering the air like random and unexpected notes in a dark jazz ballad.

The Furies are moving charred remains from the edges of the cemetery perimeter out past the gates, and I know I need to get to work.

I trudge over to the crypt, the main office in which Thane and I spent most of our days, inhaling deeply as I push open the heavy, ice-cold steel of the door.

Stepping inside, I find coffee mugs exactly where I left them, Thane's indigo-blue jacket slung over the back of her chair. It was her favourite, and I loved it too. It made her eyes storm with unrivalled intensity.

My internal reverie is shattered as my eyes fall onto the paperwork stacked neatly in my out-tray. As if that matters anymore, despite the fact I'd practically killed myself filling it all out. In fact, the thought of sorting the paperwork for this whole debacle is enough reason for me to throw up my hands and surrender to Pandora, to say, 'Here, it's your stupid job now.'

Then again, even the mass murder and universal apocalypse isn't a fair trade for that amount of paperwork— I mean, hell, I'd be expecting at least an implosion of a nearby neutron star.

I sigh, amusing myself, finding my personality returning slowly, seeping in through the cracks in the dam built strong and thick by the darkness. It's still there, but it feels brittle, the construction flaking

271

away piece by piece and fluttering down through the air to poison the once-clear waters below. I accepted the darkness, succumbed to it, and now I'm honestly having a hard time knowing how much of me is left and how much of it remains.

I grab a bundle of black jumpsuits, hauling them up into my arms, flustered and hot in the humid confines of the crypt-turned-office.

I don't know who will be resurrected first, but if there is any mercy left in this place, it will be people who can be useful, like Nita, or Souldiers from The Ashen Waste.

The last thing I need is a bunch of gluttony sinners turned gaunt pastry chefs instead of an actual army.

Sighing with an odd sense of melancholic nostalgia, I'm surrounded now by the remnants of what had once been my everyday existence, what had once been my normal.

Turning my back on it, I head out the door and into the graveyard, ready to get back to work.

"Woah—" That's all Nita says when I catch her up on everything that's been going on while she's been— well, deader than usual.

"Yeah, so I need your help. As if I don't always—" She smiles at me, sheepish as she pulls her dark curls off her neck. Her skin flushes beneath her standard-issue black jumpsuit as she examines me a moment, and I know she's wondering about the change in my appearance; my ambivalent new hair shade and worn expression.

"It's no problem. Anything else I need to know?" she asks.

"I think that's covered it. We just need fighters," I reiterate. She frowns.

"Well, you know that these Doppels will fall down like a sack of shit the second they hit the Golgotha gates— right?" she asks, cheeks reddening as she cusses. I arch one eyebrow.

"What do you mean?" I ask her, and she shrugs.

"Just that the sun is out now. That's what really keeps the Doppel bodies moving around Mortaria. The beacon helps them rise, but they're bound to stay close to it. You knew that, though— right?" She gives me a hopeful glance as though in her large chocolate eyes I am infallible.

I sigh.

"Yeah, I did. I just forgot. Everything with me has been a little fuzzy lately, ever since—" I halt, not wanting to talk about Thane. I haven't told Nita that she's gone.

"Ever since what, Luce?" She places a soft hand on my shoulder and her kindness weakens my resolve. Everyone else around me, they have this look, like they're constantly wondering in the back of their minds how long it'll be until I flip out or kill someone, but not Nita. Nita has the incredible ability to make me feel like I'm worthy of love, of friendship, even after everything I've done.

"Thane— she left me. She's back with her mother in The Higher Plains now," I admit, biting down hard on my bottom lip as my eyes sting with unwanted tears. Nita nods slowly but doesn't say anything for a few moments as this new information hangs in the air between us like a primed guillotine.

"Well, we will manage just fine without her. You were always my favourite anyway," she replies, placing a second sympathetic and warm hand on my other shoulder. I nod, not wanting to talk about it anymore, and she stares at me with intense respect.

"I need to go and check in on the others, make sure they're getting settled, see if they need anything. You okay to handle this until I get back?" I gesture around to the headstones, and she nods.

"Yes, Boss. I've got this stuff handled." Her face is assuring at the moment I need it most, so I turn on my heel, not wanting to get caught in my own dense and sticky web of emotional debris.

Turning my back on the graveyard, I move toward the fence on the right side of the endless headstone fields. Here, I locate the trap door, newly clear of the usual vermillion leaf pile, and grab onto the steel ring, hauling it up in front of me and slipping beneath the earth. I descend the concrete stairs once I hit the bottom of the ladder and close the hatch behind me, footsteps echoing out in the musty air of the long disused underground maze of crypts. We used these as cells for particularly traumatised sinners once, but as the years have gone on, people seemed to get more and more dazed and less instantly terrified by the prospect of hell being real. Haedes always guessed that television and the relinquishing of serious mass religion were the cause, and I have no evidence to suggest otherwise.

Taking a left, I duck, my platform boots meaning I'm only centimetres from hitting my head on the concrete ceiling. I hurry, taking another left and then a right, knowing the passages like the back of my hand.

Thane and I had crept around down here when work used to be slow; we'd made love in these passages, held each other, and napped in the rooms. Now, however, she's gone, as dead to me as the Sinners waiting to rise from the surrounding earth.

I reach the doorframe of the room Sephy and Xion have taken and knock once on the dense steel, waiting impatiently as the heat in the tunnel battles against the chill concrete of the walls for dominance.

The door squeals open, hinges undeniably haunted by bad maintenance. Sephy is revealed behind it.

"Oh, hey Luce. Everything okay?" she asks, voice tired.

I nod, biting my lip a moment before I fill her in.

"Yeah, everything is great. I just forgot to tell you that the Sinners here, they can't leave Golgotha, without the sun I mean—" She deflates slightly on the spot, but then straightens again almost simultaneously.

"Ah well, just more shit to add to the pile. We'll sort it. We need people on the perimeters anyway, so at least it's not a total waste of time," she suggests, and I agree, faux enthusiasm forcing my face to relax.

"I'll go now and keep watch for any potential problems. I'm feeling kind of restless down here anyway," Xion offers, and Sephy looks back over her shoulder into the tiny room that had been renovated from crypt to cupboard-sized bedroom by none other than yours truly.

"Okay, I think I'm going to rest a little. While I can. I feel like I haven't slept in days," Sephy confesses, and I try to recall the last time any of us had slept for anything even close to a considerable length of time.

"That's because you haven't. Get some rest. If you need anything I'm down the hall on the right," I offer, and she gives a weak smile.

"Thanks."

With that, she shuts the door, and I make my way toward my room, neck aching and feet throbbing. It's strange to me, this mortal weakness. I've known I'm weaker now, but being back here without the power of the sun, I feel it weighing heavier than ever. When I was in the mortal world, I'd been so laced with dark power I felt invincible. But now— now I feel well and truly human.

Fatigue comes in waves, my body protesting with aches deep in my muscles, and I contemplate taking a few hours to catch up on sleep too. Unfortunately for me, however, as I turn into my room and lock eyes on the tempting sight of my bed, my heart begins to pound a frantic rhythm in my chest.

I step through, balling my fist by my side.

Closing the door silently behind me, I turn back to face her, wishing more than ever that I was alone.

"How the hell did you get in here?" I grit my teeth, trying to stop myself from launching across the room and throttling her on top of the mattress.

"Hello to you too, Lucifer." Anubis' voice is civil, too civil, her hair flat and well-kept though her face shows signs of ageing, which I'm only too happy to acknowledge.

"You look like shit," I say, the edge to my voice as newly sharp as if it had just been struck against flint. Sparks fly, in the wake of its impact and Anubis' eyes blaze a hard jet.

"I could say the same for you— didn't think you'd go grey so fast." She smirks, and I twirl a lock of my silver hair around one finger, using all my remaining energy not to murder her where she sits.

"It's silver, actually. All the kids are doing it these days. You wouldn't understand; it's a fashion thing." I leer at her; posture erect and shoulders tense as I take her in, trying to work out why exactly it is that she's here.

Sephy said that she was desperate, but this is just a little sad.

Her body is draped in gold linen, causing her skin to appear jaundiced in the blue light from the sconces Sephy's lit throughout the compound. Her legs are crossed, delicate slender feet encased in gold beaded sandals and her arms rife with gold bangles. They jangle against one another in the silence that sits, noxious, between us.

"Why are you here?" I demand. She cocks her head, dark locks falling over one shoulder, the skin around her eyes papery with stress as she glares at me.

"I wanted to warn you and Thane. I figured I owe you that much—" She speaks as though I should be grateful, as though she hasn't completely betrayed me and ruined everything good in my life.

"Thane is dead," I announce into the chill air, skin cooling now that I've stopped fluttering from one location to the other with anxious energy.

"I— I didn't know—" She looks sad, and my laugh fills the concrete chamber, hollow as it ricochets from the walls.

"Oh, don't you even dare act like you're upset. You're the fucking reason this all happened. You have broken every single vow you took upon becoming a member of The Nexus. And for what? Huh? Tell me. I want to know what was so important you destroyed the lives of your closest friends. You got Haedes killed, Anubis!" I'm out of breath and darkness crawls under my skin, my veins screaming for violence.

"My son—" she begins, but I snort.

"Oh, fuck your son! Your son was the reason I didn't end up resurrecting Ra. Your son is better off without you because somehow, and I don't know how exactly, he's avoided becoming a raving psychopath, even with you for a mother!" I hiss, keeping my voice down for no reason I can discern. She watches me closely.

"The darkness is still within you, even with the shard's intervention. Interesting—" she mutters, and I take a step forward, wrapping my fingers around her silken throat and squeezing. Her eyes bulge in her skull, breath slipping between her fingers like water.

"I don't have time for your shit. I'm busy trying to fix the mess you made. Now, do you have a good reason for being here, or should I just kill you now? I'm sure that would be quite the cherry on top of Sephy Sinclair's day—" I whisper in her ear, feeling her pulse thrum, rapid, beneath my fingertips.

"The Demon Lords, Pandora—" she gasps, but I relinquish my grip only slightly.

"Yes, they have the shard. I know. Anything actually useful?" I demand, and she nods, skin pinching beneath my nails as she moves against my grip. I relinquish my hold, standing over her, watching as she brings lacquered dark nails to the skin, tenderly touching herself.

"Pandora wants to use that shard. She's hell-bent on it. But— you and I both know that without Xion's pendant, that thing is useless. It was clever— making a tether for a tether. I'll give you that. Except now—" She coughs, shaking her head so the mane of her hair shimmers cold in the chill light.

"Now, he's a target," I admonish, eyes steely. I already know this. She's telling me nothing I hadn't already assumed.

"Once they learn— once they know about his pendant, about the missing piece of the tether, it won't just be Pandora you have to worry about. The Demon Lords are growing tired of her. Now they have the Exilia, I fear it is only a matter of time before they try to dispose of her. The shard would be the perfect boost in power for any one of them." Her voice comes in hurried wisps, like a faucet turned on during a drought.

"Do you know where Yama and Muerta are?" I ask, not entirely sure why I haven't tied her up yet. Then again, if I know The Demon Lords

276

and Pandora like I think I do, they aren't going to give up jack shit if I take her hostage. I'm sure they don't trust her any more than I do.

"No, I went to The Indicatus Courts shortly after all this happened; they weren't there. Yama's hammer was gone too," she explains, and I wonder where they are, if they're still alive.

"Are you happy about the mess you've made? Are you proud?" I ask her, devastatingly serious in my expression as she gives a heavy exhale.

"I didn't know she would turn out the sun. I didn't think she was that reckless," she admits.

I cock an eyebrow, stare drenching her with disdain.

"Yeah well, I guess now you get to live with the consequences. I don't know, even if we get rid of Pandora, that Mortaria will ever be how it was. Everything has changed." I turn from her, feeling her sad cold eyes baring into my spine.

"I just want to get Osiris out— that's all I want now," she pleads, imploring me unsuccessfully with her tone.

"I agree. I don't think he should be punished for your mistakes. Having you as a mother is punishment enough."

She sags under the weight of my words, a limp pathetic thing. I've never thought of her so far from the Titan she once was as I do now.

"I'll do anything I can to help you."

"You can't stay here. You don't have that right anymore. Go back to The Demon Lords, to Pandora. They're your family now." I dismiss her. I don't know what the consequences of letting her walk from here freely will be, but I don't think anything she can single-handedly accomplish can be any worse than what's already happened. She's more of a risk among us than not.

I continue to stare at her, the strong features of her face twisted ugly with guilt.

She doesn't say she's sorry. I guess because, even if she did, I wouldn't believe her. She isn't sorry about the hurt or the destruction she's caused. She's sorry it didn't work out the way she wanted it to.

We stand for a moment and I contemplate giving in, holding her hostage, but then wonder if trusting her to play prisoner without ulterior motive is the biggest mistake I can make for everyone. My judgement is impaired, has been for quite a while.

I look at her over one shoulder.

"I'll be in touch," I whisper, voice distant, detached. I need to consult with Sephy before I do anything involving this traitor.

"Luce. I am sorry—" The words come like a slap around the face as I spin full circle, towering over her.

"Fuck you, Anubis. Now get the hell out before I kill you where you stand."

"You wouldn't do that." She gets to her feet, testing the waters between us as she slides past me. I clench every muscle in my body as she comes within an inch of me, my skin itching with murderous desire. I half expect her to attack me and half expect myself to lunge forward and make a grab for her skin with my bare hands.

"Wouldn't I?" I ask, raising my eyebrows, expression stony as my heart.

She looks at me as she reaches the doorway, opens her mouth to retort, but thinks better of it. Her quick footsteps echo out behind her as she makes her way back down the corridor.

I think on my own question for a moment.

Would I really kill her?

Do I still have it inside of me to be merciful in the face of such devastation?

She doesn't know the answer, and neither do I.

XION

I climb out of the wooden hatch that leads to the graveyard overhead, toting a loaded rifle in one arm, palm sweaty on the pistol grip.

Golgotha is abuzz with frantic motion, desperate, as all life seems to be. The Furies are leading newly born Doppels, skin still smeared with ichor and bloody earth, and positioning them around the perimeter of the enormous cemetery. Yew trees remain scattered every few yards, dead limbs protruding to the sky, trapped in a natural rigor mortis. It's been hard work clearing the space, and my limbs ache, my shoulder screaming from the consistent recoil of the rifle.

It felt good though, undeniably, to be acting, to be doing something. The ride here wasn't exactly easy, and yet now it feels like it was worth it. We haven't nearly taken back Mortaria, but it's a start, and an impressive one for seven people in a tiny little speedboat.

I walk over to the farthest part of the cemetery from the entrance, observing Nita as she hands yet another body a crude black jumpsuit to protect their already shattered modesty. As I wander, I look into the rushing waters of The River Styx.

Beyond it, beyond the banks and the eerie froth, I see it. An Abraxian. A demon just like me, skin black, lime tattoos glowing but only just visible from this distance. The charred black flesh, it reminds me of what I am. Reminds me of the truth.

I told Sephy I would die if the shard was shattered, but that wasn't technically true. I wouldn't die; I just wouldn't be me anymore.

I'd be a *thing* exactly like the one I'm looking at instead.

Luce warned me, all those years ago, that if my darkness ever returned the demonic energies would have become so potent, being trapped for so long, that my human half risked being entirely eclipsed by the dark.

I merely nodded, and we had taken the risk, a risk that until recently I thought worth it. Now, as I look into her face, those wide cognac eyes that have become steel dams for the damage, the stormy emotion that lies behind, I can't help but wonder.

I don't want to hurt her after everything. I pushed her to feel this way, to get in so deep, and now I'm lying to her because I'm scared I've made a huge mistake.

Not because I don't love her, but because I do. More than anything in this universe. More than my wellbeing, hers is my concern now, and I'm putting it at risk because I can't tell her the truth.

I caused Lilly so much pain, let her suffer, and then continued to defile her even after her soul had departed the mortal world. I can't do that Sephy. I won't. I won't put her in the situation of having to potentially put me down, to slaughter me like an animal. It would break her even if she would never admit it.

What's worse, the demon within me, it *knows* her. It's seen her at her weakest, knows where to exert pressure to crack her façade, knows how to hurt her. It could use my face, use my body to catch her unaware, to murder her.

I can't let that happen. Even if it means I have to die.

I won't let that part of myself, that darkness, tarnish everything between us. I just can't.

I should tell her.

279

I know I should. I know that if the shard is broken, I could alter, become dark, become a monster within only seconds. I could turn on her in only moments, and she would never even know what hit her.

And yet, when I had come to this fact, when I'd told her that the breaking of the shard would kill me, I left out the truth of the matter. Because my own truth, the one that terrifies me most, is that once she knows that I'm an unexploded bomb with an invisible timer, she won't let herself lean on me any longer. She needs to; she needs that strength.

I can't break her trust or her heart.

Not yet.

Maybe not ever.

But— if I wait until it's too late, then she'll never forgive me. No word could ever absolve me of such a sin.

I flick off the safety and shoot off the entire contents of the magazine into the shadowy dark beyond the far riverbank, watching as the Abraxian falls to its knees, dead. My rage is close to the surface at my placid weakness, and the obsidian pendant cools against my chest, a solid and slick reminder of the secret I'm shielding her from.

If only killing my inner demon was so simple.

I sigh at this thought, pivoting on the spot, and making my way around the outskirts of Golgotha. The Resurrection Flame catches my eye now and again as it continues to blaze high into the sky, the breeze causing an occasional plume.

We're all waiting, every one of us, for the announcement of our arrival to bring more demons, more violence, more death.

What will Pandora do?

What are her intentions?

I wish I knew.

The air is tense, The Furies patrolling the border with morose but intense concentration, fingers stroking the handles of their weapons in that way they always do, visible and predictable from even this distance.

"Hey." The voice travels, slightly melodic and annoyingly familiar from behind the wide trunk of a nearby yew tree. It's a Sinner, or at least I think it is. He's certainly not *alive*, and yet he isn't wearing a black jumpsuit. Instead, he's wearing a long leather overcoat and jeans.

It takes me a few seconds to work out what it is I'm looking at.

"What are you doing here?" I demand, tension pinching every muscle tight in my core as I straighten. The humid breeze draws out his silence at my question.

After a few long seconds, he reveals himself, our familial gazes burning into one another as his façade melts away. It leaves behind long greasy black hair, the familiar jawline I see every day in the mirror, and my own broad forehead staring back at me.

I want to walk away, but then I debate shooting him just for the hell of it. I go to raise my rifle, but he raises his hands, smiling with a sheepish innocence and disarming me.

I lower the gun, but I'm still not buying he's harmless.

"What are you doing here?" I repeat in a hiss, looking around to see if anyone else has noticed him.

"Well son, I think we need to talk."

24

IN A SENTIMENTAL MOOD

SEPHY

I STARE UP AT the slate-grey concrete of the ceiling; the only sound my heavy breathing. I'm trying to relax, trying to rest, to find sleep, but there's something about being in a small concrete box of a room, underground, that is causing me to panic on a level bone deep. I don't wonder what it is. I know. I wonder how I did it, for six months, lying still and confined beneath the earth.

I mean I guess being dead helped.

Turning onto my left side, I'm still unable to find relief, unable to stop my mind whirring through the many possible scenarios of the coming days. Xion's lifeless eyes, Jules' body plagued by rigor mortis, Luce's hand trailing, cold, through a pool of her own blood.

Morbid should be my middle name.

Sephy Morbid Sinclair.

I like it.

Sitting up, I lean back against the cold twisted steel of the head-board, surveying the room.

When Luce had said that old crypts had been converted into accommodation, I thought she was talking about more of a refurb than simply stuffing four-poster beds into the crypt-sized rooms. The one I'm sitting on, which is slathered in a thick blanket of red crushed velvet, is cruel black steel with adornments of the same metal twisting into gothic-style roses around each of the four posts. The detail is undeniably incredible as I can see every thorn, every petal, made from the contorted steel, and yet the rest of the room is so barren, so merely functional, that it's hard not to feel like you've been buried alive once the door slams shut. It's cooler down here at least, the earth surrounding us shifting with the rising Sinners called by the newly ignited Resurrection Flame. The thought of them brings an icy wave of nausea down over me, and I exhale heavily, knowing the unfortunate truth of the matter.

I'm not getting any sleep. Not until this is over.

Spinning, I fling my legs off the side of the high mattress before standing in the narrow space between the bed and the wall. Grabbing my gun, I pivot quickly on the spot, heading for the door and not looking back.

I make quick time through the labyrinth of underground passages, arriving at the hatch leading back up into Golgotha in less than a minute. I'm restless, legs aching with the need for motion, the need for violence. My blood is racing through my system, rapid as the now free-flowing River Styx lying just beyond the graveyard.

Anxiety thrumming through me, I ascend the ladder, pushing open the hatch overhead and pulling myself up among the bustle of newly reborn Doppel bodies in black jumpsuits.

I stare over my shoulder for a second, following the sound of The Furies' collective broken English, hard as diamond in tone but not nearly as beautiful. They instruct the Sinners on where to stand and what to look for, no falter in their circling of the perimeter as their eyes narrow and scour the surrounding land.

Luce isn't up here. She must have gone in for my idea of resting before I realised it was futile.

I scan for Xion next, closing the hatch behind me with a swift kick and locating him only seconds later. I squint, finding his bulky outline just beneath the petrified silhouette of a far-off yew tree.

He isn't alone.

What the fuck?

This is my first reaction when I realise who it is he's talking to. I grip my rifle hard, finger moving instinctually toward the trigger, as I summon a blazing Eternal Flame into one of my gloved palms.

I storm over the slowly rehydrating soil, weaving in and out of headstones. Abraxis' eyes widen as I approach, and Xion spins.

"What the hell is he doing here?!" I demand, raising my arm like I'm about to pitch a wicked flaming curveball.

"Woah, hold on Sephy! Wait. He came to warn me." My own eyes widen in disbelief as I falter in my stride. Xion's expression is one of calm, one of placid attentiveness, stoking the flames of my fury exponentially.

283

"Excuse me? He's a Demon Lord! How the hell did he even get in here? Don't we have anyone on security? This isn't a goddamn housewarming party. We're supposed to be on high alert!" I'm incredulous as I whirl around, taking in the increasingly heavy guard lining the perimeter. Sinners stare at me now, probably wondering why I'm making such a fuss.

Morons.

"I came in earlier, before all the— *security*—" Abraxis gestures, sarcastic and with careless fingers, to the peppering of bodies behind me. His eyes, dull, reek of uninspired arrogance beneath the thick, heavy curtain of his dark hair. The tree branches above him, like electrocuted limbs stuck mid-flail, cast dark shadows across his face.

"Xion, go and get the others." I bark the order, but Xion doesn't complain or retort, he looks somewhat relieved, as though he can't bear being this close to his father. Not that I blame him of course.

As he passes me, he brushes my shoulder with his fingertips, a silent apology.

Abraxis smirks.

Anger stacks up heavy in my chest, flaring hotter in my lungs, and I wonder if this keeps going on if I might turn into a badass dragon and start breathing fire.

God, I bet the heartburn would be unbearable—

"What the fuck are you smiling at?" I spit, zoning back into the moment, voice ringing soprano with irritation. I need to focus, to stop my sassy defence mechanisms from causing my mind to wander off. This— though not likely — *could* be important.

"Why, young love of course," he counters, not missing a beat. I roll my eyes.

"Wow, for The Demon Lord of Lies and Illusion, you're certainly delusional," I bite back, unable to help myself.

Raising the gun in my palm, I gaze at it half-heartedly as though I feel the need to remind him it's there and I'm not afraid to use it. He cocks a single eyebrow, broad forehead and expression ringing far too familiar and inciting the violent urges within me to grow exponentially yet again. I can't believe that a man like Xion came from an asshat like this guy. His mother must have been one hell of a woman.

"Keep floating down that river of denial, Sephy. However, if you care even slightly for my son, you are going to want to listen to what I have to say." The statement comes as a threat more than a promise, and

I tighten my hand on the pistol grip, palm becoming clammy at his insinuation.

"Why the hell do you think I want to hear anything that comes out of your mouth? You're a pathological liar by trade!" I exclaim, a smile pulling at my lips despite my fury. Surely, he can't think I'm so stupid as to believe him, so what the hell is he trying to pull?

"Look, I helped you escape before. Why would I do that only to work against you now?" he asks, and I snort, smirking and shaking my head.

I helped you escape—

Really?

"I seem to recall you standing there like a limp dick while me and Xion escaped via convection— funny how our recollections of these events are so dissimilar. Again, I suggest that you consider swapping illusion for delusion with regard to your official title."

I extinguish the flame in my palm momentarily, stroking the line of my jaw as I shift on the balls of my feet and cock my hip to one side.

"Look, whatever. I'm here for Xion, not for you." He glowers, and I almost laugh at how fearless I feel. His face had terrified me once.

What happened?

"You're here for Xion? Pfft. I doubt it. What is this great warning you have come to bestow upon us? Go on, I'm listening." I bait him, and he crosses his arms over his bulging pectorals, biceps straining against the leather of his mid-length and extremely well-worn jacket.

"Pandora has the shard. She's tried to draw the power from it already. Once she learns that she needs Xion's pendant to do that nowhere will be safe. She will hunt you two down to the ends of the universe—" he begins, but I interrupt him, bringing a calm hand up to my lips and stifling an entirely fake yawn.

"Boring. We already know this," I inform him.

His eyes bore into mine like high-powered pneumatic drill-points, their orange depths glowing white hot as his temper visibly builds beneath his ever-illusory skin.

Then, the look between us is broken as multiple footsteps can be heard approaching from behind. I spin to see Xion, Luce, and Jules trudging toward us through the fields of protruding headstones, eyes fixed fast and hard on Abraxis.

"What the hell is he doing here?" Luce asks, pupils dilating wide.

I shrug.

"Apparently, he's come to warn us that Xion is in danger, which we already know, and to tell us about how Pandora intends to try and use

285

the shard— which again we already know. So, in summary, he's here to give us an annoyingly voiced synopsis of shit *we already know*." I glower at him, musing the ways I could rip him apart.

He might have forgotten the way he stared down at me while I fought for my life against his bastard demon Kindred back in the dark colosseum, but I haven't. I'll never forget.

"I would have preferred Morgan Freeman personally," Xion comments, and I nod, masking my amusement with a scowl.

"Right? That guy has serious voice prowess. Plus, I don't want to punch *him* in his face—" I add, eyeing Abraxis from head to toe.

He steels himself on the spot, leaning against the petrified trunk of the tree on his left before crossing his ankles and trying to appear more relaxed than he actually is.

"Look, you don't understand. This is serious," he begins, running his large fingers back through his thick hair, seemingly distressed, though whether it's genuine I couldn't tell you.

I snort.

"Oh, I think I understand that. You're the one making cosy with freaking Morticia Adams up in the Exilia you stole from my father. I'm currently sleeping in a concrete underground coffin. Out of you and I, I think I understand the seriousness of this far more than you do," I spit, becoming tired of the conversation fast.

"Look, just listen. You don't understand. Now that shard has been rediscovered by The Demon Lords, the dynamics of this entire equation have shifted, and they're not in your favour, by the way."

He straightens, forcing his spine to elongate as he reaches his full height, towering over me and peering down the slope of his nose.

I listen a moment, swearing I can hear a rustle of leaves, but after a few seconds of Abraxis staring at me, goading me to reply with his smug ass expression, I realise I'm probably imagining things.

"And I should trust you because you're secretly a nice guy, who just had a string of bad luck and made the wrong choices? Boohoo for you." I shoo him with a casual wave of my hand and sense Jules shift at my shoulder. I turn back to look at him and find his head tilted, examining Abraxis. His eyes move to meet mine for only an instant, but the message from him is clear.

Calm your ass. Let him speak.

"No," Abraxis sighs, "You're supposed to trust me because if Pandora tips the balance, my Kindred are going to suffer. The world as it is, politicians, reality television—" He sees my look of confusion and steps forward, gesturing for me to listen more intently with both palms outstretched. "The law, it inspires lies. That feeds us; it makes us strong. In a world where the walls don't exist, chaos will follow, and it is the law and order of humanity, or the supposed law and order, which prompts liars. Lies from the government, lies from criminals, lies from politicians. Advertising campaigns are also an unbelievably rich source of power for me. If the world goes to shit, so do all those things. I'll be weaker than I ever have been," he adds. My eyes narrow, unsure whether or not I should believe him.

"Right," Luce says, stepping forward and looking at me. She understands what he's saying, even if I don't.

"Look, this shard— you've put yourselves in an awful position. If Pandora uses it to gain power, then we're in obvious trouble. But if she doesn't, then The Demon Lords will begin fighting between themselves for it. They're acting cool right now like it doesn't faze them, but I can see through it. They're desperate to one-up each other, and I for one, don't want to be in the middle of that war because it'll weaken all of us indefinitely. Until one of us finally manages to use the thing. Then one of us will be more powerful than ever before. Whoever it is— well, I don't even want to imagine." He pauses, breath coming heavy in his broad chest.

"But I intend on getting the shard back before that happens," I remind him, and he shakes his head.

"You don't get it, do you? You can't hide that now, if you steal it back, The Demon Lords will hunt you down, torture you, kill you even, to find its location. You've made yourself enormous targets. That shard can't remain in existence. Not with the amount of dark power it's storing," he announces, and I shrug.

"So— what if I destroy it? I mean, there must be a way to do it without killing Xion, right?" I ask, and Abraxis' eyes widen.

Luce gives me a quizzical look.

"Is that what he told you?" Abraxis looks amused, eyes darting to his son.

I turn to Xion, heart suddenly thumping against my ribs like a prisoner of war.

"What is he talking about, Xion?"

His lips part, but the answer won't come. Instead, Luce's voice breaks through the thick silence, answering for him.

"Sephy, if that shard is destroyed— Xion won't die. But he won't be Xion anymore. The darkness in the shard will go back to the soul from which it originated."

I frown.

"But it's not just *his* darkness in there. We took some of yours too—" I remind her.

"It doesn't matter; the darkness inside that thing will latch onto his soul. It'll destroy the human part of him. Dark magic that potent— only his demon side will remain. He wouldn't remember us, any of us, as he had known us as a human man. He'd become, well, an animal. Just like any other demon."

I feel myself caught suddenly between fury and distress.

"Why didn't you tell me?" I shout at Xion, placing my hand firmly on my hip and gripping harder onto the gun in my other palm even still.

"I didn't want you to think it was an option. I'd rather die. I won't become a monster. I could hurt you, any of you. I would rather die—" he repeats, and I want to be angry, want to put up my walls and hate him if only for a moment, but I can't.

As much as I don't want to, I freaking understand.

He's fought his whole life to become the man he is, to quieten the demon within. Now the only way to be the hero is by becoming it, fully, with no going back.

Fate is one cruel motherfucker.

"So— that's it? *These* are my options? Let the Demon Lords have it, and Xion dies. Let Pandora have it, and Xion still dies. Or we destroy it on purpose, and Xion becomes a demonic psychopath for good, which means— he dies?! That can't be the only goddamn way! Like, you're kidding me, right?!" I demand justice, but Abraxis only stands, face impassive, unwavering on the spot.

"I should go in and torch every single last one of those fuckers," I muse, the idea beyond appealing.

"You do that and we'll have a whole new host of problems. The Demon Kindred for one. They won't have any masters; it'll be anarchy. Not only that, but as much as I want to believe in you and your '*girl power*' thing you've got going on, there's no way in hell that you can take on four Demon Lords and Pandora alone. They have a mortal *and* a demon army. And you've got what?" he asks, looking and sounding as incredulous as I now feel at the prospect of fighting that many people and winning.

"A sparkling personality?" I remind him, smiling with faux confidence.

My lack of a real answer causes a depressed silence to fall over us all. Luckily for me, Abraxis and his stupid mouth quickly solve that problem.

"There might be— another way," he explains, and I quirk an eyebrow at him, waiting for the invariable and inevitable punch line to all this. I might have started in hysterics if I wasn't so sure this was real life.

"Well, spit it out!" I'm impatient now; despair pulling my insides in all directions, heart lodged stubbornly in my throat.

How could we have been so careless?

I wanted to save Luce. I did. But I didn't know it would come to this.

Then again, if Luce hadn't brought me back to life, she never would have succumbed to the darkness as she did. So maybe, maybe this is the Universe's sick price for my resurrection. Maybe someone who thwarted death doesn't get to be happy. Maybe I'm just doomed to suffer in life as the cost for escaping the grave.

"You could purposefully put *all* the darkness into someone you trust. I mean Xion wouldn't survive, but— but he wouldn't be damned to become pure demon either. He would be free. In a way—" He suggests this, but all I can do is laugh.

"Ha! And I suppose you have a genius suggestion for this insanely stupid plan that still kills your son?" I wonder what the hell he's been smoking as his lips purse, his posture becoming stiff and awkward.

"Well, I had thought you could trust me with it. Seeing as it's my fault he's half demon to begin with," he suggests. I look to Luce then back to Jules, lips tugging upwards against my better judgement.

Simultaneously, and despite the tone of this conversation, we all burst out laughing.

"There it is— *right there!*" Luce exclaims, her laugh genuine and loud, shaking her head.

Xion is the only one among us who isn't fully laughing, but even he can't stop his lips from turning up at the corners.

"Yeah *right*, let's willingly give the power to *you*—" I can barely even spit the words between peels of belly-aching laughter, eyes watering profusely.

Xion stares at me, his small smile diminishing, and it's then that I see it in his eyes, the plea which stops the laughter cold in my chest.

Please don't let me become a monster.

25

THORN IN MY SIDE

LUCE

I STAND, STARING AT Abraxis, trying to gauge what exactly it is he's trying to achieve. His eyes are wide but intense and his posture is seemingly relaxed, which is more than I can say for Xion who looks like he's had something hot and metallic shoved firmly up his ass. Not that I blame him. He's at serious risk now. I guess, though none of us had wanted to think about exactly how screwed he is, Abraxis hasn't given us the choice of ignorance any longer.

I wonder, like I often wonder about my mother, how he feels about his child, about the son who is only half what he is made of and the other half a foreign entity entirely. I wonder if he cares, deep down, but don't allow this trail of thought to travel across to ponderings of my own parent. I think banishment makes it pretty clear how she feels about me.

As I'm pondering this, and Jules shifts uncomfortably beside me, I feel it. A slither, a tiny ripple in the fabric of the visual. Hairs rise on the back of my neck, a shudder of familiar recognition undulating the length of my spine.

How long have they been wrapping themselves around the limbs of the yew tree?

Does Abraxis know they're there?

"Sephy. Gorgonians," I whisper, eyes bolting the length of the tree with indicative certainty.

She growls under her breath, movements shakier than I've seen them in a while. I guess hearing the truth about Xion has her rattled, which I sympathise with. I've been struggling with it myself, hoping the problem would resolve itself in time if I pretended it didn't exist.

She summons The Eternal Flame to her, a crackling, revolving ball of fury materialising within her palm and floating only centimetres from her unmarred, unphased skin.

Abraxis looks suddenly wary, and Xion lifts his rifle, confusion marring his expression as Sephy tosses the ball into the central column of the tree and narrowly misses The Demon Lord. I'm pretty sure she does this on purpose, for no other reason than the wicked glint that flashes momentarily in her eye as he startles.

The demon's writhing body catches light, becoming visible in its scaled and slithering horror only seconds before falling dead to the ground with a thud. I watch Jules flinch beside me, eyes widening as his lips part in distress.

"There's never just one—" I remind her, my mouth only inches from the shell of her ear. Something brushes against my ankles, and I'm unable to deny my disgust at the dark and grotesque despite everything I've done. Taking a sudden step backwards, my eyes dart across the area beneath my feet, desperate.

Xion shoots, unloading bullets at close range into the soil, causing the dirt to fly up like upside-down earthen rain as Jules jumps backwards and I take a wide sidestep to avoid the bullets.

Unfortunately, the fact Xion can't see them puts him at a distinct disadvantage. I watch on, feeling more helpless than ever, as Sephy manages to torch two more, their deaths silent, quick, and unremarkable. Spinning, I survey the ground, finding nothing, but have the distinct feeling that at least a dozen escaped. They will now slither across the Mortarian soil, cold-blooded and ruthless in intent, toward Gorgon, who will no doubt inform Pandora of exactly what she needs to obtain to complete and utilise the shard in her possession.

Shit.

How long had they been there?

Had they heard everything we've been talking about?

Did Abraxis know?

Was this his plan all along?

"We need to get inside," Jules says in a hurried tone, breaking the stunned silence filled only with the heavy and startled breathing of each of us. His voice is shaken, cracked and deep with the shock of what he's just seen. This alone exposes him as remarkably mortal, a fact that seems easy for the others to forget.

"Yes, go. Get underground and shut the hatch up tight. They shouldn't be able to follow you there." I point over to the entrance to the underground mess of crypts and watch as the group, including Abraxis because he doesn't seem to realise he's entirely unwelcome, hurry across the graveyard.

The back of my neck is damp with perspiration and my body aches. I hadn't been able to sleep. Not, perhaps, because of everything going on right now, but because of everything that has happened in time gone by. Thane and I often snuck off duty into that same bed to make love, to get lost in one another for a few hours when resurrections were slow. It isn't the same without her, the sheets still holding the remnants of her once pungent and lingering scent, the pillow still dented from when she'd last lain upon it.

Watching the group descend through the hatch, I wonder if Anubis has been having me watched.

Is that why she'd come to 'warn' me?

Rage splinters the last of the calm in my chest, the possibility of her easy betrayal stinging immensely. I wonder what it must be like to have no moral compass, no guilt when throwing those who had loved you, had thought of you as family, under the cosmic bus of pain and torment.

I would have noticed, surely? Even in the throes of passion, Thane noticed the Gorgonian spies on the ceiling of our bedroom, and now I'm far more attuned to their darkness than she ever was.

Trying to fill myself with confidence but somewhat failing, I pick my way across the scattering of semi-uniform headstones, eyes searching for demonic disturbance, and over to my office.

If we're going to discuss what to do next, about where we need to place our power, we're going to need a map of the area. Luckily, I have several in my desk that I use to map Sinner population across Mortaria.

Knowing which tasks needed more bodies was a constant requirement for ensuring that Yama and Muerta knew how to sentence those who had multiple sins against their name. Once it had been a more singular pursuit, but the twenty-first century was bringing sins together in a large melding pot of desire, hard times, and desperation.

I push in on the steel of the door, letting the familiar scent of coffee wash over me. I don't allow myself to linger for longer than I must, purposefully ignoring Thane's jacket and yanking open the metal bottom drawer of my desk. I pull out a map, tuck it under my arm, and promptly exit the office once more, refusing to think on all the hours Thane and I spent in silent understanding as we'd worked side by side. That was the thing about our relationship; what needed to happen between us wasn't always spoken aloud. It was, instead, sometimes a mutual understanding, a glance laced with full and unwavering comprehension of what the other person was feeling.

I wilt inside, soul gaping and wounded after so many years spent at her side.

Outside in the graveyard, the perimeter is becoming increasingly populated and more heavily guarded. Though, a fat lot of good that does now the Gorgonians have already infiltrated the space and potentially eavesdropped on conversations containing vital information. However, I suppose at least no other demons will be getting within the walls, so it's not a complete waste of time. Or at least, I hope it isn't.

The Furies pace along the line, visible to me even from afar in their tense collective stances as they call to one another and bark orders at Sinners without second thought.

I think of them, of their solitude, their rage, their inability, perhaps, to love. I envy their strength, how they rest easy with the knowledge that they can stand on their own merit and defend themselves to the last if they must.

Maybe— just maybe I can use Thane leaving as motivation to work on myself in the right way. After all, I'm sick of being placid and seemingly useless despite my supposed power. There has to be a way I can get stronger without compromising myself again.

I pull up on the hatch with vigour, looking around at the surrounding earth and checking for any sign of movement. There's none and so I lower myself, map still underneath my arm, into the hole before beginning my climb down the ladder and into the passages below.

I know the perfect place for the meeting and find the group leaning, bored, in the corridor outside Sephy's room, chatting in dulcet tones.

Sephy is hissing something at Xion but he's not responding, causing her to rage almost imperceptibly at Jules instead with only her eyes. There's no mistaking what she's pissed about though.

Xion lied to her, but I can't understand why.

"Come on, let's go to the dining room. There's a table in there. We can make a plan." I voice my idea and then pass through the narrow space left as they line either side of the corridor, taking the lead and weaving through the all too familiar maze of corridors.

The tunnels flicker cold, The Resurrection Flame spitting from equidistant gothic steel sconces on either side of the hall. I don't break stride as I reach yet another steel door identical to all the rest, leaning my full weight into it and hearing the metal scrape against the floor as it opens wide.

The inside of the room is dark, but Sephy soon rectifies that, waving a hand and lighting the place in the same chill blue as the outside corridors. There's a round mahogany table that I'd commandeered from somewhere I can't quite remember in the centre of the space. Once upon a time, Thane and I used to eat down here at this table. I think we even screwed on top of it at one point.

Sephy moves around the room, summoning The Eternal Flame to her palm and leaning up so she can feel around the edge of the low ceiling.

She nods, satisfied after several minutes of checking the place from ceiling to floor.

"We're good. No demons, well— *hidden* demons," she informs me, glaring at Abraxis as I take the map from beneath my arm and spread it on the table in front of me.

Xion, Sephy, Jules, and Abraxis gather around, the Demon Lord leaning forward and looking over the map.

"So— what's the plan?" he asks, looking between Sephy and me. I cock an eyebrow, and Sephy and I share a mystified look.

What the hell does he think he's doing?

"Um. You're not, you know, a part of the gang, dude. You're evil." Sephy smirks at him and Xion shakes his head, stifling a laugh.

"Oh, and you guys are all so righteous! What do we have — a half-demon of my own creation, the daughter of a shunned God who fucked his mortal— and married I might add— prisoner. A half God of Ancient made mortal who not so recently tried to resurrect another more brutal God of Ancient and—" He looks to Jules whose face is twisted into bored seeming offence already. "—Well, I don't know about you, but I bet there's something you've done that you're ashamed of. I mean why else would you be hanging out with this group of ambivalent misfits?"

"Sephy, can you go tie him up somewhere?" I ask her, and she nods. Jules looks at her.

"I'm going to go and uh— *help*." He looks smug, face transformed fast from affronted as he sticks his tongue out at Abraxis. I smile against my better judgement.

After everything, I really do like Jules. He's a good guy.

As the three of them make a fast and protested exit, Abraxis mumbling cuss words under his breath with a distinct lack of subtlety, I look to Xion.

"Why didn't you tell her?" I demand, and he looks suddenly ashamed.

"I don't know. Maybe I didn't want it to be true. Maybe I was hoping I'd— I don't know—" He sighs, and I push my lips together hard as he brushes his fingers back through his hair.

"That you'd what? *Die*?"

"Maybe. I guess I've spent so long fighting this thing inside me, fighting the demons of Mortaria, I guess I never really believed that the demon inside might win. After everything."

The air between us is thick and still in the silent moment that follows.

"Xion—" I begin suddenly, but he holds up a hand.

"Look, I know. It's not looking good for me right now. But, if it's between being damned or dead, I'd rather be dead. Just— remember that okay?" He implores me with his molten irises, his jaw firmly set, determined and unwavering, stoic as ever.

I know what he's saying. He's saying that he doesn't think Sephy will be able to end the demon inside him if it comes down to it.

I don't blame him, after all. Even though it had been entirely different circumstances, I hadn't been able to kill Thane either.

We stand in awkward silence for a few moments until the sounds of Sephy and Jules' quick steps can be heard growing closer. They enter, and I cock my head, finding Jules looking extremely satisfied.

"Everything alright?"

Sephy nods, looking chipper.

"Yeah— we uh, found some handcuffs in your nightstand and tied him to the headboard in your room. Hope you don't mind. I didn't have any kinky sex stuff in *my* room. I feel kind of robbed, actually." Her eyes twinkle, and my face flushes with colour as my cheeks heat. The handcuffs— I try not to recall too much detail as I struggle to remember when I last used them. I come up with nothing so smile at Sephy instead of explaining, ready to get on with things.

"Right, uh— well, that was very resourceful of you," I admonish, and she nods, clearly pleased with herself. "Anyway, now that's sorted, let's take a look at what we're up against." I lean over the map, crossing my arms over my breasts and resting my full weight on my elbows. Scouring the page, I reacquaint myself with the familiar sprawl of

296

landmarks and the web of inner-city streets, taking only a few moments to orient our position.

"So, we've got the demons which are— well everywhere, I suppose," I begin, biting my bottom lip.

"And the mortals, you know, the ones she was recruiting. I'm guessing they're pretty close to the Exilia. I can't see the demons having enough control over their urges for it to be safe for them outside," Xion adds.

Sephy doesn't look at him, instead keeping her eyes fixed firmly on the map.

I feel for her, unwillingly.

"The shard, Pandora, and the other Demon Lords— they're in the Exilia too." She stabs at the icon on the worn, crinkled map with her index finger. Jules' eyes are wide, taking it all in like a child.

"Right. So, we're here." I point at Golgotha. "And I think we can all safely assume that Xion is a target." I glance up at him, noting his expression of silent agreement.

"I'd say the chance of that is pretty high, given the fact we didn't manage to kill all the Gorgonians before they escaped." His mouth twists into a half frown, half concentrated line as his heavy brow furrows and his shoulders tense, rolling slightly forward into a moody hunch.

"So— I guess the question is how are we going to get around? I can't convect everyone, and the river is less than discreet. Also, speaking of the river, it's high, right? I mean, that's bad?" Sephy enquires, and I nod, eyes narrowing over the dark shaded ribbon, which cuts through the land with merciless yet meandering precision.

"Yeah— I mean I guess if we had Yama and Muerta here, they could tell us exactly how close she is to tipping the scales, but I spoke to Anubis this morning, and she says that they have no idea where they're hiding. Presuming they're still alive."

I drop this information before them, exposing it like it's nothing.

Sephy gapes.

"Wait. *When* did you speak to Anubis?" she snaps, folding her arms over her chest, instantly defensive.

"She was in my room earlier. Must have slipped in with Abraxis. She came to warn me, asked me to rescue Osiris too. You know her game," I add.

Xion looks concerned.

"You should have said something," he admonishes, and Sephy shoots him a glare the approximate temperature of Arctic runoff. It hits him full in the face.

"Oh, because you're Mr Forthcoming?" she snaps, incredulous. He shakes his head with unwarranted exasperation.

"That's not the point—" He begins to defend himself, but Sephy holds up a hand demanding only his silence, her eyes scanning the map and widening a second.

"Look, whatever. I've just had a thought." She chews on her bottom lip, looking down at the table with unceasing intensity as she explains her thinking. "So, Pandora has been tipping the scales by letting the demons feed on mortals, and then the victims can't be resurrected or rehabilitated here, right?" she asks, and I nod, confirming her analysis.

"Yeah, that's right. The darkness in their souls isn't being returned to The Well, so it's just, sort of— still in universal play. If that makes sense," I explain, and she grimaces.

"I've been saving people in Chicago from Demon attacks for months— but, it was all a distraction," she whispers, like someone has taken her fire and extinguished it in a single blow.

"Wait, what do you mean?" I query her, confused.

"So, how many mortals do you think she's got here right now?" She stabs at the Exilia icon with her finger, causing the crinkled paper to rustle.

"Thousands, maybe more," I conclude, estimating this figure entirely.

"We thought we'd know when she was going to do it. We thought we'd see it coming. But she never needed to move through to the mortal world to tip the scales, Luce. She has the trigger right here. The mortals she abducted, the homeless, maybe even criminals. She's kept them alive all this time, but— but if the demons are set loose at her command. It would be a slaughter. That many dead people, people who have been carrying out her dirty work, sinning here for months, it's got to tilt the scales. Right?"

I feel cold dread drip into my stomach.

Pandora could act at any time. She could rip down the walls and set The Gods of Ancient free with a single utterance to The Demon Lords. That is, if they do as she asks.

"But we don't know that. We don't know if we're close enough to the tipping point for that to work. The only people who would be able to tell us that are Yama and Muerta," I ramble, feeling undeniably sick.

I promised A.D.A.M I'd kill those mortals, that I'd keep the secret world of Mortaria just that, a secret. But what if in killing them I give Pandora exactly what she wants?

If I can't carry out my end of the bargain, how will I get Beelz back?

"We need to get this shard back, Luce. Screw everything else! What about Xion?" Sephy's eyes are wild again, but I simply shake my head.

"No, we can't. We don't have a decent plan or the manpower. We don't know what we're walking into. You could go into the Exilia and take out any number of her mortal guards trying to get the damn thing. We can't take that risk. It might be exactly what she wants you to do. What if she's trying to pin this whole thing on you? Seems like the kind of sick performance she'd orchestrate, doesn't it?" I'm definitive in the assessment, but she still opens her mouth to protest.

"But if these mortals are the trigger— then why hasn't she just done it already? What has she been waiting for?" Jules asks.

I think about this hard.

"It would have taken a while for the backup of souls to get to a tipping point like this, maybe a month or so? Maybe— maybe she's stalling until she can use the shard. What if she's trying to get power over The Demon Lords? As Abraxis said, she doesn't have any control over them — she's basically mortal without the Mortarian sun, and they're still immortal because of their status as Kindred. They've gotten where they want to be by using her, but they could get rid of her at any time and still be in a prime position to restore the Ancient Gods," I muse. Sephy's eyes blaze.

"So, we need to get the shard," she reiterates forcefully.

"No. We need to find Yama and Muerta first, Sephy. If not, we have no idea whether those mortals can be killed in the process without causing a massive universal shift. There's no point retrieving the shard if the balance tips because of it. It'll all be over." I'm breathless after the explanation, and she stares at me across the table, our gazes locked for a few moments before she relinquishes with a sigh.

"Ugh. You're right. Okay, so where do we go to look for Muerta and Yama? The Indicatus Courts?" she suggests. I give her a look of indecision.

"Anubis said that they couldn't find them there— then again, it would be stupid to assume they haven't returned just because when

Pandora was looking over a month ago they weren't there. Besides, maybe you'll find some clues about where they went."

"Right, I'll get going then." Sephy turns on her heel, hair bouncing in its high ponytail against the nape of her neck. Xion clears his throat.

"I'll come with you too," he decides, and she looks pissed, immediately opening her mouth in protest.

"But—"

"Look, if Pandora knows she needs my pendant, then this is the first place she'll attack looking for me. I'm not staying here."

She sighs, seeing his logic.

"Fine. I'll meet you upstairs in a few minutes," she concedes, storming towards the doorway without looking back.

"Where are you going?" I ask before she can disappear around the corner.

"I'm gonna go untie Abraxis. I figure he can come with. I'm not leaving him here; I want to keep an eye on him."

PANDORA

"Harder!" I gasp, leaning forward as the mortal behind me pulls on the chainmail cord yet again. The corset tightens around my waist, the cold steel of it coming into full contact with my torso. "There!" I indicate the correct tightness and hear the fumbling fingers of the incompetent behind me tying the cord steadfast against my back.

I never thought I'd find myself in an armoured corset again, especially because the last time it had been solid gold and I'd been putting it on in one of the high towers of the Solis Castra, back when I had been preparing to go to war to defend The Higher Plains. I cannot, though, feel sorry for the choice as I stare into the mirror, the tarnished steel a dull contrast to the shimmering glisten of my last garment.

It hugs my hips, my breasts, flattens my stomach and steels my abdominal muscles, forcing perfect posture. It causes my skin to appear paler than usual, and I know it's going to look just fabulous with my new wings.

A knock at the door causes me to spin, fluttering my fingers as I indicate that the Mortal man behind me should answer it before letting himself out and leaving me to accessorise.

He does so, scurrying like a rodent across the slick stone of the floor and revealing Gorgon, body snug with his Kindred, their hisses and whispers filling the chamber the second he steps over the threshold.

The Mortal leaves, and Gorgon closes the door swiftly behind him, mouth curved into a wide smile, gaze pointed as a knife tip.

"We have found the answer you seek," he whispers, though he may as well have shouted for the impact his words have on me. Joy rolls in my stomach like a tropical tide, quelling the icy waters of the fear that I am merely inadequate, that I have failed.

"And?" I sweep my dark hair up off my neck from where it falls in an intricate braid down my back, pulling it over one shoulder and twirling the loose end around my finger. I take a step toward him, breath as ever bated.

"The demon halfling. He holds a missing piece of the stone. A tether to a tether if you will. It's how Lucifer separated him from most of his demonic darkness without ripping his soul in half," he reveals. I cock an eyebrow.

"That's—"

"Very clever, indeed. I thought so too," he adds, one of his Kindred climbing around his neck, tongue flickering in and out as its scales sheen iridescent.

"I was going to say perfect. I assume that restoring the tether to its completed state will kill him, will it not?" I assume, and he nods, a small smile tugging at the edge of his lips.

"Indeed. I would assume that is why Abraxis is yet to return—" he muses.

I roll my eyes, not surprised in the least.

"Well, I suppose I shouldn't be shocked. I've known his loyalties don't lie in my court for a while now. Ever since his son managed to escape the dungeons, I have been suspicious," I recall. Gorgon nods in agreement, taking a small step toward me.

"That's very astute of you," he compliments, and I blush against my own volition, tossing my braid back over my shoulder and crossing my arms over the cold steel encasing my breasts.

"Yes, well. Trust is a luxury I cannot afford," I remind him, watching his pointed face closely. He breaks eye contact, going back to rhythmically stroking the serpentine beast coiling itself around his wrist now, his voice a sibilant caress. I don't know what to make of this. After all, why help me seize such potent power if he's not on my side, if his interests do not align themselves with mine?

"What about Anubis?" I ask him, and he shrugs.

"Still unclear. She was out of earshot, underground, so my Kindred tell me."

My lips pucker in thought.

The fireplace to my right flickers incessantly, the regular flame less illuminative than its mystical counterpart. It crackles loudly, and soon my mind has moved from the unreadable Anubis and back to the more pressing issue of the shard.

"So, we need to get the pendant, and then—"

"Connect it with the shard. If I had to guess, I'd say The Resurrection Flame might well be the way to do that though I'm not certain of course," he muses, the Gorgonian slithering around his lower leg and visibly squeezing. He doesn't look uncomfortable though. In fact, he looks unusually relaxed as the scales flicker in and out of camouflage against the velvet crush of his suit.

"So, I need the girl," I say, glee all too evident, eyes catching the firelight.

"Well, no. You just need to keep her alive until you've used The Resurrection Flame. I'd suggest the beacon in Golgotha, seeing as how she's so conveniently lit it up like a Christmas tree." He moves over to one of the four-poster bedposts and leans, his long fingers caressing the curve of it. His touch, the way he bites his bottom lip, causes me to shudder slightly, goose pimples rising against my better judgement across what was once the frigid landscape of my skin.

I shake my head, looking back into the fireplace and changing my focus. My number one priority must be retrieving the pendant and restoring the dark tether. Only then can I rest, only then can I relax and enjoy him again.

I move to storm from the room, anxiety rife in my veins as my muscles twitch with unspent energy, mind whirring with the possibility that soon such potent dark magic will be screaming through me. That it will be truly *mine*.

Looking back over my shoulder as I pull open the door and step through into the corridor outside, I find Gorgon watching my every motion, eyes narrowed, investigative to say the least.

However, I find myself failing to care or worry as I take one deep breath after the next, knowing that the next few hours, the next few days, will change everything.

His eyes meet with mine and I smile, encouraging him to join me, impatient now for my agenda to reach its climax, hungry for my long-awaited triumph.

"Come, we have much to arrange." I bark the command, unabashed. "I want the full force of Mortaria's demonic presence coming down on Golgotha in no less than a few hours. No more holding back. No more biding my time. I'm done waiting."

26

WICKED ONES

SEPHY

WE CONVECT IN UPON the black and white monochrome marble floors that now lie scattered with debris and coated in dust. There are skeletons lying in a neat line through the main entrance hall, having died waiting for their turn in front of Yama. It makes me wonder; would people behave better if they realised that hell was like a prolonged DMV experience? There would probably be a lot more saints, anyhow. Then again, I suppose anyone who had ever been on hold with the IRS would probably view this as a luxury vacation.

Xion steps stiffly from my side, Abraxis following him without pause as they both take in the surroundings, which lie dusky in the forgotten and stale air of the building's skeletal remains. I hear something move behind me and twist, well aware there could be demons, that nowhere in Mortaria is safe any longer.

Luckily, it turns out it's only Abraxis tripping less than gracefully over a fallen sconce.

"Stealthy—" I mutter, and he grunts, turning from me, his face as stoic as Xion's but far less forgiving. His father is what I imagine he might be like if he were to embrace his demon half, if he became the killer he was genetically destined to be.

Don't think about it. I scold myself, rage bubbling up and threatening to boil over; the frantic scorching fury trying to leak from my lips and scald all who hear it.

I'm hurt. More than I want to be. More than I would admit.

Xion lied to me. He didn't tell me that, at any second, he could turn fully demonic if the shard was broken. I didn't know that this shard was tied so inexplicably to his continued survival. If I had I never would have retrieved it in the first place, never would have drawn such obvious attention to its existence. It would have been better for all involved, perhaps, if it had stayed lost to us, except of course for Luce. I know deep down that Xion is selfless enough to think of this only as a consequence of a vital action, one that could not be avoided, but I however do not.

I never should have performed that ritual on Luce.

My heart feels fragile like it's been burned to ash and is held together with crappy crazy glue. He didn't tell me, and I think that's mainly because he knows there's no escaping his fate.

He will either die or he will become a fully-fledged demon without a functioning heart or moral compass. There is no happily ever after here, only loss.

And yet, I can't accept it.

There must be another way. Some loophole or trick we're just not seeing.

"Sephy, I think we should go check out the courtroom and the offices behind it," Xion suggests, his deep voice reverberating from the barren walls of the chasmic hall, the stark architecture no less startling in the heavy shadow than it had been in the light.

"Abraxis, you stay here. Watch for demons—" I instruct him, and he cocks an eyebrow, an odd smirk twisting his face and making it almost attractive as his clementine pupils sheen with unknown intent.

"And if I decide to return to Pandora?" He's testing me, folding his hands in front of his crotch and tensing slightly, waiting to see what I'll say.

I wonder if he thinks he's intimidating me.

I snort.

Pandora will know he tried to warn us the same way she will know that Xion's pendant is the final piece of the wicked puzzle she wants to complete, so I'm less than worried. Besides, it's not like he's been any use so far, not really. All he's done is bring the news that my whole life is royally fucked, and now he's hanging around like a goddamn bad smell.

"Say hi from me," I retort, shrugging, my insides numb as I realise how little I care about what he does, about what any of The Demon Lords do.

My only concern now is the shard, and the only reason I'm here and not in the Exilia right now is because Luce talked me out of it.

He could try to kill me, try to hurt me, I suppose.

Why not? I mean everyone does. So far, though, I'm still standing.

With an air of invulnerability suddenly radiating from my seemingly fragile porcelain skin, I turn on the spot, taking in the black and white stone and the high arced ceiling overhead with a sweeping and paranoid gaze before treading slowly toward the double doors at the back of the hall.

I open them, pacing fast through the waiting room, which still boasts the same array of old magazines as the last time I visited.

I hear Xion's footfall growing closer as I reach the other side of the room but still don't look back, heart growing steadily louder in my ears. Blood rushes through my veins in a helpless scream of ineptitude, and I wonder— *How can I have so much power and yet, when it comes to those I love, I'm helpless to stop them dying?*

I just want the loss to stop.

Pushing in on the double wooden doors, I reveal the courtroom where I sat before Muerta, Yama, and The Fates what feels like a lifetime ago. That was right before learning that I was responsible for the death of my parents. That Haedes is my biological father.

It's insane, but I almost wish I could go back and tell myself not to worry, that worse things, far worse things, were just over the horizon. But I can't. I can only move forward.

I still, looking out over the dust-covered benches, the debris-scattered floor, piles of bones remaining where the accused had stood before the extinguishing of the sun had ended them instantly.

The bones catch my attention, the gentility of the creamy substance seeming frail and pitiful, and I wonder why these remains have not yet been consumed by Banshees. Seems like an awful waste.

I'm taken back to the warehouse where Xion and I inspected the brutal artwork of the demonic murders, feeling sick at the thought that these hunters are leaving so much waste behind them.

"You're angry at me," Xion whispers in my ear, making me jump as I'm pulled from deep thought and back to myself. The thrum of my breathing is painful, my skin having grown too sensitive at his proximity. I hadn't noticed him approaching me from behind, too absorbed in my memories, but now it's a fact I can't escape. Pomegranate wisps of his scent taunt me, barely noticeable among the musk of the surrounding courtroom, yet undeniable.

"You caught that, huh? No fooling you." I sigh, shaking my head. I don't want to talk about this. If I do, then it means it's really happening.

"I'm sorry I didn't tell you," he apologises, but I don't acknowledge what he's said or give him a response, simply stepping forward down the narrow marble aisle created by the two lines of dark wooden benches.

"Sephy?" he calls out, voice echoing, but I ignore him still, letting my fingertips trace the wooden divide between the viewing area and the stand as I reach it.

I look over the partition, from the gallery to the judge's bench, finding the hammer that Yama had favoured as a gavel to be gone.

I move to cross the room toward it, but before I can open the wooden gate, Xion's got his hand on my shoulder and is turning me to face him.

He's too close, his face consuming my entire field of vision, inescapable in its intensity. I exhale heavily.

He isn't going to let this go.

"How could you not tell me, Xion?" I sigh, becoming more emotional than I intend far too quickly. My eyes prickle, heart beginning to sprint yet again in my chest, weighted heavy like lead.

"I didn't want you to be afraid of me. If you'd known that, at any moment, I could become that *animal*— I didn't want you to look at me like— like—" He can't get the words out.

"A demon?" I finish for him and he nods.

"Yeah. A demon."

"Why didn't you tell me about the shard, about the consequences of using it to help Luce? Why didn't anyone say anything about how important it is to you?" I glower, crossing my arms.

I try to breathe, try to relax, but I can't help but notice that the air is becoming thin around me as I continue to skirt around the deep abyss of total panic expanding fast in my gut.

"Well, I didn't think that Pandora or The Demon Lords would find out. I didn't know that this would happen— I didn't *think*. I just wanted to help Luce. I couldn't let her go on like that. It was my fault for asking her to resurrect you. I knew better," he explains, face riddled with guilt, with righteous intent. I feel unwanted empathy for him despite my desire to remain cold and furious.

"We should have kept it better protected," I scold myself now, and him, for being so careless.

Hindsight is a wonderful thing, but what would have been even better was if I'd had even a speck of foresight going into all this.

"Haedes had his tether inside a vault, inside of another vault, and it still got destroyed. I think if Pandora wanted it, she'd have found a way to get it. That box of hers is a pain in the ass," he admonishes, eyes faltering from their sureness as they slowly sweep my face, trying to determine exactly how I'm feeling. If he could enlighten me, I'd be surprised, because even I don't know at this point.

"So those are the options? What Abraxis said? Someone else absorbs the power, you get your soul ripped in two and die, or the shard gets destroyed and you turn into a monster?" I ask him, and he nods, face not full of the fear I expect. He's not afraid of death because he knows that surviving as a monster would be so much worse.

"I agree with Abraxis when he says that running with it would do no good. It would just put everyone at risk, and we have bigger problems to solve with the balance of the universe right now," he admits, and my heart shatters, the jagged shards of it cutting my insides to ribbons. "Now the Demon Lords and Pandora know that shard exists, they're not going to let it go."

"So— what? I have to let *you* go? I can't. I won't." I'm defiant now, and it makes him smile.

"Sephy, look. Promise me; promise me that if this all goes badly wrong, you won't let me end up damned. That you'll find a way to get rid of the darkness so that I'm not a threat to anybody and that nobody else uses it to hurt people?" He asks me this, propping himself on the edge of one of the benches and taking my hands in his.

"Xion— I *hate* you," I whisper, eyes sparkling with furious tears. He gives me a weak smile, devastation undiluted behind his irises.

"I'm sorry for all of it. For pushing you to feel. For the other night, back at the estate before the fire—" he whispers. "If I had known, I wouldn't have gotten so close. I never wanted to hurt you. You know that, don't you?" he asks me, and I look into his face, his forlorn and melancholy gaze, searching for the answer.

"Is this a good time for an *I told you so*?" I ask him, cocking my head and trying my hardest to lighten the mood. I don't know why because quite honestly, I'm moments away from an enormous emotional breakdown, but I can't help it. It's my last defence mechanism against the pain, the thought of losing him.

"No. It isn't. But it's the least I deserve." He seems so resigned to this as he speaks, so defeated already. But I can't accept it. I won't.

There has to be another way.

A way where Pandora and The Demon Lords don't get the power, that Xion's soul remains intact as it is and that he doesn't become a beast.

"Xion, I will find another way to end all of this. You're not going anywhere," I vow, kissing him on the nose. It's a gesture perhaps more intimate than we've ever shared, and I blush.

My rage, my fury, melts away as we stand, relishing a single moment of calm amongst the raging storm of this universal insanity. The instant in which he is here, in which he is within touching distance, leaves me with only a solid resolve and determination to fix this.

He looks at me sadly, and I feel myself getting angry again as the moment passes and he puts distance between us.

This isn't going to happen.

Not after everything.

I can't lose him.

"Well, I think it's safe to say they aren't here." Xion is sweating, taking his forearm to his forehead and wiping the perspiration away with visible effort.

We're standing in the office behind the courtroom, the one where Yama resides during his hours on duty as Judge, surrounded by thousands of thick leather-bound textbooks. All of them have been predictably alphabetised with pristine care, and he has a small model pair of golden scales upon the varnished dark wood of his desk, which I promptly blow debris and cobwebs from, examining it with hurried half-interest.

A plume of dust is cast into the air as I sit down in the high-backed desk chair upholstered in bottle-green leather, the adorning gold studs of the armrest cooling my fingertips.

"Yeah. What a bust. We're wasting time," I remind him, and he sighs.

"Sephy, calm down. As long as I have this pendant and Pandora thinks she has a chance of taking it from me, I'm safe. We need to focus. There's a lot more at stake here than the state of my soul."

But how can I?

How can I possibly focus when his life is on the line?

After everything we've been through?

He picks up a random piece of paper, ink crawling the length of the page in repetitive and scrupulously neat lines. He brings it up to his eye level, squinting as he examines the cramped handwriting.

"Hey, this is about you."

He doesn't sound all that surprised and passes me the piece of paper. I stare at the contents, underwhelmed and mainly uninterested.

The Phoenix.
A Chimera of all souls.
Will rise from her ashes.

These words jump out at me immediately; the contents always nestled deep in the back of my mind, waiting to remind me that the universe apparently has plans. The prophecy itself is perhaps the most comprehensive part of the entire document, with notes and guesses at meanings, scrawled all around it. The word that is ringed multiple times, almost angrily, is *chimera*. There are no notes beside this word, only multiple question marks.

I sigh. Staring at this mumbo jumbo is nothing but a waste of time and energy.

"Do you think the prophecy has something to do with all this?" Xion asks me, expression far too serious.

I roll my eyes.

"No. I think it's utter crap," I state my truth without apology. No words spoken by The Fates or otherwise dictate my future. I'm a rule breaker, a rebel by nature, and prophecies are no different than an archaic set of rules people live by out of fear.

I click my fingers, a gentle calm settling over me as I go to prove my point, letting a tea-light-sized flame flicker into existence before setting the paper alight from one corner. I watch it burn in my hand, embers falling out of sight, until it's entirely consumed by flame. I turn in the chair, spinning and tossing the charred and curling remains of the document into the barren sooty fireplace behind me.

I stare into the dying light of it for a few seconds before my attention is captured by the picture hanging above the mantel.

"Hey. Another map of Mortaria," I note, recognising the landmarks immediately within the gilded golden frame.

I think back to the same thing, spread on the table between Luce, Xion, and me, recalling the extremely dense population of demons now covering most of the city. That same number had once been squeezed into a space a quarter of the size.

I stare at the map for a few seconds, blinking. Yama was the most logical and to-the-point person I've ever met.

So, where would he go— logically speaking?

I continue to trace the outline of Mortaria, looking over the vast expanse of The Plains of Ichor and then at The Ashen Waste.

"I know where they are," I whisper, something clicking together too perfectly inside my head.

"Huh? Where?" Xion asks, tone urgent. I spin back in the chair, a smile taking over my face.

"The Fallen Kingdom," I announce, so sure of myself.

"What? That's insane! That's exactly where they wouldn't go! It's demon central!" He shakes his head like I've gone mad. I smirk.

"Not anymore. Not since the demons got their hunting grounds back. In fact, I'd wager it's deserted. Why would the demons stay there where there's nothing for them to feed on? Not only that, but it's miles away from their masters." My logic surprises me, and Xion stops a moment, expression turning blank for a few seconds before his irises spark with acceptance.

"Clever girl!" He growls with a sexualised approval, lips spreading into a wicked grin laced with triumph.

For a moment, this single answer to a long-asked question gives us both a dangerous taste of hope that we might not be so out of our depth after all.

He grabs me by the hand, pulling me from the chair, and together we set off to find Abraxis.

After all, who will know the layout of The Fallen Kingdom better than a Demon Lord?

The first thing that strikes me as the flames recede from Xion, Abraxis, and I, is the familiar and sick nostalgia of the smell of sulphur. I remember it from my time in the Dark Colosseum, and its familiar pungent sting causes my stomach to roll merely out of habit.

It looms, the enormous shadow of Mount Mallum, all three of us stood at the foot of it on the cracked stone stairs that ascend to the front entrance of what Abraxis calls The Halls of Antiqua.

"You really think that they'd have come here? I mean that's almost insulting—" Abraxis asks me, his eyes a heady cocktail of distaste and indignation as I contemplate rolling my eyes at him. After a split second, I remind myself he isn't worth the effort.

"I really do. Now come on, we're wasting time." I turn from him, beginning my climb up the front stone steps and pushing in on the high sprawling dark wood of the doors. The entire thing creaks like a phantom in pain as I reveal the inside of the place.

"You guys actually used to live here?" I know I sound disgusted, but it's because, well, I am. The floor is strewn with a crisscrossing trail of dried blood and gouged with the imprints of Succubi and Banshee claws.

"Each to their own. I personally like it even though Lilliana and Katerina let their Kindred run wild. They've trashed pretty much all the furniture in one way or another," he admits, our collective steps echoing out in a staccato of hurried determination.

"Charming," I mutter, looking high above me to the arched ceiling, which is pitted deep with shadow. There are stained glass windows at the end of the hall that once might have been pretty but now remain only as wicked sharp shards of kaleidoscopic ruin, teetering in their frame.

We walk the length of the hall without stopping, mainly because I don't want to take in the grim décor or evidence of violent and demonic altercations.

Finally, after a few minutes of silence, Abraxis steps in front of me, pushing a cracked wooden door open directly in front of us and peering cautiously inside.

"Nervous we aren't alone?" Xion asks him, suspicious.

"You never know. If The Demon Lords were going to convene anywhere around here, it would be in this room. If I know them, they must have been trying to come up with some sort of plan in case Pandora tries to overpower them," he explains, and I wonder what it must be like to be him. Where everyone who surrounds you is a liar, is inexplicably selfish and unwilling to sacrifice anything, no matter how small, for the other person. He lives a life without love, and although I would never admit to being in love or anything of the sort, I know that my life is full of it. I am, when all is said and done, fortunate in that regard if in no other.

He makes his way into the room, which I find to be the opposite of what I expect. There's a dim kind of illumination here, and it isn't until I see my reflection, staring back at me from every direction and made grubby by the mirrors, that I realise why.

"This is creepy," I exclaim, and he nods.

"It's so we never have to watch our backs," he explains, and I feel a wave of morose curiosity toward the way The Demon Lords live. Clearly, they are anything but a happy family.

In the centre of the space, a cracked stone table sits. I take a few steps forward, letting my fingers trace the fissure, a natural disclaimer of the division among the prior residents.

"Yama and Muerta aren't here," I conclude, thinking more carefully now. "I think this is too exposed; I mean your doors don't even appear to lock here. So— somewhere they can seal themselves away would make more sense?"

Xion is staring, curious, at his reflection as it gazes back at him from multiple angles, before turning to Abraxis with an unhindered glare. He expects him to earn his keep, apparently.

"The Dark Colosseum," Abraxis announces before adding, "The prison cells in the underground passages there where we used to keep the demons before they fought. Keeping them in close quarters used to rile them up."

I don't respond to this, merely nodding in silent disgust as I stare at the five seats positioned equidistant from one another around the table. How many discussions in this room led to my life being turned upside down? It gives me the undeniable urge to smash every mirror in the place, to set the rafters above in the broken roof ablaze and not look back.

But I don't.

Because I don't have time to think about myself anymore.

I have to save Xion.

"Okay, let's go then. We'll walk. We might spot them on the way."

We stride quickly over fertile volcanic soil, climb low crumbling walls, and refuse to pause as we cover the distance between us and The Dark Colosseum as fast as possible on foot. We remain shrouded by the silhouette of the volcano that looms like a dark reminder that living things, that creatures of the dark, are not the only power here.

The Dark Colosseum comes into view quickly as my stomach turns with sick remembrance.

I never thought I'd be here again. I'd never wanted to be here again.

But here I am.

As it is, I'm beginning to realise that what I want doesn't matter.

A familiar jingle rises from the misty recesses of my mind, making me smile.

Clorox.

For life's bleachable moments.

"What are you smirking at?" Abraxis asks me as I turn to him, expression falling dead over my skull like a limp, cold mask.

"None of your business," I retort, picking up pace and storming ahead of the two men who continue to trail behind me.

Soon, the Colosseum is upon us, the darkness of its cylindrical structure intimidating as I recall looking up from the innermost pit and into the eyes of The Demon Lords. I had been so scared then, so terrified. A child. A lamb led unwillingly to slaughter, or so it had seemed. What between then and here has changed? When did I become not the prey but the predator, hunting down Pandora and vowing to end her life even if I have to lose mine in the process? I think about this long and hard.

Once upon a time, I wanted nothing more than to be left alone, to be ignorant, for her to disappear. But now I realise that I have the power to stop her hurting others, and I have a strong feeling, as I think about Xion's vulnerability, that I can't just walk away anymore.

The moment I learned about Xion being threatened, thinking about her taking him from me, my eyes had been opened in a way that cannot be reversed. A veil has lifted, and suddenly I'm fully accountable. I have the power to stop her; I know that, and I can't waste it.

I suppose I've lost so much I thought I was invulnerable, that I could no longer be hurt, be touched, even by the likes of her. But it turns out that despite my best intentions, Xion, not the opal blade, has become my tether to this life. He's the one thing that's kept me holding on after being yanked from the peace of The Nether. I know that if I lose him, I will be changed forever. Made hard. Made invulnerable but invariably less human.

Not that I'll ever tell him that of course.

He overtakes me with his father and they lead me down a spiral of crumbling stone stairs into the pitch-black of the labyrinthian corridors below. Extinguished sconces line the walls, and a disgusting yet consistently wet drip is all that can be heard, a small but deep echo in the silence of the dark.

"Yama! Muerta!" I call out, unable to bear it any longer.

Xion gives me a wild look like I'm being insane by raising my voice.

"If they think we're demons, they might run off or hide, and I'm not really up for a wild goose chase right now!" I hiss at him, and he rolls his eyes, smirking at my stubborn retort and obvious lack of patience.

I think he finds it adorable, which pisses me off immensely.

I continue to call them, voice ricocheting from the cold dank walls like a vocal bullet as it slices the silent staleness of the air and causes the abandoned cobwebs of Phobias to vibrate ever so slightly.

I turn a corner and suddenly she's there.

Muerta, standing in the middle of the corridor, the skeletal makeup on her face aglow in the dark and making her look like nothing more than a floating skull.

"*Sephy? Xion?* Is that really you?" she calls, voice parched, and I wonder how she's fairing without the Mortarian sun.

"Yes, it's us," Xion assures her.

I watch as she turns, gazing into the shadows on her left.

The squeal of steel hinges causes me to grimace, but the expression is quickly gone as I find the source. Yama steps from within the cell on my left, his pale blue skin and golden hair unmistakable.

"What is he doing here?" he sneers, looking to Abraxis, tone solemn and riddled with condemnation. I bite my bottom lip, knowing he isn't going to approve. For Yama, there are no shades of grey, only black and white. It's both his biggest strength and most obvious weakness.

"It's a long, awful story. You need to come with me now. We don't have much time." I exhale in partial relief as Yama's eyes sheen, curious and concerned. I stare at them both, letting The Eternal Flame ignite in my palm. They're both wearing what were once beautifully embroidered clothes, Yama in a monochromatic robe, and Muerta in a jade green and brown corseted gown giving serious gypsy vibes. Now though, they're worn and smeared with blood and dirt, ragged. Just like the wearers.

Yama looks like he might object, but Muerta touches his forearm with her long, elegant fingers, indicating something unsaid but mutually acknowledged.

Once, I sat before them both on trial for my own heritage, my own destructive capabilities. Now though, I watch as their reservations melt away under the weight of what appears to be newfound respect.

They trust me, and that, after everything I've done, everything I've failed to do, is perhaps a miracle.

"Lead the way," Yama commands.

27

WHEN WILL YOU BE MINE

<u>LUCE</u>

"HERE."

Jules sets down a fine china plate with sandwiches cut into pristine triangles beside me. I sit, eyes fluttering open from where before they'd been closed, at the table in the meeting room where Sephy, Xion, and I had decided on our next course of action.

I'm trying to think of ways to get around Xion losing either his life or his humanity, but so far, I've come up with nothing.

"Uh— thanks. You, uh, didn't have to do that." I look up at Jules, who smiles down at me, guilt writhing like a cold dead thing in my gut.

"You seem exhausted. Food will help." He nudges the plate toward me further, and the expression on his face takes me back to everything I did to him when I was living at the estate.

"I guess I'm not used to this whole mortal thing," I admit, gingerly taking one of the sandwiches between my fingers and leaving dents in the fluffy white bread.

It's true; even after the sun was extinguished, I'd been so wired on dark magic I felt invincible. This constant fatigue, the hunger, the feeling of being fragile and vulnerable is not something I enjoy, nor want to get used to. "Where did you find the stuff to make this?" I ask, changing the subject, and he smiles, pleased with himself.

"I packed some food up in waterproof cooling containers and stored it in the boat before we left. I figured with you guys all being caught up with the logistics and fighting that someone would need to keep you fed and watered," he elaborates. I acknowledge him wordlessly; fond of him despite everything I've put him through. I don't deserve his kindness or his sandwiches which are undeniably delicious. Moments pass as I eat a little, and I feel him slip from my side.

"How do you do this? Being mortal?" I ask him, the suddenness of my curiosity stopping him in his tracks as he moves to leave.

"I've never known any different— I guess mortality comes with a certain level of ignorance regarding the temporary nature of life." The words are deep, well-articulated, and I wonder if it's something he's given a great amount of thought to before.

"That's very astute. I suppose mortality for someone like me is the most terrifying thing of all. Human lifespans— they're barely the blink of an eye. I mean by comparison to what I've come to expect." My lips twist into a pucker before I take a bite of the sandwich in my hand, chewing thoughtfully as my teeth sink into the thin yet tender sliced beef.

"But, don't you think that's what makes humans remarkable? Sephy— she knows that it ends, she has lost that ignorance of security that almost every mortal seems to cocoon themselves inside, and yet— she still loves. Despite herself. She still fights. She has overcome even the thought of her own futility— and that, I think, is what makes her the strongest person I've ever met."

The speech catches me off guard as more profound than anything I've ever expected to hear from a mortal, let alone one serving me roast beef sandwiches.

"You really believe in her," I remark, and he nods, expression firm set like emotional cement.

"You're not the first person to say that or to sound surprised. If I didn't, I wouldn't be here. Why— don't you?"

His question catches me off guard, the entire conversation disarming me entirely. It's deep, deeper than I thought it could ever go between me and this man I barely know. A man I tied up and smeared in rabbit's blood.

"Yes. I do," I comment, thinking about everything I've been through with the girl in question. I resurrected her, and yes, Haedes and Xion were a factor in that. However, I must also believe in her strength, or I would never have taken such a risk. "Thanks for the sandwiches," I add quickly, knowing I need to get back to trying to figure out a way to save Xion. Technically, I got him into this, and I won't let the tether that I made be the thing that kills him. I've got enough death on my hands already, not to mention the fact that he's perhaps the only family I've got left.

318

It starts small at first as I take another sandwich in hand.

Over the sound of my own chewing, I think I'm imagining it to begin with. I swallow, slick roast beef salting my gullet as I listen intently.

At first, nothing, but then I hear it again, the vibrations of a horde, demonic paws and claws pounding upon the soft yet spongy crust of the earth overhead, getting closer with each passing moment.

So, I guess they know about Xion, about the shard and the pendant.

They're coming for him, full force.

Luckily, he's not here.

I rise to my feet in a single fluid motion, moving from the room in haste and finding Jules just as he reaches the bottom of the ladder beneath the hatch. He looks over his shoulder at the sound of my footsteps, pausing a moment before his brow furrows deep. He takes in my face, fingers visibly tightening on the assault rifle clutched in his palm.

"They're coming, aren't they?" he asks me, and I don't waste time with words, merely nodding once and then watching as he begins his hurried climb toward the surface.

I follow closely behind him, making no effort to be silent or stealthy. They know we're here; they've seen the beacon, so there is no point in playing coy.

We close the hatch quickly behind us, covering it with leaves and spinning the lock closed, unsure whether The Demon Lords are aware of the underground accommodation and not wishing to give them the opportunity to find out. Most of the weapons are stored below now, moved by newborn Doppel bodies, and the last thing we need is Demon Lords toting assault rifles, they're dangerous enough without.

I can hear them unmistakably now in the too-still Mortarian air; the rumble of approaching demonic footfall. The shudder of the mass of dark power vibrates down the length of my spine and back up again to the base of my skull, the structure played by my mythical instincts as no more than a musical instrument.

My skin crawls, but I will myself to move forward regardless, knowing that the lack of sun has left me weaker than I've ever been and yet perhaps more reckless too.

The stakes are high, too high, because of my mistakes, so I refuse to be affronted by the reality of it. I need to look the demons in the eye, the very same way I've started examining my own demons, getting to know them in depth so I might keep myself from succumbing to the darkness a second time.

The perimeter of Golgotha is now fully surrounded, Sinners packed shoulder to shoulder around the entire length of the gothic steel fence. Their weapons remain trained beyond the line they cannot cross for fear of becoming no more than soulless meat sacks without the power of the sun overhead, breathing steady.

I pass them, but they don't turn to stare, not as they once would have. Have I lost the intimidating air that comes with immortality, or is it my perception of myself that's caused the change?

I wind between the headstones, Jules close behind me, The Furies coming close as they notice my approach, wordless protection instilled on three sides without second thought on their part. The air tastes like ash, chalky on my tongue, as I approach the high-rising double gates formed of twisted metal vines. I stare through the bars, finding an expected but no less daunting shadow growing closer with each passing second against the matte garnet shadow of the horizon.

I say nothing, the air tense.

Sephy isn't here, and neither is Xion.

Our two best fighters, gone.

It seemed like a good idea at the time, for Xion's safety, but now I realise that perhaps sending them both away was a recipe for disaster for the rest of us.

The Sinners shuffle audibly on either side, air becoming thick with anxious and heavy anticipation. Individual demons come into view, and we find, as the shadow recedes to show the individual monsters, that they're not alone.

Barbas, Katerina, and Lilliana lead the pack, eyes bright and glinting wicked despite the lack of direct light from any angle, as though the darkness is working for them alone.

When they reach the gates, all three of them stop only a few feet from the steel bars dividing us. We gaze at one another for a long moment.

Katerina eyes me hungrily, something like lust — though whether for sex or blood I cannot decide — flickering with all the allure of a serpent's tongue behind her irises. Lilliana is dreamy, face phantasmal and unmoving, pearlescent eyes fixed on something none of us can see as she listens to the whispers of her children. Barbas is perhaps the most focused of the three, his face still, skin thin like crumpled paper, eyes focused and stern as they scorch through the metal of the bars and into my face, merciless in their instantaneous assessment.

I straighten, unafraid.

After all, what more can I lose?

My soul, my heart, my lover and keeper of these things, have gone, or if not vanished then changed so radically that I barely recognise them as my own any longer.

So, I am suddenly fearless.

I wonder if Barbas realises this as his forehead creases, bunching up like a lady's handheld lace fan, brows knitting together with curiosity as we exchange knowing glances.

I smile a little, smug.

"Give us the halfling Xion. Or we will destroy you," Barbas orders, face spreading in a smile as his words serve to remind me that perhaps I haven't lost everything. There's still Xion. There's still my life, whatever that's worth.

"He's not here," I reply, calmly pressing my lips together as I place a finger beneath the high collar of my dress coat, the heat of stress creeping upward to flush my face.

"As if we'd believe that!" Katerina hisses, bearing her fangs in a wide grimace as her lips spread back, cheekbones more prominent than ever and cutting across the planes of her face. Eyes cast into pits of empty longing, her face takes on a desolate beauty.

The three of them stand, the shadows of the gate falling over them in harsh, dark streaks. I don't say anything for a while as we continue to stare at one another, unblinking.

I should have known they wouldn't believe me. So then, I guess this attack is inevitable. The massacre unavoidable.

I sigh, death such an inconvenience after everything I've seen, after everything I've done.

"Look, I don't know what to tell you. He's not here. Not that I'd give him to you even if he was."

I cross my arms over my breasts, fidgeting on the spot, restless for this to reach its inevitably violent climax. They don't retort, merely balling fists and looking back to their Kindred, preparing them to commence with the slaughter.

I take a few steps back from the gate, The Furies bounding forward and covering my body with their own as demonic eyes flash from beyond the bars. They encroach on the metal divide, unhindered, visibly excited at the prospect of violence.

Where's a goddamn spark shower when you need one?

The thought stirs something within me, but before I have a chance to fully understand the chaos forming some semblance of a useful idea, my attention is drawn elsewhere.

Jules reaches for and grabs my hand, pulling me back toward him with a sudden jerk and storming without warning across the graveyard. Turning our backs on the demons as I'm dragged forcefully behind him, I hear the first of the beasts bearing down on the gates, on the fences, only seconds later.

I gaze back over my shoulder, wanting to stop, to go and fight with the others.

"Jules, what are you doing?!" I hiss, his hand tightening on my wrist as I try to pull away. The world becomes a blur around me as he almost yanks my arm out of the socket rushing me away from the action.

"Sephy and Xion have risked everything to save you, Lucifer," he says, voice stern. We're running now, my breath catching sharp and thin, stinging the inside of my chest as we reach where the hatch was hidden only minutes before. "We're here because they wanted to save your soul, your life." He says this like I don't already know. Like I'm not aware that it's all my fault.

"What are you doing? I need to—" I begin, but he shakes his head, cutting me off mid-sentence.

"I won't let you risk yourself for this. They need you more than they need me." He kneels down fast, spinning the lock of the hatch open before he yanks it open. I go to move, but before I can, he's standing again, spinning me so I'm teetering precariously over the edge.

"Jules, what are you doing? This is crazy! Let go of me!" I'm utterly bewildered, but he shakes his head, placing both hands firmly on my shoulders.

"Luce, you're the only person we can trust from the original Nexus circle who we know is still alive. You need to help her. This isn't about you. It's about Sephy. She needs you." He's breathless, eyes wild, staring into my face as my lips part ever so slightly, confused as to how he has come to this most insane conclusion.

"I'm sorry," he relinquishes with a final exhale.

Then he gives me a shove, a firm one, and I lose my balance.

I fall into the concrete corridor below, my head smashing into the icy flawless grey of the floor and my shoulder taking the rest of the impact. Pain jolts through my left side like I've been electrocuted.

It's so sudden, so intense, that I cannot help but surrender to my mortal weaknesses.

The last thing I hear before I black out is the slam of the hatch, the spin of the locking mechanism, and the sharp peppered pops of gunfire followed by the high-pitched yells of a demonic massacre breaking out overhead.

SEPHY

I reappear with Xion and Abraxis flanking me, having left Yama and Muerta back at The Fallen Kingdom, awaiting my return trip.

We've convected below the earth within the cold concrete corridors of the underground accommodation back at Golgotha.

"Be right with you."

I smile at Xion, face falling fast back into placid disinterest as I turn to Abraxis. A moment passes, and I let the flames consume me once more, the air heating and compressing around me, the world dissolving in heat and fire as I am crushed into nothing and remade again, this time in the crumbling dungeons of The Dark Colosseum.

"Ready?" I ask them both, glancing first at Yama and then to Muerta. Yama's face is unfeeling, expression as cold as the ice blue of his skin, but Muerta smiles at me regardless.

At least one of them is grateful for being rescued.

They clutch onto me and I let the flames habitually rise, the sensations of compression, of heat and darkness, repeating themselves until we're standing in the room I've just come from.

Now though, it's empty.

"Sephy!" I hear my name being called, Xion's voice urgent. Leaving the two rescued Nexus members behind me, I rush from the room and out into the hallway, finding Xion with Luce in his arms. She's strewn across the floor beneath the hatch, blood pooling from her head and turning her silver hair the colour of merlot.

"What happened?!" I exclaim, looking down at her as my eyes widen with horror. Her eyelids flutter open, pupils dilating as my face hangs over her from above.

"Jules— the hatch, it's locked—" she half mumbles, voice gravelly and tight with pain.

"You guys help her. I'll go unlock the hatch," I order in a short, clipped bark, heart pounding with the punishing rhythm of panic.

Where the hell is Jules?

Why would he lock her down here?

When I reappear, standing tall on the soil of the world above, I can guess, but I just hope I'm wrong.

Bodies: Doppel and demon, lie scattered across the soil. The gates have been prized open, the once ornate spiralling steel now contorted cruelly out of shape and made sharp, capable of impaling anyone who stumbles or missteps. The ground, made flat and bloody by the massacre that has occurred here, is strewn now with broken pieces of headstone, text fragmented and indecipherable. The yew trees around the perimeter seem to have sustained the least damage, but this isn't saying much as their once rigid branches hang, splintered and dangling, from trunks that had once been free of the claw and teeth marks now scarring their bark.

I look around, finding no one.

No Jules. No Furies.

What the hell happened here?

"Hello?" I call out, throwing caution to the wind as I summon The Eternal Flame, spinning on the spot and anticipating a sudden outpouring of demons on all sides.

I jump a little at the sound and pivot fast to see the steel door of a nearby crypt opening slowly, a head poking out from within.

After a few moments of silence, wherein I take several steps closer, The Furies step out onto the soil, bloody and bruised.

In fact, as they plod down the stone steps of the crypt, they look perhaps more defeated and more bedraggled than I've ever seen them.

"Sephy— we tried. There were too many." Erlea's voice is broken, and not only because English is not her first language. Her long pale arm is spread across her abdomen where beneath, a gash peeks out, weeping heavily with thick, dark blood.

"What happened?" I ask, glancing back into the crypt from where they've come, hoping to see Jules.

"The Demon Lords, Barbas, Katerina, Lilliana, they came for him. For Xion," Erin explains, dutifully ignoring an inch-wide gash on her shoulder that's torn clean through the skin and ripped open the dense muscle beneath.

324

"Where's Jules?" I ask, staring around with wild dread flowing heavy as mercury inside my veins. The feeling is so sudden, so over-whelming, that I'm not sure that if I slit my wrists right here I wouldn't leak silver metal orbs all over the ground.

The Furies look at each other with fearful eyes.

"They took him," Ericka announces.

I feel something inside of me break.

"What do you mean? Why would they take him? He's just— he's only mortal? He— he doesn't belong here— he— he— doesn't deserve this—"

My breaths come in heavy, clipped gasps as my heart hammers, protesting for freedom from my ribcage. The world spins like a child's toy gone wrong overhead, closing in on all sides. Bile rises in my throat.

"It would be my guess that they took him to hurt you," Erlea says this in an unfeeling voice, but I barely hear it above the roar of my blood.

They took Jules.

Jules.

I spin on the ball of my foot, storming forward with careless, angry speed and torching the bodies on the ground as tears prickle my eyes and my muscles tighten, rage coiling around each one and priming it for destruction.

I don't know what else to do.

This is *all* I know how to do.

I let the fire spread, let it burn, let it rage, devouring the trees, the corpses of sinners, the bodies of demons. It scorches everything in sight, and within me, my fear is slowly ravaged to little more than ash as well, the tears of my pain falling in burning trails of salt down over my cheeks.

My terror, my pain, is replaced only now by the persistent, bone-deep knowledge that I must do whatever it takes, must risk it all, to save those I love.

I spin the wheel with furious vigour, heart and head both pounding with the gravity of the situation. Yanking it open, the metal hinges squeal and I leap down, not bothering to use the ladder and landing with a thud, knees bent in a crouch. Only a small puddle of clotted dark crimson remains where Luce had been found, and I can hear voices trailing, urgent, through the empty corridors.

I follow them to the source without hesitation, without second thought, finding everyone crowded inside Luce's bedchamber. She's lying back against a pillow, Muerta pressing bandages to her head to stop the bleeding as Xion watches on, concern marring his face deep with lines.

"You alright?" I ask Luce, who nods, blinking slowly and with each of her movements infected deep with lethargy.

"What happened?" she croaks.

The rest of the group, including Abraxis who is standing on her left and clutching one of her hands in his for reasons far beyond me, turn to face me, eyes bright with worry.

"The Demon Lords and their Kindred came looking for Xion. They took Jules and massacred the Sinners at the perimeter. The gates are in tatters. The Furies aren't in great shape either," I add as Xion's expression crumples. He runs his hand back through his hair.

"Sephy. I'm sorry—" he breathes, husky voice barely a whisper.

"Don't. I don't have time for sorry. I'm sick of waiting around for us to be picked off. You wanted Muerta and Yama; I found them. Now it's time to get that shard, and Jules, back. I'm not playing around anymore. I want this finished," I snap, turning to find The Furies approaching from behind.

"Go and get yourselves cleaned up," I bark at them, impatient. They don't seem to mind that I'm straight to the point though, merely nodding and continuing down the corridor to the supply store at the end of the hall.

I turn back, leaning against one edge of the doorframe, exhausted, as the crowded room gazes back at me.

"We need a plan. Now. Luce— what about the shard? Did you think of any way to get around the logistics of destroying it?" I'm hopeful, but she shakes her head, eyes sparkling with tears.

"I'm sorry, I didn't find anything." She looks miserable at the confession, but I try not to think about the consequences of what she's implying.

"Okay, well, we'll have to go by ear. Regardless, we need to get it back. Any ideas?" I ask them.

Xion replies fast.

"I think we need to lure Pandora and the other Demon Lords out of The Exilia— then you can go in and grab the shard," he suggests.

"Pandora won't be easy to outrun now if you do manage to bait her successfully. She's adopted Icarus' wings. She's faster than any of you on foot, and we're fresh out of other options. Except of course for you, Sephy," Abraxis offers, and Muerta's eyebrows rise slightly on her forehead.

"I *thought* I saw— I thought I was going mad." She shrugs, shaking her head slightly as Yama frowns at her. Quickly, she changes the subject.

"If you give me an hour, I might be able to help you out with speed—" she says, and I nod, taking the help where I can get it.

"You got it."

"So— what are we going to use to get Pandora out of the Exilia?" Yama asks, and I smile.

"I'd have thought that would be obvious." I stare at Xion, who sheepishly raises a hand.

"Pandora isn't stupid. She's not going to fall for that. You bait her out with Xion, she's going to know something is going on. She knows there's no way you're letting him go anywhere unprotected," Yama adds, and I know he's right. To get Pandora out of the Exilia, to get her to leave the shard behind, even protected, she'll need to have reason to believe that not only Xion is vulnerable, but also that I'm incapacitated to act against her as well.

"I also had a thought about the demons— about how we might get rid of them— reset the balance so to speak," Luce whispers, voice weak with pain. "I want to use Mount Mallum," she continues, and a slight shiver of terror run through me. Volcanic eruptions seem to be unpredictable at the best of times. How the hell is she planning on weaponizing one?

"Okay, you're gonna have to talk me through that one— but first, what about the mortals? Yama, Muerta? Exactly how careful am I going to have to be about killing them?" I enquire, heart heavy in my chest beneath such crushing, overwhelming pressure.

What I do in the coming hours, the coming moments, might change everything.

"Looking at the river, I'd say you don't want to risk it. They need to be protected." Yama's expression is stern, his brow casting dark shadows over his eyes as he looks down his straight nose at me and then back to Luce.

"Sounds simple enough. Kill the demons; don't kill the mortals; bait Pandora convincingly— grab the shard even though I have no idea what the fuck to do with it afterwards. This is fine. This is totally fine."

I mutter, almost hysterical as I realise we have about as much of a plan as Yama does a sense of whimsy.

"Do you trust me, Persephone?" Abraxis asks suddenly, breaking the short but potent silence made rich with tension. Each one of us glances at the others in the secret hope that someone is sitting on the answers, the secret fated solution to every single problem we're facing. I guess though, the problem is that this isn't a fairy tale. There is no perfect solution, only our choices here and now.

"Never. Why?" I ask, frowning at the use of my legal name but too intrigued to complain.

"Because—" he says, lips spreading wide as he grazes his jawline with thoughtful fingers, "—I think I just figured out how we can bait Pandora."

XION

The plan comes together, a spontaneous monster of an idea, like Frankenstein, hacked together from a hundred different theories, spilling in a mess from the members of our group and rising from where before there was nothing but the prospect of death. It cannot be denied either that not one of these ideas, concepts, or estimates, when brought together are terribly sound, sensible, or appealing. But still, we have a plan— sort of, and it's the best one we've got.

"It's insane, utterly mad—" I tell Sephy, eyes wild as we look over at where Abraxis had left with Yama and Muerta over an hour ago.

"You got a better idea?" she asks me, and of course I shake my head. Steeling myself, I gaze into the liquid fire of her eyes. I find desperation there, the terror of the unknown as I had expected. And yet, there's something else too, a ferocious determination to get this over with, to meet the pain head-on, to rip off the Band-Aid and swallow the bitterness of what she knows is coming.

"Why aren't they back yet?" she snaps.

I shrug, unsure.

The gates around Golgotha have been mangled beyond any quick manner of repair, and yet the demons that poured over and through them seem to have all but disappeared. It makes me nervous; makes me wonder what they're waiting for, what they're planning.

"They'll be back soon. Yama and Muerta are more than a match for Abraxis. Besides, I doubt he's going to betray us at this point, given the insanity of what he's just suggested," I remind her, feeling the pendant cool against my skin beneath the black cotton of my t-shirt. I grip it between my finger and thumb, pulling the steel chain from around my neck and handing it to Sephy.

"You'd better take this. Just in case—" I mutter, feeling the fragility of the stone as it drops, chain puddling around it, into the soft skin of her palm.

"You sure you can take this thing off without turning, you know— evil?" she asks, cocking an eyebrow with a glint of mischief suddenly alight behind her irises.

"I'm sure. I need to keep it on most of the time, it makes it a little easier to control the demon left inside, but if you don't make it back and return it to me, it's not going to matter much. If Pandora drains the shard using it, I'll be dead anyway. It's safer with you."

She looks unsettled at the grim truth of my admonishment, but before she can retort, I see the returning shadows of Yama, Muerta, and Abraxis, each of them carrying the reins of several terrifyingly beautiful skeletal stallions.

"Whoa." Sephy's eyes widen as she rushes forward over the scattered remnants of headstones, raising a hand to the bony muzzle of the horse closest to her with unharnessed curiosity.

It rears its skull, no sound other than the clatter of bone on bone escaping its non-existent lips. Hooves clatter fast into silence, the horses calming as Yama hushes them, and Muerta smiles.

"I don't understand. The sun—" Sephy begins but Muerta interrupts her, doe eyes wide with a knowing pleasure.

"These Skellions are alive under my power. Voodoo. They are the fastest horses in Mortaria, perhaps anywhere in the universe. Luckily for us, they had the good sense to follow my psychic warnings and scatter after Yama and I departed the courts. They're more than able to outrun any Banshee. There are five here; I only hope that will be enough. It is my guess the rest did not fare so well in my absence," Muerta informs her, and Sephy takes in her words, a grateful and awed expression masking her anxiety.

I look at the creatures, at their chasmic horizontal ribcages. The vertebrae, which crenulate the gradual curve of their necks and spines haunt me, causing a shudder to run up my own. I've never seen these eerie steeds before, not in all my time in Mortaria. Then again, I've never been the biggest fan of horses and these are no exception, so perhaps that's why.

Abraxis takes two of the Skellions' reins in hand.

"I'm going to connect these up to the abandoned carriage a little way down the road. It'll take a few minutes, but once that's done, we'll be ready to move." He's being surprisingly helpful, and I wonder if it's because of some unapparent sentimentality towards me, or if he's just manipulating us all for his own agenda. Either way, we're all painfully aware that we have little choice but to trust him right now. We're running out of time and, even more quickly, out of options.

I turn to Muerta as Abraxis leads two of the skeletal steeds away, the remaining three shuffling, restless, from hoof to hoof beside Muerta as condensation from no discernible source rises from their gaping nasal cavities.

"And Luce— she's well enough to make the journey over to The Fallen Kingdom? To do what needs to be done?" I ask her, and she nods.

"She should be, she's strong. We will wait for your return with the shard and then make our way across The Ashen Waste. We don't want Pandora becoming distracted by our departure or sending Demon Lords chasing after us either," Muerta informs me as Yama picks up her train of thought.

"We both agree our best bet is to wait until she's searching for you both, and then we will make our move. Hopefully, she'll be too occupied to notice."

Sephy puts my pendant over her head, tucking the stone into her cleavage and covering the chain with the thick Kevlar of her bolero before pulling her ponytail out from beneath it. Then, she pulls the sword, dangling down the outside of her left leg, from its sheath, bringing it up to the lacklustre light from the distant resurrection beacon and examining her reflection in the blade.

"Someone put out that beacon— don't forget," I remind Yama.

"Of course," he replies, leaving an uncomfortable silence in the wake of his obedience.

"Guess there's no point standing around here then. Let's go." Sephy isn't wasting any more time, but as she moves to walk away from me, I reach out, placing a soft hand on her shoulder.

"Sephy, what about— what about after?" I ask, surprisingly calm at the thought of my death. What destroys my contentedness isn't the thought of my life ending. The peace now is almost a welcome anti-climax. Instead, it's the thought of my darkness being used by someone else to end countless lives or being instilled back into my soul in such concentration that I become a monster.

"Xion— I don't know. We'll figure it out once I've got the shard back. Okay?" she suggests, and all I can do is give a small weak smile, unsure of everything other than the fact that she *has to* survive this even if I don't.

Abraxis returns to us as we stand silently among the shattered graves with nothing left to say. There is no comfort for either of us to give, no certainty we can claim. We are in freefall, and neither one of us knows when we'll land or whether we'll walk away unscathed.

"The carriage is ready." He smiles, looking at Sephy and assessing her. She gazes at me, a smile of uneasy hope replacing what has been steely determination ever since we returned to find Jules captured.

She passes the sword to Abraxis, breathing in deeply and balling her fists at her sides.

"Time to suit up. It's show time."

28

IT TAKES TWO

PANDORA

I HEAR THE DOORS of the library open at my spine as I stare out over the Mortarian landscape, the eerie glow of The River Styx an undeniable thorn in my side.

Turning on the spot, I watch Katerina take the full length of the room in only a few strides before dumping someone at my feet.

"And who is this?" I ask her, but as the man looks up at me, my question is answered.

"You're the butler. The girl's—" I recall his face from the estate, both during the ritual and subsequent blaze.

"Sephy was right. You do have terrible fashion sense," he spits, breath a hollow gasp of protest against the pain he's suffering.

I bend down so I'm on his level, finding two puncture wounds in his neck weeping blood. I look up hesitantly at Katerina, cocking an eyebrow.

"I wanted to check he was mortal— didn't think you'd care for any surprises," she adds, though I know the truth behind the act was nothing to do with me but more to do with the ravenous craving that controls her.

"I see." I look back down upon the shuddering form of the man in front of me. He looks, other than the weeping neck wound, to be relatively unharmed aside from a few superficial cuts and grazes. He's old, almost bald, disgusting, and he thinks he has the right to pass judgement on me?

I give him a quick slap across the face, watching as he closes his eyes upon contact, moving with the blow.

He's got spunk for a mortal; I'll give him that.

He stares up at me after a second, the luscious green depths of his irises the epitome of Gaia, his creator. Smiling, a small laugh sputters past the loose gate of his lips.

"What's so funny?" I ask him, eyes flashing dangerously as I hear a couple of pairs of footsteps approach through the far doors, the swift and soft echo of their soles upon the hardwood floors telling me who they belong to immediately. I hold his gaze, not allowing myself to confirm their identities as I inhale his mortal stench.

"Sephy is going to kill you." He doesn't say it as a threat but as a fact. The certainty on his face is completely infuriating.

I get to my feet to greet The Demon Lords, their shadows now blanketing us, and stare into the disinterested contempt of Gorgon, finding myself comforted by his presence. Beside him, Barbas' dead expression and paper-thin complexion are ambivalent, eyes unwavering steel as they settle on my face.

"Yes?" I'm expectant as my gaze becomes sharp as black diamond and twice as hard.

Gorgon licks his bottom lip, swallowing with deep and slow satisfaction as though he's tasting and relishing the air itself before he begins to speak.

"I think you may want to look outside. Sephy and Xion, they're getting into a carriage," Gorgon informs me.

I spin, hurrying to the balcony behind me and resting my dry, twitching palms on the railing.

Peering out, I find that if I squint, I can just glimpse a flash of red hair disappearing inside the depths of one of the carriages I thought long since rendered useless.

I cock my head, wondering how they're planning on pulling it, but before I can ask either of the Demon Lords, another sound distracts me.

"No—" Jules' gasp is almost inaudible, but I hear it, latching on to the sound like a starving predator of human fear.

I find Barbas' face, lips twisting into a thin and contented sneer as he leers over the crumpled pile of limbs and flesh belonging to the captive butler.

"No?" I repeat his sentiment, this time as a question, but he doesn't respond, pushing his lips hard together and bringing a free hand with bloody knuckles up to cover the wound on his throat. His silence speaks volumes— does he know what they're doing? Has he let slip that this is the moment where they're weakest, most vulnerable?

Would Sephy Sinclair really risk so much to rescue him? A mere mortal?

I gaze at Barbas, heart rate soaring with delicious anticipation. I've been pacing for hours, plotting, wondering how long I'll have to wait before the final series of events that will pave the way to my destined revenge unfold. The time has come sooner than I anticipated.

"What do you see?" I bark, impatient as I place my palms flat on the cold exterior of my steel corset.

"He fears for the girl. That his capture may have made her reckless— he *loves* her." The final phrase comes out riddled with disgust, mocking, as his lips curl around it, exhaling it fast like poisonous gas.

"Excellent. Gorgon, bring me my wings. Katerina, Barbas, take this mess to the dungeons." I deliver the orders as though I've been doing it my entire life, as though I haven't come from such poverty that none of them can imagine. And yet— I can't help but watch the falter in their eyes as each of them turns back to the shard. It lies ever still, useless, beneath the glass bell jar atop a marble pedestal. The sole artefact in the museum of my desire.

"Don't worry. I know this may be a trap. I'll be leaving the shard heavily guarded."

I look now to the fifteen or so mortal guards that litter the walls of the room, standing like nothing more than conveniently placed and mediocre artwork amid the gloom.

They pause even still as I let my silence echo. At their lack of obedience, my eyes narrow into sharp, cruel slits.

"Well? What are you waiting for?!"

XION

"Are you alright?" she asks me, voice bordering on real concern.

I nod, staring into the faces of the look-a-like corpses sitting opposite me, unable to look her in the eye.

"It's just not exactly a joy ride, is it?" I snap, finding the face of the red-headed body beside the one that's supposed to look like me even more disturbing. I've seen Sephy dead, and it's not something I want to revisit.

"They have to believe that we're dead. That's the whole point. Stop whining—" she says, her voice not entirely her own, the hardness of it giving away her anxiety.

Still, I cannot bear to look at her, not like this.

"I wish Muerta would hurry the hell up. What is taking her so long?" She shifts in her seat, posture overly erect as she pushes out her chest and examines the severity of her cleavage with faint approval.

"Be patient. Voodoo isn't easy. Or so I've heard," I scold her, finding the flippant attitude not at all convincing.

She's scared. We all are, but that doesn't make this level of pretending acceptable. Her temper is, as ever, convincing, despite the fact I know differently. I know that it's not how she really feels, and yet seeing her like this, it's easy to remember how unfeeling she had once appeared, how stubborn she was in the beginning.

I smile, the entire situation oddly nostalgic.

As if Muerta can sense our unrest, the carriage jolts into motion; the only sound now the bare hooves of the Skellions pounding against the ground. There are two that pull us, driverless, and the speed of them is unmistakably mystical.

The carriage wheels spin below us as I peer out of the window, the clacking of their unnaturally fast rotation matching the way the world outside the window blurs into a watercolour of bloody reds and deepest blacks. The Sea Of Shadows can be seen from my window, but soon we are turning away from it, the carriage tilting slightly as though it may topple over as the skeletal steeds take a sharp right, leaving the hellish coast behind us.

Neither of us speaks as a rhythm of harsh sounds builds around us, the clacking of the wheel spurs, the pounding of the hooves, the occasional hollow whinny from one of the Skellions as if it's breathless, even though drawing breath for them is impossible.

We don't even make eye contact, merely looking out of our windows with nervous energy running riot throughout our bodies, muscles tensing and hearts pulsating, watching the skies as the silhouette of The Exilia grows ever closer.

"Come on, come on—" she's muttering, both our eyes tentatively scouring the skies. Where once we watched for a single black raven, we now seek a much larger, more intimidating target in flight.

Twisting around another corner after what seems like an eternity of rhythmically orchestrated travel, the carriage comes now to one of the streets closest to the Exilia. We're heading to the west entrance where, what feels like hardly any time ago, I commandeered Haedes' car to pursue her, to save her.

She doesn't need saving anymore, and I know that. She's become a real power in her own right, but I don't think she can see it.

I look into the face sitting opposite me despite my own abhorrence, wondering if I'll look so grey, so lifeless and cold if I can't make it out of this alive.

I don't have time to contemplate this, to think on the fact that I'd welcome becoming at peace, dead, over becoming a rabid beast capable of massacre, because her voice fills the carriage, severing the vein of such a morbid curiosity.

"There!"

The sharp edge of her tone is made soft by the leather upholstery but is still undeniably void of the kind of determined excitement I usually gauge in situations like this.

I peer up out of my window, pulling back the drape with hesitation, finding her flying above us, a speck of black flashing dull silver as she banks left, circling overhead.

"Brace yourself—" Sephy reminds me, so I tighten my hold on the leather curve of the seat, knuckles turning white as we wait for the inevitable.

It happens just as we planned.

The entire carriage keens right, leaving us tumbling into one another. The horses make a sharp and expected skid before completing a lightning-fast U-turn in the middle of the road and starting off, hell-for-leather, back the way we came.

She straightens herself, coughing uncomfortably as I roll my eyes and laugh to myself, drawing the small velvet curtain across the window. This plan hinges on Pandora not knowing what's going on within the carriage, so I watch as Sephy does the same.

I feel every single discrepancy in the road, smooth onyx flecked through with garnets, beneath the carriage. Every tiny piece of debris, discarded bone, or shattered skull causes the entire vehicle to jostle precariously atop the axis of its wheels.

We are dragged, carriage struggling to keep its balance, skidding left around a corner, exiting the central streets of Mortaria as quickly as we'd entered. Racing on without falter or pause, the punishing rhythm of the Skellions seems unable to reach a plateau in speed as the pace continues to increase.

"Muerta was right; these things are insane—" I hear Sephy comment, voice raised above the din, but don't acknowledge her as I dare to peer out of my window, curiosity getting the better of me. That's when I see her. Among the blur of the outside world, she swoops down low.

I close the curtain yet again and feel the impact of her as she lands on top of the carriage, catalysing an increasingly wild meander in our path as the Skellions try to throw her off. We wait, clinging to the dimpled leather of the seat, breaths held.

The steeds zigzag from left to right, letting the carriage trail helplessly behind them. After a moment or two, and though I can't see, I know that Pandora must have lost her balance as the sound of her shoes atop the roof has vanished. Sephy peeks beyond the curtain this time, cautious.

"She's airborne again— I don't like this. She's so fast."

"Not ideal, considering we need to fight her on equal footing—" I admonish. Sephy bites her bottom lip.

"Her pride will be her downfall," she says thoughtfully, looking back at me and then to the bodies, which are being thrown from left to right like string-less puppets.

The growing speed of the chase causes us to fight each moment for balance, muscles tense and abdomens rigid. As we hit a pothole and lift unexpectedly from our seats, I have the sudden sick urge to grasp her hand. I shake my head, telling myself not to be so ridiculous. This definitely isn't the time or the situation to be thinking about any kind of physical contact with the woman beside me.

"How close are we?" I ask her, right before she dares to take another look.

"Not long now— another few minutes," she promises, eyes dull and reserved to the plunge we both know is coming.

As she draws in breath to say something else, the smashing of glass rings out, high-pitched and sudden. A sword thrusts through the window almost piercing my throat and causing me to lean back as far as I can, the blade skewering the thick velvet of the small drape and sending pieces of shattered glass raining down into my lap. It misses me, barely.

"Shit!" I exclaim, grabbing hold of the blade with both hands without thinking.

I know she's alongside the carriage, only inches away, and I could take the sword in through the window. Then, though, she'd see me. Instead, I give a firm shove, the sharp edge of the blade slicing through both my palms and sending her flying backwards and into our blurred surroundings.

Hopefully, that gives us at least a few more minutes.

I'm sitting, but every single muscle in my body is tense and my hands are spilling blood all over the interior. I lean forward, wiping some onto the corpse of the sinner sitting opposite me.

"Good thinking—" Sephy admonishes, blinking fast and brushing glass from the seat beside her. It tinkles into the footwell, glistening.

The horses are almost flying now the speed of them is so immense. They're streamlined to perfection without the animal urges of normal horses to slow them down. The inside of the carriage is too warm though, despite the breeze whipping through the broken window, the metallic tinge of blood and rich, stiff leather become suffocating as we fly down the road.

"Almost there—" Sephy breathes, turning to me. "Ready?"

I go to answer, but as my lips part to give her a response, the sword, slathered in the blood from my palms, protrudes through the leather behind us, blocking her from view.

We both look at it, eyes widening in shock at the sudden threat. Sephy glances out past the drape on her side.

"Hold on. Hold on right now!" she yells.

The two of us can only stare at one another.

I know what's going on outside; it's been a part of the plan all along. And yet, I'd never really given much thought to what being thrown over a cliff and into the sea inside a carriage would feel like. I guess I'd been too nervous to want to imagine it.

The sword wiggles between us, stuck in the upholstery as Pandora tries to yank it free, the edge of the cliff getting blindly closer with every passing second.

Then it happens.

I feel us run out of road and I hear the high-pitched whinny of the Skellions as their hooves meet with thin air. My stomach falls so dramatically I fear it may come out of my ass as my heart simultaneously rises, stuck in my throat. The carriage disappears from beneath me, my skull making harsh impact against the ceiling. I smell the salt of the sea breeze rushing in through the broken window on my left as pieces of splintered glass are tossed into the air from the footwell, peppering the space between Sephy and me like jagged, broken stars.

The sword between us remains, a sharp and uncrossable divide.

I stare, expression wild, at Sephy.

I find the dead look behind her eyes as we're both thrown forward, the carriage falling too fast for us to brace ourselves. We move in slow motion, her red hair fanning out like flames around her head, my hands coming up to protect my face as I am launched forward toward the dead body opposite me, the one wearing some semblance of my face.

The entire vehicle smashes into the surface of the water below within seconds, but it feels like aeons. Sea water, frothy and dark with shadow, begins to fill the carriage through my broken window in a gush of icy chill laced thick with salt. I watch the scenario unfold before taking a final and determined deep breath.

Watching, we allow the carriage to sink, dragging us both into the darkness of the oceanic abyss below.

SEPHY

My palm throbs noticeably as I stare out from behind the trees of the Sanguine Forest and across the expanse of dark obsidian sand to where the carriage has just fallen into the sea below, Skellions and all.

Pandora lands just on the edge of the cliff, body teetering on the edge with the weight of her heavy metal wings pulling her back from oblivion, staring down into the water.

She watches the carriage sink, waiting for Xion to reappear at the surface, but he doesn't, and neither do I. Well, not really me, obviously, but Abraxis wearing a mystical Sephy suit.

I look down at my palm where the gash from the sword still stings. He had tasted my blood, taken it into his mouth and swirled it around his tongue, and then— then he had rippled from the man who fathered Xion into a leggy redhead with cognac eyes. He mirrored my appearance back at me as I simply stared in wonder and disgust.

Xion had told me once that Abraxians could take on the appearance of those they had killed, but it turns out, Abraxis himself can take the appearance of anyone, provided he has a taste of their blood first. It was gross and wrong, turning him into me, and yet it was the perfect ruse. Pandora will spend the next few hours searching the ocean floor for both our bodies and the pendant that lies cold upon my chest, and I'll have the opportunity to take back the shard.

Though what I'll do with it once I have it, I still have no idea.

Luce says there's no way to stop the darkness being used for evil eventually, either in empowering someone like Pandora or being returned full force to Xion. Abraxis claimed we could store it in a willing vessel, and yet still, Xion will be dead. At peace, no doubt, free from damnation too, but dead.

It's something I can't even begin to consider.

I need him, despite everything I've tried to do to make it otherwise.

No defence I've thrown up has kept him out.

A part of me is glad.

And a part of me hates him for it.

Sighing out with the heavy desire to curl up on the ground and hide from what I know is coming, I watch Pandora pace along the clifftop, deciding at last that it's time to go.

I ball my fists at my sides, letting the flames rise around me and close my eyes, steeling myself against the burn.

I reappear on a balcony I've never stood on before, surprised. I hadn't pictured anywhere in particular but, instead, the shard and the building in general. Two French doors are open, glass spotty with dust. Glancing to the left and then the right, I find myself immediately targeted by a flock of mortal guards, all of whom I've been forbidden to kill by Yama and Muerta combined.

Great.

I locate the shard; glinting beneath a glass bell jar on top of a podium identical to the one I'd first taken it from.

I move, convecting quickly behind two of the guards and grabbing them both by the necks, slamming their skulls together and watching them slump unconscious before they can raise an alarm.

Two more guards approach, one from the left, one from the right, both with dark tired eyes and mussed-up hair, swords grasped in shaking hands slick with sweat. I know they don't want to be here and feel a momentary pang of gratitude that I don't have to kill them. After all, it's not their fault that Pandora kidnapped them.

I grab a tome-sized book, bound heavy in thick stiff leather, from a wooden table beside me, bringing it up and clubbing one of them aside the head with it. Then, taking the sword from the sheath on the outside of my left leg I slice deep, but not too deep, into the upper thigh of the only remaining guard as I spin back on my heel. He falters in his stride, and I take the opportunity to knock him out with the same book I used on his friend.

I'm left panting slightly, glaring around into the darkness of the room but finding nothing.

I thought there'd be more, maybe even some Demon Lords, but I assume there are several outside the door.

I move forward quickly, hearing a groan slip from one of the waking guard's lips and wasting no time in lifting the glass bell jar with a feeling of victory I can't help but savour. I reach out, wrapping my finger around the jagged edges of the shard and lifting it from its resting place only seconds before a familiar voice makes me jump.

I drop the glass case at the sound, watching helplessly as it falls to the ground and then shatters.

Fuck, fuck, fuck!

This is the second time now, goddamn butterfingers!

"What was that?!" I hear a suspicious tone and then the excruciating silent pause that follows while they listen, dread dousing me as I freeze on the spot.

Mercifully, the query is interrupted.

"I'll deal with this. Go down to the dungeons and ensure our prisoners are safe," she commands them.

My mind flits to his face.

Jules.

The dungeons must be where they're keeping him.

I go to convect, shard clutched in my sweating palm, relief only moments away. However, as I go to disappear, the door opens and her voice echoes out into the room.

"Sephy, wait."

I turn on the spot, biting down hard on my lip. I need to get out of here. I don't have time for this.

"What do you want, Anubis?" I ask her, primed, ready to flicker out of here in a plume of flame at a second's notice. I have no real reason to stay, not really, except for the simple fact I'm both desperate for a solution to the problem the shard presents and curious if she has it.

"You're not very stealthy. Let me help you," she implores me.

I keep my eyes dead in my face, numb.

"What are you doing here? I have to go. The Demon Lords could burst in here any second," I remind her.

"No— they've been sent for by Pandora and are headed for the clifftop. They're going to summon Cthulhu. She wants that pendant Sephy. She won't stop until it's hers." She says this like I don't already know.

I shrug.

"Good job it's safe with me then." I retort, trying to come off like I don't give a damn. Her eyes shoot to the pendant that lies, cool still, around my neck.

"Look, as soon as she comes back, she'll know something is up. She'll know you took it somehow. What if— what if we make it look like I stole it? Of course, for it to be believable, you must do something for me in return." She's bargaining, and usually I wouldn't have time for it.

However, this might buy me the time I need, once Pandora discovers the shard is missing, to decide what to do with it. How to save Xion.

"What do you want?" I spit, crossing my arms, breathing hot and rushed.

"Take Osiris with you. It'll look like I escaped with him." Her eyes fill with triumph as I sag, exhausted but unable to stop moving forward. I don't know when I'll next sleep or if I'll ever sleep again for that matter.

At least if I'm dead, I won't be this stressed.

"Fine," I retort. "He's in the dungeons, right?" She nods, hair glistening like a slick of oil in the dark.

"You better get going," I encourage. "You don't know how long it will be until they're back here." She doesn't reply this time, turning on one heel and making a swift exit toward the wide-open double doors behind her.

"Tell Osiris to meet me at The Icon. We'll be safe there." She throws the request back over her elegant shoulder and I fume.

"Selfishness becomes you—" I call after her and slip the shard of Obsidian into my pocket, taking a deep breath and convecting from the room as her silhouette disappears behind the doors.

The dungeons are the same as I remember them; dank, dim, and disgusting in both sight and smell. I expect to run into the guards here that had been sent down by Anubis, readying myself to disable them, but instead find the place empty. I guess she has less authority here than she realises, and they've decided to play hooky.

"Sephy?" The voice catches me off guard, winds me even. I turn to my left, dropping to my knees immediately as I find him strewn across the floor of a nearby cell, neck caked in dry blood.

"Jules! You're alive!" I exhale, relief flooding my gut as I take him in. He looks exhausted but nonetheless without any loss of limb.

"Yes, barely. I'm sorry about Luce— I couldn't let them take her." He's unapologetic in the statement despite the phrasing he chooses, but I nod, trying to be empathetic. He wants to help me through this.

I stare at him, sadness filling me as I realise something awful.

I can't save him yet.

If I take him, Pandora will know it wasn't Anubis who took the shard, and the whole point of this little detour will be lost.

"Jules— I can't take you with me. I'm here for Osiris." Even as I say it, I feel the weight of my words; feel the guilt that also comes from unwanted relief. At least in the dungeons, he'll be safe while Pandora and The Demon Lords are distracted. I also know they won't kill him as long as they think they can use him against us.

Maybe, as awful as it seems, this is the best place for him. It's selfish of me to think that way, but I can't help it. It's Jules.

"It's okay. I'll be here. Don't worry about me." As he says it, I watch his eyelids flutter. He's weak from pain, from lack of sleep.

"Please, do whatever you have to to stay alive," I plead.

"Sephy, I am a coward. You don't have to worry about me saving my own skin. I got this." His voice is hoarse, dry, and cracked.

"I'm sorry. I never should have let you come here," I apologise, but he merely laughs.

"Don't be so ridiculous. Someone has to look after you." He coughs, the sound ferocious as it rings out against the stone of the walls and the rusted steel of the cell door.

"Well, now I'm going to look after you. Stay here. I'll come back for you. I promise," I vow to him, and he nods, eyes half closed as though he might even fall asleep.

"I know you will. Now go, go and save Xion. Go and kill that bitch, Pandora. I know you can do it. You're the strongest person I've ever met." He crawls forward, pushing a hand between the bars. I reach for him, wrapping my warm fingers around his, which are fraught with chill, not wanting to let go but knowing I don't have a choice.

"Go on, go. I'll be all right." He's braver than I've ever realised in all the years I've known him, and I can't help but feel my eyes prickle with tears as I get to my feet and walk over to the cell next door. Jules thinks he's a coward, but the real coward is just a wall away.

"Get up," I snap. There's no time for pleasantries.

I let my eyes wander from Osiris' ragged and starved-looking form up to the door, which shows only cracks of light from the corridor behind it. The guards could come in at any moment, or demons, and we'll be screwed. Nobody can know I'm here. Nobody can know I'm still alive.

"Sephy? What about—" he begins, dragging himself to his feet, his dark eyes chasmic with hunger and pain.

"Don't ask me any questions. I'm here as a favour to your mother; that's all, and it's only because she's giving me something invaluable in return." I let the flames rise fast around my body, the world heating and contracting as I'm moved four feet to my left so I'm inside the rancid cage with what used to be a god made mortal. Now, I wonder if I can even claim him that. He looks more like a piece of roadkill that just so happens to be decadently dressed.

I clasp his forearm, and through the draped and dirty white cotton of his shirt, I feel the bones of him, brittle beneath my grasp.

"Sephy— Sephy— Sephy!" My name is hollered, echoing through the hollow labyrinth of passages, the crackling and familiar voice of someone I'd thought long dead ringing in my ears.

"Hold on," I instruct Osiris, but instead of convecting clear of the Exilia, I will myself to reappear outside the cell, pulling the weak prisoner of war behind me as I pace quickly down the corridor, searching.

I find them within seconds, their gums flashing wet in the half-light of the dungeon, a spinning wheel positioned crookedly in front of them. They're perched on three identical stools, waiting for me with somewhat miraculous elegance despite everything that has befallen them.

"Persephone Sinclair," Layla greets me as I clamp eyes on her.

"What are you doing here? I thought you were dead!" I exclaim in awe of the fact that Pandora hasn't had them killed.

"We are here to deliver you a message. A message from the heavens," Moira says though she hasn't heard my question. Anya stares at me, immense sadness behind the milk whites of her eyes.

"Well, can you hurry up? I'm kind of busy!" I snap, keeping my grip steadfast on Osiris' forearm as he wheezes beside me.

The incessant dripping of water on stone is riding on my last nerve as silence falls between us. Layla takes a deep breath as though she's about to sing.

"You are the chimera of all souls. The Phoenix." She sighs the words like she's in love, unapologetic.

"Yes, I know that!" I snap, shaking my head with impatient fury. I don't have time for this.

Moira smiles.

"And she shall be of all souls. A chimera. Of Mortal. Of God. Of Demon." The words reverberate through me, the epicentre of the quake my fast-beating heart, fissures cracking through the muscle, ripping me apart. "You must save him from eternal damnation. Only you can," she adds.

Finally, it all makes sense.

A life for a life.

Damnation for damnation.

He brought me back, and now I must save his soul by setting him free, by taking his darkness for my own.

I stare into the faces of the old women, into their knowing gazes, into the impassive lips and the weathered skin.

"Fuck you," I spit, spinning on the spot and yanking Osiris to my side.

With that, I convect from the Exilia, heart beating so fast, so heavy, I fear it might break itself in two.

29

MACK THE KNIFE

XION

AFTER A GRUELLING SWIM, we clamber up onto the glistening black sand of the beach, several miles from where we started.

Escaping the carriage had been easy, but what wasn't easy was taking demon form and swimming most of the distance underwater to avoid discovery.

My skin is charred for camouflage against the dark depths, tattoos whirling dim from lack of oxygen as I lie, gasping for breath, on the beach in my sodden clothes. I feel the adrenaline dulling to nothing in my blood, my mortal self beginning to reappear atop the face of the demon that's taken its place.

"I can see now why you like me so much—" Sephy says, looking down at what is now sea-soaked cleavage, tiny droplets of water clinging to her skin. It's completely unnecessary, as the entire duration of the swim, he had donned his demon form just like me.

"Oh, fuck off! You can stop with the whole Sephy thing now," I grumble, head lolling to one side. I've entertained him this long, knowing we have to be careful of Gorgonians listening inside or around the carriage. Now though, he's just being an ass.

I watch as her face ripples from existence, her jaw becoming squarer, forehead broader, cheekbones wider set, and lastly her cognac eyes illuminating orange. Abraxis' face now lies where hers had once gazed at me with a creepy and entirely inappropriate longing. What was once the illusion of Sephy's bulletproof corset and leather pants replaced by his leather jacket, worn dark jeans, and thick-soled black boots. Come to think of it, I've never seen Abraxis wearing anything else. Sephy might say it's a family trait, only owning one outfit, but a part of me wonders if he is really walking around naked and the clothes are merely part of his proffered illusion.

Still flat on my back, I take a moment to gaze up into the sky, an infinity of blood blanketing this world foreboding the death that lies just over its crimson horizon.

"Come on, handsome. We have to move." Abraxis wastes no time now he's back in his regular form, clambering to his feet. Water drips from his clothes and his hair as he runs a hand back through the thick black locks, which usually hang in a greasy mess way past his ears.

I push myself to stand as well, shivering despite the air around us remaining still and humid. Teeth chattering and limbs unpleasantly numb, I glance back over my shoulder to the flawless black mirror of the sea.

"What about the Skellions?" I ask him as he starts to amble back up the beach, crystalline sand shifting beneath him.

"Don't worry about that. Muerta said they'd make their way back to Golgotha in their own time," he reminds me, and I can't help but feel a pang of suspicion. He's been paying closer attention than I have, and I still can't get over the feeling that he's up to no good.

"Why are you doing all this?" I ask, suddenly unafraid of his answer.

We begin to clamber up the steep dunes of black sand, still breathless as we hurry back toward Golgotha.

"I already told you," he grumbles, black sand glittering dully beneath our equally heavy treads.

"I don't want the party line. I want the real reason. I won't tell anyone," I object. He visibly stiffens inside the wet confines of his leather coat.

We both step up and over the ground beneath us as it transitions from jet sandy dunes to flat solid earth.

"Do you know how I became a Demon Lord?" he asks, voice a low and hollow sound now as though he's in pain. I shrug, pulling a silver dagger from the inside of my jacket pocket and palming it tightly. We walk alongside the river as soon as we meet with its lazy meander, but I'm yet to see any demons. It feels wrong, but as I look around, I can't help but be grateful for the quiet. I'm exhausted.

Abraxis, taking my silence as permission, decides to give me the bedtime story I never knew I didn't want.

"So, I'm in this tavern one night. Yes, back when there were still taverns, and barmaids with hefty bosoms served pies of thick pastry with unidentifiable meat inside. Still, it was piping hot, and that was all most people cared about in those days." Abraxis' eyes are cloudy when I glance at him, wondering if he has a point.

"Sounds— nice?" I don't know what to say. He laughs.

"Uh, it wasn't. Anyway, pies aside, I was in this tavern one night. I was also, as you can imagine, quite drunk. I can't even really remember why I was there. I think I was out delivering something and I got side-tracked. Anyway, I'm quite drunk, and there's this guy in the corner of the tavern, and he's got this crowd around him, and they're dead silent."

He still doesn't look at me as he continues his story, licking his bottom lip, like we're just any other father and son comparing tales of barroom brawls gone by.

"Now, if you know anything about taverns and the kind of men who inhabit them at the early hour we're talking about, you know that causing them to fall silent is no easy feat. And I'm serious. The quiet got me so curious I went over there to see what all the fuss was about." He's so casual, the stoic façade I've always known of his Demon Lord persona seeming to have dissolved, leaving only the man who had once been mortal behind.

Our path winds through the desolate earth alongside the snaking body of the river, the pace of our steps not faltering despite the seemingly relaxed atmosphere between us.

My eyes flit from left to right, scanning for any flicker of motion, any clue to indicate oncoming demons, but there's nothing. Abraxis continues, deep voice distracting me with little effort.

"They were playing cards, these two guys. And the one with his back against the window was cleaning up — you know — he was taking them for all they had. I asked the guy standing next to me what was going on, and he told me about how this guy hadn't been beaten all week. He'd been there every single night, goading people into playing him." His gaze is fixed on something far in the distance now, but I don't know if it's an actual sight to be seen or if he's looking so deeply into his memory that he appears to be scanning the horizon for what happens next.

"So, you challenged him?" I ask, curious despite my innate hatred for the man.

"Of course, I did. I was an arrogant son of a bitch. Little older than twenty-one. I thought I knew everything there was to know about life, and also about gambling. My father, your grandfather, was a mean drunk, but he was also great at cards. It was perhaps the only thing he

348

taught me that was any use." The way he mentions my grandfather startles me. I never thought I could have had any kind of distant relatives. It had always just been me and my mother, and that was enough. I have a moment of feeling off-kilter, of feeling unacquainted with myself, but then shrug it off, continuing to listen intently.

"So, we played for a while, and I won."

"You won?" I echo him with surprise.

"I did. And afterwards, while I was standing in the alley behind the pub bent over and puking, the guy comes up to me and starts getting in my face about cheating or something, saying nobody can beat him." Abraxis shrugs like this is incidental. "You've got to understand; the police back then weren't even worth their weight in shit. If you wanted something settled, you did it privately in a back alley."

Our pace remains even, and far off in the distance I see the outline of Golgotha appear on the horizon, The Resurrection Flame extinguished.

"So, you fought?" I ask him, and he nods.

"Yeah, I stabbed him with his own knife, and then when my back was turned to walk away, he got up and stabbed me in the back of the shoulder with the same blade. But it was weird because he was smiling. It was, I remember thinking, like he had planned it from the start—" A small smile tugs at the edges of his lips now, and I cock an eyebrow.

"Who is this guy?" I demand, looking back over my shoulder to check we're not being followed.

"Loki. Actually. The Demon Lord of Lies and Illusion at the time. He was trying to find his replacement, used the card game as a ruse, and then baited me into taking his powers with a knife made of obsidian. It was a goddamn mess, but I think he was tired of this life. He wanted out badly enough to be willing to die," Abraxis adds. I nod slowly, thinking this over.

"And what about you? Do you enjoy being a Demon Lord?" I ask him, this a question I've had burning inside of me for as long as I can remember.

"Of course not. I didn't choose this. I was tricked into it, and yet the power of it, which is something I couldn't have dreamed of possessing in life due to my social standing, is something I've never wanted to give up. That was until—" He pauses as we take a left, continuing along the damp mud framing the next bend in the river.

"Until?"

"Until I discovered you. You are both the biggest mistake I ever made and the most miraculous thing I've ever done. I didn't choose this life; I was forced into it because of my own arrogance. But you—you were innocent, and I damned you to hell because of my selfishness. I loved your mother, still do, but you know I have never loved you. I pitied you. I couldn't bear to look at you as a child. It's why I was never around. I caused every ounce of suffering you both feel and created in others. I'm the reason that something that never should have been created was given the opportunity to be born and suffer." His words leave me stunned, hurt, and yet a warmth toward him I've never known blooms in my chest like a dark and forbidden star.

It turns out he hasn't been blind to my suffering all along, but ashamed of it instead.

"Why are you telling me this?" I demand, and he shrugs.

"You asked why I'm doing this. I can't let the demonic half of your soul, which I'm responsible for creating, cause anyone any more pain. Least of all you. You're just an innocent, Xion."

"You don't know the things I've done," I remind him, Lilly's face floating across the forefront of my consciousness.

"I don't need to. Anything you've done is the result of my selfishness. We don't get to choose who we are. Mortal. God. Demon. Those are the options. But we do choose how reckless we are with the power that comes along with it. I was reckless. You are the victim, the victim I never intended." He looks guilty, but after a moment, it flickers from the depths of his eyes, and I'm left wondering if I imagined it.

As I'm thinking about what he's said, something inside of me clicks, a realisation dawning on me.

Mortal. God. Demon. Those are the options.

I inhale a quick breath.

A chimera of all souls.

Sephy.

I'm supposed to store the darkness in the shard, the darkness of my soul, inside her.

It's her.

It's always been her.

The only person who could be trusted with such darkness, the only person who could contain it.

Mortaria, the only kingdom that would run best where the interests of all three beings meet at a compromise.

She was destined to be Queen all along.

Oh fuck. I can't help but think. *She's not gonna be happy about that.*

Abraxis looks at me, but neither of us speaks as we make the rest of the journey back to Golgotha in an eerily comfortable silence. There are no demons, no attacks that come unseen from the shadows, only us, side by side, almost like any other father and son, after all this time.

As we pass through the gates of the graveyard, still damp in our clothes, I find Luce, Yama, Muerta, The Furies, and — surprisingly — Osiris gathered around the three remaining Skellions in the centre of the space.

"Oh good, you made it." Luce sounds relieved.

"What is he doing here?" I ask, not acknowledging her welcome.

"Sephy made some kind of deal with Anubis. Apparently, it only works with Osiris missing from the dungeons. Don't worry about it. We're taking him with us," she admonishes, shrugging. I look to Muerta.

"Did your horses make it out okay?"

She smiles.

"You worry too much, Xion. They will be joining you here shortly." Her spindled fingers fall the length of the bony muzzle of the Skellion beside her in a gentle caress. It shifts in posture beneath her touch, relaxing as it lifts one of its front hooves from the mud and tosses its head.

"Where is she?" I ask, and Yama answers this time, watching with mild disgust as The Furies pick up several demon bones littering the ground and move to test if they would make fine clubs. I see the long wooden box on the ground at their feet and wonder what they're intending on doing with it. Then I shake my head without saying a word. I'd rather not know when it comes to The Furies and explosives.

"She's downstairs. Resting. She seemed— *off* when she got back. I don't know why. Maybe she'll tell you," Yama theorises, not smiling at me. I know he doesn't approve of our relationship, if you can call it that, but then again, it's none of his business.

"I had better be going," Abraxis says, tapping me on the shoulder.

"You're not staying for all the fun bloodshed and death? I'm shocked," I retort in a morose tone, unsurprised.

"I'm gonna disappear for a while, keep an eye on things from a distance. You never know when you'll need a friendly face these days." He alludes to a plan, but I shrug, sad he's leaving despite everything that's happening. It's not because he's going though, not really. It's

351

because I'm aware I am about to make the biggest decision of my existence and any chance of ever getting to truly know him is gone.

"Again. I'm sorry, Xion." He claps me on the shoulder, his face rippling to belong to someone else in the way I'm so used to seeing from him. He's blonde now, hair slicked back and eyes the cornflower blue of innocence.

I can't bring myself to say goodbye and wouldn't know how even if I could, so I merely watch him walk away toward The Sanguine Forest.

"I'm going to find Sephy." I sigh, the thought of seeing her face horrifying. I'm not going to be able to keep to myself what I know now about the prophecy. Not with so much riding on what we do with the shard. But I know, too, that the act itself must be her choice.

I don't want to die. I don't. I want to stay here with her. But I also can't justify letting the world burn so I can attempt to continue living or becoming a monster. I'd never forgive myself if I hurt her, or anyone else for that matter.

It's finally, after all those days of her proclaiming the insanity of *us*, that I see what she meant.

Would you save ten strangers or me?

I remember her question from that night at the bar; remember how ludicrous I'd thought it sounded. And now— now I see why she asked.

Haedes had been straddled with the same choice when it came to her, when it came to saving her that night in The Dark Colosseum.

That's why she's made to be the ruler of the most brutal kingdom in existence, to be a god even, and I'm not. She understands that there's no happily ever after here, no concern for what she wants or who she loves, and she has no hope for such things. There is only the balance of the universe, eclipsing her heart in every possible way.

Love— or the death of life as we know it, the prevailing of cruelty, and evil, and darkness. The suffering of the innocent. The end of the world.

Those are her choices.

I thought she was afraid to love me because there was something wrong with me, but now I know I was being arrogant. She was never afraid of me. She was afraid of becoming attached to living, attached to loving, because she knows, as I do now, that neither can ever last. She cannot be allowed to fall hostage to her own heart.

I descend into the hatch after yanking it open, move hastily down the ladder and stride fast to our bedroom door, dread churning rabid in my gut.

I open it and find her, curled in a ball, crying silently atop the mattress, vulnerable.

As I step, tread funereal, over the threshold, she raises her head, tears streaming down her face. Our eyes catch in a moment of pure agony, a moment neither of us can escape. A moment of fate.

A moment where I discover that she too knows exactly what's coming.

PANDORA

I stand, teetering close to oblivion on the edge of the cliff, staring down into the once again crystalline stillness of the dark ocean below.

It hadn't occurred to me at the time, as I killed Haedes and turned out the sun, exactly how much of an impact my actions alone would have not only on the people of Mortaria but on the physical land itself. Without the sun, the solar tides of The Sea of Shadows have ceased, and I wonder exactly how the individual I seek will feel about that, if indeed he's noticed.

The minutes grind on, endless and with no noticeable effect on the world around me, and yet I cannot escape the never-ending beat of my heart counting down to the death of this mortal body, its chambers forming a dark hourglass of my very own. I thought I would have all the time I needed, but now, without what I hoped would become a catalyst toward quicker action, toward furthering only my agenda and nothing more, I'm worried I have been weakened.

I need that pendant.

The darkness inside the shard will restore my immortality, and then all will be well.

"I can't say I enjoy being summoned without explanation and being made to walk several miles on foot—" Barbas' tone snakes through the air, curling fast and disappearing like ever-elusive smoke as I turn on the spot, fighting for balance against the weight of my wings.

"You'll be glad you came once I explain," I begin, but Katerina cuts me off.

"We aren't your pets, Pandora. Now what on earth is this about?" she demands, voice tinny with irritation. I sigh. I was trying to tell her before she interrupted.

"I chased down the carriage and it went over the cliff edge. I've been watching for a while now, and it seems as though both Sephy and Xion have finally met their demise.

"I did notice the resurrection beacon had gone out," Gorgon adds, lifting my spirits even further.

Shit. Yet another problem. How will I fix together the broken pieces of the dark tether now?

It's too late to worry about that now. First, I must retrieve the pendant. Without it, The Resurrection Flame is all but useless anyway.

I change the subject quickly to the missing accessory, trying to distract The Demon Lords from this flaw in what once seemed like a solid plan.

"I need the pendant, and short of sending one of you diving, you all should know why I called you here. We need to summon him. Only you can do it. You know he'll respond to you." My stare is impatient, hard, and imploring all at once, the perfect fusion for persuasion.

Lilliana speaks next, the slow throbbing of her carotid artery becoming more rapid as some thought or memory dances behind the dark glass of her pupils.

"You want us to call on Cthulhu?"

"No, I want you to summon The ," I correct her. Barbas snorts.

"Call him that and he'll never help you." He looks smug, but I'm too busy for contests of ego. Instead, I only have the time to be curious and focused on how to achieve my goal.

"And why doesn't he like to be called Kraken?" I enquire.

Katerina speaks once again, her voice high pitched even still, but this time, somehow hypnotic.

"Davy Jones, that's his mortal name, was chosen as Leviathan's Demon Lord long ago. He was old and withered by the sea, lonely as anyone could be, for no woman would have him. He was given the powers of persuasion— to sexually entrap women, and yet the one thing Leviathan never told him was that should any woman ever fall in love with him, they would know his true face. He fell in love with a Norwegian virgin who enjoyed stealing down to the harbour to answer his call, his allure, and he loved her in return. Yet, when she saw his true face, she cast him out as 'The Krake' and ran through the village of her hometown exposing him as 'an unhealthy animal' and something twisted, something evil and wrong. She felt he was the devil, and she was not about to keep that fact to herself. Thus, the nickname The Kraken was born. It's the one he's most famous for, but Davy Jones was his mortal name, and now he preferably goes by Cthulhu," Katerina explains, and I nod, listening.

"He fled here, sick of mortals, sick of their heartlessness, vowing to end all those who tried setting foot in his kingdom, either here in Mortaria or in the mortal world. It was because of this Mermaids came to be. His demons have been trying to break through to the mortal seas for centuries," Gorgon adds, and I think back to when I had first learned of Persephone Sinclair. Just before I felt the shift in the tides of the ocean, felt Leviathan and his Demon Lord straining against the barriers between this world and the next, longing to break free. Judging by the fact they're still here, I'll bet they failed.

"Can you do it?" I ask them, and they nod, a solemn look passing between them as they step forward and onto the very edge of the cliff-top at my side.

I stare left, to the non-existent layer of shimmering sand that comes into existence and then thickens into a beach, before turning back to watch as the four of them hold and close their eyes.

Lilliana's lips move soundlessly and a sudden breeze rips up off the surface of the dark tideless expanse.

It takes a few minutes, but eventually, the chain of Demon Lords beside me open their eyes.

"He's coming—" Lilliana informs me, expression absent as ever. We watch and wait, surveying the ocean with scrutiny, my heart pounding.

I am only minutes away from possessing the shard. Minutes away from certain victory and total power.

Thrilling isn't enough of a word to cover it.

At first, there's a ripple, barely noticeable, but after only a few moments, the water is frothing like the mouth of a rabid dog, white-capped foam bubbling into existence. The salt of the air fills my nostrils as I inhale deeply, puffing out my chest within the steel confines of my corset and widening my stance, ready to greet this new Demon Lord who until today has been only a myth on the tip of my tongue, an idea lurking in the darkest corners of my mind.

They erupt from the depths, flying upward like vines of thick suckered flesh, aubergine and onyx in colour, sheening, slimy, and slick with water. I watch this raw display of power, letting the new breeze toss loose strands from my braid around my face in dark ribbons as I watch the tentacles slow, less foreboding and more focused as they form a staircase.

I watch as he appears, at first nothing more than a glimmering mound damp with the sea, but soon he is risen from the depths, standing erect and tall, his torso broad, his eyes dead and cold like the deep.

He takes a step onto the first thick tentacle, and I watch it stiffen beneath his weight, the wooden leg that follows his first encrusted with polyps formed of crustaceans and urchins suckered into the very grain of his prosthetic, now a part of him.

As he grows closer, I think he appears to have an abnormally long face, but with each tentacle rising higher from the water, bringing him further from the sea and closer to the cliff edge, I find that actually where his facial hair would once have sprouted, tentacles of his own now reside. They flop, wet and flaccid around his lips, dangling precariously from his chin and moving with a mind entirely their own. I cannot help but stare at him with every outstretched tentacle he walks over to reach me, trying to see the man behind the monster. His eyes are dull green like algae and the rot of the sea after many years, his skin yellow and scaly, head free of any hair.

He's wearing what I imagine was once a fine-looking silk jacket, but the navy blue of the fabric is mottled by small resident crustaceans and riddled with holes. He catches me looking and smiles, revealing broken shells instead of teeth. They're razor sharp behind the flat fish-like lips, which seem to be pulled too tight over his skull. Beyond, his tongue is black, a sea slug forced to do his verbal bidding for all time.

It is grotesque, and I see now why the woman who had nicknamed him The Kraken had been so shocked. It's shocking, even to me, and I've seen my fair share of monstrosities.

"What do you want?" his voice is cracked like lightning hitting a cresting wave, spittle flying into the air. I blink, swallowing hard as I try to ignore the saliva hitting my porcelain skin, giving him a soft and what I hope will be perceived as sweet smile.

"I am looking for a pendant. It was lost in a carriage along with two troublemakers. A redheaded girl and a man with olive skin and a thick build. I was hoping you and your children would help recover it for me." I'm not apologetic in my request or even coy. I'm direct and sense the sudden stillness of the other Demon Lords as Cthulhu examines me intensely.

"Who is she?" he barks at Barbas, who uncrosses his hands and drops them to his sides, stepping forward and getting as close to the edge as physically possible.

"Lovely to see you again, old friend. You are looking well. This is Pandora. It is her mission to bring down the walls between dimensions and set free our gods once more," he explains, and I'm startled at the sureness in his tone, at the lack of snark or sarcasm.

"And what do I get in return for this favour?" he asks me, bringing up a hand to scratch one of the tentacles which lies just to the left of his lips, dirty fingernails and pruned skin causing it to writhe from his grasp.

I'm fascinated, and so it takes me a moment to realise he's waiting for an answer.

"I will give you continued domain over this and the mortal seas should I succeed. The Circle of Eight's Kindred will be no match for the Gods of Ancient. The seas will be merciless and cruel, a thing to be feared once more under your command." It's the only thing I can think to offer given my current predicament. Promises of future power, a power which has not yet been set free.

I'm nervous as he ponders this, but after two short moments, he nods.

"One moment," he emphasizes his consonants, the vowels coming out too soft in contrast and giving his voice the edge of a subtle caress.

He closes his eyes, and I wonder if he's lucky enough to have telepathic links to his Kindred like Lilliana. It would make sense, seeing as the summons that brought him here was via thought and not spoken.

We wait a few minutes more, the silence becoming awkward as Katerina fidgets at my side and we have only one place to stare, that being directly into Cthulhu's face. To look away could be construed as an insult, and that's the last thing I need.

"We have found the carriage you describe," he announces at last, licking his bottom lip with his blackened tongue. I notice now it is spotted with tiny whelks as my attention focuses in on the details of his flesh, my revulsion all the while protesting further examination.

"And?" I press him, unnerved by the stillness of the tentacles keeping him elevated to my eye level.

"The bodies of which you spoke. A redheaded girl and a man— but no pendant on either of the corpses." His eyes suddenly open, and my heart sinks.

"What about around the wreckage, somewhere on the sea floor?" I ask him, desperation obvious in my voice. He closes his eyes again, grunting with impatience.

I look down into the water below, finding the increasingly visible shadows of his demonic children circling the space where the carriage sank. He's silent for even longer this time, but slowly he blinks, once, twice, before shaking his head, tentacles waving sloppily from his chin.

"No pendant," he repeats, looking faintly amused. I scowl, heart beginning to fall heavy within my chest.

"But it has to be there. It just *has to* be! It's a pendant with dark magic stored inside— made of obsidian." I give him the details, but he merely shakes his head, eyes turning cruel as his lips curl back in a shell-formed and snaggle-toothed snarl.

"Do you question my knowledge of my own domain? You asked; I answered. There is no pendant here." As his words echo out, their tone final and definite, the breeze picks up slightly, catching me from behind. I'm coerced toward the edge of the cliff, the crumbling edge far too close for comfort.

Is he doing that? I wonder, bowing my head now in respect.

"I am sorry. I meant no disrespect. Thank you for your help."

I turn from the edge of the cliff, hearing him snort with irritation. I don't see him fall back into the sea, but I hear the recoil of the tentacles and the subsequent splash of his submersion.

My nerves are fraying, my temper and patience worn too thin. The pendant is my only shot at gaining true power for myself, and those two brats have hidden it from me and purposefully perished in a lovers' suicide.

So now— now I will do the only thing I can think of, the only thing left to secure the loyalty of The Demon Lords, no matter how uncertain the outcome will be for us all.

I will summon the mortals I have been so carefully collecting over many months, their souls like secret weapons sealed tight inside their too-fragile bodies.

The pendant might be gone, but Sephy is dead, a noticeable consolation prize, so then who is left to stop me?

Then, undeterred by any halfling or pathetic red-headed demi-goddesses, I will call on the demons, which bow now to me, loyal and vicious, heartbeats wild and lusting for a kill.

And, I will have myself a massacre betwixt them. A slaughter to end the universe as we know it.

At long last, the scales will tip at my hand. Tonight.

30

HOW DEEP IS YOUR LOVE

THE DISH WHICH HAD once held The Resurrection Flame smoulders behind us, the bodies of those Sinners who had risen again, only to be torn apart by a demon horde hours later, crunching underfoot. I wonder momentarily about Nita, about how she died, if it hurt. I hope not.

The Skellions are magnificent, but as I look around at Muerta, Yama, Osiris, Erin, Ericka, and Erlea, I find our next problem.

"There aren't enough mounts to transport us all," I note aloud, counting. Three steeds that can take two passengers at a push, and there are seven of us including me.

"What do you suggest? That we leave someone behind?" Yama asks, his face unfeeling. The thought hadn't even occurred to me, not even for a moment.

"No. I want all three Furies for protection. You two need to come along with, and I'm not letting Osiris hang around here unsupervised. Just give me a minute. I'll come up with something." I'm merely hopeful as I make this statement because the truth is I have no clue what I'm doing. I could use a carriage, but it's less than stealthy and would struggle to navigate the thick ash blanket of The Ashen Waste. I could use a Gondola, but the river doesn't stretch as far as I need it to.

Then, I have an idea. It's grasping at straws, and I have no idea if I'll be able to pull it off, but it seems like the only plan that might actually work. I look over into the shadow cast by the thick canopy of The Sanguine Forest, hoping that its dense cover will provide what I need.

"You finish packing. Meet me by the river over there. I'll be back," I vow, and both Yama and Muerta look concerned.

"Lucifer—" Muerta begins to warn me, her tone deep. But I ignore her, mind made up as I stroll through the mangled gates of Golgotha.

Carefully, I pick my way across the soil flooded with the eerie overflow from the river without looking back.

It might be insane, but all of this is, and insane hasn't stopped me in the past. In fact, insane seems to have worked pretty well for me so far. I'm still here and relatively unchanged, if you don't consider the rising body count beside my name and the small brush with potent and addictive dark magic.

The rushing current of the River Styx laps at the toes of my boots, the water level equal to the highest peak of the banks on either side. The scales are precariously close to tipping, and I wonder then why I haven't seen any demons since I climbed from the underground crypts and up into the decimated remains of the graveyard, my head throbbing and bandaged.

Odd— I note, brushing the bottom of my chin with my finger. I will just have to hope that I cross the demon I'm looking for, otherwise I have no idea how I'm going to get myself to Mount Mallum at any kind of speed.

I take a step into the rushing current, pushing off from the bank and letting the souls of the dead, of the sinful, wash over my skin and drench my clothes. It's like a baptism of death, the souls thick like honey running through my fingers and catching, slightly more viscous than the water in which they're immersed.

The current is strong, threatening to pull me downstream, but I resist, steeling my muscles and trying to find traction on the swampy consistency of the riverbed beneath me. I use my arms to wade, feet propelling me forward, clothes sodden and heavy as my dress coat floats around me like a cloud of dense black ink. My hair becomes limp and drenched on my shoulders, the froth of the rabid current coating my face in a slick mask of both sweet and salty river water, the fluid beading fast on my skin and trailing from my face like the tears of those souls so desperate to rise and to move on from their lives.

Finally, after a good few minutes of tensing myself against the current, abdominals tight and legs aching, I reach the other side. Relief floods me as my fingers bury deep into the dirt of the opposing riverbank, breathing coming in deeper, more fulfilling waves than the short wisps I'd struggled to inhale during the trek.

Pulling myself up onto the adjacent riverbank, across from where I began, I flop down, face first, into the soil, breathing ragged as I give myself a single minute to collect what's left of my strength.

I stagger to my feet, clothes heavy with water, and quiet myself, slowing my breathing and returning my heart rate to normal. I make pace over to the first line of bloody scarlet trees, the dark bark providing what is hopefully adequate hiding spots for waiting Banshee.

It doesn't take me long to find one, though I'm honestly surprised there aren't more. The demon in question is gnawing on what looks like a stick but could well be a bone strewn with earth and dead leaves. I make myself known as I step forward, letting the shadows rescind around me.

The demon stirs, noting my presence, glancing upward with a predatory gaze that lingers, white eyes piercing through my skin and into the skull beneath, assessing my qualities as a meal.

I hold out a hand, fingers stretching forward and assessing the space between us, the sickly-sweet ichor breath of the Banshee reaching out in a scorching caress. It rises to its feet, tossing the bone in its jaws aside and emitting a low feral growl, unblinking and hungry.

We stare at one another, eyes locked, and in that moment I feel it snaking through my veins like liquid sin, the allure of what I knew was lying in wait, calling to me.

It's been evicted but not destroyed.

Sit. I command the demon, watching it trying to shake off my influence but failing as its front paws elongate and the head of the beast bows low, wet snout touching the earth.

I walk forward, the tendrils of our connections braiding thicker with each step. Taking one clump of fur between my fingers, I haul myself up into the hold of the Banshee's spine before I can lose my nerve, resting my elbows between its rising shoulder blades and feeling the racing heart and pulsations of its thick, hot blood beneath my body.

Go.

The single command is enough, and as I bury my fingers deep in its matted fur, I see black veins rippling close to the surface of my skin. My pupils dilate, darkness spidering through me from somewhere I thought gated and locked, lost beneath my skin.

The trees fly past us, the only sound the thudding of paws on bloody earth and the joint beating of our hearts, the undulations of the monstrous body causing me to rock back and forward with increasing vigour.

We burst through the front line of trees, the Banshee leaping over a fallen tree trunk and skidding to a halt right by the edge of the river. The eerie white glow spotlights the both of us from below, my face cast into ghostly pallor and my pupils dilating even wider at the darkness running through me with increasing potency. The group; Muerta, Yama, The Furies, and Osiris stare at me across the flowing current of the river, eyes wide, shocked. I ignore their reactions though, merely jerking my head to the right and gesturing for them to follow.

Beneath the long extinguished dark orb of the sun, one Banshee and three Skellions make their way toward Mount Mallum with the intention of changing everything Mortaria has ever known.

SEPHY

We stare at one another, a single moment an eternity.

He breaks the connection, moving to close the door behind him, sealing us inside the flame-lit concrete chamber. There's nowhere to hide now. Nowhere left to run.

"Don't say it—" I warn him, tears streaming down my cheeks in hot salty rivers sprung from the trickle of emotion at the epicentre of my heart, unbidden and vulnerable.

"Sephy— It's *you*. The prophecy—" Xion, utterly ignoring my desperate plea says it, the words which fracture everything between us.

"I said don't say it!" I roar, the flames in the torches surrounding the four-poster bed exploding against the walls. My eyes are murky with tears that refuse to stop falling, my voice thick with pain. "Why the hell did you say it, are you stupid or something!?" I bellow, heart in my throat as I leap to my feet.

"No— I just, I don't want to lose myself. Sephy—"

"What about *me*?! You think I want to lose your stupid big feet and lack of tact, and what about your microwaving skills? How am I going to live without those? Dammit Xion, I can't do this whole life thing without your stupid ass!" I curse at him, collapsing back down onto the mattress as the full force of what he's asking me to give up hits me.

"Don't you see, Sephy? If you don't do this, you *will* lose me. Everything about me you know, everything about me you find charming or even annoying, will be gone. I'll be a monster."

I look into his eyes, and the truth of what he says stuns me breathless.

"Xion, *no*. I won't do this. Absolutely not!" I protest, gulping down air and crossing my arms over my chest as fury threatens to vanquish my tears, my reason, altogether.

"We don't have much time. This is the only way." His face isn't hard or definitive anymore, which would implore my continued stubbornness; but is instead soft, kind, his humanity never more obvious as the stars behind the molten gold of his irises threaten to burn themselves to dust.

"I can't. I won't. I'm *not* killing you." I shake my head, repeating myself, clawing at the red velvet of the sheet that lies between us. My heart feels like it's been pierced by a scorching hot blade, fresh from the kiln of universal torment that seems to follow me wherever I roam.

"But don't you see? It's perfect, Persephone. I don't have to become a monster, and nobody will be able to hurt others with the darkness I've been trying to quell my entire life." His voice is weak, and at the same time, more persuasive than I've ever heard it.

"It's *not* perfect," I whisper, watching him as he takes a single step toward me, swallowing hard. The scent of him, of rich pomegranate, swirls in the air, enrapturing me in the desperate knowledge that I cannot let him go.

I've known the truth for a while; it had been made even more obvious to me that night back at the estate.

And it's all his fault.

I told him.

I warned him, but he didn't listen.

I wonder though if either of us could have stopped this, like a moth to the flame that will eventually eviscerate its dark wingspan, grounding it forever.

Is this fate?

"But— it's the best solution we have. Please." Xion grasps my hands in his, getting down on his knees and looking up into my eyes, the warmth of his palms making me unwillingly relax, unwillingly weak.

"It's not the best solution for me, Xion. I— *I love you.* I love you more than I've ever loved anyone." The confession is like an earthquake, starting with the smallest movement of my lips as the truth falls from me, but rumbling outwards and through us both. Xion's eyes grow wide, his head cocking to one side, and a shiver of unexpected honesty runs through me, devastating as any natural disaster.

"I know. I love you too." He kisses my knuckles.

"I've never told you before," I mumble, feeling my face flush, vulnerable. He's holding my heart, formed of glass that's been twisted and made unrecognisable by the emotional heat between us, in his shaking palms.

"You didn't have to. Your actions tell me everything. You came back for me. You always do," he whispers, reaching up and placing his lips on my forehead, his fingers cupping the nape of my neck and pulling me up off the mattress into his arms.

"Please, don't make me do this," I whisper against him, tears drenching his shirt with salty misery.

"But it's the closest to redemption I'll ever get. Don't you see that?" he asks me, eyes glistening in the dimming light of the torches as my rage diminishes.

"But I don't want to live without you, Xion. That's why you brought me back, isn't it? So we could be together, so we could have a life together—" I ask him, confused as to his sudden seeming desire to end his own life.

"I thought so, at the time. But now I realise it wasn't just about me. I can't imagine a world without Sephy Sinclair in it. Without your stubbornness, your passion, or your strength. The universe needs people like you." He places his hands on my shoulders, looking down at me. I want to slap him, but at the same time, I'm paralysed by the prospect of losing him forever.

"But what about me? I need you." I protest, voice hoarse under the strain of my own internal conflict.

"No. You don't. You never have. You don't need anyone. That's one of the reasons I love you so much. When you kiss me, when you touch me, I know it's because you want to be there, by choice. You've never needed me, Persephone. It's me who's needed you—" he admits, a finger tracing the arc of my cheek and wiping away the salt trails left behind by my ever-spilling tears. "You showed me that a part of myself I thought had died, that I thought was irreparable, was in fact stronger than I'd ever known. Because of you, I know now that there is something of me I want to save. My humanity." The speech isn't what I want to hear, but despite this, a part of the message gets past all my defences in that way only Xion's words can. He's kind, and gentle, and sweet, and honourable— all of those things, the things making him human are at risk of being destroyed forever if I don't do what he's asking.

The Xion I love is doomed either way, and he wants it to be me. Wants me to be the one to save his soul, to preserve the man he has fought to become. The man I love.

"Don't let me lose myself because of this. Please. I'm asking you, Persephone. As the person I love. *Please.*" I look into his eyes, but I can't answer him. Instead, I do something entirely inappropriate.

Twining my fingers around the nape of his neck, I pull him to me, kissing him deeper than I've ever kissed anyone.

The act reverberates through me, and I feel the beat of his heart, the thrum of his pulse, the groan strangled in his throat as he reciprocates, desperate now more than ever.

The torches dim to a candle-lit ambience as I continue to kiss him, not wanting to think, not wanting to talk, just needing to show him everything that has gone unspoken between us for far too long.

Our lips scorch against one another, and his strong hands come up to cup my chin while the stubble of his jaw line creates a beautiful friction against my raw fingertips as I lock him against me.

We don't speak, don't have to. In fact, the act is incredibly silent, and yet he speaks volumes to me as he pushes me back against the pillows and clambers onto the mattress, whipping his shirt over his head and kicking off his shoes. His pupils dilate as he takes me in, eyes connecting with mine and telling me the story of us with a single glance. Everything we've been through, everything we've suffered, we've felt, melds together in a torrent of quiet gasps, desperate trailing fingers and ravenous kisses atop the red crushed-velvet sheets.

I let him pin me to the bed with his weight, our noses touching, still fully dressed beneath the heat of his carved torso. My fingers run through the thick tangle of his dark hair and he traces my jawline and then my neck with his lips, with his tongue. I cage him against me, afraid of letting go, afraid of ever leaving this room.

It's terrifying, exhilarating, revolutionary as he unbinds my corset and tears off my pants, his fingers tracing a map of everything we've seen across my skin. The devastation, the pain, the love, the lust, it rises with the curves of my breasts, dips over the peaks of my hip bones, and caresses my abdomen before rising to trace my throat alongside his warm lips as he hardens against my stomach.

It becomes a sensual blur, a wildfire of sensation that rips through us both as his pupils grow ever wider, his increasingly concentrated irises capturing the firelight of the sconces and blazing back into me, the heat of our passion coming alive in his face. He unbuttons his jeans, towering over me as I wait, breathless, eyes still full of tears, lips plump and tender.

Slipping out of the last of his clothes, he lunges at me, aggressively kissing me like it's the end of the world, because for us, it is. The end of everything I've been afraid to want, everything I'd tried to guard against, and yet here I am, wanton and raw, heart torn open and bleeding profusely. The agony of it makes the pleasure only more unbearable, more precious, more meaningful.

He settles over the top of me, biting my bottom lip and caressing the side of my face with gentle fingers.

"I love you, Persephone," he whispers in my ear before pulling back and kissing me deeply again. He eases into me slowly and I inhale in a sharp and involuntarily gasp. Tears trickle from the corners of my eyes, down my cheeks and onto the velvet beneath the silken skin of my back, hair splayed in an ironic crimson halo around my face.

"I love you too. I'll never love anyone again. There's only you." The confession might be seen as melodramatic, but I know it's true. No man could ever compare to him, could ever see through me as he does. No one could ever handle this level of all-consuming passion laced with stubborn independence.

He's the love of my life, and I wish I'd told him sooner.

I thought that telling him would make it real, would destroy me. But it was already real, beyond words, beyond flowers, hearts, or greeting cards. It was in every small action, every breath, every worried thought or painful act. Every sacrifice, every risk, has been for him.

He brought me back to life, but he also brought me fully to life for the first time in my entire existence. I have never felt this passionately, this definitely for anyone, and I know now that even if I hadn't resisted, I'd be in the exact same position. Broken but undeniably alive.

It turns out no matter who you are, you can't help who you fall in love with. Yet, I'm glad it was him. I just wish it wasn't like this.

We make love slowly, deeply, looking into one another's eyes; tears flowing freely down my face the entire time. He kisses me through it all, through the pain, through the pleasure, through the emotional depth I didn't know I was capable of.

When it's over, as we fall apart against one another, our jagged broken edges made smooth like the missing pieces of a puzzle, I still can't let him go. We start all over again, never wanting to stop, to admit defeat, never wanting it to end. The intense flame of everything we are, of everything we mean to each other, has always been volatile, explosive, full of heat and all-encompassing passion.

Unfortunately for both of us, a flame that burns this bright, this hot, can never burn for long.

After it's over, I let him hold me in a way I've never allowed before. I can't bring myself to want to move, to break our embrace. I kiss his shoulder lightly, look up into his eyes as he stares down at me, sated, eyelids heavy and limbs warm as they entwine with mine. My lashes flutter, my gaze taking in the planes of his face, the kindness in the curve of his mouth, the softness in the molten gold of his eyes, the spark of recognition just beneath the glassy surface of his pupils that identifies something in me I didn't know was there.

It's then I know why I hadn't been able to stop myself from crying the entire time we'd been making love.

I want to save the man I love.

More than anything.

And I know that, to do so, I have to kill him. I have to let him go so that what is good in him is not destroyed forever.

"I'll do it; I'll save your soul," I whisper to him. He closes his eyes, sparkling with tears now too.

It doesn't make any sense, but I love him so much, want him to be content so deeply, that I'm somehow willing to unravel my own life to save what he's fought to become. To stop his darkness from making the world a worse place. I am saving him from himself even if in the process I'll destroy myself.

Perhaps then, that's what love is.

Selflessness. Sacrifice. Pain.

I want to be angry, but I can't waste this moment. I'm right here, in his arms, and there's nowhere I'd rather be.

The minutes slip like diamonds through our fingers, precious, rare, and irreplaceable.

"Xion, will you tell me now?" I ask him. He cocks an eyebrow, pulling me closer as I splay my fingers across his pectorals, letting them tease through his chest hair.

"Tell you what?" he asks, kissing me on the forehead as though any moment where he isn't showing me how deeply he cares is one entirely wasted.

"I want to know about your plans for the future, our future." I nuzzle deep into him, letting the warmth and the scent of him cocoon me like a blanket.

"Sephy, I don't know— that's— Are you sure?" He looks bewildered as I lean up and his fingers trace a meander down my back, causing my eyelids to flutter and my bottom lip to quiver.

"Please," I say, kissing him fully on the mouth.

He holds me close to him, deepening the kiss for a few moments before he finds my gaze again, eyes brimming full of the tears I had thought would have long since dried up by now.

"Okay, babe. All right, hush now." He's never called me babe before, and though my independent self shudders, I accept the term, heart giving an unwilling flutter against my consent.

"Please—" A single tear falls from my eye as I wrap myself tighter in his arms. "Just lie to me."

31

THE POWER OF LOVE

XION

SHE STARES UP AT me, legs curled beneath her on our pristine couch.

"I can't believe after all the packing and unpacking we're finally here."
Sephy is beaming, turning to look out over the skyline of Chicago, the city
she loves, from the panoramic glass window of our brand-new penthouse
apartment.

I let my eyes linger on her as she sits, seemingly content at last, beside me.
I, however, am unable to believe I'm here for a different reason, but it isn't
the view; it's her.

I lean forward, the scent of cinnamon enrapturing me with its nostalgic
charms, raising my hand to cradle the back of her head, fingers trailing
absently through the silken flames of her hair. I wrap my arm around her
shoulders, and she turns away from the glittering lights of the city over which
we hover, pupils dilating now as she stares directly up at me.

"I am so glad we did this," she concludes, chin tilting up as her lips rise
to meet mine. Everything inside of me sparks and sputters into a liquid burn
that covers every inch of my skin.

As the kiss breaks, my heart hammering as ever in my chest, her eyelids rise,
revealing a glisten of mischievous intent, as prominent and unmistakable as
a newborn sun.

She uncurls her legs from beneath her, rising fluidly onto her bare feet
before stepping across the hardwood floors and over to a glass cabinet.
Standing against the left-hand wall, it rises, concealing the space behind it
that is plastered in aubergine and cream wallpaper, modern yet undeniably
her, undeniably us. The light flooding the open plan space is stark yet warm,
spotlights inlaid into the ceiling having dimmed intuitively to capture the
ambience of our first night living together as a couple.

She fiddles inside the cabinet for a few seconds before a needle scratching against vinyl sounds, and then the soulful funk of **The Bee Gees** *seeps out into the room, encapsulating me in a bubble of memory.*

"I love you," I sigh, watching as she turns and presents me with a hand. I oblige, spritely as I spring up from the soft hold of the couch cushions, crushing the distance between us in only seconds.

I twist my arms around her body, claiming her as mine, revolving slowly and staring with wonder into the face I cannot get enough of.

"And I love you, Alex Johnson." She meshes her fingers together behind the nape of my neck, letting herself dangle ornately in my arms.

"So, what do you want to do on our first night living together as a couple?" I ask her, feeling the music seep into my muscles, into my bones, as I pull her closer so we're flush. The heat of her and the intensity of her gaze are so unwavering it feels like nothing can break us apart.

"I can think of a few things—" She rests her head on my pectoral, and I feel her smile against me.

We dance, swaying and circling across the floor, enveloped and safe in the promise of a future that can never be.

"Tell me another—" she demands, smiling as we devour a thick white baguette, nibble on grapes and apples, and drink wine from the bottle, naked atop the sheets of the bed. Neither of us is willing to acknowledge what lies beyond the closed door, the fate of us. "You know I'm really glad Jules thought to bring food. I mean I assume it was Jules. You found this in storage with the weapons, right?" she asks me, and I nod, remembering my naked dash down the winding corridors in search of sustenance as a grin spreads over my face.

"Luckily for us, yes. Jules really does think of everything," I respond, and she looks momentarily sad. I reach across the sheets, covering her hand with mine.

"You'll make sure you save him?" I ask her, knowing the answer already but scared she's forgotten what's happening beyond these four walls. She nods, not speaking, like the wrong word will shatter the illusion of whatever the hell it is we're doing right now.

"Tell me another." She picks up a grape from the wooden platter between us, the sheet dropping slightly from where she's wrapped it around her porcelain curves. She pops it in between her raw lips, holding it there and crawling forward, careful not to tip over the wine between us.

"Grape?" she asks me with a seductive glance, and I lean forward, kissing her and feeling the fruit slip between us. It bursts inside my mouth, the juice slicking over my tongue, tart, before rolling in sugary waves down my gullet.

"Mmm—" I groan, senses in overdrive.

Is this what it means to know you're about to die? That everything becomes more vibrant, tastes more fabulous, that sensations become more irresistible? Or is that just Sephy, just the knowledge that after everything, the fact she loves me too is out in the open between us, an airborne drug that will not cease in its attempts to make everything about this so agonisingly addictive?

I don't want to die.

But I don't want to be damned or damn the world either.

If I could, I would stay, lie forever by her side, holding her while she sleeps, but I have to make the right choice, not the easy one. If I let this darkness inside of me hurt other people, hurt her, then everything I've ever done, everything I've ever fought to become, will have been for nothing.

Sephy wouldn't want to love me that way, and I wouldn't want to be loved that way. I want to be worthy of her, and perhaps, dying is the only way to do that now. We've both been selfish, especially me, but now it's time to put what I want aside because the universe, the fate of everything we hold dear, demands it to be so.

It's not fair.

But nobody ever promised that life would be.

I want to be the man she deserves, even if that means that my soul is ripped in half in the process.

What can I say? I guess after everything, I've realised that death isn't the worst thing that can happen to a person.

Not even close.

She stares at me, her beautiful face etched forever into my mind like a long aching brand.

"Please Xion, tell me another—"

SEPHY

372

I'm more intoxicated than I have ever been, drifting on a sea of plans for a life I didn't know I wanted. A life I cannot mourn because it never happened, and yet grief blooms unstoppable in my chest like an invisible but fatal wound that refuses to close.

He tells me about the movies we would see, the popcorn we would share, the foreign beaches we would visit, and the restaurants we would frequent. He talks about cosy weekends spent in bed, satiating great hungers both for food and sex. He makes the domestic, everything I never wanted, seem shiny and new like a designer dress I never thought would flatter me, yet it does.

I want it. Want him. Want those nights spent in front of the fireplace, cuddled up together with a good book and fine whisky. I want him to be there to creep up on me in the shower and take me, limbs slick with foam, up against the tiled wall. I want to make him breakfast in bed, want to cook with him and dance to our favourite music.

The want is too much. The desire a puncture in my heart slowly filling with concrete as the inevitable draws closer, the hole letting the cement leak through, creating a heavy and immovable dread in my stomach too.

"Sephy, I think we should go. We've been down here a while. We can't leave it much longer, there isn't time." His words are like an ice bath, chilling me through so every limb freezes, refusing to move.

"But I—" I try to stall, but I know that the time for us to bask in what could have been is over now.

The wine bottle is empty, the fruit and bread nothing but crumbs and scattered cores.

Bodies sated but not content, we both move to the edge of the bed, and I allow my mind to fall into the numb clutch of routine motion, unable to comprehend what it is we will do next.

I dress slowly, methodically, the chain of the obsidian pendant still hanging warm around my neck, the metal assimilated too easily with the temperature of my skin. I pull on my pants, the obsidian shard still heavy in my back pocket, and then move to Xion so he can lace up the back of my corset. Every time his dextrous fingers graze against me, I unwillingly shudder at the sensation, the touch of his skin to mine like flames licking ice.

Xion places his jacket over his shoulders, and it takes me back to stealing his leather jacket back at home but refusing to acknowledge the real reason I was doing it. It seems stupid now. Everything I've done to deny this, to flee it, seems redundant and petulant.

"Ready?" he asks me, and I shrug.

"No. I'm not ready. But it doesn't matter, does it? Let's go."

I sigh, taking his hand in mine and squeezing it tight.

We walk from the room, ascending through the hatch via the ladder and away from the safety of the four walls that had sheltered us from the warzone overhead.

"We should convect," Xion suggests, looking back over one shoulder and up to the looming darkness of the Exilia's sharp silhouette.

"I don't want to. I'd rather walk, I need time." I voice my unwillingness to comply with the universe even still as he shakes his head, the side of his mouth quirking in a smile.

"Stay here—" He darts off into the over-ground crypt that had once served as an office and returns with a thick blanket of jet velvet clutched in one palm. He passes it to me, the material slipping too easily through his fingers, reminding me of sand in an hourglass, every fleeting second reflected too clearly in the surrounding world.

"Your hair is a dead giveaway." He smiles as I wrap the cloak around myself, fastening a silver clip in the shape of a Celtic knot beneath my throat.

"I've been thinking about just dyeing it or something to make covert ops more covert in the future—" I muse, and he shakes his head, disapproving.

"Don't. It wouldn't be you." He says it like he knows me, but I wonder how that's happened when I'm losing touch with who even I thought I was. The Sephy Sinclair I was before Mortaria wouldn't have fallen in love, and she certainly wouldn't have killed the man in question to save the balance of the universe or to save his soul.

Selflessness is a new look on me, and I'm not sure how I like it.

How am I going to carry on without Xion there to keep me anchored, to keep me grounded? How can I possibly live without him after everything I've vowed never to feel but ended up succumbing to anyway? I am a fool for loving him, and fate is going to make sure I never forget it.

He grabs my hand in his, intertwining his fingers with mine and pulling me forward across the bone-scattered soil of Golgotha, the cloak fluttering in heavy folds around my ankles as I pull the hood over my head, blanketing myself in mystery.

I peek up at him as we pass through the gates, wondering what he's feeling.

Before, when I thought I had time, I would have pondered but not asked, but now I simply say it.

"Are you okay?" I voice the query almost as soon as it materialises inside my head. He peers down at me around the edge of my hood, hand squeezing mine.

"No. You know— if there was a way I could stay with you, if there was a way to stop this darkness inside of me from destroying everything, I would do it. Please don't think I want this. I don't. I just can't become a monster, Sephy. I can't let more people die so I can stay here and love you. I couldn't live with myself."

I know what he means, I couldn't live with myself either knowing that being with him was causing suffering to others or fear in either of us. Once upon a time, I would have said fuck it and settled for the immoral but easy choice, but after all the pain my resurrection caused, I know I can't live with that kind of guilt.

"I just, this, all of this— it's so cruel." I feel myself choking up as I realise that once again I've been peeled from the thin layer of security I've got left and stripped naked, vulnerable, raw. I pull the hood of my cloak further forward, hiding my grief.

The universe seems to be trying to teach me a lesson, and it's that whatever means anything to you doesn't matter. Nothing and no one is safe.

Xion doesn't reply to my statement, perhaps because he knows there's nothing else to say. It's a fact.

Life is cruel, end of story.

And yet, as we convect from one side of the riverbank to the other, I wonder if I'd take back falling in love to prevent this hurt.

Never.

I don't think I could. What has just passed between us is arguably the most miraculous thing that's ever happened to me, and I wouldn't trade that for anything. Not long-lasting numbness, or an escape from the grief I know is coming. Grief might be the final act of love I have to give. If I wasn't torn open, splayed bare, by losing him, I guess it would mean I never really loved him the way I know I do.

"Sephy?" Xion says my name so it hangs between us like a question.

"Yes?" I whisper, the smoke of The Eternal Flame replaced in my nostrils by the metallic tinge of the Sanguine Forest as we approach the first line of trees.

"Just— don't let this be in vain. Once this is over, you can't break down. You have to stop Pandora. You need to save Mortaria and restore the balance." He implores me to be the one thing I'm not sure I can be in this situation: strong. So, I bite my bottom lip, nodding despite my doubt that I'll ever feel any kind of strength again without him here.

The rest of the journey to the clearing, which had once held The Hollow, passes in scarlet silence as the ruddy earth squelches under-foot. No demons bother us though I feel them stirring on all sides; waiting, though for what I couldn't say.

I don't know why The Hollow seemed like the right place to do this. Perhaps because our first trip through the tree's portal was right after I saw Xion's true face for the first time. It was that day that I understood his strength, not demonic but human.

Though that might be true, I also wonder if maybe it's really because I need the strength of Haedes close by, need to remind myself that the woman he had bled for, the woman he had grown The Hollow for to begin with, is dead too. The love of his life died, and he survived. Somehow, I have to as well, following in footsteps I had never imag-ined could become a roadmap for my fate.

I am surprised, however, to find the tree nothing more than a hacked-down stump. Splintered branches litter the soil, the metal grate that once wrapped around the base and the plaque dedicated to my mother a twisted and unrecognisable mass of shadow only a few yards away.

"They cut it down." I don't know why this makes me so angry, but it does. Nothing is sacred, not to her. She's single-handedly dismantling my family, my heritage, one person at a time.

Momentarily, I think about the fact that in killing Xion, perhaps I'm playing into her hands, giving her the satisfaction of knowing she's ripping my world apart. But then I stare at him, at his kind eyes, and remind myself that this isn't about her or me. It's about him.

I turn to face him and he takes my hands in his.

He looks down into my eyes, and I place a hand on the side of his face. He leans into my palm, the stubble of his cheek grazing my soft callouses. I take this same hand, using it to cast a line of fire in a circle around us, creating a boundary between us and any lurking demons.

The flames flicker in his irises, turning the gold hot and languid as he gazes down at me.

"Can I get a kiss for the road?" he asks me, and I tears immediately spring to my eyes.

I can't do this.

"Xion I— I don't know if I can—" I stutter, and he places a hand on my jawline, tilting my head and pulling my lips up to his.

The kiss is devastating, the longing, the unrequited possibility of us becoming a physical presence as his free hand cups my lower back and he pulls me into him, bending me back and kissing me raw among the firelight.

It's unlike any kiss I've ever experienced, pure, unhindered emotion without a hint of lust, only love. I don't want it to end, the taste of him washing over me and coating my tongue, his arms making me feel so indescribably wanted and safe that I cannot deny that he is and will always be my home.

How have I wasted the time we had being so unsure?

How have I ever doubted this?

I feel it in every fibre of my marrow, in every beat of my heart. I belong to him, and him to me. Gasoline and match, spark and timber, we blaze for one another, two halves of something incredible and rare. A fast-burning wildfire, beautiful from every angle yet destructive as all hell.

I love him, and because of that, because of my loyalty to everything he has fought to become, I must set him free, preserve his goodness and everything that has made me fall harder than I ever saw coming.

Perhaps I'm not killing him; perhaps I'm saving the man I love and killing the demon, killing the darkness within him.

It isn't enough for me, but it has to be.

It's the only thing left to do.

He lets me go, my hood falling back from my face and leaving me exposed. I let my hand rest above the place where my palm branded him inside the Exilia dungeons what feels like a lifetime ago.

I remove the pendant from around my neck, taking a deep and heavy breath, tears spilling down my cheeks yet again as the taste of pomegranate fades from my tongue.

Dropping my hand from his, I pull the shard from my back pocket while the flames around us rise higher and higher and the moment becomes thick with tension.

Detaching the obsidian pendant from the chain, I look up to Xion, wanting to say something but unable to find the right words. His stare says he already knows, so I take a final deep breath, summoning The

Resurrection Flame to me and letting the two pieces of the tether meld together under the mystical cobalt heat.

Xion grabs me around the waist, pulling me into him and looking down into his eyes.

"Xion I—" I want to say I love him, but he smiles, placing my hand over his fast-beating heart.

"I know. I'll always be yours," he whispers. A tear falls from my eye and dribbles, salty and hot, down my cheek. His eyes are sheening with unshed tears too, his entire expression broken beyond repair.

I take the shard in my free hand as he holds me, his heartbeat persistent under my right palm as my left-hand shakes uncontrollably.

I'm sobbing silently, my red hair blowing around me in the spark-peppered air of the flaming ring, eyes blazing with the surrounding firelight as I stare up at him.

I don't know how to do this.

I can't.

I'm about to drop the shard, but before I do, Xion's hand covers mine, steadying me.

"Goodbye, Sephy."

His last words echo in the space between us as I feel him guide the shard of obsidian to the place above my own heart. He slices through my pale flesh with the razor-sharp edge, causing a sharp inhale from us both, drawing blood.

I watch the light leave his eyes as he gazes at me with more love than I ever thought I needed, dying in my arms.

He falls to his knees, pulling me with him as I feel the darkness transferring into my veins, setting them on fire with an icy burn that takes my breath away.

I collapse, tears falling fast onto the floor as the flames surrounding us extinguish, leaving me vulnerable and alone.

Bloody dirt cushions me as I rock backwards and forward, a wail escaping my lungs as something inside me breaks forever. I cradle his body in my lap, the heat slipping from me faster than I expect. I can't let go, not willing to acknowledge this is really happening as the darkness continues to thrum, stinging the insides of my veins and making me over, reforming me dark and new.

Somewhere between agony, grief, and newfound power, I lose consciousness, his body still intertwined cold with mine among leaves scorched black.

32

EMPEROR'S NEW CLOTHES

PANDORA

MY BOOTS SLAM AGAINST the cold stone floor of the Exilia as I lead The Demon Lords through the cavernous entrance. The stone underfoot is wet with river run-off, the current of the River Styx frothing and bouncing against the crystal-carved banks. They etch through the space, a permanent glowing tattoo on the otherwise flawless flesh of the palace.

Desecration of the body. The thought occurs to me as my eyes sweep across the ravenous water, remembering hours spent, knees perched upon prayer pillows in a cold and spiritually desolate church, praying for resolution, for a divine saviour. I smile now, knowing the truth of the matter. Only I can bring about my salvation.

Gorgon and Barbas carry the metal bulk of my wings as we storm up the skeletal staircase, Barbas' illusion holding as ever strong.

The eyes of Sinners sweep me, and I wonder if they can sense that their end is approaching with increasingly merciless speed. I inhale the scent of their humanity as I pass, making my way up to the library without breaking my stride as I take a right at the top of the staircase, my silhouette cast, fast-moving and divinely curvaceous, upon the surrounding walls.

When I reach the double doors of the library, I find them unguarded, causing my fingers to curl inward, digging with familiar fervour into the silken flesh of my palm. I inhale, a scent far too familiar, the identity of which is fast confirmed as Katerina emits a low feral growl from the deepest part of her feverish and hungry throat.

I unsheathe the sword at my hip, watching as the full length of the blade catches firelight from surrounding sconces and turns molten before I storm forward on the balls of my feet. Slamming the double doors open with both palms, a cool breeze whips my hair back from my face.

The scene which confronts me is underwhelming. No massacre, no damage to the room, shelves tipped, or drapes torn asunder. Instead, the bodies lay neatly on the floor, small but gaping head wounds leaking pitiful amounts of blood onto the rich wood beneath.

They aren't even dead.

Just unconscious.

My eyes flit from the still, puppet-esque limbs and over to the shattered glass of the bell jar that encased the shard before flying to the pedestal where it had sat.

The stone surface is barren; the shard gone.

My rage builds, teeth grinding with unintentional fervour as every single muscle in my body tenses in protest. My knuckles turn white around the hilt of the sword before, in four silent jab-like slashes, I decapitate the unconscious and entirely useless guards, letting their blood spill over the floor like cheap wine.

Spinning on the spot, I find myself statuesque and cold as I look each Demon Lord directly in the eye with unwavering fury, an accusation born like wildfire from the gorged dark of my pupils. The sword hangs at my side, dripping still-warm blood onto the floor.

"Which one of you took it?" I demand, biting down so hard on my bottom lip that I feel the skin burst. Blood spills upon my tongue like the precious juice of long-awaited fresh fruit as Katerina's lips pull back slightly, saliva visibly slicking her incisors as her nostrils flare.

"Pandora, you can't honestly believe one of us took it?" Gorgon looks incredulous like butter wouldn't melt in his mouth, as he sets the dull matte feathered wings down on the banquet-sized table beside him with a clunk.

"Why shouldn't I? It is clear that each of you has your own agenda when it comes to amassing power." I remind him that I'm not as stupid as they clearly all think I am, examining my nails with faux boredom as my heart races in my chest.

"And you think that if it had been one of us, we would have bothered leaving the guards alive?" Barbas enquires, the statement causing my paranoid certainty to waver, teetering on the knife's edge between self-destruction and deliverance.

My lips pucker, tightening with doubt as I ponder his statement, looking back over my shoulder to the empty pedestal.

"Gorgon. Go and check the dungeons. I want to know if anyone is missing," I bark. He bows his head slightly before moving silently from the thick tension of the library and disappearing seamlessly into the shadow of the corridor beyond.

"No matter. The time for squabbling over power is past. I am tipping the scales. Tonight," I announce, and Lilliana's plump lips spread over her teeth, face becoming demonic and gaping as her eyes sheen alabaster with malicious anticipation.

"But— how are you intending to do that?" Katerina asks, sweeping past me and trailing her fingers provocatively over my bare shoulder. She takes the sword gingerly from me with her other hand, raising the blade into the air and running her finger along the edge.

"I will be allowing your demons to feast on the entirety of the mortal army we've built. Their deaths should tip the scales," I explain, watching as she raises her index finger to her lips, sucking it clean with relish.

"You want to sacrifice your army?" She looks confused, but I nod only once, certain as I turn my back on Barbas and Lilliana to face her.

"But of course, what use are mortals against the likes of the Gods we're bound to face in taking down Zeus?" I demand. She shrugs, biting her bottom lip and relishing the salty metallic tinge of blood on her tongue.

"Very well, my Kindred will be happy to oblige in the purge—" She smiles, the vermillion of her irises pluming outward like clouds of bloody ink suspended in clear yet deadly acid.

"So, you're just giving up on the shard?" Barbas enquires, cocking one eyebrow so it forms a question mark above the dull steel of his irises.

"It will be of little consequence once The Gods of Ancient are again free at my hand, Barbas. I expect them to reward me appropriately. If they do not, then they are no better than Zeus, and I want no part in this world any longer." The words slip from me and his eyes narrow.

"Fearlessness becomes you," he says, expression deadpan. The sentiment is not meant as a compliment, merely a tired observation, and yet my heart swells.

I've had so much taken from me, and at last, my fear of inadequacy has been vanquished, my choices made crystal clear. Death is no longer an adversary, only a welcome alternative in the face of continuing to draw breath beneath the rule of unworthy gods.

I step over the dead bodies, giving a swift kick to one and simply ignoring the others as I make my way over to the balcony.

"This is where we make our stand," I inform them, not looking back but expecting their undivided attention nonetheless.

"You want them lining the main street of Mortaria?" Lilliana's voice comes closer as I clutch the balcony railing and observe the stolen city beyond. My fingers caress the cool stone, blood chill in my veins and my heart marching funereal, sure now that this is what I'm supposed to do.

"Yes. I want to bottleneck the mortals. They will have nowhere to run," I explain, detached from the massacre ahead.

"Very well, you want all of our Kindred?" Barbas asks, more pliant, more amenable than I've ever known him.

"Yes. Once the walls between dimensions fall, I'll need the full force of the demon army ready to move. They should be strong from the feast on fresh mortal blood and I want The Higher Plains to know that we mean business." The thought of Zeus' surprised expression, his bulging muscles and furious forehead pulsing with hot and full veins brings a slight smile to my lips.

"And what of Sephy Sinclair?" Katerina asks, looking back over her shoulder to where the shard had once been.

Before I can answer, Gorgon's tones slither through the air upon his return.

"Osiris is gone, but the rest of the prisoners are still in their cells. I would assume that it was—" he begins, but I cut him off, spit flying from my lips and onto the balcony, spattering the stone dark with my fury.

"Anubis!" I hiss, balling my fist and spinning to snatch my sword back from Katerina's lax fingers.

"That would be my guess, yes." Gorgon's voice is fractured with irritation as his usual smooth tone is broken by ragged and angry syllables sliced short by his anger.

"As for Sephy Sinclair, she is dead," I announce to Katerina.

"So, what now?" Gorgon asks, straightening inside his worn suit jacket. I smile, contentment expanding throughout my gut like pure wicked sunlight.

"Gather the demons, gather yourselves. We're about to be infamous. Barbas. I want the mortals down in the courtyard in twenty minutes, the demons approaching in thirty." I nod to them as not one of them questions me any longer.

I glance at my wings, then look at Katerina and Lilliana.

"Help me into my wings and fetch me some wine," I order Katerina, Lilliana, and Gorgon.

Barbas turns from us, leaving the room with all the silent prowess of a hawk in flight among light falling snow.

"You're sure we don't need to worry about the Sinclair girl?" Katerina gives me a final look, asking for reassurance. I grin as I remember the carriage flying over the cliff, forced into the dark ocean depths by my relentless pursuit.

I nod, confident at Cthulhu's confirmation of the red-headed corpse resting peacefully on the sandy floor of his dark nautical kingdom.

Turning on my heel, I look back out over Mortaria, feeling the stir of demons being called by their masters and the foreboding change carried on the winds of this place.

I speak, confidence lacing my every breath.

"That girl slipped from the clutches of death once already. Nobody is powerful enough or stupid enough to try it twice, let alone succeed."

LUCE

The city passes us in a blur of bright hungry eyes, dull decaying flesh, and the mist laced howls of soulless beasts. I keep my head down, eyes closed, guiding the Banshee with only my mind's most hypnotic cadence.

It's not as easy as it was before, the connection more tenuous and exhausting the longer I strain to keep it woven, like an invisible umbilicus threatening to tear away from the inside of my skull with each passing moment. The Banshee rears at times, causing my fingers to bury deep into its fur for balance, nails sometimes piercing the skin. The scent of its blood, not quite human but instead rich like honey-glazed marrow, swims in the air as we race headfirst through the humidity of the Mortarian city outskirts, leaving the silhouette of the Exilia far behind.

Passing from crystal roads to dirt paths, I hear the laboured hollow breaths of the Skellions as their hooves grind, immortal ivory against earth and rock. The Skellion on my left is carrying Yama and Muerta, with Ericka and Osiris saddling another to my right, and Erlea and Erin trailing behind the thick deep impact of demonic paws on increasingly sweet soil.

The Banshee and I are barely one as we approach The Plains of Ichor, the unending gyration of its steep hackles and powerful back legs thrusting us forward at increasing speed. The smell of ichor gets stronger and my power wanes even further, like a once glorious moon engulfed in the shadow of the night. The beast beneath me shakes its head like it's trying to dislodge a rodent caught in its teeth.

I soon realise though, only too late, that it is not the ichor that is disrupting my mental connection with the Banshee but instead someone else.

Come to me, my child—

Lilliana's voice is the serrated blade that severs our connection once and for all. The Banshee digs in its claws and halts, the sudden disruption of forward momentum causing me to fly from the animal and into the sickly-sweet moist soil ahead.

"Luce! Are you alright?" I hear Yama's voice rumble over the flat plains between us and dig my hands into the dirt as I make unhindered contact with the earth. The vibration I perceived as sound continues as the ichor seeps into my dress coat. I exhale in a sigh, exhausted beyond what I'd thought possible as I get to my feet.

It's then that I realise the vibrations I sense underfoot aren't a remnant echo from Yama's concern at all but rather the thunder of demons coming directly at us.

"Shit!" I point to where demons are rushing from The Icon, a mixture of uncamouflaged Gorgonians, ragged-looking Banshees, salivating Succubi, and skittering Phobias. I reach into my coat pocket, gripping the hilt of one of my discreetly stowed knives as they move closer and closer, unceasing in speed or intent.

The Skellions shift beside me, and I turn quickly to see what has become of the Banshee I've ridden this far north, only to find it has gone from sight.

What? I steel myself for the fight, for the battle, knuckles bulging around the hilt of the lightweight military-grade dagger in my palm, silver hair blown back from my face by the oncoming horde.

The first line of demons doesn't slow, nor does the second, and as Erlea, Erin, and Ericka draw weapons, closing ranks around Yama and Muerta, I steel myself in place.

They're soon upon us, but as I raise a knife to clash with tooth and claw, with slippery scale and tattered fur made matte with the bodily fluids of not-so-fortunate victims, I find no such challenge.

We stand, rooted to the earth by leather boots, by the bone of Skellion steeds, by faith in the ability of each of us to defend the other to the last, and yet, there is no need. The demons do not fight; they do not so much as glance our way. Instead, they fly past us, the only danger coming as Gorgonians rush past my ankles, heading the way we've just come from and toward the Exilia.

Pandora.

The name is a curse to me now, and yet we have so much in common. She said so herself. We could have been allies, had it not been for the fact that I have some miraculous shred of moral compass remaining.

"Pandora is going to tip the scales. We need to get moving." I spin, my demonic steed long gone with its brethren, letting out an exhale of hot breath into the syrup of the air.

"How are you going to—" Muerta enquires, but I can only shrug.

"I could use the exercise," I say quickly, but she frowns, looking from me to Osiris and then whispering something into the periwinkle shell of Yama's ear.

I watch as he dismounts the Skellion, passing the reins to his ex-wife.

"Get on." He gestures to the place in front of Muerta where he's just been astride the skeletal stallion. I step forward, not bothering to argue as Muerta gives me a hand up onto the horse.

I watch as Yama moves fast over to Osiris, who then dismounts. The two of them take several steps off into a deserted ichor field to carry out a discussion I can no longer hear.

"We need to talk about protecting the mortals," Muerta speaks into my ear, Spanish accent barely more than a whisper.

I scan the ominous outline of Mount Mallum up ahead, feeling my lungs constrict, anxiety crushing them like a vice.

"I know what you said, but I can't. I won't do it," I whisper back, voice a hiss.

"Why? You have nothing left to lose. I'm guessing that Thane's absence is no coincidence." Her words make me stiffen as she curls her bony arms around my waist, passing me the reins without another word.

"Not that it's any of your business, but she left me, yes. Because of the magic, the darkness. You told me it was getting out of control, and I didn't listen. You were right."

"I didn't want to be right, and just because I was doesn't mean that Thane should have left. Love— well, it's for better or worse, isn't it?" Her question illuminates a place inside of me I long thought was lost to the dark. Thane left and it was my fault, but it was also her choice. She chose to leave because she didn't like half of who I am, half of my nature.

Perhaps then, that isn't my fault.

"Are you saying— are you saying that I shouldn't be ashamed of who I am?" I ask, the heat of her breath and the scent of tequila and spice wafting through the silver veil of my hair between us.

"Never. You should be cautious, be aware of the dangers, but never be ashamed. You cannot help how you were made. What is done, is done. You must accept and make the best of it, even if that means learning to succumb to and control your Ancient side." Her words are like a soothing balm to a long open wound, stitching two halves of me back together with tenuous silver thread.

"I thought you were against my darkness?" I breathe with quiet curiosity, my voice cracking as I realise I'm afraid of what she'll say next.

"Lucifer, I never wanted this for you, but it is what you are, what you have become. You must embrace it or it may very well destroy you, and I don't want that. We are family, remember?" she reminds me, and I swallow hard, relishing the heat of her torso as it seeps into my spine.

"I will ride with Ericka. Osiris is going to make his way to The Icon. He has something to take care of there before it is too late." Yama's voice is definitive and unyielding, cutting through the emotions that have been tossed up anew into the air between Muerta and me like long-ignored dust.

My gaze travels to Osiris.

Yama mounts the Skellion beside us in his place, monochrome robes billowing around him and coming off as nothing less than regal as I try to read the Egyptian god's face.

"Are you going to be all right on your own?" I ask, unable to help acknowledging the long-standing comradery between us, even after everything with his mother.

"You know— I think I finally am." He gives a sad smile, the rich hue of his skin glinting ever so slightly in the dark merlot blanket of gloom from the sky hanging overhead.

I give him one last look then squeeze the Skellion between my thighs.

My hair whips back from my face as we charge forward, fast and unstoppable, toward The Ashen Waste and then beyond to the waiting volcano.

The Ashen Waste flies past us, demon free, barren on all sides, a blur of ambivalent dove grey. The quiet is eerie, my heart rising further into my throat with each hoofbeat of the Skellion that carries Muerta and me across the soft grey expanse of land, edges and horizon dulled by the ash peppering both the air and ground.

We reach the entrance to The Fallen Kingdom faster than I ever would have imagined only a few months ago, and I allow my eyes to rise, finding the height of the volcano, which lies behind the crumbling Halls of Antiqua, intimidating to say the least. As the Skellions slow, onyx shadows falling over their ivory bones and turning them stark in contrast, Muerta sighs behind me.

"Luce, we still need to talk about Necromancy. I know it is not something you have ever attempted before, but it's in your blood. Your father was a master, it's how the Sinners rose before the Mortarian sun existed." She gives me a history lesson I don't need as we pass by the crumbling external walls riddled with rotting vegetation.

"I am aware, but Necromancy takes years of practice. I doubt I'll even be able to reanimate a corpse let alone raise something sentient." I feel the weight of my past more than ever as my nostrils flare, the scent of sulphur spiteful in the air.

"You don't need sentience— you only need bodies to stand between the demons and the mortals. I honestly believe this is our best chance. It could mean the difference between the dimensional walls crumbling or holding fast." Her voice is sweet and imploring as I dismount the Skellion with a swift and careful swing of one leg. My feet hit the ground and I hold up a hand to Muerta, helping her dismount as well, her ragged skirts fluttering around her slim ankles as both leather clogs impact the ash below.

Turning in the foot-deep ash, I find the rest of the group dismounting their steeds as well, Erin and Erlea struggling with the heft of the wooden box containing the rocket launcher I intend to use to set all hell loose. The leather of their coordinated outfits makes them look thinner than I've ever noticed before, each body bony, angular, a weapon in its own right. Watching them with interest, I'm glad to have them with me, even if the demons are nowhere to be seen.

"Look, I just— I don't think it's a good idea." My mouth twists in a doubtful pucker, eyes continuing to gaze at The Furies who mount the long crate on both their shoulders, carrying it like a coffin.

Shouldn't the volcano, the distraction, be enough to ward off the demons? To stop Pandora?

"Regardless, you think about it. I will help you, Voodoo and Necromancy cross over quite largely in principle, so I can guide you through it. The time for caution is long since over, Luce. The dead might be our last hope of stopping Pandora and The Demon Lords before they can tip the scales." Her tone is stern, eyes piercing pools of varnished mahogany as her gaze brands itself into the forefront of my mind. Yama closes the distance between us, standing beside Muerta, and they both look down at me, reminding me of my mother.

"You have a responsibility to the universe, Lucifer. Whether acting with darkness or light, the burden you carry remains the same. Immortality comes with a price, and that price is impossible choices such as this. It's time you decided whether you are willing to risk it all for the greater good." He sounds like a fortune cookie, but I cannot help but notice the similarity between his words and those that had fallen from Thane as she'd walked in and out of my visions of The Othrysian Orchard. This is what she was trying to tell me. I have gifts, a lifespan, that most people would happily kill for. This is the trade-off.

"You think Sephy can take care of Pandora if we focus on protecting the mortals?" I ask Yama, but he looks uncertain at best.

"I think that Persephone Sinclair is a wildcard. We must ensure our success and only hope that she can triumph in her quest against Pandora and the others. We are the gods; the fate of worlds lies on our shoulders. She is a mere Demi-God and an inexperienced one at that. Our faith must not lie with such a volatile entity. Now come, we have a mountain to climb." Yama points to the hulking natural beast of volcanic rock and acidic vents, and Muerta looks to me with a torn expression, her thick lashes casting jagged shadows over her alabaster cheekbones.

The six of us, the cavalry of light against the overwhelming dark, begin our journey toward Mount Mallum, silence falling over us as anxiety builds like a wave, threatening to break at any moment and chill us all to the bone.

As we pass over cracked stone, through air laced with the scent of death and past rotting blooms, I feel relief, thinking on Yama's words.

He's wrong, and I know it.

Sephy Sinclair *is* the last stand, the final defence of Mortaria, the universe's strongest and most relentless game piece on a chessboard that's been host to a slow-moving and predictable game for centuries.

Now though, the Queen is fast moving across the board, darting from light to dark, approaching checkmate without pause.

I, personally, after everything I know of her, cannot help but have faith that she will burn the Mortaria of Pandora's dark dreams to the ground, even if she has to end her own life to do it.

33

NOT AFRAID ANYMORE

<u>SEPHY</u>

THE WORLD RETURNS TO me in pieces, dull-edged and transparent, the richness and sting of emotion long gone. I reach up to the sky, spreading my fingers wide, watching the dark veins sprawl beneath my skin, a map of the sins committed by the man I loved.

He remains in my lap, cold, a lump of flesh no longer Xion but meat for the hunt.

I sit up; synapses firing and fizzling like a lit fuse, my muscles taut steel, blood scorching dark honey running through my veins.

I feel it around me as the world blurs, energy pulsating in the roots of long-dead trees, the sky lit with invisible vermillion lightning made evident only by the darkness eroding a path through my soul, a ceaseless and aggressive tide of pain and power, reshaping me to something untouchable, something inhuman.

At their footfall, the hairs on the back of my neck stand to attention, my heart slow, steady, unphased and untouched by fear.

After all, what more can I lose?

I stare down into Xion's lifeless face, letting my electrified fingertips run through the coarse grain of his facial hair, his eyes open and milky from the tendrils of death that have taken him from this place. Tears spring to my eyes but do not fall, suspended in the numbness of my infected heart, icy and impossible.

The Banshee charge from behind the surrounding lines of trees, and I rise fluidly to my feet, muscles languid, waiting to take them out. Xion's body slips from my grasp, lying limp on the floor as I watch hungry eyes dart toward it. I stand, feet wide and defensive as my fingers curl so my knuckles protrude, raw and white in the calm air.

The demons don't stop though; whether that's because they're afraid of me, or too busy heading somewhere else, I couldn't tell you. Either way, it's time to move. What's done is done, and I have no desire but to ensure what's just happened here is not in vain.

I spin, emotionless as I glide across the ground toward Xion, his body nothing more than a cold void in my newly acute vision of the surrounding world.

I could convect, but I'm afraid it might damage his body, do something to him more than what's already passed. It is with this in mind that I take his chill and pliable fingers in mine and begin to drag him.

As I give the first heave, leaves are pulled along beneath his weight, revealing something glinting in the dull light of the forest.

It takes me a few seconds to register what it is, but then I realise.

In loving memory.

The plaque, which Haedes had mounted to The Hollow's surrounding gothic cage in memorial of my mother, stares back at me.

I blink once, then twice, the darkness infusing my muscles with the strength I require to complete the task at hand.

As it is, I should be sobbing, wailing, crying, but I can't. Instead, I'm only numb, shocked, sure this cannot be real, that in a few moments, I'll wake to the low rumble of his voice, the warmth of his arms.

Acting without any further thought, I move through the motions of what I know must be done, heaving Xion over the ruddy ground of The Sanguine Forest and not looking back.

My teeth grind; sweat forming on my brow and in the crook of my neck, dribbling with scorching insistence down my back and arms, drenching me beneath the kevlar of my corset. My breath is a furious rasp; unable to process anything that's happened, unable to make any sense of the world around me, only able to keep moving forward, blindly and with feverish determination.

It continues for well over a mile until I'm forced to slump by a tree trunk and let Xion's arm fall limply to the ground at my feet. I run my fingers across my forehead and they come away damp with salt water. I'm panting, skin rippling dark just beneath the surface, muscles laced with intense ache.

The world blurs as I sink to my knees in the dirt, the scarlet canopy overhead whirling in a bloody and kaleidoscopic typhoon. I gaze up to the sky, closing my eyes a moment and allowing the darkness to wash over me. I let it soak into my skin, let it flow, jet ravines guiding the liquid sin between my bones, flooding around joints and allowing it to immerse my nerves fully, a soothing balm for my grief.

The resulting rage, the consequent injustice of it all, gives me the strength I need.

I get to my feet once more, unsure how after everything I'm still standing at all. Sweat cools against my skin, refreshing me despite how it was formed.

Staring down into his face, I find the lifeless gaze staring back at me, a new wave of emotionless nothing blanketing everything jagged inside.

"Don't look at me like that. This is your fucking fault!" I spit through gritted teeth, hand jerking forward to slam both his eyelids close, the last curtain-fall of the final act of a life cut far too short.

So now it's inside me, this thing he fought for as long as he can remember, a demon in wait, a darkness unrestrained and set loose in my body like onyx flames, engulfing every gentleness I found at his side, extinguishing the light.

I can see now why Luce succumbed. It's freedom — this darkness. A carelessness, a key befitting the lock of moral guilt that binds us to do what's right.

Fuck what's right.

I played by the rules, I tried to be the hero, and this is where it got me. Soaked in my own cold sweat and dragging the body of my lover through damp earth beneath a merciless sky the colour of arterial blood.

I take up Xion's hand once more, yanking it with more force than I knew I was capable of.

I hear something pop, his shoulder coming loose from the socket.

If I was in my right mind now, the sound might bring with it a flood of tears, a wail rising in my throat like a plume of dry volcanic ash. As it is, however, I can't bring myself to feel anything, to do anything other than what I know is absolutely necessary, and so continue to heave him through blood-stained earth and back to Golgotha, to where he and I will rest at last, even though peace would be far too much to ask.

I haul him up into the hold of the mattress, resting his head against the pillows from where I'd gazed into his loving expression only hours before. The scent of cinnamon-glazed pomegranate blooms in the air around me, a funereal bouquet of nostalgic sentimentalism that threatens to defeat my resolve. I pull the sheet of red velvet up and over his body, shrouding him in a soft bloody crush of fabric, hiding his corpse from view and erasing his face like he never existed.

His body covered, the memory of him and me flits in front of my mind's eye. It refuses to close, and I allow myself to collapse against the cool concrete of the wall, staring down at the mound of flesh on the bed.

My hand rises, covering my mouth as it widens into a silent scream, my eyes filling with tears, my knees crumpling beneath me.

He told me not to fall apart, but how can I stand strong without him; how can I swallow my grief and rise above the tidal wave of pain he's left behind, my heart shredded beyond recognition?

I wasted so much time being unsure, being afraid.

Why did I do that?

The floor impacts my knees as my hair, now tipped onyx like it's been charred, falls around my face. I place both hands, fingers splayed wide, onto the floor, tears falling fast and spattering against the cool stone, my shoulders shaking beneath the crushing weight of worlds.

Perhaps this wouldn't be so bad if you weren't such a fucking heavy-footed asshole.

You've stamped your big ass footprints all over my goddamn heart, I muse, lips spreading wide in an unexpected smile as I let my head fall back, staring up to the ceiling.

I laugh against my better judgement, shaking my head, tears streaming down my face, a jumbled mess of emotional debris sharper than black diamonds. My heart stirs beneath the rubble, a grenade with its pin unceremoniously yanked, threatening to detonate at any moment.

Pulling my knees up to my chest, I rest my forehead atop them, squeezing my fingers, watching the veins of darkness beneath my flesh ripple and dance, fading in and out of existence as each sob reaches deeper into the well of my sorrow, drawing out the tears from a seemingly bottomless abyss.

I close my eyes; giving into everything I've been fighting trying to get back here, trying to keep the last of him safe. The demons have had enough of him; they won't get his body too.

The thought stirs something inside of me, the weight of my conviction imploding in on itself in a dark hole that threatens to swallow me. I watch as the black veins dominate the porcelain fragility of my muscle-strapped arms, determined resolve returning, the sharpest edges of it laced with rage.

I sniff, wiping my eyes, fists balling as I picture her face, realising there's still work to be done.

I look at the mound of him, too afraid to draw back the sheet for one last goodbye. Instead, I walk over to the door, locking the steel barrier between the body of my lover and the hell of the outside world. I take one last deep breath, straightening and allowing the darkness to steel my nerves, turning my emotions to ice and flooding my gut with a welcome arctic chill.

I light the torches around the room with a flick of my wrist, cobalt flames rising in an exaggerated explosion from each sconce. I don't look back, merely closing my eyes and allowing the same cold blue flames to lick at my skin, convecting me to the other side of the door and into a desolate dark of a future without him.

Outside in the corridor, I wave a hand, igniting the sconces scarlet with Eternal Flames that lick high and serpentine upon the walls. I turn robotically, striding down the hall and away from the room storing Xion's remains. Taking a sharp right, I listen to the thud of my heart matched only by my quick and hard pace upon the concrete of the floor, each step laced with purpose.

My fingernails bite into the skin of my palms as I become acutely aware of the sparks flying between synapses oiled slick and volatile with dark power. The door of the storage room meets with my shoulder as I fall into it, pushing it open without breaking stride. I look around at the space stacked full of wooden crates, reaching out and feeling the rough raw grain of the wood protesting against the flesh of my fingertips as I rip lids from boxes. Rummaging through the contents without care, straw flies through the air and settles scattered on the floor.

Matte gunmetal grey and the sheen of black plastic glints in the low light as I stash as much firepower as I can on my person, using the belt slung low around my leather pants to its full potential as my hips swing heavy with artillery.

I bite down on my bottom lip, feeling the flesh split and relishing the blood upon my tongue, the copper spice of it perhaps the only sign that I'm still human. My muscles vibrate with unsated strength, and the guns, bullets, swords, knives, and explosives weigh no more than lethal feathers in my grasp.

My hair flies around me as I spin on the spot, returning to the entrance of the storeroom and slamming the metal door shut behind me as the charred tendrils of flaming hair flare out around my face, eyes heating with reckless intent.

As I make my way out of the labyrinth of corridors, I wonder if this has been my destiny all along. To become so damaged, so desperate to escape the pain of my sad existence, that I'll recklessly ride into battle alone.

I know it's crazy, suicide perhaps, but I can't help but feel that it's exactly what I've always been meant for. I'm no longer afraid, no longer conscious of the larger picture, only desiring to find Pandora at the end of my narrow sights and rip her limb from limb. She's taken everything from me, and now it's time I take my revenge.

Xion won't die in vain, even if I have to sit on a throne and preside over hell to give his sacrifice meaning.

I yank myself up the length of the ladder, pushing up on the hatch sealing the compound underground with one hand. It flies open, slamming into the hard earth on the other side.

Standing at the mouth of the void, I wrench the steel trap door closed, the clang of metal-on-metal echoing in my ears long after I've spun the lock fast shut.

I inhale, watching the trails of light that meander below the earth like the roots of cosmic trees, the dark flowering fruits that I know are the souls of Sinners. The web of energy is intricate, ebbing, and I wonder how it could be that I never noticed it before.

I wonder what I must look like.

Do I look like Luce had?

Black chasmic pupils and a map of sin spreading like cancer beneath my skin?

I guess none of that matters now.

Whether I look like evil reincarnate or not, there's no one I care about left to look at me with any kind of admiration, any kind of love or lust, anyway.

With a jerk of my head, I dislodge the thought, eyes falling onto the stark and jagged silhouette of one of the two Skellions who've returned from The Sea of Shadows.

I close the distance between us, feet slamming into the earth, leg muscles twisting taut and unwavering in their intent.

The skeleton of the stallion is dressed in a thick crust of salt and charcoal seaweed, crustaceans I don't recognise clinging to the inside of the steed's hollow ribcage. Its hooves are dressed in black crystal ballet shoes of crushed obsidian sand stuck to the bone with the adhesion of the last remaining seawater. They shimmer as it raises its left front leg, hollow eye sockets daring me to ride.

As you wish. I sigh, eyes gleaming as I raise my head to the sky and let the humid air dry the last of my tears.

Gritting my teeth, my gaze glides over the jagged outline of the Exilia as I launch myself up and over the unsaddled back of the Skellion, its vertebrae locking me in place upon the curve of its back. It may have no saddle or stirrups, but the reins of woven black leather still hang loosely around its neck, the bridle slack against the muzzle of its skull.

I take them in my palm and yank them tight, the leather burning as I grip it tighter than is necessary but unable to stop myself relishing the pain. I put my free hand on the hilt of the sword that presses flat against my outer thigh like the caress of a sleepy post-coital lover, comforted by the blade.

I look back to the hatch, where below Xion's body lies, dead, and then shake my head, putting all thoughts of my humanity aside and urging the Skellion to depart at a canter.

My world passes in a blur as the Skellion gallops through the deserted landscape, the eerie glow of the river an earthbound north star, guiding us home.

Funny how the darkness has turned me into the badass female equivalent of Poe. Where's Thane's raven ass when you need her? I smirk to myself, unfeeling as my weaponry clatters against the thick leather of my pants, the momentum of the Skellion's gyrations reassurance that I'm moving forward without falter toward my fate, toward watching Pandora die right before my eyes.

I yank back hard on the reins, hearing the hollow laboured pant of the steed coming in hard wisps beneath me as we kick up ruddy river-soaked earth, my heart steady, fearless as we get closer to the outskirts of Mortaria with every hoofbeat and the next steady fill of my lungs.

The buildings rise on either side, the deep hollow pounding of bone against garnet studded onyx causing me to slap the rear of the steed. The horse whinnies as we gallop faster than I've ever ridden before, hair streaming back from my face.

My eyes dilate as we skid around the corner, turning onto the main street. The horse halts without warning and I grip the reins, guiding it so I'm facing The Exilia.

Pandora stands, wings spread wide and metallic, upon the balcony that looks over the city. Between her and me are perhaps thousands of human captives, and between me and them lies an army of demons, standing in wait for the kill order that will change everything. They hang in the street, surprisingly civilised, jaws dripping down onto the onyx stone and leaving it reflective with bloodlust.

I watch as Pandora's eyes zoom in on my face, her mouth falling open.

"Impossible!" she bellows, fists crashing down onto the edge of the railing separating her from the sky. I smile, lips spreading wide as I jerk my chin upward, squaring my shoulders and elongating my spine, defiant— *alive*.

She screams something unintelligible and I grin, yanking down hard on the reins of my steed and smiling maniacally, unhinged and unafraid. The Skellion rears up, a whinny of phantasmal and haunting emptiness splitting the silence that follows her mangled command, before lurching forward.

I push myself down low to its back, muscles tightening as it hits top speed in mere moments. The crowd of demons grows closer, but I don't dwell on them. Instead, I place both hands around the spindled neck of the horse, bringing my knees up to rest atop the curve of its bony spine and pushing myself up to stand. Moving one leg back so I'm balanced, I surf on the back of the Skellion as it charges headfirst into the churning mass of teeth, jaws, and claws.

The wind whips my hair back, my supernatural balance steeled by the darkness running through my veins. I watch the veins on my arms becoming more visible than ever, twisting around me like oxymoronic Abraxian tattoos as I summon fire to my palms and begin to throw projectiles as fast as I can.

Soon though, we run out of road. The bony projectile that the steed has become meets with the front line of the demonic forces and is taken down within moments.

I fly through the air, stomach falling through the barren cavity of my body as I cartwheel and land, one kneecap smashing into the ground, body rolling slightly to disperse some of the impact.

The demons surround me, thousands of them. I look back over my shoulder and find Pandora, eyes bright, smiling down at me.

So then, this is it? I wonder, spinning on the spot.

This was reckless, stupid, impulsive, crazy, and suicidal, and yet I know it's exactly what I needed to do.

Contented, I unsheathe my sword, ready to go down fighting.

I just hope I've bought Luce enough time, my death enough of a distraction to give her the precious minutes she needs to end this thing once and for all.

Smiling, I summon The Eternal Flame to me and prepare for the violence I know is coming. However, before the first demon can launch itself at me, everything begins to blur.

I can't stop it, couldn't have predicted it, and so fall to my knees, fire extinguishing. My sword falls from my hand in a clatter of limp metal against dark crystal as I slump face-first against the floor, splayed out and vulnerable.

As the demons close in around me, I hear it. A female voice so familiar it cannot help but make my lips turn up in the corners, deeply amused.

The very last thing I hear echoes over and over throughout my mind as I fall into unconsciousness.

Do you believe in life after love?

34

IMMORTAL

LUCE

WE PICK OUR WAY over crumbling dark rock for what seems like years, the rate of ascent steeper and more gruelling than I anticipated. My hands are charred black from the climb where I've been forced to use all available limbs to scale the mountain's craggy silhouette. I mean you know it's a volcano, but until you're a speck on the side of the thing, I guess it escapes you just how massive it actually is.

"If we ever try to climb a volcano again remind me to bring someone who can convect—" I pant, wiping sweat from the back of my neck. The Furies glare at me silently, the three of them struggling beneath the weight of the wooden crate containing the rocket launcher and its ammunition. I give them an apologetic grimace, pulling the high collar of my dress coat away from the nape of my neck, struggling for air.

The heat coming off the volcano is immense, as I suppose I should have expected.

"Are we really doing this?" I ask Muerta, who has her ragged burlap skirts hoisted over her knees, thigh-high pinstriped stockings visible as her old-fashioned leather clogs navigate the side of Mount Mallum with unexpected grace and nimbleness.

"It would appear so," she retorts, a sharp exhale pushing through the plumpness of her full lips.

"Have you ever known this thing to erupt?" I ask her, suddenly curious.

"Not in the time I've been here— I wonder if that'll mean we're in for a more ferocious eruption. I suppose I know relatively little of volcanoes—" Muerta's eyes rise, their mahogany sheen reflecting the craggy charred peak that looms overhead.

"Well, I guess it's a good thing we're going to blow one up then." I wince, boots struggling for traction, as the climb becomes steeper and less stable than I'd thought possible.

"Do you think Thane would approve?" Muerta asks, catching me off guard as my heel dislodges a small layer of crumbling pumice stone. I look back over my shoulder as it skitters down the mountainside and past The Furies who continue to climb, silent beneath the weight of the crate they're carrying, breathing ragged and strained with effort.

"No. I don't. Should I care?" I ask.

Turning back to meet her gaze, the wind takes loose strands of my hair in its caress, turning it fluid in the air like quicksilver. Brushing it aside and out of my eyes, I hear the way my voice becomes slightly fragmented as I pose the question.

"Once upon a time, I'd have said yes. I thought she was your north star, your guiding light, but now I'm not so sure. Things are shifting, and beyond this, beyond Pandora and the Demon Lords, something more is stirring in the distance. Perhaps— perhaps you are what the darkness needs to bring it to heel," she muses, not meeting my gaze as her fists tighten in the material of her unevenly hemmed skirt.

"What are you saying, Muerta?" I am tired, exhausted in fact, my heart thudding loudly in my chest at the sudden reappearance of Thane in my otherwise occupied psyche.

"We always thought it was the light that would triumph over dark— but perhaps the only light that can truly defeat it, truly rein it in, is light which coexists with it. Don't you think?" she enquires. I roll my eyes.

"I don't know. I'm a bit busy to have this conversation right now. First, we blow up the volcano, then we worry about the philosophy of the universal dichotomy of light and dark— don't you think?" I repeat, cocking my head. She smirks so the skeletal makeup following the bony architecture of her skull looks ever so slightly possessed.

"Well, when you put it like that— but still, you must decide about the possibility of Necromancy. We must ensure success, Lucifer." She nags me like the mother I never had and no longer desire, and I exhale heavily, relieved to find the peak of the mountain growing visibly closer at last.

"Look, I'll do what I have to. If I wasn't willing then I'd have just stayed in Chicago. They have much better take-out choices," I mutter.

"Splendid."

We continue the rest of the climb in silence, Muerta's desire for answers sated for now at least.

My mind is cast next to Xion, to everything he's prepared to sacrifice to resist giving over to his darker nature. It's strange, now that I think about it, a creature for whom the gods have such disdain, choosing light far more easily than I have myself, one of their own. I only wish I had his resolve, his righteousness. Perhaps if I did, I wouldn't be clambering up the side of a stupid volcano.

The air becomes thick with smoke, sulphur, and scorching heat, the rock looser and more easily dislodged, the path ahead more tumultuous and terrifying with every single step. The instability of this part of the mountain becomes increasingly apparent each time I hear rock skitter down the steep descent or watch as gases burst from the ground causing each of us to leap back in horror. Sweat continues to bead on my brow, my heart pounding as I'm certain that one of us is going to end up dead.

I reach the peak after another ten minutes of ragged breathing and aching muscles, and gaze down, finally, into the bowels of the volcano.

It's underwhelming, this break in the rock that reveals what lies within the wide vent. However, the gooey centre, the molten magma that teems and bulges in a way entirely primal, is anything but.

"Well— that's a weapon if I ever saw one," Muerta comments, the glow of shifting molten rock lighting the undersides of both our faces, the heat rising from the magma chamber almost unbearable. It sets our pallor alight, making our serious expressions appear demonic beneath the mauve weep of the sky.

A few minutes later, The Furies arrive, panting.

They set down the wooden crate on a ledge, each one perching like a well-trained hawk upon a jagged spike of volcanic rock, trying to catch their breath. Ribcages expand and relax, each one of them emitting a cough at the thick chemical composition of the surrounding air. I can't blame them, and bring up my collar to cover my mouth, trying to gain some respite from the no doubt dangerous concoction. It stings my lungs, makes my eyes water, and feels as though it's stripping the inside of my nose of its outermost layer of skin.

The heat warms the back of my legs as I turn, clambering away from the edge of the vent and toward the crate, still guarded closely by The Furies. Bending, I crouched in the narrow space between the body of the volcano and the end of the ledge's crumbling outcrop, tearing the wooden lid from the box. I find the bazooka nestled deep within the straw packing the space, ammo shells snug beside it.

"Ladies, mind helping me lift this up to the cone?"

The three women glare at me but don't verbally complain, rising with perfect balance and composure atop the precariously loose rock supporting them. The glorious multitude of their skin tones reflective with sweat, the taut muscles beneath straining as they haul themselves up the side of the peak to assist me.

It takes several minutes of heavy breathing, grunts from resulting pulled muscles, and careful placement of feet atop crumbling dry earth, but I soon find myself at Muerta's side again. Looking down into the neon orange glow of molten lava that bubbles lazily around fifty feet below where I'm standing, anxiety erupts in my stomach.

"You know that once you fire that thing, we are going to have to get the hell out of here, right?" Muerta asks, and I nod, biting down hard on my bottom lip with concentration.

"Oh, I fully intend on throwing this aside and making myself scarce."

I frown as I go through what's about to happen in my head, the nerves beneath every inch of my silken soft skin suddenly known to me as vulnerable. Erlea and Ericka place the Bazooka upon my shoulder and Erin loads the rocket into the broad cylindrical chamber. I shift; adjusting my footing beneath the gunmetal grey bulk that weighs more than I'd thought and feeling far greater appreciation for the Furies.

Hearing rock crumbling beneath my tread, I swallow hard.

Don't look down. I remind myself, blinking a few times to dislodge the tears forming from the sting of the spitefully pungent fumes.

"Ready?" Muerta asks me, and I shake my head.

"Nope, and to top it off, I'm realising that this is a completely stupid idea. Who the hell came up with this?" I release the safety, looking around at the other women. Gulping down air like it's in short supply, The Furies move in at my spine, ready to steady me should I lose my balance.

"That would be you, Lucifer—" Muerta reminds me with a wide, uneasy smile.

I shake my head, closing one eye as I peer down the sights and lower the barrel of the rocket launcher so it's aiming directly into the mouth of the volcano. Cruel jaws of black pumice surround the welling hot magmatic saliva below, primed and gaping.

"Oh yeah— right—"

Me and my big mouth— I curse myself as I place my finger over the trigger, pulse rapid in my ears, heart pounding in my chest.

My hand trembles as the breeze moves silently around me, threatening to send me tumbling down the mountainside with a single gust.

I take a final deep breath, closing my eyes and tensing my entire body before grimacing as I decisively squeeze the trigger. There's a split-second delay where I secretly hope the rocket launcher hasn't worked, but that notion is soon destroyed as I'm thrown backwards by the force of the recoil.

The Furies do their best to stop me from getting hurt, but despite their efforts, the rock beneath my heels gives way and I tumble several feet down the mountain. The rock smashes into my skin, tangles in my hair, but I'm too distracted by the fact my entire body is on fire with the impact of the fall.

My fingers scream as I reach out, weapon tumbling listlessly from my shoulder, and find traction enough on a rocky outcrop to finally stop my fall.

My legs dangle as the sudden stop in my descent causes my shoulder to pop out of joint, and I cry out, squeezing my eyes shut and trying to catch my breath as all air is pushed from my lungs.

The Furies hurry down the mountainside toward me, Erlea reaching me first and grabbing me by the wrist, the three of them hauling me up so I'm on semi-stable and steeply inclined ground. As soon as my feet touch the ground, a second impact causes the earth beneath me to reverberate.

"Move!" I scream up at Muerta as the rocket detonates inside the throat of the earthen monster, causing the explosion we'd planned but had not expected to be quite so immense.

Smoke flies up into the sky along with rock that soars through the air as though it weighs no more than feathers, the sound of the volcano stirring causing my very bones to shudder.

My feet move so fast with panic that soon I'm barely in control of my body. I fear if I try to slow down, I'll be sent hurtling off the side of the volcano and fall to my death with no brakes to rely on and no plateau in the mountainside steepness for miles. The tread of my boot skids over layers of pumice, lifted and scattered like confetti in my wake, and then I hear the thundering cracks of the mountain beneath my feet shifting as it wakes from a dormancy far too long.

Glancing back over one shoulder, I see plumes of smoke and magmatic debris propelled into the air like from a god's most ferocious exhalation, the mountain clearing its throat as it warms up to serenade the sky with plumes of ash unlike anything in Mortaria's living memory.

"Don't look back!" Muerta's voice carries through the air, which thickens with fresh chemical spray bursting from newborn cracks, as I continue to scramble down the side of Mount Mallum, leaving The Furies, Muerta, and a growing landslide of debris to follow haphazardly behind.

The descent passes in a blur of fighting for balance, eye-watering smells, and increasing heat on my spine. Finally, though, I find Yama's face waiting at the bottom of the mountain, golden hair alight with the glow of magma that will soon douse the surrounding area.

"Hurry!" he shouts, voice barely audible as the ground beneath my feet shakes of its own violent volition. This time the seismic tremor is stronger, causing me to stumble and hop before crashing into his broad chest. Taking only a second to grab his hand, I yank him behind me.

"Where to?" I demand a solution and he scowls.

"You mean you don't know where we're going?!" He's furious as he glances back over his shoulder, face mixed between his will to run and to stop a moment, clear his head, and find a reasonable solution to an unreasonable and unpredictable problem. In the split second he's looking behind us, weighing this up, Muerta grabs his free hand in hers and then connects herself to a chain of furious women, making the decision for him as she shoves us into motion.

"I hadn't really thought about that!" I admit, pupils filled with reflection of the gargantuan column of smoke still being ferociously blown into the sky.

"We need to get underground! Come, The Halls of Antiqua!" Yama squeezes down on my palm, making sure I've heard him as a flaming projectile of rock flies left of us. Skidding across the blood-stained cobbles of The Fallen Kingdom's main street, it smoulders on impact. The piece of rock smokes in the middle of the road as we wind around it, but I can't help but stare, shocked at what I've done.

Shit!

I charge the length of the street, wondering what on earth had made me think I could blow up a freaking volcano and get away unscathed. My feet pound against the stone as I hear yet more boulders crashing into the earth around us, flaming bright against the darkening Mortarian sky.

After a few minutes, my shoulder aches from pulling Yama behind me, the balls of my feet are throbbing, and my skin is blazing with the increasingly hot surrounding air. It doesn't matter though; this is no time for my mortal inadequacies.

Determined, I launch myself forward, slamming into the back doors of The Halls of Antiqua and feeling relief wash over me as they fly open beneath my weight. The darkness of the place engulfs us, the sound of spewing earth impacting the ground echoing around me on all sides and causing the broken chandeliers overhead to shake as shifting plates deep beneath our feet cause my femurs to quake.

Once everyone is inside, Muerta bars the doors behind us and I pause to stare back at her. Without falter or hesitation, she storms through the space between us, grabbing my free hand and yanking me behind her this time.

We pass through the mirrored walls of The Demon Lord's meeting room, tiny pebbles jittering atop the broken stone table, and into the main corridor. The round stained-glass windows cast dappled pools of fiery light onto the bloodstained black floors, but I don't have time to wonder about the cause as the ground beneath my feet becomes a more ferocious demon in its own right, trembling and vibrating so fiercely I fear it might crack open and swallow me whole.

I'm thrown forward; ears ringing as the sound of shattered glass and crumbling rock come together in a violent crescendo of natural destruction. My head smashes into the floor, skull cracking harshly against the cobblestone and reminding me of the fact I've already sustained one such blow today. Glass rains down like jagged hail as Muerta's hand is ripped from mine.

"Ow—" I moan, fighting the urge to spew my guts all over the glass-speckled floor. If I don't have brain damage or at least a severe concussion after this is all over, it'll be a miracle.

"Come on, we have to get underground!" Muerta yells, pulling herself to her feet.

I glance up at the ceiling, finding thick plumes of ash creeping in through the now hollow circular windows. The ash cloud of the volcano's first eruptive stage is growing, creeping fast into the building as the carcass of it is pelted with flaming bits of stone.

I follow Muerta's raven locks as they shimmer, bouncing around her shoulders, and glance back over my shoulder to find Yama and The

Furies close behind. She leads me off to the right of the main corridor, down a flight of unsteady broken stairs, and toward a steel trap door. She yanks it open without a single thought for what could be inside.

"Get in!" she screams, finding my expression cautious as the room shakes around us. I inhale deeply, taking the last of the steps in my stride and jumping down into the darkness below without pause.

I bend at the knee, absorbing the impact from the fall and finding myself engulfed in darkness almost immediately.

I watch as the remaining five bodies follow suit, falling in after me via the single beam of light before Yama makes his descent and closes the hatch behind us.

The walls and ceilings reverberate, threatening to collapse, and I eye what I think are thick wooden beams holding up the ceiling. Standing up straight, I reach up, placing my hands against the low-hanging concrete of the ceiling, wondering what it would feel like to be buried alive.

I guess I didn't give Sephy enough credit for crawling out of her own grave. That had to suck.

"Lucifer. We must do it, now!" Muerta implores me, hand finding mine in the darkness and giving a frail squeeze as The Furies and Yama mill about in the dark, eyes glinting as they turn to me, expectant. My vision adjusts slowly, becoming accustomed to the dim as I find the faces of Yama and Muerta watching me intently.

"All right." I sigh, not giving myself any time for doubt or anxiety.

Muerta pulls me to my knees, the contact of them against the cold concrete causing shivers to run up my skeleton and rattle my skull.

"How do I do this, Muerta? I don't have any ingredients— nothing—" I hiss, heartbeat wild beneath my ribs.

"Lucifer, the darkness is inside of you. Use it."

Moving my hand to the concrete beneath us, she lets her palm rest above mine as we both bear down on the earth, propped up on all fours like the most basic of animals.

"Reach down into the earth— what do you feel?" she asks, but I shrug, impatient.

"I don't— I don't feel anything— the volcano—" I stutter, and before I have a chance to finish the sentence, her hand contacts with the back of my head.

"Concentrate! Reach out through the earth, through the web of death created by the river— follow it and use that energy. You must harness it. Then, direct it into any remains you can sense. You will know them; they are empty masses," she explains.

I breathe heavily, hair falling around my face.

"Luce, concentrate now!" Yama barks, his voice deep and harrowing as I take a final cold inhale and close my eyes, letting my fingertips splay out against the slick coolness of the floor and opening my mind, travelling downward into the makings of Mortaria.

I find it, a single strand of silver magic intertwined with flecks of obsidian light that represent the absence of goodness. I follow it, mind racing through the tremoring soil of Mortaria, the web of dark souls that lies underground more complex than I've ever realised before.

I feel the darkness stirring inside me, awakening and turning vicious, consuming as it had been before I'd been stripped of my potency. I try to keep a handle on it, to rein it in like a wild stallion bucking left and right, but I find myself fighting with each passing second just to keep control. I feel them, veins spidering beneath my skin, eyes flooding with the dark.

Letting the power flow, I give over to it as I move with increasing pace along the maze of sin-filled souls, finding myself eventually surrounded by dark holes, voids of magic or life.

They are empty masses—Muerta's voice echoes in my head, and I realise I've found corpses, remains— bones.

What now?

A puppeteer over life and death despite my best intentions, I follow my instincts, letting the strands of darkness fall through my phantasmal and incorporeal fingers, testing my power.

Tracing the outline of the ebbing magic, I watch as it dances under my influence, wasting no time in guiding the cord of influence into the darkness of the corpses overhead. The cord grows in length, climbing through the chasmic void of death and branching off, neurons of magic firing and creating momentum where before there was nothing.

Detached from my physical self, I'm awed by the power within my reach. I thought I was helpless, but it turns out that I'm only helpless if I let the darkness control me. I can command it, but only if I try, only if I train my instincts to work for me, not against me.

I continue to glide through the soil, the magic within my soul stretching its wings after years of cowering behind bars of my own making. Following the trails of energy, I redirect into the bodies of the dead.

Slowly, in the silence of the Mortarian streets, the calm of The Obsidian Shore, and the barren forest floors scattered with dead vermillion leaves, my dark influence spreads, and the dead begin to rise, ready to serve me and me alone.

PANDORA

I watch from the balcony, heart hammering as the demons close in around the redhead, who is proving to be a far bigger pain in the ass than I'd originally intended.

The Demon Lords, having heard my garbled cry of attack to the masses below, are clustered behind me, giving the span of my metallic wings a wide berth.

After a few moments of demonic bodies crowding in around her, I breathe a sigh of relief.

If she wasn't dead before. She is now.

But how?

How did she survive the plunge into demonic oblivion?

Stupid girl.

How on earth did she think she was going to single-handedly defeat so many demons?

Does she believe herself that powerful?

Foolish is the last sentiment with which I grace her memory.

Spinning, I almost take out Barbas with the tip of my left wing, as I face The Demon Lords.

"Well, that was rather anti-climactic," I exhale, voice tumbling from me like raw silk as the words threaten to snag, unravelling in my throat.

"You assured us she was dead." Barbas' voice is rife with disdain, expression flat as a pancake.

"That's the thing about Demi-Gods, especially redheads. They're tricky—" A voice echoes throughout the library, phantasmal and annoying in the breadth of only a single sentence.

"What the!?" Gorgon exclaims, taking several steps forward into the gloom of the room.

She steps forward from the shadow, cognac eyes twinkling with malice.

"Don't you recognise me, old friend?" Sephy asks, examining her nails with casual reserve.

She takes another pace toward him, high heeled boot meeting with the wood underfoot and causing the floorboard to creak, only thickening the tension in the air.

I look back over my shoulder, a wing partially eclipsing the horizon from view. I find the demons still crowding around the epicentre of her demise. But then, there's something else.

Where before there was an obvious divide between the mortals and the demons, a layer two bodies thick, a barrier, ripples into existence, disguises shred like wrapping paper. The bodies of what had seemed like mortals turn Abraxian, skin charred and glowing neon with whirling multicoloured tattoos, shielding the bodies of the mortals at their backs.

What the hell is going on? Demons— defending humans?

Then, as I watch the redheaded halfling take yet another step forward, I know the truth of this illusion, her burly gait uncharacteristic and all too telling.

"Abraxis." I nod curtly, watching as the plump and luscious lips of one Miss Sephy Sinclair shimmer out of smooth and juicy existence, becoming chapped and thinning as Abraxis' form reappears in a shudder from beneath her face.

"How kind of you to notice." He bows, smirking.

I take the opportunity of his dropped gaze and draw my sword from the outside of my thigh, clutching the weapon as a natural extension of my arm. I charge through the open double doors, wings only inches from clipping the edge of the wide doorframe, and lunge for him in a blind and unexpected bolt of rage that supercharges my muscles.

Before the blade can contact the face that's deceived me, my path is blocked by a blur of fast-moving white and bronze.

The fine tip of my sword's mid-class length is caught between the clanging curves of two Khopesh, the sickle-shaped blades glinting a dull gold before the face of Abraxis' protector.

"Osiris. What a pleasant surprise," I snarl, baring my teeth as my lungs push against the harsh metal confines of my corset. Struggling against him, something catches my eye as another shadow emerges through the gaping doorway.

"Oh, and of course, where would Si be without his mummy?" I grunt, trying to hold my footing.

The fallen Titans of Hermopolis come forth, Abraxis smiling as Anubis draws a large, curved dagger of her own, the handle of the blade gilded with thick multifaceted rubies, drops of blood made crystalline by the feign of her magnificence.

"Got it, Si?" Anubis asks her son, giving me a curt glare.

"You bet—" Osiris pants, spinning and tossing the end of my blade into the air.

The force of it causes me to stumble backwards, but before I can catch my balance, the room seems to suddenly shake as well. I wonder if it's some kind of trick, but as the books within tall wooden bookcases begin to fall from their shelves, splaying open their pages and leaving knowledge vulnerable on the floor, I realise that it's not me but something else entirely.

"Get out of my way!" I barge past Lilliana, who is seemingly unphased by the tremor as she watches the books fall as though they're mere leaves tumbling from autumnal trees.

Clamouring toward the balcony, I take hold of the thick railing, gaze settling far in the distance on the cause of the earthquake.

No.

My plans are dwarfed in but a second as I watch the rising vents of smoke born from the far-off silhouette of Mount Mallum, Mother Nature having awoken and found the dark kingdom of her nightmares made flesh under the thrall of another.

"What's happening, Pandora? Is that the volcano?!" Katerina's tone is laced with fear, but when I fail to reply to her the hem of her long skirt brushes against my ankles as she spins, hurrying back to the rest of The Demon Lords.

"Mount Mallum is going to erupt!" she cries, causing me to tear my gaze from the spewing mountaintop to find The Demon Lords crowded at my back, eyes filled collectively with fear.

It would appear I've found something that finally brings them all to heel. The only problem is that thing isn't me.

"It makes no difference. We move ahead as planned." I wave a hand, brushing the problem away as though it has no more weight than a feather.

Barbas shakes his head.

"I'm out. Fuck this shit. You don't know what the hell you're doing and I'm not getting myself killed for your sorry revenge ploy," he spits.

I smirk.

"And how exactly are you going to flee from Mortaria? There is no way out. The Hollow is gone. The only way out— lies with me." I palm my back pocket, searching for the box but find it missing. Spinning on the spot, I glance to the floor and then hear a laugh that chills my stomach into a glassy frozen pit.

"Looking for this?" Abraxis asks me, strolling from within the library and out of the double doors, box clutched firmly in between his index finger and thumb.

He grins at it, satisfied.

"How—" I begin to chastise him, but he shakes his head.

"I'm the Demon Lord of Lies and Illusion, Pandora. You don't think I can pick a pocket or two? I'm almost insulted." He spins on the spot for mere bravado, looking at the box with more satisfaction than I can stand.

"You don't even know how it works," I remind him, heart fluttering, a trapped moth blinded by the light of my desire for revenge.

"I don't need to. I just need to know that I have it and you don't." He smirks.

I watch as his eyes flit next to his fellow Demon Lords.

They turn to him, eyes fixed on the box clutched in his palm.

"Fetch—" He winks, tossing the box into the musty air before him.

It's as though, in this moment, he's unleashed all hell. The Demon Lords turn visibly rabid right before my eyes as another tremor shakes the Exilia beneath my feet, an ancient beast shedding the chains of dormancy.

I growl, bearing my teeth and lunging forward toward Abraxis, sword raised in my hand, temperament thoroughly unhinged by his complete and utter betrayal.

He ducks beneath my attempt to skewer him straight through, twisting beneath the span of my wings and smiling, his head turning to stare into the depths of the gloom blanketing the room.

I'm distracted momentarily by his diverted attention, following his gaze and finding The Demon Lords clambering over one another, trying to save themselves from the oncoming eruption as they scramble for the box.

Another tremor draws me back to myself as Abraxis darts sideways, becoming lost in the tangle of violence between Demon Lord and Titan. I watch on, the sky pregnant with explosive potential as another tremor causes me to fall sideways, balance made near impossible under the weight of my wings.

The sound of shifting rock can be heard, echoing across the land and washing over me, an ever-expanding turret of smoke billowing up and spreading to darken everything that cowers below.

I take a second to gaze down over the main street of Mortaria, at the demons becoming restless and the mortals shrieking in terror as Abraxians clash with what had once been their brethren in battle.

This can't be a coincidence. I muse, wondering who is responsible.

Could this be some kind of intervention from The Higher Plains?

The thought makes my innards tremble with delight.

Unfortunately for me, I don't have time to wonder about the logistics, I need to retrieve my box, need to ensure my survival above all else.

I spin, wings catching air and slowing my rotation, as I head back into the tirade of petty bickering and violence among those who had once seemed formidable opponents.

Another tremor, a loud explosion sounding in the distance.

Barbas, Katerina, Lilliana, and Gorgon still, their bloodied hands and gouged skin becoming eerily statuesque, frozen with terror.

Shit.

"Fuck this!" I hear Gorgon exclaim, recoiling from the action and giving me a fleeting look as he turns on his heel and sprints from the room, lithe, exactly like the snake I've known he was all along.

"Coward," I say aloud, watching as Katerina, Lilliana, and Barbas follow his path from the room, giving a quick glance back over their shoulders to me before following suit.

The Demon Lords, those I had expected to stand with me against Zeus, flee, giving me evidence that darkness lends itself to survival, brutal and dirty as it is, above all else.

Although, one Demon Lord and two Titans remain.

We stand, the four of us, at a crossroads of indecision and appraisal.

My eyes fall, creating a domino effect of gazes descending to the same spot on the floor between us. Here, the box stares up at the last of us, the possibility of it too delicious to resist.

Anubis moves first, diving forward.

She's too fast for me, but as I soon see, her actions are in vain.

I hear it before I see it, the crunch of stone underfoot.

Anubis' body crumples, only feet from the Othrysian portal box, dead.

Osiris shifts, revealing what had once been a ruby and gold scarab brooch crushed beneath his boot. I cock an eyebrow, muscles steeling themselves for the moment I will leap into action, mouth open slightly.

"You surprise me—" I say to Osiris, tone unimpressed, tightening my grip on the sword in my palm.

"It was time," Osiris retorts, glaring at me as the tension reaches boiling point.

Another second passes, a tremor suddenly rocking the room in its entirety. Osiris takes the moment I'm off balance and launches forward, but instead of surrendering, I use the unexpected momentum of the quake, and I'm too fast, swinging my sword back and skewering him between his third and fourth rib.

I hear him cry out, the blade slipping too easily through his torso.

Sweeping forward, I scoop up the box in my free hand and straighten, holding the sword to Abraxis' throat before he can move a single step toward the door.

"And here we are— seemed inevitable, didn't it?" I ask him. He merely chuckles.

"I suppose. Though I wouldn't be so sure of yourself. She's going to kick your ass, and I'm going to love watching every second," he spits, grinning as the point of my sword buries into the place just below his Adam's apple.

"She's dead! Fool!" I narrow my eyes, another quake rippling through the floor and causing my wings to clatter, each metallic feather trembling as though afraid of the surrounding air.

"Is she though? You know they call her The Phoenix. Phoenixes don't burn, Pandora. They rise—" He cocks an eyebrow as though he knows something I don't.

Mortal screams sound, echoing through the air of the library that's becoming fast rich with the scent of burning. The sound of demonic whimpers can also be heard, causing the hairs on the back of my neck to rise ceremoniously.

Have the Abraxians, in such small number, really managed to overcome the rest of the demon Kindred so quickly?

"I think that's your cue." He looks back over my shoulder, eyes widening.

I twist toward the balcony, curiosity far too overwhelming to fight. When I turn back around, he's gone.

A scream escapes my lips, fury coursing like poison through my veins as I storm back across the wooden floorboards, knuckles white on both my sword and the box that started all this trouble.

When I reach the railing, I stare down into the increasingly smoky air over Mortaria, finding myself shocked beyond what I'd thought possible. I thought it was the Abraxians, but it seems now they're the least of my worries.

An army approaches, swords in hand, soulless and with nothing to lose.

The dead walk once more, and they're headed straight for me.

35

BELIEVE

<u>SEPHY</u>

THE SONG CONTINUES TO echo inside my head as I find myself standing in a red-lit corridor, the end of which is capped by a fluttering velvet curtain. I shiver, the air a melding of chill damp and scorching heat, the world appearing grainy before my eyes like I'm watching an old movie that's been recoloured very badly.

Finding a neon sign overhead, bathing me in its unapologetic glow, I blink once, then twice, familiarity rushing through me as I realise where I am.

I've been here before, but I was very drunk indeed.

"*Sephyyyy Tequilaaaaaaaa!*" The voice splits the air like a razor blade as the corners of my lips quirk into a reluctant smile. I step forward without hesitation, the heels I now seem to be wearing clipping the floor with a fast-paced rhythm that matches the music seeping through the curtain.

The black dress from Luce's nineteen-fifties style ball covers my body, the velvet hugging me and the hem fluttering around my fast-moving ankles as I come to a pause right before the curtain, eager and with a pounding heart.

My fingers reach out, pulling back the fabric and exposing me to the full volume of Cher, the lyrics of *Believe* wrapping themselves around my limbs and infecting me with the impulse to swing my hips.

Then I see him, for the first time in what feels like forever, and I completely crumble into the stormy depths of his grey irises.

"Hey, baby girl—" Haedes greets me, wearing a brilliant white zoot suit with black trim. Propped up on one elbow, he cups his chin atop the macrocosm of the thousands of tiny dots decorating the bar, fedora tilted so the brim hangs provocatively over one eye. His hair is starlight cobalt, shimmering slightly, his skin as flawless and statue worthy as it ever was before my first untimely death.

"Hey." My heart is in my throat, the weight of everything I've lost coming to hit me full force as I stand in the middle of Sugar Skullz, eyes brimming with sparkling tears, as if I haven't cried enough already.

"Drink?" he asks, sensing my desperate need for one.

He turns, grabbing something before holding it up to show me, a vermillion glass bottle made mosaic by adorning broken ceramic tiles that follow its seductive curve.

"Please—" I breathe, taking several steps forward across the sticky dark sheen of the floor and sliding onto one of the barstools that had been so fun to spin on that night, right before I'd thrown up on Xion.

Xion.

Oh god, is every thought going to be serrated with his memory now? Is this what I have to look forward to? I should smile at the memory, but the expression seems to be on hold for the indefinite future, making my soul wilt, a sunless sky of grief eclipsing what had once been a fiery bloom in my chest.

I watch as Haedes sets down the tequila bottle in front of me before he rummages under the bar, looking for shot glasses, but ignore his effort, taking the bottle in my palm and uncorking it with my teeth, as ever, ladylike.

"So, it's that kind of day, is it? Right, better get my own. One second." He spins, caught seemingly off guard as I take the salty fluid into my throat and swallow deep, the burn of it chasing away the tears that threaten to fall and leaving only emptiness behind.

After a few seconds, Haedes returns, clutching a bottle identical to mine except in puce green.

He takes a seat next to me, just as he had done the night when we visited before, and watches as I take another swig.

"Woah, easy there!" He chuckles, but the joy of the sound doesn't reach the rest of his face.

His eyes are riddled with melancholy.

"If you knew the day I've had, you'd be getting me another." I gesture to the bottle and he sighs, uncorking his own bottle with practised bravado and setting the rim to his lips. He takes a deep drag, swallowing as a small pocket of air bursts in the back of his throat, the sound of long-awaited refreshment the only thing that permeates the tension between us for a long moment.

"I do— I do know. I've been watching. That's why we're here," he mumbles, the sentiment barely audible over the deep seductive flow of Cher's voice.

"And where is here? What the hell is this? You know I'm supposed to be fighting right about now? I mean, you couldn't have picked a less crucial moment to interrupt me for a drink?" I demand, one eyebrow cocked as my mouth is filled with saliva at the thought of another sip.

"We're in The Nether. This is the only way I could help you, so I took it— although I admit the timing was less than desirable. You went charging off to fight an army of demons on your lonesome. I didn't exactly have much time to make my move."

He doesn't look at me as he takes another swig of tequila from the bottle clutched in his palm, free hand drumming its long fingers down on the patterned glass in time with the song, which seems to be stuck on repeat.

"So, I'm dead?" I ask, detached in every regard.

"Not exactly. This is what's known as a Kindred vision. While everyone else was picking theirs, I've been banished, so now I'm choosing you." He clears his throat casually as though he's just announced he's ordering takeout.

"So, what the hell does that mean? Aren't you supposed to have like— I dunno— whole armies of Kindred or something?" I demand, and he smirks.

"I don't want or need hoards. I only want and need one. You. Besides, me making you my one and only Kindred will help offset the darkness you've just absorbed. I'd have been stupid not to have done it, given the circumstances." He pauses, taking a sip from the bottle but stopping himself from swallowing as he swills the alcohol inside his mouth, thoughtful. "I'm sorry about all this. I never wanted this for you," he apologises after the spirit finally disappears down his gullet, but I shrug, the sentiment washing off me.

"Doesn't seem to matter much what anyone wants these days though, does it?" I ask him, wanting to hear what he has to say more than I let on as I take another mouthful of tequila, eyelids half closing in a kind of ambivalent sleepiness.

"No. If it did, your mother would still be with us, God rest her soul—" he adds thoughtfully.

"And so would Xion. I— I never knew I could love like that until him," I admit, the walls that had existed between my long-lost father and me seemingly insignificant now in the face of everything that's happened.

"Seems cruel, doesn't it? The way the universe teaches us the value of our power through the loss of those we love." Haedes sighs, and I blink back yet more tears, which cling to my eyelashes.

"I promised him I wouldn't let the sacrifice be in vain. That means I have to be Queen, doesn't it? There's nobody else, right? It has to be me?" I ask, eyes staring into the mirror beyond the bar, my face made up in thick eyeliner and victory red lipstick but undeniably hollow, barren of emotion beneath.

"You know I wanted your mother to be Queen, to rule by my side. Together, we could have done incredible things. It seems fitting that both of us will rule together through you," Haedes replies.

I feel my shoulders hunch forward.

"That doesn't make me want to sit on that throne," I announce, and he smiles.

"I never wanted to rule Mortaria either. At least, not the way Zeus and Poseidon thought I should. I wanted to be free of them, of the expectations of The Higher Plains altogether. It's why I hated the idea of The Nexus Council so deeply. It wasn't arrogance, hard as that is to believe; it was fear. Fear that my brothers would try to bully me into running things the way they wanted via members of the council," Haedes admits, eyes glancing at the side of my face from beneath the curve of the brim of his hat.

"So, I'm screwed?" I surmise, caring little for his tale of woe.

"Seems that way. Then again, you do have a choice. You know you could walk away, I won't try to stop you, not that I could—" Haedes places a soft hand on my shoulder, the chill of his marble-esque skin the opposite of what you'd expect from a god with his powers.

"I was so selfish once." I sigh, taking a considerably smaller but no less salty sip from the bottle in front of me.

"Do you regret becoming the person you are now, after everything?" Haedes asks, and I think on this a moment, moving just enough for the fiery tendrils of my hair to tickle my shoulders and the space above my breasts.

"No. I don't. I don't think— I don't think Xion would have loved me if I hadn't changed so much. He was so righteous even for a half-demon, and I was so self-centred. He made me selfless. It was him. He did this."

"That bastard," Haedes snorts, and I smirk against my better judgement.

I go to reply, but before I can come up with something witty and quintessentially me, a loud yowl followed by a sudden furball launching up onto the bar makes me jump, leaving my heart pounding against the underside of my ribs.

"Woah! I thought you said we were in The Nether?!" I exclaim, looking deeply into Cassie's eyes. She meows proudly, padding her paws up and down on the counter and winding between the vermillion and puce glass of the liquor bottles.

"We are. Cats, particularly house cats with all their base instincts sated, can travel through time and space at will. Some cats have been recorded being in as many as nine places at once. I guess that's where the nine lives thing comes from." I cock an eyebrow as Cassie gets bored of trying to steer our attention from one another, leaping off the bar and skulking off into the back room.

"I didn't take you as a fan of cats—" I muse, and he shakes his head.

"I'm not, but Thane— well, her mother Nemesis is in a relationship with Hecate. That woman is the definition of a well-groomed crazy cat lady. They have the creatures walking in and out of their house at all hours," he explains, and I nod, not interested but glad of something less crucial to talk about.

"How is she, Thane, I mean?"

"She's hurting. She hasn't said much about Luce, but I'd have to be blind not to see it. How's Luce?" he counters, taking a deep pull on the bottle as his fingers trace its green curve absent-mindedly.

"I don't know. The darkness, it changed her. I didn't get it, the pull, but I guess I do now. It's like having a veil lifted; you can see where all the power around you lies, see how to take it." I remember the thrumming darkness that pulsed beneath my feet in Golgotha, the urge I'd felt to harvest it, claim it as mine.

"If it wasn't alluring, there'd be nothing particularly remarkable about resisting, I suppose," Haedes muses, stroking the line of his jaw with a curved index finger.

"I think understanding it is important, especially if I'm going to rule." The words sting me internally, but I know they are necessary so take another mouthful of tequila, attempting to numb the gaping wound of my reluctant surrender to fate.

"Quite right you are—"

"Did you at least try to get us some kind of assistance?" I ask without bravado, raising one eyebrow into the shape of a question mark.

"Of course, I did. I went to Zeus and The Aetherial Court. He sent Hercules to assess the situation," Haedes rolls his eyes, and I swallow hard.

"Hercules? Really? I never saw anything of him," I admit.

Haedes smirks.

"I'm not surprised. Zeus thought I was being overdramatic, trying to save face due to being killed and having to return to The Higher Plains. Stupid asshole. It wouldn't surprise me if Hercules gave him the same information I did, and he still didn't listen—"

"Hmm—" I think about this as the current rendition of *Believe* comes to a close.

Haedes, taking one final swig from his bottle, rises with languid prowess from the barstool beside me and holds out a hand.

"Care to dance with dear old dad?" he offers, and I spin slightly on my perch, laying a palm directly into his.

He pulls me to my feet, hand coming to expertly cradle my wildly curvaceous silhouette as it hooks around my waist. The scent of burning sandalwood drifts from him, making my head fuzzy. Cher's voice starts up again, and he pulls my body flush to his.

I rest my head on the shoulder of his pristine white jacket, and we sway, dancing alone in the middle of the karaoke bar.

"Do you believe in life after love?" he croons to me, pulling back so I'm forced to look into his face.

"I suppose we'll find out," I respond, and he sighs.

"Sephy, what you did, riding off like some martyr— You know that as your father, I can't condone that kind of behaviour. What you tried to pull is suicide." he condemns me, and I feel the tears I've been chasing with liquor return.

"I just— it's not fair. I loved him. He was—" My bottom lip trembles and Haedes pulls me closer.

"Shhh. I know— more than you can imagine. But Sephy, you're extraordinary. Part god, part mortal, part demon, and now part Kindred soul of mine— the universe needs you. Needs your loss, your rage. You have to fight for those who aren't strong enough to fight for themselves. It's not fair, but it's who you are and the cards you've been dealt. I know you can do this, and so did Xion. It's why he trusted you with the darkest part of himself."

"If you give me the old Ben Parker speech, I will slap you," I threaten him, face deadpan as thick heavy tears roll down my cheeks.

We continue to dance; Cher's voice soothing something inside of me I didn't realise was fixable.

"Watch this—" he whispers in my ear, holding me away from him and taking his fingers from my waist with a flourish before tracing them down my arm. Where he makes contact with my skin, the flesh turns red hot then cools to the blackness of earth. The neurons beneath my flesh— which becomes slowly translucent— fire, flaming through my muscles and showing the power that lies just beneath my surface. It's a ripple, mystical and scorching, and I accept it without fighting.

"This is the final part of becoming a Kindred, Sephy, my blessing, bestowed to you in an ashen touch—" he explains.

I roll my eyes.

"Only you could do something so monumental with Cher blaring in the background."

"Hey, I make no apologies for how I choose to bless you. You'll be returning with a definitive edge, so to speak. You should be grateful I had the good sense to include The Queen in this most momentous occasion." He twirls me under his arm, unable to stop his feet from tapping and his hips swinging with feline elegance as he does so.

"A definitive edge? What does that entail exactly?" I ask, more curious than I want to admit.

"How should I know? It's my first time." He gives me a wicked glance, the implication of his Kindred blessing virginity hanging with an oddly amusing air in the space between us.

"So, I get to be a guinea pig too, fabulous." I can't help but feel hard done by. People in their homes in the millions, clambering to be seen by the world, and all I want to be is invisible— and probably drunk while I'm at it.

"Any advice for me before I go?" I ask Haedes, and he pauses a moment thinking hard, his face seeming torn. He doesn't want to let me go.

"Pandora—" he begins, and I interrupt, eager for information.

"Yes?"

"Kick her ass," he finishes, face deeply lined with amusement.

"I was hoping for a secret weakness or something, but don't worry, I'm on that. She has some serious shit to answer for."

"Oh, and— there's a bow buried deep in my vault. It can't be used to kill, but it never misses a target. Aphrodite left it at my place once; couldn't bring myself to throw it away. Might come in useful though," he adds as though he's no more than ordering a side of onion rings.

"Okay— well, is this goodbye?" I ask, stepping back out of his arms.

The song blaring from the speakers dies, leaving us in pregnant silence.

"Never." He smiles, holding out his arms. I weaken, my knees sagging beneath the velvet sheath of my gown. Within moments, I've staggered the length of the space between us, and I'm in his arms, sobbing.

He doesn't say anything. He only strokes the silken flaming locks of my hair, kissing my forehead and rocking me slowly from side to side. We stand like this for a while, and I wonder how long I could theoretically stand here.

Are the demons devouring my body as we speak?

Or is this outside of time, of the constant and unending march toward an inevitable end point, no matter how far off in the distance that end may seem?

I let myself be weak for a final moment, relishing Haedes' embrace, the last of this ashen touch we've been afforded, before stepping away, drying my tearstained cheeks, and taking a deep steadying breath of spirit-laden air.

"So, uh— how do I get out of here?" I ask, trying to sound casual as ever. He smiles.

"Take my hand—" he commands, and I do as he asks without pause, ready for the pain, ready to rise.

He pulls me into him, giving me a final kiss, which lands warm on my cheek, before twirling me out from him in a rhythmic pirouette of magical intent. As I spin, dancing in the silence, the bar around us dissolves.

I return to Mortaria, ready at last to fight for the Kingdom my father has left me.

423

36

THE PHOENIX

SEPHY

I'M COILED, SPRUNG, READY to strike as I come back to myself.

I hear them stirring beyond the dome of my power, and yet I feel no pain, bear no wounds.

My eyes are screwed shut, an unfamiliar heat ebbing over my skin. I blink, eyelids fluttering open, eyelashes trembling as excruciatingly pure violet light floods through my retinas, shocking my brain.

Stretching out from where I've been lying, curled up on my left side, I discover that I've been protected by myself without any recollection of trying to do so.

The purple flames curve, an orb of shimmering, hungry tendrils capturing my now conscious form and keeping me from the encroaching demons.

I sit up, hands gloved by violet tongues of flame, hair alight, my muscles rich with unspent power, blessed, *Kindred*.

My sword beckons, flaccid and impotent upon the stone on my left, begging to be clutched, to be held.

Reaching for it, the weight is welcome in my calloused palm, the edge as sharp as my newly awakened senses.

The emotional release of my father's arms has cleared my mind, giving me crystalline, laser-tipped focus as I clamber to my feet. The orb of fire flickers to nothing but thin air as I rise, hair crackling fiercely as the flames lift my locks around my face in an obvious challenge.

I look up, ignoring the demons that circle me, no longer concerned by them, seeking only Pandora. I locate her within seconds, stood high above me on the balcony of the Exilia, looking out over the street.

I smile.

The chill of encroaching corpses catches my attention, the clang of clashing swords upon the ivory of bones reanimated growing closer from the corner of my eye. I can only think this is Luce's doing, but dwell on it no further as the demons that have been lying in wait for my demise become quickly and fortunately distracted.

Too bad.

Pandora watches me as I lift a single hand, sending flames flying along the path I wish to clear without accelerant or chemical aid. My will now is enough, my soul itself a lit match amongst the gasoline of my emotional turmoil.

I tread along the flaming stone, reflection cast formidable upon the onyx, speckled bloody, lit aflame with my power, with my intent to take back what's rightfully mine.

I watch Pandora's face contort, confusion melding into pure rage as her lips pull back over visibly gritted teeth and her jaw tenses.

She takes several paces back, retreating into the depths of the darkness behind her, the gleam of her silver-corseted torso blazing orange with the encroaching fires of Mount Mallum as she prepares to leap.

I still, demons cowering on my left and right, retreating at my back, purple flames engulfing any creature stupid enough to get too close. The ground beneath my feet trembles, and I look now to the sky. Smoke, thick and black, the beginnings of a bigger threat, billows through the air, blanketing the sanguine sky and plunging the world below into almost total darkness.

My flaming hair, my gloved and blazing arms, remain bright, acting as a welcome torch as pieces of debris begin to crash in around me on all sides.

As I track the path of a large piece of flaming rock, she reappears, launching herself from the balcony in a blur of polished silver and dull steel, muscles roped with strain as she throws herself into the sky, putting her faith in metal and magic alone. My nostrils fill with sulphur, the acidity of it stinging my eyes, rank and suffocating as it billows relentlessly across the scorching sky.

Eyes watering, pulse thumping in my ears, I stare up and into the skies ever still, my narrow gaze tracking her as she takes flight among the full force of the Eruption's prelude. Her silhouette is jagged yet fluid among the chaos, a meshing together of mortal and machine.

It forms then, malleable and fluid like liquid mercury inside my grey matter, squirming, the influence of such synaptic quickfire flowing down through my nerves and seeping into my blood, into my muscles, with volatile intent.

They spread, roaring, spitting flames from my spine, not burning but tickling me with a welcome and familial caress. The wings of a Phoenix erupt from me, spreading wide, my hair glowing brighter as the force of the self-induced explosion causes the air around my entire body to stir, enticed and alive with newfound potential.

Well, that's just plain badass— I muse, making a small leap from one foot like a ballet dancer wishing to temps-leve into the arms of her male partner. The partner here isn't visible, but I know he's there.

Haedes, his blessing, his magic, catches me, wings of fire spreading from me and beating hard against the thick smoke that encroaches on every side as though they were not made from fire at all but feathers.

My body flushes with heat, with excitement, and without pause, the wings made from this brand-new violet flame allow me to rise, magnificent, into the air.

I smile, unable to help it as air rushes past my cheeks, making them fill hot with blood, my heart pounding with exhilarated pleasure as I squint, searching for her within the increasingly thick gloom of volcanic ash and dust.

As I rise higher and higher through the smoke, I get glances of the world below, the army of what appear to be reanimated skeletons, flesh dangling precariously from their bones, jaws agape with no muscle or flesh to keep their skulls as one. They pile into the narrow street, fighting to trap the mortals against The Exilia by thickening the waning barrier of Abraxis' forces that lie between them and the vicious mess of teeth and claws threatening to tip the balance between worlds.

As if Haedes is watching, which I know he probably is, music erupts across the span of the sky, covering Mortaria with its familiar, motivational, and hard-core beat.

The Phoenix by Fall Out Boy bursts through the smoke, echoing loudly in my ears and causing me to throw my head back, a laugh erupting from deep in my chest as a smile manifests, inescapable, upon my lips.

I swing my hips, wings acting of their own accord, flawlessly in tune with my needs.

Well, at least it isn't Cher— I muse, wrinkling my nose against the burning air.

"Thanks for the fighting music!" I yell out to no one in particular, then remember his one request of me.

Kick her ass.

The smile on my lips widens into a grin.

Yes, Sir.

The smoke from Mount Mallum covers everything, thick, billowing, a raging entity as bone-dry ash and scorching dust fills my lungs and continue to make my eyes water in an unceasing onslaught. My nose is filled with the pungent burn of the earth tossed skyward as I hover, rising even higher above Mortaria, searching for her in the black.

A flicker here, a glint of silver there, the music continues to rage on throughout it all, unrelenting, urging me to violence.

I spin three hundred and sixty degrees, smoke pluming around me. The only sounds noticeable the falling debris from the volcano, which leaves trails behind it like shooting stars turned flailing inferno in the sky, and the crackling of the flames keeping me airborne.

"You know there's a special place in hell for people like you—" Her voice comes to me from over my shoulder as I tighten my grip on the sword in my palm, spinning to stare into the pale, cruel face, the eyes devoid of mercy of kindness.

"I know—" I raise my sword, surging forward, watching as she mimics my motion and the sharp edges of our weapons clash in mid-air, the metal coming alive with the light of falling embers. "—A throne."

She pushes her blade from mine with a small and guttural grunt, hoping that the force of it will disorient me. But instead, I merely fall backwards, feigning defeat before my wings catch the hot air beneath them and I barrel roll back on myself.

Turning a somersault, I return, wings beating steady along with the rush of blood singing in my veins, to my previous height, only this time I'm behind her.

"Nice wings—" I comment, tapping one with my sword so she tilts slightly before rolling back around to face me. The smoke is so thick we could be fighting thin air rather than each other for all the visibility it allows, but I know I can use this to my advantage.

My wings are divine, a gift from the gods; hers are not.

"You too. Daddy give you those?" she sneers, lunging forward as a large piece of rock falls too close past my left shoulder.

I fly backwards to avoid them both, smoke filling my lungs as I make a deep and sudden inhale and surprise jolts through my system, jarring my senses like the first off-key guitar riff in a heavy rock ballad.

"I'd like to think I earned them," I call back, and she laughs.

"Of course, you would."

I close my eyes, listening, trying to wait for her to retort, to goad me yet again, hoping the direction of the sound will give me a better grasp on her location. My heart thuds against the inside of my ribcage, a phoenix that refuses to burn to ash, only this one has been robbed of flight, trapped within my chest, and allowed to rage on without fear of scorching itself black.

"They'll never accept you as one of them, Sephy. Never—"

I spin, finding her encroaching to my left as her hollow voice echoes into nothing. I raise my sword just in time to smash into her oncoming blade, blocking the unseen attack.

"And I'll never be one of them, thankfully. I'm a chimera of all souls, one of a kind. Which is more than I can say for you!"

I twist in mid-air, bringing my knee up to smash her in the stomach, my wings casting an eerie violet glow on both our faces. Her purple irises go almost translucent beneath the mystical haze of my proximity as her pupils dilate, the shock of the impact of my kneecap in her abdominals causing her to falter and fall, losing altitude as she disappears beneath the thick layer of smoke that is lit only now and again by a passing trail of falling fire.

I fall after her, and as I find myself at a level where the smoke has not yet infiltrated, I see what is happening below.

All-out war.

The dead fighting demons with lifeless determination to protect the living. Abraxians murdering what had once been their dark allies. The sound of it is deafening, rising above even the increasing tempo of the music pouring from nowhere. I hear the precise rabidity of it as I circle overhead, a hunter of the skies now. The gnashing of teeth within snarling jaws, with lips that pull back in demonic sneers laced thick with digestive enzymes, claws that gash the stone beneath as they reach out to claim a pound of flesh but miss, finding no flesh to be had upon the reanimated skeletons of Lucifer's very own necro-maniacal army. It's a dark rabid crescendo of primal energy, unceasing for even a moment.

428

I gape at the scale of it, at the chaos, but before I can even think about landing to get involved in the fight, something, or should I say someone, makes her presence known, tackling me from behind.

The force of impact knocks the air from my lungs, and for a long, terrifying moment, I think I might have been fatally wounded by a fast-moving and unseen blow.

We tumble, a whirling cacophony of wings, flame, steel, and blade, crashing into the street below.

The fighting continues to rage around us as we impact the onyx sidewalk, Pandora finding the upper hand as she lands on top of me, the weight of her steel, steampunk-style wings increasing the weight of her otherwise lithe form and crushing me into the pavement. My head slams back into the stone, pain flooding my senses in increasingly disorienting seismic waves from the epicentre at the back of my skull.

"Why won't you just stay dead?" she exclaims, eyes wild as she pulls her arm back, blade turning lilac as it reflects the flaming tendrils of my hair back at me.

"What can I say, there's not enough tequila in The Nether to incline me to stay." As I'm throwing out this witty and entirely brilliant retort, she plunges the sword downward, aiming directly for my jugular.

Willing my hands alight, I catch the blade between flat palms, stopping it only centimetres from the throbbing pulse that ebbs just beneath the skin of my throat. I exhale heavily, not realising I'd been holding my breath, waiting for the blow that might well have ended my life.

I let my palms heat, the flames growing hotter as I urge them on with every passing second, straining against her. She watches, pausing in her curiosity, outraged as I melt her sword into a glowing blob of molten and unrecognisable steel twisted useless beneath my fire. The heat is conducted along the length of the sword, and I watch as Pandora drops the handle as it becomes too hot to hold.

Jerking to her feet with surprisingly well-balanced poise, she turns on the spot, taking off at a sprint in the opposite direction and launching once more into the sky. Smoke covers her tracks, masking her path as elusive.

I'm left behind only to watch her outline eclipsed, splayed upon the street below, panting as adrenaline rushes through me, a ravenous chemical demon devouring all sources of potential firepower and converting them into action without thought or pause.

I let myself relax, taking a deep breath and allowing the pain radiating from the back of my skull to dull as my head lolls sideways. Here, my eyes rest upon the twisted and discarded sword Pandora had attempted to kill me with, and I watch the cooling metal as it returns to solid form upon the pavement beside me, eyes widening as I raise my arms over my head.

I watch them as they blaze, the fire crawling over my skin like an old friend.

Closing my eyes, I let the flames engulf my entire body, convecting into the open air of the sky for the first time.

It works exactly as I intend.

I reappear, flaming violet wings spreading either side of my spine and beating hard to stabilise my weight amid bulging plumes of smoke that continue to flow, heady with the smell of the impending eruption, over the city.

I squint through the haze of heat and smoke, seeing something glimmer a few feet from me.

Diving forward, I make my way toward it, but rather than finding Pandora, I'm instead confronted with the highest peak of the Exilia's massive silhouette, the smoky quartz that makes up the bulk of the building almost indistinguishable from the surrounding air but for the sheen of its facets.

"Sephy—" Her voice is a taunt through the dim light, a laugh following closely behind the echo of her haunting call. "Where's the halfling now? Where's Xion? I expect he'll be here to rescue you at any moment." She's snakelike in the way her words constrict around my heart, causing the flames that encase my skin, my hair, my clothes, to flare explosively, rage making wildfire of the flickering purple tongues.

"I save myself," I spit at her, knowing full well that Xion has already saved me, already reminded me that loving someone is worth the pain that goes along with it. He allowed me to rise from the pain of my tragic past, reminded me that I'm a warrior, a fighter. Reminded me what it means to be Persephone Sinclair.

Fuck this bitch.

I cuss, listening to her high-pitched hysterical laugh as I spin in mid-air, hunting her as I inhale the air for a whiff of my prey.

A break in the smoke reveals the tip of one of her wings, but also an enormous piece of flaming rock hurtling toward me.

I drop through the smoke, this single glimpse enough, disappearing as though I'm no more than a ghost, before ascending once more with my sword clutched in hand and smashing into her torso with the blunt edge of my left shoulder.

The heat from falling embers surrounds me, prickling my bare skin as scalding hot ashes scatter through my hair like melancholy hellish snow.

Thrusting upwards with my sword, I aim for her face, ready to end it. She rotates sideways, swinging her wing to dislodge the weapon from my hand. She makes contact, and the blade flies through the air. She grabs it with unpractised ease, hooking the handle around an outstretched index finger as her body starfishes across the distance between us.

I watch her clutch at my sword, thinking of the one I had melted only minutes before— has she learned nothing?

Steel can't succeed in the face of fire.

Then it hits me.

Her pupils dilate as she takes in my face, preparing to rush my unarmed form. Her wings turn a dull bloody burgundy as a patch in the smoke clears, allowing the sanguine weep of the sky to shine muted through the dark.

I inhale, watching as she crosses the space between us with a lithe effortlessness, sword primed to strike.

For what I have planned, I'll need to keep her close.

I know that what I'm about to do is going to hurt but take comfort in the fact that it will be nowhere near as much agony as shattering my own heart only hours prior.

Closing my eyes, I open my arms, beckoning her forward and bracing myself for impact. The sword pierces through the corset at speed, running clean through my torso, gutting me.

I wrap my arms around her, embracing her and pulling her close. Bending ninety degrees at the waist, I continue to fake my surprise, my limpness, as I clutch at her. I gasp, bringing my hands to grasp Pandora by the shoulders as I take a tortured and agonising inhale.

"Can you feel it?" She smiles salaciously, the malice in her eyes sharper than razor blades, colder than the innermost circle of Dante's hell.

Blinking, I adjust my grip on her again, faking helplessness as I reach behind her, pulling her closer still, burying my shaking face into

431

the dark tendrils of her hair. She smells like violets and tonic mixed in with dried blood as I take a final inhale, preparing to end this.

I will my palms to heat as hot as they'll go, feeling the hot fluid leaking from the wound around the sword that remains embedded in my abdomen and knowing I'm running out of time.

"Can you?" I ask her, smiling. The steel of her wings turns fluid, scorching hot and malleable in my hands. I trap her panicked limbs as she tries to get away from me, but I'm frozen in place, bound to her by the sword that starts wrapped in her fingers and ends protruding through my back. Even in the final moments, she still won't let go, refusing to fall until she's ripped the blade from my body, until she's caused me one final ounce of pain.

"Goodbye, Pandora—" I smile, whispering in her ear as I push back from her. I stare on, watching the falling angel among the smoke, her skin reflecting a pure and glorified light. It's not from her flesh though, not from the soul that was long ago charred black and baptised in blood.

Her wings are aglow, molten from my touch, melting in mid-air.

The expression on her face turns from triumphant to confused and, finally, to all-encompassing terror as she begins her descent back to the hell she's created below. She flails, reaching for any kind of foothold, fingers falling through thin grey air, eyes meeting mine as she tilts backwards, picking up speed like a dark falling star.

If I was merciful, if she hadn't taken so much from me, ripped me open and laid me bare before the hell fires of tragedy that will forever burn in my soul, I might extend a hand.

As it is, however, she killed my dog, so she can go to fucking hell.

Watching her fall until she disappears through the smoke, I take a few moments, breath painful, before I place both flaming palms on the hilt of the sword protruding just beneath my ribs. I let the steel warm from the handle, the heat running through my torso and becoming slowly unbearable as the blade becomes white-hot. With a scream escaping unbidden from my lips, I yank the entire length from beneath my ribs with a jerk, watching it re-emerge, wet with boiling blood the colour of a throne's rich upholstered velvet.

My insides twist, burning, and I think I might faint, might give in to the agony. Instead, though, all I can think about is the fact I have to protect the balance, must prevent the scales from tipping.

The wound is at least, for now, cauterised.

The volcano emits yet another rumble in the distance, and I feel the very air around me tremor, a tidal wave of pent-up kinetic energy set free from deep within the earth. The magmatic curtain is about the rise on the show of a lifetime, and this smoky pre-show, this tectonic warm-up, is most certainly coming to an end.

37

THE WINNER TAKES IT ALL

SEPHY

I SOAR ABOVE A burning world, smoke rising as though from the pyres of a million long-dead dreams of what my life could have been.

It's a mess. This world. This place that's so vital to the continued balance of everything I've ever known, and yet it's my job to fix it.

I can't do that alone.

Beneath the swirl of the hot, snowy ash and the flaming spew that continues to consume the sky, I find them standing tight in the face of demonic onslaught. The dead have ringed the living, forming a wall three skeletal bodies thick, with Abraxians popping up every now and again, fighting my cause.

Good job, Luce— I think as I observe the undead, knowing I'm going to need her skills, along with those of the other Nexus members for that matter, if I'm going to get everyone safe and inside before the imminent volcanic eruption. Luce vowed to end the lives of the mortals, but she and I now know there's more hanging on their collective survival than any of us thought.

The wound in my abdomen continues to burn, as much as I try to ignore it altogether, reminding me that I'm still human, still at least part of who I had once been.

So, what will we do now?

Shaking my head, I try to keep my mind clear of worries about the future but fear falling too deep into the grief — the open wound — of my too recent past as well.

I bank left then right, the flaming tendrils that form the fiery feathers of my wings crackling and shedding violet embers among the deepening melancholy grey of the sky.

I make my way across the city, away from the clatter and din of fighting, over the barren expanse of The Plains of Ichor and, too soon, find myself soaring high above the peak of The Icon, the gold of it no less impressive among the encroaching gloom.

I pass overhead, wondering about Anubis, about how I'm ever going to be able to trust her after all this, about whether I even have the right to toss her from The Nexus Council.

What rights *do* I have?

I'm no god, no ruler, not really. I was just in the wrong damn place at the wrong damn time, and I know it's only a matter of days, if not weeks, before everyone around me begins to see that as well.

The Ashen Waste blurs beneath me as the smoke thickens into a wall of chemicals, smoke, and heat, causing me to cough as the debris I'm having to dodge gets larger the closer I come to the peak. I know this isn't the climax of the eruption, and from what I do know of Volcanoes — from my limited experience of watching Dante's Peak — once it gears up for the big pyroclastic cloud portion of the performance, I'll want to be far away from here at least.

I fly on for what seems like forever, no way to judge what distance I'm covering as the smoke closes in on all sides, obscuring the world above and below completely.

What did I expect?

That Luce would be on the side of the volcano waving a white flag?

Stupid. Think Sephy— I chastise myself, clearing my mind and picturing her face clearly among the emotional haywire of my grey matter.

The flames rise and I spin, corkscrewing through the air as the blazing wings sprouting from my spine fold to embrace me, allowing them to engulf me on every side, the kiss of their fire the only such embrace I will know from now on.

I rematerialize in darkness, the purple flames of my hair lighting the narrow confines of the room that closes in around me.

"Sephy—" Muerta's voice is a whisper broken by shock as I stare out from amongst the blaze of my body, nodding.

My eyes rest on Lucifer, who is positioned on all fours upon the slick cool stone of the floor. Her eyes are covered by a film of abyssal black, silver hair falling around each side of her phantasmal face, paler than ever now in the light from my Kindred flame. Her fingers are bent at the knuckle, arachnid in shape, muscles riddled with tension.

"Luce— I'm here. You did amazing." I compliment her with gentle eyes, but she continues to stare into the darkness opposite her. Yama shifts, and The Furies stare at me from beside him, sweat-slick faces glistening and astonished at my new power.

I take a deep breath, inhaling the scent of rot, of dried blood and decay that spills from each wall of the place. The scent of acrid burn, of scorched earth and natural volatility has not yet impregnated the room, but I know that if we hope to avoid the power of Mount Mallum once it reaches the crescendo of its organic rage song, we need to move.

"Can someone get her back? We need to take cover in the Exilia if we have any hope of saving the mortals Luce has worked so hard to protect."

Muerta nods, not questioning my authority as she reaches out through the dank air to touch Luce on the shoulder. However, right before her skin makes contact, the darkness in Luce's eyes recedes to pinpricks, her glacial blue irises freezing over the space fast. She comes back to herself, slumping back onto her heels and breathing like she's just run a race.

"The demons are retreating. I let the army drop from my influence. The mortals are no longer under attack, but still vulnerable as there aren't many Abraxians left to defend them. We need to move!" she exclaims in a rush of breath.

Her neck is visibly damp with chill perspiration as she raises her head to the ceiling and rises to her feet in a single fluid jerk.

"Oh, hey Sephy. I saw you. Nice trick with Pandora's wings by the way. Where's Xion?" she demands, eyes innocent and wide with wonder as lilac light plays across the hollows and curves of her skull. Getting to her feet, she takes a step toward me, wavering slightly as though balance is a tipsy afterthought. Muerta steadies her as The Furies step forward from the shadow, and Yama moves toward Luce's back, towering a head over everyone else.

I blink once, then twice, staring into their curious expressions and embracing the sting of having to explain Xion's absence.

I can't, can't speak, can't break down, so instead I simply say, "Okay, let's go."

I grab Luce and Muerta by the wrists and pull them toward me, not waiting before allowing the flames to ripple into existence around us, air compressing and transporting us back to The Exilia.

The structure around us tremors slightly, the floor visibly blurring with motion as the fire relinquishes.

I sigh out, my injury twinging in a sudden and unexpected acute shocking pain. I double over as I drop the wrists of the two women on either side of me, and Muerta looks down at me, concern riddling her face's reflection in the pristine crystal of the floor.

"Sephy, are you alright?" Luce asks, placing a hurried hand on my bare shoulder.

I flinch.

"Fine, just a scratch." I gasp, straightening and feeling the wound pull tight.

Pain ripples through me in a porcupine wave.

"You need to go down to the dungeons. Free The Fates and Jules. Then, go and open the gates. Start getting everyone off the main street and inside. Can you do that?" I ask her, gaze intense and face pinched tight with fatigue.

"Of course. Go and get the others." She nods, giving me a forced smile, her pale skin stretching thin over her cheekbones with obvious strain.

I nod back, smiling at her with the only remaining energy I can muster, seeing in her eyes that she knows the truth about Xion.

She knows he's gone forever.

The flames encroach and recede, tickling my flesh, and before I can blink, I'm staring into the tawny gaze of Erin, moving soundlessly to transport The Furies back to the Exilia, to safety, as quickly as I can.

Finally, I return with Yama, the last of the group who journeyed to Mount Mallum. Everyone is gathered atop the staircase, which flickers back to stone from bone.

The powers of the Demon Lords are waning.

"What are we waiting for?" I ask, looking at Luce and finding her and Jules exchanging worried and curious glances. My hair is still alight, my arms and hands gloved with flame, blood, and ash. The scent coming off me is that of burnt hair, and I'm pretty sure my face has seen better days too. Regardless, this isn't a beauty pageant. Thank Christ. If it were, Mortaria most certainly would have been doomed. I am not the girl you ask to give a speech about world peace.

"Luce and I were just saying how there are a few demons that haven't gotten the message from the rest of them. The majority have fled, but there are still some blocking the gates. We need to shift them, and fast, before we can get the mortals inside to safety," Jules explains, hopping from left to right with his knees pushed together in an awkward pose.

"What's wrong? Why are you standing like that?" I demand, and he rolls his eyes.

"I need to use the Little Butler's room," he announces, round cheeks flushing.

I have to stop myself from snorting.

"Okay, you go and pee. I'll go and sort out the demons. Luce, Furies, you get the hall ready to receive everyone, and make sure the gates are closed once they're inside, okay?" I order them. They nod without complaint, long lustrous hair peppered grey like they've been cleaning some kind of haunted house that's been deserted for years.

"What do you want us to do?" Muerta asks me, gesturing to herself and Yama as her enormous hazelnut eyes gleam, serious and yet undeniably exhilarated.

"Go make sure The Fates get settled and search the rest of the Exilia. I don't want to find a Demon Lord or random demon hiding inside any of the closets," I declare, finding it hard to remember at this moment that I'm speaking to gods made flesh. More staggeringly, they're taking instruction from me like I know what I'm doing.

That remains to be seen— I muse, turning and heading for the staircase that descends into the wide-open lobby ringed with what had once seemed immense columns. Now though, I'm wondering how well they're going to hold up in the face of a pissed-off volcano.

I don't pause, hearing a few half-hearted summons travelling through the air toward me before they fizzle into silence passing over one shoulder.

They have questions, but I'm too wired, too full of rage, and too afraid to stop what I'm doing, to still for even a moment, to turn back and answer them.

I pass beneath the columns as a shudder wracks the crystal beneath my feet, but don't stumble, continuing to walk among the chaos, hair swept back from my face and dirty with blood, soot, and ash beneath the violet blaze capturing every strand.

I don't have a weapon. I don't need one, and I know that I have a job to do. As long as I keep putting one foot in front of the other, everything will be all right; nothing can hurt me now.

Nothing and nobody.

I've already lost everything, and so now I have morphed into a Phoenix, unstoppable.

I convect, saving time, to a point just inside the gates.

I'm impatient, itching to hit something, itching to feel my muscles burn, my ligaments tear, and my knuckles bloody among the frenzy of whatever demons are stupid enough to have remained here.

I push the gates forward, fingers white as they wind around the wrought steel bars, opening The Exilia to the mass of screaming mortals as the sky continues to burn and loom overhead, an unbiased threat to all life.

The bodies, hot and frenzied with panic, push past me, so instead of trying to fight the current of mortals, I convect once again to where I'm most needed, finding myself face to face with the tail end of the demonic horde that threatens to tilt the balance of the universe.

I throw my hands out to my sides, watching as they glow brighter, the purple flame-tipped scarlet like a newly forged blade. They come in a microcosmic onslaught, taking me as immediate and sole target, distracted from the mortals who flee to safety behind me while the world falls into chaos around us.

Towering over us, the volcano readies to release the pyroclastic cloud that will wipe out anything in its path.

I close my mind to the threat, to the smoke and the ash, to the fire and the smell of burning flesh, focusing on the target right in front of me, the one thing I can control.

My mind becomes a blur, surrendering to the instinct of the fight, as the first monstrosities launch themselves towards me without the etiquette to pause and snarl or, at least, make this somehow dramatic. It isn't climactic or grand but simply dirty, primal, and straightforward.

There can only be one winner, one person left standing, and I know with certainty that will be me.

My hands reach forward, ablaze, grabbing a Succubus around its scrawny neck and twisting hard, decapitating it, and watching its remains slump, burning, to the ground.

I crouch, allowing Gorgonians to slither only too willingly into my waiting hands, tearing their reptilian bodies in two and throwing them asunder with equal relish, my heart beating steadily beside my lungs, a constant and unending drumbeat, a funereal march of destruction.

Banshees draw up to the plate, and I spread my fingers, awaiting their jaws with outstretched and seemingly vulnerable palms full of fire, tearing their top and bottom layers of saliva-rich fangs apart and listening to the skull crunch and snap beneath my fury.

My whole body is tense, numb to the ache and the exhaustion of grief, as I murder demon after demon, my moral conscience, my squeamishness, or incapacity for pure lethality impaired beneath the smouldering heavens as loss smothers my mind in its warm, inescapable folds.

The roar of the volcano, the tremble of the earth, doesn't reach me, for I am lost in automated and endless death, taking life after life, my muscles clenching and unclenching, face and forearms spattered hot with thick rivulets of blood that shower down on me like violent rain upon the twisted steel of my popping veins.

My fingers burn from the clawing motion, from the yanking of bone from socket, of flesh from muscle, but I can't stop.

I'm invulnerable, immortal, free, powerful, and I don't want it to end.

I won't go back to being the hunted.

Another shudder wracks the ground, a deafening rumble falling on my uncaring ears as I hear only the crack of a Succubus skull separating from vertebrae and the legs of Phobias being torn from their bodies, leaving only helpless masses of black arachnid incompetence behind.

Pieces of shit! I scream internally, hands meeting with the paws of a Banshee that's decided to launch itself through the air at me.

Suddenly my knees weaken, and the world begins to spin.

If I was unacquainted with exhaustion, I might think it was Haedes' pulling me back to The Nether for a lecture on how not to be a suicidal maniac in times of great peril. However, as part mortal, I'm all too familiar with this weakness, with this lack of control.

My gut is throbbing, alive with my pulse from where I've only just pulled my own white-hot sword. My legs suddenly resort to the consistency of Jell-O, betraying me, and my breath becomes but shallow wisps in my ears.

The Banshee tackles me to the ground, the stench of ichor and death permeating all five of my senses as the air thickens with it, the drool of the animal dripping down hot and sticky onto my chest.

Its jaws open wide, and I stare back into the abyss of its throat, fight gone, surrendering to what I've known is inevitable.

I lay back, exhaling heavily, but before I can close my eyes to welcome the pain, a sound causes me to startle on the ground, my muscles jerking independently of my mind as the shock causes them to twitch like they've been electrocuted.

Where before the demon was leering over me, its skull is now blown apart, flesh and brain matter spattered over its shoulders. The body collapses on top of me, and I feel myself go completely limp, the flames that have encapsulated me since I awoke Kindred finally extinguishing.

He drags the body from mine, the stink of its fur coating me in a thick layer of grime, before he pulls me up into his arms, slinging his shotgun to one side.

"Come on. You've done enough." Jules' kind voice is the last thing I hear as he turns his back on the destructive scene that's overtaking the city of Mortaria.

Then, I give in, unwillingly, to the pain, to the reality of everything that's happened, and unconsciousness steals me from the fight.

I stir, pain radiating from my core, eyelashes tickling the frail skin beneath my eyelids.

Suddenly, I remember everything that's happened.

The volcano, the eruption, Pandora, Haedes, Xion.

Xion.

My heart shatters anew as my eyes open, staring up into the canopy above the gold and chocolate-encrusted four-poster bed in my Exilia suite.

"What's—" I begin to panic, pulling myself upright and wincing as I feel, perhaps for the first time, the full extent of everything I've been through.

"Woah— no. Lay back down. *Right now.*" The voice is way more authoritative than usual, causing me to pause.

Jules reaches out and places both hands on my shoulders, pushing me back into the too-soft clutch of a mountainous pile of down pillows resting against my back.

I exhale heavily, blowing a loose strand of red hair from my eyes and gritting my teeth against the ache that extends through each of my limbs.

"What the hell do you think you were doing, Sephy? The mortals were safe— you could have—" Jules looks outraged, worry and anger melding together in the forge that lies behind the dark intensity of his pupils.

"I know," I reply, bitter.

441

He looks at me, eyes wide, dropping the hands that still rest on my shoulders as he shuffles on the side of the velvet-strewn mattress.

His palm encloses my hand, which lies bruised and bloody beside me.

"Sephy, where's Xion?" he asks me, swallowing hard and causing his Adam's apple to bob. He doesn't blink, clearly worried about upsetting me.

Fortunately for him, I don't have the energy left to cry again.

"Dead. He sacrificed himself." The sentence falls from my lips, fractured. My voice is hoarse, my throat dry and cracked from all the debris and smoke I've inhaled.

"I see." The silence that follows from him is unbearable.

"What's going on with the mortals? The volcano—" I go to swing my legs over the side of the mattress yet again, but Jules shoves me back against the headboard, face twisted with ironclad disapproval.

"Everyone is fine; everything is taken care of. The main part of the eruption has passed, and the others are handling it. You slept through it all, which proves exactly how exhausted you are because it was extremely dramatic. You need to rest. You should see yourself," Jules scolds me, and I bite down hard on my bottom lip. I feel, all of a sudden, like a naughty child being scolded by a parent.

"I can't just sit here, Jules," I protest, but again, he merely shakes his head.

"You can, and you will." There's no waver in his tone as he gets to his feet. "Now, what can I get for you? A bath?" he suggests, but I can only shrug.

"I guess. I hurt everywhere," I admit, looking down over my bare arms. Scratches, grazes, bruises, and deep cuts litter my skin, turning me a multitude of dark colours in turn.

"Right. Stay here. I'll be right back," he promises, turning a prompt one-hundred-and-eighty degrees and hastening from the room, closing the brass sliding panel back in place to protect whatever semblance of privacy I still possess.

I lie in the bed, looking at the door, remembering Xion appearing behind it wearing a tuxedo and with a black mask adorning his face.

I cast my eyes away, to the fire burning in the hearth, but see only the missing outline of Cerb silhouetted on the rug.

I can't be here.

Checking the door remains closed, I get unsteadily to my feet, stiff and nauseated with pain, not thinking, only feeling the depth of everything I've lost as I convect from the room in a blaze of anguish.

I reappear, shivering, my body seeping into the fluctuating depths of feverish shock.

The place is empty, quiet, the only light that of the blazing skies outside the panoramic window beside the bed.

Xion's apartment is cold and stale, the surfaces, the air, the hazy scent of pomegranates and cinnamon melding together and wrapping me in its nostalgic charms. My heart grows heavy within my chest, and I do the only thing I know how to, taking each breath as it comes.

Limping past the couch where I'd devoured microwaved meals, then past the bed where I'd asked him to hold me and he'd given me some insane analogy about a cow being slaughtered, I blanche, each memory serrated.

Mental.

That was us. Down to the core, two completely insane people that somehow found themselves at home in the domain of one another's crazy.

I kick off my shoes, padding through the empty bedroom, past the closet with a hundred identical leather jackets, and into the bathroom. The tub to my left holds bittersweet memories, his foamy embrace and my fear about getting in too deep.

Because being afraid stopped me drowning in him— *not*.

I wasted so much time.

The mirror reflects my image and I startle, barely recognising the girl staring back at me, wide-eyed and horrified.

She's bloody and bruised, dark circles rimming her eye sockets, skin startlingly pale in contrast with her vivid red hair.

I strip without ceremony, finding the wound that is causing me the most agony to be beyond horrifying to look at. My clothes become a discarded pile of black fabric in the corner of the room as I turn my back on an image I can't stomach. Against my consent, my eyes continually wander to my ravaged stomach.

Blood smears the edges of the puncture just beneath my ribs where I'd drawn out the hot blade. My torso is spattered with bruises, my shoulders the colour of blueberries, and my collarbone streaked brown and red tipped with sickly yellow the colour of day-old vomit.

I shiver in the barren tiled confines of the room, turning on the ball of my foot and closing the plug in the bottom of Xion's infamous spa tub.

I spin the faucet, bones in my fingers and wrist crunching in protest as steam begins to moisten the surrounding air and my muscles try to relax without my permission.

I drop in hands full of Epsom bath salts and sea mineral soak that I find in the cabinet under his sink basin, waiting impatiently and unable, even still, to stare at myself in the mirror. I know I'm lucky. These wounds would have killed any normal human, but I can't help but feel as though the world has turned on me, made me victim to its cruel indifference. Then again, as I peek back over my shoulder, daring to take in the painful mural of my spine, I realise it's not the cuts and bruises that bother me so deeply but rather the gaping Xion-sized wound that wraps around every one of my limbs in turn.

As the steam billows and the scent of sea salt and bergamot fills the air, I fight the will to turn pliant and jellyfish, the pain growing more intense with each step I take towards the bath. It becomes too much, so I step into the depths of the steaming half-full tub and sit, wincing as the salt-infused waters coat my skin and wound.

Shit. Shit. Shit.

Talk about salt in the wound.

This was an extremely stupid idea— I muse, teeth bared as I wince and wonder what the hell I was thinking. I suppose I was hoping the Epsom salts would stop my muscles aching for long enough that I might get some rest, some sleep, but I guess that was too much to ask as well.

Turning on the jets, I let the water froth and bounce, rising around my torso. I lean against the edge of the tub, stretching out my legs and closing my eyes, letting the smell of the bath soak fill my nostrils.

My mind finds some semblance of calm, some reprieve between the onslaught of the jets and me turning off the faucet as the water level rises to my throat. The water covers me like a blanket, the sound of the bubbles rushing from the jets soothing my battered psyche at last.

LUCE

The main hall is crowded with scared mortals, but short of telling them that we will do our very best to protect them, I'm not sure what else I can say. They sided with Pandora, but I know, as do Muerta and Yama, that the urge to survive for such creatures muddies the waters of their judgement. They will do what they must to cling to what remains of their abysmally short lives, and I suppose they cannot be blamed for that.

It takes a few hours, but eventually the tremors emitting from the volcano lessen into mere rumbles that can be felt but no longer rattle the crystal chandeliers dangling overhead.

As the mortals are squared away into a myriad of makeshift beds that consist of little more than blankets and pillows from every room that have been scattered on the floor, I manage to finally steal away.

I'm only too relieved to hear the echoing snores of exhausted mortals becoming little more than ambient white noise before dissolving into silence.

I'm exhausted, my mind racing, heart slow but steady in my chest. What has happened here is nothing short of revolutionary, life-changing, and I'm yet to come to terms with the fact that I just successfully prevented the end of the world as we know it.

I brush a silver strand of hair behind my ear, feeling an unending relief that is yet to subside.

I am one lucky bitch, that's for sure.

It's not lost on me, as I creep away and ascend the spiral staircase, that I've escaped blame for the demise of several dimensions. Nor is it lost on me the personal cost paid by those closest to me.

My heart wilts at the thought of Xion's sacrifice, mind still reeling with the shock of losing someone who had seemed so permanent in my life. He had been stronger than me, more righteous than I could ever dream of becoming. He had the makings of a god in every single way I do not. So perhaps, it is he who should have survived while I perished instead.

I reach the top of the staircase and walk into the door of my suite that is, suspiciously, unlocked. Inside, I feel strangely out of place, finding no Thane or Beelz in wait but, instead, two people I don't expect.

"Hey, what are you two doing here? And more importantly, how did you even get in here in the first place?" I demand, finding Abraxis kneeling beside the bed Thane and I had once shared.

"Osiris, he was wounded. I brought him here to rest. Also, why does everyone in this damn dimension underestimate me? I'm the goddamn Demon Lord of Lies and Illusion, servant of Delyria. You think I can't pick a freaking lock?" he explains with unexpected passion.

I still find my eyes narrowing despite his casual tone though, suspicious of his motives despite everything that's happened.

"Did you do this?" I ask, sweeping across the floor, dress coat fluttering around the backs of my knees as I pull it from my shoulders and drape it across the foot of the mattress, staring down at the wounded man before me.

"No, Pandora. There was a fight over her box. Osiris killed his mother, and then Pandora skewered him when he made a play to keep it out of her hands," Abraxis explains, and I blink once then twice.

"He— he *killed* Anubis?" I ask, not sure if I've heard him right. His features are alarming to me as I stare at him, not only because I've watched his face ripple in and out of form so many times, but because of the stark resemblance he currently holds to his late son.

"Yes. Crushed her tether. She's gone." He doesn't say it with sadness, merely as a fact. I shuffle, uncomfortable on the spot.

"Xion, he's dead. He sacrificed himself, gave his power to Sephy."

Jules told me that Xion had sacrificed himself, but until I'd seen Sephy in the room beneath The Halls of Antiqua, I could not have fully understood what this meant.

Now, the two pieces of information slide together with an inaudible but perfectly timed click.

I could feel it in her soul, the demon that had long lain dormant in him. I also feel Haedes, his blessing, coursing through her veins, helping to keep the darkness at bay so she might use it when she needs to, without being consumed as I have been.

Osiris stirs atop the black velvet sheets.

"I'm sorry about Xion." Osiris' words are fraught with pain, his fists balled as he attempts to turn onto his left side.

"Shh. Don't worry about that now. Rest." I run my fingers back through my hair with one hand, resting the other on his stiff, corpse-like leg, trying to comfort him.

Sephy had been afraid his loyalties did not lie with her, but in killing his own mother, all doubt has been vanquished from my mind. I continue to stare down at him, awed by his decisiveness and fast action in the face of losing someone he naturally cared for very deeply.

Abraxis gets to his feet, his silhouette made hard by the dark leather of his duster, black greasy hair sheening beneath the glorious light of the chandelier overhead. I get a faint but stale whiff of her as he rises; blackberry and pine, my stomach tightening and my heart beginning to pound.

Abraxis licks his bottom lip, sensing my discomfort.

"We have something to discuss," he says, taking several steps from the edge of the bed and walking past my antique armoire. He stills after a few more purposeful strides, statuesque before the bloody view beyond the ceiling-high glass doors that lead out onto the balcony.

"And what might that be?" I ask, eyes flicking between his face, the left side of which is soaked red from the light outside, and the view beyond the balcony railing, smoke still swirling like dark heavy mist in the air.

"You don't belong here anymore, and I can't rule the demon Kindred alone— you know just as well as I that while they're most certainly rabid killing machines, they're necessary to keep the balance of the worlds in check. Evil is necessary; if it wasn't, choosing good wouldn't be so miraculous." He states this without emotion, staring not at me but out over Mortaria. The city no longer glistens sharp and jagged, instead blanketed mute and grey by ash and debris. I remember the unending shudder and the noise of the pyroclastic cloud as we had cowered, made sublime and insignificant as the earth had raged violently against the sky and city for hours. I've never felt anything like it, and even now I cannot forget how it had dwarfed me, humbled me almost entirely.

The scent of burning seeps beneath the door, wafting slowly into the room and taking it over.

As I follow Abraxis' gaze, contemplating the wasteland the city has become, I remember Muerta's words back at the volcano. She too had thought I could use the darkness within myself to tame the demon kindred.

Maybe she and Abraxis are right.

Looking back over one shoulder, I ponder on everything that's happened.

Haedes, Thane, Xion, Anubis— everyone I thought of as family are gone now. This place is no more a home than a jumble of belongings I've accumulated over several lifetimes, the relationships that came of them now over.

Sephy can take care of herself.

There's nothing left for me here.

Abraxis and I stand next to each other for a while, watching the falling embers flutter through the sky, followed by ash, followed by smoke.

"So, you're saying I'll be a Demon Lord? Like you?" I ask him, finally accepting that this is perhaps what I've been heading towards all along.

"No, Lucifer. Demon Lords are chosen by the Gods of Ancient. Moloch never chose you, but regardless, here you are. You, my dear, are a conqueror." He bows his head, giving a flourish of one hand without looking at me even still.

"So, what are you saying?" I press him for an honest answer, for the truth of the matter, impatient as ever.

"I'm saying you'll be their Queen."

38

YOU'RE THE VOICE

SEPHY

THE SMELL OF HIM, the warmth of the sheets in which I'm cocooned, allow me to awaken in relative comfort. Then I bear it, the moment I've been dreading, waking up to realise he's gone all over again. It doesn't seem real, not when I can still smell him on the pillow cupping my neck, on the sheets slathering my body.

I crawled into his bed, naked, wearing only the bandages that bind tight around the wound from the sword that pierced straight through my abdomen. Weak from the frothing lather of his spa tub, sleep had come easier than I'd expected, my mind turning liquid, malleable, and weak in the aftermath of the fight with Pandora, the eruption of Mount Mallum.

Death.

So much death.

I wrap the sheet tighter around my body.

Cringing, my shoulders creak when I move to sit up, protesting my usual carelessness of motion. I gingerly place both feet on the floor, pulling the sheet with me as I stand, and the room spins a few moments before I manage to take a few pained and shaky steps toward the window overlooking the city.

Everything is blanketed soft by a layer of ash, the sky still full of smoke but with patches of vermillion triumphant among the murk. I can almost smell the burning through the window though it might be my memory of flying amongst it for a prolonged period.

I flew.

Like *actually flew.*

With wings and everything.

Could I do it again?

I stand, looking out over the city in the firm clutches of an aftermath, the streets deserted, lights extinguished, as my stomach gives an angry rumble.

The last time I'd eaten was in bed with Xion what feels like a lifetime ago.

Trying not to think about the fruit and baguettes scattered among our entangled naked limbs, I turn from the panoramic view and scurry through to the kitchen. The torches on the walls remain extinguished, the dwelling cast in an eerie red glow from the silent world outside.

I enter the kitchen, heels cooling and relieved from the ache of running for I don't know how long in heels far too high. Stomach rumbling in an encore, I turn to the fridge.

I pull open the door, but no light comes on, and the contents smell rancid.

Without Sinners, the reserves that have carried Mortaria this far are predictably empty just when I need the microwave the most. I guess the last of the Doppel-generated power must have finally run out.

I sigh, shaking my head.

I need to recuperate, but the city needs me more.

Someone has to clean up the mess Pandora made.

Looking around the kitchen for any kind of edible food, I come up empty so settle for grabbing a lukewarm bottle of water from the back of the refrigerator and sipping leisurely as I walk back through the apartment. My breathing is heavy, lungs still rough with the smoke I've inhaled as I approach the bed again, lost and wandering around the remnants of what is now to fade and become yet another painful memory.

I sit on the side of the mattress, water filling the gurgling chasm inside me as my eyes trail over the room, landing on the bedside table and lingering.

Curious about the dead man I've yet to retrieve from Golgotha, I rifle through the drawers in the black acrylic nightstand. I find a few empty deodorant bottles, a copy of the Holy Bible that makes me snort, and then, beneath it all, something altogether more significant.

A birth belonging to one Mr Alex Johnson. Born in 1952 at some maternity clinic in Detroit. I hold the paper between shaking fingers. This might be the only real evidence that Xion's mortal past ever really existed.

Seems kinda flimsy, I muse, placing the sheet of official-looking parchment back in the drawer and slamming it shut.

I open the next drawer down; underwhelmed by the normal crap you accumulate in the course of living, but find myself confronted this time with something I don't expect.

A dagger.

Not opal, like mine, but made from the darkest obsidian I've ever seen. I stare at the weapon, lifting it carefully from the depths of the nightstand. Wrapping the sheets tighter around myself, I watch the blade turn deep aubergine as it melds with the red light falling in through the opposing window. The hilt is solid silver, and I remember seeing it before.

My memory is cast back to that night, the night everything had changed. The Banshee had come through the window of my old ballet studio, throwing the meeting I was being bored to death by into utter chaos. Xion had come to aid a damsel in distress, who didn't exist, and this was what he had wielded in doing so.

I turn the knife over in my palm; it's beautiful, and the significance of the stone, the cause of both his deliverance and demise, is not lost on me.

I place it down, closing the drawer, which is otherwise empty, and let the sheet drop from where it is cinched around my breasts. I walk around the edge of the bedframe, pulling open the closet and finding myself halfway to tears as my eyes fall on the jackets hanging, clones of one another in every regard.

I let my fingers reach out to stroke the soft leather, inhaling the mix of it and his unforgettable musk. My heart breaks all over again, and yet I can't let the tears fall. I don't have time for this pain, for this heartache.

Xion told me not to fall apart, to do what was necessary, and to keep everything moving forward, and that's exactly what I'm going to do.

I select a white V-neck t-shirt which is way too big for me, grab one of the many leather jackets from its hangers, and dump the pile of contrasting fabrics on the bed. Then, I walk through to the bathroom, pick up my pants from yesterday, and swipe the first aid kit off the side of the sink basin where I'd left it hanging open after getting out of the bath.

Throwing the rest of the clothes into the pile with the stuff from Xion's closet, I reach for the hair elastic that I shoved absent-mindedly around my wrist at some point among the chaos of the last few— hours? Days? Weeks? It's impossible to know without a watch or any kind of natural guide how much time has passed. I don't even know how long I was asleep.

I remove the elastic band without a second thought, bringing my ratty and barely dry tresses up into a loose bun before fastening it in haste. Then I unbind the dressings that are soaked through with fresh blood and yellowish fluid, weeping thick from the wound and no doubt signalling infection. I guess that's what you get when you self-cauterise a wound with a sword that's seen thousands of demons beheaded. They aren't exactly the most hygienic of species.

Sighing, I throw the bandages and gauze padding onto the floor beside yesterday's discarded boots, reaching back for the first aid kit and setting to work removing the adhesive medical strips keeping it closed. Cleaning the cut stings like a bitch, but I can't deny I feel better knowing that I've applied some antibacterial cream, fresh gauze, and bandages as I fasten the fresh dressings around my torso with medical tape.

Standing, I feel the wound pull and wince, but don't allow myself to pause as I turn and begin to dress. I don't have a bra, nor the desire to wear one over what are probably several slow-healing broken ribs that have bloomed into new and dark floral bruises just beneath my breasts overnight.

Throwing on the t-shirt, I move to squeeze back into the leather pants I've been wearing ever since we left Bermuda.

You could have had fresh clothes if you'd stayed at The Exilia, I remind myself as I snuggle into the familiar embrace of Xion's leather jacket and move to pull on my shoes. I ponder the choice I've made, this being seemingly the most difficult of the two, but remind myself I would have been waited on. I would have been fussed over, been given time to think, been removed from everything that's so routine it allows me to carry on, regardless of the fact I'm broken inside beyond repair.

No.

Coming here was the right decision.

It's given me a brief window of time to pull myself together, to recalibrate and recharge, to rest surrounded by the last remnants of the only person who has ever truly made me feel safe.

Letting out a heavy sigh, I grab the obsidian blade from among the crumpled sheets, spinning on the spot as I pocket it in the innermost folds of the leather jacket's silk lining.

The apartment is barren and cold without him in it, but as I allow my eyes to sweep over the empty coffee table, the nightstands sporting only bedside lamps, and the closet full of many identical clothes, I realise that Xion could have been a ghost. Without the birth certificate that's been stowed back safely in the top drawer where I found it, it wouldn't have been difficult to deny that he ever really existed.

No family, no belongings, not really. The only things he seems really to have left behind is a rackful of identical leather jackets and a redhead with a smashed-up heart and chimera soul.

I don't have time to dwell though, to grieve, I have a job to do and people relying on me to do it. So, without real thought, without a real goodbye, I convect from Xion's apartment for what I know will most likely be the very last time.

I reappear in front of the double doors that look out over the entrance of the Exilia. The river is rushing noticeably higher in the distance, and so it is with this I feel a sudden relief that I've returned before anything else can change for the worse.

"Sephy!" Luce's voice breaks through the wave of relief that blankets my senses, scurrying forward wearing a silver pantsuit with a plunging neckline that reveals she too has decided to forego a bra entirely.

"Hey, how long was I gone?" I ask her, placing a hand on my hip so I don't feel so completely out of place, so redundant, without anything to keep my hands busy. I have no shield from the reality of what's passed, no weapon to strike it down. The only way to deal with all this is to plunge right in, to delve straight through, to feel the pain. People are going to ask questions, want explanations, sticking unclean fingers into new and unclosed wounds, making them fester.

"Not too long, about eleven or so hours. You look better," she compliments me, and I nod in response, not wanting to make small talk.

"Yeah, I uh, I went to Xion's place. Took a bath, patched myself up," I reply, not sure what else to say.

Her pupils dilate, eyes shiny with tears, his name fresh pain between us. I drop my gaze, and so, gracefully as ever, Luce changes the subject.

"So, the mortals are all in the throne room resting. I— I don't know what I'm going to do about the promise I made to the Colonel. I need Beelz if I want to stay here." She looks concerned, worried that changing tact and talking about business, about war, is the wrong thing to do, that it's insensitive. I, however, am grateful.

This is something I can fix, something with a glaringly obvious solution.

"Easy. We keep them here, indefinitely. Put them to work helping us fix the city. We go back to the Colonel and tell him everything has gone according to plan. This isn't their jurisdiction, remember? They don't have to know they're still alive, and besides, I'll kill anyone who tries to claim otherwise." I give her a small smile, and she sighs, relieved.

"Right. Perfect. Thanks—" she murmurs, cheeks flushing with rosy and unhindered gratitude.

"Okay, I need to talk to them. Make them see that what I'm doing is to help them, not keep them trapped here," I think aloud, and Luce nods, eyes travelling from mine to beyond my left shoulder.

I turn, tracing the path of her gaze, and find Jules walking toward us.

I feel instantly guilty. I left without saying a word after I'd left him stuck in the dungeons while I was off sleeping with Xion one last time. Apparently, when disaster strikes, I'm a crappy friend.

"Sephy, you're back. You look better!"

Jules. Kind, sweet Jules who had blown open the skull of a Banshee and saved me with a single pull on the trigger of his favourite shotgun. He doesn't blame me for disappearing on him apparently, which is far more courtesy than I probably deserve.

"Jules, sorry about last night. Did I look that terrible? Everyone is saying I look better. All I did was bathe and take a nap," I apologise, a sheepish expression creeping over my face as he gives a tiny smile in return, green eyes glistening with a natural empathy I've never even been close to possessing.

"You had Banshee brains in your hair— and you looked like you'd been human shish-kebabbed." Jules shuffles from left to right, clearly uncomfortable.

Nobody knows what to say to me, and I can't blame them; I wouldn't know what to say to me either.

"Well, before you go and talk with the mortals, you'll want to wait until they're fed. Any luck, Jules?" Luce presses him for an answer. His gaze lingers on me, searching for some subtle marker that I might be okay before he turns to her and puckers his lips in annoyance.

"The pantry has been completely ransacked. Seems like Pandora and the Demon Lords didn't think to restock it at any point during their stay," he informs her. She rolls her eyes, shoulders slumping.

"Well, they turned out the sun and therefore killed all our trade routes with the mortal world, so that's hardly surprising. Still, the people are getting cranky. We need to sort something and soon." She looks stressed, fingers playing with a loose lock of silver hair that falls into obscurity upon the glistening fabric of her jumpsuit.

As the discussion reaches a symbiotic plateau between the three of us, my stomach gives an audible rumble. My oh-so-filling bottle of water has done truly fuck all to help my rabid appetite.

"Okay, food first. Jules, should we go on a McDonald's run?" I ask him, plucking the first fast food place I can think of out of thin air.

"You want to order two thousand meals from McDonalds?" He looks incredulous, but I simply smirk.

It's insane and totally something I would do.

"Sure, why not. You've still got my debit card, right?" I ask him, and he nods, returning my smirk as he rolls his eyes.

"Only you would think that the answer to feeding two thousand refugee mortals comes from the land of golden arches."

I let myself laugh. Though I'm not happy or contented, I cannot resist being myself in this moment as I remember the banter that's always been so rife between us.

"Hey, enough with the grumpy face, or I'll order you a happy meal; and even worse, I'll ask for a girl's toy for you—" I threaten him.

Luce continues to look between us, mystified.

The smell of deep-fried potato is still thick in my throat and alluring in my nostrils as I make the final convection trip back with Jules. Our arms are stacked with cardboard boxes that are crammed full of paper McDonald's meal bags, the smell of all that food making me salivate profusely. They rustle invitingly as Jules sets his down and I do the same, grabbing food for myself before we move to hand it out to the masses.

"Right. Get me a few mortals out here. We can carry these inside now. That's the last of them," I instruct The Furies who had rushed over from tea with The Fates as soon as they learned they would be able to relive their McDonald's experience all over again. They turn in sync, and I wonder momentarily what tea between them and the three much older Fates must have sounded like. I mean, I'm sorry, but I just can't picture what they'd have to talk about other than the perks of indefinite sisterhood.

The Furies return after a few minutes, and in the meantime, Jules and Luce separate out food for Muerta, Yama, and themselves.

A group of twenty or so Mortals emerge swiftly through the double doors, which The Furies close fast behind them, and immediately begin sniffing the air. Their eyes widen, each one of them turning to stare at me as if they've been summoned so I can incinerate them.

"Food's here." I smile, trying for reasons quite beyond me to put them at ease. "Everyone grab a box," I order them and watch on as they oblige without argument, moving with hurried and stilted steps to secure a single box of food each.

"Make sure everyone gets one. No fighting. I got equal amounts of everything because I wasn't about to take two thousand orders, got it?" I look for their confirmation as they line up behind me; silent and observatory with wide eyes even still.

They eventually nod into the tense silence between us, none of them speaking, fear flickering behind their dark pupils as the wafting scent of McDonald's fries forms a heavy cloud of greasy heat around us.

"All right then." I nod to The Furies who open the doors in front of me and then lead in the procession of fast food into the hall, my wound twinging as the steel heels of my boots ring out against the quartz of the floor.

I smile at the Mortal crowd, who turn to see what the commotion is about as they stand from crumpled blankets strewn on the floor where they're huddled together in small groups, skin spattered with smoke and in some places blood and bruises.

"Dinner time!" I yell out, voice an echoing high-pitched boom. I feel a warm sense of pride fill my gut as their eyes turn surprised, glittering with the hope of a hot meal. "Vegetarians, the last box in the line is yours." I point back to a young Indian man who has only just made it through the wide-open doors before they close swiftly behind him, Jules and Luce gliding forward to escort him on either side.

Reaching the very front of the crystalline and chasmic space, I'm confronted with the throne Pandora had constructed after I melted the existing one into a puddle of liquid gold the last time I was here. My stomach turns in slight horror as I realise it's been soldered together, forming a jagged seat out of the Hollow's broken limbs. She had dominated this land, not ruled it. This throne says that clearer than words ever could.

I keep my food clutched to me as I pivot on the spot, looking back over the hall as Mortals begin to pour toward the people handing out paper bags. They don't push, surprising even to me, but rather form orderly queues despite the symphony of empty bellies that are audible even from the very front of the room.

It takes a few minutes, but soon all that can be heard are muffled groans of satisfaction and the rustling of greaseproof paper in slick fingers.

"Everyone listen up," I call out over the ambient noise of jaws moving, of lips licking smudges of various sauces clean.

All eyes in the room turn to me.

"So, we need to talk. I'm the person who's going to be taking over Mortarian rule—" I begin, yanking the Big Mac from its box deep within my paper bag and bringing it to my lips. I take a bite, and someone in the crowd clears his throat before I have a chance to swallow.

"I'm sorry, but who the hell are you? Where's Pandora?" the brave individual asks while I'm still chewing.

My eyebrows rise, but before I can answer, the voice of another man, though this time one I'm familiar with, cuts clean through the air.

"She's Sephy Sinclair, she saved us. I saw her." Jono, the man who I've helped survive the city streets of Chicago during the long winter months, becomes visible among the myriad of faces in the crowd. I nod at him with a grateful smile, swallowing.

"Yeah, I'm Haedes' kid, in case you didn't know. As for Pandora—" I wave a hand, setting the throne beside me unceremoniously ablaze with casual indifference. "The bitch is dead. I killed her. Luckily for you."

A collective gulp ripples through the crowd as the very last remnants of Pandora's rule crackle heartily behind me. I take another bite of my burger.

The jaw of the mortal who had questioned me stiffly closes as his gaze drops to the floor.

"Everybody sit. I'm not gonna stand here and bark at you like some dictator. I'm part mortal. All of you are mortal too. You're not Sinners here. I have no power over any of you. I merely want to keep you safe," I admit, taking a seat on the single step that raises the platform holding the throne above the rest of the reflective floor. The group follows my lead, dropping to the blankets under their feet and continuing to eat, eyes locked on my face.

457

"Here's the thing. A.D.A.M., the group responsible for keeping this crap secret from the general public back home, they want you guys dead. You've seen too much; you know too much," I announce.

Startled murmurs break out amongst the masses of dirty-faced refugees.

"Look, I'm not going to let that happen, but you can't go back. I know that you've been working for Pandora, working against me and my agenda, but I also know that you were victims of her demons in the first place. She brought you here against your will, and now you face death if you leave. I just want to make everything as easy and as comfortable for you all as possible. However, that's going to require some help on your part—" I swallow and take another chunk of bun and beef into my mouth, half my Big Mac gone already.

"What are you saying, exactly? Do you need us to fight?" Jono looks scared now, and so I shake my head feverishly, swallowing fast before panic engulfs the rest of the crowd.

"No, but until we have more Sinners available, we will need help cleaning up Mortaria. The city is covered in ash and debris right now; roads are blocked. We need to start cleaning up if we ever hope to regain what's been lost here, if we ever hope to start correcting the imbalance between good and evil created by Pandora," I explain as calmly as I can, but Jono looks worried even still.

"But, what about the demons?" he asks, to which I have no answer. I flounder in silence for what feels like a lifetime, but as I let my mouth hang open, searching for an answer, Luce steps in to save me.

"I'll be moving to The Fallen Kingdom to manage the demonic presence in Mortaria. The volcanic eruption has rendered most, if not all, dead. They will be reintroduced by myself and Abraxis at a controlled rate, and once again confined to The Ashen Waste beyond the wall. You have nothing to fear," she explains. My forehead creases in concern for her.

She's going to take over the role held by the Demon Lords for all these years with her past involving the darkness?

"How do we get more Sinners?" someone calls out, and I inhale, the next problem I have to face coming and smacking me right in the face.

"I might have a solution to that—" The voice comes from the other end of the hall where one of the doors has been opened and closed quietly without my notice.

Standing, smiling across the room at me, is my asshole cousin, Hercules.

"Excuse me."

I get to my feet, stuffing the last of my burger into my face and chewing angrily, grabbing the fries, which remain untouched, before cutting directly through the onlooking crowd.

I gesture for him to step outside with me, and he rolls his eyes, blonde feathered hair annoying as all hell.

"What the *fuck* are you doing here?" I snarl at him as the door closes behind us and the hall erupts into discussion about my little speech.

"I came to help." Hercules looks outraged, his stupid muscles bulging, his torso bound in thick popping veins beneath a chest plate of solid gold.

"Oh, you come to help, *now*? *Gee* thanks so much, you're *such* a hero, Cuz!" I grab a few fries and slip them into my mouth, hoping that keeping both my hands and mouth busy will stop me from doing something I probably shouldn't but most certainly won't regret.

"Hey, don't blame me. There's been a lot of important stuff happening with The Aetherial Court since your resurrection. Mortaria is Haedes' problem, remember?" Slightly out of breath, I watch as his gaze falls to the red cardboard carton clutched in my shaking hand. "Ooh are those—" he reaches out to take one, but I slap his hand away.

"Uh, fuck off. Assholes who show up after the war is won in their unmarked golden armour don't get freaking fries!" I scowl, taking another handful and relishing the salty golden crunch of them as they practically melt on my tongue.

"Jeez, sorry. Look, I came to tell you about Aphrodite's bow—" The words spark my memory, the missing piece.

It can't be used to kill, but it'll hit whatever you point it at.

Perfect.

"Again, too goddamn late. Haedes and I already discussed this. I just thought I'd better feed the living before tending to the dead," I snap, furious beneath my lying and hopefully chill seeming façade.

"You know someone needs to show you your place, Sinclair," Hercules snarls, getting closer to me than is necessary.

He towers around four inches taller than me, but I look up into his face, unafraid.

He inhales, the air thick with potential violence between us.

Is he afraid of me behind it all?

Or is he as good of a fighter as legend has made him out to be?

Reaching up, I place my greasy fingers around his enormous nose and twist.

"Got your nose—" I whisper in his ear as I lean forward slightly, feeling his exhale and smiling, knowing that I've intimidated him even if he doesn't want to admit it.

I walk away, still munching my fries, not stopping as I call back over my shoulder.

"Oh, thanks for the uh— *help*. Try sending it in by mail next time. I'm sure it'll arrive faster that way."

"Are you sure this is going to work?" Jules asks me, handing over the bow it's taken him over two hours to retrieve. Haedes collected *a lot* of crap in his time here.

"Nope," I admit, shrugging and taking the bow in my palm, admiring it.

"You think the sky is clear enough for this?" Luce asks, and again I only shrug.

"Dunno," I relinquish, unable to tear my gaze away from the instrument lying heavy in my palms. It's made from rose gold, embellished with yellow gold in parts. It sheens, the string pliable as I give it a little tug. Adornments that are completely unnecessary to function curve around the frontmost part of the weapon, vines with heart-shaped leaves climbing around the upper and lower limbs in three-dimensional and stunningly detailed decoration. The arrow rest is the blockiest part of the entire piece, and as Jules pulls out a matching golden quiver stocked full of arrows, I see why.

"Well, they're impressive—" I comment, finding the arrows twice as long as I expect as I pluck one from its shimmering brothers.

"You don't want to take the whole quiver?" Jules asks me, but I shake my head.

"I'm a good shot, but even if I wasn't, this thing supposedly hits whatever you aim it at."

I continue to examine both parts of the weapon, both bow and arrow, loading the latter into the former and taking a practice aim out over the city as I pull back the string to test pliancy.

We're collected on the balcony of the library, which remains in disarray from where Pandora and The Demon Lords had scrapped. Anubis' body is gone from where Luce claims Osiris killed her, probably cleared away by Muerta and Yama on their rounds of the Exilia earlier, but spatterings of blood still mar the carpet, though from a dead body or Osiris' wound, I couldn't tell you.

"Okay, let's try this then. Watch out." I exhale, nervous, clutching the weapon to me and concentrating on my intense sudden will to rise into the air.

It doesn't take much, the *edge* that Haedes mentioned clear when it comes to how easily I now summon flame to me and then again with how effortlessly I can manipulate it.

Violet flames explode from my spine, causing Jules to jump as the wings stretch wide. I grin at his surprise.

Hair flaming, the elastic holding it in a topknot snaps and my fiery red locks are unleashed over my shoulders as I rise into the air, feet lifting effortlessly from the Exilia balcony.

The air is still thick with the smell of smoke, but most of it seems to be thinning as the red of the sky causes my bow and arrow to turn from pink to scarlet where before there was no sky to be seen for miles.

I ascend through clouds of smoke and over the highest peak of The Exilia, wind catching my hair and stoking the flames that surround my head in a halo of raw power.

I find myself strangely at peace as I come to face it, that enormous black orb hanging dead in the sky.

I don't pause, don't wait as I load the arrow, setting the tip alight with that very same violet flame that's keeping me suspended high above the city below.

My city.

I'm done waiting, done surrendering, done being victimised. I have power now, demonic power, Kindred power, and I know that whatever happens in the future, I will be okay.

How do I know this?

Because I lost the man I loved, the life I loved, and I'm still standing, still ablaze, still Sephy.

Despite it all.

I survived.

Taking aim, I suck in a deep breath, close my eyes, and let the arrow fly.

39

I'M EVERY WOMAN

<u>SEPHY</u>

I LEAN OVER THE library balcony, gazing up to the blazing violet sun that can be seen through a thin haze of the only remaining atmospheric evidence that a volcanic eruption ever occurred.

It's been one week, and I haven't slept. Whether that be because I've been undertaking tasks I'd never considered being in my future, or because the sun and my newfound Kindred status means I don't need to, I couldn't tell you.

What I can tell you, though, is that the past seven days have felt like a lifetime.

I rub my fingertips along my arms, inhaling the familiar muggy Mortarian air, which now holds only the faint aroma of burnt bacon and is a vast improvement from when I last stood here.

The city centre has been mainly restored to what it was, and I can see Mortals scurrying in the main street below with brooms, rakes, and masks covering their mouths, hauling the last of the ash and debris out of the road and across the onyx sidewalk. A lot of the windows on the outermost buildings have been smashed clean through from the force of the pyroclastic explosion, so we still have a long way to go in cleaning up the streets on the outskirts of town, which remain peppered with broken glass even still. I guess it's going to take time, though, and seeing as nobody around here is ageing anytime soon, it's at least one luxury we can definitely afford.

I wanted to help, but Jules has forbidden it, saying I'm not healed enough to be hauling rubble despite the fact my wound is now but a faint pink line beneath my sternum and no longer requires bandages.

The streetlamps blaze a heady cobalt, and the Exilia has said a quick and painless goodbye to the likes of Yama and Muerta. The sinners are rising in Golgotha again, and Muerta has been assigning them on sight alone back at the teeming graveyard while Yama gives her quotas to fill where sinners are needed most. Over the horizon on my right, I can see the outlines of our first successful trade ships returning from a desperately needed supply run to the Mortal world. Power is also coming back slowly, and while the Exilia never lost electrical power, almost all the outer city blocks were plunged into medieval darkness by the lack of Sinners toiling on treadmills.

As for Osiris, he and The Furies have gone to tackle the mess of The Ashen Waste, working to clear a path so that Abraxis and Luce might return to whatever remains of The Fallen Kingdom with an army of Doppel bodies ready to begin a seriously needed clean up. We're thinking about rebuilding, especially if Luce is planning on living there because I honestly can't see how the city of stone will have survived. If it has, it certainly won't be habitable.

I think of Abraxis, on the eyes that cause my heart to leap into my chest every time they catch mine, the familiarity and eerie reminder of what I've lost splintering me. I can't bear to be in the same room with him, not when he's wearing his preferred face, but Luce has been dealing with him instead, for which I'm grateful.

I guess that brings me to today.

They're going to retrieve his body.

Xion's body.

The words don't compute, the fact that his remains are lying in the underground crypt where I left them but he is gone. It's shocking and unbelievable even after seven long days of my newfound purgatory have passed in torturously slow moments and agonisingly drawn-out breaths. I try not to think about it, merely moving forward and doing what needs to be done.

So, as Luce and Abraxis go to retrieve his body, to prepare for tomorrow's funeral, Jules and I will return to whatever remains of The Sinclair Estate to deal with A.D.A.M. and retrieving Beelz.

"Ready to go?" Jules' voice permeates the dusty air of the library, quieter than usual, but still, I start, spinning to find him crossing the threshold of the doorway at the far end of the room.

"Sure—" I reply, voice lacklustre, exhausted in spirit but not body.

"Might I suggest you leave that here?" He gestures to the knife that I didn't even realise I'm still holding, turning it rhythmically between my fingers, a comfort with its fiery sharpness.

"I've been thinking about that. I don't know where to put it. I'm not leaving it in the vault. It's like a giant neon sign saying, '*Oh look something extremely valuable.*'"

I recall the fact that the door of the thing is still blown wide open. I'm going to have to get it fixed at some point, so I suppose that's one more thing to add to my eternally growing to-do list, right after *resurrect city's population* and *cremate dead lover*.

Yay.

"Why don't you store it inside a book? Doesn't look like anybody uses this library much, Pandora excluded," Jules suggests, and I shrug.

"Bring me a big one then." I sound less than enthusiastic because I am. I feel like a robot, someone simply walking through the motions, a puppet on a string.

I wait, listening to Jules rummaging around behind me for a few minutes before he returns, a forced smile twisting his lips into an upturned curve.

He passes me a copy of The Holy Bible, making me smirk.

Placing the blade down on the balcony railing, I raise the book over my shoulder. A small sputtering protest attempts to fall from Jules' lips before I bring it down on top of the knife with a smash.

"What the hell?! What did you do that for?" he asks me as I lift the heavy leather-bound volume and stare at the cracked remnants of what had once been my tether. The stone has split into three equally jagged parts, broken beyond repair.

"Nothing else will be used against me, Jules. I mean it." I sweep the debris from the railing, watching the shattered pieces of the opal blade fall into oblivion below.

"But— what if—" he begins to ask something he appears unsure he should mention, and I cock an eyebrow, wondering what it is he could possibly say.

"What?" I ask, impatient as I pass the book back to him. He dips slightly as he takes it in his palm, the weight of it more than he was prepared for as he continues to stare at me in a state of shock.

"What if you wanted to get rid of your powers, you know, in the future? To become more or less mortal again?" The suggestion surprises me. I hadn't thought about it, and with the difficulty I've had recently playing around with tethers, I have no desire to even consider going back. I'd probably kill everyone in the process.

"Jules— it's time I accept who I am. And that isn't a mortal destined for a regular life. I'm Haedes' daughter, and I belong here. This is where I was conceived, and it's where I found the love of my life. As much as I hate it, it's home. I can't run from that, or who I am, anymore." The confession falls from me, unhindered like the waters of The Spring of Souls that had been pent up for far too long. The silence between us becomes thick as Jules stares at me, eyes glistening with unwelcome pride.

We stand, awkward for a few moments, as I stare out over the city, thinking hard about what I've just said for perhaps the first time. I can't deny the truth of it because it's probably the most honest moment I've had with myself since before I said goodbye to Xion.

"Ready?" he asks me, changing the subject and bringing welcome relief among the tension.

"Sure, let's do this thing. You called them?" I enquire, voice monotone, and he nods.

"Yep, they'll be meeting us at noon," he responds, face serious and anxious right before the flames consume us both.

The Sinclair Estate is chill with weak sunlight, the sky a periwinkle blue scattered with wisps of cloud that don't seem to have the willpower to move with any great speed. The grass around us is black, but not from my convection despite Jules hurrying to stamp out the blue flames. The entire lawn is charred, debris scattered across what was once a pristine blanket of emerald.

"*Oh my God*, your mother must be turning in her grave right about now," Jules mutters under his breath, and I smirk. He thinks she'd be pissed about the lawn when the house is little more than a smouldering pile of brick and smashed marble?

"Yeah well, I don't think she'd be happy about the house either," I point out and he shakes his head.

"She hated this house, though. Said it was too ostentatious. The saving grace for her marriage was the surrounding grounds," Jules informs me, stepping over the blackened grass which crunches, dry and sharp, beneath his highly polished black shoes.

I follow him with an absent mind as he approaches the remnants of what had once been my childhood home.

The entire front façade is gone, chunks of mocha stone from the front steps mixed in with chequered marble from the entrance hall littering what can only be described as an enormous landfill of burnt rubble. The once grand double doors lie in charred splinters, the staircase no longer ascending but falling haphazardly into the basement.

465

"I don't expect you've given any thought to what you want to do about all this?" Jules asks me as I kick a piece of debris into the pit of the basement below with my left boot. Watching it skitter, the sound of the mocha stone echoes through the thin summer air as it tumbles away into the dark.

"Actually, I have. I can't sell it. I wouldn't do that to Mom and Dad. They're here. So, I thought I could put the land to good use instead. I mean, I obviously won't be living here anymore." The thought depresses me, which is surprising because of the amount of time I've spent feeling trapped by the highly polished balustrades and plush carpets of the place, not to mention the live-in psychotic uncle.

"So? What did you decide?" Jules asks, picking up a charred silver service tray and smiling at it with sad nostalgia before he tosses it aside. It lands with a bell-like clang, dislodging a charred photograph that's utterly unrecognisable and causing a mini landslide in its wake as more rubble falls into the basement.

"I'm going to turn it into a halfway house for troubled kids. The Alex Johnson Halfway house—" I say the second part slowly like it's sacred or something.

Jules' eyebrows rise fast on his forehead.

"Alex Johnson?" he asks, tentative, as he takes a deliberate step towards me over some broken glass.

"Yeah, it was Xion's name before— you know, the demon stuff. I don't know; I just keep thinking about how he disappeared from the face of the planet, nothing to prove he was ever here except a dead girl and the birth certificate that he took with him. I wonder if he could have lived a better life, been able to carry on some semblance of normality, if he had the proper help, if he had somewhere to go—" I muse, and Jules nods, smiling with a sweet endearment behind his eyes.

"I think that's a great idea." He places a hand on my shoulder, taking another exact step to weave between two piles of shattered marble.

"Good, because you'll be dealing with the contractors for the rebuild." I smirk at him and his face instantly falls.

"You know, I saved your life. Don't forget that, Sephy." His eyes narrow, expression turning wry.

"It's not a punishment. Think of it as a very underwhelming reward. You're the only one I trust with my family's land. It's the last traces of the Sinclair family we're dealing with here, my legacy." I know it sounds corny, and Jules rolls his eyes.

"Yeah, yeah. Try to butter me up all you like, but I know the drill. As if dealing with the interior decorators wasn't bad enough while you were dead." I watch his eyes glaze over with the memories, expression becoming comically haunted.

"Yeah well, imagine that it's my last dying wish or something. Imagine I'm dead again—" I wink at him and he quips back, the words flying out of his mouth before he can stop them.

"Ah, yes, those were the days—"

My expression falls, feigning horror, and he gives an uneasy laugh. "Too soon?"

"Nah, I'm only messing with you. After all, what's left to do but laugh? I can't cry anymore, Jules." He opens his mouth to reply, sadness blooming in the emerald pastures of his irises, but before he can say anything, the rattle of tyres on alabaster gravel can be heard growing louder.

He pulls his cell phone from his pocket.

"They're early," he comments in a dull-set tone, not looking at all amused.

"Let's get this over with then," I reply, watching a black SUV with tinted windows lead a larger armoured vehicle seamlessly down the driveway.

Turning my back on what used to be the main house, Jules and I pick our way back across the patchy blackened grass to greet the Colonel, my shoulders stiffening as the passenger side door opens and the familiar smash of rubber soles on gravel makes me internally flinch.

"Miss Sinclair, how wonderful to see you so— alive." The Colonel's thick red moustache twitches as spittle flies from his lips, his hands coming fast to rest across his lower back as he takes several large steps toward me. I let the wind catch my hair a little, balling my fists beneath the overhang of the sleeves of Xion's leather jacket.

"Look, cut the crap. Where's Beelz?" I demand, exhaling heavily and feeling my temper begin to boil beneath the seemingly cool exterior of my expression.

"Right here. What do you have to tell me about the mortals?" he asks, left eye twitching slightly as his thick ginger eyebrow rises.

"Taken care of. You don't have to worry about it," I reply swiftly, without pause, wondering if he can sense the half-truth of the situation.

"And what, I'm just supposed to trust your word?" The Colonel asks me as the driver of the SUV climbs out of the car, probably due to some unseen hand signal or something equally as cliché. He slams the car door shut behind him, pulling what looks like a taser rod from behind his back.

Gritting my teeth, I let my skin ripple from mere flesh to the mystical surface on which flame will flourish, the tongues of scarlet licking hungrily at the air, my hair catching light only seconds later.

"I don't know; how much do you want to keep your hair?" I ask him, cool and collected despite the anxiety pooling in my gut. I'm powerful, sure, but these guys have weapons, a lot of them, and enough bodies to put me in a difficult situation if they try.

"All right, no need for that Miss Sinclair. I merely have to ensure that you, or rather Lucifer, has kept her end of the bargain. I'm just doing my job." He looks rather irritated, which doesn't fail in making me smile.

"I assure you it's been taken care of. Now, give me back my panther." I cock an eyebrow, crossing my arms and letting the flames encircling my head diminish to a mere fizzle in the early morning.

"Very well." He reaches into the back of his belt for his walkie, bringing it up to his lips and barking, "Bring out the panther!" Then, he clicks off the transmitter button and turns back to stare at the armoured van that's parked, ominously, behind his Jeep.

After a few tense seconds, the back doors of the vehicle fly open, slamming against the rear bumper and causing the air to ring with the sound of thick metal on metal. The sounds that follow are painful to the ear, high pitched, sharp, and feral, but the source is no mystery as a man with a plastic stick ending in a loop that's fastened tight around Beelz's throat appears. I watch him with disgust as he approaches in a scurry, holding the pissed-off animal at as large of a distance as he can manage.

"Give me that!" I snap, storming forward and snatching the plastic rod from his white knuckles and tossing it down. Beelz watches me, clementine irises glowing with rage as I kneel so I'm on her eye level.

"Beelz, just— stay still, okay?" I whisper, placing my hands up, palms open so she can see I mean no harm. She looks at me and blinks twice, the feral purr still running like a hot motor in her throat, before licking her lips and giving a slight nod of approval.

I crawl forward across the gravel, feeling the eyes of The Colonel and his animal-handling lackey burning into my back. With tentative care and making sure to hold eye contact with the Panther at all times, I slowly loosen the white carbon fibre loop from around her throat and hook it over her ears before tossing the thing aside with obvious fury.

"You know there was no need to treat her that way. She lived in The Estate with me for over a month, and I never once had a problem. She's perfectly house trained," Jules scolds them, face stiff with disapproval, and yet I know this is a polite mask for the anger he's really feeling. I can tell by the way his posture has stiffened and his trigger finger hangs curved, twitching, by the pristine outer seam of his ironed pant leg.

"She bit one of my colleagues. He nearly lost a leg from the knee down." The Colonel defends his actions, but it doesn't placate me.

"Get off my property," I snarl, not caring for excuses.

Beelz would only ever bite if provoked; Anubis has proven that. I have to wonder, then, what kind of sick tests they've been trying to run on her for the duration of her entrapment.

Jules doesn't speak, but merely takes a step close to me as I scratch the place between Beelz's ears, a show of solidarity. The Colonel and his crew of merry morons don't respond, at least not vocally, simply turning away from us and piling back into their vehicles.

I don't watch them go, remaining focused on Beelz and relaxing only once I've heard four metal doors slam shut and the tread of thick heavy-duty tyres passing fast over gravel fade into nothing.

"I hate those guys," I mumble, more to Beelz than to Jules, but I hear him agree in a similarly low tone.

"Yes, they're heading for a serious shock if they think they can keep ordering people like you around."

I smile, grateful for his faith in my power.

"I think I'm going to go and say goodbye, you know, to Mom and Dad, before we leave," I decide quickly, the white marble of the mausoleum catching my attention from far off in the distance.

"Take as much time as you need." Jules turns his back on me promptly, moving back to examine the rubble of the house and no doubt dreading dealing with the rebuild as the truth of its utter decimation hits him full force again.

I expect Beelz to follow him, mainly because in the time she's spent with us he's usually the one most likely to be handling food, but she doesn't. She trots after me across the lawn, sniffing the air with inquisitive calm, a low purr just audible if you listen hard enough. The sound is oddly comforting, and my muscles unfurl as I let it wash over me.

With the sound of her large paws padding soft against the earth behind me, I stride over to the mausoleum; heart lighter than it has been in a while.

I suppose it's not because I miss my parents any less, but it's because I feel like now, they would be proud of what I've decided to do with my life. I've been through so much, all of it difficult, but I know that I'm where I've always been heading at long last, as sad as that makes me.

Ascending the cold steps bathed in diluted sunlight, my heels click against the marble and echo out into the small empty chamber built atop their remains.

I stare down at it, glad that at least this part of the estate was left unscathed by the demonic invasion and resulting explosion, the brass plaque sheening as though it's only just been polished. I bend down, Beelz' dark matte shadow falling lithe over the memorial, picking out my parent's names as the engraved letters turn darkest black, the last absolute permanence of what I've lost only exaggerated as I trace my fingers over the swirling letters of the word *Sinclair*.

I hear it first from Beelz, in the rumble of her purr becoming louder beneath the glossy sheen of jet fur blanketing her agile skeleton, in her deep inhale of the surrounding air, nostrils opening and closing in snake-like slits.

I watch as she tilts her head, emitting a low growl between bared teeth.

She creeps forward, toward the back door of the Mausoleum, slinking low to the ground.

The hairs on the back of my neck stand on end, heart thumping uncontrollably in my ribcage as I step over my parents' names and move toward the solid marble door at the rear of the tiny room.

I ready myself to summon fire for a fight, wondering if perhaps a Demon Lord has returned to try and finish what Pandora started.

I turn the cool handle, pushing the back door of the construct wide open and looking out into the crowded line of trees that mark the edge of the dense forest. Here, the high sun leaves mainly shadow, light barely penetrating the thick overhead canopy at all and resulting in a chilly gloom.

"Hello?" I call out, knowing immediately that I deserve a slap.

I'm acting like a freshman sorority pledge in a slasher flick.

Something rustles beyond the treeline, in the bushes, and Beelz lets out another low growl, pressing close to the outside of my calf as she slinks closer to the doorway.

It moves, a blur of massive black and brown fur, lolling out of the woods and directly towards me, tongue hanging out of one side of his mouth.

"Cerb!" I exclaim, eyes widening, my whole body coming alive.

How is this possible?

I watched him killed by Banshees. Or at least, I thought I had.

As he comes to meet me, I bury my face in his neck, immediate tears springing to my eyes at the familiar rising and falling of his chest, breath ragged and excited in my ear.

"Oh my God!" I squeal, collapsing to my knees as I let my full weight fall onto the dog's shoulders and clutch him to me, sobbing uncontrollably.

"I thought you were dead!" I gasp in his ear as he nuzzles the side of my face, licking at my earlobe.

"Sephy?!" I hear Jules' concerned tones growing closer, but can't reply, only having the energy to cling to my dog and cry. I hear him hurry into the mausoleum, and as he finds me, I turn to look at him, tears streaming down my cheeks.

"I— I thought he was dead—" I stutter, looking into the face of the animal, his dopey grin. He's the same as he ever was except for a few obvious traces that he's been injured. His left eye is cloudy and white now, and a large, jagged scar slashes from his brow to the right side of his upper lip. A chunk of his ear is missing too, and there's an enormous bite mark on his back leg that I notice as I run my hands down the length of his torso and down to his paws, checking for more wounds.

"He— he survived the demons—" I'm still crying, choked up entirely by the rediscovery of my childhood friend who I thought had been forever lost.

"Well— I'll be damned," is the only reply Jules can come up with as he drops down to his knees, holding out a hand and stroking Cerb's face. The dog lays on his back, as much a puppy as he ever was, and we go about rubbing his belly, watching him squirm and yap with delight as we bask in this rare miraculous moment.

Cerb has survived, and with his homecoming, with his incredible and death-defying return, I feel a little as though part of my heart has slowly started to heal as well.

LUCE

I'm sitting in my apartment, the silence palpable, sipping red wine from an ornate glass with a stem that looks like it belongs to a thorned rose. My fingers are placed carefully between the glass protrusions; elegant and poised externally in a way my insides will never hope to match.

I take more wine from the glass-blown flower, thoughtful as I stare into the blazing hearth, melancholy after the day's long duty.

A knock on the door startles me, causing my eyes to tear from the flickering, dancing flames that rise high from the coals beneath. The wine jumps slightly as I turn my attention to the door from the couch where I'm sitting. Placing the wine glass down on the glass coffee table in front of me, I call out, shattering whatever calm, or loneliness, had been rushing over me in waves only moments before.

"Come in." My voice is high in pitch, tongue slick with merlot, heartbeat slow in my chest.

The door opens only seconds later, revealing Sephy and Beelz. My spirit lifts at the sight of her orange eyes, glowing, her black fur made warm by the firelight from the hearth as Sephy ushers her in and closes the door behind her.

"You found her!" I smile, reaching out and watching as Beelz trots devoutly forward, head lolling sideways to meet my palm full-on. I cup her face lovingly.

"Hi, Beelzy. I missed you," I croon, her rough tongue licking my hand as her eyes sweep my face, gaze superior as ever. After a few silent moments of feline appreciation, her eyes dart around the apartment and then linger as she makes a slow assessment.

She senses the emptiness just as I do.

You won't find her here. I think. *She up and left us, and she isn't coming back.*

"How did everything go?" I ask Sephy, watching as Beelz goes to claim the bed in the back room as her own once more. I bet she's missed the velvet sheets.

I look up at Sephy as she stands, restless, amid what I once thought of as my home. Now it's a mere reminder of what I've lost.

"It was fine. Plus, I found Cerb. He survived that attack on the estate. I mean he's banged up, but he's alive. It's a freaking miracle." She sways from side to side, anxious in expression, like she can't wait to leave.

I wonder.

"When is the last time you slept?" I ask her, trying to recall any time in the last seven days that she hasn't been convecting all over creation trying to fix what Pandora and The Demon Lords have left broken.

"Eh, sleep is for weenies." She shrugs, something she's been doing a lot to avoid having to come up with answers she either doesn't have or want to give.

I smirk at her, worried more than I want to admit as I mask my concern for her with hospitality instead of a lecture. I, of all people, know how well lectures work on people like Sephy and I.

"Do you want a glass of wine?" I ask, and she lets out a sigh.

"I shouldn't. I have to—" She begins to make the excuse, but I get to my feet, grabbing her by the elbow. She lets me, and I give her a small shove onto the upholstered red velvet of the couch I'd sat on with Xion not so long ago, talking about her.

"You need to stop for a hot damn minute and have a glass of wine with me." I stride from the living space, a silk kimono robe embroidered with golden seven-pointed stars woven among poison ivy, belladonna, and foxglove draping my tall form as it trails silently along the floor behind me. It had been a gift from Haedes from somewhere in Japan to celebrate him officially making me a member of The Nexus.

Pulling the silk tie around my waist, I realise that perhaps I've chosen it because it's one of the only pieces of nightwear I own that wasn't gifted to me by Thane on one of numerous Valentine's days, anniversaries, or impromptu romantic evenings alone.

Rounding the counter, I catch Beelz making herself at home amongst the bedspread and wonder how she'll find The Fallen Kingdom once we've relocated. It certainly won't be as luxurious as this, so I doubt she's going to be very happy.

I take down a glass identical to my own then move over to the empty bottle sat open further along the countertop. I pour Sephy a glass, adding something extra from one of the kitchen drawers with subtle finesse, before returning to the sofa where she's kicked off her shoes and is hugging one of my plush scarlet cushions to her chest. She stares into the fire, face paler than I've seen it in a long time, eyes ringed with dark circles further exaggerated by the firelight.

"How was it today?" she asks me, taking the glass from between her fingers as I sit down beside her. I watch her take a large sip without pause, the wine staining her lips a little as she swallows it fast, cognac eyes intense in the ambient terracotta light.

"How do you think?" I ask her, pushing my silver hair back behind one ear and reaching to retrieve my own glass before taking a quick sip.

She looks thoughtful for a moment.

"You knew him— better than I did. I feel now as though even though I loved him, I barely knew him as a person. I mean, not really. We never talked about his past, about what he liked, his family. It was all so— intense. I feel like there should have been more," she expresses, pushing her lips together so they drain of colour.

"I don't think that those things — his past, his favourite movie — I don't think it matters. You both understood one another on a level that goes far beyond that." I remember watching him talk about her, the soft determination to protect her laced thick with adoration and admiration for the warrior she is.

"I didn't want him to die—" Her voice becomes thick as she whispers the words. I reach out, placing a hand on her shoulder.

"I know, but in ending his life, you saved his soul Sephy. He loved you. He didn't want to lose the person who fell in love with you, and he didn't want you to have to destroy the love you had for him to do what was right. You didn't do what was easy, but you did the right thing. You loved him until the very end and in death. You made the statement that you and he both deserved more and that what you have, it was worth preserving, worth protecting from any darkness that could taint it."

The two glasses of wine I consumed before Sephy arrived have loosened my tongue.

"I miss him," is all she can say, a single tear falling down one cheek.

"I miss him too. More than I thought possible," I admit, my own eyes filling with tears at the thought of his body lying now with Abraxis and Osiris, who are preparing it for tomorrow's funeral.

"Luce, will you do something for me?" Sephy asks me in earnest, her eyelids drooping slightly as she takes another sip of her wine. I nod, knowing soon she'll be asleep under the influence of the potion I've slipped her. It might be unethical, but she needs to stop, to recuperate, to gather all her strength for the long walk she'll take behind his coffin tomorrow.

"Anything. What is it?" I promise, and she smiles, head lolling back against the sofa cushions, red hair warm and splayed out behind her.

"Will you tell me about him? Everything you know—" She yawns, and I smile, Xion's face flitting through the forefront of my mind as though it's being created by an old-school projector.

"Of course," I vow, covering her free hand with mine and feeling the heat of her skin warm me.

Her eyes cloud over with musty sentimentalism that I've never seen in her before and she squeezes my fingers, smiling as her eyes sparkle bright with pain.

And so, by the firelight on the night before we lay him at last to rest, I tell her the stories that made up the life of the kindest man I've ever known.

40

PROUD

<u>SEPHY</u>

STIRRING FROM UNCONSCIOUSNESS, I hear a motor-like purr, followed by an exhale of hot breath. I open my eyes, fingers crawling through the velvet sheets and gripping the fabric. I'm met by a pair of bright orange eyes, glaring at me amid the black duvet.

"Good morning, Beelz," I murmur, heart immediately sinking, heavy as lead. Today's the day I've been dreading, the day I say goodbye forever. I didn't think I'd be able to sleep the night before, let alone pass out in Luce's bed.

I sit up, blinking.

The wine.

"Hey, good morning," Luce calls through the wide-open sliding doors that usually partition this room from the rest of the suite.

"Did you *drug* me?" I bring my fingers up to touch my bedhead, wincing at the obvious hideousness of it.

Luce doesn't reply, just gets a smug smile that stretches over her lips, turning her face feline in its contentment.

Swinging my legs over the side of the mattress, Beelz leaps up, disgruntled by even this slight movement. I stand; body stiff from the total unconsciousness it has experienced, but my muscles and my mind feel undeniably rested.

I tread through to the living area where the scent of batter and chocolate hits me full force, causing my stomach to rumble.

"Thanks— for whatever it is you gave me—" I shrug, slumping down on the couch and curling my legs beneath me. I'm still dressed in yesterday's clothes; minus the leather jacket I've been refusing to part with since I first adopted it back in Xion's apartment.

Luce flutters around the kitchen, still dressed in the black and gold robe she'd been draped in last night. I wonder if she's slept because if she has, it wasn't next to me. Beelz saw to that.

"No problem. You needed it," she calls through from behind the counter where she's bustling with silverware and plates.

"You know I never apologised— for how hard I was on you. When you were going through all the darkness stuff." I yawn, feeling particularly amenable as the intoxicating scent of chocolate continues to waft around me in a heady and comforting cloud.

"You were right to be pissed. I was out of control." She shrugs, eyes a stony pale blue, mouth pressed into a hard line as she rounds the counter. She's carrying a plate stacked with pancakes and in the other hand some oxidised black cutlery. Sitting down beside me, she presents the plate to me, which I take, eyebrows rising on my forehead at her evident triumph of cooking breakfast single-handedly.

"Yeah, but I didn't understand. When I absorbed Xion's darkness, I knew though. It takes everything in you that's self-loathing, that's telling you that you've been victimised or made to feel that life has treated you unfairly, and it uses it to make you want to hurt. You've been victimised a lot, or I mean from what I've been told. I get it now." I look down at the pancakes, mouth flooding with saliva, as she gazes at me thoughtfully.

"Oh! I almost forgot!" She rushes back through to the kitchen, returning with a pouring jug of syrup.

"Oh my God. You really are the devil." I smirk at her as she adorns the still-warm pancakes with a thick cape of golden maple syrup.

"Guilty! Though this is the first time in a few decades I've cooked food and not rabbit intestines for a potion. I hope they're all right." She smirks at me, watching as I tuck in.

The pancakes are light as air, the chocolate melted ever so slightly so it dissolves into a gooey paste on top of my tongue.

Setting the jug of syrup down on the coffee table between the couch and the hearth, she slumps back onto the couch beside me, robe slipping back from her thighs to reveal her flawless long legs, pale beneath.

"Can you believe we have to say goodbye to him today?" I ask her, knowing that skirting around the subject of what's coming is no longer any use.

The funeral is today, and in a few hours, I'll be heading out to light the pyre.

"No. I can't. Though I do have a few details to hash out with you. Last minute stuff." She looks uncomfortable, and I feel a stone form from the pancakes. Until now, they've been gliding down my throat without hesitation.

"Like what?" I ask, fork hovering between my plate and lips.

"Well, the Sinners and the Mortals. They want to pay their respects," she begins, and I swallow hard, licking my bottom lip as anxiety riddles my gut.

"Luce, I can't set that pyre aflame with the entire city watching. It's going to be hard enough doing it anyway," I admit, knowing I must sound weak. She doesn't judge me though, merely shaking her head, eyes warm with understanding.

"Oh no, but Abraxis suggested we have Nightshade pull the coffin through the city from Golgotha. Give them a chance to pay their respects. There's been a lot of demand for it; people want to say thank you. He touched more lives than he realised." I nod, knowing I can't deny him this. He was a hero, and he deserves a funeral befitting his sacrifice.

"Okay, so we head to Golgotha, and the cart is waiting for us there?" I ask, taking another tentative mouthful to distract myself.

"That's right. Also, I didn't want to bother you with outfit choices and stuff so trivial, so I ordered your outfit from the tailors. It arrived this morning, but if you hate it, we can find something else, I'm sure."

I exhale, realising that I've been stressed about this tiny detail without knowing it.

"Thanks. I'm sure it'll be fine. It's not like I'm ever gonna want to wear it again." I suck melted chocolate from the fork, not making eye contact with the woman in front of me.

"There's something else too," she gets to her feet, moving through to the kitchen and returning with a brown cardboard box wrapped with black ribbon.

"A funeral day present— that's uh, a little morbid don't you think?" I ask, trying to be funny, but she doesn't laugh, instead pursing her lips together. Passing me the box, she watches with narrow eyes as I open it.

Inside, within a bottle green velvet drawstring bag, a small silver tiara drops out into my palm.

"Really?" I ask her, cocking my eyebrow, cognac eyes deadening.

I'm not exactly the tiara-wearing type.

"I know. I know it's not exactly *you*— but hear me out. This is the first public event you'll have attended since most of the Sinners came back from the beyond. It asserts your intention to take the throne, and more importantly, Haedes had it made for your mother." My eyes widen as I realise the implications of the gift and so place my now empty plate on the coffee table beside the syrup, silverware clattering. I then move to examine the silver headpiece more carefully.

The setting is beautiful, in what looked originally to be silver, but the rigidity of it suggests platinum to me as I scrutinise it more thoroughly. It's adorned with pear-shaped emeralds, a three-fold centrepiece placed lovingly among platinum-bound branches to emulate the leaves of the mortal world she'd left behind.

It's as though she was the life to his death, the Spring to his Fall.

"Okay, I'll wear it. But on one condition," I bargain, looking deep into her eyes and feeling a kind of sisterhood, a comradery, I've never allowed myself to entertain before.

"Sure, what is it?" she asks me, and I feel the loneliness of this day encroaching with long outstretched icy fingers from beyond the door of the suite.

I don't want to be alone right now, don't want to feel his loss. I know that watching him burn will be hard enough.

"Can I get ready here? I mean, I have no idea how to wear something like this, but you seem to be well-versed in this kind of thing." I know it's a flimsy excuse, but if she sees through it to the core of my vulnerability, she is kind enough to look past it. Her face twists into a smile, rife with a maternal air I didn't realise I had been longing for.

"Sure, I'd be honoured," she replies, placing a hand over mine and giving it a firm squeeze.

She doesn't say anything, but it passes between us, unspoken but intrinsically meant.

I got you.

I stare at my reflection in Luce's vanity as she pulls two thick locks of my fiery red hair back into a knot at the back of my skull. I haven't had anyone brush my hair like this since Jules found me on the front steps of The Sinclair Estate, drenched in rainwater and bloodied from fighting my way out of my own coffin. Before that, well, I guess it was my mom.

"My mom used to brush my hair out like this, in front of her bedroom vanity, when I was a kid," I recall, breaking the silence between us.

My mind is flooded with grief, with pain, and so talking about something, even my dead mother, feels better than pondering the fresh and bitter wound of a future without Xion.

"Mine didn't. She— well, we didn't have a regular mother-daughter relationship exactly." Luce brings out two long hairpieces and spears the knot at the back of my skull with them, half my hair now held in place by what looks like two jagged clock hands and the rest tumbling over my shoulders and down my spine.

"Who— I mean, not to sound rude, but which—" I don't know how to ask the question without offending her, but it's difficult to keep the figures, which for so long I thought were nothing more than myth, straight in my head.

"Hecate. My mother is Hecate. She was raped by my father, Moloch, and then fell pregnant with me. I grew up knowing that story better than I knew any fairy tale." She looks sad, running her long dark fingernails through my hair.

Tilting her head, she ducks down and stares at me in the mirror. "Perfect!" she declares over my right shoulder.

Moving from behind me, she goes through to the sitting area to retrieve the tiara. Returning with it clasped between her forever elegant fingers, she moves in a way that makes the emeralds glint deep lush hues in the dim, unchanging red light of mid-morning. It seeps through the drawn gossamer drapes that hang, uninterrupted on either side of the glass doors leading to the balcony, a stubborn reminder that the world beyond these four walls will wait for nobody.

I stare into my eyes, rimmed dark with what Luce assures me is the world's most cry-proof mascara and eyeliner, finding my cheeks alive with rouge and my mouth pink, glossy, and unfeeling.

Setting the tiara among my locks, I feel the teeth of it pinch against my skull. It's heavier than it looks, and once she's done fiddling with it, she gestures from behind me, indicating in the mirror that I should stand.

Nudging the stool back, I rise to my full height, heels clicking a little as I teeter, taking several small steps back to bask in her approving gaze.

"Awesome, and how do I look?" She twirls, radiant. Her body is encased in a simple black velvet gown that ties around her throat in a complex knot of fabric. I stare, envious, at her perfect figure. I'm sure, next to her, I must look like a sack of dog shit wearing a wig.

"Luce, you're a goddess," I say it as fact, but she takes it as a compliment, her thick lips pulling back over gloriously white teeth in a stunning and otherworldly smile that doesn't reach her eyes.

Looking down at myself with self-conscious dread, I feel the high velvet collar of the dress coat suffocating me as I begin to panic, knowing we have to leave soon. It's double-breasted with sheening black steel buttons, the seven-pointed star of the Nexus council flocked onto the back with grim and shadowy permanence.

It's a political statement, what I'm wearing, which makes me simultaneously angry and sad.

Today should be about Xion.

Then again, as Luce has reminded me over and over, Xion left me here and trusted me to keep Mortaria going, to restore the balance, and that starts with my first public appearance, which just so happens to be today.

"All right, are you ready?" she asks me, beckoning Beelz to her side.

I shake my head.

"No."

"Me neither," her voice falls into a broken whisper as she crosses the distance between us, Beelz following in her shadow.

I stand tall, taking a deep breath as she wraps her hands inside the crook of my arm and rests her head on my shoulder. I stiffen, swallowing hard behind the blackness of my coat's high collar.

We don't say anything, we don't have to. Just hang in the moment, wishing we could be going anywhere else, but knowing there's only one place we need to be.

I convect from the room, Beelz and Luce at my side.

We reappear beside the cold steel bars of Golgotha's main gate. Still twisted entirely out of shape from the demon attack where Jules had been taken captive.

I look beyond the contorted metal, finding Sinners still rising in the graveyard beyond as Nita, Luce's long-standing and trusty assistant, has offered to keep things moving during the ceremony. After all, we have so much to do it didn't make sense to have Mortaria stop totally for the funeral.

The world keeps on turning, as impossible as that seems without him in it.

Luce pulls me by the crook of my arm across the path strewn with dead leaves from the nearby skeletons of Elm trees, and we are greeted by a group of familiar faces.

Jules, with Cerb sitting obediently beside him, steps forward first, giving me a swift hug before passing me the leash.

"I thought you'd want him here," he explains in a low voice.

I smile tightly, eyes tearing up already as I whisper "Thanks," in return.

Abraxis, Muerta, and Yama are also gathered around the back of an ornate gothic-style funeral carriage, consisting of a glass box upon four enormous black spoked wheels. Nightshade stands at the front, bridled, and connected to the vehicle via glistening reins, ready for her slow trot through the city streets.

I don't near her, finding it difficult to breathe as my eyes rest on his coffin, sealed away behind the glass walls that sheen red, reflecting the Mortarian sky.

It's him, lying inside.

Xion.

I have to say goodbye.

This is it.

I take an unsteady breath, suddenly feeling afraid, not ready, like I want to run.

Jules puts his hand in mine before I can move, taking Cerb's leash and watching as Luce places her lace-gloved fingers through mine.

"We will be with you the entire way," Luce promises me, but I don't feel better for it. I feel dizzy and cold, shaken to my core.

This can't be real.

It just can't.

But it is.

Yama, wearing black and silver robes that hang asymmetrically from one shoulder, takes Muerta's hand, her body cloaked in black as well, her skeletal form only distinguishable beneath due to the thick corset pulling her waist tiny among the billowing folds of black cotton. They walk with Abraxis, who is wearing an entirely black suit and looks smarter than I've ever seen him, taking several steps before waiting behind us. I catch Osiris out of the corner of my eye as he joins us too, wearing a ceremonial black tunic and matching wide-hemmed pants, his eyes trained fast on the floor as he brings up the rear.

It looks like I'm leading the procession, Beelz, Cerb, Jules, and Luce walking with me the entire way in solidarity.

My family keeps me standing, keeps me moving forward in a way I can never repay.

With unspoken command, which I'm convinced comes from Muerta, Nightshade lurches forward. The sound of her hooves on the road is empty and the air is cold as a slight breeze chills my face, blowing my hair back from my shoulders.

We begin to walk, one step after the other, following the coffin in silence.

The walk is agonising, my shoulders aching as though the coat I'm wearing is solid lead. I let the tears fall, silently streaming down my face, heart breaking all over again at the realisation that there's no going back.

Xion is gone.

He's dead, and there's nothing to do but move forward without him.

It seems impossible.

We turn onto the outer street that leads into the city, pulling us at last away from the coastal road we've been walking ever since leaving Golgotha.

Then I see it, eyes widening.

There they stand, lining the streets, every single one of them clutching a lit candle to their chests, waiting for us.

"Oh my—" I gasp, tears streaming anew down my face as Luce and Jules tighten their grip on me, Beelz and Cerb walking calmly in unison just ahead.

"I told you; he touched more people than he knew," Luce whispers to me as we begin to walk up a slight incline, passing the first rows of buildings, most of which are still under repair, and finding faces mirroring my grief back at me on either side. The whole city must have turned out, Mortals, Sinners, Gods, Goddesses, Demi-gods, Demon Lords, and even a very badass butler, all brought together by one man, to say goodbye, to honour his memory.

Xion was a hero, and this is what he deserves.

I just wish he was here to see it.

I smile through my tears at the onlooking crowd as we pass them, watching eyes fill with admiration, with sadness, some with pity. Nobody speaks; nobody moves as the silence is filled only with my footsteps and the clipping of Nightshade's hooves against the stone of the city streets. We walk among them, their faces, their recognition of his goodness, of his heroism, his sacrifice, somewhat healing as I

483

realise that he was righteous until the very end. It means he has been taken from me, but if he had stayed and chosen the selfish way, he wouldn't be Xion, the man I fell deeply in love with.

I saved his soul, saved the rarest part of him.

I miss him, heart aching inside my chest as we turn onto the main street of Mortaria, The Exilia Multum looming in front of us.

The people continue to crowd the sidewalks, holding their candles, watching the coffin as it passes. y metronomic heartbeat slows, torturously, in my chest.

We plough through the streets at an abysmally slow pace behind the carriage until, finally, the gates at the end of the street open, and Nightshade takes a gentle left, drawing the coffin into the grounds.

I don't hear the gates close behind us, don't hear my own tears falling to the ground as we finally reach the place where I will cremate his body, ensuring that nobody can ever use him to hurt me again, because of the applause which echoes out across the sky from beyond. The people clap, a roaring tidal wave of respect, of acknowledgement of everything he was. It's solitary act that unifies them across life and death, hands pounding together, unstoppable, in his memory.

It takes around half an hour after the applause finally dies into nothingness for the pyre to be ready. I walk fast, the rest of the small group of ceremony guests in tow, toward my mother's gardens.

I remember wanting to cry in his arms here, remember being afraid of my own heart, but you know it makes sense to me now, spreading his ashes here, cremating him among the pomegranate trees. My mother brought this place to life amid so much death, so many odds against her, and like this garden, our relationship had blossomed, bloomed in the most unlikely of soil and against all the odds that said we should never even have existed as half-breeds, let alone fallen in love.

The garden comes into focus around me too fast as Jules and Luce remain behind me, following closely in my footsteps as I pass through the gothic steel of the gates wound fast by tendrils of poison ivy. It stands in the centre of the gravel at the far end, an enormous pyre, and among the wood, his body is shrouded in black fabric so I don't have to watch his face crack and burn. The Fates are waiting, wrapped in what seems like miles of black fabric with beaded silver shawls hanging from their sagging shoulders, hair pristine and faces plain as they stand beside the pyre.

Yama, Muerta, The Furies, The Fates, Osiris, Abraxis, Luce, Jules, and I finally reach the end of the garden, the sound of trickling water breaking the tension from the fountain that allows the grass to grow green and the trees to climb high.

I exhale, a shuffling of bodies filling the void, taking a few moments as we take our places atop the lawn. My cheeks are tearstained, my heart shredded and raw, and yet still, I stand here, knowing that once again I must be the one to do the hard thing, to carry out the impossible.

Xion said that falls on me because I'm a warrior, and maybe he was right. Maybe that's why he trusted Mortaria in my young and inexperienced hands, why he thought it should be me on the throne.

I wish I had his faith, could see what he had seen in me.

I guess the only way to know if I can be who he thought I was is to try.

So, I will. For him.

The funeral begins, but I don't hear a word. Instead, I'm lost in memories and wondering why I hadn't seized the time I had with him with both hands and clung on for dear life.

I had been stupid, thinking I could stop myself falling in love. I thought if I resisted, if I pretended it wasn't true, it wouldn't hurt as badly when it ended. It turns out that perhaps it hurts worse because I feel like a complete fool, and I'm left wondering what could've been if I'd just said yes.

I examine his mass among the wood and beneath the shroud, Xion's profile definite, and I remember looking up into his face with crystalline clarity as I stand, a spare part to a funeral that's happening around me without me really being present.

After a few moments of silence, of me staring intensely at the pyre, Jules reaches out and touches me on the shoulder.

"Sephy, it's time—" he prompts, and I return to the hell I'm living through, finding the watchful and concerned eyes of those who have stood by my side these last few weeks, through death, and bloodshed, and war.

I think back to the discussion we'd had about how Xion would be buried.

I was on autopilot for most of the planning, dead to the world and caught up with my memories, but one thing I had been adamant about was that he was to be cremated under my flame, not buried. I didn't want him torn apart by demons or resurrected like I'd been. I didn't want him to rot. I wanted him to be free. In taking the dark half of his soul into himself I had vowed this unspoken promise, and now it's time for me to hold up my end of the deal.

I take a small step forward, hands shaking just as they had done when I'd clutched the shard to me the last time I'd been in his arms.

I place a hand on the side of the pyre, whispering "Goodbye," as a tear escapes me, and allow my palm to heat.

The flame doesn't explode from me, nor is it red or blue.

Instead, the violet flame simply flickers into being, a slow-burning yet beautiful sight as it lights my face, turning it ghostly and exuding the numbness, the fatality of the grief that's raging inside.

I step back, crying, eyes illuminated as the pyre goes up in flames and the silhouette of his body is consumed, burning beneath the scorching heat of my power.

Jules clutches me as I stumble back, still shaking, folding me into his chest and letting me sob until his suit jacket is soaked right through.

Bodies stir around me, moving away, leaving him, but I can't. I won't.

I stand in Jules' arms, Luce by my side, until the flames extinguish and all that remains is a pile of ash.

I don't remember what happens the rest of the day.

I walk through the motions, shake hands, sip down wine like it's air.

I'm there, but my mind isn't.

My mind is stuck at Xion's side, watching the last of him burn in violet flames, courtesy of my very own ashen touch.

41

THE BLACK PARADE

SEPHY

THE SOUND OF RAPPING knuckles on heavy brass startles me into consciousness.

Head pounding, I reach under my pillow, wrapping my fingers around the hilt of the obsidian blade I'd found in Xion's apartment.

Rolling over, silk pyjamas clinging to me beneath the velvet sheets, I hurl the blade without looking.

It smashes into the brass of the door, pinging off to the left and landing with a clatter on the floor. I groan, allowing my pillow to cradle my head.

I really need to stop doing that— I muse as the brass door slides open, revealing Luce, who looks mystified.

"What the hell? Why did you throw a knife at the door?" she asks me with a cocked brow, glancing between my bedhead and the obsidian dagger that lies on the floor to the left.

"Eh, it's a long story," I admit, knowing that what I've just said isn't even the half of it.

"Ready to become Queen of The Underworld?" she asks me, spreading her arms wide with bravado.

Cerb stirs from sleep at the intrusion, used to my early morning knife throwing and, yawning, rises to his feet. Shaking out his masses of fur, he leaves a cloud of the stuff to hang in the air, fine individual strands silhouetted against the hearty flames dancing in the fireplace on the opposing wall.

"Oh Christ, don't remind me," I complain, putting my head under the pillow and pulling both sides down over my ears.

I don't get the reprieve I'm hoping for though as Luce yanks the pillow off my head and smacks me with it.

"Get up! We have shit to do to make you not hideous! Besides, Leeah will be here any minute," she adds in this little titbit and I roll over, staring at her incredulously.

"Excuse me? You invited that red-headed harlot here? Today of all days?" I exclaim, eyes wide as I suddenly find myself much more awake.

"My gift to you. I have a lot to do before the ceremony. I'm still packing, remember?" She rolls her eyes, running her fingers through flawless silver hair. She too is wearing pyjamas, as well as having chosen to wear the same embroidered black and gold robe she seems to be favouring lately.

"Ugh. This whole day is just shit," I mutter, and she sighs, exasperated.

"Most girls dream of becoming a Queen, you know," she reminds me, and I sit up, standing fast and allowing the room to spin a moment.

She turns from me, staring out of the window and over the city as I blink several times, slowly trying to banish sleep.

"Yeah well, I'm not most girls," I remind her in turn, thinking about what today really means. It means the end of my freedom. Once that crown is sitting on my head, the whole of Mortaria, its ability to resurrect and reform Sinners, lies in my flaming hands.

That means my freedom is essentially dead in the water, a pitiful limp thing you wouldn't even feed to your cat.

"Right you are. Anyway, I must be getting to the throne room. Rumour has it that Hercules is waiting for me there, I just wanted to make sure you're awake and suffering at a reasonable hour." She grins, and I pout.

"I may be awake, but you have to go deal with Mr Muscle, so have fun with that—" I quip back, and she strides quickly past me, touching my shoulder as she goes.

"Oh look," she says, reaching the door. "Look who it is! Have fun!" Scurrying away, the leggy redhead with a spattering of freckles that are just a little too adorable for me to be comfortable with is revealed, Jules at her side.

"Uh, hey, Sephy." She steps across the threshold awkwardly, Jules ushering her forward as he places my breakfast tray on top of the unmade sheets.

"I think you mean, *Your Highness*," Jules smirks at me and I glower back.

"Oh, fuck off."

"Gladly, Annie is going to teach me how to make a baked Alaska the traditional Mortarian way." His face lights up, a glimmer I've never seen before dancing in the back of his eyes as he departs the room.

I round the bed, ruffling the fur on top of Cerb's head as I move to take a slice of toast from beneath the silver cover keeping my breakfast warm. I butter it haphazardly, standing and leaning over the tray, my back to Leeah who stands awkwardly in the corner.

It could be me that's intimidating her, but it has only been ten days since Xion's funeral, so my guess is that she doesn't quite know what to say to me in the aftermath of his death.

I turn, taking a bite of the wholemeal bread and crunching loudly, licking butter from the corner of my mouth.

"So—" I say, and she smiles, stepping forward from where she's leaning against the far wall. I notice that she's clutching a kit bag, no doubt full of beautification tools, and is wearing high-waisted black pants that flare at the bottom over a black button-up blouse that's tucked into her tiny waistband.

"I'm sorry about Xion." Her fire-engine red hair is swept up in a black bandana, curled like something out of a nineteen-fifties show where the housewife always has dinner on the table and the husband expects her to greet him at the door.

"Me too," I reply, shrugging. "I'm sorry about that night, the party. I was a bitch to you," I apologise; humbled by everything that's happened.

I guess if I'm going to be a Queen, I should start acting like it, and who better to begin with than the leggy redhead who I'd been so threatened by. It's funny now, thinking how afraid I'd been that Xion might like her, might replace me. It seems utterly childish and stupid; especially now that I know what we had was more than surface tension, more than lust. It was deep, with roots that wrapped around my heart and become a permanent part of its shadow-casting architecture.

"That's okay, I get the impression Luce knew what she was doing setting me and Xion up." She smirks, and I smile at her, grateful for her acute observation.

"She really is the devil," I comment, and we both laugh, shattering the tension between us once and for all.

Leeah takes several steps forward, cautious in motion as I swallow the last of my toast, taking her fingers and placing them on my chin.

She tilts my jaw up to the light falling from the topaz-encrusted chandelier overhead.

"You're going to look like a badass," she muses, eyes narrowing as she sees some vision I'm not privy to.

"I like the sound of that," I admonish, sighing as a weight lifts, ever so slightly, from my shoulders.

If Luce uses Leeah as a stylist, then she must be good, so at least I won't be crowned looking like a freaking poodle.

"Great," she says, leading me over to the vanity that stands a few feet from the left side of the bed. "Shall we begin?"

My outfit, the one that Luce has had designed, arrives in a black dress bag from what boasts to be Mortaria's most prestigious tailor. Leeah eyes the crest embroidered on the left side of the black plastic; a look of approval evident on her face.

Luce has organised most of this thing, honestly. I haven't had a say in the type of throne I'll be sitting on or the crown I'll be wearing. I've never even seen the orb and sceptre. The only thing I know is that Yama is conducting the ceremony, and shortly afterwards, Luce is departing for The Fallen Kingdom and taking a handful of Sinners with her. Abraxis was supposed to be involved in the move, but ever since Xion's funeral, he's seemingly disappeared off the face of the planet.

There has also been discussion about replanting The Hollow, watering it this time with my own blood, but it seems safer to leave any unpredictable access points between this and the mortal world sealed for now, especially with the Mortals adjusting to spending what will be the remainder of their lives here, cut off from everything they've ever known.

Leeah uses sparkling black clips to pin my hair back in a stylish knot at the back of my skull, my face painted fierce. My eyes are rimmed smoky as though the cognac irises within are smouldering embers, scorching the surrounding flesh with intense heat. My lips are a deep red, bordering on the shade of arterial spray, and the angles of my skull have been contoured with various powders and presses. It's not over the top, but it's enough to make me look like a warrior, like a Queen, and for that I'm grateful to Leeah.

Pressing a final jewel-encrusted black clip into my hair, she nods with approval, picking up a canister of hairspray and setting the style in place.

"I think you're about done," she informs me, turning to stare at the bag that is hung on the back of the door now, curious.

"Shall we take a look?" I ask, sensing her eagerness to discover what it is I'll be wearing.

I hold my breath, praying for Luce's sake that it isn't a dress, as I cross the room.

Taking the bag down from the door, I hook it over the railing that forms a square between the four posters of my bed. Unzipping the bag, I unhook the cover from the hanger, revealing the outfit inside.

Oh my.

It's perfect.

Black leather pants and a double-breasted black military jacket that will hang over a black and gold corset. It's simple, not a dress, and to quote Leeah, *badass.*

"Oh wow. That's perfect." She sighs with appreciation, reaching out with polished natural fingernails to touch the fabric. Fine gold chains hang over one of the shoulders of the jacket, and I find similar gold embellishments on the back of the pants as I turn them around, suspended in mid-air.

"You had better get dressed. You don't have much time—" Leeah points out, and I stare half-heartedly at the breakfast tray still atop the sheets of the bed. I haven't eaten anything since the single slice of toast I'd forced down earlier this morning, and right now I have no desire to try eating anything else.

"Okay, well uh, thanks. I can take it from here."

Leeah nods, soundlessly repacking her bag as though she's on autopilot and has done this exact day a million times before. Finally, grabbing the hairspray and stowing it in her case, she shuts the clasp and smiles at me.

"Good luck, Sephy. You look awesome!" she unleashes the compliment, but I don't reply as she leaves the room, closing the door behind her.

Alone, except for Cerb who is once again asleep in front of the fire, the walls close in. Pacing over to the balcony, I fling open the double glass doors without pause and step out into the muggy Mortarian morning.

I look out over the city. It's busy, bustling with excitement, with fraught energy as carts hurry in and out of the gates leading to The Exilia. Beside them, gondolas full of guests, I suppose those sinners with prestige, float lazily down The River Styx toward the main entrance of the palace.

I sigh, realising that the air out here is no less suffocating than it was in my room. There's no escape from this. It's been my fate, as much as I have tried to escape it, since the day I signed those stupid papers back at The Sinclair Estate.

I turn, walking defiantly through the suite of chocolate diamonds and shimmering topaz, yanking the clothes from the hanger, and setting about unbuttoning my pyjamas. My face is made, the mask Leeah put in place protection from what perhaps I only know to be true.

I have no fucking clue what I'm doing.

After selecting underwear from the wardrobe on the left side of the bed, I stalk back across the chocolate gleam of the polished floor, Cerb's eyes following my movements with half interest.

Dressed in my undergarments, I yank on the leather pants, making sure not to get tangled in the mess of gold chains that swing from the central belt loop above my ass, and then buckle myself into the ornate corset before slipping, snug, into the military-style jacket. I apply some of my signature cinnamon perfume around my collarbone and behind my ears, admiring the simple onyx studs that Leeah said would be a nice nod to Haedes. Fastening a black velvet choker that connects with tight gold chains around my throat, I admire myself, wondering what the crown will look like with all of this. I didn't enjoy wearing my mother's Tiara yesterday; it bit into my skull and left a dull ache that I can feel even now, but maybe it's not supposed to fit like a snug pair of pyjamas. Maybe it's supposed to hurt, to nag at your nervous system, a screaming reminder of the responsibility you're carrying for more lives than you can count.

Way to freak yourself out, genius— I think, realising as I take one last look in the mirror that my heart is racing in my chest, blood thrumming in my veins.

I can't stop though.

If I stop, if I think it through, just like with Xion's absence, it'll swallow me whole, and fear will root me to the spot. I will never leave this room. And so, recklessly, I charge headfirst into what I know is coming, striding from the room and taking step after hurried step toward the throne.

When I reach the entrance hall, a large crowd of people is gathered at the top of the quartz steps.

Upon hearing the solid gold, crucifix-shaped, stiletto heels of my knee-high leather boots, they immediately turn in unison.

A collective inhale tells me the look I'm sporting has the intended effect, and my confidence grows a little brighter like a lone candle fed pure oxygen inside my chest.

Luce and Jules push through the crowd, and I watch as Dolly and Annie, freshly reborn in Golgotha shortly after the eruption had passed, begin to usher people through the double doors that then close soundlessly behind them.

A small group of individuals is left as Cerb catches up to me, coming to stand by the side of my left thigh, clearly more interested in the excitement than sleeping.

Luce, Jules and — annoyingly enough — Hercules stand, staring up at me as I descend the crystal ramp that leads off the main entrance hall to both my suite and the library.

"You look *amazing!*" Luce pulls me into her arms, the scent of red delicious apples wafting from her.

"Thanks to you." I smile at her, ignoring Hercules as he rolls his eyes.

"I knew you'd rock the 'General' look." She winks. Hercules sighs.

"Yes, can I help you?" I ask him, irritated before he's even dared to open his mouth.

"I just came by to congratulate you and bring you a gift from Haedes. Yama has it, for the ceremony—" He shrugs, holding out a hand for me to shake.

"Are you trying to be nice?" I ask him, feigning shock as I press a hand to the place above my heart, the gold chains that hang from my left shoulder cooling the skin of my palm.

"Maybe." His gaze doesn't betray the truth of why he's here, and I refuse to take the hand he's offered. It hangs there like the following silence, unaddressed in mid-air.

"That's, maybe, *Your Highness*," I retort, a glint in one eye. He glowers slightly, before composing himself, giving a small bow and walking off down the stairs.

"Wonder where he's off to," Luce muses aloud, and I shrug.

"Who cares?"

"Don't underestimate him, Sephy. He's got more connections than you'd think," she warns me, but I shrug.

"Does he have an army of pissed-off mortals and even more pissed-off dead people? Because if not, I don't think I'll be worrying myself anytime soon." Jules smirks at my cocky retort, but Luce's eyes remain fixed on my cousin's back as he boards a gondola and disappears down the river without further hesitation.

"Shall we then?" I demand, not wanting to dwell on Hercules any longer.

Luce nods, as does Jules, who takes my hand and raises it to his lips, placing a kiss on the back of my hand.

"Wait here, the doors will open when we're ready for you. Then just walk down to meet Yama." Luce gives me these instructions sparingly, and suddenly I'm wondering if we should have had a rehearsal or something.

I told everyone I didn't want to be bothered with the coronation prep or Xion's funeral arrangements. I'd been too busy trying to get everything back on track with the Sinners and the small matter of clearing up after a volcanic eruption. Now though, it seems something I should have realised was more important than I'd thought.

I wait, feeling like a spare part, behind the gargantuan double doors, twitching from my left foot to my right, heel jiggling incessantly.

I check myself, straightening my jacket, smoothing my fingers over my hair for loose strands, ensuring that my fly is zipped up because nobody wants to see my bright red lacy thong while I'm being crowned.

Finally, as I wet my glossy lips nervously, I hear the doors begin to move.

Standing up straight, I take a deep breath, blinking a few times and noticing butterflies mauling the insides of my gut.

I'm about to be made Queen.

Shit. Shit. Shit, is all I can think, my face flushing red as I silently hope that the thick layer of foundation Leeah had applied covers it.

The doors swing open without apology, revealing me to the waiting throne room.

The lights of the main chandeliers have been extinguished, and the black shimmering runner, which is peppered with gold leaf and looks like a liquid milky way, is illuminated only by black gothic candelabras that stand a good foot over me. The candlelight flickers, intense, illuminating the faces of those guests who've been chosen to attend.

I hadn't wanted guests, hadn't wanted all this, but Yama and Luce had both agreed that not opening The Exilia for the coronation would look like I was hiding something. After everything, trust is perhaps the most important thing to instil in the people I'll be ruling over.

I step into the firelight, nervous, finding Yama in robes of uninterrupted gold at the end of the runner, waiting with a serene smile plastered on his blue lips.

Eyes examine me, my red hair aglow in the dim as I pace down the runner, keeping my head held high, shoulders set back, and eyes set on my destination, trying not to run but keeping up a pace as fast as decency will allow.

All I can think as I meet Yama at the end of the walk from hell is *please have whisky.*

He does not, but he does sidestep me, revealing a throne I recognise. It had been Haedes', an exact replica of the throne I melted, determined that Pandora wouldn't sit where he sat.

Now though, I will sit in his place.

It seems right.

As messed up as that is.

Yama licks his bottom lip, black velvet gripped in his palm. He gestures for me to step up, gaze encouraging, before turning me gently and indicating that I should put my arms into the ceremonial Nexus robe that he holds outstretched. Once the snug floor-length black robe, finished with skeletally stark adornments down the spine, hangs in a slimming silhouette from my body Yama turns from me. Eyes glistening, he addresses the guests that watch us intently.

"Welcome. Today we crown a new Queen," he announces, looking down at me, concern obvious in his stare.

Do I look that nervous?

I made him promise me to cut the shit and keep the ceremony short. I have no intention of being on show longer than necessary.

"Ready?" he asks me in a curt whisper, and I nod.

Stepping past me, he gestures now to the golden throne, the seat padded with red velvet.

I take a step forward, sitting as I turn to face the crowd.

Here, I find The Fates in the very front row, staring up at me with excited if not entirely gormless expressions.

"Repeat after me," he commands, face stiff with authority.

I nod, swallowing.

"I, Sephy, The Phoenix."

"I, Sephy, The Phoenix." I cringe internally at the title. I hadn't wanted one, obviously, but then there'd been this whole stupid argument about titles.

Yama continues, sensing my brazen hatred for this entire debacle.

"Solemnly vow to uphold the values and protection of the people of this realm and any other whom may look to those of The Nexus for help. To place those needs of my people, the souls in my care, before those of myself, and to understand that my life and death now belong to the service and wellbeing of the place Mortaria holds in maintaining the universal balance of good and evil."

I ponder the implication of this vow, having never heard these words spoken before, but then realise something incredibly frustrating.

I've already carried out this promise, more than once in fact, without even having made it.

With this in mind, I repeat the vow back to Yama, voice tinny with nerves and shaking as the vast number of eyes staring up at me seem to take on a kind of scrutinous intensity I'm not prepared for.

He turns, Muerta passing him two objects.

I'm surprised as they are given to me, the underwhelming nature of their design. They do not sparkle or gleam. The orb is made up simply of a lump of coal, the sceptre a crooked branch from what I assume was once The Hollow.

I clutch them to me and Yama jerks his head slightly, signifying something. I just don't know what.

Then it occurs, as I stare at the uncharacteristic lump in my left hand, that coal is an odd but perfect choice.

I will my hand to light, the purple flames devouring the coal and setting it ablaze. I hold the lump of flaming rock in my palm, and Yama smiles before pivoting back to his ex-wife once more.

When he spins back to face me with effortless speed, my eyes are immediately drawn to what he's holding.

This must be what Haedes asked Hercules to deliver.

A small smile forces itself onto my face as the thoughtfulness of the gesture touches me, the crown glistening scarlet in the gentle light from hundreds of flickering candles.

I stare at it, the gold of the setting so familiar, the enormous rubies that mimic the leaves of The Sanguine Forest. It's similar, very much so, to my mother's tiara, and yet it's me all over. It's Mortaria, and

Haedes, and me, Persephone Sinclair, made solid in metal and precious stone.

I bow forward, coal still crackling violet in my palm as Yama sets the crown atop my head. It's heavy, not that I had expected it to be anything else, and as I lean back, posture forced straight by the throne, the master of ceremonies turns to address the crowd.

"I present to you, Sinners of Mortaria, Her Royal Highness, Queen Sephy, The Phoenix." He stands aside, gesturing to me like I'm a prize pony.

The crowd stands from their seats, putting their hands together and applauding me.

As they do so, music explodes from nowhere— except I know exactly where it's come from.

Haedes.

My Chemical Romance, yet another thoughtful choice considering his predilection for Cher and all things utterly fabulous, begins to chime out into the hall, sombre and regal.

The Black Parade continues to fall familiar on my ears as I get to my feet.

I will the orb of coal in my palm to extinguish, and it does, leaving behind a shiny crystal substitute flaking with black coal dust. I pass Yama the sceptre and orb in turn, walking back down the aisle and out into the entrance hall.

Yama had wanted a reception, but I said no.

Luce and I have instead come to a compromise with him on how I will greet my new subjects, and so I wait for her as she is the first to emerge through the double doors, ready for me.

"Ready?" she asks, eyeing the crown that's nestled tight among the red locks of my hair.

I smile, exhaling heavily with relief.

"Yep, totally—" The ceremony had been a necessity but a painful one. However, the next part of the day was what I'd been ultimately and solely looking forward to.

I grab her arm, and we convect, reappearing just behind the metal gates of the Exilia where Nightshade stands, waiting for me.

Annie moves forward, producing a stool and change of shoes, black riding boots to exchange for the killer heels that are already starting to pinch.

Luce helps me out of my shoes, laughing as my crown tilts on my head, and she has to set it right, complaining that I need either a larger head or a smaller crown as I step into the flat leather riding boots, the material soft as butter yet supple and supportive where I need it.

Nightshade is dressed to match me, black and gold reigns and saddle adorning her glossy, lithe body, mane glistening and braided with delicate metal chains.

Placing a hand on her muzzle, I close my eyes, inhaling the scent of her, glad for the familiar amongst everything new.

"Ready girl? It's been a while," I whisper, kissing the side of her face.

She exhales heavily, teeth exposed as her lips pull back slightly, rearing back like she's ready to go.

Annie places the stool beside her, and I clamber up onto Nightshade's back, the saddle snug between my thighs. Luce passes me a pair of leather riding gloves once I'm seated, and I slip the black garments on over my fingers, thanking her as I do so.

I look down at them, at Luce and Jules, who finally join us from the entrance hall along with Yama and Muerta, their smiling faces looking up at me and proud, causing my heart to unwillingly swell.

My Chemical Romance continues to play, drifting through the air and out over the streets up ahead.

I swallow hard, watching as the gates are opened before me, and Nightshade and I set off at a trot.

The main street of Mortaria is packed, but not in the way it had been for Xion's funeral. This isn't a quiet, sombre crowd but a crowd buzzing with excitement. They're singing along to the music, those who don't know the words humming, fists pumping in the air.

I appear at the end of the street, smiling, and they erupt into a roar of approval.

I blush, smiling, my heart soaring.

Sinners, placed methodically along the curb, step forward from where they've been running crowd control while the ceremony has been taking place, and move in synchronised time to form two perfectly straight lines.

As I approach the tunnel of Souldiers, they each raise a single golden sword to the heavens, creating an arch of sharp and merciless blades for me to ride through.

The sky is finally totally clear of ash, any signs of the past trauma of this place gone, the lilac sun blazing once more over everything I've fought and sacrificed to protect.

Nightshade and I ride through the streets of the kingdom I can now safely call my own, and I know, somewhere, Haedes is looking down, hips swinging, feet tapping, with a smile on his face and a song in his heart.

42

9 TO 5

<u>PANDORA</u>

"NAME?" MY VOICE COMES out in a drone-like bark.

My manager turns toward me from behind the pastry case on my left, giving me a disapproving glare as soon as she hears my tone of voice. I smile at her, hatred seething within my chest as I have to physically stop my fingers from crushing the paper coffee cup in my hand.

"Hercules, with an H." The words fall on deaf ears as I take the marker to the side of the cup, scrawling the name on autopilot without even thinking about it.

God, this is menial.

Then, I stop.

Staring at the name I've just written, my head snaps up, and I come face to face with his baby blues.

He looks wrong in mortal clothing, his muscles hidden behind a black windbreaker and wrapped in dark denim jeans. He smiles at me as I take in his face, lips slightly parted as I sway on the spot. Has the mundane green apron driven me to madness, the hiss of the milk-steaming wand finally pushed me over the edge?

"Dora! Customers are waiting!" My manager, and unfortunately also my roommate, Sally hisses in my left ear, bringing me unapologetically back to myself as I stand, feet aching in black Posturepedic work shoes that make me want to weep. They are truly hideous.

I smile back at Sally as she whisks past me to take out the trash, or something equally as pointless, hating her but undeniably reliant on her generosity.

I found myself, boxless and bruised, in a New York alleyway next to a bunch of unholy-smelling green dumpsters.

After I shed my disfigured wings, she'd found me, dressed in leather pants and steel corset, assuming I'd been beaten up by a boyfriend who was, and I quote, into some 'kinky medieval sex shit'.

Then, for reasons beyond me, she'd taken me in without protest. She'd fixed me up with this job too, which, as much as I hate it, is currently the only way I'm affording my half of the weekly grocery run.

"I'll take a venti, caramel mocha with whipped cream." He orders his drink, causing me to stare down at the cup in my hand.

Ugh, sickly sweet and completely over the top, just like the drinker.

Then I realise something else.

Shit. Wrong size.

Because apparently, as well as having absolutely massacred coffee by adding a bible's worth of extras which have to be added *just so*, we also have to take the size of the order in freaking Italian—

I throw the cup away, grabbing another from the obtrusive stack behind me and jotting down the order and his name once more before sliding it routinely along the counter.

Then something else hits me; I'm about to be on my own, the graveyard shift in the city that never sleeps.

Awesome.

I shuffle along the counter, grabbing milk from the fridge under the coffee machine and beginning the routine I've barely just mastered.

"So, how are things?" Hercules asks, head popping up in between the machines right where the syrups are stored.

"Fine. Yourself?" I ask him, and he smirks.

"Better than you. I just came from Sephy Sinclair's coronation, actually." He drops in this little detail, and it eats at me like a vial of sulphuric acid dropped scalding hot down my throat. I try not to let it show, staring with a forced and nonchalant expression at the neon sign behind his head, a Mermaid holding her own tail.

It still makes absolutely no sense to me because Mermaids don't have anything to do with freaking coffee.

"What are you doing here?" I demand, sick of his games.

He smiles.

"Getting coffee." He smirks as I heat the milk, burning myself on the nozzle of the milk steamer.

"No, what are you really doing here?" I demand, cocking one eyebrow and brushing a loose lock of greasy black hair off my forehead with the slick base of my palm as I add caramel syrup to his cup.

"Well, seeing as you asked so nicely, I have a gift for you. Well, two, actually." He looks smug as I pour shots of coffee into the bottom of the almost empty paper cup and then add the bubbling milk, procuring a lid and cardboard sleeve for the beverage before passing it to him.

"Thanks." He places the coffee down on the side, undoing his black puffy jacket and pulling a small black velvet bag from within his innermost pocket. He passes it to me, smiling, and I stare down at it, heavy in my hand, mystified.

By the time I look back up, he's gone. I also realise I completely forgot his whipped cream.

"Hey, Sally. Bathroom break. Will you cover me?" I ask her as she returns from out back.

She rolls her eyes but nods, jerking her head towards the back and mouthing, 'Quickly!' to me as I rush past her, bag clutched in my hand.

Bustling past racks of enormous drying coffee mugs, still warm from the dishwasher, and then past the staff lockers, I duck into the dingy bathroom.

Black matte tiling on all surfaces is illuminated by a single hanging bulb that swings slightly as I lock the door behind me. A mirror reflects my pallid and bedraggled appearance, smeared cloudy with watermarks from the sink underneath, showing only exactly how far I've fallen this time. The air of the place is rife with the chemical scent of citrus, and it stings my nostrils, causing my lips to pucker in distaste.

Putting the partially clean toilet seat down, I sit atop it, crossing my legs and taking a deep breath before opening the bag.

I let its contents fall into my hands, gripping the two objects so hard my knuckles go white.

I stare at them. A lifeline delivered by the son of the man I risked it all to take down.

I examine what he's given me, a smile creeping onto my face after far too long working in a Mortal city with no hope of escape.

My box and I are finally reunited, and beside it, a single but jagged shard of onyx lies in my palm. What's more, once I've examined it in the dim light from the underwhelming dangling bulb overhead, I come to believe that it had once belonged to a very important hourglass.

An hourglass that had been shattered by my very hand.

The jagged onyx shard reflects the wicked gleam in my eye, causing my face to erupt, finally, in a smile.

EPILOGUE

HAEDES

"YOU DO KNOW ZEUS is going to kill you?" Thane reminds me as we stand at the edge of the innermost grove of The Divine Pastures, side by side.

My hands are shoved deep into my suit pockets as I muse on everything that's happened.

Sighing as her words reach me, I shake my head. This is the third time she's told me as much in the last thirty minutes alone, and honestly, the last several attempts didn't work at discouraging me, so I'm not sure why she doesn't just shut up.

Staring up at the descending plati-sun overhead, I watch the sky morph into a heavy indigo dusk before I turn my attention, intense now, to the individual blades of grass that continue to weave their timeless magic soundlessly before my very eyes. The air is warm, fragrant, and enrapturing in every regard, something sorely missed during my time in Mortaria.

"Eh, I'm sure I'll live." I muse; smug as she stares at me, shocked. Her black spiky hair looks wild, her face gaunt. She's lost weight since returning here, for which in my opinion there is no excuse.

If you ask me, the food is quite heavenly, pardon the pun.

"What makes you so sure he won't just toss your ass out of here?" she asks me, cocking one eyebrow and pursing her lips.

I shrug, shifting my weight from one foot to the other as a tangerine coloured flutterby flutters predictably by.

"I think this whole debacle with Sephy has made him see the power in my skills. The Eternal Flame is the only way to truly destroy a soul, and I think there's a battle on the horizon. Zeus is going to need all the help he can get," I reveal, and she frowns, keeping half an eye on the grass. glowflies of every colour dance through the shadows surrounding us, the sun setting fast toward the horizon beyond the thick weave of trees that make up this place.

"A battle?" she asks me, and I nod, frowning slightly as I cross my arms and lean against the silver threaded bark of a nearby tree. The scent of nightbloom and lightflower is rife in the air now as the day comes to a final close, calming to some but not to me.

Instead, the pungent perfume is putting me on edge.

"Two of the three realms have now changed hands after hundreds of years under the same rule. You know what happened with The Circle of Eight and their Kindred, and now Pandora has tried to mess with the balance using Mortaria. Something is up. Not that anyone will take me seriously of course, hence why I haven't brought it up." I exhale, running my hands through my hair. "Until there's some link, some event that ties them all together, they're just random events that coincided," I add, answering her next question before she can ask it.

"Maybe I'm just being paranoid," I say, knowing she probably thinks I'm insane.

But rather than her face morphing into incredulity, she looks thoughtful instead.

"I see what you're saying. Is that why you did this?" she asks me, gesturing to the pasture.

"No, I did this because he deserves to be here," I reason, not thinking about the fallout. I've stolen Zeus' staff and granted entrance to The Higher Plains to an individual who had not so long ago been half-demon.

It surprised me, finding his soul even able to be fully restored, but then I realised that a question that has been nagging at me for years has finally been answered.

The purple flame, the flame that powers the Mortarian sun, it doesn't destroy souls or resurrect bodies; it restores the soul, makes what is broken whole again.

Sephy hadn't realised it, but in burning Xion's body atop his funeral pyre, she had healed what had been the tattered remains of the soul she herself had torn apart by absorbing his darkness. So now, now he's eligible to ascend, to live here as a Titan, and I will be the one to approve him for residency even if it pisses off the entire Olympian population.

I know it's going to be hard, that everyone will wonder what the hell I'm doing, but they don't *know*. They haven't lived among demons, among darkness. They don't know that shades of grey, that ambivalence, are what's real rather than the dichotomy of black and white, of good and evil, that Zeus insists to be the way of worlds. To be what separates us from them.

Thane gives me a knowing smile, and I return to thinking about the responsibility I'm taking on, fighting for Xion's place here.

"You know it's crazy, but I think it's awesome you're doing this. Whatever will Sephy say when she finds out you made him a Titan?" Her eyes glisten with excited curiosity.

I shake my head.

"She can never know, Thane. I'm serious. She gave him up willingly. I won't let her long for someone several dimensions away. She has too much to focus on. She must never know he's alive, that he's here. It would be too painful. You know more than anyone what it's like to love someone in another world that you can no longer reach. It would destroy her." I'm firm, staring her down.

She's silent for a long time after, leaning against the tree opposite me, this one veined with gold, and I wonder if she's thinking about Luce, about everything she gave up when she walked away from her mortal body. I know she thinks it was brash now, not that she would ever admit it, but watching Luce's struggles, I've seen pride grow within her gaze that I know she thought she would never feel again.

The silence engulfs us, the fear that something dark is just on the horizon, potent within our minds as we wait and watch, a body remade among the lush grasses that spread out in a rich carpet before us.

The sun sets on another day in Olympus, and we continue to wait with bated breath as a new Titan is born.

THE END

READY TO MEET THE NEXT QUEEN OF FANTASY?

KEEP READING FOR A SNEAK PEEK OF INDIGO DUSK- BOOK 1
IN THE THIRD TRILOGY OF THE QUEENS OF FANTASY SAGA
OR DOWNLOAD KAIRI'S STORY HERE!

ALSO BY

QUEENS OF FANTASY SHORTS AND NOVELLAS

TIDAL KISS SHORTS AND NOVELLAS
Beyond The Shallows
Waiting For Gideon
Vexed

ASHEN TOUCH SHORTS AND NOVELLAS
Death Blooms
A Touch Of Smoke And Snow

AETHERIAL EMBRACE SHORTS AND NOVELLAS
Ambrosia Nights

EXTRAS
Infiniflash Fiction Volume One

OTHER GENRES FROM KRISTY NICOLLE

DYSTOPIAN ROMANCE:
Something Blue- A Dystopian Romance Standalone

POETRY:
I Am Arcana- A Tarot Inspired Poetry Collection
Starsong- A Zodiac Inspired Poetry Collection

To keep up to date with the latest release dates, spin offs, and exclusive content, head on over to kristynicolle.com

ACKNOWLEDGEMENTS

Another day, another beloved character doomed, another trilogy finished. Funny, seems like only yesterday that I was saying that about The Tidal Kiss Trilogy. I want to thank my tribe; Mark, My Parents, Leeah Minick, Jaimie Cordall, Dawn Yacovetta, Rose Lintz, The Tidal Telltails, my utterly foxy PA Winter's Rage and everyone else who stuck it out through the ups and downs of this novel. With crappy health and even more bipolar weather, this book was a struggle from start to finish, and without each and every one of you the damn thing wouldn't have been finished, so thank you! I'm kind of sad, and kind of excited to say that this trilogy is done, I think most readers would agree that this trilogy is the most intense thing I've written so far, and my energy levels upon its completion surely reflect that. I'm exhausted, and definitely need a nice long vacation with pyjamas, cocktails and a quiet nook with a book. To all my readers, I hope you've loved this story as much as I have. It's been brutal, tragic, laugh-out-loud hysterical and definitely full of sass, but regardless I have enjoyed writing every single word! So, onwards— to the final trilogy of the Queens of Fantasy Saga!

I'll see you in Aetheria!

ABOUT THE AUTHOR

30-Year-Old British Author of Award-Winning Indie Fantasy Romance, Kristy Nicolle is escaping the pain of Ehlers Danlos Syndrome by crafting intricate and immersive worlds for her readers. She lives in Norwich, Norfolk, with her long-time life partner Mark, and can often be found writing in her local coffee shop - *Botany and Beans*, with a peppermint mocha, surrounded by beloved witchy paraphernalia and plants she knows only too well she'd kill at home.

FOLLOW KRISTY NICOLLE ON SOCIAL MEDIA OR FIND HER AT KRISTYNICOLLE.COM

www.ingramcontent.com/pod-product-compliance
Lightning Source LLC
Chambersburg PA
CBHW021836010726
47493CB00005B/1430